TI

OMNIBUS

# THE RUSKIN BOND OMNIBUS

*Edited by*

**Ruskin Bond**

Rupa . Co

First Published 2004
Third Impression 2005

Published by

Rupa . Co

7/16, Ansari Road, Daryaganj,
New Delhi 110 002

*Sales Centres:*

Allahabad Bangalore Chandigarh Chennai
Hyderabad Jaipur Kathmandu
Kolkata Mumbai Pune



Typeset in 11 pts Revival by
Nikita Overseas Pvt Ltd
1410 Chiranjiv Tower
43 Nehru Place
New Delhi 110 019

Printed in India by
Rekha Printers Pvt Ltd.
A-102/1 Okhla Industrial Area, Phase-II
New Delhi-110 020

# Contents

## GHOST STORIES FROM THE RAJ

## NIGHTMARE TALES

## HAUNTED HOUSES

## SCARY STORIES

# GHOST STORIES FROM THE RAJ

# Introduction

The *raison d'etre* for telling a ghost story was probably best summed up by the Fat Boy in *Pickwick Papers*, when he said: "I wants to make your flesh creep!"

But it isn't always as simple as that, and not all ghosts are frightening.

The other night I woke up around midnight with bright moonlight streaming in at the window and lighting up the bedroom. Someone, or something—a vague, nebulous figure—was standing beside my bed, looking down at me. It could only have been a ghost. I waited for the spectre to say something but it remained silent; nor did it move away.

"Hello," I said. "And what can I do for you?"

No answer. Not even a gesture, either of goodwill or ill-will. A most ineffective ghost.

"Do you have a message for me?" I asked. "Anything you'd like me to do for you?"

No response. It just stood there, shimmering in the moonlight.

"Well," I said, "I've got better things to do than just lie here holding a one-sided conversation." And I turned over and went to sleep again.

The ghosts in this collection are far more alarming. Most of them were observed, experienced or imagined by British writers during the period 1840 to 1940: a century of ghosts!

For the British, coming from a land where haunted houses and castles were the norm, were fascinated by the wonderful variety of supernatural manifestations that they found in India: *churails* (the ghosts of wayward women, whose feet always faced backwards), *munjias* (the spirits of Brahmin youths who died before marriage), *bhoots* who took up residence in peepal trees, or mischievous *prets* (Indian poltergeists) who sometimes entered the homes of living people and created havoc in their lives.

The stories of this period tell us something about colonial attitudes—ranging from the paternalistic to the cynically indifferent—but we must remember that they were written purely to entertain, to enliven a dull railway journey, a sleepless night, a rainy day in the hills, a long sea voyage, or a period of recuperation from a tiring illness. Ghost stories are meant to frighten you, but at the back of your mind you know it's all a nightmare from which you are going to wake. In other words, it's a "safe" fear and you can enjoy the process of being frightened.

The human imagination is a wonderful thing, and I shall conclude this brief introduction with a 'factual' experience of my own, which was certainly hair-raising.

Some years ago, a neighbour of mine, an old English lady who lived alone, died of heart failure and was laid out on her bed for the night, as it was too late for the funeral. A friend and I decided that we would take turns at her beside, and at about midnight I sat down on an easy chair in the bedroom to undertake my part of the vigil. There had been the usual power failure, but we had lit candles and I could see the features of the corpse quite clearly.

For some reason I couldn't take my eyes off her face. Her eyes were closed, but after a while I was sure I could make out a slight smile on her lips. This smile gradually grew wider until it became a rather menacing grin. I was frightened out of my wits. Was I about to see her rising from the dead? As the grin grew even wider, I got up from my chair, ready to flee the room. Just then there was a loud report, like a pop-gun going off, and her false teeth shot out of her mouth and rolled off the bed.

We had forgotten to remove her false teeth. *Regor mortis* having set in, the rigidity of her jaws had forced her mouth into that terrifying grin, ejecting the teeth with considerable force.

Not a ghost story, but a ghostly one all the same.

Happy hauntings!

## *The Wondrous Narrative of John Cambell*

### Gunfounder to the Mogul Emperors, 1654–1667

AMONGST THE MSS. TREASURES IN THE BRITISH MUSEUM ARE a number of contemporary manuscripts relating to Englishmen who dwelt or travelled in India during the Seventeenth Century. Ranking high amongst them in interest, if not in veracity is one called the Richard Bell MSS. from its having been inscribed by a traveller of that name in the years 1669–1670.

The document purports to contain an exact account of the travels and adventures of one John Cambell who met Bell at Alleppo in 1669 whilst on his way home overland from India and continued the journey in company as far as Rome, meeting with more wondrous adventures on the way. During this journey the narrative was written to the dictation of Cambell and completed at Rome on the 20th December 1670 the joint signatures being attested by Joseph Kent, the English Consul.

How this manuscript came into the collection of Sir Hans Sloane, from which it passed into the British Museum in the year 1780, there is nothing to show, nor why it should have remained unknown to all but the curators until it was discovered by that indefatigable antiquary Sir Richard Temple in the year 1905 and published in the Indian Antiquary of that year, which we have permission to use. Concerning Cambell, Sir Richard Temple thus writes:

"Some of Cambell's statements explain why travellers' tales have become a byword and synonym for pure invention. There is no chronological sequence and anachronisms are frequent. Indeed were it not for the testimony of Manucci who mentions several of the persons alluded to by Cambell it would be difficult to attach any credence at all to the narrative. However, the records of the English in India of this date are so scanty that any account by an eyewitness is worthy of reproduction, and especially so, when, as in this case, out-of-the-way information is blended with accounts of magical occurrences wondrously described." To this William Irvine, the Translator of Manucci, adds:

"This is a wild and utterly unchronological narrative, by the side of which the wildest flights of Manucci read as sober sense. But there are some grains of fact, as the men whom he mentions Robert Smith, John White, Thomas Roach and William Gates are all mentioned by Manucci as with Shah Jehan and Aurungzebe when Cambell was with Murad Baksh and Dara Shekoh, Smith and Roach also appear in the Surat Records in 1667 and 1672 and the son of the latter is mentioned in 1704."

In these, both men are mentioned as having considerable influence at court notably Smith "who has the ear of the Mogul". They were also men of considerable wealth, apparently for these first two letters concern large sums they had advanced to the Company's merchants at Agra on private accounts and of which they were applying to the Company to recover for them. They do not figure very creditably in the pages of the Venetian adventurer Manucci, who was himself a gunner in the service of Dara Shekoh, a son of Shah Jehan, for he alleges that they tried to rob him of the effects of Lord Bard after the death of the latter to whom Manucci had been page. Though Manucci is circumstantial enough it seems that he exaggerates for these men were then high in the service of Shah Jehan and acted by his orders.

However, there seems little doubt but that, like all such men in the service of Indian princes at this period, *might* meant right. From the opening decade of the Seventeenth Century Europeans were entertained in considerable numbers at the Mogul courts both by the reigning Emperors and their sons, each of whom had his personal army, the artillery of which was worked or supervised by European master gunners, mostly runaway seamen from the vessels of the various East Indian Companies, Dutch, English, and French, or ex-pirates wrecked or marooned on the coasts.

So early as 1612 William Hawkins headed some 60 of all nations in a procession to the Catholic Church at Agra the occasion being the baptism of two nephews of Jehanghir willing to embrace a new faith in the hope of those Portuguese brides which had been promised them. However as the brides were not forthcoming, the bargain was cancelled. These Europeans comprised all sorts of trades and professions, such as jewellers, lapidaries, surgeons, doctors, painters and sculptors, though the great bulk were always artillerymen and military artificers, of whom at the period of which we write there were over 200 in the various services.

All received high pay for the time ranging from Rs. 200 to 300 a month, the captain gunners, such as Roach and Smith, drawing much more. The salary of John Whelo, master gunner, in 1712 is recorded as equal to about Rs. 2,000 a month by the Dutch ambassador, so probably Smith and Roach may have been paid almost as liberally if not quite. As a special inducement for European gunners to enter and remain in such service the Mahomedan rulers as to spirituous liquor were relaxed in their case, they being permitted not only to distil, but to sell such liquor to non-Mussalmans, the privilege was valuable for Manucci records that he himself drew Rs. 300 a month for the use of his. Of the origin of the privilege he tells the following amusing story:

"Finding that his own gunners were of no use and hearing that Europeans were very expert at the art, Jehanghir ordered his Governor at the Port of Surat to procure him a master gunner, from the English who were the very first to arrive at this port. They sent him a most skilful gunner who was assigned Rs. 500 a month. But this man, like all the other Englishmen, was very fond of spirituous liquor, and, this being forbidden by the Mahomedan religion, he was consequently very unhappy. Therefore he set about to obtain his heart's desire so, one day when Jehanghir ordered him to fire a shot at a great sheet stretched on sticks on the opposite bank of the river, he intentionally missed every shot."

"At this the Emperor was much put out thinking the man unskilful, and sending for him asked him the reason for such bad shooting when he had such a reputation for skill. The Englishman replied that there was no lack of skill, but that he was unable to see straight unless he had drunk spirits. On this the Emperor directed some to be brought from the elephant stables where there was no lack of it on account of it being kept to give to the elephants to increase their courage in battle or fighting with each other. When the Englishman saw the spirits he was highly delighted, and seizing the bottle put it to his mouth with the same eagerness as a thirty stag would rush to a crystal spring."

"Then at one draught he swallowed the lot licking his moustache for the few drops that clung to it. The Emperor was astounded at the pleasure of the Englishman who expressed his satisfaction by all kinds of gestures. He then went to his gun and after rubbing his eyes told the Emperor they were now clear, and directed that the sheet should be taken away and an earthen pot on a stick put in its place. At the very first shot he knocked the pot to pieces. Therefore in consequence of this amazing skill derived from spirituous liquor, the Emperor gave the Europeans the sole privilege of distilling liquor with which none were to interfere. He said that the Englishmen must have been created at the same time as spirits as without them they were as fish out of water."

The only appearance of Cambell in the records of the East India Company is a mention of his arrival at Bundar Abbas in

January 1669 in poor condition having been robbed of Rs. 8,000 and a quantity of jewels whilst on his way through Sind to Tatta whence he took boat for Bunder Abbas. The letter goes on to say that Cambell had served the Mogul for a number of years and concludes by stating that he had been advanced money and since departed for Alleppo with a recommendation to the English Consul there. It is difficult to decide Cambell's real nationality. In his own account and the mention by the Factor, with whom Cambell claimed relationship the name is thus spelt, and he also writes concerning rich relations in England. But against this is set a statement that though he put the English coat of arms on all the guns he cast for the Emperors, on the trunnions he cast a lion rampant, which was the Scotch crest.

Whatever else he may have been, however, John Cambell ranks very high amongst tellers of travellers' tales of the Baron Muchausen or Sir John Maundeville school. Though he emulates the worthy Sir John in the matter of two headed men and men with eyes in their necks or foreheads, Cambell far excels him in the matter of monstrous beings of unmortal origin who slay whole armies in a single afternoon, of chance met wizards who transmute the money in his pouch to base metal or completely empty it from a distance with other as wondrous feats. But most of all does Cambell revel in tales on Jinns and Demons who pay visits in state or drop in casually on an afternoon or evening for theological and family discussions, and reward their entertainers, or unwilling hosts with revelations of the hiding places of vast treasures.

But with all Cambell's extravagance much that is useful may be extracted from his wonderful tales, for undoubtedly he did serve the Moguls and equally did he make extensive travels in India, Persia and Asia Minor. We have spent much time in reducing his chaotic tale to some chronological sequence and a measure of actual fact, the clue seeming to be in that the narrative was written over a period of eighteen months or so, at many different places, and haphazard, just as the facts were recalled to the mind of the dictator, or his imagination most lively. Judging by internal evidence both narrator and scribe seem to have indulged rather freely in the beverage so relished by Jehanghir's gunner. It must also be remembered that in those days when works of fiction were unknown actual travellers were relied on for tales of the wonderful. Nobly some of them met the demand.

However, the overture is finished, the lights grow dim and on the silver screen of the narrative appears a burly bearded figure whose blackly burnt visage is relieved by blue eyes twinkling with broad humour and perchance a tongue bulging a cheek of brass. A moment's pause. Cambell composes his face to prim decorum and then, over the fancy bridged gulf of some 250 years sounds this wondrous narrative of marvellous experiences.

"You should know that, in the year 1609. Jehanghir being then the Great Mogul, one Asaf Khan being then his Counsel in chief (Commander in chief) had gotten great treasures by his war with the Gentues (Hindoos). It was always their pride to adorn their Pagodays and places where they keep their Gods with images of golden cows and such other creatures as they worship and to embellish these places with precious things of great value. This Asaf Khan plundered them all and by such means got great store of Treasure which he buried in his house at Old Dilly.

After he died, the Emperor by torturing all his generation got six elephant loads of treasure valuing £500.000 though suspicion caused that to this day much remayneth behind, though where, unknown. The only one of his generation now remayning called the Lord Jaffir Khan, a Colonel of Horse (mansabdar) being in great distress of money, comes to the undermentioned, Mr. Robert Smith, Mr. Thomas Roach, Mr. John White, Mr. William Gates and I John Cambell, telling us that if we would lend him a certain sum he would pawn to us his house in Old Dilly a good pennyworth (valuable).

We having lent him this sum, along comes an old Brahmin once servant to him who buried the riches telling us 'within this house is great treasure which ye, being Xtians may dig, for the Emperor not calling you to account as he would us, should we dig and find he will kill us and all our families. But ye may dig and fear nothing.'

So hearing, we agreed with the Lord Khan to dig giving him one share and each taking one. This house was in Old Dilly, we living in Johnabad (Jehanghirabad, the city of Jehanghir). It is as big as Whitehall and Scotch yard (Scotland Yard) together being built Castle wise and very strong. Then for three months we dug and found nothing for they had built house upon house until in the end we came to near nine fathom deep. In this time two of our labourers were struck dead, some broke arms and legs, others lamed and many hurried out (ran away). Presently the Emperor Aurungzebe hearing of our digging sent word to know what we were about.

To which Thomas Roach replied we were digging for stone to build a house withal, this making colour (a blind) and so that passed. Finding more men we continued one more month digging until finding naught, I John Cambell demanded back my money again. Then said the Lord Jaffir Khan.

'Fear naught. I will bring magicians, and if then we find not, you may again have back your money.'

Then he brought three magicians to whom we shewed how far we had digged. After this they did something we understood not casting spells or what not, and then told us.

'Take up this stone,'

This we did and under it found a great brass pot full of money. Said the magicians.

'Meddle not with this now. Leave it until the next day when we will come again to guard you from the Divells, under whose care it be.'

But we obeyed them not, for which we paid dearly. That night we were very merry judging we had found the prize we sought, until in the middlemost of our mirth there came into the courtyard, which was very great, a vast number of labourers with mattocks, spades, and other digging implements, all of *silver* with which they threw up a great mound for a platform. This done, others came and spread carpets after which came nine seeming men bearing a canopie of state having staves of silver which they set upon the top of the mound. We being struck dumb at such sight, remained silent for the space of one hour.

It being the 12 of then night in came a Great Divell in the shape of man, he sitting in a Golden Chair borne on men's shoulders.

He had over him an umbrella with a Gold Staff and Red silken covering, and with him came many other seeming men attending upon him. At this we were all sadly amazed I John Cambell falling into a swoon but soon recovering. Then all we five Xtians having with us Bibles, fell to reading very seriously keeping in our midst the Lord Khan for fear of the Divell. Seeing this, to us said this Divell:

'Lay by your bibles and give me this man who is my *gholam* (slave).'

We kept silent. Then came a great ill-shaped monster into our midst and tried to hawl away the Lord Khan. On this Mr. Smith, our Minister (Elder of their church) stept out and laying his bible on the Monster, made him give up his hold. Mr. White questioned the Great Divell why came he into our house. On this he answered:

'I am Murteza Ally, now the Governor of this part of the Divells world. What do you Xtians here?'

To which Mr. Roach answered: 'We are here of our right. We gave money for this house.'

Then said the Great Divell: 'Let be get you gone from here and with you your bibles leaving my *gholam*, and you shall have all your money back again and three times more.'

To this answered Mr. Roach: 'We know there is much money here. We shall have all or nothing.'

And so consented Mr. Smith, Mr. White, Mr. Gates and I John Cambell. At these bold answers the great Divell raged furiously and told us:

'Ye may thank Isa Musa (Christ) that I cannot withhold this treasure from you ye being Xtians. But ye shall pay dearly for it in the end!'

(Which said threatening came to pass, for a slave girl belonging to Mr. Roach, discovered to the Emperor that we had been digging for treasure and only by great payments did we come free of trouble.) At last said the Great Divell:

'Take your bible away from the Lord Khan and give him to me. He is my slave.'

But we would not whereon up came another ill shap't Monster who demanded the Lord Khan, saying he had been servant to the Lord Khan who buried the treasure and by him slain to prevent discovery. When we would not yield him he raged, saying furiously:

'Then ye shall have nothing.'

On this Mr. White calling him Divell, demanded his departure whereat he again raged, saying:

'I am no Divell but a poor slave that was killed to guard this treasure. Have a care what you say. Why come you here to cast guns and make war. Get you gone to your own country.'

Then said Mr. Roach: 'We will not go save with this treasure.'

So saying we all commenced to read our bibles aloud. On which they all vanished away leaving us swooning from which we recovered not until the coming of the day. When we had awakened we found at our heads something of that for which we had digged being a Golden Image in the shape of a cow with three strings of jewels hanging from it. This discovery we kept secret, melting the gold down to ingots. The next day, I John Cambell going from my house in Johnabad to Old Dilly, was met by a Divell seeming man, riding on a horse which said to me:

'Go no more to Old Dilly to dig or 'twill be the worse for you,' and vanish't away.

'The same night came the Divells to the house of Mr. Roach wherein was the Lord Khan, and cast both over the walls though no harm done, save to the Lord Khan who was bruised full sore. But they molested none of us after so long as we kept our bibles with us, nor even the Lord Khan after we laid a bible on his chest. So, being warned in such fashion we went to the house no more by night but digged only by day, and the dwelling in a tent without the walls. On one afternoon when so engaged there came the Great Divell without attendance and remained by Mr. Smith reasoning (debating?) for three hours by the clock in which time he came and went three several times. He in this discourse told us that his kind have no manlike feelings nor pain, and said they delight much in guarding treasures and dwelling in great gardens, living in ancient and holy trees. To Mr. Smith he said:

'Why do you give your bible to my people (Mussalmans)? Ye are Xtians. Keep ye to your own religion. Meddle not with that of others.' To which Mr. Smith made reply:

'Our religion is free to all that desire it. Begone thou in the name of the Father, the Son, and the Holy Ghost.'

At this the Great Divell said: 'I am Emperor of Emperors, and have great armies and riches at my command. But I have no power over Xtians. Get you gone to your own country.'

But Mr. Smith, again reading from his bible, said 'Avaunt thee Satan!' At which the Divell gave a great howl and vanish't away, coming no more that day. But in the evening when we were all being merry in the house of Mr. Smith, there came suddenly in a Great Sarpent, the colour of Gold which took three turns on its belly and then vanish't quite away. After that there came in a great number of Divells all in terrible shapes some being seeming Tygers some Lyons and divers, other Monsters, most terrible to behold. But we steadfastly reading in our bibles all this time they made us no harm but presently all vanish't away and came no more leaving us in peace to dig the treasure.

'What we got was great but much more remains. When we had got all we desired we cleared (filled in?) the ruins making a fair Garden for the Great Divell according to promise made by Mr. Smith, which said garden at this day he is still making (1668). But for many days after, Mr. Smith who had most wrestled with the Divell, was sore sick vomiting blood and having no rest at night until he prayed in this wise.'

'God pardon me. I will have no more discourse with Divells', at which he became well again.

"All this happened in the year 1665. The next year Mr. William Gates and the rest went to war in the South, I remaining at Johnabad to cast more guns for the wars. Mr. Gates was killed in the wars with Sivajee, and did afterwards make an appearance to me which I regarded not deeming it a wham (dream). So again, one night when I lay abed about 12 of the night, a Ghost came to my bed and gave me a great blow on the chest saying:

'Arise, Do you not know me?'

At this I was sore afraid and said: 'Get you gone in the name of the Father, the Son, and the Holy Ghost.'

Then said the Ghost: 'I am no Divell but William Gates that lieth dead at Bijapur. Rise you up and follow me or 'twill be the worse for you.'

'Though all the doors were locked yet we passed clear through them the Spirit going before, I following until we had gone about 200 yards. Then staying, it said:

'I have here buried some money and cannot rest until I shew you where it is, Guard you (take heed?)'

And with that he stamp't hard on the ground and so vanish't away. I fell down in a swoon awakening not until next morning at which time I found a stake in the ground at my head I made relation of what had passed to Mr. Smith, after which we both digged at that place and took up an earthen pot in which was much money, put there by Mr. Gates. This we sent to the poor of the parish of Stepmey wherein Mr. Gates was born, which must have pleased the Spirit, for it came no more. I would have kept the money for myself, but Mr. Smith advised otherwise.

In the year 1668, I John Cambell took leave from the Mogul and went on my travels wherein I had much wondrous adventure.

*From Indian State Railways Magazine (April 1933)*

# *The Men-Tigers*

by Lt. Col. W.H. Sleeman

RAM CHUND ROO, COMMONLY CALLED THE SUREEMUNT, chief of Deoree, here overtook me. He came out from Saugor to visit me at Dhamoree, and not reaching that place in time came on after me. He held Deoree under the Peshwa, as the Saugor chief held Saugor, for the payment of the public establishments kept up for the local administration. It yielded him about ten thousand pounds a year, and when we took possession of the country he got an estate in the Saugor district, in rent-free tenure, estimated at fifteen hundred pounds a year. This is equal to about six thousand pounds a year in England. The tastes of native gentlemen lead them always to expend the greater part of their incomes in the wages of trains of followers of all descriptions, and in horses, elephants, & c.; and labour and the subsistence of labour are about four times cheaper in India than in England. By the breaking up of public establishments, and consequent diminution of the local demand for agricultural produce, the value of land throughout all central India, after the termination of the Mahratta war in 1817, fell by degrees thirty per cent.; and among the rest that of my poor friend the Sureemunt. While I had the civil charge of the Saugor district, in 1831, I represented this case of hardship; and government, in the spirit of liberality which has generally characterized their measures in this part of India, made up to him the difference between what he actually received and what they had intended to give him; and he has ever since felt grateful to me. He is a very small man, not more than five feet high; but he has the handsomest face I have almost ever seen; and his manners are those of the most perfect native gentleman. He came to call upon me after breakfast, and the conversation turned upon the number of people that had of late been killed by tigers between Saugor and Deoree, his ancient capital, which lies about midway between Saugor and the Nerbudda river. One of his followers, who stood behind his chair, said, "that when a tiger had killed one man he was safe, for the spirit of the man rode upon his head, and guided him from all danger. The spirit knew very well that the tiger would be watched for many days at the place where he had committed the homicide, and always guided him off to some other more secure place, where he killed other men without any risk to himself. He did not exactly know why the spirit of the man should thus befriend the beast that had killed him; but," added he, "there is a mischief inherent in spirits; and the better the man the more mischievous is his ghost, if means are not taken to put him to rest." This is the popular and general belief throughout India; and it is supposed, that the only sure mode of destroying a tiger, who has killed many people is, to begin by making offerings to the spirits of his victims, and thereby depriving him of their valuable services!* The belief that men are turned into tigers by eating of a root is no less general throughout India.

The Sureemunt, on being asked by me what he thought of the matter, observed, "there was no doubt much truth in what the man said; but he was himself of opinion, that the tigers which now infest the wood from Saugor to Deoree were of a different kind—in fact, that they were neither more nor less than men turned into tigers—a thing which took place in the woods of central India much more often than people were aware of. The only visible difference between the two," added the Sureemunt, "is that the metamorphosed tiger has *no tail*, while the *bora*, or ordinary tiger, has a very long one. In the jungle about Deoree," continued he, "there is a root which, if a man eat of, he is converted into a tiger on the spot; and if in this state he can eat of another, he becomes a man again—a melancholy instance of the former of which," said he, "occurred,

---

* When Agrippina, in her rage with her son Nero, threatens to take her step-son, Britannicus, to the camp of the Legion, and there assert his right to the throne, she invokes the spirit of his father, whom she had poisoned, and the manes of the Silani, whom she had murdered.

I am told, in my own father's family when I was an infant. His washerman, Rughoo, was, like all washermen, a great drunkard; and being seized with a violent desire to ascertain what a man felt in the state of a tiger, he went one day to the jungle and brought home two of these roots, and desired his wife to stand by with one of them, and the instant she saw him assume the tiger's shape, to thrust it into his mouth. She consented, the washerman ate his root, and became instantly a tiger; but his wife was so terrified at the sight of her old husband in this shape, that she ran off with the antidote in her hand. Poor old Rughoo took to the woods, and there ate a good many of his old friends from the neighbouring villages; but he was at last shot and recognized from the circumstance of his *having no tail*. You may be quite sure," concluded Sureemunt, "when you hear of a tiger without a tail, that it is some unfortunate man who has eaten of that root—and of all the tigers he will be found the most mischievous."

How my friend had satisfied himself of the truth of this story I know not, but he religiously believes it, and so do all his attendants and mine; and out of a population of thirty thousand people in the town of Saugor, not one would doubt the story of the washerman if he heard it.

I was one day talking with my friend, the Rajah of Myhere, on the road between Jubbulpore and Mirzapore, on the subject of the number of men who had been lately killed by tigers at the Kutra Pass on that road, and the best means of removing the danger. "Nothing," said the Rajah, "could be more easy or more cheap than the destruction of these tigers, if they were of ordinary sort;

but the tigers that kill men by wholesale, as these do, are, you may be sure, men themselves converted into tigers by the force of their *science*; and such animals are of all the most unmanageable."

"And how is it, Rajah Sahib, that these men convert themselves into tigers?"

"Nothing," said he, "is more easy than this to persons who have once acquired the science; but how they learn it, or what it is, we unlettered men know not. There was once a high priest, of a large temple, in this very valley of Myhere, who was in the habit of getting himself converted into a tiger by the force of this science, which he had thoroughly acquired. He had a necklace, which one of his disciples used to throw over his neck the moment the tiger's form became fully developed. He had, however, long given up the practice, and all his old disciples had gone off on their pilgrimages to distant shrines, when he was one day seized with a violent desire to take his old form of the tiger. He expressed the wish to one of his new disciples, and demanded whether he thought he might rely upon his courage to stand by and put on the necklace. 'Assuredly you may,' said the disciple; 'such is my faith in you, and in the God we serve, that I fear nothing!' The high priest upon this put the necklace into his hand with the requisite instructions, and forthwith began to change his form. The disciple stood trembling in every limb, till he heard him give a roar that shook the whole edifice, when he fell flat upon his face, and dropped the necklace on the floor. The tiger bounded over him, and out at the door; and infested all the roads leading to the temple for many years afterwards."

"Do you think, Rajah Sahib, that the old high priest is one of the tigers at the Kutra Pass?"

"No, I do not; but I think that they may be all men who have become imbued with a little too much of the high priest's *science*—when men once acquire this science they can't help exercising it, though it be to their own ruin and that of others."

"But, supposing them to be ordinary tigers, what is the simple plan you propose to put a stop to their depredations, Rajah Sahib?"

"I propose," said he, "to have the spirits that guide them propitiated by proper prayers and offerings; for the spirit of every man or woman who has been killed by a tiger rides upon his head, or runs before him, and tells him where to go to get prey, and to avoid danger. Get some of the Gonds, or wild people from the jungles, who are well skilled in these matters—give them ten or twenty rupees, and bid them go and raise a small shrine, and there sacrifice to these spirits. The Gonds will tell them that they shall, on this shrine, have regular worship, and good sacrifices of fowls, goats, and pigs, every year at least, if they will but relinquish their offices with the tigers and be quiet. If this is done, I pledge myself," said the Rajah, "that the tigers will soon get killed themselves, or cease from killing men. If they do not, you may be quite sure that they are not ordinary tigers, but men turned into tigers, or that the Gonds have appropriated all you gave them to their own use, instead of applying it to conciliate the spirits of the unfortunate people!"

From *Rambles and Recollections of An Indian Official* by Lt. Col. W.H. Sleeman of the Bengal Army, Vol I.

# *Haunted Villages*

by Lt. Col. W.H. Sleeman

ON THE 16TH, WE CAME ON NINE MILES TO AMABAE, THE frontier village of the Jansee territory, bordering upon Duteea, where I had to receive the farewell visits of many members of the Jansee parties, who came on to have a quiet opportunity to assure me, that whatever may be the final order of the supreme government, they will do their best for the good of the people and the state, in whose welfare I feel great interest, for I have always considered Jansee among the native states of Bundelcund as a kind of oasis in the desert—the only one in which man can accumulate property with the confidence of being permitted by its rulers freely to display and enjoy it. I had also to receive the visit of messengers from the Rajah of Duteea, at whose capital we were to encamp the next day; and finally, to take leave of my amiable little friend the Sureemunt, who here left me on his return to Saugor, with a heavy heart I really believe.

We talked of the common belief among the agricultural classes, of villages being haunted by the spirits of ancient proprietors, whom it was thought necessary to propitiate. "He knew," he said, "many instances where these spirits were so very *froward*, that the present heads of the villages which they haunted, and the members of their little communities, found it almost impossible to keep them in good humour; and their cattle and children were, in consequence, always liable to serious accidents of one kind or another. Sometimes they were bitten by snakes, sometimes became possessed by devils; and at others, were thrown down and beaten most unmercifully." Any person who falls down in an epileptic fit, is supposed to be thrown down by a ghost, or possessed by a devil. They feel little of our mysterious dread of ghosts—a sound *drubbing* is what they dread from them; and he who hurts himself in one of these fits is considered to have got it. "As for himself, whenever he found any one of the villages upon his estate haunted by the spirit of an old patel, (village proprietor,) he always made a point of giving him a *neat little shrine*; and having it well endowed and attended, to keep him in good humour: this he thought was a duty that every landlord owed to his tenants!" Ramchund, the pundit, said, "That villages which had been held by old Gond (mountaineer) proprietors were more liable than any other to those kinds of visitations—that it was easy to say what village was and was not haunted; but often exceedingly difficult to discover to whom the ghost belonged! This once discovered, his nearest surviving relation was, of course, expected to take steps to put him to rest; but," said he, "it is wrong to suppose that the ghost of an old proprietor must be always doing mischief—he is often the best friend of the cultivators, and of the present proprietor, too, if he treats him with proper respect; for he will not allow the people of any other village to encroach upon their boundaries with impunity; and they will be saved all the expense and annoyance of a reference to the Adawlut (judicial tribunals) for the settlement of boundary disputes. It will not cost much to conciliate these spirits; and the money is generally well laid out!"

Several anecdotes were told me in illustration; and all that I could urge against the probability or possibility of such visitations appeared to them very inconclusive and unsatisfactory; they mentioned the case of the family of village proprietors in the Saugor district, who had for several generations, at every new settlement, insisted upon having the name of the spirit of the old proprietor of another tribe inserted in the lease instead of their own, and thereby secured his good graces on all occasions. Mr. Fraser had before mentioned this case to me. In August, 1834, while engaged in the settlement of the land revenue of the Saugor district for twenty years, he was about to deliver the lease of the estate made out in due form to the head of the family, a very honest and respectable old gentleman, when he asked him, respectfully, in whose name it had been made out? "In yours to be sure; have you renewed your lease for twenty years?" The old man, in a state of great alarm, begged him to have it altered immediately, or he and his family would all be destroyed—that the spirit of the ancient proprietor presided over the village community and its interests; and that all affairs of importance were transacted in his name. "He is," said the old man, "a very jealous spirit; and will not admit of any living man being considered, for a moment, as a proprietor or joint proprietor of the estate! It has been held by me and my ancestors immediately under government for many generations; but the lease deeds have always been made out in his name; and ours have been inserted merely as his managers, or bailiffs—were this good old rule, under which we have so long prospered, to be now infringed, we should all perish under his anger." Mr. Fraser found, upon inquiry, that this had really been the case; and, to relieve the old man and his family from their fears, he had the papers made out afresh, and the *ghost* inserted as the proprietor! The modes of flattering and propitiating these beings, natural and supernatural, who are supposed to have the power to do mischief, are endless.

While I was in charge of the district of Nursingpore, in the valley of the Nerbudda, in 1823, a cultivator of the village of Bedoo, about twelve miles distant from my court, was one day engaged in the cultivation of his field on the border of the village of Burkhara, which was supposed to be haunted by the spirit of an old proprietor, whose temper was so froward and violent that the lands could hardly be let for anything; for hardly any man would venture to cultivate them lest he might unintentionally incur his ghostship's displeasure. The poor cultivator, after begging his pardon in secret, ventured to drive his plough a few yards beyond the proper line of his boundary, and thus to add half an acre of the lands of Burkhara to his own little tenement, which was situated in Bedoo. That very night his only son was bitten by a snake, and his two bullocks were seized with the murrain. In terror he went off to the village temple, confessed his sin, and vowed not only to restore the half acre of land to the village of Burkhara, but to build a very handsome shrine upon the spot as a perpetual sign of his repentance. The boy and the bullocks all three recovered, and the shrine was built; and is, I believe, still to be seen as the boundary mark!

The fact was, that the village stood upon and elevated piece of ground rising out of a moist plain, and a colony of snakes had taken up their abode in it. The bites of these snakes had, on many occasions, proved fatal; and such accidents were all attributed to the anger of a spirit, which was supposed to haunt the village. At one time, under the former government, no one would take a lease of the village on any terms; and it had become almost entirely deserted, though the soil was the finest in the whole district. With a view to remove the whole prejudices of the people, the governor, Goroba Pundit, took the lease himself at the rent of one thousand rupees a year; and in the month of June went from his residence, twelve miles, with ten of his own ploughs, to superintend the commencement of so *perilous* an undertaking. On reaching the middle of the village, situated on the top of the little hill, he alighted from his horse, sat down upon a carpet that had been spread for him under a large and beautiful banyan tree, and began to refresh himself with a pipe before going to work in the fields.

As he quaffed his hookah, and railed at the follies of men, "whose absurd superstitions had made them desert so beautiful a village with so noble a tree in its centre," his eyes fell upon an enormous black snake which had coiled round one of its branches immediately over his head, and seemed as if resolved at once to pounce down and punish him for his blasphemy! He gave his pipe to his attendant, mounted his horse, from which the saddle had not yet been taken, and never pulled rein till he got home. Nothing could ever induce him to visit this village again, though he was afterwards employed under me as a native collector; and he has often told me, that he verily believed this was the spirit of the old landlord that he had unhappily neglected to propitiate before taking possession!

My predecessor in the civil charge of that district, the late Mr. Lindsay, of the Bengal civil service, again tried to remove the prejudices of the people against the occupation and cultivation of this fine village. It had never been measured; and all the revenue officers, backed by all the farmers and cultivators of the neighbourhood, declared that the spirit of the old proprietor would never allow it to be so. Mr. Lindsay was a good geometrician, and had long been in the habit of superintending his revenue surveys himself; and on this occasion he thought himself particularly called upon to do so. A new measuring cord was made for the occasion, and with fear and trembling all his officers attended him to the first field; but in measuring it the rope, by some accident, broke! Poor Lindsay was that morning taken ill, and obliged to return to Nursingpore, where he died soon after from fever. No man was ever more beloved by all classes of the people of his district than he was; and I believe there was not one person among them who did not believe him to have fallen a victim to the resentment of the spirit of the old proprietor. When I went to the village some years afterwards, the people in the neighbourhood all declared to me, that they saw the cord with which he was measuring, fly into a thousand pieces the moment the men attempted to straighten it over the first field.

A very respectable old gentleman from the Concan, or Malabar coast, told me one day, that every man there protects his field of corn and his fruit tree by dedicating it to one or other of the spirits which there abound, or confiding it to his guardianship. He sticks up something in the field, or ties on something to the tree, in the name of the said spirit, who from that moment feels himself responsible for its safe keeping. If any one, without permission from the proprietor, presumes to take either an ear of corn from the field, or fruit from the tree, he is sure to be killed outright or made extremely ill. "No other protection is required," said the old gentleman, "for our fields and fruit trees in that direction, though whole armies should have to march through them. I once saw a man come to the proprietor of a jack tree, embrace his feet, and in the most piteous manner implore his protection. He asked what was the matter. 'I took,' said the man, 'a jack from your tree yonder three days ago, as I passed at night; and I have been suffering dreadful agony in my stomach ever since. The spirit of the tree is upon me, and you only can pacify him.' The proprietor took up a bit of cow-dung, moistened it, and made a mark with it upon the man's forehead *in the name of the spirit*, and put some of it into the knot of hair on the top of his head. He had no sooner done this, than the man's pains all left him, and he went off, vowing never again to give similar cause of offence to one of these guardian spirits."

"Men," said my old friend, "do not die there in the same regulated spirit, with their thoughts directed exclusively towards God, as in other parts; and whether a man's spirit is to haunt the world or not after his death all depends on that."

From *Rambles and Recollections of An Indian Official* by Lt. Col. W.H. Sleeman of the Bengal Army, Vol I.

## *The Return of Imray*

by Rudyard Kipling

IMRAY ACHIEVED THE IMPOSSIBLE. WITHOUT WARNING, FOR no conceivable motive, in his youth, at the threshold of his career, he chose to disappear from the world—which is to say, the little Indian station where he lived.

Upon a day he was alive, well, happy, and in great evidence among the billiard tables at his Club. Upon a morning he was not, and no manner of search could make sure where he might be. He had stepped out of his place; he had not appeared at his office at the proper time, and his dogcart was not upon the public roads. For these reasons, and because he was hampering, in a microscopical degree, the administration of the Indian Empire, that Empire paused for one microscopical moment to make inquiry into the fate of Imray. Ponds were dragged, wells were plumbed, telegrams were dispatched down the lines of railways and to the nearest seaport town—twelve hundred miles away; but Imray was not at the end of the drag-ropes nor the telegraph wires. He was gone, and his place knew him no more. Then the work of the great Indian Empire swept forward, because it could not be delayed, and Imray from being a man became a mystery—such a thing as men talk over at their tables in the Club for a month, and then forget utterly. His guns, horses, and carts were sold to the highest bidder. His superior officer wrote an altogether absurd letter to his mother, saying that Imray had unaccountably disappeared, and his bungalow stood empty.

After three or four months of the scorching hot weather had gone by, my friend Strickland, of the Police, saw fit to rent the bungalow from the native landlord. This was before he was engaged to Miss Youghal—an affair which has been described in another place—and while he was pursuing his investigations into native life. His own life was sufficiently peculiar, and men complained of his manners and customs. There was always food in his house, but there were no regular times for meals. He ate, standing up and walking about, whatever he might find at the sideboard, and this is not good for human beings. His domestic equipment was limited to six rifles, three shot-guns, five saddles, and a collection of stiff-jointed mahseer-rods, bigger and stronger than the largest salmon-rods. These occupied one-half of his bungalow, and the other half was given up to Strickland and his dog Tietjens—an enormous Rampur slut who devoured daily the rations of two men. She spoke to Strickland in a language of her own; and whenever, walking abroad, she saw things calculated to destroy the peace of Her Majesty the Queen-Empress, she returned to her master and laid information. Strickland would take steps at once, and the end of his labours was trouble and fine and imprisonment for other people. The natives believed that Tietjens was a familiar spirit, and treated her with the great reverence that is born of hate and fear. One room in the bungalow was set apart for her special use. She owned a bedstead, a blanket, and a drinking-trough, and if anyone came into Strickland's room at night her custom was to knock down the invader and give tongue till someone came with a light. Strickland owed his life to her when he was on the Frontier in search of a local murderer, who came in the grey dawn to send Strickland much farther than the Andaman Islands. Tietjens caught the man as he was crawling into Strickland's tent with a dagger between his teeth; and after his record of iniquity was established in the eyes of the law he was hanged. From that date Tietjens wore a collar of rough silver, and employed a monogram on her night blanket; and the blanket was of double woven Kashmir cloth, for she was a delicate dog.

Under no circumstances would she be separated from Strickland; and once, when he was ill with fever, made great trouble for the doctors, because she did not know how to help her master and would not allow another creature to attempt aid. Macarnaght, of the Indian Medical Service, beat her over her head with a gun-butt before she could understand that she must give room for those who could give quinine.

A short time after Strickland had taken Imray's bungalow, my business took me through that Station, and naturally, the Club quarters being full, I quartered myself upon Strickland. It was a desirable bungalow, eight-roomed and heavily thatched against any chance of leakage from rain. Under the pitch of the roof ran a ceiling-cloth which looked just as neat as a whitewashed ceiling. The landlord had repainted it when Strickland took the bungalow. Unless you knew how Indian bungalows were built you would never have suspected that above the cloth lay the dark three-cornered cavern of the roof, where the beams and the underside of the thatch harboured all manner of rats, bats, ants, and foul things.

Tietjens met me in the verandah with a bay like the boom of the bell of St Paul's, putting her paws on my shoulder to show she was glad to see me. Strickland had contrived to claw together a sort of meal which he called lunch, and immediately after it was finished went out about his business. I was left alone with Tietjens and my own affairs. The heat of the summer had broken up and turned to the warm damp of the rains. There was no motion in the heated air, but the rain fell like ramrods on the earth, and flung up a blue mist when it splashed back. The bamboo, and the custard apples, the poinsettias, and the mango trees in the garden stood still while the warm water lashed through them, and the frogs began to sing among the aloe hedges. A little before the light failed, and when the rain was at its worst, I sat in the back verandah and heard the water roar from the eaves, and scratched myself because I was covered with the thing called prickly heat. Tietjens came out with me and put her head in my lap and was very sorrowful; so I gave her biscuits when tea was ready, and I took tea in the back verandah on account of the little coolness found there. The rooms of the house were dark behind me. I could smell Strickland's saddlery and the oil on his guns, and I had no desire to sit among these things. My own servant came to me in the twilight, the muslin of his clothes clinging tightly to his drenched body, and told me that a gentleman had called and wished to see someone. Very much against my will, but only because of the darkness of the rooms, I went into the naked drawing-room, telling my man to bring the lights. There might or might not have been a caller waiting—it seemed to me that I saw a figure by one of the windows—but when the lights came there was nothing save the spikes of the rain without, and the smell of the drinking earth in my nostrils. I explained to my servant that he was no wiser than he ought to be, and went back to the verandah to talk to Tietjens. She had gone out into the wet, and I could hardly coax her back to me, even with biscuits with sugar tops. Strickland came home, dripping wet, just before dinner, and the first thing he said was:

'Has anyone called?'

I explained, with apologies, that my servant had summoned me into the drawing-room on a false alarm; or that some loafer had tried to call on Strickland, and thinking better of it, had fled after giving his name. Strickland ordered dinner, without comment, and since it was a real dinner with a white tablecloth attached, we sat down.

At nine o'clock Strickland wanted to go to bed, and I was tired too. Tietjens, who had been lying underneath the table, rose up, and swung into the least exposed verandah as soon as her master moved to his own room, which was next to the stately chamber set apart for Tietjens. If a mere wife had wished to sleep out of doors in that pelting rain it would not have mattered; but Tietjens was a dog, and therefore the better animal. I looked at Strickland, expecting to see him flay her with a whip. He smiled queerly, as a man would smile after telling some unpleasant domestic tragedy. 'She has done this ever since I moved in here,' said he. 'Let her go.'

The dog was Strickland's dog, so I said nothing, but I felt all that Strickland felt in being thus made light of. Tietjens encamped outside my bedroom window, and storm after storm came up, thundered on the thatch, and died away. The lightning spattered the sky as a thrown egg spatters a barn door, but the light was pale blue, not yellow; and, looking through my split bamboo blinds, I could see the great dog standing, not sleeping, in the verandah, the hackles alift on her back and her feet anchored as tensely as the drawn wire-rope of a suspension bridge. In the very short pauses of the thunder I tried to sleep, but it seemed that someone wanted me very urgently. He, whoever he was, was trying to call me by name, but his voice was no more than a husky whisper. The thunder ceased, and Tietjens went into the garden and howled at the low moon. Somebody tried to open my door, walked about and about through the house, and stood breathing heavily in the verandahs, and just when I was falling asleep I fancied that I heard a wild hammering and clamouring above my head or on the door.

I ran into Strickland's room and asked him whether he was ill, and had been calling me. He was lying on his bed half dressed, a pipe in his mouth. 'I thought you'd come,' he said. 'Have I been walking round the house recently?'

I explained that he had been tramping in the dining-room and the smoking-room and two or three other places, and he laughed and told me to go back to bed. I went back to bed and slept till the morning, but through all my mixed dreams I was sure I was doing someone an injustice in not attending to his wants. What those wants were I could not tell; but a fluttering, whispering, bolt-fumbling, lurking, loitering someone was reproaching me for my slackness, and, half awake, I heard the howling of Tietjens in the garden and the threshing of the rain.

I lived in that house for two days. Strickland went to his office daily, leaving me alone for eight or ten hours with Tietjens for my only companion. As long as the full light lasted I was comfortable, and so was Tietjens; but in the twilight she and I moved into the back verandah and cuddled each other for company. We were alone in the house, but none the less it was much too fully occupied by a tenant with whom I did not wish to interfere. I never saw him, but I could see the curtains between the rooms quivering where he had just passed through; I could hear the chairs creaking as the bamboos sprung under a weight that had just quitted them; and I could feel when I went to get a book from the dining-room that somebody was waiting in the shadows of the front verandah till I should have gone away. Tietjens made the twilight more interesting by glaring into the darkened rooms with every hair erect, and following the motions of something that I could not see. She never entered the rooms, but her eyes moved interestedly: that was quite sufficient. Only when my servant came to trim the lamps and make all light and habitable she would come in with me and spend her time sitting on her haunches, watching an invisible extra man as he moved about behind my shoulder. Dogs are cheerful companions.

I explained to Strickland, gently as might be, that I would go over to the Club and find for myself quarters there. I admired his hospitality, was pleased with his guns and rods, but I did not much care for his house and its atmosphere. He heard me out to the end, and then smiled very wearily, but without contempt, for he is a man who understands things. 'Stay on,' he said, 'and see what this thing means. All you have talked about I have known since I took the bungalow. Stay on and wait. Tietjens has left me. Are you going too?'

I had seen him through one little affair, connected with a heathen idol, that had brought me to the doors of a lunatic asylum, and I had no desire to help him through further experiences. He was a man to whom unpleasantness arrived as do dinners to ordinary people.

Therefore I explained more clearly than ever that I liked him immensely, and would be happy to see him in the daytime; but that I did not care to sleep under his roof. This was after dinner, when Tietjens had gone out to lie in the verandah.

'Pon my soul, I don't wonder,' said Strickland, with his eyes on the ceiling-cloth. 'Look at that!'

The tails of two brown snakes were hanging between the cloth and the cornice of the wall. They threw long shadows in the lamp-light.

'If you are afraid of snakes, of course —' said Strickland.

I hate and fear snakes, because if you look into the eyes of any snake you will see that it knows all and more of the mystery of man's fall, and that it feels all the contempt that the Devil felt when Adam was evicted from Eden. Besides which its bite is generally fatal, and it twists up trouser legs.

'You ought to get your thatch overhauled,' I said. 'Give me a mahseer-rod, and we'll poke 'em down.'

'They'll hide among the roof-beams,' said Strickland. 'I can't stand snakes overhead. I'm going up into the roof. If I shake 'em down, stand by with a cleaning-rod and break their backs.'

I was not anxious to assist Strickland in his work, but I took the cleaning-rod and waited in the dining-room, while Strickland brought a gardener's ladder from the verandah, and set it against the side of the room. The snake-tails drew themselves up and disappeared. We could hear the dry rushing scuttle of long bodies running over the baggy ceiling-cloth. Strickland took a lamp with him, while I tried to make clear to him the danger of hunting roof-snakes between a ceiling-cloth and a thatch, apart from the deterioration of property caused by ripping out ceiling-cloths.

'Nonsense!' said Strickland. 'They're sure to hide near the walls by the cloth. The bricks are too cold for 'em, and the heat of the room is just what they like.' He put his hand to the corner of the stuff and ripped it from the cornice. It gave with a great sound of tearing, and Strickland put his head through the opening into the dark of the angle of the roof-beams. I set my teeth and lifted the rod, for I had not the least knowledge of what might descend.

'H'm!' said Strickland, and his voice rolled and rumbled in the roof. 'There's room for another set of rooms up here, and, by Jove, someone is occupying 'em!'

'Snakes?' I said from below.

'No. It's a buffalo. Hand me up the two last joints of a mahseer-rod, and I'll prod it. It's lying on the main roof-beam.'

I handed up the rod.

'What a nest for owls and serpents! No wonder the snakes live here,' said Strickland, climbing farther into the roof. I could see his elbow thrusting with the rod. 'Come out of that, whoever you are! Heads below there! It's falling.'

I saw the ceiling-cloth nearly in the centre of the room sag with a shape that was pressing it downwards and downwards towards the lighted lamp on the table. I snatched the lamp out of danger and stood back. Then the cloth ripped out from the walls, tore, split, swayed, and shot down upon the table something that I dared not look at, till Strickland had slid down the ladder and was standing by my side.

He did not say much, being a man of few words; but he picked up the loose end of the tablecloth and threw it over the remnants on the table.

'It strikes me,' said he, putting down the lamp, 'our friend Imray has come back. Oh! you would, would you?'

There was a movement under the cloth, and a little snake wriggled out, to be back-broken by the butt of the mahseer-rod. I was sufficiently sick to make no remarks worth recording.

Strickland meditated, and helped himself to drinks. The arrangement under the cloth made no more signs of life.

'Is it Imray?' I said.

Strickland turned back the cloth for a moment, and looked.

'It is Imray,' he said; 'and his throat is cut from ear to ear.'

Then we spoke, both together and to ourselves: 'That's why he whispered about the house.'

Tietjens, in the garden, began to bay furiously. A little later her great nose heaved open the dining-room door.

She sniffed and was still. The tattered ceiling-cloth hung down almost to the level of the table, and there was hardly room to move away from the discovery.

Tietjens came in and sat down; her teeth bared under her lip and her forepaws planted. She looked at Strickland.

'It's a bad business, old lady,' said he.'Men don't climb up into the roofs of their bungalows to die, and they don't fasten up the ceiling-cloth behind 'em. Let's think it out.'

'Let's think it out somewhere else,' I said.

'Excellent idea! Turn the lamps out. We'll get into my room.'

I did not turn the lamps out. I went into Strickland's room first, and allowed him to make the darkness. Then he followed me, and we lit tobacco and thought. Strickland thought. I smoked furiously, because I was afraid.

'Imray is back,' said Strickland. 'The question is—who killed Imray? Don't talk, I've a notion of my own. When I took this bungalow I took over most of Imray's servants. Imray was guileless and inoffensive, wasn't he?'

I agreed; though the heap under the cloth had looked neither one thing nor the other.

'If I call in all the servants they will stand fast in a crowd and lie like Aryans. What do you suggest?'

'Call 'em in one by one,' I said.

'They'll run away and give the news to all their fellows,' said Strickland.

'We must segregate 'em. Do you suppose your servant knows anything about it?'

He may, for aught I know; but I don't think it's likely. He has only been here two or three days,' I answered. 'What's your notion?'

'I can't quite tell. How the dickens did the man get the wrong side of the ceiling-cloth?'

There was a heavy coughing outside Strickland's bedroom door. This showed that Bahadur Khan, his body servant, had waked from sleep and wished to put Strickland to bed.

'Come in,' said Strickland. 'It's a very warm night, isn't it?'

Bahadur Khan, a great, green-turbaned, six-foot Mohammedan, said that it was a very warm night; but that there was more rain pending, which, by his Honour's favour, would bring relief to the country.

'It will be so, if God pleases,' said Strickland, tugging off his boots. 'It is in my mind, Bahadur Khan, that I have worked thee remorselessly for many days—ever since that time when thou first earnest into my service. What time was that?'

'Has the Heaven-born forgotten? It was when Imray Sahib went secretly to Europe without warning given; and I—even I—came into the honoured service of the protector of the poor.'

'And Imray Sahib went to Europe?'

'It is so said among those who were his servants.'

'And thou wilt take service with him when he returns?'

'Assuredly, Sahib. He was a good master, and cherished his dependants.'

'That is true. I am very tired, but I go buck-shooting tomorrow. Give me the little Sharp rifle that I use for black-buck; it is in the case yonder.'

The man stooped over the case; handed barrels, stock, and fore-end to Strickland, who fitted all together, yawning dolefully. Then he reached down to the gun-case, took a solid-drawn cartridge, and slipped it into the breech of the .360 Express.

'And Imray Sahib has gone to Europe secretly! That is very strange, Bahadur Khan, is it not?'

'What do I know of the ways of the white man, Heaven born?'

'Very little, truly. But thou shalt know more anon. It has reached me that Imray Sahib has returned from his so long journeyings, and that even now he lies in the next room, waiting his servant.'

'Sahib!'

The lamplights slid along the barrels of the rifle as they levelled themselves at Bahadur Khan's broad breast.

'Go and look!' said Strickland. 'Take a lamp. Thy master is tired, and he waits thee. Go!'

The man picked up a lamp, and went into the dining-room, Strickland following, and almost pushing him with the muzzle of the rifle. He looked for a moment at the black depths behind the ceiling-cloth; at the writhing snake under foot; and last, a grey glaze settling on his face, at the thing under the tablecloth.

'Hast thou seen?' said Strickland after a pause.

'I have seen. I am clay in the white man's hands. What does the Presence do?'

'Hang thee within the month. What else?'

'For killing him? Nay, Sahib, consider. Walking among us, his servants, he cast his eyes upon my child, who was four years old. Him he bewitched, and in ten days he died of the fever—my child!'

'What said Imray Sahib?'

He said he was a handsome child, and patted him on the head; wherefore my child died. Wherefore I killed Imray Sahib in the twilight, when he had come back from office, and was sleeping. Wherefore I dragged him up into the roof-beams and made all fast behind him. The Heaven-born knows all things. I am the servant of the Heaven-born.'

Strickland looked at me above the rifle, and said, in the vernacular, 'Thou art witness to this saying? He has killed.'

Bahadur Khan stood ashen grey in the light of the one lamp. The need for justification came upon him very swiftly. 'I am trapped,' he said, 'but the offence was that man's. He cast an evil eye upon my child, and I killed and hid him. Only such as are served by devils,' he glared at Tietjens, couched stolidly before him, 'only such could know what I did.'

'It was clever. But thou shouldst have lashed him to the beam with a rope. Now, thou thyself wilt hang by a rope. Orderly!'

A drowsy policeman answered Strickland's call. He was followed by another, and Tietjens sat wondrous still.

'Take him to the police station,' said Strickland. 'There is a case toward.'

'Do I hang, then?' said Bahadur Khan, making no attempt to escape, and keeping his eyes on the ground.

'If the sun shines or the water runs—yes!' said Strickland.

Bahadur Khan stepped back one long pace, quivered, and stood still. The two policemen waited further orders.

'Go!' said Strickland.

'Nay; but I go very swiftly,' said Bahadur Khan. 'Look! I am even now a dead man.'

He lifted his foot, and to the little toe there clung the head of the half-killed snake, firm fixed in the agony of death.

'I come of land-holding stock,' said Bahadur Khan, rocking where he stood. 'It were a disgrace to me to go to the public scaffold: therefore I take this way. Be it remembered that the Sahib's shirts are correctly enumerated, and that there is an extra piece of soap in his wash-basin. My child was bewitched, and I slew the wizard. Why should you seek to slay me with the rope? My honour is saved, and—and—I die.'

At the end of an hour he died, as they die who are bitten by a little brown *karait,* and the policemen bore him and the thing under the tablecloth to their appointed places. All were needed to make clear the disappearance of Imray.

'This,' said Strickland, very calmly, as he climbed into bed, 'is called the nineteenth century. Did you hear what the man said?'

'I heard,' I answered. 'Imray made a mistake.'

'Simply and solely through not knowing the nature of the Oriental, and the coincidence of a little seasonal fever. Bahadur Khan had been with him for four years.'

I shuddered. My own servant had been with me for exactly that length of time. When I went over to my own room I found my man waiting, impassive as the copper head on a penny, to pull off my boots.

'What has befallen Bahadur Khan' said I.

He was bitten by a snake and died. The rest the Sahib knows,' was the answer.

'And how much of this matter hast thou known?'

'As much as might be gathered from One coming in in the twilight to seek satisfaction. Gently, Sahib. Let me pull off those boots.'

I had just settled to the sleep of exhaustion when I heard Strickland shouting from his side of the house—

'Tietjens has come back to her place!'

And so she had. The great deerhound was couched statelily on her own bedstead on her own blanket, while, in the next room, the idle, empty ceiling-cloth waggled as it trailed on the table.

# *The Summoning of Arnold*

by Alice Perrin

ONE OF THE MANY LESSONS THAT THE GREAT MOTHER India instils into the hearts of her white foster children is to sympathise with one another's troubles and misfortunes however trivial or however serious.

Therefore, when Mrs. Arnold, the Collector's wife at Usapore, was suddenly ordered home by the doctor, and Arnold could not get leave to go with her, it was sympathy with the husband's lonely unhappiness that made Williamson offer to move over to Arnold's bungalow and see him through the weary separation.

The offer was gratefully accepted, for the Arnolds had not been married long, and the man was missing his wife, and worrying about her ill-health to the verge of melancholia. So Williamson established himself in one half of the large, echoing bungalow, though there was no doubt that the move was somewhat inconvenient to himself! in fact, he admitted as much to me afterwards, when he was telling me of the horrible thing that happened while he was there.

But, being a thoroughly unselfish, good-hearted fellow, he thought little of his own inclinations and only endeavoured to prove a cheery companion, and help the other on from one English mail day to the other.

Arnold simply lived for the mail, and yet when his wife's letters did come he would be almost afraid to open them, in case she might be worse, or anything bad had happened. Williamson sometimes found it very difficult to keep his friend's spirits up to the mark, circumstances being unfavourable from every point of view. To begin with, Arnold himself was not in the best possible health, having had typhoid fever the previous year; he had the work of a large and turbulent district on his shoulders, no light burden; Usapore itself was a dismal, sandy little civil station; and, to crown it all, there seemed every prospect of the rains failing (which would mean a famine), and the heat was already beyond description.

However, the two men played mild tennis in the afternoons and whist in the baking little club in the evenings, and when they were alone they talked about Mrs. Arnold's last letter, and Arnold read bits of it aloud to Williamson, and always wound up by groaning over ' his infernal luck.'

'Why didn't I take leave six months ago when I could have got it?' he would reiterate; 'and then Lilla wouldn't have been ill, and

I should not have felt such a worm myself. But I hung on to escape the hot weather. I've never felt really fit since I had typhoid, and I believe it has played the dickens with my heart. And then this anxiety about Lilla is simply driving me mad. I'm in such a funk that she makes light of things not to worry me, and doesn't tell me what the doctors really say.'

But, in spite of these forebodings, Mrs. Arnold's letters continued to be very fairly satisfactory. She declared that she was better, that the air of Dover, where she was staying with her mother, was certainly doing her good, and the doctor hoped that in a few weeks she might be able to drop the *rôle* of invalid.

This sort of thing went on for several mails, and sometimes Arnold was in boisterous spirits, looking forward to his wife's return with the advent of the cold weather, while at others he plunged into the lowest depths of depression.

Then at last, one fatal evening, the English mail brought a letter from Mrs. Arnold saying that directly she could bear the move she was to go up to London to see a specialist. She besought her husband not to be anxious, the only reason for such a step being, she assured him, that the doctor thought she gained strength too slowly, and that, on the whole, it would be wiser to have the best advice.

Of course Arnold was in despair. That night, after eating no dinner, he sat outside on the plot of scorched grass in front of the house and surrendered himself to the gloomiest of views; and when bed-time came he refused to go in, saying he knew he should not sleep.

So Williamson lit another pipe and made up his mind to stay there too because it was the kind of night in India when, if a man is not happy, he probably begins to wander about the compound with a revolver to shoot pariah dogs that bark and keep him awake, and sometimes, instead of a dead dog, it is the man who is found shot, through the roof of his mouth. So Williamson watched Arnold very carefully, and tried to induce him to talk instead of sitting huddled up in his chair, with his hands hanging down at his sides.

'Buck up, old man!' he said encouragingly. 'If there'd been any bad news you would have had a telegram.'

'She may not have seen the London man yet,' replied Arnold. 'She said in her letter she thought it would be a fortnight before she could go.'

'Well, it's more than a fortnight since that letter was written. You look at the black side of things too much. Besides,' he added awkwardly, 'she wouldn't like it if she could see you now, Arnold. You know her one wish is that you shouldn't worry.'

Arnold straightened himself wearily.

'I know, I know,' he said, as if ashamed of his weakness. 'But when you care about a woman with all your heart and soul, Williamson, it's hell when you think there's any danger of losing her. Lilla is everything in the universe to me, and the parting from her was awful—our first parting! I wonder how a man manages to live out his life if his wife dies and he was really devoted to her—' He paused, and there was a dreamy silence, broken presently by the harsh scream of the brain fever bird rising to a desperate pitch and then subsiding.

'You'll laugh, perhaps, when I tell you,' he went on hesitatingly; 'but when she left me she said that if she died she would come straight to me first, and I gave her the same promise on my side. If anything happens to Lilla she will come herself and tell me. She will come and fetch me. I believe this with every atom of my being.'

❖

Williamson did not laugh. He felt a little cold thrill run down his back, and actually caught himself looking nervously over his shoulder. He was not a superstitious man by any means, but Arnold's voice sounded so unnatural; the surroundings looked so weird in the increasing light of the rising moon, which threw the long black shadow of a clump of bamboos across the dried-up patch of uneven grass; and the magnetic stillness in the thick, hot atmosphere was severed at intervals by the desperate cry of the brain fever bird, as it flew restlessly from tree to tree.

Williamson mentally called himself an ass. 'You'd better go to bed, Arnold,' he said bluntly; ' and if you apply for sick leave I'm sure you'd get it.'

Arnold laughed a little.

'Oh, I'm all right,' he said, 'and with a famine coming on I can't well ask for leave unless I'm actually too ill to work, which I'm not, and I don't think any doctor could honestly give me a certificate.'

Williamson thought otherwise, and determined to speak to the civil surgeon the next morning. In the meantime it was midnight, and if Arnold would only go to bed so much the better for them both.

'Come along,' he urged; 'you'll sleep all right if you go to bed now. The air will cool down very soon.'

They rose and went to their rooms, and shortly afterwards no sound was to be heard in the house or compound but the monotonous cry of the bird that would not rest.

Williamson undressed and threw himself on his bed. He listened at first to satisfy himself that Arnold was not moving about, and once he got up and crept to his friend's door, but there was only silence, so he went back to his room, and presently fell into an uneasy sleep.

An hour or two later he was suddenly awakened by the loud sound of a voice calling. He sat up, the echo of what he had heard still ringing in his ears : '*Lilla! Lilla!*' He could only conclude that Arnold had been shouting his wife's name in his sleep, so he waited a few moments, and the brain fever bird's discordant shriek rose and fell in the air. Perhaps that was what had disturbed him, the cry was not unlike the two syllables repeated over and over again.

He listened intently, and finally got up. He put on his slippers, and, taking his hand lamp, made his way to Arnold's open door. He did not speak, for if Arnold were asleep, it would never do to wake him, but he moved the curtain quietly to one side and looked into the room.

The punkah was swaying slowly to and fro, and Arnold was lying on his back, covered with a sheet. He seemed all right, but still Williamson was not quite satisfied. He carefully advanced, then stopped and looked apprehensively about him, sniffing the air, for it was full of a strong and unmistakable odour of chloroform.

The fear seized him that Arnold had committed suicide, and he hurried to the bedside. The smell of chloroform was overpowering, and, half choked with the fumes, he shouted at Arnold, and shook him desperately. There was no movement, no response. Faint and giddy, he rushed from the room, roused the servants and sent for the doctor, who, when he came, confirmed Williamson's fear, and said that Arnold was dead.

'Where is the bottle?' he said, when all restoratives had failed and hope was at an end.

'I couldn't see any bottle,' said Williamson, feeling as though he were in a nightmare. 'I looked, but I couldn't see anything. The smell was awful when I came into the room, and only a few minutes before I could have sworn I heard him shouting in his sleep. That was what woke me. It must have been hideously quick work.'

'It would have been,' said the doctor; 'his heart was so weak, it would not have taken very much to kill him.'

'Then you ought to have made him go on sick leave.'

'I suggested it when his ordinary leave was refused, but he said he wasn't bad enough, and I don't know that he was, if he had let himself alone. And then, with the prospect of a famine, a man can't conscientiously bolt unless he's in a hopeless way;' then, after a pause—'Had he a medicine chest anywhere?'

'I don't think so, but we'll look.' They looked, but found nothing, and they also questioned the punkah-coolie, who could give them no information beyond the fact that he had fallen asleep, and he thought the sahib had shouted to wake him.

So the doctor said it was one of those mysteries which would probably never be explained. Arnold had certainly killed himself with chloroform, but had taken some extraordinary precaution beforehand that the bottle should not be discovered.

But early next morning a telegram came from London for Arnold, which was opened by Williamson and the doctor. It told them that Mrs. Arnold had died while under chloroform, during an operation that had proved absolutely necessary.

'There !' cried Williamson, losing all self-control and beating his hands together like a maniac. ' That explains it! That's why there was no bottle—no trace of one! She came to fetch him—he said she would! He told me so only a few hours before. Oh! my God!'—and he sank into a chair, shuddering and shaking.

The doctor fetched some brandy.

'My dear fellow!' he said soothingly, 'pull yourself together. You're over-strung. Drink this and go and get some sleep, or I shall be sending you home on sick leave next.' Which he afterwards had to do, for Williamson was very ill, and for some weeks it was doubtful whether he would get over it. But he did recover, and was sent home, and just before he sailed he told me this story.

From *East of Suez* (1926)

# *Chunia, Ayah*

by Alice Perrin

'I HOPE YOU CLEARLY UNDERSTAND THAT I DO NOT BELIEVE in ghosts?'

The little grey-haired spinster paused and regarded me with suspicion, and, alarmed lest I should, after all, lose the story I had been so carefully stalking, I vehemently reassured her on the point, whereupon, to my relief, she continued,—

'It certainly was a most extraordinary thing, and even now I hardly know what to make of it, though it happened a long time ago. One cold weather when I was in India keeping house for my brother, I received a letter from a friend, begging me to pay her a long-promised visit. She wrote that her husband was going into camp for a month to a part of his district where she could not accompany him, so that she and her little girl would be all alone, and I should be doing her a great kindness by coming. So the end of it was I accepted the invitation, though I greatly disliked leaving my brother to the tender mercies of the servants, and after a long, hot journey arrived at my destination at five o'clock one evening.

'My friend, Mrs. Pollock, was on the platform to meet me, and outside the station a bamboo cart was waiting, into which we climbed, and were soon bowling along the hard, white road at a brisk pace. Mary at once began to relate anecdotes of her little girl, whose name was Dot—how tall she was for her age (twenty months!), how much she ate, what she tried to say, what the ayah said about her, and so on.

'Now I must confess that I am not very fond of children; I like them well enough in their proper place (if that is not too near me), but I do not know how to behave towards them, and am always nervous as to what they will do or say next. Therefore, fond as I was of Mary herself, the subject of her conversation did not particularly interest me. When we arrived at the house, she actually inquired which I would do first—see Dot or have some tea! I boldly elected for tea, as I was exceedingly tired and thirsty, and I also reflected that if I did not at once make a determined stand, I should be Dot-ridden for the remainder of my visit.

'After tea I was taken to my room, and Mary brought her treasure to me for exhibition. She was the most lovely child I had ever beheld, with a grave, sweet face that quite won my unmotherly heart, and for once my prejudices completely melted away. Mary put her into my arms and stood by in an ecstacy of pride and delight as I proceeded to tap the pin-cushion, rattle my keys and perform various idiotic antics in my efforts to amuse Dot, who, I felt sure, would set up a howl in a few moments. But she watched my foolish attempts to be entertaining with an attentive gravity that was quite embarrassing, and charmed though I was with the little creature, I felt relieved when she held out her arms to go back to her mother.

'Mary called for the ayah to come and take the child to her nursery, and a woman with a sullen, handsome face entered and took her charge away. I remarked that the ayah looked bad-tempered, upon which Mary assured me that she could trust the child anywhere with her, and that she was a perfect treasure.

'The next morning I was awakened by a soft little pat on my face, and, opening my eyes, I found Dot holding herself upright by the corner, of my pillow.

'"Why, little one, are you all alone?" I said, lifting her on to the bed, and then I discovered that her feet were wringing wet.

'She held up one wet little foot and examined it carefully, and then pointed to the bathroom door, which was open, and from where I lay I could see an over-turned jug and streams of water on the floor—evidently Dot's handiwork. I put on my dressing-gown and took the child to her mother, explaining what had happened, and Mary hastily pulled off the soaking little shoes and socks and called for the ayah, who presently entered, and stood silently watching her mistress.

'"What do you mean by leaving the child in this way?" exclaimed Mary, angrily, and gathering up Dot's shoes and socks, she threw them to the ayah, bidding her bring others that were dry. One of the little shoes struck the woman on the cheek, for Mary was annoyed and had flung them with unnecessary force, and never shall I forget the look on the ayah's face as she left the room to carry out the order. It was the face of a devil, but Mary did not see it, for she was busy rubbing the cold little feet in her hands.

'"Mary," I said impulsively, "I am sure the ayah is a brute. Do get rid of her. I never saw anything so dreadful as the look she gave you just now."

'"My dear," answered Mary, with good-humoured impatience, "you have taken an unreasonable dislike to Chunia. She knew she was in the wrong and felt ashamed of herself."

'So the matter dropped; but I could not get over my dislike to Chunia, and as my visit wore on, and I became more and more attached to dear little Dot, I could hardly endure to see the child in her presence.

'My month with Mary passed quickly away, and I was really sorry when it was over, more especially as on my return home, my brother was called away unexpectedly on business, and I was left alone. I missed Dot more than I could have believed possible, for I had become ridiculously devoted to the small, round bundle of humanity, with the great dark eyes and short yellow curls, and my feelings are not to be described when the letter came from Mr. Pollock giving me the awful news of the child's death.

'I read the letter over and over again, hardly able to believe it. The whole thing was so hideously sudden! I had only left Mary and Dot such a short time ago, and when last I had seen the child she was in her mother's arms on the platform of the railway station, kissing her little fat hands laboriously to me in farewell, and looking the picture of life and health.

'Poor Mr. Pollock wrote in a heart-broken strain. It appeared that the child had strayed away one afternoon and must have fallen into the river, which ran past the bottom of the garden, for the little sun-hat was found floating in the stream, and close to the water's edge lay a toy that she had been playing with all day. Every search had been made, but no further trace could be found. The poor mother was distracted with sorrow, and Mr. Pollock had telegraphed for leave, as he meant to take her to England at once. He added that the ayah, Chunia, had been absent on three days leave when the dreadful accident happened, or, they both felt convinced, it would never have occurred at all. Mary, he wrote, sent me a message to beg me to take the woman into my service, as she could not endure the idea of one who had been so much with their darling going to strangers, for the poor woman had been a faithful servant, and was stricken and dumb with grief.

'I telegraphed at once that I would take Chunia willingly. I forgot my old antipathy to her, and only remembered that I should have someone about me who had known and loved the child so well. When the woman arrived I was quite shocked at her altered appearance. Her face seemed to have shrunk to half its former size, and her eyes looked enormous, and shone with a strange brilliancy. She was very quiet at first but burst into a flood of tears when I tried to speak to her of poor little Dot, so I gave it up, as I saw she could hardly bear the subject mentioned.

'She helped me to undress the first night, and then, instead of leaving the room, she stood looking at me without speaking.

'"What is it?" I inquired.

'"Mem-sahib," she said in a whisper, glancing over her shoulder, "may I sleep in your dressing-room to-night?"

'I willingly gave her permission, for I saw that the woman's nerves were unstrung and that she needed companionship. Then I got into bed, and must have been asleep for some hours when I awoke thinking I had heard a shrill voice crying in the compound. I listened, and again it came, a high, beseeching wail. It was certainly the voice of a child, and the awful pleading and despair expressed in the sound was heart-rending. I felt sure some native baby had wandered into the grounds and was calling hopelessly for its mother.

'I lit a candle and went into my dressing-room, where to my astonishment, I saw Chunia crouching against the outer door that led into the verandah, holding it fast with both hands as though she were shutting someone out.

'I asked what she was doing, and whether she knew whose child was crying outside. She sprang to her feet and answered sullenly that she had heard no child crying. I opened the door and went out into the verandah, but nothing was to be seen or heard, and I had no reply to my shouts of inquiry; so, concluding that it must have been my fancy, or perhaps some prowling animal, I returned to bed, and slept soundly for the rest of the night.

'The next evening I dined out, and on my return was surprised to hear someone talking in my dressing-room. I hurried in, and again found Chunia kneeling in front of the outer door imploring somebody to 'go away' at the top of her voice. Directly she saw me she came towards me excitedly.

'"Oh! mem-sahib!" she shrieked, "tell her to go away!"

'"Tell who?" I demanded.

'"Dottie-babba," she wailed, wringing her hands. "She cries to come to me—listen to her—listen!"

'She held her breath and waited, and I solemnly declare that as I stood and listened with her, I heard a child crying and moaning on the other side of the door. I was mute with horror and bewilderment, while the plaintive cry rose and fell, and then flinging the door open, I held the candle high above my head. There was no need of a light, for the moon was full, but no child could I see, and the verandah was quite empty. I determined to sift the matter to the bottom, so I went to the servants' quarters and called them all up. But no one could account for the crying of a child, and though the compound was thoroughly searched nothing was discovered. So the servants returned to their houses and I to my verandah, where I found Chunia in a most excited state.

'"Mem-sahib," she said, with her fists clenched and her eyes starting out of her head, "will she go away if I tell you all about it?"

'"Yes, yes," I cried soothingly, "tell me what you like."

'She silently took my wrist and dragged me into the dressing-room, shutting the door with the utmost caution.

'"Stand with your back against it," she whispered, "so that she cannot enter."

'I feared I was in the presence of a mad woman, so I did as she bade me, and waited quietly for her story. She walked up and down the room and began to speak in a kind of chant.

'"I did it," she sang. "I killed the child, little Dottie-babba, and she has followed me always. You heard her cry to-night and last night. The mem-sahib angered me the day she struck me with the shoe, and then a devil entered into my heart. I asked for leave, and went away, but it was too strong, it drew me back, and it said kill! kill! I fought and struggled against the voice, but it was useless. So on the second day of my leave I crept back and hid among the bushes till I saw the child alone, and then I took her away and killed her. She was so glad to see me, and laughed and talked, but when she saw the devil in my eyes she grew frightened, and cried just as you heard her cry to-night. I took her little white neck in my hands—see, mem-sahib, how large and strong my hands are—and I pressed and pressed until the child was dead, and then the devil left me. I looked and saw what I had done. I could not unclasp her fingers from my skirt, they clung so tightly, so I took it off and wrapped her in it—"

'The woman stopped suddenly. I had listened in silence, repressing the exclamations of horror that rose to my lips.

'"What did you do then?" I asked. Chunia looked wildly round.

'"I forget," she murmured; "the river, I ran quickly to the river—"

'Then there came a shriek from the dry, parched lips, and flinging her arms above her head she fell at my feet unconscious and foaming at the mouth.

'Afterwards Chunia was found to be raving mad, and the doctor expressed his opinion that she must have been in a more or less dangerous state for some months past. I told him of her terrible confession to me, but he said that possibly the whole thing was a delusion on her part.

'I went to see her once after she had been placed under restraint, but the sight was so saddening that I never went again. She was seated on the floor of her prison patting an imaginary baby to sleep, croning the quaint little lullaby that ayahs always use, and when I spoke to her she only gazed at me with dull, vacant eyes, and continued the monotonous chant as though she had not seen me at all.'

'And the child you heard crying?' I ventured to ask.

'Oh! How can I tell what it was? I don't know,' she answered with impatient perplexity. 'I can't believe that it was the spirit of little Dot, and yet—and yet— *what was it?*'

From *East of Suez* (1926)

# *Caulfield's Crime*

by Alice Perrin

CAULFIELD WAS A SULKY, BAD-TEMPERED INDIVIDUAL WHO made no friends and was deservedly unpopular, but he had the reputation of being the finest shot in the Punjab, and of possessing a knowledge of sporting matters that was almost superhuman. He was an extremely jealous shot, and hardly ever invited a companion to join him on his shooting trips, so it may be understood that I was keenly alive to the honour conferred on me when he suddenly asked me to go out for three days' small game shooting with him.

'I know a string of jheels,' he said, 'about thirty miles from here, where the duck and snipe must swarm. I marked the place down when I was out last month, and I've made arrangements to go there next Friday morning. You can come, too, if you like.'

I readily accepted the ungracious invitation, though I could hardly account for it, knowing his solitary ways, except that he probably thought that I was unlikely to assert myself, being but a youngster, and also he knew me better than he did most people, for our houses were next door, and I often strolled over to examine his enormous collection of skins and horns and other sporting trophies.

I bragged about the coming expedition in the club that evening, and was well snubbed by two or three men who would have given anything to know the whereabouts of Caulfield's string of jheels, and who spitefully warned me to be careful that Caulfield did not end by shooting me.

'I believe he'd kill any chap who annoyed him,' said one of them, looking round to make sure that Caulfield was not at hand. 'I never met such a nasty-tempered fellow, I believe he's mad. But he can shoot, and what he doesn't know about game isn't worth knowing.'

Caulfield and I rode out the thirty miles early on the Friday morning, having sent our camp on ahead the previous night. We found our tents pitched in the scanty shade of some stunted dâk jungle trees with thick dry bark, flat, shapeless leaves, that clattered together when stirred by the wind, and wicked-looking red blossoms. It was not a cheerful spot, and the soil was largely mixed with salt which had worked its way in white patches to the surface, and only encouraged the growth of the rankest of grass.

Before us stretched a dreary outlook of shallow lake and swampy ground, broken by dark patches of reeds and little bushy islands, while on the left a miserable mud village overlooked the water. The sun had barely cleared away the thick, heavy mist, which was still slowly rising here and there, and the jheel birds were wading majestically in search of their breakfast of small fish, and uttering harsh, discordant cries.

To my astonishment, Caulfield seemed a changed man. He was in excellent spirits, his eyes were bright, and the sullen frown had gone from his forehead.

'Isn't it a lovely spot?' he said, laughing and rubbing his hands. 'Beyond that village the snipe ought to rise in thousands from the rice fields. We sha'n't be able to shoot it all in three days, worse luck, but we'll keep it dark, and come again. Let's have breakfast. I don't want to lose any time.'

Half an hour later we started, our guns over our shoulders, and a couple of servants behind us carrying the luncheon and cartridge bags. My spirits rose with Caulfield's, for I felt we had the certainty of an excellent day's sport before us.

But the birds were unaccountably wild and few and far between, and luck seemed dead against us. 'Some brutes' had evidently been there before us and harried the birds, was Caulfield's opinion, delivered with disappointed rage, and after tramping and wading all day, we returned, weary and crestfallen, with only a few couple of snipe and half a dozen teal between us. Caulfield was so angry he could hardly eat any dinner, and afterwards sat cursing his luck and the culprits who had forestalled us, till we could neither of us keep awake any longer.

The next morning we took a different route from the previous day, but with no better result. On and on, and round and round we tramped, with only an occasional shot here and there, and at last, long after midday, we sat wearily down to eat our luncheon. I was ravenously hungry, and greedily devoured my share of the provisions, but Caulfield hardly touched a mouthful, and only sat moodily examining his gun, and taking long pulls from his whisky flask. We were seated on the roots of a large tamarind tree, close to the village, and the place had a dreary, depressing appearance. The yellow mud walls were ruined and crumbling, and the inhabitants seemed scanty and poverty-stricken. Two ragged old women were squatting a short distance off, watching us with dim, apathetic eyes, and a few naked children were playing near them, while some bigger boys were driving two or three lean buffaloes towards the water.

Presently another figure came in sight—a fakir, or mendicant priest, as was evident by the tawny masses of wool woven amongst his own black locks and hanging in ropes below his shoulders, the ashes smeared over the almost naked body, and the hollow gourd for alms which he held in his hand. The man's face was long and thin, and his pointed teeth glistened in the sunlight as he demanded money in a dismal monotone. Caulfield flung a pebble at him and told him roughly to be off, with the result that the man slowly disappeared behind a clump of tall, feathery grass.

'Did you notice that brute's face?' said Caulfield as we rose to start again. 'He must have been a pariah dog in a former existence. He was exactly like one!'

'Or a jackal perhaps,' I answered carelessly. 'He looked more like a wild beast.'

Then we walked on, skirting the village and plunging into the damp, soft rice fields. We put up a wisp of snipe, which we followed till we had shot them nearly all, and then, to our joy, we heard a rush of wings overhead, and a lot of duck went down into the corner of a jheel in front of us.

'We've got 'em!' said Caulfield, and we hurried on till we were almost within shot of the birds, and could hear them calling to each other in their fancied security. But suddenly they rose again in wild confusion, and with loud cries of alarm were out of range in a second. Caulfield swore, and so did I, and our rage was increased ten-fold when the disturber of the birds appeared in sight, and proved to be the fakir who had paid us a visit at luncheon-time. Caulfield shook his fist at the man and abused him freely in Hindustani but without moving a muscle of his dog-like face the fakir passed us and continued on his way.

Words could not describe Caulfield's vexation.

'They were pin-tail, all of them,' he said, 'and the first decent chance we've had since we came out. To think of that beastly fakir spoiling the whole show, and I don't suppose he had the least idea what he had done.

'Probably not,' I replied, 'unless there was some spite in it because you threw a stone at him that time.'

'Well, come along,' said Caulfield, with resignation, 'we must make haste as it will be dark soon, and I want to try a place over by those palms before we knock off. We may as well let the servants go back as they've had a hard day. Have you got some cartridges in your pocket?'

'Yes, plenty,' I answered, and after despatching the two men back to the camp with what little game we had got, we walked on in silence.

The sun was sinking in a red ball and the air was heavy with damp, as the white mist stole slowly over the still, cold jheels. Far overhead came the first faint cackle of the wild geese returning home for the night, and presently as we approached the clump of palms we saw more water glistening between the rough stems, and on it, to our delight, a multitude of duck and teal.

But the next moment there was a whir-r-r of wings like the rumble of thunder, and a dense mass of birds flew straight into the air and wheeled bodily away, while the sharp, cold atmosphere resounded with their startled cries. Caulfield said nothing, but he set his jaw and walked rapidly forward, while I followed. We skirted the group of palms, and on the other side we came upon our friend the fakir, who had again succeeded in spoiling our sport. The long, lanky figure was drawn to its full height, the white eyeballs and jagged teeth caught the red glint of the setting sun, and he waved his hand triumphantly in the direction of the vanishing cloud of birds.

Then there came the loud report of a gun, and the next thing I saw was a quivering body on the ground, and wild eyes staring open in the agony of death. Caulfield had shot the fakir, and now he stood looking down at what he had done, while I knelt beside the body and tried hopelessly to persuade myself that life was not extinct. When I got up we gazed at each other for a moment in silence.

'What are we to do?' I asked presently.

'Well, you know what it means,' Caulfield said in a queer, hard voice. 'Killing a native is no joke in these days, and I should come out of it pretty badly.'

I glanced at the body in horror. The face was rigid, and seemed more beast-like than ever. I looked at Caulfield again before I spoke, hesitatingly.

'Of course the whole thing was unpremeditated—an accident.'

'No, it wasn't,' he said defiantly, 'I meant to shoot the brute, and it served him right. And you can't say anything else if it comes out. But I don't see why anyone should know about it but ourselves.'

'It's nasty business,' I said, my heart sinking at the suggestion of concealment.

'It will be nastier still if we don't keep it dark, and you won't like having to give me away, you know. Either we must bury the thing here and say nothing about it, or else we must take it back to the station and stand the devil's own fuss. Probably I shall be kicked out of the service.'

'Of course I'll stand by you,' I said with an effort, 'but we can't do anything this minute. We'd better hide it in that long grass and come back after dinner. We must have something to dig with.'

Caulfield agreed sullenly, and between us we pushed the body in amongst the thick, coarse grass, which completely concealed it, and then made our way back to the camp. We ordered dinner and pretended to eat it, after which we sat for half an hour smoking, until the plates were cleared away and the servants had left the tent. Then I put my hunting-knife into my pocket, and Caulfield picked up a kitchen chopper that his bearer had left lying on the floor, after hammering a stiff joint of a camp chair, and we quitted the tent casually as though intending to have a stroll in the moonlight, which was almost as bright as day. We walked slowly at first, gradually increasing our pace as we left the camp behind us, and Caulfield never spoke a word until we came close to the tall grass that hid the fakir's body. Then he suddenly clutched my arm.

'God in heaven!' he whispered, pointing ahead, 'what is that?'

I saw the grass moving, and heard a scraping sound that made my heart stand still. We moved forward in desperation and parted the grass with our hands. A large jackal was lying on the fakir's body, grinning and snarling at being disturbed over his hideous meal.

'Drive it away,' said Caulfield, hoarsely. But the brute refused to move, and as it lay there showing its teeth, its face reminded me horribly of the wretched man dead beneath its feet. I turned sick and faint, so Caulfield shouted and shook the grass and threw clods of soil at the animal, which rose at last and slunk slowly away. It was an unusually large jackal, more like a wolf, and had lost one of its ears. The coat was rough, and mangy and thickly sprinkled with grey.

For more than an hour we worked desperately with the chopper and hunting-knife, being greatly aided in our task by a rift in the ground where the soil had been softened by water running from the jheel, and finally we stood up with the sweat pouring from our faces, and stamped down the earth which now covered all traces of Caulfield's crime. We had filled the grave with some large stones that were lying about (remnants of some ancient temple, long ago deserted and forgotten), thus feeling secure that it could not easily be disturbed by animals.

The next morning we returned to the station, and Caulfield shut himself up more than ever. He entirely dropped his shooting, which before had been his one pleasure, and the only person he ever spoke to, unofficially, was myself.

The end of April came with its plague of insects and scorching winds. The hours grew long and weary with the heat, and dust storms howled and swirled over the station, bringing perhaps a few tantalising drops of rain, of more often leaving the air thick with a copper-coloured haze.

One night when it was too hot to sleep, Caulfield suddenly appeared in my verandah and asked me to let him stay the night in my bungalow.

'I know I'm an ass,' he said in awkward apology, 'but I can't stay by myself. I get all sorts of beastly ideas.'

I asked no questions, but gave him a cheroot and tried to cheer him up, telling him scraps of gossip, and encouraging him to talk, when a sound outside made us both start. It proved to be only the weird, plaintive cry of a jackal, but Caulfield sprang to his feet, shaking all over.

'There it is again!' he exclaimed. 'It has followed me over here. Listen!' turning his haggard, sleepless eyes on me. 'Every night that brute comes and howls round my house, and I tell you, on my oath, it's the same jackal we saw eating the poor devil I shot.'

'Nonsense, my dear chap,' I said, pushing him back into the chair, 'you must have got fever. Jackals come and howl round my house all night. That's nothing.'

'Look here,' said Caulfield, very calmly, 'I have no more fever than you have, and if you imagine I am delirious you are mistaken.' He lowered his voice. 'I looked out one night and saw the brute. It had only one ear!'

In spite of my own common sense and the certainty that Caulfield was not himself, my blood ran cold, and after I had succeeded in quieting him and he had dropped off to sleep on the couch, I sat in my long chair for hours, going over in my mind every detail of that horrible night in the jungle.

Several times after this Caulfield came to me and repeated the same tale. He swore he was being haunted by the jackal we had driven away from the fakir's body, and finally took it into his head that the spirit of the murdered man had entered the animal and was bent on obtaining vengeance.

Then he suddenly ceased coming over to me, and when I went to see him he would hardly speak, and only seemed anxious to get rid of me. I urged him to take leave or see a doctor, but he angrily refused to do either, and said he wished I would keep away from him altogether. So I left him alone for a couple of days, but on the third evening my conscience pricked me for having neglected him, and I was preparing to go over to his bungalow, when his bearer rushed in with a face of terror and besought me to come without delay. He said he feared his master was dying, and he had already sent for the doctor. The latter arrived in Caulfield's verandah simultaneously with myself, and together we entered the sick man's room. Caulfield was lying unconscious on his bed.

'He had a sort of fit, sahib,' said the frightened bearer, and proceeded to explain how his master had behaved.

The doctor bent over the bed.

'Do you happen to know if he had been bitten by a dog lately?' he asked, looking up at me.

'Not to my knowledge,' I answered, while the faint wail of a jackal out across the plain struck a chill to my heart.

For twenty-four hours we stayed with Caulfield, watching the terrible struggles we were powerless to relieve, and which lasted till the end came. He was never able to speak after the first paroxysm, which had occurred before we arrived, so we could not learn from him whether he had been bitten or not, neither could the doctor discover any scar on his body which might have been made by the teeth of an animal. Yet there was no shadow of doubt that Caulfield's death was due to hydrophobia.

As we stood in the next room when all was over, drinking the dead man's whisky and soda, which we badly needed, we questioned the bearer closely, but he could tell us little or nothing. His master, he said, did not keep dogs, nor had the bearer ever heard of his having been bitten by one; but there had been a mad jackal about the place nearly three weeks ago which his master had tried to shoot but failed.

'It couldn't have been that,' said the doctor; 'he would have come to me if he had been bitten by a jackal.'

'No,' I answered mechanically, 'it could not have been that.' And I went into the bedroom to take a last look at poor Caulfield's thin, white face with its ghastly, hunted expression, for there was now nothing more that I could do for him.

Then I picked up a lantern and stepped out into the dark verandah, intending to go home. As I did so, something came silently round the corner of the house and stood in my path. I raised my lantern and caught a glimpse of a mass of grey fur, two fiery yellow eyes, and bared, glistening teeth. It was only a stray jackal, and I struck at it with my stick, but instead of running away it slipped past me and entered Caulfield's room. The light fell on the animal's head, and I saw that it had only one ear.

In a frenzy I rushed back into the house calling for the doctor and servants.

'I saw a jackal come in here,' I said, searching round the bedroom, 'hunt it out at once.'

Every nook and corner was examined, but no jackal was found.

'Go home to bed, my boy, and keep quiet till I come and see you in the morning,' said the doctor, looking at me keenly. 'This business has shaken your nerves, and you imagination is beginning to play you tricks. Good-night.'

'Good-night,' I answered, and went slowly back to my bungalow, trying to persuade myself that he was right.

From *East of Suez* (1926)

# *A Ghost in Burma*

(A Story Based on Fact)

by Gerald T. Tait

IT IS A REMARKABLE FACT THAT GOOD FOOD AND DRINK SEEM to have the power of stimulating the mind and memory, and in consequence, some of the best stories, whether they belong to the humorous series or whether they be yarns, are told after dinner. The following was no exception to the rule and we heard it at a friendly gathering of exiles on leave, united after many years of absence and many years of wandering in strange lands. Peter Kane, burnt mahogany by the tropical sun, tall, broad shouldered, who had spent the greater part of his service in wild corners of the Empire, had been listening for some time with a smile on his face, to a discussion on ghosts. Finally he broke into the conversation.

"Would you fellows like a true yarn on ghosts?" We naturally all assented. I have set it down in his own words and you may or may not believe it according to the amount of imagination or superstition, call it whatever you like, in your make up. As far as we were concerned, knowing Peter we believed the story.

"It happened years ago. I was only a young railway engineer then just out from Home. Ever since my early childhood the name "Burma" was magic to my mind; it typified all that represents the mysterious East, and you can imagine my joy on learning that I was appointed to that country of my dreams. My luck as I believed then was in the ascendant, for on my arrival, I found I was to join a survey party working towards the Chinese border lying beyond the river Salween. What more could a youngster wish for? A wild country, inhabited by few but very wild tribes, plenty of work, plenty of sport, and before us the unknown, the unexplored. As one grows older and more settled, I must confess one's ideas of luck differ somewhat and nowadays, luck to my mind is to get nearer home. However, for a youngster the outlook was ideal. I landed in Rangoon late in October and made my way by rail to Mandalay whence the survey expedition was to set forth. I can hardly describe the joy it was to me to see this country; I literally drank it all in and asked for more. From the very start, Rangoon with the great Shwe Dagon covered with gold, the multi-coloured crowd around its base, the orange robed priests, the pilgrims, the vendors, the beggars, crowded my brain with one confused mass of colour. Then in the train, I seemed to spend my time moving from one side of the carriage to the other. Everything struck me as picturesque, the paddy fields with those solemn white or gray paddy birds picking their way daintily through the slush, the smiling Burmans up to their knees in mud planting out the rice, little thatched roofed huts clustering around groves of great darkleaved trees, the whole country green and fertile.... So much for childish enthusiasm.

My stay in Mandalay was short; indeed we left two days after my arrival. The party consisted of Paddy Greene as Chief, a short, plump, cheery, fairhaired Irishman with always a twinkle in his eye, an amazing brogue and a divine voice when he sang. Then Tom Inglis, neither handsome nor ugly, just average looking exactly alike the hundreds of thousands of other men of the same class who have followed the same footsteps through Public School and University; entirely dependable and sound, never rattled. Next followed John Alaistairs, dark haired and morose; and lastly myself just a raw youngster without any particular distinction. The remainder of our staff consisted of native surveyors and a full complement of ubiquitous coolies.

The first portion of our journey was by train to railhead, situated about 100 to 150 miles from the Chinese frontier as the crow flies. In actual fact for us, this distance was just about double; for the country to be surveyed was extremely hilly and covered with dense and impenetrable jungle. The only existing trade routes being tracks following the crests of the ridges rising anything up to 5,000 feet above the bottom of the valleys. These tracks, however, were not for us. The road we had to travel followed not the ridges but the valleys and the slopes slightly above them. Those who have visited this part of the world and strayed from the beaten track, will readily understand what I mean when I talk about impenetrable jungle. Imagine a solid barrier of trees rising to 120 feet, covered with thick foliage close planted, with between them colossal bushes with thorns three or more inches long and clumps of thick bamboo; the whole woven into a solid mass by myriads of creepers, some with stems like a ship's hawser, the only relief from the monotonous green being patches of brightly coloured orchids; slopes amazingly steep and studded with rocks and boulders hidden by the undergrowth but more than noticeable when stumbled upon. Advance through this country meant about two miles a day with luck, every foot of path hewn by the axes of the special jungle-clearing coolies, and every foot stubbornly contested by the forest. To crown everything a dim semi-religious light filtered by the dark mantle of leaves overhead. Observations could only be made by laboriously climbing tall trees. A heartbreaking country but possessing an undeniable thrill in spite of the damp heat and the mosquitoes.

I must confess that at times I felt depressed and had it not been for Paddy and his tonic-like nature, I really don't know how we would have carried on. Alaistairs was more than a wet blanket and would alone have depressed a regiment. Inglis on the other hand seemed utterly undisturbed by his surroundings and might just as well have been walking down Piccadilly for all the effect they had on him.

You may think that I am drawing out this description unduly. I do it, however, with a purpose so that you will more fully grasp the inexplicableness of the subsequent find and events.

Our work went on and we crept further and further into the unknown depths towards the Salween. Finally after about two and a half months we stepped out on to the crest of a ridge almost devoid of trees, overlooking the surrounding country and in particular the Salween itself. The change from the monotony of our foregoing road to this open and wildly beautiful vista, swept away all feelings of depression.

We have now reached the setting for our drama. I will describe it so that you fellows may picture it in your minds.

The river flows with a rushing roar at the foot of immense perpendicular rocky walls forming a deep trench varying from 90 to 400 feet across. The bed of the river consists in a series of steps anything up to a mile long with a drop of ten or fifteen feet between each, turning the swift waters, sometimes into cascades, sometimes into rapids filled with boulders. The sides of this trench rise up to 1,000 or 1,500 feet above the level of the river. From the top the ground, covered with enormous rocks piled up into confused masses, stretches inland a few miles but rises to 5,000 and 6,000 feet, thus forming a valley about eight miles across with slopes set at 60 degrees. This valley receives numerous tributary streams, most of them contained in deep gorges cutting the main valley at right angles. The whole country is covered with dense jungle and tall rough grass. The few flat spaces to be seen are small golden sand banks on the edges of the side streams where, throughout the day, myriads of butterflies of every size and colour, dance and scintillate. Also here and there, small plateaux just above the level of the waters of the main stream, where the trench shallows and where the mantle of vegetation has slightly retreated. It is here, by the way, that are sometimes to be found the temporary shelters put up by the nomadic tribes of this country Moi, Khas and Tac-Cui, strayed from the neighbouring wilds of Laos. These patches show up brilliant emerald due to the wild plantains and the wild paddy thereon.

Through this decor of savage beauty we made our way to the banks of the river.

Two days were wasted looking for a place to cross.

The third morning on turning a bend, we suddenly came upon an amazing sight. On the opposite bank, perched upon an almost overhanging rock, stood a square bungalow, for all the world like the ordinary P.W.D. rest-houses found throughout India and Burma. We could hardly believe our eyes. The strangeness of this find in the middle of this dense jungle defied words. Our native followers themselves, we could see, were just as surprised as ourselves. One fact stood out very clearly. We had to examine this bungalow. A place was found, about half a mile down stream where the river was fordable and we finally reached the bungalow by two in the afternoon.

The East is a curious part of the world particularly in respect to the propagation of news and messages generally. Now remember our coolies had never been anywhere near this part of Burma before, nor had they ever heard of this bungalow; further, for weeks we had not seen any local natives. Yet one and all refused to approach saying that it was haunted. I asked them how they knew and the only reply I could obtain was "We have just been warned not to stay here." They were very insistent that it was not their fault, but how could they act against direct orders. As to "Who" gave the orders they would not say. No amount of questioning elucidated a further reply and finally they remained sullen and dumb.

This was most annoying for the idea of resting once more in civilised surroundings appealed to us tremendously. After a short discussion we decided to remain on the spot for three days provided of course we succeeded in propitiating our coolies. Before going any further, let me describe the general lay-out of the building.

Square, perched on a bare rock overlooking the Salween, it had a verandah running around on the three sides to landwards. The fourth side, an absolutely flat wall with just one window in the centre, overhung a 1,000-foot drop straight into the river below. In the very middle of the whole building, was an open courtyard with a large brick cube in the centre about 10 feet aside. The bungalow was in a fair state of repair yet unoccupied.

We were all as keen as mustard to investigate and entered, led by Paddy. In spite of our coolies' fears it seemed a very ordinary kind of habitation. The only odd thing about it was the brick cube in the courtyard and this particularly attracted Paddy's attention. For the time being, however, he said nothing and would pass no opinion as to its *raison d'etre*. Try as we would we could not evolve a theory as to how this building had been erected and by whom. We settled on our various rooms, Paddy, Inglis and myself chosing the room overlooking the river; Alaistairs preferring to be alone in a room off the courtyard. I could scarcely tear myself away from our window for the view was really magnificent with its sheer drop of a thousand feet into the roaring torrent below.

It took a good deal of persuasion to induce the coolies to carry our stores indoors and they only finally agreed to do so on the understanding that they would be allowed to sleep outside in the open glade roughly 300 feet across separating the building from the jungle. The joy of a rest in the cool verandahs with a sight of the blue sky above soon made us forget the fatigue of the journey. It was only towards evening that we once more began to take notice of our immediate surroundings. Paddy was the first to break the silence. "That brick cube in the courtyard puzzles me," he said, "I cannot for the life of me imagine what it was for." "I should say it was put up by the owner to hide a well," I suggested hopefully.

"Don't be an ass," he replied. "You may not believe me but that cube, unless I am very much mistaken, dates back some 5,000 years before the bungalow was ever built."

To say we were astonished is to say the least of it. We all sat up, thinking he was pulling our legs. Inglis, however, took the statement quite calmly. "How do you make that out?" he asked. Paddy replied:– "Being an engineer, the subject of building and building materials throughout the ages has always been of particular interest to me. Did any of you closely examine that cube? I think not. If you do you will find that its walls are built of plano-convex bricks, not made in moulds but fashioned by the hands of the maker on a flat surface, the top being left convex. This I may say is an absolute characteristic of the oldest Sumerian periods dating back to about 3,000 B.C. Remains of similar workmanship have been found in Mesopotamia at Kish and in India at Mohenjo-Daro. Furthermore, if you look at the surface you will see on some of the bricks curious small regular carvings which are nothing else but cuneiform writing. Unfortunately I cannot read it. This find would be of extraordinary interest to archæologists, if ever they believed us."

With one accord we rose and made for the courtyard. Paddy proceeded to explain the find to us on the spot. It undoubtedly tallied with all he said. Here then was yet another mystery.

Conversation at dinner that night consisted mainly in a lecture by Paddy and in theorising by the rest of us, needless to say, without any tangible results. We finally turned in at about ten and settled down to a good night's rest.

As far as I am concerned I fell asleep as soon as my head touched my pillow and I slept without a break until suddenly awakened by an unearthly shriek. It took me a minute before I came sufficiently to my senses to realise that it was not a dream. I jumped up to find Paddy and Inglis groping for their torches.

"What on earth was that," I cried.

"It seemed to come from Alaistair's room," replied Inglis, as we set off at a run. We found Alaistairs sitting up in bed. He apologised on seeing us saying that he had had a nightmare and dreamt that cold hands were grasping his neck. On being assured that he was safe we trooped back to bed again laughing at the alarm. The next day passed quickly and uneventfully. Alaistairs seemed quite cheerful for a change and pooh-poohed the idea of changing rooms.

Paddy spent the most of his time in examining his precious brick cube and making sketches of it. Night set in with its usual tropical rapidity and once more we settled down to sleep. This time I must confess the memory of Alaistairs' shriek kept me awake. I tried hard to sleep but without success; finally I could not stand it any longer and got up and went to the window in hopes of getting in little fresh air. The moon was not quite full but its light was sufficiently strong to show up the country for miles. Far below the sound of the rushing of water rose, here a woodpecker tapped unceasingly, there a night-jar or screech-owl disturbed by some jungle beast raised its voice in protest. I stretched my arms out and breathed deeply.

Now I want you particularly to note my position. I was standing leaning out of the window with only plain whitewashed perfectly flat walls without many crevice or ledge, stretching above, on both sides and below, where even a lizard would have had difficulty in finding purchase, while all round me was the gaping void of the precipice.

There I was breathing deeply when to my horror I felt my arms grasped by two cold and clammy invisible hands, coming apparently from straight in front of me. I let out an appalling yell. Inglis and Paddy jumped out of bed.

"For God's sake come," I shouted, "Something has got hold of me."

Inglis was the first to reach me. He caught hold of my arms and said "Hold on old man, I'll help you." His fingers crept up my extended arms. "Paddy, he is right, I can feel a hand."

My hair stood on end for nothing could be seen. “Catch hold of him,” said Paddy who by this time had joined us, “and we’ll pull together.”

Their united effort was successful, the cold hands gradually slipped and then let go. I was once more free, unhurt but mighty scared. Paddy fetched some brandy and then examined the walls, but without success for it was a physical impossibility for any human being or even a monkey to hang on to that smooth surface. Having sufficiently recovered Paddy suggested looking up Alaistairs. We entered his room but to our surprise found it empty. Inglis was the first to make the discovery. Poor Alaistairs lay face downwards on the top of the cube, dead; his throat, showing the distinct markings of two hands. Dawn soon came. We organised a very complete search but it revealed nothing, not so much even as footprints in the dust on the top of the cube.

That is my story.”

There was a short silence among us. Then someone asked: “What about the Sumerian cube, did you report it to anyone?”

Peter Kane gave a short laugh, “My dear fellow no one believed us; even Paddy’s sketches were declared fakes. As for poor Alaistairs, we reported him as having died from fever contracted on the way out. You see, supernatural deaths are not popular with the powers that be.”

Had the Sumerian cube anything to do with his death? Was it by chance an ancient sacrificial altar? How came the bungalow at that spot?—are questions yet to be answered.

From *Indian State Railway Magazine* (December 1928)

## *'There are more things—'*
## A Tale of the Malabar Jungles

by H.W. Dennys

IT WAS DORA TORRINGTON WHO STARTED THE SUBJECT AS WE lay in deck chairs near the tennis court enjoying that pleasant hour in late summer between sunset and the dressing gong. She was of the restless, wealthy type who are never happy unless mixed up in the very latest craze. It had started with Women Suffrage, and now consisted of a mania for a religion which, from her conversation, we gathered was a cross between Spiritualism and Christian Science. Her position as hostess gave her privileges, and her audience tried not to appear bored as she dwelt on a lecture she had recently attended.

"He was such a dear little man," she rambled, "all bald-head and forehead, and he gave us *such* an interesting talk on the subject of 'Faith.' Do you know he said that the Bible was quite correct,—literally I mean—when it says that faith can remove mountains, and he gave us all kinds of weird stories to prove what he said. Then he went on to say that he saw no reason why, if we had sufficient faith, we shouldn't be able to do even more than that, and actually *create* things! Wouldn't it be too thrilling if we could think of wanting a new car so hard that it suddenly arrived."

Her audience stirred. The idea had possibilities.

"Think too," said Vera, whom I would have you know is my wife, "of being able to concentrate so hard on Tim that half his face suddenly disappeared behind a beard. It might make him look quite distinguished, though I'm afraid," she added sadly, "it could never make him good-looking."

I stiffened. Humour of this type struck me as being crude and certainly unjust. I was about to launch a snappy counter-attack, when a grunt from the chair on my left diverted my attention.

Peter Mainwaring, who occupied it, was apparently the only one present who hadn't treated the idea as a joke, and as I glanced at him was mumbling to himself with a far away look in his, eyes.

I postponed my snappy reply, and gave him a dig with my elbow to bring him back to earth.

"What's biting you, Peter?" I enquired. "Bring it out and let the public enjoy it."

"It's not so foolish or impossible as you all think, because I've seen it," was the unexpected reply.

Ten pairs of eyes focussed themselves on Peter curiously, who finding himself the centre of attention, grew flurried and evidently regretted his remark.

"I scent a story," quoth pretty Yvonne Elder, removing her graceful young self from the edge of a table to the comfort of a deck chair. "Let's have it Peter before we go in to dress."

Peter, who had just returned from a shooting trip in India, and had been more than usually silent of late, glanced round enquiringly. We were unanimous in assent. Peter's stories, few and far between, were invariably good. As he is a far better story-teller than I shall ever be, I will give it in his own words.

"It was three months before I left for home," he commenced, "and whole yarn sounds so utterly incredible, that I'll pardon you all if you think I was mad or suffering from D.T.'s at the time. Sometimes I begin to think so myself."

For three months I had been wandering all over India slaughtering away to my heart's content, and had been more than usually successful. It was in Madras on my way down to Colombo and Home, that I met a man by name of Frobisher. We were in the bar of the Madras Club at the time, and hearing that I had been out big game shooting, he asked me if I had visited the West Coast in the course of my travels. As a matter of fact, it was about the only part that I hadn't visited, and told him so.

"Why Heaven's man," he said, "you've missed the best part of India for game. You can get elephant, tiger, bison, bear, panther, crocodile—any blinking thing you like down there."

It was off the beaten track for me, but his enthusiasm fired me. After all, I thought, I might as well do the thing properly while I was about it.

"I have a great friend down there," he continued, the light of the chase in his eye. "I'll give you an introduction to him if you like, though I haven't seen him for years now. He is as keen a sportsman as you and I'm sure would show you all the best places."

I hesitated and was lost.

"Thanks very much," I replied. "I think I'll try it. Can you tell me where your friend lives?"

"He's at a place called Munaloor, about sixty miles inland and all on his own. He plays at growing rubber, but has ample private means, and spends a large portion of his time out shooting. He's a bachelor and middle aged, but I warn you he's a bit of a crank in many ways. I expect you'll hit it off all right though."

The following day there came a note round to my hotel from Frobisher, containing the letter of introduction and a brief note wishing me luck and deploring his inability to come with me. As a post-script was another warning about his friend's eccentricies. God! if I'd only known then what those eccentricies were!

I won't bore you with my journey across the Coast. I went over by car, taking it easily and thoroughly enjoying the four hundred mile trip. At the small Club on the coast where I stayed the night before starting off inland, I made enquiries about my perspective host, whose name, I had learnt, was Anderson. Information was very vague—an unusual thing in a part where Europeans are few and far between. Anderson was not a member of the Club, and very rarely, it appeared, ever visited the town. I gathered he was a bit of a hermit, who spent his entire time on the Estate and was rarely seen by anyone. He was twenty miles from his nearest neighbours, and discouraged any attempt at social intercourse. My informants were rather tickled at the idea of my paying him a visit, but wished me luck.

All this didn't sound too encouraging, but the next day I set out hoping for the best. The first thirty miles of road proved excellent, but after leaving the main road, which carried straight on to the Nilgiris towering above me, and taking a branch road, the surface got steadily worse and worse. For the first few miles there were paddy fields and cocoanut groves, but as I went further, these gradually disappeared until eventually I was driving over what was little more than a footpath, with dense jungle on either side. Twice I skirted fairly large rubber estates, but after leaving them I saw no sign of cultivation or human residence at all with the exception of a few odd clusters of wretched grass huts, occupied by a local jungle tribe.

I had not left the coast until fairly late, and on account of the condition of the road, it was dusk by the time I reached Munaloor Estate. To my surprise it was beautifully kept and evidently run on scientific and up-to-date lines. The coolies quarters were filled with contented looking natives, who regarded me and my car with evident surprise. Everywhere were signs of prosperity. The misgivings which I had felt before began to melt. The man who ran a show like this couldn't be the bear that rumour described.

A turn in the road and a steepish climb brought me to his Bungalow, and as I twisted my way up the drive, amidst masses of tropical flowers. I experienced an odd feeling of elation and apprehension at its appearance. That doesn't sound possible, but it's the only way I can describe it.

The Bungalow itself was a big one, but of the most bizarre and fantastic construction imaginable. Eastern and Western architecture seemed to have blended, and the result, though undoubtedly attractive, was so unusual as to give one a curious sense of discomfort. It was a two-storeyed building; long, rambling and highly decorated. Minarets and domes formed the roof, and were painted gold. A large low verandah composed the front, but was rendered gloomy by numerous large and over-decorated pillars. The whole building was painted cream instead of the usual white, and, coupled with the golden minarets, proved, as I have said before, a trifle overwhelming. I hadn't time to take in more details however, before I pulled up in front of the verandah and met my host.

Here I received another shock. I don't know quite what I had expected him to be like, but I certainly wasn't prepared for what I saw.

He was a giant of a man in every sense of the word. Six foot three at least, and almost too broad for his height. A shaggy mass of black hair covered his enormous head, while a vast black beard concealed half his face. But it was his eyes that really fascinated me. Glaring at me from under bushy black eyebrows they made me feel rather like a rabbit fascinated by a snake. There was a compelling power in them that was almost frightening, and they weren't looking any too sociable then.

It was he who broke a rather awkward pause.

"Who are you, and what do you want? I don't like visitors here."

His voice was as large and deep as his frame would indicate, and the opening wasn't exactly promising. I removed my fascinated stare and delved in my pocket.

"I have a letter of introduction here from Frobisher, whom I understand is a friend of yours. I am on a shooting trip, and wondered if you could be so kind as to put me on to some good spots."

At the mention of his friend, the giant's whole manner changed at once. His beard, which had literally seemed to bristle before, relaxed, and a singularly pleasant smile creased round his eyes, which were about all that were visible of his face.

"Friend of Frobisher's, are you? I'm afraid I must have seemed rather rude but I'm shy of strangers. Come along in and have some tea; my Boys will bring in the luggage and see to the car."

He took the letter and led the way inside. Here yet another surprise awaited me. I should have been prepared for it, but somehow I wasn't. Eastern voluptiousness and Western comfort were the dominating features. Thick Persian rugs covered the floors; low divans took the place of the customary "long chairs," and were buried under masses of multi-coloured cushions; rich and highly coloured hangings and tapestries, obviously collected from all portions of the East, covered the few spaces on the walls that were not occupied by sporting trophies, and draped the numerous doors. Even the lighting—and he had electric light out there in the jungle,—was unusual. Cunningly concealed, and softly coloured bulbs, threw a diffused light over the place, and I could have sworn that there was a kind of incense burning somewhere. The centre room, into which he brought me, extended the whole height of the building, and had as ceiling one of the golden domes,—painted gold inside also,—and a balcony formed by the second storey which ran all round it. I felt rather as if I had stepped straight into a Drury Lane production of the "Arabian Nights," and half expected to see scantily clad dancing girls enter. And the extraordinary part was that he seemed to fit into the picture in spite of his European clothes.

He must have seen my look of astonishment, for he smiled again.

"I'm afraid you must think this a bit out of the ordinary"—I rather liked that. 'A bit out of the ordinary,'—I should damn well think so, "but think you will find it fairly comfortable."

I have to confess that it was. After tea, a grave and bearded servant,—no South Indian he, but a Pathan from the North,—led me to my room, where I found my dinner jacket, which by luck I had brought, laid out, and a hot bath in a sunken marble bathroom awaiting.

Dinner that night I rather dreaded. I had visions of us reclining on divans and eating our food off golden platters, but I found that I had no need for alarm, as my host was apparently perfectly normal in that respect, and after a preliminary cocktail, we sat down at a gleaming ebony table with glittering glassware and spotless linen.

Anderson, looking really magnificent in his dinner jacket, with which he wore a scarlet "cumberbund," chatted agreeably of his views on life.

"I don't like visitors," he said, "partly because they would not understand all this," with a gesture towards the ornate surroundings, "but chiefly because I find the average human being is almost entirely devoid of brains,—and I can't stand idiots. I have planned out my own method of living, and have my own particular hobbies and vices. Ordinary people might object to them. For instance, I keep what is termed a harem, and dabble in what would probably be called 'black art.' Well-meaning busy bodies would doubtless attempt to reform me if they knew about it, so for the sake of peace I shut myself off from the outside world."

I felt singularly small. I have no pretence to intellect, and whatever may be my public opinion on "harems" and "black art," I don't somehow agree with them in practice. But this black bearded giant completely overwhelmed me with his personality. One of his hobbies was a study of the natives of South India, and his stories of their different habits and customs kept me enthralled throughout dinner and the coffee and liqueurs which followed. Only once again did he refer to "black art."

"The jungle tribe of this part," he said, "are one of the most primitive races in the world and yet have control over powers of which the rest of the world knows nothing."

I was interested and asked for details, but he shut up at once.

"No, no, not now. We must be up early to-morrow if we are to do any shooting, and I don't want you to go having nightmares. I have a little wooden shack about fifteen miles from here which I use for trips of this kind and make my headquarters. It is quite near a settlement of the jungle tribe I was referring to, and I find them very useful as 'shikaris' and general porters. If you have any breeches and putties. I advise you to wear them to-morrow as the jungle is teeming with leeches at this time of year. In the meantime we had better be getting to be if we are to be up at four-thirty in the morning."

Peter paused awhile here and took a sip of the whisky and soda by his side, while the rest of us settled ourselves more comfortably in our chairs in anticipation of the second half of his story.

"I am sorry to have taken so long over the preliminaries," he resumed, "but it is essential that you should try and grasp the character of this man to follow what happened during that shooting trip."

It was gloriously fine when we set out early next morning after a small breakfast. The rains had just finished and Nature was at her best and brightest. The sun, which rose shortly after we left the Bungalow, seemed to shine on a cleansed and refreshed world and even as it dispelled the morning mists, had not as yet enough power to cause any discomfort. My host, as he strode along beside me, informed me that he kept this shack prepared all the year round, so that we could stay out as long as we wished.

"There are ibex on those hills," he continued, pointing to the towering outskirts of the Nilgiris, on whose sides the pearl grey mists were slowly dissolving, "but they are wily creatures, and we will be lucky if we get one."

He chatted away cheerily of the various adventures he had had out shooting and it was evident that he was a great "shikari." Soon after this we left the friendly rubber trees and the narrowness of the jungle path and the density of the under growth, put an end to further conversation.

The West Coast jungle is different to that of the rest of India. An extremely heavy rainfall, and a damp, sticky heat, make for luxuriant growth and as we pushed our way along, with giant trees and exotic creepers and flowers around us, I felt strangely awed by the magnificence of it all. My companion was evidently more wideawake, for as I dreamed, there came the sharp crash of his gun, and a jungle fowl, which had rashly chosen that moment to fly across the path, fell almost at my feet.

"Something for the pot," he smiled, handing it over to one of the coolies who was carrying our kit.

As I have said, it was only fifteen miles, but fifteen miles through the jungle takes some doing, and I was glad enough when we came into the little clearing which contained the natives' grass huts and was told that the shack was only a few hundred yards ahead.

Anderson stopped awhile and chatted with the natives, who to me resembled apes more than men, and I noticed a curious look in their eyes, which later I realized was a mixture of awe and fright. He was apparently something of God to them, and although he seemed to speak kindly enough, I could detect the ring of authority in his voice and read abject submission in their eyes and manner.

The hut proved to be, as he said, only a bamboo and thatch affair, but was furnished inside in the same weird manner as his Bungalow. He evidently believed in doing his shooting in comfort,—in fact he admitted so to me, but somehow I couldn't help wishing, even that first night, that the place wasn't quite so comfortable.

It all seemed so unreal: so fantastic, and there was a definite feeling of repulsion about this lonely hut in the depths of the jungle—a feeling akin to that which had struck me when I first saw his Bungalow,—only more pronounced.

For a complete week, however, it seemed as if my apprehensions were unfounded. We had excellent sport in every way, and I was lucky enough to bag two fine bison bulls and an ibex. Anderson was the perfect host and kept me amused night after night with his strange philosophy and endless stock of yarns.

It was on the evening before we started back for home that things happened, and I feel quite creepy even now at the thought of them.

We had had a fairly strenuous day and had returned just before nightfall, with a sambhur stag and a huge boar "tusker" by way of trophies. After an excellent dinner we were lazing amongst the cushions of his divans chatting desultorily. I remember that it was I who brought the subject up first. We happened to be talking on religion, and remembering Anderson's references to "black art," I asked him casually if he thought there was anything in the doings of some of the famous Spiritualists.

He eyed me as if weighing me up, and evidently finding the inspection satisfactory, burst forth:

" 'Anything in it.' Of course there's something in it—there's everything in it, but those idiots at home are merely blundering around the edges of the subject. They think, when they make tables knock, and shapes materialize, that they are invoking spirits,—the poor brainless fools. They are toying with the greatest power on earth, and know nothing of it. They don't realize their danger, and never will until someone accidently stumbles on the truth,—and then he probably won't live to tell it."

I was keenly interested and even rather excited.

"I'm afraid I can't quite follow what you are talking about. What is this 'power' to which you refer?"

The light of fanaticism was burning in the man's eye, but his reply was sober enough.

"It is something that took me years to discover, and even then I only found it in the end by accident. I think I have mentioned before that these Tiamurs,"—referring to the jungle tribe near whose settlement we were living—"have powers that no one else on earth possesses. From them I accidently learnt the secret, but given the necessary clue, have raised that power to be something more than it will ever be to them and have gone many stages further than they ever will. You won't understand the full psychological details, so I am going to put it as simply as I can. You may have read in the papers of an experiment conducted which proved that the human eye has a slight power of attraction. In this case I believe, it was demonstrated that the 'rays', or whatever you like to call them, issuing from a man's eye, were powerful enough to move a small object suspended from a hair, and cause it to oscillate slightly. I, at that time, was dabbling in so-called Spiritualism and I recall finding, after reading that article—which seemed to draw no great public attention—that it fitted in with a theory which I had already begun to form. Then suddenly out here, I hit on the truth. I won't trouble you with how it happened, but will tell you of the stage which I have now reached. It's a difficult thing to explain, but I'll do my best."

I shifted to a more comfortable position amongst the cushions and waited for this remarkable man to continue.

"The human brain is a marvellous affair—far more wonderful than even the leading psychologists dream. They do not know, for example that from the moment of birth until death, the cells of our brains are ceaselessly sending out what, for lack of a better word, I will call 'rays'. Neither do they know that these 'rays' have the most extraordinary powers. They succeeded in proving that the eye could move matter, but there they dropped the subject. Little did they realize that the eye was then merely concentrating those brain 'rays' and that given time and practice, the brain is capable of moving far more than a mere scrap of metal dangling from a hair."

He must have seen the doubt in my eyes, for he pointed to an ordinary walking stick leaning against the wall at the other side of the room.

"Watch," he said curtly.

I looked; rubbed my eyes and looked again. It was true and I wasn't dreaming. *The walking stick was moving slowly across the room,—upright and of its own accord!*

I was too spellbound even to be frightened, and turned my gaze to his face. His eyes were fixed on the stick and the pupils had narrowed down to mere pin-points. Almost could I imagine those "rays" of his issuing from his brilliant eyes.

He took the stick as it reached him and threw it over to me. I examined it with care. It was solid enough in all conscience.

He regarded me with shining eyes.

"Frightened?"

I shook my head dumbly. I was—but I wasn't going to admit it.

"No," he said, continuing his talk as if there had been no interruption, "there is nothing to be frightened of in that, but it's when we reach the next stage that in the hands of amateurs, the danger arises. Shall I go on?"

I nodded, still incapable of speech.

"Even the Tiamurs can do *that*, and so can our scientific and spiritualistic friends at home,—on a minor scale. They can even go a step further and use those rays to *make* matter—but they don't realize it. When they see a ghostly face in a darkened room, or feel beastly animals crawling or flapping their wings, they think they have invoked some long dead spirit. What they really see, however, is the creation of their own minds, or rather of their sub-conscious minds. Science has long ago proved that the entire universe, including you and me, is composed of atoms. Constantly they are trying to smash atoms, or some such foolishness, little knowing that from the human brain alone the necessary power can be generated. 'Rays' that are sufficient to attract the atoms which compose an object, are also invested with further powers,—those of disintegrating and re-assembling atoms in any form that the brain may desire. The 'ghosts' that spiritualists see are the result of their inadvertent use of this power, and therein lies their danger. I have the advantage that I know what I am playing with—they don't."

He paused a while and I began to wonder whether it was all a ghastly nightmare or not. Before I had time to speak, he had commenced again.

"So far have I got, my friend, but here temporarily I have to admit defeat. I can create something out of nothing. I can make a stone where there was no stone before, *but* those creations remain a part of me, and one the relaxation of my will power they depart into the void out of which they came. If I could separate them from myself. I would achieve the ambition of my life, and control a power sufficient to rule the world." And he finished triumphantly. "*I am on the verge of obtaining that power.*"

I stared at him fascinated: horror incredulity and terror on my face. He looked at me in amusement.

"You evidently don't believe me. I will have to give you another demonstration."

I shook my head beseechingly, but he was too engrossed with his subject.

"Think of some definite object, will you," he demanded. "Not too large for convenience's sake. The brain, like a wireless set, has its receiving as well as its transmitting apparatus. If you think hard enough of anything, my brain will receive your thoughts and reproduce the object of them for you. All I ask of you is to remain where you are and not touch either me or it."

My curiosity overcame my terror, but for the life of me I could find nothing suitable to think of. Finally in despair, I started thinking of one of the beautiful champagne glasses that we had used in his Bungalow that first night. It was a lovely thing of purest glass with a long tapering stem and delicately tinted lip, and the memory of it was still strong in my mind. I glanced at Anderson as I thought. He was half sitting, half lying on a divan some eight feet away, and separated from me only by a low lacquer table. His eyes, as on the previous occasion, were wide open, but with the pupils contracted to mere pin points while their gaze was concentrated on the table between us. I shrank back in mortal terror from what I felt was going to happen, but my eyes were fascinated—fixed. It happened! Before my very eyes it happened! In the subdued light of that little room, the fruit of my brain was born out of the very air, and as if prove its reality, Anderson stretched out a huge arm and rapped its edges until it rang. It was too much for my frayed nerves. I put my arms before my face as if to ward off a blow and to shut out the sight of that slender glittering "thing".

"Stop, stop," I almost shrieked. "It's—it's blasphemy."

The next thing I can remember distinctly was the fizz of on opening soda water bottle, and looking up from the shelter of my arms, found Anderson standing beside me pouring soda into a good stiff peg of whisky.

"Here drink this my son," he said quite gently. "I was a damned fool to go showing off my parlour tricks. They are things I have never shown anybody,—except the Tiamurs, and even they don't like them."

I grabbed at the whisky gladly enough and Anderson became his usual courteous self, but I was thankful when dawn broke next morning, and after a sleepless night I was able to get away from the scene of those nightmare experiments into what seemed the clear, uncontaminated air of the jungle.

Anderson enquired solicitously after my health, and again expressed regret at having scared me so.

"I'm afraid that I was carried away by my enthusiasm," he said. "I will be grateful if you will keep all that you have seen and heard to yourself,—at any rate unless you hear from me."

I promised him readily enough. I didn't want to be considered more of a liar than I was already.

The morning was clear and fine, but even in the pleasant twilight of the jungle I was still feeling nervous, and hurried on determined to set off for civilization in the car that day rather than spend another night with Anderson. In order to travel quicker, we had left our guns with the luggage coolies and after some three hours brisk tramping, were some way on ahead of them.

As we were crossing a small track of swampy ground. Anderson leant forward and examined some marks in the mud.

"I see that our old friend the 'rogue' elephant has just come along here," he remarked. "He can't be very far ahead either, as the water is only just beginning to filter into his tracks."

"How do you know he is a 'rogue,'" I asked, "Is this another exhibition of your supernatural powers?"

Anderson laughed good naturedly.

"No. I happen to know that he is the 'rogue' from the fact that one of his feet is slightly deformed and smaller than the others. He has been hanging around the countryside for some time, and besides doing a lot of damage to the Estate, is reputed to have killed several coolies. I hope we don't meet him with only walking sticks in our hands. I've half a mind to wait for our rifles."

I succeeded in persuading him to come on, but a few minutes later bitterly regretted my impetuosity.

We had passed into one of those occasional small clearings in the jungle where thick grass was growing shoulder high. We had got nearly three-quarters of the way across it when suddenly from the other side, came the shrill, unmistakable 'trumpet' of an angry elephant, and the next instant the jungle parted and the enormous bulk of a solitary tusker came charging down towards us.

A charging elephant is an unpleasant sight even under the most favourable circumstances but when one is standing defenceless in a clearing with the nearest tree some seventy-five yards away, the unpleasantness becomes acute.

"Run," came Anderson's voice curtly, "For your life."

I needed no bidding; I was already running, but I had only gone a few yards when I somehow sensed that my companion wasn't following. I glanced over my shoulder as I raced along, and the sight which I saw pulled me up dead in my tracks.

Alone out there in the clearing stood Anderson, waiting the charging elephant, and as I watched, I saw him raise a heavy rifle to his shoulder and aim deliberately at the only vulnerable spot of a head-on elephant,—the centre of its forehead. Came the ear splitting crash of a 450 Express and the elephant, staggering forward a few paces, fell head foremost to the ground, almost on top of the prostrate figure of Anderson, who had crumpled up on the report of the rifle. I dashed back horror-stricken, but was too late. They were both dead when I reached them."

Peter paused again and finished his drink.

"But I thought," said Yvonne, "that you had left your rifles behind."

Peter hesitated.

*"We had,"* he said slowly at last. *"When I reached his body all that was lying at his side was his walking stick."*

There was a deathly silence as Peter's voice completed the tale.

"We carried him back to the Bungalow, and the Doctor whom I brought back next day after an all night run, declared death due to heart failure. I didn't tell him the full yarn—I didn't want to be ridiculed—so, as the natives weren't saying anything, I let him have his own way. Any rate it would have done no good. Poor Anderson had achieved his ambition and in doing so had saved my life and lost his own."

Peter fished in a pocket and pulled out a small battered lump of lead: obviously the spent bullet of a high velocity rifle. We crowded round to examine it.

"I found that next day in the dead elephant's brain," he said simply.

From *The Madras Mail Annual* (1930)

# *The Aryan Smiles*

by J. Warton and N. Blenman

IT SHALL EVER BE ONE OF MY GREATEST REGRETS THAT I DID not go with Michael Clancey on the evening he met his untimely death. If I had not been able to prevent it, I might, at least, have consoled a pious widow and daughter with the thought that his soul still lingered for the charity of their prayers, and that his end had not been the awful one of suicide. Not that they inclined to the latter view, but they feared it, while, with the mentality of simple Irish Catholics, they naturally acquiesced in the superstitious explanation of a very bizarre incident.

Whereas I might, then, have been able to bring into the light of human reason at least one of these happenings in a community where too ready a credence is placed in the damnable Black Arts of the Orient, it is to a mind, sceptical and materialistic as mine, the more galling to have to relate only the remarkable facts concerning the loss of a very dear friend.

"Mike," I had said, "I can't go with you to-night, much as I would love to have a drive"—and much as I liked his company; for we used to spend many an evening chatting of our military days, and Mike, bluff and quick-tempered, had been the most popular man in the Battery.

We had come to India together, and like so many soldiers in the old days, we had been glad to take up quieter occupations and to remain in the country. The growing railway systems offered a good field for employment, and my friend had joined the Southern Punjab and Delhi Railway; on this comparatively small section of railroad, he had had a somewhat meteoric career. As Station Master of Delhi, and a man not yet forty-five, he had reason to exult in his change of professions, for he might otherwise have been plain Farrier-Sergeant Clancey.

I had been lucky to get in with a firm of piecegoods merchants.

One of our more important men was up from Calcutta, and as I had a semi-business dinner to attend that evening, I did not feel quite up to the conviviality which Michael Clancey would be sure to lead me into: although there was time for a little outing before dinner, I had preferred to entertain him at my bungalow. After an half-hour's tete-a-tete and a couple of mild whiskies on the verandah, he had climbed into his dog-cart alone, cracked his whip and turned sharply out my gate. It was a sultry July evening. Before going in to dress, I stood outside for a few minutes listening to the fine even patter of his Waler's hoofs get fainter and fainter down the long quiet road. I had seen and heard the last of Mike Clancey for ever, but did not know it then.

It must have been 7-30 when he left me; an hour later I was at the hotel at which I was to dine. Four of us sat down to dinner.

We were well into our cigars when I received the following note. On top of the small envelope was written "Urgent, Please deliver at once." Excusing myself, I read:—

"Dear Mr. Warton,—Mr. Clancey's syce, who is the bearer of this, will tell you more than I can. Being a friend of Mr. Clancey's, I am sure you will question the man at once. I am nervous about it myself, and shall tell you the reasons for my anxiety if you would call over now.—Yours sincerely,—Marie Smythe."

Mrs. Smythe was one of the Railway colony. I think her husband was the Plate-Layer. My friend was boarding with the Smythes at the time while his wife and daughter were in the Hills.

Somewhat disconcerted at receiving this vague note, I crumpled it into my pocket, and, leaving the company as nicely as I could, went downstairs to hear what the groom had to say. He had come down in his master's dog-cart; the horse was champing and sneezing over his head while he gave me a story, which, coupled with Mrs. Smythe's note, was sufficiently alarming, although the whole affair bore a very queer aspect indeed.

For a time I wondered whether it warranted my leaving the dinner party. I told the syce to wait, however, and went back to my fellow-diners for a few minutes and even had another drink. Being uneasy all the time, and as it was nearly ten o'clock, I decided at last to go. Saying boldly that a friend had been suddenly taken ill, and receiving from each one a laconic "I'm sorry!" as he rose to shake hands, I bid my companions "Good-night."

Sitting by the syce, while he drove me to Mrs. Smythe's, I got him to recount his brief story.

"The Sahib went out first at seven o'clock," he said.

"Yes, yes," I put in, "he came to see me."

"Well, he returned home, called for the whisky, sat a while on the 'chabutra', and then we drove off towards the Roshanara Gardens. Sahib often went there before dinner 'to take the air'. He would walk round the Gardens, leaving me to hold the horse. This evening, I thought it rather late for the master's usual drive. However, it was still lightsome when he pulled up in the Gardens. He alighted and went off in the direction of the Tank. Holding the reins, I sat down on the gravel walk. But the Sahib being longer than I thought he would, I eventually took the horse and buggy a few paces off on to the lawn, where I secured the reins to a small tree, gave the animal his fodder from the cart, and began to smoke myself.

"In this way, Sahib, I had consumed two or three 'biris', strolling about some times to see if the master was in sight; and the horse meanwhile had finished his bag of hay.

"There was no sign of the Sahib, and we must have been out more than an hour—he usually dined by half-past-eight—so I walked all round the Gardens. After waiting another short while, I drove back to the 'kothi' without him, then inquired at Smythe Memsahib's, who sent me back to the Gardens at once to look for my master; but I did not stay there more than a few minutes. To tell you the truth, Sahib, we poor country folk are very frightened. And what was the use of waiting? So I went again to the Memsahib, after having called first at your house; and then she gave me the letter to you."

To such a narrative I had no comments to make, and waited rather curiously for Mrs. Smythe's account, which she gave me in the presence of her husband.

"We stayed dinner very long for Mr. Clancey," she said, after apologising for having called me away. This, she said, she would not have done but for the fact that Mr. Clancey had been rather unwell during the day.

"Oh," I remarked, "I didn't know that. He seemed all right when I saw him this evening."

"It's a funny thing, Mr. Warton," she went on. "A kind of fits, perhaps; though I have never seen anything like it before. At breakfast Mr. Clancey complained of feeling very hot. He said his skin was burning. I suggested 'prickly heat'; but he assured me it wasn't that, and began to eat quite heartily. Suddenly we saw his face go as red as a turkey-cock's; he jumped from the table, tearing off his collar and unbuttoning his coat. 'Fiends alive, Fiends alive, Mrs. Smythe!' he shouted, grabbing at his clothes. 'I'll go home!' 'No, go into the bedroom, Mr. Clancey,' I said. 'What's the matter?' throwing off his coat, he went inside, supported by my husband."

"With his shirt off", added Mr. Smythe, "he ran straight to the bathroom, and ducked his head in the tub. 'I'm on fire, Smythe,' he cried. 'Splash it on hard!' and we drenched him to the waist with mugfuls of cold water, you could see the very blood glowing under his skin, but it soon got back its natural whiteness, and he sat down with us and finished his meal."

Mrs. Smythe continued the account.

"We saw him again at tea time," she told me. "He had just come from his round at the Station, as usual. He ate very little, but drank an enormous quantity of tea, saying there was nothing like tea for cooling the system. It has been a very hot day, as you know, and we did not think too much of Mr. Clancey's discomfort. However, I took his temperature before he went home; he had no fever."

"In that case," I said, rising impatiently, "it might be that poor Clancey is lying in an apoplectic fit, or something of the kind—I wonder whether this man looked properly!—I had better go to the Gardens and see."

Smythe offered to accompany me, and we set off to the Roshanara Gardens. On the way I had more details of my friend's misfortune.

"My wife had not time to tell you," began Smythe; "but what has been troubling her most is damn queer—the sort of thing you might have no patience with; I have little time myself for these tales—But I may as well tell it to you. Now, these queer symptoms of Clancey's, when he complained of his flesh being on fire—these may be anything at all. But he told us blandly that he thought it was the jogi's curse."

"The jogi's curse?" I said.

"Yes," reiterated Smythe, "the jogi's curse. And when he said this, my wife became very solemn, telling him it was not right to jest about such things. But let me explain.

"Now, you know how hot-headed Clancey is. It appears that last evening he maltreated one of these religious mendicants—he told us about it at dinner. He was driving through the Station garden when he noticed this sadhu fellow on the grass-plot. The man had set up a few bricks, lit a fire, and was preparing his evening meal. What Clancey said to him I don't know, and he probably had good reason to be annoyed, for he has practically made that garden with his own hands; but he should not have struck the fellow,—though he told us about it very sadly afterwards. As a matter of fact, he is too fond of that horsewhip of his, using it on the Station staff at times; in spite of it, they are fond of him. Anyhow, he says the jogi was insolent, that he laughed and went on with his cooking. The Station Master riled that his authority should be so flouted, dismounted from his dog-cart, whip in hand, and ordered the trespasser out of the garden; when he still would not go, Clancey lashed the smiling Hindu three or four times across the back. The jogi poured some water on to the fire, and, drawing out the moistened ashes from his 'chulah', threw it in handfuls over his naked body, applying the emolient especially to his smarting wounds. Then, holding up his skinny hands and pointing heavenward, he muttered something which Irishman took to be oaths and curses. He says the man finally gathered up his things, spat on the ground, and went away, but not without looking round at Clancey and saying: 'The Almighty has a Lash of Retribution! Its thongs are Flames of Fire!"

"But," I protested, "Clancey wouldn't understand all that."

"I believe one of his babus overheard, and translated it for him," explained Smythe.

"An eloquent piece of nonsense!" I said. "But, of course, it's just possible Clancey has been ailing from the weather. It has been a particularly hot day."

In this part of India the Monsoon is often very feeble. Here we were at the end of July, and still panting for the rain. The sky, however, had been overcast all day, which made the heat the more unbearable.

It was pitchy dark in the Gardens; but with the aid of a couple of railway lanterns, we eventually went over the grounds very thoroughly by eleven o'clock. During this search Smythe and I walked right under a huge peepul tree that grew on the verge of the Tank. Under this tree we missed the light from the second lantern, and, calling to the syce who carried it behind us, we saw that he stood at some distance away. He said that he would not go under that tree for love or money, and begged that we would not ask him to do so. So Smythe took the lamp from him, and we passed on after examining the ground under the tree, as we did with every other dark patch and corner of the Gardens.

There was nothing for it now but to begin a long vigil on the spot where my friend had left his dog-cart, when he had commenced his walk. About midnight Smythe went home to his wife, so I was left with the syce for company. He sat cross-legged on the grass near me, while I reclined on the cushion seat which had been removed from the trap.

Feeling the urge to engage him in conversation, there was one question that came to me at once. (The more important matter of his master's encounter with the jogi we had already thrashed out; he had been with Clancey at the time and corroborated that story). In fact, the question I put to my companion now was just an idle one, for I guessed the likely answer, knowing the minds of these rustic folk regarding such things as phantoms and spooks. The tree he had been so afraid of, I thought, is probably haunted by a she-devil, the well-known 'churail'. Anyhow, "Syce", I said, "why wouldn't you come under that peepul tree with us?"

"No Hindu would, Sahib," he answered, "unless he were a stranger in Delhi."

"No? And why not?"

"How shall I tell you? You white people laugh at these things. But you must have heard it when you were under the tree."

"Heard what?"

"Didn't you hear him smoking his hookah?.... T-oo-r-r-.... T-oo-r-r-r?"

"What?" I said. "In the branches of the tree?—That was a night-bird of some kind!" And I laughed.

"For this reason," he said indignantly, "I did not wish to say anything about the cursed tree."

However certain I felt that this simple-minded Hindu had mistaken the croaking of some nocturnal creature for the bubbling and gurgling drawl of a hookah, I was ready to hear any old story, and cajoled him into telling me a rather good one.

"In the first place," I said, "why do you call it a cursed tree? The peepul is sacred to you Hindus."

"Yes," he agreed "but this particular peepul has been cursed. It came about in this way: In the time of the Emperor Aurungzeb, a certain 'pir' took up this abode under this tree, and began to persecute the poor Hindu people who used to come to the sacred tree to offer their 'poojahs' and to bathe in the Tank. He would throw away the flowers, sweets and fruits of their sacrifices, desecrate their altars, and beat the devotees off if necessary".

"The Hindus," I commented, "were very meek to allow the high-handed behaviour of this Mohamedan!"

"You know the fanatical Muslim Aurungzeb was," he said. "The poor Hindus could hope for no redress. And so things went on at this peepul tree, till, making a virtue of necessity, the Hindus of the neighbourhood abandoned their sacred tree to this wicked man. In fact, their veneration grew to loathing—it was considered to have been defiled. And when, eventually, the holy pir was buried on the spot where he had made his home, under the tree for some forty years, the curse was thought to be complete, and no Hindu would think of sacrificing under this peepul. One night, they say, a band of daring youths (Hindus) went to the pir's grave, exhumed the recently-interred body, and threw it into the Tank, where it remained. Since then, Sahib, the soul of that wretched pir haunts the old peepul. I heard him to-night, worse luck! You heard him too. And he is always there at the top of the tree at night, pulling away at his hubble-bubble."

"Humph!" I said, and thought I would like to go over to the tree and throw a few stones at the croaking bird which had given rise to the syce's funny story. I might have made the test, but that we had to take shelter presently under an open pavilion near by, for the long-promised rain had come at last, though at an awkward time. A high wind blew the sand into our faces, there were quick flashes of lurid lightning, and we had only just enough time to unyoke the Waler before we realised that we were exposed to an Indian sandstorm. I thought the horse would have kicked down the wooden posts of the pavilion, and that the zinc roof would have been blown over our heads, while we struggled to make the animal share the small shelter with us. Soon the elements became calmer, and so did the horse. But suddenly, as if from nowhere, there was a bluish-yellow flash and a crashing report. Looking in the direction of the sound, I heard a splashing.

"Sahib," whispered the syce, with his hand on my arm, "that is the peepul tree! It has been struck!"

These sandstorms are fiercer than they are lasting, so in a few minutes we were able to go out and examine the tree, the syce keeping at a very safe distance. Almost half of it had seen torn down and lay immersed in the water of the Tank. The other part stood gaunt and lifeless on a charred and blackened trunk. This was easily discernible, for the bark of the peepul is of a glistening light grey colour.

I had had enough of strange stories, and now had come an uncanny experience. How this fitted into a chain of apparently occult influences was shown the next morning. After an anxious night of waiting and watching, informing the police, and having no rest, we began dredging operations at the Tank; the clue for the search was Clancey's horsewhip.

Like a lost fishing-rod, it was seen to be sticking up out of the weeds close to the fallen tree. The syce recognised it at once;

he said the Sahib always took the whip with him in these little walks.

About mid-way the body of my poor friend was brought out, with all the ordinary signs of drowning apparent. The water was certainly weedy; yet Clancey could swim well. But how and why he got into the water shall never be known. And just before his body was found, one of the men brought up a vessel covered over and filled with a loamy black soil form the bottom of the Tank; when the mud was removed, the object revealed itself to be an old copper hookah.

"Throw it back!" cried the syce. "It belonged to the wicked pir!"

Whether he was right or not will also never be known.

From the *Indian State Railway Magazine* (June 1933)

# *Panther People*

by C.A. Kincaid

ALEC BRIGGS, A TALL POWERFULLY BUILT MAN IN THE middle thirties, was driving through the Dharwar forest one cold weather morning in an ancient but still quite efficient touring car. He was superintendent of forests in the Kanara District and was on his way to confer with other forest officers, English and Indian, in Dharwar. He had come up the Ghats[1] and had a bare twenty miles to go before he reached the open plain. He knew the road well; only a few weeks before he and an English friend had driven along it and at a bend had suddenly come face to face with a tiger. The tiger had stepped with a low growl to one side; Briggs

1. The mountains on the western boundary of the great central plateau of India.

pressed the accelerator and the car shot past. A mile or so farther on they had met two or three forest women picking up sticks for fuel. Greatly excited, they had shouted to them to get into the car and escape; a tiger was close by. The women had declined the invitation with a smile. "The old tiger," they said, "why, we see him every day. He is quite harmless; he never hurts anyone." Indeed in their indulgent contempt they even neglected to call him 'they'—the royal privilege to which all tigers are entitled. Briggs smiled at the recollection and looked at the trees which surrounded him on all sides and, but for the road to guide him, would have soon engulfed him in their midst.

Just then out of a small clearing in front stepped an Englishman. He had no topi and he was dressed in a suit of a curious grey material, old but well cut and serviceable. Briggs wondered what on earth the man was doing in this wild haunted forest. He threw the gear lever into neutral, pressed his brake and pulled up close to the newcomer. As he came nearer, Briggs noticed his curious build. He must have stood six feet two, but his legs and his arms were quite short; indeed, out of all proportion to his great height. On the other hand, his body was beautifully formed with a strange catlike grace that quite made up for the shortness of his limbs.

Briggs addressed him courteously and said: "Hullo! What's the matter? Can I help you at all? I expect you have lost your way."

The stranger answered in a pleasant well-bred voice: "No, I have not got lost. I know this forest well; besides I have a useful bump of locality. I am on a shooting expedition. I was just walking to my camp. Still, as it is some way off near the edge of the forest, I should be glad of a lift."

"Right-o!" said Briggs, cordially. "Come along inside. I'll tell you what. We'll drive to a glade I know of a couple of miles ahead and there we'll have breakfast. I have a tiffin basket at the back and I shall be very glad indeed if you'll join me."

"It is most awfully kind of you. My name is Savile. I used to be in the 82nd, but I retired three years ago and now I am just loafing about and shooting when I get the chance."

The car did not take long to carry the forest officer and his guest to the glade of which the former had spoken. Briggs opened the door and got out; he lifted the tiffin basket from the back to a convenient mound. The basket was amply furnished, for its owner liked to do himself well when on the march. Two large flasks held hot tea. Polished white dishes, cups, saucers, plates and cutlery of all kinds offered every aid to the consumption of cold chicken and tongue, ham, pressed beef, currant cake and fruit that awaited the hunger of the travellers.

Briggs carved the chicken and gave his newly-found friend an ample portion. Savile snatched the plate so greedily that Briggs thought to himself 'the poor devil must be starving.' Certainly Savile polished off his helping in no time and was quite ready for a second before Briggs, stout trencherman though he was, had really started on his first. Then Savile said in his clear well-bred voice: "Are you not afraid to go through this forest alone?"

"No," said Briggs with some surprise, "why?"

"Well, of course, it may only be idle gossip; but I have heard from some trustworthy natives that there are panther people about."

Briggs began to wonder whether his guest was not an escaped lunatic; so, instead of asking him incredulously what the devil he meant, he said as calmly as he could: "No, I have never heard that; but what are panther people exactly?"

"They are men and women who have the power to turn themselves into panthers at will; or perhaps they may be panthers that have the power to turn themselves into men and women. After all it does not matter much, for it comes to the same in the end, doesn't it?" And Savile smiled whimsically.

Briggs began to grow deeply interested: "You surely have never met such people, have you?"

"Well, yes. I was so unfortunate some four years ago as to marry one of them."

This was more than Briggs could stand: "I wish the deuce, old chap, you wouldn't try to pull my leg. You cannot expect me to believe such a yarn as that."

Savile's courteous manner never changed. "Well, such a statement does seem rather tall in cold blood; but if you like I'll tell you my story and then you can believe it or not, as you please...."

"Yes, do."

"Some eight years ago I had just got my majority and I thought it was time to marry. Subalterns, you know, are expected to remain bachelors. Married captains are not always popular; but majors are more or less required to have wives. So I began to look for a suitable lady."

"When a man begins to look for a wife, it is wonderful how soon he finds a lady who seems to be his long-looked-for ideal. I met my soul's mate at Dhulia in Khandesh, where her father held a post on the railway. After her marriage she insisted on spending our honeymoon shooting the great jungles of Western Khandesh; and she never seemed so happy as when we were camping in the forest. After our honeymoon we went to Mhow, where my regiment was stationed and the rainy season passed very pleasantly with polo, cricket and tennis—the usual military life, you know. My wife was a bit of a flirt; but I did not mind that. She had only just come out when I married her and I realised that she was wild to enjoy to the full the new life she had just begun to know."

"Among her favourite squires was a Civil Servant, a man called Trevelyan, who was in the Political Department and was officiating as first assistant to Sir William Thompson, the Agent to the Governor-General in Central India. Trevelyan was a good-looking, well-set-up man and I liked him personally so much that I never dreamt of being jealous of his friendly relations with my wife. When in November we received and invitation to spend ten days at Christmas in the Agent's camp at Bundelkhand, I guessed, and rightly, that Trevelyan had got us the invitation. My wife was delighted at the idea of camping in Central India. I was overjoyed at the thought of bagging my first tiger."

"Well, to make a long story short, we reached our destination on Christmas Eve. Although there were not many guests there was an abundance of large and luxurious tents, while a huge *shamiana*,[2] divided into two parts, served as a dining room and a drawing room. The Agent to the Governor-General had invited eight guns and three of them, including myself, had brought their wives. A big drive was fixed for Christmas Day and H.H. the Maharaja of

2. Large state tent.

Ortha, who owned the jungle where we were camping, had done some splendid staff work. He did not take part in the shoot; but I saw him one day when he came to call on the Agent."

"Did you know him?" asked Savile, pausing.

"No," said Briggs, "I am afraid my acquaintance with Maharajas is somewhat limited."

"Well, if you had seen him once you would never forget him. He stood six feet high and was very handsome; his bearing was such as can only be found in a Rajput chief who claims descent through two hundred generations from the divine Ramachandra himself. However, I must not begin telling you about Hindu divinities and Rajput descents or I shall never finish. I must get on with my story.

"My wife and I had separate tents—it was her wish always to sleep alone as she said I snored so badly that I disturbed her—and our tents stood at the edge of the encampment. On Christmas Day we all met cheerfully in the big tent for tea and eggs and toast and to wish each other a Merry Christmas; then we set out. Most of the way we were carried on the Maharaja's elephants—interesting at first but slow after a bit, for their maximum speed is some two miles an hour. When we got near the place where the tigers were supposed to be lying up, we got off the kneeling elephants and walked to the *machans* assigned to us. I was rather a junior, so I was given an outside place and never really expected to shoot anything: nevertheless, in big game shooting luck lies upon the knees of the gods.

"Suddenly I heard the heavy, dull footfalls of a great beast and into the open space below my tree stepped a magnificent male tiger. It was in the prime of life, brilliantly striped and wearing its deep winter fur. I took careful aim at the point of its shoulder and fired. It fell; I gave it a second barrel and then, reloading, waited, hoping for another animal. Then I heard two shots with a little interval between them; they came from the direction of the A.G.G.'s *machan* and I guessed that he had secured a tiger too. I was right. When the beaters came up, we compared our experiences. There had been a tiger and a tigress in the beat. I had got the one and my host the other."

"You were jolly lucky," murmured Briggs, "to bag a tiger in your first beat."

"Yes; I was, and there was no lighter-hearted guest in the A.G.G.'s camp that evening at dinner; but now I am coming to the sinister side of the story. I am afraid I am boring you?" Savile paused on a note of interrogation.

"No, please do go on: I am deeply interested."

"Very well. Next morning as we sat in the big tent at our tea and toast, a young fellow, Howard of the Central India Horse, rushed in greatly excited. Addressing Sir William Thompson, he cried: 'I say, Sir, a panther came into our camp last night. There are pugs[3] close to my tent and just outside Trevelyan's!' His statement brought answering cries of 'Rot!' 'Not really!' and we all ran out to see the panther's tracks. Yes; there they were. There was no doubt about it. The beast could not have been very large, six foot six or seven foot at most judging from its footprints.

---

3. Tracks.

"After talking the subject threadbare, we turned to other topics. That day we beat another part of the jungle but drew a blank. Next morning Howard again brought news of fresh panther's tracks in the camp. This time they were visible outside my wife's tent. I began to get seriously alarmed. Trevelyan, too, looked so shocked at the news that I thought he was going to faint. Whether Sir William noticed his assistant's weakness or not, I do not know; but, if he did, he covered it by saying: 'I tell you what. One of you fellows must sit up for the panther this evening close to the camp. We'll tie up a goat and it will probably come about five or so this afternoon. It must be desperately hungry and quite unafraid of men, or it would not enter my camp at night. Will you sit up for it, Savile?'

"I agreed readily, and after tea, on our return from another drive in which Jowers, the Superintendent of Police, bagged a bear, I went and sat up in a tree a couple of hundred yards from the camp. A goat was brought and tied up, but there was not sign of a panther. No monkeys chattered; no birds struck warning notes; even the goat seemed perfectly calm and collected. It grazed for a while and then lay down quietly; so far as I could judge, it fell fast asleep.

"I was disgusted, as you can imagine. At the same time I could not get out of my head Trevelyan's appearance at *chota hazri*. I had begun indeed to regret having accepted Sir William's invitation. The first and second evenings Trevelyan had been too attentive to my wife for my liking, but the third day he had seemed to avoid her and all the fourth day he had appeared to be terrified of her.

"Just before dinner time I slipped out of my tree, went to my tent and changed for dinner."

"I am generally a very sound sleeper; but whether I had eaten or drunk too much, I found myself wide awake at two o'clock in the morning. I was about to turn over when I saw in the bright moonlight—it was nearly full moon—a panther pass close by the *chicks* (screen) of my tent. It was warm and I had not let down the *kanats*.[4] I did not know quite what to do. I was frankly afraid. I thought the best thing was to wait a minute or two and then peep out. I did so, and putting my head through the tent door, I looked about for the panther. It had vanished! Then I went to my wife's tent. It was empty! Her nightdress lay on her bed and her slippers under it. For a moment I thought that she might have paid Trevelyan's tent a visit and the blood rushed to my head; but I grew calm again as I saw that all her clothes lay on her chair. I decided not to make myself ridiculous by rushing into Trevelyan's tent. I would get back to bed and wait until my wife returned and ask her. Once, however, under the bedclothes, I fell asleep and did not wake until my wife came into my tent fully dressed to ask me whether I was not going to have any *chota hazri*. I pulled on my clothes as quickly as I could and went to the dining room.

"There I found more excitement. Fresh tracks had been noticed outside my tent this time and again outside Trevelyan's. I looked at Trevelyan. His appearance was ghastly; rising from his place, he excused himself, pleading fever. I asked my wife later why she

---

4. Canvas door of tent.

had left her tent in the night: she looked me in the face and, laughing, asked me what I meant. When I told her that I had entered her tent and found her bed empty and her nightdress lying on her bed, she said: 'My dear boy, you must have been dreaming. Is it likely that I should walk about the camp at 2 a.m. stark naked?' I could find no answer and for a time I really thought that I must have been dreaming. I resolved, nevertheless, to keep awake the following night, rifle in hand, and shoot the panther should it come again into camp. I told no one, not even my wife, of my intention. I was afraid that everyone else would want to sit up, too, and the panther would be scared.

"After dinner I drew my chair close behind the *chick* of my tent and, as before, I did not lower the *kanat*. I kept awake until one, and then I must have dropped off to sleep. About two I awoke with a start and saw in the brilliant moonlight the same panther walk just in front of my tent. I rose as quietly as I could and, peeping outside, saw it entering Trevelyan's tent. I had my rifle in my hand; I opened the breech quickly to make quite sure the cartridges were there, and then went on tiptoe after the invader. I was terribly afraid it might be a man-eater and would kill Trevelyan before I got there.

"When I reached his *kanat* I pushed it gently on one side and saw the panther standing by Trevelyan's bed. He was sitting up with a look of terror on his face. It seemed to me as if the next moment the panther would spring on my friend and carry him away. I raised my rifle carefully and noiselessly and, aiming at the panther's heart, fired. It sank in a heap on the ground. I rushed in and said: 'Thank God, old chap, I was in time.' To my surprise he did not thank me nor indeed did he speak at all. With an agonised expression he pointed with his finger to the dead animal. I looked and saw a change come over the panther. Its fur disappeared; its forelegs lengthened and became arms; its body shortened, its face lost its bestial shape and became human. Lastly, to my horror, the beast that I had shot changed into the naked corpse of my wife. I turned to Trevelyan and said 'In Heaven's name, what is the meaning of this?' He replied, as if half out of his wits, 'I have behaved like an infernal blackguard, Savile. While pretending to be your friend, I have made love to your wife. On Christmas Day I made her promise to come to my tent that night. This she could do, unseen as I hoped, as you had separate quarters.'

"'You damned sweep, Trevelyan!'

"'Yes, that is just what I was—and well, I was suitably punished. Your wife came about 2 o'clock when I was asleep. I woke up to find her standing by my bedside clad only in my old overcoat. As I put out my arms, she kissed me. I took her into my embrace and she offered no resistance; but when she was about to go I noticed that she had brought no clothes. I asked her what she would do and how she had come. She could not have crossed the open space in the moonlight, mother naked. She laughed and said that she needed no clothes. She stood by the bed without a stitch on and then before my eyes changed slowly into a panther. I was too horrified to say a word and I watched her leave my tent and walk back to her own. I went to bed but I could not sleep. I lay wide awake until morning. Indeed since then I have not slept at all and every night she has come. I have seen her enter as a panther, change into a beautiful woman, and again into a panther. I daresay you have noticed how ill I have looked. I have been on the verge of madness; and now, thank God! you have shot the monster and I am free.'

"Before I could reply, the A.G.G., the Superintendent of Police, Howard and two or three other men crowded into Trevelyan's tent, Howard crying joyfully—'Well, did you get old Spots?—Who fired? Then a hush fell on the group when they saw me, gun in hand, and close in front of me the dead body of my wife, with a hideous expanding bullet wound in her side. The A.G.G. said in a grave, quiet voice: 'Please explain what has happened, Savile.' I replied 'Ask Trevelyan, Sir, he will explain.' Sir William turned to Trevelyan, but he only burst into a fit of maniac laughter: 'He thought he was shooting a panther and he has shot his own wife! Ha! Ha! Ha!'

"Sir William again turned to me said 'You *must* explain, Savile!'

"'It is quite true, Sir, what Trevelyan said. I saw the panther enter his tent. I followed it and, seeing it about to spring on him, I shot it, and now it has turned into my wife. I cannot understand it.'

"'You can hardly expect us to believe that tale, Savile,' said the A.G.G., his lips grimly set. 'I must ask Mr. Jowers, the Superintendent of Police, to do his duty.'

"Jowers stepped forward and arrested me. I was sent back under police guard to Mhow and there I was allowed to engage counsel. I briefed Lawrence and told him the whole story; but it was clear from his expression that he did not believe a word I said.

At last he cried in despair—'Look here, Savile, I am your counsel and, as such, bound to believe what you tell me. Frankly, I cannot; and if I, your advocate, cannot, how can you expect a judge and a jury to do so? So I tell you what: let me conduct your case in my own way. You had plenty of grave and sudden provocation. You were armed as you were sitting up for the panther; and seeing your wife enter Trevelyan's tent at night, you rushed blindly after her, and in a fit of ungovernable rage shot her dead. In France you would be acquitted; even in India the offence will be adjudged culpable homicide not amounting to murder, and you will get two years at the outside.'

"What could I do? My only witness, Trevelyan, had gone raving mad. If my own counsel scoffed at my story, what chance had I with a jury? I should certainly hang. I agreed to plead guilty to a charge of culpable homicide not amounting to murder. After a few formal witnesses had been examined and I had made a statement such as Lawrence had advised, I was convicted on my own plea and sentenced to three years' imprisonment—Lawrence had been unduly optimistic. I got a month or two remission for good conduct and after two and three quarter years in Yeroda jail near Poona, here I am. I have no job and no money."

Savile stopped and rose to his feet as if to stretch himself, and Briggs began to wonder whether it would be possible to squeeze him in as a temporary subordinate in the Forest Department so as to give him a chance to make a fresh start. As he wondered, he saw, or seemed to see, a curious change come over Savile; his yellow coat appeared to be developing round black spots; his fingers that were slender and shapely seemed to be growing into long curved claws; his ears were slipping back to the top of his head and becoming small and pointed; his whole face was jutting out and becoming bestial. Suddenly Savile said with a harsh snarl quite different from the clear cultured voice, in which he had told his story: "And so you will give me all your money, or by God...."

Briggs' brain worked like lightning. He realised that, strong as he was, he would have no chance against the feline monster into which Savile was rapidly turning. Then he remembered that the only animal that a panther fears is a wild buffalo. He pretended to look at something over Savile's shoulder and cried—"Look, look! Buffalo! Buffalo!" Savile swung quickly and nervously round to see. At that moment Briggs sprang to his feet, and with all his strength hit at Savile's jaw. As Briggs rose Savile turned round his head, just in time to receive a tremendous blow on the point of his chin. He collapsed and fell. Briggs, leaving his tiffin basket and its contents where they lay, sprang into his car and pressed the self-starter. Plugs refused to fire, with the result that the car rolled on with only four out of six cylinders working. After a minute or two Briggs looked round anxiously and to his horror saw that the monster—now definitely a panther—had recovered from the blow and was racing after him. He tried to make his car move quicker, but no matter how much he pressed the accelerator, the panther gained on him. At last he felt a shock at the back of the car, and looking round saw the head and forequarters of the panther struggling to climb over the folded hood. He snatched at the cranking handle that lay on the seat at his side and with all his might struck at his enemy's head. The blow caused it to let go the back of the car and it fell to the ground, evidently hurt. Briggs drove on a few hundred yards to where the road rose steeply. He had to drop into second speed and then he looked back again. Once more the panther was following him as hard as it could. In his nervous anxiety to get on, Briggs went back too soon into third speed, with the result that the engine stopped altogether.

"Good God!" muttered Briggs, as the sweat rose on his forehead. "If the self-starter does not work I am lost. I shall never have time to crank up the engine with the handle."

He pressed the self-starter. It gave its usual roar, but no sound came from under the bonnet. Briggs' heart sank into his boots. He pressed again, and this time his heart rejoiced in the answering purr of the working engine. The car again moved forward and in a few seconds reached the top of the slope. Briggs changed into second and then third and, gliding down the hill at full speed, he soon left the panther behind. He looked round and saw his pursuer, just where the road swung outward in a great curve, leap inward to the jungle. He realised then that he was by no means out of danger; for, by taking a short cut through the jungle, the monster would follow the chord while he followed the arc of the semi-circle. An ordinary panther would not have thought of doing so; but it would certainly occur to Savile's diabolic intelligence.

Briggs drove his car as hard as he could; nevertheless, when he reached the point where he expected his enemy to emerge, he unconsciously slowed down to hear, if he could, the soft padding, the only sound a galloping panther makes no matter how thickly the jungle may be strewn with dry leaves. Suddenly he caught the sound quite close to him. In a paroxysm of fear he stamped on the accelerator. This time the old car reacted splendidly. With all its six cylinders working it bounded forward at sixty miles an hour; it was only just in time. suddenly a great yellow body sprang from the forest edge with outstretched paws, missing the back of the car by only a few inches. The road now ran quite straight; the forest began to thin as Briggs neared the outer fringe of the wood. All of a sudden he heard behind him the same well-bred tones in which Savile had entertained him at breakfast.

"Well, goodbye, old chap, and thanks awfully for the lift and the breakfast."

Briggs looked round and there, some three hundred yards away, he saw Savile, just as before, in his yellow well-cut, well-worn shikar suit. Savile spoke again, but this time with a note of irony in his cultured voice which the high trees on each side of the road transmitted like a speaking tube:

"And if you hear of a nice, cushy job, you'll be sure and let me know, won't you? The Dharwar forest will always find me."

With these words and a wave of his hand Savile strolled out of sight into a clearing close by. Briggs drove the rest of the journey in a state very near insanity. He kept repeating to himself interminably the problem suggested by Savile: "Are panther people men who turn themselves into panthers; or are they panthers who turn themselves into men?"

After another hour and a half of furious driving he reached Dharwar. There he drove to the house of his host, the Forest

Superintendent of Dharwar, and when the latter came out to welcome him Briggs asked him excitedly: "I say, Buchan, for God's sake tell me are panther people men who turn themselves into panthers, or panthers who turn themselves into men?"

Buchan, who was a shrewd, kindly Scotsman, did not exclaim as many might have done: "My dear Briggs, what on earth are you talking about?" He saw that Briggs had gone through some very severe experience; so although he had never heard of panther people, he said, like a mother soothing a fretful, questioning child:

"I expect they are men who turn themselves into panthers; after all, a panther would be too stupid to turn itself into a man, wouldn't it?"

There was just enough appearance of logic in this inadequate answer to satisfy Briggs for a moment. Buchan pressed his advantage by adding: "I expect you are very tired. Here, take this whisky and soda and run off for a bath. It's all ready for you; and then we'll have tea and you will tell me the whole story."

Briggs had his whisky and soda and the alcohol and the soothing tones of his host helped to restore his sanity. After he had tubbed and changed, he returned, and during tea he told Buchan his amazing adventure. He then repeated his question as to the origin of panther people.

"Well," said Buchan, "I agree with Savile that it does not really matter, although, judging by his wife's case, it would seem to be the exclusive privilege of humans to turn themselves into panthers. An Indian would say that Mrs. Savile's spirit entered her husband's body after he had shot her; but that only raises the further question whence Mrs. Savile acquired her science. On the other hand, Savile may have invented the story so as to keep you in the forest while he worked up power to change himself into a wild beast. Like your self-starter he may have found it hard to start his internal engine. I tell you what. When you are returning to Dharwar I'll go with you and I'll take with me my six-shooter—none of your popgun pea-shooter Browning automatics—but a real man-stopping Colt six-barrelled revolver and I'll have a cartridge in every barrel. If your friend Savile turns up he'll get something that will check his deplorable versatilities."

Buchan chuckled and Briggs laughed.

As a matter of fact Buchan got no chance of displaying the man-stopping powers of his heavy Colt, for neither of them ever set eyes on Savile. Enquiries at Yeroda jail showed that no Englishman of that name had been imprisoned there. Of course the name 'Savile' may have been assumed; or perhaps Buchan was wrong and Briggs' undesirable acquaintance was really a panther which had somehow or other discovered the art of turning itself into a man, and not a man who knew how to turn himself into a panther.

From *Indian Christmas Stories* (1936)

# *The Old Graveyard at Sirur*

by C.A. Kincaid

WHEN I WAS JUDGE OF POONA SEVERAL YEARS BEFORE the Great War, my tours of inspection used at times to take me to Sirur, the old cantonment some forty miles from Poona that had housed the Poona Horse ever since the conquest of 1818. Not far from the officers' mess and their mud bungalows was the old cemetery. It was no longer used, but it contained the graves of officers of former generations who had succumbed to cholera, enteric fever and the score of other diseases that in eastern lands lie in wait for the English soldier. In the centre rose a tombstone considerably bigger than the others and I often noticed the Indian troopers salute it as they passed. I was loth to question the officers of the Poona Horse, although I knew one or two of them fairly well. It was none of my business and I thought that they might think me impertinent if I probed the matter. One day, however, after seeing several men salute very rigidly with eyes turned towards the central monument, I could no longer control my curiosity; and, meeting a Captain Johnson, an excellent and understanding gentleman, I blurted out:

"Excuse my stupid curiosity; but would you mind telling me why your troopers salute so regularly and so correctly the graveyard. Although they very rightly honour their living superiors, I find it strange that they should salute the dead as well."

"Oh they don't salute the graveyard; they salute old Colonel Hutchings. He commanded the regiment in the eighteen-twenties. He comes out, so they say, and sits on his tomb. It is that big one in the centre. He sits on it and every now and then his wife joins him."

"My dear chap, what are you talking about? They are both dead as doornails. Do you mean their ghosts sit on the tombstone? Have you seen them yourself?"

"Well, I don't know," said Johnson, looking rather confused. "I thought I did once or twice; but it was no doubt my imagination."

"I say, do tell me: who was this Colonel Hutchings? Why does he sit on his tomb? Who was his wife? Why does she sit on his tomb, too?"

"Look here," said Johnson good-humouredly. "I know what an infernal prober you are; but I have neither the time nor the knowledge to stand your cross-examination. You are going into Poona shortly; send for old Rissaldar Major Shinde. I'll write you down his address. He knows all about Colonel Hutchings; he tells us the story after mess sometimes when we ask him to Sirur, as we do once a year at the time of our annual regimental sports. He retired ages ago, but his memory is as fresh as ever."

As Johnson spoke he wrote down the name of the Rissaldar Major and his address in Shukurwar Peth, a well-known quarter in Poona city.

Shortly after my return to headquarters, I sent a line from the Sangam, the judge's official residence, to Rissaldar Major Shinde. I begged him kindly to call on me at 9 a.m. any day that he might be free. I mentioned Captain Johnson's name and told him frankly that I wanted to hear all he could tell me about the cemetery at Sirur, and especially Colonel Hutchings' tomb. Two mornings later a fine old Maratha gentleman drove up in a tonga and was shewn in with every sign of respect by the judge's macebearer.

After shaking my visitor cordially by the hand, I thanked him for coming, and said: "Your name is Shinde, is it not? Are you a member of the family of H.H. the Maharaja of that name?"

"I, Sahib, am a Shinde of Kizarnagar; and you, who have studied our history will remember how the great Madhavrao Shinde would have given up all his titles to be one of my family; but that is another matter. I read in your letter that you wanted to hear about Colonel Hutchings Sahib. He was in a sense more nearly related to me than H.H. the Maharaja; for he married a lady of our family."

"Married a lady of your family? What do you mean, Rissaldar Sahib? He was an Englishman and he could not have married a lady of your family. Nor would her parents have allowed her to marry a Christian no matter who he was."

"Yes, indeed, Sahib, he did, and that was the cause of the trouble. If you care to listen, I shall tell you the story."

"Oh, please do."

"Colonel Hutchings Sahib, so my father used to tell me, was stationed at Kirkee before the Peshwa fought the English in 1818. Hutchings was then a handsome young Captain Sahib and was, it appears, very attractive to our women. One day he and a squadron of horse, mostly recruited from Musulmans and Mhars and all ready to die for their English leader, were riding along the banks of the Muta Mula below where the great dam and bridge now are. It so happened that one of the Shindes of Kizarnagar had died, and, as was then the custom of our family, his widow had given out that she would become a *suttee* and burn with her lord. She was, however, quite a young girl, probably not more than fifteen years of age. When she saw the pyre ready for her to ascend, she lost all control of herself and began to scream and struggle like a maniac. Her mother and married sister tried to soothe her and offered her opium, so that she might be drugged and not feel the pain of burning. But no, Sahib, the widow woman would not listen. One of her brothers wished to stun her with a blow from one of the logs from the pyre; but her mother was reluctant to have this done; for the women of her family—she was a Ghatle from Kolhapur—had never before flinched from the flames. She thought that it would be a disgrace if her daughter did not sit erect on the pyre with her husband's head on her lap and a candle held upright in each hand.

"Just then Hutchings Sahib rode up. The widow, seeing a foreigner, called to him for help. Hutchings Sahib was then a brave young soldier. He did not understand that he was about to insult our holy religion. All he saw was a young and pretty woman, calling to him to save her from a painful death. He turned to his squadron and said: 'Well, brothers, will you help me to carry her out of danger?' Of course those Mlecchas and untouchables were only too pleased. So he charged the crowd. Unarmed, and taken by surprise, they offered little resistance. The dead man's brothers did indeed shew fight; but they were cut down and one of them killed. A couple of Mhars lifted the widow woman in front of Hutchings Sahib's saddle. He turned his horse, rallied his squadron and rode back to Kirkee. There he got a Portuguese padre Sahib, who lived with the Portuguese troops of the Peshwa's army, to marry him to the widow. Thus when the Peshwa's minister complained to Elphinston Sahib, the resident, and demanded the woman back that she might complete the *suttee* ceremony, Elphinston Sahib said that as she had by her second marriage become an Englishwoman and a subject of the king of England, he would not give her up.

"The Peshwa's government told our people and added that owing to the widow woman's remarriage they could do nothing for us. We were furious. The *suttee* ceremony had been stopped. All the merit that would thereby have been acquired by our dead relative had been lost. The widow had been carried off, our kinsmen had been killed, and we were to get no redress. Well, we resolved that if the Peshwa would not help us we should help ourselves.

We vowed that we should kill Hutchings Sahib and the widow woman also."

"You say 'we', Rissaldar Sahib, but you could not have been alive then."

"Quite true, Sahib. I was not born until many years afterwards. I am only seventy years old now. By 'we' I mean the Shindes of Kizarnagar."

"I understand; but do go on, Rissaldar Sahib, with your story."

"As the Sahib pleases. We vowed, as I have said, to kill Hutchings Sahib. It was not, however, easy. Hutchings Sahib and the widow woman lived in a house almost surrounded by the troopers' lines; and as a rumour had spread that we sought their lives, the lines were well guarded and no one allowed inside. One day, it is true, two of our people got through the gates, but before they could do anything they were caught, beaten half dead and thrown out. This added fuel to our hatred; still we could do nothing, for not long afterwards the Peshwa fought the English and they beat him at Kirkee and Ashta. In the end he surrendered and the English, as the Sahib knows, took his country. The Poona Horse were stationed at Sirur. Hutchings Sahib had fought very bravely in the war and he was promoted to command the regiment and to be a Colonel Sahib. He, of course, went to live there too and the widow woman went with him; and all the time we were eating our hearts out with ungratified hatred. It must have been six years after he had risen to command the regiment and was about to return to England that our chance came. We had long hung about Sirur in vain, for he was very cautious. One day, however, when he went a little way out of Sirur in a *palki,* either to shoot blackbuck or chinkara, four of our men rushed out of their hiding place in the dry bed of a river. Slashing the *palki* bearers' legs with our swords, we made them drop the *palki* and then we fell on the Colonel and killed him. His gun was unloaded, but he made a great fight and with his sword wounded two of our men before we could finish him. This was our undoing; for the *palki* men ran back and told the widow woman. She told the police that the murderers must have been Shindes from our village. The police went there and, finding two of our men with unhealed wounds, arrested them. They were identified by the *palki* bearers and hanged. We were now resolved to kill the widow at all costs; but a day or two after the execution she took opium, died and was buried besides the Colonel Sahib. The officers raised the big monument that you have seen over both of them; but they have carved on it only the name of Hutchings Sahib; for they were ashamed of his marriage to a woman not of his race. Ever since the Colonel Sahib sits from time to time on his tomb. Sometimes, although more rarely, the widow woman sits beside him; so the troopers always salute as they pass the tomb. Everyone of them has at one time or another seen him in the spirit."

"So that is the tale, Rissaldar Sahib, thank you ever so much for it."

"There is no need for thanks, Sahib. It is I who should thank you for your courteous hearing. Moreover, that is not all the story, there is more to tell; only no doubt the Sahib is weary and I shall come again some other day."

"Oh no, Rissaldar Sahib," I said quickly, afraid that I should lose the rest of the yarn. "Do go on. So far from tiring me, your words have made me feel young again."

"The Presence is too kind. Well then I shall continue. Many, many years afterwards we Shindes heard that the son of Colonel Hutchings Sahib's sister, a young man called Furley Sahib, had been posted to the Poona Horse. I was then a youth of twenty years and it was arranged that I should enlist as a trooper in the same regiment and, when the chance came, kill Furley Sahib. I must admit that I was not very eager to do this. The quarrel was all so old and I realized that if my plan succeeded, I should probably be hanged; and that if I failed I should have had to work and train as a soldier for nothing. I did not want to be a soldier. I wanted to stay in Kizarnagar and farm our lands. Still my father and my elder kinsmen put such pressure on me and said so many times that it would be a family disgrace if I did not avenge the honour of the Shindes, that at length I gave way. I joined the Poona Horse as a trooper and after some time I contrived to get myself appointed as an orderly to Furley Sahib. He was a fine young man and I had no feeling of dislike towards him; but I could not escape from the task laid upon me. While I was pondering how to kill him—either by arsenic in his tea or by an open attack on him—war broke out with Afghanistan. Furley Sahib immediately got himself transferred to the 2nd Bombay Cavalry and I asked him to take me with him. I was sure that in a battle I could shoot him without anyone noticing me. Furley Sahib was pleased at my request and we went together by train until we caught up the 2nd Bombay Cavalry near the frontier. I shall not weary the Sahib with a long account of what happened. The Sahib knows the history of the war better than I do. It is enough to say that the 2nd Bombay Cavalry were sent with a body of Indian infantry and the 66th English regiment under General Burrows Sahib to hold Kandahar. Stuart Sahib occupied Kabul. One day Burrows Sahib's scouts told him that Ayub Khan and some five thousand Afghans were assembled in the hills only six or seven miles away. Burrows Sahib decided to attack Ayub Khan and disperse his force before it grew to a great army; for the Afghans were streaming to join Ayub Khan from all quarters. Next morning Burrows Sahib and his brigade moved out against Ayub Khan; but we soon learnt that the scouts had either lied deliberately or had themselves been misled. We went more than twelve miles before we saw the Afghans and then we found that they numbered fifty thousand and not five thousand. Nevertheless Burrows Sahib gave orders to attack; indeed he could hardly have done otherwise, for the enemy were advancing against him at great speed. We of the 2nd Bombay Cavalry were on the right flank and three of the squadrons were commanded by three Monteith brothers, who that day shewed themselves to be real soldiers, very brave and skilful. Suddenly we heard a buzzing noise far away to the left. This was the first rush of the Afghan Ghazis and their shouts reached us in the distance like the hum of bees swarming at the end of the Deccan cold weather. Burrows Sahib formed his infantry into squares and they shot so steadily that the Ghazis were stopped and forced to take cover. Then some minutes later the Ghazis rallied and again charged with the same humming sound.

Again Burrows Sahib formed his men into squares and broke the Ghazi rush with musketry fire. Then that accursed Ayub Khan brought up his guns from behind the hills and before our footsoldiers could deploy into open order, he fired with fury at our squares. Under cover of this fire the Ghazis again charged and our men, confused by the cannonade and with great gaps in their ranks, were not able to stop them as they had done before. Burrows Sahib ordered a retirement; but under the heavy cannon fire and the attacks of the Afghans our infantry broke and it seemed as if our entire army would be destroyed. It was then that the three Monteith brothers shewed such courage and skill. Every time the Ghazis tried to get round the infantry, we of the 2nd Bombay Cavalry charged, each squadron led by a Monteith Sahib. Thus the infantry were able to get back safe to Kandahar. It was during the cavalry fighting that I thought that my chance had come. Lifting my carbine, I took a steady aim at Furley Sahib's back. No one noticed me, as all the troopers were watching the Ghazis and our infantry; I was just about to pull the trigger when I was knocked off my horse by a most violent blow. Some vile Afghan had fired a jezail in our direction and the shot hit me in the chest, just as I was about to shoot Furley Sahib. At first he did not notice my fall, but when the retreat began he saw me on the ground and, lifting me up, put me on the saddle in front of him and so brought me alive to Kandahar. There he looked after me and I soon recovered. By doing this, Furley Sahib wiped out our quarrel, and from that time on I became his devoted friend; and no words of my kinsmen had any influence with me."

"I suppose you were in Kandahar when Lord Roberts marched from Kabul to relieve you."

The old Rissaldar Major drew himself up and saluted on hearing the famous soldier's name: "Yes, indeed I was; the great Roberts Sahib came all the way from Kabul with the speed of Hanuman himself. In the meantime, however, Ayub Khan had tried to take Kandahar by storm and had been beaten back with heavy loss. Many of the Afghans had deserted and we had killed and wounded some ten thousand; so that Lord Roberts Sahib's task was easier than that of Burrows Sahib. Still he did his work thoroughly and so routed that demon of an Ayub Khan that he never fought the English again. That is my whole story."

"Well, thank you ever so much for it; but what happened to Furley Sahib?"

"He got safely through the Afghan War; afterwards he returned to the Poona Horse and rose to command it. It was he who gave me my last promotion and made me a Rissaldar Major. He was like a father to me and after his retirement he wrote to me every Christmas. I felt it deeply when he died, two years ago."

The old man suddenly stopped speaking and his eyes shone with a suspicious moisture.

"Do you think I could photograph Colonel Hutchings on his tomb?" I asked.

The old Rissaldar thought for a moment and said "Yes, I think it is possible. The best time would be at midnight. Two days hence the moon will be full; if the Sahib were to go to the cemetery then, he might catch the Colonel Sahib."

"Splendid! You must come too. I shall drive you there."

"Very well, I shall be happy to do anything that will give the Sahib pleasure."

At nine p.m. two days later the old Rissaldar presented himself at my bungalow ready for the drive to Sirur. As I was about to take the wheel, I noticed that he had no overcoat. It was March and the nights were still chilly and my car was an open one.

" You cannot drive without an overcoat, Rissaldar Sahib; you must take one of mine, otherwise you will catch your death of cold." So saying I ordered my servant to fetch a discarded ulster. I wrapped it round the old warrior and gave him a spare muffler as well to keep his throat warm. He accepted them gratefully. Motorcars did not then move as fast as they do now and it was just on midnight when we reached the Sirur cemetery. We got out and looked at the graveyard from a distance. Seen by the full March moon, it was an awe-inspiring sight.

"Let me go alone, Sahib," whispered the Rissaldar. "Hutchings Sahib may not wish to shew himself to a stranger."

I agreed and the Rissaldar entered the graveyard, while I, concealed among the shrubbery, waited outside. Acting on my instructions, he placed the Kodak on a tomb some thirty feet from the Colonel's monument, gave the film a long exposure and, dropping the shutter, rejoined me. We drove back to Poona and in the small hours parted excellent friends, the Rissaldar returning me my ulster and muffler. I told him to come back in a week's time so that we might examine together the developed proof. Seven days later the peon about nine a.m. announced the Rissaldar. A packet of proofs had arrived the day before, but I had not opened it. I wished to do so in the old man's presence. Among the proofs was that of the Sirur cemetery. I handed it to the Rissaldar without looking at it closely. He cast his eyes over it and exclaimed: "There he is, the Colonel Sahib, there he is! and the widow woman is there, too. I saw them both in the cemetery."

I took the proof from my friend's hands and, sure enough, there, seated on the plinth of the monument, was the shadowy form of an Englishman in old-fashioned dress.

"I see the Colonel Sahib; but where is his wife whom you will call the widow woman?"

"I call her the widow woman," said the Rissaldar Major severely, "because in our caste there is no widow remarriage and she had no right to marry again. Still I see her; she is there coming from behind another tombstone to join him."

I looked where the old soldier pointed and there did seem to be something that might have been the late Mrs. Hutchings. About the Colonel himself there could be no doubt whatever; and I still treasure the photograph of the graveyard, doubly strange because of its weird appearance by moonlight and the uncanny figure of the Englishman sitting on the plinth of the central monument.

I took out my note case and tried to induce the Rissaldar to accept a hundred rupees; but I was severely snubbed. He said with dignity: "A Shinde of Kizarnagar does not accept money for doing an act of courtesy that any gentleman might do for another."

From *Indian Christmas Stories* (1936)

## *The Munjia*

by C.A. Kincaid

IT WAS A STUFFY SEPTEMBER AFTERNOON IN NASIK. RAIN HAD not fallen for some days and even before that it had been far below the average. Indeed, there had at one time been so great a dread of a famine that the priests of Ramachandra's temple had for twenty-four consecutive hours kept their most important idol from resting by pouring cold water over it at short intervals. The suggestion had been made by the English judge, who was immensely respected as a learned Sanskrit scholar. He had supported his suggestion by so many quotations from the Vedas and Puranas (the Hindu gospels and epistles), that the priests had, although with diffidence, followed the Englishman's advice. Its value had been fully vindicated; for within the twentyfour hours a heavy thunderstorm had burst. A week's steady downpour had followed and the earth, soaked with six inches of precious rain, had lost its iron crust and although still thirsting had become soft enough for the early monsoon sowing.

Thus for the present there was no immediate danger of a famine, but sporadic cases of plague had occurred and one of the unlucky sufferers was a young Brahman boy of great promise called Mahadev Joshi. He was a Deshastha Brahman and his school career had been brilliant. He had carried off all the prizes that the Nasik High School could offer. From school he had entered the Deccan College near Poona and there had taken a brilliant first class in mathematics. He had distinguished himself at games as well, and Dr. Selby, the principal of the Deccan College, who loved Mahadev as his own son, had offered him the post of junior professor in mathematics; but the young Brahman was attracted to the Bar, for which his penetrating intellect and perfect knowledge of English were admirably adapted. He presented himself for the High Court pleader's examination and passed it with exceptional brilliancy. Weary of study and anxious to see his parents and friends he had returned to Nasik, the beautiful town near the source of the Godavari river. There, after three weeks of delightful, restful idleness, he had contracted plague. There was nothing strange that he should have done so, for his family house was an old *wada* or mansion dating from the time of the Peshwas and was overrun with rats. The rats were infested with fleas, the fleas settled on the bare feet of the members of the family and thus spread infection; first a servant, next a distant cousin, caught plague. They did not die of it, but they helped to spread the disease; so that when young Mahadev came to the old family house for a holiday, run down from overwork and too little sleep, he was a likely victim.

Mahadev's father Balwantrao and his mother Saraswatibai nursed their sick son with anxious devotion. The father was weighed down by the natural fears that any father would feel for the life of his brilliant son. In the mother's anxiety was a more sinister element. Mahadev had been invested with the sacred thread at the age of twelve and thus had been initiated to the Brahman caste. By the rules of orthodox Hinduism—and Nasik is very orthodox—Mahadev should have been married at fifteen. This is what his mother most ardently wished; indeed the question of his marriage had been fully discussed and he was betrothed to Narmadabai, the pretty daughter of the leading criminal pleader of Ahmadnagar, but old Balwantrao Joshi, greedily ambitious for his son's school and college successes, put off the marriage on various pretexts. His wish was to keep the boy unmarried until his examinations were over. These had now been successfully passed and Balwantrao had drafted wedding invitations that a Bombay printing press would print on cards in big gold letters.

Nevertheless the marriage ceremonies had not begun when Mahadev fell ill, and Saraswatibai was tortured with the thought that if her son died unmarried he would die a "munjia" — a Brahman boy invested with the sacred thread but still a bachelor. She held the vulgar belief that in that event Mahadev's soul would become a vile, evil spirit. Deprived of rebirth because of his parents' sin in delaying his marriage, her darling son would haunt a *pipal* tree and, feared and cursed by every human being, would rush at intervals from his dwelling place and play a horrible trick on some unfortunate person walking close to his tree. His only chance of escape was to possess some wayfarer's body: but she knew how difficult that was. She, therefore prayed and prayed to Vishnu and Ganpati, to Shiva and Parvati and to every other god she could think of—even the graceless Saturn—that her son might recover at any rate live long enough to marry Narmadabai.

The sick boy was well looked after as well as any English patient would have been. The civil surgeon was called in consultation and under his supervision the local practitioner wrote out correct prescriptions. Unhappily there are no specific remedies for plague. What is needed is a perfectly sound constitution, helped by good nursing. Mahadev's mother and sisters were present at his bedside night and day; so he did not lack good nursing. Thanks to their "ceaseless vigilance, the buboes under his armpits grew smaller, and smaller and the sick boy smiled and even laughed, his gaiety spreading joy through the whole household. Then one day he sat up for his morning tea, his mother's arm round his neck; he was bending his head forward to sip it when suddenly he fell forward, knocking the cup and saucer out of her hand. She turned to the towel stand close by for a towel to dry her son's hands and chest; as she did so, Mahadev's body twisted round and fell, so that he hung half in bed and half out of bed. In wild despair Saraswati called to her husband.

"Come, come" she screamed. "Mahadev has fallen, he is very ill!"

Old Balwantrao was deeply immersed in an article in the *Kesari* newspaper condemning vigorously some measure or other proposed by the Government of India. Nevertheless he dropped his paper and ran up the uncarpeted wooden stairs which led to the sleeping rooms. There he saw Mahadev hanging motionless out of bed and Saraswati lying prostrate on his body. He murmured in Marathi "Kay zalen? Kay zalen?" (What has happened? What has happened?) Going to the bedside he lifted his son back into bed and felt his wrist. Afterwards he put his hand on Mahadev's heart. Both pulse and heart were still. With the calm self mastery of the Deccan Brahman, Balwantrao said in even tones: "As it seems to me, Mahadev is dead." Saraswati, half mad with grief, screamed at her husband: "Yes, he is dead and thanks to your wicked ideas, he is dead unmarried, a 'munjia', and he will live on as an evil spirit long after we have died and have been reborn."

"Nonsense! Nonsense! Why believe in such childish tales, 'munjias' do not become evil spirits—that is a mere fable. In any case," he added by way of compromise, "if Mahadev does become a demon we can always appease him by offering him rice and grain, or even a fowl now and then."

No words of Balwantrao, however soothing, could lessen the poor mother's grief. Had her darling son died married she would probably have borne her sorrow and survived; but the dreadful thought that her beloved son should, from being an universal favourite in school, college and in Nasik society, become a hateful phantom, proved too much for Saraswati. When Balwantrao and the male mourners returned from the burning ground whither they had taken Mahadev's body, they found his mother lying face downwards at the bottom of the stairs. A cerebral hemorrhage had overtaken her as she was walking up to take a last look at her son's room. She had fallen backwards and broken her neck in her fall. A day later her body was carried to the same burning ground wherein Mahadev's had already been consumed.

Poor old Balwantrao shaved his head and moustaches and observed the usual twelve days' mourning. He sought refuge from his grief in the devotion of his daughters and in the study of sacred Sanskrit books; and he gave little thought to the question that the other townspeople were feverishly asking each other; "Where will the 'munjia' take up his abode?"

For many days after the death of Mahadev the Nasik townsmen put red painted stones at the foot of various *pipal* trees in the neighbourhood of the town. One or two trees near Nasik were, it was believed, already occupied by 'munjias' and they received due homage and small daily offerings of rice. It never occurred to any of the citizens that the new 'munjia' would go any distance from the city. They did not bear in mind that Mahadev, who had often mixed with Englishmen and liked them, might well establish himself near the quarter where they lived. One evening two or three tongas, filled with respectable Brahmans of Nasik and their wives and families, set out about 10 p.m. to catch the midnight express from Nasik Road Station. The train reached Bombay at 8 a.m. next morning and night travel saved the passengers, all of whom slept well in trains, the hot day journey down the Ghats and through the Konkan plain. The third class carriages can be very stuffy by day and Indian children suffer a good deal from the heat.

The road to the station ran west of the Nasik golf course, used alike by Bombay visitors and Nasik residents. Between the road and the links stood a giant *pipal* tree. It was full moon and the travellers were laughing and talking together, holding in their hands endless bundles of bedding and balancing their sterns precariously on innumerable tin trunks and brass waterpots. As the tongas passed the *pipal* tree the ponies took fright and galloping madly off the road and across the open country, they did not stop until they had overturned the tongas into a ravine a mile away. No fewer than two children and a young woman were killed outright. One man had a compound fracture of the leg, a second had his arm broken and everyone, including the drivers, was badly shaken and injured. The ponies were put on their feet, shivering with fright, but beyond a few slight cuts were not badly injured. The police were sent for; the dead were transported to the mortuary near the Civil Hospital. The injured were handed over to the care of the house surgeon and next day the police inspector held an inquest. There was, however, little to record save the bare facts of the accident. The oldest Brahman assured the inspector that he had heard a bloodcurdling shriek and that in the moonlight he had seen a monstrous diabolical figure issue from the *pipal* tree and deliberately scare the ponies. In his judgment the phantom was the soul of Mahadev, the 'munjia' that had taken up an abode in the *pipal* tree on the golf course.

The Brahman was corroborated by one or two of the women and one of the older men; nevertheless the inspector refused to put into his report anything about the 'munjia'. He had experienced the unpleasant scepticism of English officials and he knew well that any reference to such a phenomenon would only be treated by his English superior as "damned native superstition" and that he himself would get a "wigging" for writing rubbish in an inquest report.

The refusal of the inspector to record the evidence of the elderly Brahman was fully understood by the Nasik townsmen and they were not annoyed by it. After all, what could the superintendent do, even if he knew that a 'munjia' haunted the *pipal* tree? He might have the tree cut down, but that would only infuriate the demon who lived in it. Mahadev's soul would seek some other hiding place and issuing therefrom would cause worse trouble than ever. No; the townsmen's course was clear. They knew now where the 'munjia' dwelt and it was for them to propitiate him by worshipping him as a god, by placing beneath his tree stones painted with the royal red of divinity, by offering him daily small portions of rice and by burning nightly in his honour small single-wick lamps full of country oil.

Such attention might well have soothed the irascible spirit of any ordinary 'munjia'; but Mahadev, whose acute intelligence had survived his body, knew well that such offerings, although pleasing, got a 'munjia' nowhere. His only chance of obtaining a speedy rebirth and thus advancing towards the end of his eighty million earthly lives was to enter and possess some other human body and then cause its destruction. There were several ways of possessing a human body, but only one was easy and that was to enter the mouth when its owner yawned. Mahadev, no longer anxious to do anyone harm now that offerings were made at the foot of the *pipal* tree, hovered about the neighbourhood, hoping to take advantage of some passing Indian and to possess his body when he yawned. Unfortunately every Indian is well aware of the risks run in yawning and always snaps his fingers in front of his mouth so as to scare away evil spirits.

For a whole month Mahadev's spirit fluttered close to the faces of passing wayfarers, but not one gave him a chance. They did not often yawn; but when they did they never failed to snap their fingers and to scare him away. At last seeing a solitary Englishman yawn cavernously in the distance it occurred to Mahadev that he might possess an Englishman's body, since he could not enter an Indian's. At first the thought was hateful to him. Although he had often met Englishmen and liked many of them, he had always remained orthodox in food and the thought of occupying the body of a "beef-eating" foreigner was simply hateful. Nevertheless he decided at last that it was better to enter an Englishman's body and drive out his soul than remain for ever an 'anima sine corpore,' gibbering dismally in a *pipal* tree.

When, however, he lay in wait for Englishmen playing golf, he found another obstacle in his way. When they yawned, especially if they were not alone, they put a hand in front of their mouth, thus blocking the entrance quite as effectually as by snapping their fingers. Still Mahadev had seen one Englishman yawn without covering his mouth, so he hoped that he would see another; and so it happened. After several days' vain waiting, Mahadev saw the Assistant Judge Colin Travers pass close to the *pipal* tree. Travers had come out of court late and had, therefore, found no partner at the clubhouse. He was tired with work and had a yawning fit. As he passed the *pipal* tree he yawned for about the tenth time. He was carrying in one hand a mashie and in the other a bag of clubs, so he had no hand left with which to cover his mouth. It opened to its fullest extent and offered a wide aperture by which Mahadev could enter. The 'munjia' dived between the double row of strong, white teeth, down the throat; and while Colin Travers was laying down his bag of clubs and wondering whether he should play his next shot with his mashie or his iron, the evil spirit that had been Mahadev drove out Colin Travers' soul and occupied the vacant body.

The physical shock to Travers was so great that he sat down helplessly at the foot of the *pipal* tree and gasped feebly for breath. Once, however, he recovered his physical powers he became the tool of Mahadev's spirit and obeyed without hesitation the 'munjia's' slightest whim. Indeed, why should he have objected? His own soul was lost and had no longer any control over his body; on the other hand Mahadev's soul completely dominated it. Now what Mahadev wanted was that his new body should be destroyed. His own spirit would then be free for rebirth. There were two ways by which the 'munjia' could achieve his end. He might either kill himself or he might commit a murder and get hanged. Now in the Hindu belief suicide (athmaghat) is a grave sin and Mahadev had already committed sin enough by entering the soul of an Englishman. In his next life he would certainly have to pay for that crime by not being born a Brahman. If he committed suicide as well, heaven alone knew what dreadful fate might befall him. He might be reborn as a Mhar or even as a Mang. His only resource, therefore, was to commit a murder and so get condemned to death. Having formed this resolve, he picked up his clubs and walking towards the assistant judge's bungalow, entered it. The servants seeing, as they thought, their master Colin Travers, salaamed and made way for him. The 'munjia' did not know Mrs. Travers, but he hoped that he would find her in. She was sitting in the dining room with a friend, a lady missionary from the medical mission beyond Godavari. Hearing her husband's step, she called 'Is that you Colin? I thought you were going to the Club. Miss Smith the medical missionary is here. She will be delighted to see you. Do come and talk to her."

"Oh! do, Mr. Travers" echoed Miss Smith.

The 'munjia' noticed a thrusting dagger on the wall just inside the outer door. Travers had secured it when trying some dacoits. The 'munjia' took it off the wall, felt its point and walked into the drawing room. He bent over Mrs. Travers, as if to kiss her, but she recoiled in horror at the expression of his eyes.

"Good gracious, Colin, what is the matter with you? You look different! You have become somebody else!"

The false Colin did not answer, but deliberately drove his; thrusting dagger into her heart. The unfortunate missionary rose to flee, but the 'munjia' overtook her and killed her with a thrust in the back. He then threw the dagger on the ground, walked to the office of the superintendent of police, Alfred Dawkins and said calmly: "I have come to give myself up for a double murder, please arrest me."

The superintendent had for several hours been trying to pen a report about the criminal tribes in his district. He had a store of sound practical knowledge of their ways and customs and he could have told at a glance to what section any wandering beggar belonged; but his penmanship was not equal to his experience. In his efforts to cover two sheets of foolscap with material that a skilled writer could have expanded into a thick book, the unhappy superintendent had chewed his wooden penholder almost down to the metal. He was too preoccupied to grasp what Travers had said: but delighted to escape for a moment from the intolerable drudgery of writing sonorous official phrases, he rose to his feet and said cordially: "By Jove, Travers, do come in; sit down and have a whisky and soda! Here, boy, bring in two chota pegs. I suppose you have come to speak to me about the police enquiry in that coining case? Or let me see—would it be about the murder of little Krishnabai by that up-country watchman?"

"No indeed, I have not come about either of those cases, Superintendent Sahib," said Travers, using unconsciously the Indian form of address, " I have just committed a double murder and I have come to give myself up."

"Committed a double murder? What the devil are you talking about? If you have come to pull my leg, old chap, I really have no time now and you'd better try your luck some other day; but don't go away until you've had your chota peg. It's no fun drinking alone, is it? Ha! Ha!" and the jolly policeman laughed heartily.

"No, Superintendent Sahib, I am not joking," replied Travers earnestly. "I really have committed a double murder and please come and see for yourself."

After a quarter of an hour Dawkins, clad in white uniform and followed by four constables, joined Travers.

"Now come along and show me this mare's nest of yours."

Travers did not reply and the two walked together in silence during the ten minutes needed to go from the superintendent's house to that of the assistant judge. On reaching it, they were met by a mob of excited servants, who shouted: "The Sahib has killed his Memsahib and the doctor Memsahib! The Sahib has killed his Memsahib and the doctor Memsahib!"

The superintendent began at last to think that there was something in Travers' story and entering the assistant judge's bungalow became certain of its truth.

Turning to one of the constables, Dawkins told him to fetch the deputy superintendent of police, Khan Sahib Mahmud Khan, and instruct him to hold an inquest. With two constables behind them he and Travers walked to the Khan Bahadur's house. The latter, a retired Parsi Deputy Collector, nearly fell over backwards when he was asked to record Travers' confession.

"The fact was," stated Travers, " I was both tired of my wife and jealous of her. I wanted to get rid of her; I also wished to punish her for the way she flirted with....with (the 'munjia' did not know the names of any of the regimental officers, so he finished lamely) with certain military gentlemen. Coming home I saw her sitting in the drawing room, so I decided to kill her. I took a dacoit's dagger from off the wall and going up to her, I stabbed her. Then that foolish woman, Miss Smith began to talk, you know how these medical missionaries jabber—so I killed her too."

The confession was carefully recorded. Travers was placed in the lockup for the night; and next morning he was taken before the first class assistant collector, to whom the superintendent had telegraphed. He recorded the Crown evidence as briefly as possible; and when Travers pleaded guilty to the two charges of murder and admitted the correctness of his confession, the magistrate committed the accused to take his trial in the High Court of Bombay.

On the morning of Travers' trial there was great excitement in the Presidency town. The sessions hall of the High Court of Judicature was packed to overflowing; indeed hundreds of would-be spectators were turned away. Travers' trial was the first on the list of criminal trials. The judge to whom the sessions had been allotted sat in state in his red robes under the sword of justice. On either side sat the Sheriff and the Chief Presidency Magistrate. As Travers was English, the jury of nine selected to find on his guilt or innocence were also English. He had refused to engage a barrister, so one of the European members of the Bar, who knew him personally, undertook voluntarily his defence. It was impossible for his counsel to do much, because Travers from the beginning insisted on pleading guilty; the medical evidence, too, confirmed the accused's protest that he was absolutely sane. The barrister for the defence could only rely on the passage in Travers' confession that he was jealous and attempted to reduce, the charge from one of murder to one of culpable homicide; but as the Advocate-General pointed out, Travers' jealousy of his wife was no excuse for the assassination of Miss Smith. The judge summed up shortly and the jury after an absence of barely ten minutes brought in a verdict that Travers was guilty of murder, but added to their verdict a strong recommendation for mercy. Why they did so, they would probably have found it hard to explain. Their real reason, no doubt, was that in their belief no sane man could have behaved like Travers. If Travers was sane, then all the facts had not been put before the court.

The judge was glad of an excuse not to pass sentence of death on a man whom he knew personally and whom he had until recently always esteemed; so much to Travers' obvious disgust, he passed a sentence of penal servitude for life. The accused was led away and the judge called the next case.

Travers was sent to jail and from the first was an object of special interest to the superintendent, Captain Jameson of the Indian Medical Service. Jameson had never met Travers before, but he felt that there must be some terrible secret underlying his conduct. The prison staff took their cue from the superintendent, Travers responded to kindness and the jail officials all thought he was the nicest as well as the most intelligent prisoner, whom they had ever had at Euroda. It was however, only the lull before the storm. The 'munjia' had not the slightest intention of remaining imprisoned in Travers' body a moment longer than he could help. If two murders did not suffice to procure a death sentence, then he would commit three. The third would certainly bring him release, for murder by a life convict can, under the Indian Penal Code, only be punished by death. One day Travers asked if he might have a pair of Indian clubs for morning exercise, as, so he said, his health was suffering from lack of it. He had always been accustomed to swing them for half an hour every morning. Jameson was delighted to grant this trifling indulgence and as he had a spare pair in his bungalow, he brought them over the same evening and gave them to Travers.

Travers broke into profuse thanks, so as to disarm any possible fears on the superintendent's part. Picking up the clubs, he swung them once over his shoulder and then brought down with all his force the right hand club on the top of Jameson's head. The unfortunate officer fell with a broken skull; and a second blow, as he lay on the hard stone flagged courtyard shattered it to pieces.

"Now," thought the 'munjia' in triumph, "I am bound to be hanged."

No one, however, came forward to arrest him. The guards were all too bewildered to take any action. Then the joy of battle inherited from Travers' Norse ancestors acted physically on Mahadev's soul. "After all why await trial? Why not go on killing until death comes of itself?" With a club in each hand Travers fell on the unfortunate Maratha guard, who scattered in every direction. Running after them at great speed, Travers overtook several and with mighty blows clubbed them to death. The Indian convicts locked into their cells were in an ecstasy of delight. They applauded each murderous blow with yells of:

"Shabash Sahib! Maro Sahib!" (Bravo Sahib! Hit them Sahib)!

After Travers had killed half a dozen sepoys, those on duty at the outer gate ran up the staircase into the central tower, whence they commanded all the open spaces of the great prison. From this vantage point, they took careful aim with their rifles and fired deliberately at Travers. It was not easy to kill him, because he was moving about and also because in his berserk rage, he did not seem to be affected by the bullet wounds. At last he collapsed suddenly from loss of blood. As he lay motionless the guards fired a volley at him. He gave a convulsive movement, tried to rise and fell back dead.

At last the 'munjia' had won the desired release. Mahadev's soul left Travers' body and took its place in the line of Hindu souls waiting for reincarnation.

All the Englishmen who had known Travers were deeply shocked at his crimes and death.

"Such a terrible end to a most promising career," they said. "Travers might have risen to anything. He must have been mad but it was a dreadful end."

Yes, they were quite right; it was a dreadful end, a terrible end. Yet what happened to Travers might have happened to anyone—to you or to me.

From *Indian Christmas Stories (1936)*

## *The Pool*

by John Eyton

SOME THREE HUNDRED YEARS AGO A LITTLE WHITE TEMPLE nestled in a fold of the hills, like a mushroom in a green dell. It stood on the bank of a dark pool; wooded hills towered over it to the west, and barren hills rolled away to the east. It was a very holy place; men believed that the foot of God had touched earth here and had made a valley. So from time immemorial it had been a place of pilgrimage. Men journeyed to the hills to see it, and the steps leading down to the pool were often thronged with travellers in white garments, women in saris of red and blue, sadhus in orange and in yellow.

The water was dark—born of a deep-laid spring, which was never dry, and whose overflow ran away in a little tinkling rill into the deep woods. It was believed that the pool was bottomless—for what could resist the foot of God?

Animals came to drink quite near the temple with out fear—dark, great-eyed Sambar stags—little barking deer of the colour of autumn leaves—mottled leopards. There were bright birds too about it—proud pheasants, and jays of vivid blue; big butterflies of dark green and blue, with swallow tails; and red dragon-flies haunted the reedy edges.

It was ever a place of great silence and of rest. A very holy man watched over the temple, sitting all day long, legs crossed, arms folded. He was said to be a hundred years old. His face was wizened and shrivelled and puckered in a thousand wrinkles. His head was shaven, and his forehead bore three upright lines of yellow paint. He wore but a single blanket of faded orange.

Such were the temple and the pool, and the priest of the pool.

There came an evil day for that peaceful place. A horde of wild Mohammedan fanatics from below swept over the hills and descended like a scourge on the pool. The little old priest ran up the path towards them, his arms outstretched, adjuring them to spare the ancient holy temple. A swarthy man of great stature lifted his sharp sword and swept off the head of the little priest; others plunged their swords into the frail body, and they threw the wreck of it into the pool. They burned the temple and destroyed the peace of the place..... Then the pestilence passed on.

Thereafter, green rushes covered the whole face of the water, save where the spring welled up in the middle. Men feared to approach the pool, where pale figures were seen at night, and where a despairing cry was sometimes heard. The peace returned;

the place was left to the animals and the birds and the butterflies. But the memory of it never died.

Time passed, and the surrounding hills came into the hands of an Englishman, a retired Colonel named Brown. He was not an unkindly man, but he had a strong belief in the absolute superiority of his own race, and in the inviolability of property. He was tall, with white hair and moustache, and a face whose natural redness was enhanced by the white suits and hats which he wore. He made a pleasant estate in the hills; built a roomy bungalow; put up neat cottages; planted orchards, laid out paths everywhere; in fact, subdued the jungle with a system admirably English. Incidentally he cleaned up the pool, which lay just beyond his boundary. The villagers refused to do the work, but he imported labour, and cleared out the rushes and dredged up the mud. In the course of the work they found a number of blackened stones and rudely carved figures, which the Colonel gave to the Lucknow Museum. Evidently there had been some sort of a temple on the spot, which lent colour to the village talk. Then the spring was analysed and found to contain good water; so the supply was utilised, pipe-lines being laid on to the gardens. The villagers resented the whole proceeding, but they always did resent innovation. Colonel Brown was justly proud of his improvements.

Then the most annoying thing happened. The Colonel was walking round the estate one afternoon when he distinctly heard the mournful chant which accompanies funeral procession. It was the usual thing—a sentence endlessly repeated by two alternate groups, first in full tone, then faintly, like an echo. It came from the direction of the pool. When he had turned the corner he saw the awful truth—a little party of men walking swiftly down the path and bearing a stretcher on which lay a body swathed in white. Mourners trotted behind intoning their sad chant. They were actually going to burn a dead body near the spring-head! It was monstrous. They did it too; he saw the smoke curling up from the valley, and found logs of charred wood at the fringe of the pool the next morning.

That afternoon was the beginning of the Colonel's troubles. First he put a chowkidar on the place, and the chowkidar was beaten by day and saw bhuts by night and ran away. But the burning went on, in proportion to the mortality of the village. Then the Colonel summoned the head men, who talked nonsense about the place being holy from time immemorial. He dismissed them with a purple face and a few home truths. Next, he applied to the civil authorities, who declined to interfere, since the pool was not actually on the estate of Colonel Brown, and had certainly a reputed sanctity. Lastly, he wrote to the *Pioneer*—last resource of wounded pride—and complained of 'the new spirit of pandering to the native, regardless of the position and rights of landlords,' and wondered what the Government was doing.

In spite of all, the burning continued. People refused to burn anywhere else. They believed that here was sanctity for their dead.

Then worse befell. One morning the Colonel observed through his field-glasses a little strip of red rag floating from a tree on the margin of the pool. This would not appear to be of importance; but the Colonel knew India. That red rag meant a priest, and a priest meant pilgrimage. Never was proud banner a surer challenge than was that little strip of red rag. The red rag affected the Colonel after the proverbial manner. He descended on the place, breathing unutterable things.

All he found was a solitary figure sitting under the tree which flaunted the red rag. It was a man of middle age, clad in a blanket of faded yellow; his head was clean-shaven, and his forehead bore three upright lines of yellow paint. He sat motionless, with set, staring eyes. The Colonel asked him his business... no answer; Then he made a sort of set speech on the rights of man... still no answer; then he began to shout, but the priest still ignored his presence. He failed to make any impression on that holy man. Angry as he felt, he knew better than to lay lands on a priest—so he marched off, speechless with rage. They would build a temple next, he knew, if they were given a chance. So he stalked home and wrote a perfect sheaf of letters and appeals on the subject.

That evening the Colonel began a nasty attack of malaria. It is possible that he had been bitten by a mosquito on the occasion of one of his numerous visits to the pool, which was still a swampy place, hot and stuffy. However this may be, the mosquito which bit the Colonel knew his business. He was in bed a fortnight. His wife barely managed to pull him through the attack which was unusually malignant. When he could get about again, his first walk was in the direction of the pool....

There, like a mushroom in a green dell, nestled a little new white temple.

With the reader's indulgence, the author begs leave to draw a picture dating some three hundred years hence....

Colonel Brown is long forgotten. The Englishman, and his Government, and his rights, and his laws have faded away as a ripple dies on water—as a wind stirs in the trees and is gone. But on the bank of the dark pool a little white temple still stands, and still the pilgrims come... for such is India.

# NIGHTMARE TALES

# Introduction

"Only mad dogs and Englishmen
Go out in the mid-day sun."

It was an Englishman, Noel Coward, who wrote the above lines. And no doubt it was an Englishman who invented the sola-topee (or pith helmet), enabling him to step out into the heat of an Indian summer's day, to manage the Empire for Queen (or King) and country.

First here as traders and merchant adventurers, later as rulers (first for the East India Company and then for the Crown), the British colonial—whether in the Army or the administration—never really came to terms with India. It was always a foreign and hostile environment, and the Englishman was constantly baffled by local customs, religions, and life-style. India was seldom, if ever, "home".

Outside the station bungalow lay a world of magic, witchcraft, intrigue, dust storms, monsoon floods, temples and mosques, scorpions, poisonous snakes, dacoits, mosquitoes, murder and general mayhem, with which they had sometimes to cope.

Probably, the only thing Indian that they accepted whole-heartedly was Curry and Rice.

Many wrote about the India they had to contend with, none more vividly than Rudyard Kipling, a journalist who was at his best writing about the ordinary British soldier. Others were administrators, Army officers, tea-planters or railwaymen who took time off from their varying duties to write about jungle adventures, or the supernatural (always in vogue), or the perils of life on the Frontier. Occasionally, the memsahib put pen to paper. Most of them kept diaries; others, like Alice Perrin, Flora Annie Steele, and B.M. Croker, were accomplished novelists and short-story writers.

Time and again, their themes were of the unknown, the uncanny, the supernatural, the black arts—the white man threatened by the powers of darkness and often succumbing to that darkness. This is what gives their stories a nightmarish quality and makes them readable today when other, more mundane literary efforts have been forgotten.

Of course, the real threat came from that fierce mid-day sun and the various afflictions—cholera the most deadly—that it helped engender.

# The Uncharted Islands

By *E.H. Visiak* and *John Gawsworth*

Heddlestone,
April 27th, 1763.

Reader,

The manner of my preservation, with two companions, from the uncharted islands, as well as other particulars, may seem to many incredible; and some, perhaps, will not stickle to brand the whole relation as a fabulous tale.

I can only say, and I do aver it, that herein I have set down nothing but what really fell out in my experience, described nothing but what I really saw in my brief sojourn on one of the group; which is a misfortune one way, leaving some things inevitably obscure.

As to what happened to us after our escape in our ship, 'tis beyond the drift of my relation, since nothing further transpired concerning the islands themselves. Indeed, like one drunk, our ship drove in fair weather and foul, with only her topsails aboard, our course (if a course it can be called), being generally westward. At length after several months, and when both our drink and victuals were near consumed, we drove blundering ashore, by the mercy of God, upon one of the Nicobar Islands.

Here, was a Dutch ship about to sail and we went on board of her.

From Amsterdam we got us a passage to Plymouth; and so came I home to Heddlestone, where I dwell unto this day.

Richard Roach.

## I

No remarkable passage in our voyage befell after our going from the Indian Seas on January 10th, 1724, at a latitude of 40° S., and entering the Southern Ocean. Accordingly, I pass to the period when we did anchor close in shore 'twixt some uncharted mountainous islands (the subjects of my tale) and our Captain did adventure ashore alone.

Upon the first night in this anchorage, as I well remember, I was pacing softly up and down, feeling—nay, possessed and overcome by a sense of solemnity and awe and adoration. It seemed to me, indeed, that the deck, and the night, were haunted by a presence, immanent, inscrutable, ineffable.

I looked about me. The illumining moon made the faces of the sleepers one in peace and in glamour with the face of a man who had died dreaming of his childhood. A watchman stood silent at either bulwark amidships, in the bows, and on the poop. The decks lay in a wonder-work of moonshine and shadow. The sea-birds slept, and nothing moved on the moon-gazed expanse of the shore. Only the breakers lapped and gurgled beneath the broken bulwarks, and an eerie and dolorous sound came intermittently from a mountain on the nearest island.

The hour was about midnight. I continued to pace the decks; but, as I came aft, the watchman there turned and beckoned to me. He was the man who had begged Captain Blythe to let him accompany him on shore; and he said in a whisper:

"Take my place here, will ye? I'm a-going ashore. The Cap'n thinks as I'm afeared. He'll come to no good out yonder. There's devils there, I tell 'e! I heard tales of this-yere coast; and I know 'tis so. But I'm a-going to follow him. Look'e here, do you see this?" As he spoke, he pulled out a silver locket that hung from a cord round his neck. "There's a piece of the holy cross in there, which is a certain-sure protection—a certain-sure protection," he repeated impressively, "against devils. So I'm a-going to protect the Cap'n—d'ye see? I'm a-going ashore, while you takes my place."

He stared at me with wide, blue eyes that shone as clear as glass, and clutched hold of my arm with his horny hand. There was an intensity and urgency in his voice, and on his face a look past description. To have scoffed at such sincerity, though never so homely expressed, were unworthy and really profane. On another occasion, and in another mood, perhaps, I might have scoffed (for I was only a boy); but now I heard him seriously, agreeing to take his place, yet endeavouring to dissuade him from going. But when I found him resolved, it was borne in upon me (I know not how against my inclination) that I should accompany him. So I told him I would go with him, and that we should wake one of the others to act as watchman. He demurred, hinting at all manner of ghostly objections; but I overbore them by mention of his infallible relic. So we proceeded to rouse up one of the sleepers, who, after some natural vexation at his awakening, consented, for a reward, to take watch.

Then, the seaman, being armed with a great blunderbuss (not to speak of his infallible relic!), and I with a pistol, we went ashore, and advanced towards the sandhills, going with the utmost vigilance. But I began to be much afraid, a prey to panic imaginations, full of repentance for having set forth, ashamed to return. Nor was the seaman, apparently, one whit more courageous—which did not tend to hearten me! Continually glancing about him, his face tense or twitching, he seemed beside himself. His motive in venturing was plain: he desired to vindicate his courage; and, despite his timidity—or rather, because of it—he really did do so. But what my motive had been, unless it were sheer perversity, I am not philosopher enough to determine.

We scaled one of the outer sandhills, which were very high and like in character to a hummocky mountain range, and began to struggle over the shifting slopes, while the dreadful groaning sound grew sensibly louder. Suddenly the seaman gave a shuddering cry. "Look!" said he, pointing to the sand; and, there, among the long, straggling grass, almost at our feet, was a human skull.

It was the first time in my life that I had seen such a thing, save in sculptured representations in churchyards; and, being part in shadow, it appeared to grimace at me in the moonlight. I clutched the seaman's arm; and his blunderbuss went off.

The stupendous report was echoed from the mountains; and (the blunderbuss having been charged with small shot and bearing slopingly upon the ground) there went up about us a great column of sand-dust which enveloped us for many moments. But when it cleared, and I had cleared the sand out of my eyes (for I was near blinded with it), instead of one skull, I saw three, together with bones sticking forth where the shot had uncovered them in the sand. I showed them to the seaman, who was still rubbing his eyes. The blast of sand had stung my face a good deal, but he had received the brunt of it, and he raged, indeed, very passionately, taking no notice of the skulls.

"You cursed swab," he cried, picking up his blunderbuss, which had leaped from his hand, and looking fearfully round, "you've gone for to do a brave thing, you have! What was you feared of, you swab, you? If a skull scares ye, or a skelinton, what'll you do when you comes across them as made the skull be here? I wish I hadn't took you along, that I do! What if you've roused 'em on us? Look round. Do you see any of 'em? What's that yonder, by the wood there?"

He pointed to the shoulder of a long, ragged wood that stood as a hedge beyond the sandhills. But I saw nothing, save straggling trees, the dense-leaved branches of which were strangely contorted. And, when I had told him so, he seated himself upon a knoll of sand, and bade me keep watch while he cleaned his gun; which he proceeded to do with his neckcloth. When he had removed every grain of sand from the muzzle (lest, as he told me, it should burst on firing), he charged it; then, gave it to me to hold while he unloaded, cleaned, and recharged my pistol. This done, and the blunderbuss returned to him, he had a look at the skulls and bones in the sand.

"It do scare me!" said he presently.

"What scares you?" asked I.

"Them," said he, pointing, apparently, to the skulls.

"But you said, didn't you, that I ought not to be afraid of a skull?"

"It's not the skulls I'm feared on, though it's them, too. It's *them*," said he, pointing, "Don't you see them shells?"

I had seen them, without thinking them worth notice. "Why,

they are but shells. It looks as if someone had been feasting off shell-fish here. There's nothing dreadful in that."

"Oh, a'n't there? And, who's been a affeasting off the skulls and the skelintons, think ye?"

His meaning came to me with a thrill of horror. "Cannibals!" I cried. "You think there are cannibals here!"

"Ay," said he, getting to his feet. "Cannibals, and worse, and I shouldn't wonder. But the sound's stopped!"

It was true. The groaning sound was no longer audible. We waited, hearkening intently, but it did not recur. It had become, as it were, native to the scene for us; and its cessation was even the more daunting, as a syncope and sign of death. The seaman looked furtively at me; and I think the thoughts that flitted through my mind were in his also. Here was justification—or, at least, pretext—for returning to the ship: since the seaboard appeared to be deserted, and the sound which had directed us inland ceased, the reason of our venture might be said to have ended; and the Captain was even then returning in all likelihood, if, indeed, he were not already safe on board. Fear is selfish; and these considerations in me doubtless, discovered a shallow heart. Love and gratitude (such as I ought to have had for such a benefactor and friend as Captain Blythe had been to me) are not so soon contented; and I should have been moved by quite another fear.

"We can do nothing here," said I. "We don't know where to go now the sound's stopped; and the Captain has probably returned by this. You don't want to meet with cannibals, do you?"

The words were ill-chosen. "D'ye think, then, as I'm afeared?" cried he, drawing himself erect and puffing his chest out. "No. Do you return, but I goes on! It shall never be said, nor thought (what's more!), that Joseph Yates flinched from his dooty, nor turned aside from the path what was set afore him. Cannibals or worse, I goes on! Cannibals, or devils, or monstrosities, or goblins, or ghouls; it's all one to me: I goes on!"

Fanning up his courage thus with a bravado, he started off across the sand-hollow; but, coming abreast the wood, he stopped dead, and I also, arrested by a dim glimpse of a face in the moonlit skirts of the trees.

It was a dreadful face, very high and narrow in the forehead. A sort of dusky red it seemed to be; and there were broad bands of blue round the eyes and joined across the bridge of the nose as monstrous spectacles. It stared at us for a moment, with sloe-black, venomous-looking eyes, and then withdrew—or rather, vanished; for it made no sound, not a rustle of the undergrowth.

"Ah, what was that?" I cried; but the seaman took the locket from his neck, and held it swaying from the string, muttering papist prayers. His face gleamed ghastly in the moonlight; and, ceasing to pray, he stood mumbling and licking his dry lips. As for me, I felt verily, that, if I made no effort, I should go stark mad; and I began to beseech him instantly to go with me back to the ship. "Let us run! At once! At once! I can't go alone. Oh, put away that locket——"

I broke off; for, from beyond the wood, there came a weird humming sound, being all upon one low note; which grew nearer and louder, coming soon in a sort of short, rapid measure, pronounced with demoniac violence, and sometimes accented with a prolonged, hoarse, rasping hiss, which yet was not a hiss, but something far more dreadful.

Still the seaman made no move; and a sort of numbness stole over me, so that I stood, as it were, conscious in a swoon. And, mercifully it was so, or my reason could not have endured; for, of a sudden, there came a sound that tore the night, the sound of many bestial and savage voices yelling and snarling as in a frenzy of unspeakable hate.

I heard it, I say, as in a trance; and an impulse, which was the veriest instinct, sent me dashing into the thicket of the wood, burrowing under the fern, as a child, affrighted by some imagined terror of the night, buries himself beneath the bedclothes. The seaman followed suit, dropping his blunderbuss; and we lay almost together in the undergrowth, panting and gasping, worming our bodies deeper and deeper. But we went too far—at least, I did—taking no heed of the direction, which lay across the angle of the wood; and, unwittingly poking my head into the moonlight, I lay staring and staring through an opening in the branches.

There was a throng of dusky red, savage figures advancing beside the wood; and, from the kilts of long grass (as it seemed) about their naked bodies, the plumes of feathers upon their heads, and their weapons of a sort of long axes, or of clubs, I might have taken them for mere savages. But their faces were as infernal masks, hideously contorted, and striped or patched black, bloody, and blue; their eyes rolled until the whites alone were visible; their tongues hung lolling from their mouths. They went in a close column four deep, dancing and leaping, twisting their axes and clubs, and rolling their eyes all in time; and there stood, a little on one side, a figure clad to the ankles in a glossy dark cloak, who seemed to be the leader, yet had unquestionably a feminine appearance, though her contorted face was no whit less hideous and dreadful than the others. It reminded me for all the world of a frightful Hindu idol depicted in the book of missionary travel which, home at Heddlestone, I had taken from my grandfather's library. This creature it was that spied me in the thicket; and, uttering a weird screech, she pointed directly to the place where we lay.

Instantly, the night became hushed and silent, the massed lines of terrors standing motionless. Then, while I waited in numb suspense, two of them sprang from the ranks. One seized me as with a grip of iron; and, dragging me forth, laid me prostrate at the leader's feet; the other dashed headlong after the seaman, who had escaped. I looked shudderingly up at the face of the leader—and was amazed! For, her contorted muscles had relaxed; her features had become smooth and delicately shapen, the twisted mouth straight, the pupil-less eyes full, dark, and lustrous; and, though the copper-dark skin was daubed with red, and there were lines of blue about the lips, it was the face of a young and comely woman!

Now, she spoke a word in a strange tongue; and there stepped forth a creature whose nose and chin were flaming yellow on a red ground. Brandishing his long-hafted axe, he roared out a string of words, and was answered from the ranks by a ferocious clamour, while I shut my eyes, expecting death, wondering in a daze whether the pain would be greater than I could bear; and when the leader gave a sudden and sharp cry, I made sure that the time had come. Yet, still it tarried; and, on opening my eyes, they met those of the woman, who gazed steadfastly down upon me, and with such a look as heartened me with with a gush of hope.

But there arose a stir and hubbub in the ranks, which immediately began to be broken up, the creatures coming crowding round us; and one of them, whose massive form was daubed with red from head to foot, began to speak in harsh, grating tones, addressing the woman, and apparently reproaching and railing at her, pointing fiercely at me, the while, with a sort of broad double-bladed axe of transparent green stone in shape like a battledore. The others formed a ring about us; and he began to run up and down as he spoke, taking several paces in either direction, but always with his face towards the woman. His axe shone in the moonlight with great beauty as he brandished it; and I found myself watching the sheeny arcs it made, as a babe watches a bright and moving object. He ended suddenly, dropping his axe, which hung suspended from his wrist, and stood as if waiting for the woman to reply.

But she did not so much as look upon him, or upon any of them, gazing fixedly upon the ground. Then, still silent, she took two paces and a stride, stepping right over my prostrate form; and, lifting her head erect, she looked around with a defiant and majestic gesture, crying:

*"Tapu!"*

Suddenly, one of those who stood outermost gave a shout; and, in the stillness that followed, I caught a distant humming sound like to that which had frightened me in the beginning. The woman spoke sharply and rapidly; and immediately the column formed again; the terrible staccato chorus broke forth anew, interspersed with yelling sounds, which, if it were possible, were even more daunting than before. Dancing and leaping in time, with twisting axes and clubs, and with their eyeballs hideously rolling, the army—for there were hundreds of them—advanced evidently to battle.

But the woman remained standing by; and when the last rank had passed, she made a sign to me to begone, pointing urgently and vehemently towards the sandhills. I rose, and was in the act of starting off, when, chancing to look towards the receding army, I saw that the creature whose nose and chin were painted yellow, had left the ranks and came running towards us; and on that, I stood still: perhaps, I saw instinctively that flight would not serve against so swift a runner; perhaps, my courage failed. It failed indeed, when he came near enough for me to see his face, gleaming in the moonlight; for it was set in a look of appalling ferocity; and my skull ached in horrid anticipation as I saw his long axe brandished terribly as if his very hand itched to deal the blow that should cleave it.

When he came up, however, he stood and began to harangue the woman in savage tones. But she, stepping quickly between us, confronted him in silence. She was the most majestic, barbaric, and imperious-looking figure that it is possible to conceive. Nor, would she so much as vouchsafe to answer a word; and presently, with a fierce exclamation that sounded like a threat, he turned, not without dignity, and set off to rejoin the army, running as swiftly as he had come.

Then again, the woman signified flight; and this time I fled, running across the plain like mad, and scrambling desperately up the unstable slopes. Yet, had I but small fear of pursuit, concluding, from a sudden and loud conclamation of savage voices, that the opposing armies were now embroiled. I was much mistaken—as I knew presently, when, on perceiving that the voices were nearer, I looked sideways back as I came upon a high sandhill, about half-way to the sea, and saw, with a dreadful shrinking at heart, a great multitude pursuing me, being those very armies by whose conflict I had trusted to make my escape. A panic terror seized hold of me then; and I went staggering and plunging blindly in the sand. My limbs kept giving under me; my feet felt as heavy as lead. The ship was in sight, and but two sandhills separated me from the shore; but the pursuers were scarcely a quarter of a mile away, and gained upon me every minute. Suddenly they began to utter, all together and repeatedly, an eerie and exceeding mournful cry, *"Haere mai," it came, "Haere mai, haere mai"*; a great, weird, floating, wailing cry. The night was full of it. The mountains echoed it.

But I heard it as a deadly summons; and when a figure moved in the shadow of an adjacent sandhill and made a spring towards me, the ghostly bright moonlight changed to thick darkness, and, the wailing became a roaring as the sound of many waters about my ears. The figures clutched hold of me even as I swooned, and I heard a voice that I seemed to know.

When I came to myself, I was sensible of a chill of water about my body and splashing up upon my face, and, of being borne along through inky black, breaking waves. Close in front of me was the ship, her masts and sails towering; and spurts of pistol fire came from the low-sunk decks where the men crowded, shooting off their pistols. I turned my head—to look straight into the eyes of Captain Blythe!

His face was stern-set with effort; but he gasped out a word of assurance to me as he gave a mighty stroke. Two or three more brought us close under the ship, at the place where the bulwarks were broken away, and we were hauled speedily on board. I was so weak at first that I had to support myself by the bulwarks. But the Captain appeared to recover his strength and his command in the same moment; and the first thing he did was to stop the firing. "To make enemies of them were madness!" cried he. "Hold your pistols ready, men; but don't fire unless I bid ye."

He spoke with a sternness that prevented all demur, and, at the same time, controlled the men from panic. The shore was thronged with a seething, dusky multitude, from whose clutches, apparently, we had escaped but very narrowly. They stood gazing upon us; some of them waving spears or staves or axes. I observed that they formed two separate parties which appeared to have consorted, the members of one party being not daubed with paint.

Suddenly, on the nearer shore, there fell a commotion as the throng opened right and left to admit of the passage of a tall, gaunt figure (being a head and shoulders taller than anyone near), who, in common with the rest, was naked except for his great kilt. He came, stepping stately and slow, bearing a long, slender, pointed stick; and was followed by an old, small, wizened form—yet strong and wiry-looking withal—who held one of those battledore-shaped axes. Their dark faces, plain in the moonlight, looked fierce and grim; and they bore themselves with a remarkable statuesque carriage of their plumed heads. They took their stations together beside the waves; and, when the small, wizened figure had waved his axe (which he did very haughtily)—as a signal to the crowd to withdraw still further—and a wide space was made for them, in a silence broken only by the splash of the gentle breakers, he began to address us, speaking—or rather, roaring—in a harsh, deep voice, running up and down, meantime, about ten paces in either direction, and brandishing his axe. What he said was quite unintelligible to us; yet, ever and again, I caught, or imagined I caught, a word or a phrase that sounded like a sort of barbarous English.

He ended with the strange wailing cry, thrice repeated, that had filled the night as I fled among the sandhills. *"Haere mai! Haere mai!"* he wailed, making a gesture of beckoning to us, but with the palm of his hand held downwards. The other followed suit; and at the third repetition he lifted his long stick and waved it in the air; whereupon the multitude cried as with one voice, *"Haere mai! Haere mai! Haere mai!"*

It was more weird and impressive than I can tell; and, as it ceased, dying in the distance with a great, ghostly echo, from high up in the mountains there boomed forth that dreadful groaning sound which had frightened us in the beginning at our coming to land.

The men, lining the bulwarks, stood perfectly spell-bound; as I did also. But the orator waited evidently for some response; and, standing up in a breach of the bulwarks, Captain Blythe made him a low bow. Immediately, upon a wave of the axe, those who stood in the forefront of the crowd sank down in a crouching posture; but the two chiefs (as we took them to be) remained arrogantly standing. The wizened chief turned, and spoke a word. Almost immediately after, two or three savages set off running along the shore to a small shed, which, lying in the shadow of a great boulder, had slipped our notice. They hauled out a canoe, and returned, dragging it swiftly over the sand to the chiefs, who, when a man had taken his place to paddle, got in also.

And then, a terrible thing happened. The tall chief, who had seated himself in the stern, suddenly rose up, pointing vehemently with his stick at something in the bottom of the canoe. But, having looked upon it, the other leaped clean ashore over the side. The three savages who had brought the canoe stood ready to launch her; and, one after another, he seized them by the hair, and thrust with great blows at their temples with the point of his axe; so that they fell flat upon the sand, and lay still.

It was a most dreadful sight. Our men cried aloud at it. All together they cried, cursing and swearing. One, indeed, lifted his pistol to take aim at that murderous savage. But the Captain was on the alert; and, stepping swiftly to the man, "Don't fire!" cried he," not on your life! Do you wish to destroy us?"

The chief himself began to address the crowd, running up and down as before and brandishing his axe, venting upon them, apparently, the dregs of his spleen. Then, moving along the front, he proceeded to muster a company of twenty or thirty of them; and they marched away towards the canoe-shed, the chiefs walking on their flank beside the sea, to disappear from view beyond the great boulder, which stood at an elbow of the shore. The rest remained where they were, gazing at us, chattering among themselves, or shouting to us, smiling, gesticulating, waving staves, axes, or clubs. But they left a clear space about the canoe and the corpses.

Thus half an hour passed, while we watched, waiting for we knew not what; and now, remembering so tardily the woman who had twice intervened to save my life, I looked to see if I could spy her in the throng; but I could not. I wondered, too, what was become of the seaman who had escaped when I was taken in the wood. Suddenly, an enormous canoe, painted bright red, and having a very high, carved prow, came sweeping round the promontory, driven by fully twenty paddles; and the two chiefs sat in the stern. Steering close to the shore, scarcely beyond the breaking waves, she came swiftly on, intending, evidently, to board us on the landward side; so that our men made ready to fire their pistols in case the Captain gave them the word.

He never gave them the word; for, when the canoe had brought alongside, with surprising speed and precision, and was made fast with lashings, the wizened chief arose, and climbed over upon our main deck, coming alone, with fearless dignity. His greenstone axe hung suspended from his wrist; and he held a long staff of black wood, with a big, carved head. So, he crossed the deck, stepping stately and slow, his kilt rustling, the crisp, curled strips like pipe stems. His face looked extraordinary, being completely tattooed (as those permanent devices on sailors' arms) in a grotesque and harmonious pattern of curving, spiralling lines, arching upon his high, sheer forehead, circling under his eyes, and sweeping from the nostrils of his aquiline nose down on either side of his chin, curling about his lips, and running in scrolls upon his cheeks. His white hair hung matted in a sort of mane, with two feathers stuck at the back; and from his ear there dangled the dried skin of a purple bird.

I felt horror for the savage who had perpetrated those barbarous murders; and, the men regarded him under lowering brows.

Yet, his sunken, bright, sloe-black eyes beamed and glowed with a look that I can only describe as a prodigious and animal good-humour. He advanced to the Captain, smiling upon him, for all the world, as a benevolent elder might smile upon a little child. *"Haere mai!"* said he, *"haere mai! hoe mai! hoe mai! e te pa-ke-ha, haere mai!"*

*"Haere mai!"* said I at a venture. The Captain turned, and looked sternly at me; but the face of the chief was wreathed in a smile that spread as a great ripple. Then, stepping to me, before ever I knew what he was going to do, he bent forward and began to rub his nose against mine.

It was an attention, needless to tell, which was very unwelcome to me; and, recoiling from him, I retreated to the bulwarks. On this, the men, who stood round, burst out laughing. But there arose in the canoe a great roaring of many threatening voices; and, gripping his axe, the chief looked fiercely and haughtily round, glaring positively like a tiger. What the upshot of it had been I know not, had not the Captain acted with that address and readiness in which he seemed never to be wanting. He immediately threw himself into an appearance of the most violent anger with me and with the men, dissembling so well as to deceive all of us, raging up and down the deck, tearing at his beard, gnashing his teeth, rolling his eyes. The astounded men quailed before him; and the chief stared at him, astonished out of his rage. And, awakened by the clamour, our moon-struck mate, Wallis, who had lain quiet until now, began, of a sudden, to rave as a dog howls at a noise. At length, stepping close up to me, the Captain said in a low, urgent voice, "Do as I bid you, lad! At once, cast yourself flat on your face before him!"

This I performed without a moment's pause; and a great shout as of approbation arose from the canoe. When, at a word from the Captain, I got to my feet, the chief was evidently appeased. He smiled again, and began to talk in his strange tongue. The Captain returned his smile, but kept shaking his head to intimate that he did not understand, and the more he did so the more eagerly talkative the chief became.

The madman, meanwhile, continued to rave; and the chief, pointing to where he lay bound under the bulwarks, evidently enquired concerning him. The Captain answered by tapping his forehead. The chief seemed to understand, for, he kept nodding. Yet, he continued to point to the maniac, and suddenly cried out wildly.

"Him mad," answered the Captain, and the chief nodded vehemently, now muttering.

"Him lunatic," said the Captain, making his last endeavour, and pointed from Wallis to the moon with an expressive gesture.

For a moment the chief looked puzzled. Then, with a cry as of great wonder, he shook his head backwards and forwards repeatedly, and, stepping to the raving maniac, stood gazing earnestly at him for a long time, every now and again looking up to the moon.

The moon was setting. As it set, Wallis grew calmer, relapsing into lethargy.

The chief signified presently, with a sweep of his long staff, that we should all go over into the canoe, and when the Captain demurred, pointing to Wallis, he stepped to the bulwarks on the landward side; then, setting his hands to his mouth trumpet-like, holloed out an order in a harsh, grating voice that might have been heard half a mile away. A number of savages immediately set off running swiftly towards the sandhills; whereupon, turning about, he crossed his hands upon his staff, let his chin sink at rest upon them, and stood as if waiting.

We waited also. The Captain, erect by the bulwarks, a pistol in one hand, the other stroking his long beard, his eyes sunken in the shadow of his knit brows, stood as a man poised betwixt thought and action. The men, also holding pistols, stood lounging about the deck, some of them smoking their pipes, discoursing in low voices as their eyes roved from the canoe to the shore, to the statuesque figure of the chief, or to the Captain. The mate, Wallis, lay quiet on his mattress. The voices of the savages came in a confused roaring as they chatted together in the canoe and on the shore.

Thus, about half an hour passed, when the party of savages appeared upon the sandhills, bearing between them a stretcher, or palanquin upon their shoulders; and, as they brought it to the shore, to set it down there, the chief turned to the Captain, and lifting his staff, pointed with it from the mate to the palanquin, and stood waving from the ship to the canoe.

Then the Captain made up his mind, and gave the command. So, having lowered the maniac into the canoe, we all climbed over into her, and were set on shore.

It was the hour before dawn then, and darkly in the waning starlight those strange savages environed us, with confused and barbarous voices, yet seemed fantastical and remote. They did not press upon us or jostle us. Nor, did they stare upon us, as our yokel English are wont to stare at strange and far-come foreigners. Their forbearing courtesy, indeed, was of a piece with the dignity of bearing remarked in the two chiefs, and, though in a lesser degree, observable in all.

We were to go on a journey inland. So much, with expressive gestures, the wizened chief gave us to understand. And, when the maniac, Wallis, had been lifted into the palanquin, we set forth, going in a body with the chiefs, and accompanied by the whole multitude, who began to be very merry, talking and laughing together. Yet, when the maniac, on a sudden, began to rave very violently (being troubled, I suppose, by his rough passage over the sandhills), they fell silent, even those on the outskirts, and a hush and tension came over them as of awe. But the bearers were ready to set their burden upon the ground were it not for the fierce, restraining presence of the wizened chief. The maniac was no less than a demon to them, and they proceeded, indeed, in great trepidation.

Having gone the distance of about three miles, first over a sandy plain, then over undulating country set with dusky clumps of bush, we approached that great, ramified mountain range which had been visible from the ship, now reared in gloom and majesty above us, and began to ascend a great fern-clad hill that rose to the level of the wooded spurs. The maniac was quiet now; and the savages chattered and laughed in the darkness, gay and tireless as a troop of holiday-makers. At last, when our men had begun to murmur for the toil of the way and for hunger (their thirst they had quenched at a stream), there appeared above us a steep terrace. A ladder depended from it, and having mounted it, we saw, about the summit of the hill, a great fence, or palisade, prodigiously high and strong, being made of the trunks of large trees whole. A shrill clamour proceeded faintly from beyond as of the voices of women and children, accompanied by the barking of dogs. Dawn was come, and the gigantic pales loomed weird and sinister in the wan light, higher pales at intervals being shaped at their tops as hideous human heads, with their tongues hanging out.

There was a ditch in the terrace, about six feet deep, with a drawbridge over it, which we crossed, passing thence, through a narrow entry in the palisade, over a second ditch with a second palisade beyond it, through that over a third drawbridge, and thence beyond a third palisade. Whereupon we found ourselves upon a sort of village green, luridly and smokily lit with torchlights and with fires. Long, wooden houses stood clustered round it and about, having thatched, sloping roofs, which overhung very handsome porticoes, or verandahs, carved in scrolls and grotesque figures that gleamed weird and dreadful in the lurid light; while at the apex of every roof there stood a hideous mask below an image bestuck with feathers. Three or four of these houses were very large.

So much I saw vaguely, having eyes rather for the inhabitants of the place, women and children, for the most part, who came crowding about us, crying the melancholy *"Haere mai!"* And, an ancient woman, who sat doubled on the roof of a hut near us, was wailing it most drearily, rocking her bent body in a rhythm. The crone's voice was broken and bitter beyond tears; and I thought that doubtless, some dreadful calamity was fallen upon these people.

Yet, the younger women, at least, seemed to be dressed rather for joy than for sorrow, having garlands of flowers in their flowing dark hair. They wore very handsome, long, woven cloaks, with hanging strips, and some of them were even comely, and almost as light of skin as Europeans. But their lips and chins were blue with tattoo-marks; which put me in mind of the woman who had saved my life beside the wood. I was looking for her among them, when the throng who had accompanied us, on a sudden, made a rush forward, sweeping us along with them towards one of the great houses that stood at the farther end of the green.

But, having spoken briefly to the bearers of the maniac (directing them, I suppose, where to take him), the wizened chief drew the Captain and myself apart, and led the way to another large house. This we entered, bending singly in a very low doorway within the verandah, to find ourselves in a sort of hall, dimly illuminated by a fire, and to be confronted by the most horrid and affrighting figure that imagination of man, or of devil, could conceive.

It was about eight feet in height, and it stood in quivering shadow at the foot of the first of three massive pillars that rose to the ridge of the roof. Beast or hydra or devil (whatever it was), it appeared to grin and mop at us, lolling out its long tongue, so that I started back from it in a scare.

But, seizing hold of my arm, the Captain said, quickly, " Have no fear, lad. It is but an image, a carven image," and I saw that it was so. The Chief stood staring at us in perplexity. Then, looking to see that we followed, he stalked onward to the centre of the hall.

What with my fright, and the close, murky atmosphere (for, though the fire gave but little smoke, there appeared to be no outlet for it), I turned sick and dizzy. Yet, I pulled myself together, to behold, without fear, the gigantic and monstrous figure of a man, having a prodigious head and bushy hair, that stood before the central pillar, while another nightmare image—half beast, half devil—loomed shadowy from before the third pillar.

The walls were wainscoted with yellow reed-work, very delicately plaited, and; ranged at intervals along them, there stood great slabs of dark wood carved in scrolls. Scrolls were painted in scarlet and black and white upon the pillars, and upon the rafters that sloped above the slabs inward to the ridge of the roof.

But, smiling in very pleasant, friendly fashion, the chief signified to us to be seated upon one of the mats which lay here and there upon the rushes with which the place was thickly strewn.

So we sat us down, wondering what would happen next. Soon after there entered two savages, one bearing plates, or rather baskets, of steaming food, the other a vessel shaped like a globe. The chief, smiling at us, made a gesture of eating with his fingers, and immediately after withdrew to the door, walking with his staff, with portentous dignity.

"Well," said the Captain when he was gone, "I don't know how 'tis with you, lad, but I am near famished, and I shall not stick for a matter of knives and forks."

With this, he tasted the dish, as I did also, and we ate of it very heartily. 'Twas cooked eels laid upon a mess of sweet potatoes and a food like a biscuit, piping hot, and mighty good, too.

When we had finished, a savage stepped to us; and having looked with care to see that not a crumb or particle of food remained fallen upon the mat or among the rushes, he bore the empty baskets from the house.

"Has that fellow something to drink, I wonder?" said the Captain presently; and, turning, beckoned to the savage, who remained. He came and stood holding the globe forth above the Captain's head. But when he made to take it, the other appeared to hesitate, stepping a pace back. Then, as the Captain continued to stretch forth his hands, he gave it to him. It looked like a big brown cannon ball, but there was a hole in the top of it.

The Captain sat staring upon it for a space, bending his brows. Then, holding it in one hand, he tilted it slowly over above the hollowed palm of the other until some liquid began to trickle from it. Having tasted this, he told me that it was water. So, he poured out some more of it, and drank, using his hand for a glass, and passed the thing to me; and I, having drunk also after the same manner, returned it to the savage. He, who had watched us with a very puzzled look in his great, merry black eyes, bore it immediately from the house.

Presently, two more savages came in, each bearing a sort of oval block, being hollowed out at one side, and having set them near us, they returned as they had come. They scarce were gone when there entered, one after another, near a dozen more. But these were not as the others (whom we took for slaves). For, they had feathers in their hair, and pendants of greenstone or birdskin hanging from their ears. Their faces were tattooed all over in the manner I have described, and along with them were the wizened chief and his gaunt comrade.

They came, all of them, without speech, with slow and stately steps, holding their heads stiffly erect, and moving with such dignity and haughtiness as put me quite in awe.

Without so much as a look at us, they passed to the farther end of the house, and returned, each bearing one of those oval-shaped blocks, to dispose them in a circle about the fire, which was contained in a sort of oblong box of stone. Then, sinking down upon the mats, each laid his head upon his wooden pillow, and was still.

"I could wish for a softer bed," said the Captain in my ear, "but travellers cannot be choosers."

Hereupon, he drew one of the blocks to him; and, having folded his handkerchief and placed it in the hollow, he laid his head upon it, and, having his pistol beside him, composed himself to rest.

I asked him whether I should watch while he slept, but he told me to try to sleep. "Have no fear,' said he, 'They could have murdered us before had they wished to, instead of feasting us. And, if they would murder us, it will be all one whether we watch or no."

So, I laid me down also, and, after shuffling awhile, I found I lay easy enough. However, I was not difficult to content, and was too drowsy for fear. Drowsiness swept over me as a tide, casting me, almost on the instant, into deep sleep.

That night I dreamt a monstrous dream; and it seemed to me that our ship had anchored off the island on a dark midnight.

Then rose up a dreadful figure on the shore, and stretched forth an arm of stone, and with a stone hand laid hold on the ship and lifted her aloft, and dropped her all shattered into the crater of a volcano—that same mountain we had heard emitting an eerie and desolate sound. Whereupon, with a blast of sulphureous fire, the ship was blown an appallingly great height into the air.

With that I awoke; but though the phantasy of my dream passed away, I knew, as by an instinct, that something monstrous had, indeed, happened on the island. I looked round. Save for the Captain, the great hall was deserted. It glimmered in a mesh of misty pale amber sunlight which shone in magic harmony upon the delicate green of the wainscoting, the dark, carved slabs, and the painted scroll-work—black and scarlet and white—of the pillars and rafters. I looked round—*in one place the wainscoting was rent in a long fissure.*

Scarce had I seen the thing but I was on my feet, and standing over the Captain. "Rouse up!" cried I, terror in my staring eyes. "An earthquake! Haste! Come on! If there come another, we shall be entombed."

He took up his pistol and we hasted out. The hour was morning. Past the carved giant we went, past the gargoyle, to the door, which opened as a sliding-panel. As we stepped forth upon the verandah, we were near dazzled by the brightness of the morning, so that at the first we did not spy the old wizened chief who sate squatted upon a mat in the verandah. He wore a great caped cloak of glossy dark-brown feathers; and, but for his mane of matted grey hair we had not known him. For, he sate perfectly motionless, having his back towards us, and did not turn his stiff reared head, nor gave any sign at our coming.

For a moment we stood, puzzled whether or not to take any notice of him. Then the Captain drew me onward. But, turning as we passed from the verandah, I had a glimpse of his face, which was as still as if it had been cut in stone; a still, impassive face, austere and inscrutable. The double-edged blade of his greenstone axe projected from beneath the folds of his cloak.

There were twenty or thirty savages on the green, for the most part servants or slaves (whom we began to distinguish by their long, undressed hair, devoid of feathers). These great, brawny fellows were standing stock still, as if listening intently.

About us the air was hot and heavy, and seemed to throb in our ears.

Suddenly there fell a jag of lightning; and the thunder scarce had ceased to roll but, flash upon flash and jag upon jag, the lightning came continuous, as if it would seam and sear and melt the firmament. The earth did crack and crack as it came to ground.

There came a sudden, mighty flaw of wind, and then fell the rain.

It fell in flows and cataracts, crashing down like an avalanche, the natives standing motionless all the while. Yet, the outrageous tempest held not long, ceasing as suddenly as it had begun. Hereupon, the savages on the green returned to their occupation, which had been lifting the carcasses of very fat pigs. Staggering under their burdens, they flung them down in heaps before three cloaked figures who sate houses at the other side of the enclosure.

The Captain and I, to see whether the ship was affected or no, then left the palisade by way of the drawbridge and, clambering down the ladder from the terrace, made our way out on to the fern-clad hillside. Everything around us was shattered and tumbled together, and the path quite gone.

"I am apt to think, lad," said the Captain, "that 'twas no earthquake; the lightning struck the place."

"Nay," I replied, "the earth shook. 'Twas certainly an earthquake. Did you not see the fissure in the wainscoting?"

" 'Twas no earthquake, but what ..." he broke off, for there came a dreadful, subterraneous rumbling sound. The ground did heave beneath our feet. I was thrown staggering down.

The dread portent ceased. The earth fell quiet. But from behind the palisade above us a blast of flame belched forth.

"Great Heaven! My men!" cried the Captain. And, sensible that he could do nothing to aid them, added, "Quickly! Quickly! To the beach!"

Hereupon, he began to hurry me along faster and faster.

The air became sulphureous and laden with dust and ashes. A rumbling, low and ominous, sounded intermittently from the region of the palisade-volcan. The woods beneath us were full of the crying of terrified beasts, and presently, from afar, what sounded like the shouts of English voices.

The sky became tinged with a ruddy glow. A fierce roaring sound arose. I looked up, to see that all about the palisade-city, which continued to belch forth fire, the fern-clad hillsides were kindled and roaring in a holocaust.

Scouring hard behind the Captain, I presently descended with him a gully, coming safe to the shore. There we repaired to a canoe, hewn all out of a great tree trunk. In the stern was a leathern sack full of a kind of bread, and a jar of water. I helped hale her down the narrow strip of shore to where the breakers were now foaming and gnashing like creatures possessed.

And, now began the island to quake and to be shaken to pieces. The cliffs split in flaws and fissures, with stupendous sounds; the roar that came to us from the woodland bespoke a deluge of fire over which, no doubt (for 'twas not within view), the volcan reared high its infernal plume.

"Quickly! Quickly, lad!" cried the Captain, when the canoe was gotten down. "Get you in! Get you in!"

"Hold hard!' cried another voice, and turning our heads, we beheld the long-lost Joseph Yates running towards us.

In a moment he was up with us, and clambered aboard next to me.

Now, there came a dreadful thundering of the cliff and fragments of rock bounded about us like hail. So, without delay the Captain launched us forth, running out through the breakers and giving the canoe at the last a mighty impulse before swinging himself aboard.

Tossed in the turmoil of the boiling sea, the canoe blundered out, vaulting nimbly over the surges. We clutched her sides, seared and scalded and near stifled with the smoke and fiery spume and dust that blew whirling down upon us from the erupting and burning island. Giddiness overcame us. We fought against it hard, with shut eyes, bringing the whole force of our wills on the resolve to endure and live.

Suddenly, there was a strange silence.

The roar of the holocaust in the woods was abated, the wind coming about from the sea; the cliffs, for a space, had ceased to thunder.

Struck out of ourselves with amazement, we forgot our peril and listened.

Straining our eyes upon the livid-looming cliffs vaulted with fire, we looked to see the cause. A sheet of light came, a tongue of flame, that, serpent-like, wound coiling down. For a moment the lull in the Inferno-storm continued. Then, on a sudden, there came an astounding loud report; and, wave upon wave and sheet upon sheet, a sulphureous blue flame swept, coiling and writhing, down the face of the cliff.

It leapt upon the beach, it lapt it round in entwining, clinging wraiths; it encircled the canoes with tongues of flame; and then came the end!

A giant boulder crashed from the summit of the lofty cliff head-long down, and rebounding upon a spur of rock that projected almost to the place where the canoes lay, crashed them utterly. And, hard upon the falling boulder, there came an avalanche, an avalanche of molten stone.

It roared down the cliff; it swept over the shore. At its touch the sea reared madly up in an appalling great wave, hissing out clouds of steam that veiled the livid light.

And, upon us then there had fallen a dreadful fate: to be whelmed in burning lava!

We saw it coming, the wave of torment and of death. We gazed with a horrid fascination on its livid front, livid and black and shimmering like silver slime; and that instant was swollen thousand-fold with agony.

In the next, by a sudden strong rebuff of the clashing seas, our canoe was jerked slanting up, and cast upon the fo'c'sle of our tossing ship.

She had lashed away from her moorings, and unchecked by any custodians, had blundered round to save us.

# Thrown Away

By *Rudyard Kipling*

To rear a boy under what parents call the 'sheltered life system' is, if the boy must go into the world and fend for himself, not wise. Unless he be one in a thousand he has certainly to pass through many unnecessary troubles; and may, possibly, come to extreme grief simply from ignorance of the proper proportions of things.

Let a puppy eat the soap in the bath-room or chew a newly-blacked boot. He chews and chuckles until, by and by, he finds out that blacking and Old Brown Windsor make him very sick; so he argues that soap and boots are not wholesome. Any old dog about the house will soon show him the unwisdom of biting big dogs' ears. Being young, he remembers and goes abroad, at six months, a well-mannered little beast with a chastened appetite. If he had been kept away from boots, and soap, and big dogs till he came to the trinity full-grown and with developed teeth, consider how fearfully sick and thrashed he would be! Apply that notion to the 'sheltered life,' and see how it works. It does not sound pretty, but it is the better of two evils.

There was a Boy once who had been brought up under the 'sheltered life' theory; and the theory killed him dead. He stayed with his people all his days, from the hour he was born till the hour he went into Sandhurst nearly at the top of the list. He was beautifully taught in all that wins marks by a private tutor, and carried the extra weight of 'never having given his parents an hour's anxiety in his life.' What he learnt at Sandhurst beyond the regular routine is of no great consequence. He looked about him, and he found soap and blacking, so to speak, very good. He ate a little, and came out of Sandhurst not so high as he went in. Then there was an interval and a scene with his people, who expected much from him. Next, a year of living unspotted from the world in a third-rate depôt battalion where all the juniors were children and all the seniors old women; and lastly, he came out to India, where he was cut off from the support of his parents, and had no one to fall back on in time of trouble except himself.

Now, India is a place beyond all others where one must not take things too seriously—the midday sun always excepted. Too much work and too much energy kill a man just as effectively as too much assorted vice or too much drink. Flirtation does not matter, because everyone is being transferred, and either you or she leave the Station and never return. Good work does not matter, because a man is judged by his worst output, and another man takes all the credit of his best as a rule. Bad work does not matter, because other men do worse, and incompetents hang on longer in India than anywhere else. Amusements do not matter, because you must repeat them as soon as you have accomplished them once, and most amusements only mean trying to win another person's money. Sickness does not matter, because it's all in the day's work, and if you die, another man takes over your place and your office in the eight hours between death and burial.

Nothing matters except Home-furlough and acting allowances, and these only because they are scarce. It is a slack country, where all men work with imperfect instruments; and the wisest thing is to escape as soon as ever you can to some place where amusement is amusement and a reputation worth the having.

But this Boy—the tale is as old as the Hills—came out, and took all things seriously. He was pretty and was petted. He took the pettings seriously, and fretted over women not worth saddling a pony to call upon. He found his new free life in India very good. It does look attractive in the beginning, from a subaltern's point of view—all ponies, partners, dancing, and so on. He tasted it as the puppy tastes the soap. Only he came late to the eating, with a grown set of teeth. He had no sense of balance—just like the puppy—and could not understand why he was not treated with the consideration he received under his father's roof. This hurt his feelings.

He quarrelled with other boys and, being sensitive to the marrow, remembered these quarrels, and they excited him. He found whist, and gymkhanas, and things of that kind (meant to amuse one after office) good; but he took them seriously, too, just as seriously as he took the 'head' that followed after drink. He lost his money over whist and gymkhanas because they were new to him.

He took his losses seriously, and wasted as much energy and interest over a two-goldmohur race for maiden *ekka*-ponies with their manes hogged, as if it had been the Derby. One-half of this came from inexperience—much as the puppy squabbles with the corner of he hearthrug—and the other half from the dizziness bred by stumbling out of his quiet life into the glare and excitement of a livelier one. No one told him about the soap and the blacking, because an average man takes it for granted that an average man is ordinarily careful in regard to them. It was pitiful to watch The Boy knocking himself to pieces, as an over-handled colt falls down and cuts himself when he gets away from the groom.

This unbridled license in amusements not worth the trouble of breaking line for, much less rioting over, endured for six months—all through one cold weather—and then we thought that the heat and the knowledge of having lost his money and health and lamed his horses would sober. The Boy down, and he would stand steady. In ninety-nine cases out of a hundred this would have happened. You can see the principle working in any Indian Station. But this particular case fell through because The Boy was sensitive and took things seriously—as I may have said some seven times before. Of course, we could not tell how his excesses struck him personally. They were nothing very heartbreaking or above the average. He might be crippled for life financially, and want a little nursing. Still, the memory of his performances would wither away in one hot weather, and the bankers would help him to tide over the money-troubles. But he must have taken another view altogether, and have believed himself ruined beyond redemption. His Colonel talked to him severely when the cold weather ended. That made him more wretched than ever; and it was only an ordinary 'Colonel's wigging'!

What follows is a curious instance of the fashion in which we are all linked together and made responsible for one another. *The* thing that kicked the beam in The Boy's mind was a remark that a woman made when he was talking to her. There is no use in repeating it, for it was only a cruel little sentence, rapped out before thinking, that made him flush to the roots of his hair. He kept himself to himself for three days, and then put in for two days' leave to go shooting near a Canal Engineer's Rest House about thirty miles out. He got his leave, and that night at Mess was noisier and more offensive than ever. He said that he was 'going to shoot big game,' and left at half-past ten o'clock in an *ekka*. Partridge—which was the only thing a man could get near the Rest House—is not big game; so everyone laughed.

Next morning one of the Majors came in from short leave, and heard that The Boy had gone out to shoot 'big game.' The Major had taken an interest in The Boy, and had, more than once, tried to check him. The Major put up his eyebrows when he heard of the expedition, and went to The Boy's rooms where he rummaged.

Presently, he came out and found me leaving cards on the Mess. There was no one else in the ante-room.

He said, "The Boy has gone out shooting. *Does* a man shoot *tetur* with a revolver and writing-case?"

I said, "Nonsense, Major!" for I saw what was in his mind.

He said, "Nonsense or no nonsense, I'm going to the Canal now—at once. I don't feel easy."

Then, he thought for a minute, and said, "Can you lie?"

"You know best," I answered. "It's my profession."

"Very well," said the Major, "you must come out with me now—at once—in an *ekka* to the Canal to shoot black-buck. Go and put on *shikar*-kit—*quick*—and drive here with a gun."

The Major was a masterful man, and I knew that he would not give orders for nothing. So I obeyed, and on return found the Major packed up in an *ekka*—gun-cases and food slung below—all ready for a shooting-trip.

He dismissed the driver and drove himself. We jogged along quietly while in the station; but, as soon as we got to the dusty road across the plains, he made that pony fly. A country-bred can do nearly anything at a pinch. We covered the thirty miles in under three hours, but the poor brute was nearly dead.

Once I said, "What's the blazing hurry, Major?"

He said quietly, "The Boy has been alone, by himself for—one, two, five,—fourteen hours now! I tell you, I don't feel easy."

This uneasiness spread itself to me, and I helped to beat the pony.

When we came to the Canal Engineer's Rest House the Major called for The Boy's servant; but there was no answer. Then, we went up to the house, calling for The Boy by name; but there was no answer.

"Oh, he's out shooting," said I.

Just then I saw through one of the windows a little hurricane-lamp burning. This was at four in the afternoon. We both stopped dead in the verandah, holding our breath to catch every sound; and we heard, inside the room, the '*brr—brr—brr*' of a multitude of flies. The Major said nothing, but he took off his helmet and we entered very softly.

The Boy was dead on the bed in the centre of the bare, lime-washed room. He had shot his head nearly to pieces with his revolver. The gun-cases were still strapped, so was the bedding, and on the table lay The Boy's writing-case with photographs. He had gone away to die like a poisoned rat!

The Major said to himself softly, "Poor Boy! Poor, *poor* devil!" Then he turned away from the bed and said, "I want your help in this business."

Knowing The Boy was dead by his own hand, I saw exactly what that help would be, so I passed over to the table, took a chair, lit a cheroot, and began to go through the writing-case; the Major looking over my shoulder and repeating to himself, "We came too late!—Like a rat in a hole!—Poor, *poor* devil!"

The Boy must have spent half the night in writing to his people, to his Colonel, and to a girl at Home; and as soon as he had finished, must have shot himself, for he had been dead a long time when we came in.

I read all that he had written, and passed over each sheet to the Major as I finished it.

We saw from his accounts how very seriously he had taken every thing. He wrote about 'disgrace which he was unable to bear'—'indelible shame'—'criminal folly'—'wasted life,' and so on; besides a lot of private things to his father and mother much too sacred to put into print. The letter to the girl at Home was the most pitiful of all, and I choked as I read it. The Major made no attempt to keep dry-eyed. I respected him for that. He read and rocked himself to and fro, and simply cried like a woman without caring to hide it. The letters were so dreary and hopeless and touching. We forgot all about The Boy's follies, and only thought of the poor Thing on the bed and the scrawled sheets in our hands. It was utterly impossible to let the letters go Home. They would have broken his father's heart and killed his mother after killing her belief in her son.

At last, the Major dried his eyes openly, and said, "Nice sort of thing to spring on an English family! What shall we do?"

I said, knowing what the Major had brought me out for,—"The Boy died of cholera. We were with him at the time. We can't commit ourselves to half-measures. Come along."

Then began one of the most grimly comic scenes I have ever taken part in—the concoction of a big, written lie, bolstered with evidence, to soothe The Boy's people at Home. I began the rough draft of the letter, the Major throwing in hints here and there while he gathered up all the stuff that The Boy had written and burnt it in the fireplace. It was a hot, still evening when we began, and the lamp burned very badly. In due course I made the draft to my satisfaction, setting forth how The Boy was the pattern of all virtues, beloved by his regiment, with every promise of a great career before him, and so on; how we had helped him through the sickness—it was no time for little lies, you will understand—and how he had died without pain. I choked while I was putting down these things and thinking of the poor people who would read them. Then, I laughed at the grotesqueness of the affair, and the laughter mixed itself up with the choke—and the Major said that we both wanted drinks.

I am afraid to say how much whisky we drank before the letter was finished. It had not the least effect on us. Then we took off The Boy's watch, locket, and rings.

Lastly, the Major said, "We must send a lock of hair, too. A woman values that."

But there were reasons why we could not find a lock fit to send. The Boy was black-haired, and so was the Major, luckily. I cut off a piece of the Major's hair above the temple with a knife, and put it into the packet we were making. The laughing-fit and the chokes got hold of me again, and I had to stop. The Major was nearly as bad; and we both knew that the worst part of the work was to come.

We sealed up the packet, photographs, locket, seals, ring, letter, and lock of hair with The Boy's sealing-wax and The Boy's seal.

Then the Major said, "For God's sake let's get outside—away from the room—and think!"

We went outside, and walked on the banks of the Canal for an hour, eating and drinking what we had with us, until the moon rose. I know now exactly how a murderer feels. Finally, we forced ourselves back to the room with the lamp and the Other Thing in it, and began to take up the next piece of work. I am not going to write about this. It was too horrible. We burned the bedstead and dropped the ashes into the Canal; we took up the matting of the room and treated that in the same way. I went off to a village and borrowed two big hoes,—I did not want the villagers to help,—while the Major arranged—the other matters. It took us four hours' hard work to make the grave. As we worked, we argued out whether it was right to say as much as we remembered of the Burial of the Dead. We compromised things by saying the Lord's Prayer with a private unofficial prayer for the peace of the soul of The Boy. Then we filled in the grave and went into the verandah—not the house—to lie down to sleep. We were dead-tired.

When we woke the Major said wearily, "We can't go back till tomorrow. We must give him a decent time to die in. He died early *this* morning, remember. That seems more natural." So, the Major must have been lying awake all the time, thinking.

I said, "Then why didn't we bring the body back to cantonments?"

The Major thought for a minute. "Because the people bolted when they heard of the cholera. And, the *ekka* has gone!"

That was strictly true. We had forgotten all about the *ekka*-pony, and he had gone home.

So we were left there alone, all that stifling day, in the Canal Rest House, testing and re-testing our story of The Boy's death to see if it was weak in any point. A native appeared in the afternoon, but we said that a *Sahib* was dead of cholera, and he ran away. As the dusk gathered, the Major told me all his fears about The Boy, and awful stories of suicide or nearly-carried-out suicide—tales that made one's hair crisp. He said that he himself had once gone into the same Valley of the Shadow as The Boy, when he was young and new to the country; so he understood how things fought together in The Boy's poor jumbled head. He also said that youngsters, in their repentant moments, consider their sins much more serious and ineffaceable than they really are. We talked together all through the evening and rehearsed the story of the death of The Boy. As soon as the moon was up, and The Boy, theoretically, just buried, we struck across country for the Station. We walked from eight till six o'clock in the morning; but though we were dead-tired, we did not forget to go to The Boy's rooms and put away his revolver with the proper amount of cartridges in the pouch. Also, to set his writing-case on the table. We found the Colonel and reported the death, feeling more like murderers than ever. Then, we went to bed and slept the clock round, for there was no more in us.

The tale had credence as long as was necessary; for everyone forgot about The Boy before a fortnight was over. Many people, however, found time to say that the Major had behaved scandalously in not bringing in the body for a regimental funeral. The saddest thing of all was the letter from The Boy's mother to the Major and me—with big inky blisters all over the sheet. She wrote the sweetest possible things about our great kindness, and the obligation she would be under to us as long as she lived.

All things considered, she was under an obligation, but not exactly as she meant.

# The Mark of the Beast

By *Rudyard Kipling*

East of Suez, some hold, the direct control of Providence ceases; Man being there handed over to the power of the Gods and Devil of Asia, and the Church of England Providence only exercising an occasional and modified supervision in the case of Englishmen.

This theory accounts for some of the more unnecessary horrors of life in India: it may be stretched to explain my story.

My friend Strickland of the police, who knows as much of natives of India as is good for any man, can bear witness to the facts of the case. Dumoise, our doctor, also saw what Strickland and I saw. The inference which he drew from the evidence was entirely incorrect. He is dead now; he died, in a rather curious manner, which has been elsewhere described.

When Fleete came to India, he owned a little money and some land in the Himalayas, near a place called Dharmsala. Both properties had been left him by an uncle, and he came out to finance them. He was a big, heavy, genial, and inoffensive man. His knowledge of natives was, of course, limited, and he complained of the difficulties of the language.

He rode in from his place in the hills to spend New Year in the station, and he stayed with Strickland. On New Year's Eve there was a big dinner at the club, and the night was excusably wet. When men foregather from the uttermost ends of the Empire, they have a right to be riotous. The Frontier had sent down a contingent o' Catch-'em-Alive-O's who had not seen twenty white faces for a year, and were used to ride fifteen miles to dinner at the next Fort at the risk of a Khyberee bullet where their drinks should lie. They profited by their new security, for they tried to play pool with a curled-up hedgehog found in the garden, and one of them carried the marker round the room in his teeth. Half a dozen planters had come in from the south and were talking "horse" to the Biggest Liar in Asia, who was trying to cap all their stories at once. Everybody was there, and there was a general closing up of ranks and taking stock of our losses in dead or disabled that had fallen during the past year.

It was a very wet night, and I remember that we sang "Auld Lang Syne" with our feet in the Polo Championship Cup, and our heads among the stars, and swore that we were all dear friends. Then some of us went away and annexed Burma, and some tried to open up the Soudan and were opened up by Fuzzies in that cruel scrub outside Suakim, and some found stars and medals, and some were married, which was bad, and some did other things which were worse, and the others of us stayed in our chains and strove to make money on insufficient experiences.

Fleete began the night with sherry and bitters, drank champagne steadily up to dessert, then raw, rasping Capri with all the strength of whisky, took Benedictine with his coffee, four or five whiskies and sodas to improve his pool strokes, beer and bones at half-past two, winding up with old brandy. Consequently, when he came out, at half-past three in the morning, into fourteen degrees of frost, he was very angry with his horse for coughing, and tried to leapfrog into the saddle. The horse broke away and went to his stables; so Strickland and I formed a Guard of Dishonour to take Fleete home.

Our road lay through the bazaar, close to a little temple of Hanuman, the Monkey-god, who is a leading divinity worthy of respect. All gods have good points, just as have all priests. Personally, I attach much importance to Hanuman, and am kind to his people—the great gray apes of the hills. One never knows when one may want a friend.

There was a light in the temple, and as we passed, we could hear voices of men chanting hymns. In a native temple, the priests rise at all hours of the night to do honour to their god. Before we could stop him, Fleete dashed up the steps, patted two priests on the back, and was gravely grinding the ashes of his cigar butt into the forehead of the red stone image of Hanuman. Strickland tried to drag him out, but he sat down and said solemnly:

"Shee that? 'Mark of the B—beasht! *I* made it. Ishn't it fine?"

In half a minute the temple was alive and noisy, and Strickland, who knew what came of polluting gods, said that things might occur. He, by virtue of his official position, long residence in the country, and weakness for going among the natives, was known to the priests and he felt unhappy. Fleete sat on the ground and refused to move. He said that "good old Hanuman" made a very soft pillow.

Then, without any warning, a Silver Man came out of a recess behind the image of the god. He was perfectly naked in that bitter, bitter cold, and his body shone like frosted silver, for he was what the Bible calls "a leper as white as snow." Also, he had no face, because he was a leper of some years' standing and his disease was heavy upon him. We two stooped to haul Fleete up, and the temple was filling and filling with folk who seemed to spring from the earth, when the Silver Man ran in under our arms, making a noise exactly like the mewing of an otter, caught Fleete round the body and dropped his head on Fleete's breast before we could wrench him away. Then he retired to a corner and sat mewing while the crowd blocked all the doors.

The priests were very angry until the Silver Man touched Fleete. That nuzzling seemed to sober them.

At the end of a few minutes' silence one of the priests came to Strickland and said, in perfect English, "Take your friend away. He was done with Hanuman, but Hanuman has not done with him." The crowd gave room and we carried Fleete into the road.

Strickland was very angry. He said that we might all three have been knifed, and that Fleete should thank his stars that he had escaped without injury.

Fleete thanked no one. He said that he wanted to go to bed. He was gorgeously drunk.

We moved on, Strickland silent and wrathful, until Fleete was taken with violent shivering fits and sweating. He said that the smells of the bazaar were overpowering, and he wondered why slaughter-houses were permitted so near English residences. "Can't you smell the blood?" said Fleete.

We put him to bed at last, just as the dawn was breaking, and Strickland invited me to have another whisky and soda. While we were drinking he talked of the trouble in the temple, and admitted that it baffled him completely. Strickland hates being mystified by natives, because his business in life is to overmatch them with their own weapons. He has not yet succeeded in doing this, but in fifteen or twenty years he will have made some small progress.

"They should have mauled us," he said, "instead of mewing at us. I wonder what they meant. I don't like it one little bit."

I said that the Managing Committee of the temple would in all probability bring a criminal action against us for insulting their religion. There was a section of the Indian Penal Code which exactly met Fleete's offense. Strickland said he only hoped and prayed that they would do this. Before I left I looked into Fleete's room and saw him lying on his right side, scratching his left breast. Then I went to bed cold, depressed, and unhappy, at seven o'clock in the morning.

At one o'clock I rode over to Strickland's house to inquire after Fleete's head. I imagined that it would be a sore one. Fleete was breakfasting and seemed unwell. His temper was gone, for he was abusing the cook for not supplying him with an underdone chop. A man who can eat raw meat after a wet night is a curiosity. I told Fleete this and he laughed.

"You breed queer mosquitoes in these parts," he said. "I've been bitten to pieces, but only in one place."

"Let's have a look at the bite," said Strickland. "It may have gone down since this morning."

While the chops were being cooked, Fleete opened his shirt and showed us, just over his left breast, a mark, the perfect double of the black rosettes—the five or six irregular blotches arranged in a circle—on a leopard's hide. Strickland looked and said, "It was only pink this morning. It's grown black now."

Fleete ran to a glass.

"By Jove!" he said, "this is nasty. What is it?"

We could not answer. Here the chops came in, all red and juicy, and Fleete bolted three in a most offensive manner. He ate on his right grinders only, and threw his head over his right shoulder as he snapped the meat. When he had finished, it struck him that he had been behaving strangely, for he said apologetically, "I don't think I ever felt so hungry in my life. I've bolted like an ostrich."

After breakfast Strickland said to me, "Don't go. Stay here, and stay for the night."

Seeing that my house was not three miles from Strickland's, this request was absurd. But Strickland insisted, and was going to say something when Fleete interrupted by declaring in a shamefaced way that he felt hungry again. Strickland sent a man to my house to fetch over my bedding and a horse, and we three went down to Strickland's stables to pass the hours until it was time to go out for a ride. The man who has a weakness for horses never wearies of inspecting them; and when two men are killing time in this way they gather knowledge and lies the one from the other.

There were five horses in the stables, and I shall never forget the scene as we tried to look them over. They seemed to have gone mad. They reared and screamed and nearly tore up their pickets; they sweated and shivered and lathered and were distraught with fear. Strickland's horses used to know him as well as his dogs; which made the matter more curious. We left the stable for fear of the brutes throwing themselves in their panic. Then Strickland turned back and called me. The horses were still frightened, but they let us "gentle" and make much of them, and put their heads in our bosoms.

"They aren't afraid of us," said Strickland. "D'you know, I'd give three months' pay if *Outrage* here could talk."

But *Outrage* was dumb, and could only cuddle up to his master and blow out his nostrils, as is the custom of horses when they wish to explain things but can't. Fleete came up when we were in the stalls, and as soon as the horses saw him, their fright broke out afresh. It was all that we could do to escape from the place unkicked. Strickland said, "They don't seem to love you, Fleete."

"Nonsense," said Fleete; "my mare will follow me like a dog." he went to her; she was in a loose-box; but as he slipped the bars she plunged, knocked him down, and broke away into the garden. I laughed, but Strickland was not amused. He took his moustache in both fists and pulled at it till it nearly came out. Fleete, instead of going off to chase his property, yawned, saying that he felt sleepy. He went to the house to lie down, which was a foolish way of spending New Year's Day.

Strickland sat with me in the stables and asked if I had noticed anything peculiar in Fleete's manner. I said that he ate his food like a beast; but that this might have been the result of living alone in the hills out of the reach of society as refined and elevating as ours for instance. Strickland was not amused. I do not think that he listened to me, for his next sentence referred to the mark on Fleete's breast, and I said that it might have been caused by blister-flies, or that it was possibly a birthmark newly born and now visible for the first time. We both agreed that it was unpleasant to look at, and Strickland found occasion to say that I was a fool.

"I can't tell you what I think now," said he, "because you would call me a madman; but you must stay with me for the next few days, if you can. I want you to watch Fleete, but don't tell me what you think till I have made up my mind."

"But I am dining out tonight," I said.

"So am I," said Strickland, "and so is Fleete. At least if he doesn't change his mind."

We walked about the garden smoking, but saying nothing—because we were friends, and talking spoils good tobacco—till our pipes were out. Then we went to wake up Fleete. He was wide awake and fidgeting about his room.

"I say, I want some more chops," he said. "Can I get them?"

We laughed and said, "Go and change. The ponies will be round in a minute."

"All right," said Fleete. "I'll go when I get the chops—underdone ones, mind."

He seemed to be quite in earnest. It was four o'clock, and we had had breakfast at one; still, for a long time, he demanded those underdone chops. Then he changed into riding clothes and went out into the verandah. His pony—the mare had not been caught—would not let him come near. All three horses were unmanageable—mad with fear—and finally Fleete said that he would stay at home and get something to eat. Strickland and I rode out wondering. As we passed the temple of Hanuman, the Silver Man came out and mewed at us.

"He is not one of the regular priests of the temple," said Strickland. "I think I should peculiarly like to lay my hands on him."

There was no spring in our gallop on the racecourse that evening. The horses were stale, and moved as though they had been ridden out.

"The fright after breakfast has been too much for them," said Strickland.

That was the only remark he made through the remainder of the ride. Once or twice I think he swore to himself; but that did not count.

We came back in the dark at seven o'clock, and saw that there were no lights in the bungalow. "Careless ruffians my servants are!" said Strickland.

My horse reared at something on the carriage drive, and Fleete stood up under its nose.

"What are you doing, grovelling about the garden?" said Strickland.

But both horses bolted and nearly threw us. We dismounted by the stables and returned to Fleete, who was on his hands and knees under the orange bushes.

"What the devil's wrong with you?" said Strickland.

"Nothing, nothing in the world," said Fleete, speaking very quickly and thickly. "I've been gardening—botanising you know. The smell of the earth is delightful. I think I'm going for a walk—a long walk—all night."

Then I saw that there was something excessively out of order somewhere, and I said to Strickland, "I am not dining out."

"Bless you!" said Strickland. "Here, Fleete, get up. You'll catch fever there. Come in to dinner and let's have the lamps lit. We'll all dine at home."

Fleete stood up unwillingly, and said, "No lamps—no lamps. It's much nicer here. Let's dine outside and have some more chops—lots of 'em and underdone—bloody ones with gristle."

Now a December evening in Northern India is bitterly cold, and Fleete's suggestion was that of a maniac.

"Come in." said Strickland sternly. "Come in at once."

Fleete came, and when the lamps were brought, we saw that he was literally plastered with dirt from head to foot. He must have been rolling in the garden. He shrank from the light and went to his room. His eyes were horrible to look at. There was a green light behind them, not in them, if you understand, and the man's lower lip hung down.

Strickland said, "There is going to be trouble—big trouble—tonight. Don't change your riding things."

We waited and waited for Fleete's reappearance, and ordered dinner in the meantime. We could hear him moving about his own room, but there was no light there. Presently, from the room came the long-drawn howl of a wolf.

People write and talk lightly of blood running cold and hair standing up and things of that kind. Both sensations are too horrible to be trifled with. My heart stopped as though a knife had been driven through it; and Strickland turned white as the tablecloth.

The howl was repeated, and was answered by another howl far across the fields.

That set the gilded roof on the horror. Strickland dashed into Fleete's room. I followed, and we saw Fleete getting out of the window. He made beast-noises in the back of his throat. He could not answer us when we shouted at him. He spat.

I don't quite remember what followed, but I think that Strickland must have stunned him with the long boot-jack or else I should never have been able to sit on his chest. Fleete could not speak, he could only snarl, and his snarls were those of a wolf, not of a man. The human spirit must have been giving way all day and have died out with the twilight. We were dealing with a beast that had once been Fleete.

The affair was-beyond any human and rational experience. I tried to say "hydrophobia," but the word wouldn't come, because I knew that I was lying.

We bound this beast with leather thongs of the punkah-rope, and tied its thumbs and big toes together, and gagged it with a shoehorn, which makes a very efficient gag if you know how to arrange it. Then we carried it into the dining room, and sent a man to Dumoise, the doctor, telling him to come over at once. After we had despatched the messenger and were drawing breath,

Strickland said, "It's no good. This isn't any doctor's work." I, also, knew that he spoke the truth.

The beast's head was free, and it threw it about from side to side. Anyone entering the room would have believed that we were curing a wolf's pelt. That was the most loathsome accessory of all.

Strickland sat with his chin in the heel of his fist, watching the beast as it wriggled on the ground, but saying nothing. The shirt had been torn open in the scuffle and showed the black rosette mark on the left breast. It stood out like a blister.

In the silence of the watching we heard something without mewing like a she-otter. We both rose to our feet, and, I answer for myself, not Strickland, felt sick—actually and physically sick. We told each other, as did the men in *Pinafore,* that it was the cat.

Dumoise arrived, and I never saw a little man so unprofessionally shocked. He said that it was a heartrending case of hydrophobia, and that nothing could be done. At least, any palliative measures would only prolong the agony. The beast was foaming at the mouth. Fleete, as we told Dumoise, had been bitten by dogs once or twice. Any man who keeps half a dozen terriers must expect a nip now and again. Dumoise could offer no help. He could only certify that Fleete was dying of hydrophobia. The beast was then howling, for it had managed to spit out the shoe-horn. Dumoise, said that he would be ready to certify to the cause of death, and that the end was certain. He was a good little man, and he offered to remain with us; but Strickland refused the kindness. He did not wish to poison Dumoise's New Year. He would only ask him not to give the real cause of Fleete's death to the public.

So Dumoise left, deeply agitated; and as soon as the noise of the cartwheels had died away, Strickland told me, in a whisper, his suspicions. They were so wildly improbable that he dared not say them out aloud; and I, who entertained all Strickland's beliefs, was so ashamed of owning to them that I pretended to disbelieve.

"Even if the Silver Man had bewitched Fleete for polluting the image of Hanuman, the punishment could not have fallen so quickly."

As I was whispering this the cry outside the house rose again, and the beast fell into a fresh paroxysm of struggling till we were afraid that the thongs that held it would give way.

"Watch!" said Strickland. "If this happens six times I shall take the law into my own hands. I order you to help me."

He went into his room and came out in a few minutes with the barrels of an old shotgun, a piece of fishing-line, some thick cord, and his heavy wooden bedstead. I reported that the convulsions had followed the cry by two seconds in each case, and the beast seemed perceptibly weaker.

Strickland muttered, "But he can't take away the life! He can't take away the life!"

I said, though I knew that I was arguing against myself, "It may be a cat. It must be a cat. If the Silver Man is responsible, why does he dare to come here?"

Strickland arranged the wood on the hearth, put the gun barrels into the glow of the fire, spread the twine on the table and broke a walking stick in two. There was one yard of fishing-line, gut, lapped with wire, such as is used for *mahseer*-fishing, and he tied the two ends together in a loop.

Then he said, "How can we catch him? He must be taken alive and unhurt."

I said that we must trust in Providence, and go out softly with polo sticks into the shrubbery at the front of the house. The man or animal that made the cry was evidently moving round the house as regularly as a night watchman. We could wait in the bushes till he came by and knock him over.

Strickland accepted this suggestion, and we slipped out from a bathroom window into the front verandah and then across the carriage drive into the bushes.

In the moonlight we could see the leper coming round the corner of the house. He was perfectly naked, and from time to time he mewed and stopped to dance with his shadow. It was an unattractive sight, and thinking of poor Fleete, brought to such degradation by so foul a creature, I put away all my doubts and resolved to help Strickland from the heated gun barrels to the loop of twine—from the loins to the head and back again—with all tortures that might be needful.

The leper halted in the front porch for a moment and we jumped out on him with the sticks. He was wonderfully strong, and we were afraid that he might escape or be fatally injured before we caught him. We had an idea that lepers were frail creatures, but this proved to be incorrect. Strickland knocked his legs from under him and I put my foot on his neck. He mewed hideously, and even through my riding boots I could feel that his flesh was not the flesh of a clean man.

He struck at us with his hand and feet-stumps. We looped the lash of a dog whip round him, under the armpits and dragged him backwards into the hall and so into the dining room where the beast lay. There we tied him with trunk straps. He made no attempt to escape, but mewed.

When we confronted him with the beast the scene was beyond description. The beast doubled backwards into a bow as though he had been poisoned with strychnine, and moaned in the most pitiable fashion. Several other things happened also, but they cannot be put down here.

"I think I was right," said Strickland. "Now, we will ask him to cure this case."

But the leper only mewed. Strickland wrapped a towel round his hand and took the gun barrels out of the fire. I put the half of the broken walking stick through the loop of fishing-line and buckled the leper comfortably to Strickland's bedstead. I understood then how men and women and little children can endure to see a witch burnt alive; for, the beast was moaning on the floor, and though the Silver Man had no face, you could see horrible feeling passing through the slab that took its place, exactly as waves of heat play across red-hot iron—gun barrels for instance.

Strickland shaded his eyes with his hands for a moment and we got to work. This part is not to be printed.

The dawn was beginning to break when the leper spoke. His mewings had not been satisfactory up to that point. The beast had fainted from exhaustion and the house was very still. We unstrapped the leper and told him to take away the evil spirit. He crawled to the beast and laid his hand upon the left breast. That was all. Then he fell face down and whined, drawing in his breath as he did so.

We watched the face of the beast, and saw the soul of Fleete coming back into the eyes. Then a sweat broke out on the forehead and the eyes—they were human eyes—closed. We waited for an hour but Fleete still slept. We carried him to his room and bade the leper go, giving him the bedstead, and the sheet on the bedstead to cover his nakedness, the gloves and the towels with which we had touched him, and the whip that had been hooked round his body. He put the sheet about him and went out into the early morning without speaking or mewing.

Strickland wiped his face and sat down. A night-gong, far away in the city, made seven o'clock.

"Exactly four-and-twenty hours!" said Strickland. "And, I've done enough to ensure my dismissal from the service, besides permanent quarters in a lunatic asylum. Do you believe that we are awake?"

The red-hot gun barrel had fallen on the floor and was singeing the carpet. The smell was entirely real.

That morning at eleven we two together went to wake up Fleete. We looked and saw that the black leopard-rosette on his chest had disappeared. He was very drowsy and tired, but as soon as he saw us, he said, "Oh! Confound you fellows. Happy New Year to you. Never mix your liquors. I'm nearly dead."

"Thanks for your kindness, but you're over time," said Strickland. "Today is the morning of the second. You've slept the clock round with a vengeance."

The door opened, and little Dumoise put his head in. He had come on foot, and fancied that we were laying out Fleete.

"I've brought a nurse," said Dumoise. "I suppose that she can come in for ... what is necessary."

"By all means," said Fleete cheerily, sitting up in bed. "Bring on your nurses."

Dumoise was dumb. Strickland led him out and explained that there must have been a mistake in the diagnosis. Dumoise remained dumb and left the house hastily. He considered that his professional reputation had been injured, and was inclined to make a personal matter of the recovery. Strickland went out, too. When he came back, he said that he had been to call on the Temple of Hanuman to offer redress for the pollution of the god, and had been solemnly assured that no white man had ever touched the idol and that he was an incarnation of all the virtues labouring under a delusion. "What do you think?" said Strickland.

I said, " 'There are more things ...' "

But Strickland hates that quotation. He says that I have worn it threadbare.

One other curious thing happened which frightened me as much as anything in all the night's work. When Fleete was dressed he came into the dining room and sniffed. He had a quaint trick of moving his nose when he sniffed. "Horrid doggy smell, here," said he. "You should really keep those terriers of yours in better order. Try sulphur, Strick."

But Strickland did not answer. He caught hold of the back of a chair, and, without warning, went into an amazing fit of hysterics. It is terrible to see a strong man overtaken with hysteria. Then, it struck me that we had fought for Fleete's soul with the Silver Man in that room, and had disgraced ourselves as Englishmen forever, and I laughed and gasped and gurgled just as shamefully as Strickland, while Fleete thought that we had both gone mad. We never told him what we had done.

Some years later, when Strickland had married and was a church-going member of society for his wife's sake, we reviewed the incident dispassionately, and Strickland suggested that I should put it before the public.

I cannot myself see that this step is likely to clear up the mystery; because, in the first place, no one will believe a rather unpleasant story, and, in the second, it is well-known to every right-minded man that the gods of the heathen are stone and brass, and any attempt to deal with them otherwise is justly condemned.

# The Ninth Year

By *R. Edison Page*

To every regiment of Indian Native Infantry there are nine English officers; and in every nine years one of these must die. Promotion comes by a man's retiring, or by his removal to the Staff, to another regiment, or to civil employment; but once at least in nine years it comes by death. This is the belief: it may be founded on long-armed coincidence; or it may be that the High Gods of the East do indeed exact this toll.

The history of the Fazlabad Infantry, for nearly a generation, in no way discredited this belief. The Adjutant had been murdered on parade seven years to the week before the Second in Command broke his neck at polo; and eight years later the Senior Wing Officer died of sunstroke. Since then more than eight years had passed, and Death had let them be. They gave him every chance: they lived hard; they fought hard; no jungle was so full of fever but they hunted through it; and between Seidkhasana and Mannargudi no more reckless set of men rode to pig in the dawn.

Fate was not kind to Hubert Selby, nor for that matter to

the regiment, when it sent him to join the Fazlabad Infantry. He was one of those large, soft-fleshed young men who never so much exercise hardens; and he took very little. He kept only one pony, for hacking; and detested every sport. But he dressed with a too conspicuous care; smoked a few cigarettes rather for pictorial effect than for pleasure; and drank very mild pegs. His complexion was white and opaque; his eyes, of a dull black, were prominent; his hair was black, and always sleek; what there was of his soft and scanty moustache was carefully trimmed; and the supercilious reserve of the woman-hunter was spread over his regular features like a varnish.

His occupation was playing cards; and though he was no gambler, he was skilled in all games of chance. His recreations were reading French novels, and what is called in the army "Dolly-mopping." He was an incompetent officer, and as lazy as he was incompetent.

It was natural that he should not be beloved by his brother-officers. He was not disagreeable with them: indeed, it would have taken a tougher man than Selby to be disagreeable with them; he learned even, painfully, not to be supercilious with them; but truly he was of another race. And, it is given to few to like a man whose pursuits they despise, whose work falls on their shoulders by day, while he empties their pockets by night.

At the beginning of the ninth year after the death of Captain Davies, Selby became senior Wing Officer. In his new post also he did as little work as he could; and the mischief to which he devoted his abundant leisure, was the seeking an intrigue with a native woman of some position. This is the most dangerous of all games; for the Eastern methods of purging honour are sudden, secret, and deadly, while the Zenana lies without the pale of the Law of the British Empire. In the course of his search he had one or two narrow escapes, and no success worth the risk; but so far from teaching him wisdom they only whetted keener that amorous curiosity which is the moving principle of the woman-hunter's nature.

One evening, at the end of the hot weather he rode out on his patient prowl; and turned his pony's head along the bank of the canal towards the bathing-ghâts, to take his pleasure watching the women bathe. Among the common folk in India there is no prejudice against mixed bathing, as long, to all seeming, as the bathers are not overburthened with clothing. About a mile from his goal he came upon a little country-house provided with a bathing-ghât of its own. The native of India is for the most part careless of privacy; in building the ghât the owner of the house had shown himself careless of the fact that it was necessary to cross the public road in going to and fro from it; and Hubert Selby came suddenly round the trees upon Rukmini changing, upon the edge of the ghât, the dripping Sāri in which she had been bathing—women of position bathe wholly covered—for a dry one. The setting sun poured its level rays across the plain, and burnished her wheat-coloured skin to gold; the admirable contours of her rounded limbs and bosom stood out clear and faultless against the purple background of the fields. Selby checked his pony, and sat staring at her beautiful face, his lips parted, in a breathless admiration. Then she saw him; caught the Sāri before her face with a little cry; and sank down, covering herself entirely with it from his eyes; but not before the vermilion streak down the parting of her hair had shown him that she was a married woman.

Then he found his voice, and poured out at the little pyramid of drapery every burning word of the Indian lover he could remember. In the suddenness and surprise of the event he was somewhat incoherent; but his flattering sincerity was plain enough to Rukmini. He came soon to the end of his vocabulary; tired even sooner of pouring out his protestations at a motionless, silent Sāri; and was on the very point of dismounting when he saw some men coming down the canal bank, and started discreetly his pony on again. But he had lost his desire to visit the bathing-ghâts; he looked back to see Rukmini scuttle across the road into the house; turned his pony's head; and cantered home across the fields. His mind was full of the vision; and a hundred schemes for obtaining access to the beautiful creature ran through his mind. Even in his first extravagance he knew that he must be wary; for the size of her ornaments had left him in no doubt that she was the wife of a rich man: "of some beastly old bunniah," he said to himself; and likely to be carefully guarded.

These hundred schemes, most of them impossible to absurdity, kept his mind at work until he had dressed for Mess. He came to it to find everyone at the pitch of joyful excitement: the Colonel had returned suddenly from Simla, before his leave was up indeed, with the news that the regiment was to hold itself in readiness to join the Shingarhi field force immediately the order came from headquarters. Everyone was very cheerful, and very noisy; no one stinted himself liquor; and after dinner a chance remark set going Burkle, the racing Adjutant, a young man whose irrepressible sporting instinct found occasion for a bet in everything on the earth, or off it.

"By Jove! So it is!" he cried. "The ninth year's running; and nobody's gone to grass! What's the odds that we don't all of us escape old catch-em-alive-oh! this journey? I'm betting that we do."

To their high spirits it seemed a very proper matter for a wager; half a dozen bets were offered and taken; and the usual wrangling about conditions followed. Then the fired imagination of the ingenuous Adjutant soared to proposing a sweepstake of a magnum of champagne apiece; but the Colonel dashed it from its height by demanding, with a somewhat brisk asperity, to be told what a dead man would do with eight magnums of champagne.

During the days that followed everyone was busy indeed, bringing the regiment to the pitch of efficiency for the field. His lack of popularity, and his laziness in time of peace invested Selby's appointment to the duty of staying behind, in command of a small depôt of recruits and the unfit, with such a propriety that no one was at the pains to condole with him; much less did anyone come forward, trembling lest he should accept it, with the quixotic offer to give up to him his chance of gaining a little glory at a great risk of a couple of inches of telegraph wire in the stomach. And, for himself, he forewent that chance of glory and the hardships of the campaign with an even mind, assured of leisure and freedom to devote himself to the chase. In spite of the press of work he found time to ride now and again past the house on the canal; and one evening he was sure that the veiled, motionless woman who had watched him from the flat roof was the pretty creature he had surprised.

As he rode back into the Lines, in a pleasant satisfaction, he met the Colonel; and a little while after the Colonel said to the Adjutant, "I wonder what mischief that young brute Selby is up to. I saw him ride in just now, licking his lips for all the world like an old maid's fat tom-cat who's been stealing cream."

"There's no telling with that kind," said the Adjutant with an excellent air of worldly wisdom. "It maybe a woman; it maybe that he's invented a new kind of Blind Hookey."

Resigned almost to cheerfulness, Hubert Selby saw the regiment march away in a fine gaiety to fight the Waziri in his dismal mountains. Its going left his evenings also, unoccupied by cards, free for the chase; two hours' leisurely work discharged his duties for the day. His idleness fed his fancy full. He learned soon that the house belonged to a well-to-do native who was absent, that only his wife, her woman, and an old man left in charge of them dwelt in it. He cast about for the necessary, the almost inevitable old woman. There is an Eastern proverb that one old woman will corrupt more women in a month than ten rakes in a year. Since his quarry did not live in the town, where old women abound, he had some difficulty in finding one. But at last, his sweeper learned from the lady's sweeper what old women visited her house; and Selby chose from among them a poor widow. This go-between brought to her task the usual rapacity, and a readiness for mischief only natural in an Indian widow who is treated like a dog by all around her till she loathes the human race. She brought to it, indeed, that last cunning, the cunning of the maltreated slave; found Rukmini softened by her husband's absence and Selby's assiduity, flattered by having awakened this passion in one of the Master-race; played upon her carefully trained animal propensities, uncontrolled by any moral sense, till she overcame her religious scruples against the defiling touch of a white man; and earned her rupees.

Late one night Selby, assured that the old man in charge of it had been drugged, stole out of the Lines down to the house on the canal. There were no windows to the women's quarters; but he was not so inactive but that he could climb into the branches of the pipal tree which overhung the roof, and let himself down through one of the big air-holes in it, which serve as windows and ventilators, and are covered with stone slabs in bad weather, into Rukmini's chamber.

In that dim light, in that heavily-scented, intoxicating air, with the sense of danger strong upon him, he found her even more beautiful and alluring than he had thought from his brief sight of her. The hours he spent with her passed in a luxurious dreaming which made his life by day infinitely tiresome; the secrecy and her beauty glutted his craving for cheap romance; and for weeks she held entirely his fancy. Then he began to tire, or rather to awake. Her dwarfed intelligence and her dwarfed soul rendered the interchange of any but the simplest ideas between them impossible; he grew aware that after all, she was no more than a charming animal; and her charm for him had gone. The unrestrained expression of her exuberant, exacting fondness, her furious outbursts of groundless, senseless jealousy alike wearied him. Then his aroused caution quickened the weakening of his passion: he learned that she was the wife of the Subadar Golaba, a native officer of his own regiment. He learned it by chance and so late, because having made up his mind that she was the wife of "Some beastly old bunniah," he had never thought to ask, and because it is a point of honour with a Hindu woman never to utter her husband's name.

He was relieved, indeed, to hear that the regiment was on its way back; its return promised an early ending of the intrigue. But he made shift to be profuse in the expression of his bitter regret; for he feared lest Rukmini, in her reckless passion, might confess all to her husband, if she suspected ever so faintly that he had tired of her. Her grief at their coming separation was piteous; but in his weariness of her he was hard put to it to show an equal sympathy.

They were indeed, and it was a poor consolation, both of them assured that their intrigue had been kept a secret. Therein they were wrong. A course of datura in his hookah of nights, while it deepened his sleep, had disordered the digestion of the old man in charge of the house; and he had cast about for the cause of his dyspepsia. He had not been long finding it. When he did, he was very careful to fill his hookah himself, and from a hidden store of tobacco which could not be tampered with. Then, feigning the deep sleep of the drugged, he watched; learned little by little all that was to be learned; and bided his time with old age's pulseless hatred of those who had tricked him.

Some days before the return of the regiment, he borrowed a little money at 80 per cent from a grain-dealer, and set out to meet it, anxious indeed, to tell his version of the story of how he had been baulked in the discharge of his duty, to his patron, before anyone else who might have learned the secret, told theirs—an advantage called in the vernacular *pesh-bandi,* first move, and important in India above all countries. He met the regiment three days from home; sought out the Subadar; and made a clean breast of his failure. The Subadar fell upon him and beat him, but less severely than the old man had expected; then went to the Colonel, and obtained leave of absence on the plea of bad news from his home. He spent three days collecting kinsfolk and connections by marriage, and arrived with them at the house on the canal as the Fazlabad infantry marched into the Lines.

The old man had been missed; but in her grief at the coming loss of her lover, and in her yet more desperate grief after he had bidden her farewell, a grief so intense as to raise her veritably to a higher plane of humanity, Rukmini had paid no heed to his disappearance. The old woman who had brought them together, who had lain across the threshold of her chamber to guard her secret, was wiser, and fled to hiding. Rukmini lived the few bitter, empty days in a firm assurance of her safety; but when she saw her husband and his train of relatives come trooping into the courtyard, a dreadful, sickening fear, more for her lover than herself, gripped her heart. She had barely the time to realise their danger; for, when she rose to greet her husband's mother, the women-folk of her kin fell upon her with cursing and reviling; and smothering her screams of anguish with a cushion, beat and tore and bit her till she lay senseless, a poor mangled wretch, with no trace of beauty left. Her husband and two brothers rescued her from their claws; and while his mother dismissed suavely and kindly her women-servants, who with the evil wisdom of their class fled in haste, throwing away the sweetmeats which had been given to them, they gagged her; stripped her of the rags of her garments and any ornaments the women had left; and bound her to a charpoy to await death.

At Mess that night the English officers were but little less cheerful than they had been on the night which brought them word to prepare for active service. They had gained glory and medals; they had come, without the loss of one of them, through Ghazi rushes, awkward, scrappy skirmishes in the dark, and perpetual sniping; and the last night of the ninth year was running. Burkle, the Adjutant, with his unfailing, sporting accuracy, had made out that it expired at two o'clock on the morrow; and he was talking about it with a cheerfulness unpleasing to those of his brother-officers who would have to pay, and to those of them who had suffered in health from wounds, bad food and water, or the hardships of the campaign, and remembered uneasily the gamble on death with which they had gone forth to war.

Selby was even more cheerful than Burkle. Though he drank but little, a curious, wild gaiety, quite foreign to his reserved, supercilious habit, was on him. It might have been relief that he too had come well out of his danger, the ended intrigue; it might have been pleasure at the thought of getting back to the cards he had so missed. He was at a loss to find words to express his joyous contempt of the silly superstition; he welcomed every poor joke with extravagant laughter; he made poor jokes himself. The others began to believe that in their absence he had began to turn into a decent fellow. Even after his gaiety had been a little dashed by the refusal of all of them to play cards that night, on the ground of weariness, he went off to his quarters singing, very much out of tune, the chorus of a comic song.

Between three and four in the morning there was a clamour in the Lines and a hurrying to and fro. A terror-stricken native who had been cooling Selby's sleep with a punkah, roused Burkle to tell him that his master had been murdered; Burkle had rushed into his quarters to find him bathed in blood, and sobbing out his life from a gaping gash in the chest, which had cut his left lung nearly in half. At the sight of Burkle the wistful, helpless wonder had left the dying man's face; it had been contorted in the effort to speak through the blood which choked the channels of his speech; he had gasped "Ruk—Ruk—" and died.

They turned out the men, and sought high and low for the murderer. They never found him, nor a trace of him; they could not guess even the motive of the crime. His servant, seeing that his master slept, had left the punkah to get a drink of water, which meant an absence of any time between ten minutes and an hour; he had come back to find his master dying. They were inclined to believe his story. There were no signs of disturbed attempt at robbery; there was no clue among the dead man's papers. Burkle could only say that his last words were something about "rook"; and the thought sprang to their minds, though no one uttered it, that it was an appropriate word in his dying mouth. Investigation in the Lines and in the Bazaar brought no scrap of evidence. They buried him at sunset, tried to persuade themselves, and assured one another that he was a very decent fellow.

Two days later, a funeral procession wended its slow way from the Subadar Golaba's house to the burning-ghât. He was burying his young wife who had died after a very short illness; and he showed an unusual lack of restraint in his grief. No one, no Englishman at least, thought to connect the two funerals.

# A Man's Theory

By *Alice Perrin*

John Orchard was one of those irritating people who are born with a talent for what is commonly called 'knowing best.' As a child he was detested by his companions because he invariably tried to correct and improve their methods of playing games; as a youth he was loathed by his contemporaries because of his pedantic ways and opinionated self-complacency; as a man he was unpopular because he never hesitated to contradict, and lay down the law (the annoying part being that he was so often right), and, after he married, his wife's affection for him changed to hatred, this story will explain why.

He was a prig of the first water, and a very successful prig, too. He did splendidly at school so far as learning was concerned. He conducted himself with caution and credit at college. He passed first of his year into the Indian Civil Service, and, apparently, knew more about the country and the natives before he went out than did many men with twenty years' experience of both. He comported himself with the calm self-confidence of a being of mature age; he was well-read, clear-headed and far-seeing, and his first twelve months in India promised exceeding well for his future career.

During the second year of his service he was transferred to a large military station, and there poor Mr Orchard led the life of a dog, owing to the 'roasting' he received from the subatterns of the various regiments. He was dragged from his bed in the small hours of the morning and made to ride his washerman's donkey round his own garden. He was tossed in a tablecloth after a big club dinner, together with the glass and crockery, remains of dessert and wine-dregs. He was insulted, buffeted, laughed at, chaffed, until he was utterly and completely miserable, and with tears of rage and mortification in his eyes besought his commissioner to transfer him to a more congenial atmosphere. Many men would have profited by the experience, and emerged wiser, if sadder, individuals, but Orchard's trials merely had the effect of planting in his breast a deadly and eternal hatred of all things military, and of making him more dictatorial and opinionated than ever.

He was sent to a very small civil station, where his talents and position found some recognition; that is to say, he could argue and assert as much as he pleased in the little club, without danger of contradiction, except of a deferential nature. He gave dinner-parties to the few ladies the place could boast of, and showed them the proper way to manage servants and order meals. Having private means of his own, he was much respected, and the delightful manner in which he had arranged his rooms was greatly admired. He was also good-looking (in a rather common-place, uninteresting way), and he had not been settled in his new quarters more than six months before he discovered that he found considerable favour in the eyes of the civil surgeons' pretty little daughter. Mary Forde took him at his own valuation, and thought him perfect. She was a single-hearted, unselfish girl, who, being motherless, had been educated under the care of a maiden aunt at Bedford, until she was old enough to join her father in India. Orchard was the first man who had paid her any serious attention, and it is doubtful if he would have done so, had he not one evening suddenly caught the admiring gaze of her soft blue eyes fixed upon him, while he was expounding his theories on whist to a man who had been an adept at the game when John was yet a schoolboy.

He began to think about Mary Forde. He considered that a man with money of his own, and good prospects, might safely marry early in life without harming his career. It gave him more social standing, and established a home, provided that the girl was healthy, good-tempered and obedient. In his own case he was fully aware that, matrimonially speaking, he could do vastly better for himself than propose to Mary Forde, but, at the same time, he was genuinely attracted by her quiet manner and sweet face, and felt convinced he might do a great deal worse. He gave himself six weeks to consider the matter, during which time Mary was miserable, doubting whether he really meant to propose, and torturing herself with the conviction that if he did she was not nearly good enough for him.

At the end of the allotted time he drove to the civil surgeon's house one morning before breakfast. (John was exactly the kind of man who would propose before breakfast.) He found Mary busy in the garden among the roses, and half an hour later she was his promised wife.

The wedding took place some three months from that date. He chose her trousseau (he had excellent taste), he selected her ayah, he made all the arrangements for the ceremony, and allowed her no voice in any matter at all. She meekly acquiesced in everything, so certain was she always that John knew best, a theory that coincided entirely with John's ideas.

They were married in April, and shortly afterwards were transferred to one of the hottest and driest stations in Northern India. There was no question of Mary going to the hills, for, as John replied to an interfering friend who had suggested such a proceeding, 'a wife's place was with her husband'. *His* wife, thank goodness, was young and strong, and if he could stand the heat she could, too. And, indeed, Mary would have been the first to cry out against such a plan had she been given any choice in the matter.

She bore the hot weather remarkably well, thus justifying John's opinion, and it was not until after her baby was born, the following summer, that she began to show any symptoms of flagging.

"Better send her to the hills," advised the doctor.

"Nonsense," replied Orchard; "she will pick up directly the child is a little older. She shall wean him in three months, and a baby is always better in the heat. In two or three years we shall take him home and leave him there."

Mrs Orchard's slender hands clasped the small bundle closer to her. Leave him at home when he was so little, and would forget her! Awful thought! But if John said so, it would have to be. She had begun to recognise of late that his will was cruelly inexorable. At any rate, he was quite right about the hills now, she would feel stronger later on, and she could never desert her husband. Still, during the long, stuffy nights, when the sheets of her bed felt as if they had just been removed from the front of a roaring fire, when the hot winds howled all day, and sometimes all night, and John would not allow wet grass screens in the doorways because he considered them unhealthy, she longed and craved for a breath of cool, pure air. She lay awake night after night gasping for breath, and patiently patting and soothing the child, that cried and whined continuously with the irritation of prickly heat and mosquitoes. It was a pet theory of her husband's that babies should never be carried up and down, or even moved from their beds when they cried at night.

"Get the child into good habits from the beginning," he would say, "and it will save an infinity of trouble afterwards, besides laying an excellent moral foundation for his future character. A child should never be allowed its own way in anything."

Therefore, when John junior yelled and screamed in the night-time, his mother was obliged to lie and listen to him until John senior was sound asleep (nothing ever seemed to disturb his rest), and then followed hours of patient croonings and pattings, and pacings up and down the room until the little fellow fell unwillingly asleep and was unconsciously restored to his cradle.

The days and nights grew drier and hotter and more unendurable. Mrs Orchard became thinner and paler and unnaturally nervous. The sight of a rat in her bedroom one night sent her into hysterics, and it took all her husband's sternest rebukes to calm her down. She slept little and ate less, and wore herself out during the day housekeeping and looking after the child—now nearly six weeks old. She had no English nurse, because John considered a good ayah far better for a young baby, and he was no doubt right; but Mary could never feel any confidence in an ayah, and consequently did far more for the child herself than was really necessary.

So continued her sleepless nights and busy days, until she could hardly drag one foot after the other, and at last, one evening when they were sitting together in the drawing-room after dinner, John noticed the change in his wife.

"You want a tonic" he announced, "and you must get more sleep at night. The child must be put into another room with the ayah. You must have got him into ridiculously bad habits, allowing him to disturb you so. Once a baby is in its cot it ought to go to sleep without any fuss. Children in England sleep all night through."

"But, John, dear, the nights are so awful out here at this time of year. No one can sleep" ("except you," she might have added), "and poor baby is a mass of prickly heat."

"He is a self-willed little beggar, and he must be taught how to behave himself. I can't have him wearing his mother to a skeleton." Now, Mary, don't move, as a fretful cry arose from the bedroom. "He knows you will go and pat him to sleep if he makes enough noise, and he's only trying it on."

"But the ayah has gone to her food, and he is alone," she said anxiously, half-rising; but her husband laid a restraining hand on her arm. The fretful cry went on.

"He will stop in a minute," he said, with his smile of superior wisdom, "when he finds you take no notice."

Mary lay back in her chair unwillingly, and sighed. The night was stifling, the crowds of motley insects were buzzing and beating round every lamp in the room, while the lizards licked them down wholesale. There was a dense haze of dust and heat in the air, and outside the stars were scarcely visible, while the harsh hum of crickets and the barking of weary dogs were the only sounds that cut through the dark, hot stillness. The cries from the bedroom increased gradually until baby was roaring lustily. John Orchard put out a warning hand.

"Don't move," he said again, in a voice of authority. "Discipline can't be commenced too early, and the sooner he learns that he cannot have his own way the better for us all. The young man has a fine temper of his own, I must say!"

"Oh, John, I *must* go to him. Something is wrong. He never cries like that for nothing."

"Doesn't he? I've heard him often enough. The only difference is that he has never before howled like that without your going to him. I'm determined you sha'n't be a slave to that child, Mary. It's nothing but sheer temper, a regular cry of rage."

He took up the newspaper and read calmly. Mary began to cry. She dared not openly disobey her husband, she had never done such a thing even over the smallest matter.

Presently, the screams grew less violent, and changed to a feeble wail.

"What did I tell you?" said John, triumphantly. "After tonight you will have no more bother with him. Now he has stopped. He's tired of making such a row and has gone to sleep."

He looked up from the paper and found that Mary had noiselessly left the room. The next moment he heard a shriek (certainly not from the baby) followed by a crash.

"Damn!" he muttered, and, rising, reluctantly from his chair, he crossed the hall and entered the bedroom, which was quite dark, and as he advanced his foot struck against something that clattered. It was the hand lamp that usually stood on the bedroom mantelpiece.

"Mary?" he said doubtfully, with fear creeping through his veins.

There was no answer. He fetched a lamp from the hall, and saw his wife lying on the floor by the cradle, a huddled, unconscious heap. He held the light aloft and peered into the little bed. The baby face was white and still, the tiny fists tightly clenched. From the child's neck a narrow red stream trickled across the sheet, and on the pillow, hesitating whether to go or stay, and with its head and paws dyed crimson, sat a large grey rat.

# The White Tiger

*By Alice Perrin*

He was called the White Tiger by the villagers of the district because his yellow skin was pale with age, and his stripes so faded and far apart as to be almost invisible.

Having grown too large and heavy for cattle killing with any ease, he had lately become a man-eater, and terrible were the stories told by those who had seen him, and escaped the fatal blow of his huge paw. He was described as being the size of a bull-buffalo, with a belly that reached the ground, and a white moon between his ears, true tokens of the man-eater, as every native of India knows. He was said to have the power of assuming different shapes, and to lure his prey by the imitation of a human voice, and certainly his craft and cunning were such that not even Mar Singh, the local shikaree, had ever been able to trap him, or obtain a shot at him with his famous match-lock gun. And, Mar Singh had seen the tiger often, knew his favourite haunts and lairs, and could point out the very trees upon which he preferred to sharpen his murderous claws.

The brute continued to levy his terrible tax on the scanty population of a remote district, until the women and children were afraid to leave the village, and the men went out to work in the fields fearing for their lives.

At last, the increasing number of victims attracted the attention of the local authorities, and a reward of a hundred rupees was placed on the head of the White Tiger, with the result that Mar Singh, who clothed himself in khaki with a disreputable turban to match, and was regarded in his village as the wariest of hunters, redoubled his efforts to bring about the destruction of this awful scourge. Also, now that the fame of the White Tiger's misdeeds had penetrated to headquarters, it was more than likely that a party of 'sahibs' would appear on the scene with elephants and rifles, in which case, though the tiger would be doomed, the reward would be distributed amongst the mahouts and the beaters, and Mar Singh himself would only receive a share.

So, night after night he perched in the branches of the trees above the favourite routes of the enemy, and from sunrise to sunset he haunted the outskirts of the jungle, and hung about the drinking-pools in the bed of the shrinking river, for, (unlike his cattle and game-killing brothers) the man-eater may be sought for at all hours. But to no purpose, the White Tiger seized a plump human victim once every few days, and Mar Singh's vision of the reward grew faint.

"The striped one is surely an evil spirit, and no beast at all!" said Mar Singh, who never uttered the word tiger if he could help it, for fear of ill-luck.

He had come in weary and crestfallen from a long day's search, having actually caught a glimpse of the White Tiger, and followed the tracks of the huge, square pugs to the edge of a thorny thicket, without the chance of a shot that could have taken effect; and he was pouring out his irritation and disgust to Kowta, his half-brother, who sat at the door of the family hovel contentedly smoking a hookah.

"Without doubt," agreed Kowta, "and therefore, would it not be wiser to let the sahib slay the Evil One if he be able?"

"What sahib?" asked Mar Singh sharply, pausing in the act of cleaning the precious match-lock gun, which was the envy and admiration of the village.

"Then thou has not heard the news?" said Kowta, innocently. "A sahib has pitched his camp within one day's march of the village, and they say he has come to hunt the White Devil."

The dreaded blow had fallen, and Mar Singh danced with rage.

"I will give him no news of the tiger. I will tell him nothing, and see, too, that thou remainest silent, Kowta, when he sends for information, else will it be the worse for thee!"

Kowta twiddled his big toe in the dust, always a sign of hesitation with a native, and Mar Singh scented trouble. He knew that Kowta was heavily in debt to the village usurer, and that sahibs often paid well for news of a tiger's movements. He was also aware that Kowta was jealous of his standing and reputation in the village, which would be increased ten-fold could he but destroy the tiger and earn the magnificent reward.

He changed his tone.

"See, brother," he began insinuatingly, "the utmost that the sahib would give thee might, perchance, be ten rupees, and thy share of the Government reward would scarcely be more than two. What are twelve rupees compared with forty, added to half the whiskers and claws of the Evil One, and perhaps, the lucky bone as well? All this will I give thee when I slay the beast, as I most assuredly must do if the sahib doth not interfere."

Kowta puffed stolidly at his hookah and was maddeningly silent.

"Also," continued Mar Singh, eagerly, "consider the trouble that a sahib's camp brings upon a village. His servants, being rascals, will order supplies in the name of the sahib, and pay us nothing for them, and the police will annoy us if we complain. We shall be forced to beat the jungle, and many will be hurt and some killed, if not by the tiger then by other wild beasts, also——"

"But how am I to tell that thou wilt give me the forty rupees and half the claws and whiskers? Whereas, a sahib holds to his promises, as we all know."

"I swear it!" cried Mar Singh with fervour, "by the skin of the White Devil I swear to deal well by thee!"

So, after some further argument, Kowta reluctantly agreed to take his brother's side, and Mar Singh unfolded a scheme by which Kowta was to proceed to the tents of the unwelcome Englishman, and pose as the shikaree of the district, possessing an intimate knowledge of the tiger's habits. Mar Singh would keep Kowta well-informed as to the movements of the tiger through the medium of the postman who ran from village to village with news and letters, and the sahib, at all hazards, was to be led in the wrong directions, until he grew weary of the fruitless chase, and withdrew from the district with his camp and elephants.

Kowta, therefore, proceeded to don the khaki costume, which he had long coveted, and the next morning he started on his diplomatic errand, while Mar Singh betook himself to the jungle to watch the movements of the White Tiger, that he might warn Kowta by the evening runner as to which locality must be avoided the following day.

Kowta enjoyed himself immensely at the camp. He arrived at sundown, and was interviewed by the sahib himself, to whom he gave voluble, but entirely false, information concerning the tiger, and promised to lead him direct to the animal's lair in the morning. The sahib, being young and new to the country, retired to bed in happy anticipation, and Kowta repaired to the kitchen tent, where, surrounded by the servants, he sat smoking his hookah and relating blood-curdling tales of the doings of the White Tiger.

Natives seldom sleep till far on in the night, and therefore, the gathering was at its height when the jingle of bells told of the postman's approach, and Kowta, explaining to the company that he was expecting news of his dying grandmother, went out into the moonlight to meet him. The chink-chink of the bunch of bells grew louder, and mingled with the regular grunts of the runner, and Kowta, stepping forward into the sandy path, checked the man's rapid trot.

"Oh, brother!" he saluted, "what word from Mar Singh, shikaree?"

"Kowta, there is no word from the mouth of Mar Singh, thy brother, seeing that but an hour after thy departure he was slain by the White Tiger on the outskirts of the grazing plain, and Merijhan, the cow-herd, saw it happen. I bring the evil news to thee fresh from thy village."

For a moment Kowta was paralysed by the horror of the dreadful and unexpected news. Then he asked questions, and learned that his brother's body had been recovered by a party of villagers who had sallied forth with drums and fire-works and had driven the beast from its prey. The mangled remains now lay in the family hut, and Kowta's presence was required to make arrangements for the funeral.

Kowta slipped some coppers into the postman's willing hand, and charged him to keep silence as to the catastrophe when delivering letters in the camp. Then he collected his belongings, and left a plausible message for the sahib to say he had been summoned to his grandmother's deathbed, but would return with all haste the following day. He set out in the moonlight along the narrow jungle path, bordered by tall grass higher than his head, and walked rapidly, though the heat was over-powering, until, just as the dawn broke, he came within sight of the village. He strode through the fields of tobacco and young wheat, and saw the bright green parrots flashing to and fro in the vivid yellow light; partridges ran from beneath his feet, calling shrilly as they disappeared behind the clumps of dry grass; and he could hear the jungle fowl in the distance crowing to the rising sun. Everything was awake and glowing with life, and the dark interior of the hut, where the women were wailing and the atmosphere seemed charged with death, formed a sharp contrast to the outside world.

The mangled body of the dead man, torn and chewed by the tiger, lay on the string bedstead, surrounded by a noisy group of mourning relatives. There was nothing for Kowta to do but arrange for the remains to be taken to the burning-ground in the evening and to attempt to pacify the wailing throng, until, as the fierce, hot noon came on, they gradually dispersed, and even the widow of the dead man sought a siesta in a neighbour's hut, while Kowta sat down on the threshold of his home to think.

An idea had been slowly forming in his brain which brought with it a wave of exultation. Why should not he compass the destruction of the White Tiger, and so earn the whole reward. He was in debt to the moneylender, and he also greatly desired a plot of land that was for sale just outside the village, and the hundred rupees would not only free him from debt, but would also purchase the coveted little piece of ground. It was true that Mar Singh himself had never succeeded in shooting the White

Tiger, but then his difficulty had always been the want of suitable bait, whereas *now*—Kowta glanced back into the shadow of the hut and shivered, remembering the native belief that the soul of the tiger's victim becomes the servant of the slayer, and is bound to warn the master when danger threatens.

Mar Singh's spirit might or might not be in bondage to the White Tiger, but, in any case, the hundred rupees was worth some risk, and with proper precautions there should be little or no danger, seeing that the match-lock gun had been recovered uninjured. Kowta rose and looked up and down the little village street. Not a breeze stirred the giant leaves of the plantain trees, not a bird uttered a note, not a voice broke the breathless calm, every creature except himself was wrapped in slumber.

He made up his mind. He would attempt the plan, and afterwards, whether he succeeded or failed, he could deny all knowledge of the disappearance of his brother's body, and encourage the suggestion which would naturally arise, that the sorcery of the White Tiger had spirited the corpse away. So, he gathered the wreck of Mar Singh into a bundle, wrapping it in his own white cotton-waste waist-cloth, and with the loaded match-lock over his shoulder, went swiftly through the sleeping village and out into the fields, invoking on his errand the blessing of Durga, the goddess who rides the tiger. Thence, he took a narrow jungle path with tangled shrubs closing over his head, and as he emerged from this on to the bushy, broken ground leading to the river, he gathered a leaf from the nearest tree and muttered—

'As thy life has departed, so may the striped one die.'

He walked up the pebbly bed of the dwindling stream till he reached a pool of clear water, in the wet margin of which were printed countless tracks of animals that had drunk there during the night. Wild pig, jackal, fox, hyena, all had slaked their thirst, but the White Tiger had not been of the company. A hundred yards off lay another pool, and around it Kowta found a solitary track—the big, square pugs of the beast who, by common consent of the other jungle inhabitants, had been given a wide berth, and allowed to drink alone.

The marks were not more than a few hours old, and Kowta followed them cautiously, grasping the gun and dragging his other burden behind him along the gravelly sand. The footprints led him to some rocky boulders, on the summit of which a family of monkeys sat peacefully hunting for fleas, a sign that the tiger was not on the move, else would they have been crashing and chattering in the nearest trees, and pouring forth torrents of abuse. The pugs led on round the rocks to a shady thicket of thorn bushes in a deep ravine, and Kowta felt that he had tracked the White Tiger to his lair.

He laid his brother's body close to the edge of the thorny thicket, and then cast about for a safe retreat within easy shot, but no climbable trees were at hand, the cover consisting of low, scrubby bushes. The only suitable place of concealment seemed to be the nearest rock, behind which it would be easy to hide and yet command a good view of the bait.

The odour of the dead body tainted the air as the sun blazed full upon it, which suited Kowta's purpose well, for tigers prefer their food as carrion, and hunger would soon bring the beast forth. Kowta lay down behind the rock and waited. A hot, high wind was blowing, and the sand from the riverbed, getting into his eyes, made them smart, but he paid no heed to the discomfort, and only watched the thicket intently for the least movement.

He held his breath when, presently, something rustled and crept out—merely a mangy little jackal with loosely-hanging brush, who sprang four feet into the air as he came suddenly on Mar Singh's body. Then the animal uttered the long, miserable wail known as the 'pheeaow cry,' and ran back into the thicket, causing Kowta's heart to beat high with hope, for he knew the jackal was a 'provider,' one that gives notice to the tiger when food is to be found.

Now, without doubt the Evil One would steal forth, and nothing could then prevent a shot at such close quarters taking effect. A pea-fowl screeched wildly, and Kowta could hear the agitated flapping of its wings, that also was a token that the tiger moved. The monkeys set up a clatter and scuttled from the rocks. He was coming—the White Devil, the evil-striped one!

Kowta waited breathless, his pulses throbbing in his ears, thinking of the hundred rupees and the plot of ground that were now almost his own, and gazing fixedly over the sickening, twisted limbs of the mutilated body only a few yards from him.

The tension was terrible, and the cracking of a dry twig behind him sounded almost like the report of a gun, he felt a surging in his brain, and, as another stick snapped, some irresistible power compelled him to turn his head.

There, five yards behind him, crouched the White Tiger, that with silent steps and awful cunning had stalked him from the village. The ears were flattened to the broad head, the long white whiskers bristled and quivered, the wicked yellow eyes glared, and held the man helpless, spell-bound with horror, waiting for the spring that came with a hissing, growling roar, as the White Tiger claimed yet another victim.

# The Face of Bronze

By *John Eyton*

John Sanderson belonged to the Survey Department of the Government of India. At the time of this history he was thirty years of age—a sallow young man, with untidy light hair, a long, clever, clean-shaven face, and the earnest grey eyes of a dreamer. He was a member of a solitary service, which suited his character, and though for months he went without sight of another white face the deprivation did not worry him. He loved his work, with all the spirit of an explorer; had plenty of imagination; a quiet love of adventure; and a great stock of sleepy dreams. It was a lonely temperament—with just a latent strain of morbidity. He had made few men friends at Cambridge, and it was said of him that he would run a mile to avoid a woman.

In India his habitual abstraction intensified. He grew to depend entirely on himself for companionship. He had a few book friends and loved beautiful things, so long as they were inanimate. He had only been home on leave once, and had spent the whole time intervening between two visits to his mother in walking about the North of Scotland by himself. He always loved hills.

On his return from leave he was given a job after his own heart; he was sent to make certain verifications on the Durand Line. It was ticklish work, and he was more than once sniped at, because he would insist on avoiding his escort. Nevertheless, he was extremely happy in those barren hills. Moreover, he was just the very man to find what he did find there.

It happened quite by accident. He had been out late, and had only an hour in which to walk back to his little camp. The obvious course was to call up his escort, which was playing a game of chance on the top of a hill, and to take the rough path by which he had come. Being Sanderson, however, he completely forgot the existence of his escort, and decided to take a short cut.

His way led down the steep, stony bed of a dry nullah. He scrambled down with difficulty, using one or two stunted bushes to help him until he got half-way down. Then, a bush came bodily away, and he fell heavily about ten feet, dislodging a small avalanche of stones. The fall was very sudden and it gave him a considerable shock, so that he sat for some time, looking vaguely round him. Then, among the stones, his eye noted an object whose texture was not that of a stone. It was smooth, of a greenish colour, and had a metallic look—whereas the stones were rough and red. He shifted his position and picked the thing up. Then, he had a surprise.

He looked at it for a long time, turning it over and over. It was a very perfect thing—the head of a woman in bronze. True, it had been broken or twisted off at the neck, but the face was uninjured. The features were beautiful—straight eyebrows, straight nose, finely moulded chin; but he did not stare at the features. The extraordinary impression of life in the face held him. Cast in bronze as it was, and coated over with the green of age, he had a feeling that it lived. He could see the bloom on the cheeks, which were soft and rounded; he could look into the eyes; and the soft sweet lips were just about to smile. Sanderson sat there an hour, forgetful of everything—a lonely figure among the rocks, in the shadow made by the setting sun. Yet, it was only a little bronze face—half life-size.

He took it home carefully, wrapped in his handkerchief. At the very outset he risked his life for it, since it was unhealthy to be out after dark in those parts without an escort. He merely toyed with his roast chakor at dinner. Instead of recording the results of the day, he sat in a deck-chair in the ill-lit tent, an empty pipe twirling in his mouth, and gazed and dreamed. It would not be too much to say that he fell in love with his prize. For him the face lived; he saw it in dreams—alive.

Thereafter, Sanderson abandoned himself completely to the face of bronze. His work he got through automatically, nor did he shirk any of it. For the rest, he concentrated the whole of his dreamy and somewhat morbid nature on the face. He would sit looking at it for hours on end—imbuing it with life, making stories about it, worshipping it. It seemed to mesmerise him; he did not doubt its power over him, nor did he try to fight the influence, but surrendered his mind to it.

He knew it was Greek; no other nation could have produced so magical a thing. Greek coins had been found from time to time in the ruins of Akra, and little Greek statues around Peshawar and the Khyber—relics of the days of Alexander and his generals. But this was a thing apart; he looked on it as a treasure reserved for him—the most beautiful face in the world.

He revisited the spot where he had found it, and made a very careful search; but he could not find the missing portion. There was not a trace of a ruin—just a brown, bare hill-top, a slash of a nullah in the side, and a trickling stream below. He soon gave up looking for the history of the face; it was sufficient in itself—more than sufficient. A friend might have laughed him out of his intense concentration, inducing a tardy sense of proportion. But he was entirely on his own—a day's march from the nearest outpost.

It was after he had returned from the search in the nullah that the first dream came—rather, the first connected dream—for the face itself had appeared to him nightly. It is not proposed to explain the dream; psychology may hint that it was a figment born of an overworked imagination. It is simply given as a fact—for what it is worth.

He saw the interior of a rough tent—an affair of two uprights, cross-pole, and sloping sides. It was but dimly lit by a wick floating in a saucer of earthenware. On one side was some sort of a rough couch, with tumbled rugs and skins on it; there were skins on the floor, too, which otherwise was bare. Behind the couch, in the corner, was a pile of indistinct objects, in which metal glinted. The flap of the tent was down.

There was a man in the tent—a man with curly, dark hair, clad in a tunic of some dark material. His legs were bare almost to the hips, and they looked long and shapely. His face was invisible because he was lying at full length on the ground with his head between his hands, looking down as if he were reading. Altogether, Sanderson had an impression of a handsome, well-built youth. More he could not gather because he never saw the face. The youth was lying between the entrance and the light—face to the light and back to the entrance. He never moved. A long time passed before the tent-flap stirred and someone came silently in, and stood in the shadow, looking down on the youth as he lay. Sanderson knew rather than saw that the figure was a woman, wrapped in a dark cloak. … Then he awoke.

He had the impression of an actual experience rather than of a dream. This experience was consecutive and intensely vivid. It actually happened. He saw exactly the same thing several nights running, and brooded over it all day. The scene never altered; the youth never moved nor showed his face. Sanderson always awoke with the shadowy figure of the visitor before his eyes, and with a sense of some cruel thing impending. Then, one night he knew more.

The beginning was the same—the dark tent and its shadowy corners; the lissom figure on the ground; the stirring of the tent-flap; the soundless entrance; the waiting figure. But this time the figure moved, as if gathering strength. The right arm was raised, throwing a great bar of shadow across the tent. But the youth never looked up. Then came a swooping movement; something glittered in the hand of the woman, and she stooped and struck the youth between the shoulders. His head fell forward and lay still; his hands dropped; he was dead.

The woman glided swiftly forward and picked up what lay between the youth and the light. It was a head and shoulders of bronze—half life-size. She raised it above her head and fled from the tent into the darkness. Then she threw it far away … down … and herself fell huddled to the ground.

Sanderson awoke in terror—a wild fear which was akin to madness. He had only one idea—to get away; back to men and women and the sound of laughter and the welcome of little lighted shops in busy streets. He could not be alone again, nor chance seeing again what he had seen. In that last act he had been no mere spectator. In some strange way he had lived the scene, powerless to avert the horror which he felt. … His face of bronze—he could never look upon it again. He dare not see it again. It would bring back the silence—the waiting—the knowledge. He would cover it up and bury it in the place whence it came. Then he might have peace. ...

With eyes averted, he opened the box in which he had put his treasure. His hand felt for it. Then, he gave a cry of surprise—the head of bronze was not there.

# The Dancing Fakir

By *John Eyton*

Jackson was an incorrigible drifter. He was generally referred to as 'that Jackson,' having no known first name, Christian or otherwise. In the bazaar also he was 'that Jackson,' without the appendage of Saheb. The bazaar knew his kind too well. Yet, he was an Englishman of a sort—the sort that drifts.

Once, in better days, he had spent two seasons with a third-rate variety company in one of the Calcutta music-halls. He had shown really marked ability as a mimic, and could take off a native to the life; his patter songs were popular; even when drunk, as was frequent, he could keep a wonderfully serious face. But one night he returned from a strange revel in the Chinese quarter, and proceeded to divest himself of his clothing on the stage—slowly and impassively. It took six men a considerable time to remove him. He had a rooted idea that he was a Dancing Fakir, and with a dead-white face he made rings round the manager and his minions, until he fell insensible among the footlights. His theatrical career ended in that faint.

Jackson drifted on. The Calcutta race-course knew him for a time in various capacities—none of them above suspicion. At one time he was concerned with bicycles, which he stole for another to hire out. This led to three months in jail. After his release he drifted from Calcutta to Bangalore, and thence to Bombay, where he helped in a motor garage, having a smattering of mechanics and a turn for touting. From Bombay too he passed. There was a story of a drunken assault on a Parsee by a pale, pock-marked Angrezi dressed in a dirty white cotton suit, an old khaki topi, and canvas shoes, who passed by a selection of names—Williams, Duveen, Riley, Smithers, and Jackson. The police got track of him in the bazaar, in a street where his predilection for the rawest arrack made his capture seem a certainty; but he escaped. It was thought that he had disguised himself as a native. The reward for the tall, stooping man with the pale, clean-shaven face and the pock-marks was never claimed. Jackson had passed on. He was never heard of again.

The apotheosis of Jackson was in this wise.

He became a Fakir. Perhaps, his success at the Calcutta music-hall suggested this unusual course. His remarkable knowledge of native idiom stood him in good stead, and he found the part easier to play than he would have supposed. His patter, with the impassive face, procured him free meals—even free drinks on the wooden platforms of country liquor shops. He never gave himself away, however drunk; for the more drunk he was the more he believed himself a Fakir. In a Fakir a certain wildness is expected; his dancing was looked upon as an idiosyncrasy, and gained him a reputation. He cultivated long hair, which he made tawny with henna; he wore nothing but a yellow cloth round his middle, and brown beads round his neck;

a wild, wispy beard was also grown gradually, and dyed red; and white dust on his brown, naked body, and red caste-marks barring his forehead were easy. No one ever recognised Jackson. He had no name now. His wanderings are unknown; he must have seen much—enough, at least, to make him forget that he had ever been Jackson.

Little wayside shrines knew him; he could puff out vile smoke from the earthenware pipe, and spit, and make strange guttural noises with any beggar priest in India. He ate no meat, but he throve on grain and milk, gifts of villagers; the Dancing Fakir became a finer figure on this fare than ever was Jackson. There is reason to believe that he drank less and less spirit. His diet must have stayed the craving. At any rate his physique improved vastly; he was really tall now, without the stoop; there was scarcely a taller Fakir in all the thousand villages he visited.

Though his wanderings have not been chronicled, it is certain that he was at Bijapur at the time of the riot. It was Ramlila time—a season of religious festival and plays and fairs. Bijapur was gay with people in their brightest clothes. The steps of the temple above the river were thronged. There were bathers in scarlet and in yellow; women in blue and in red; coloured strips of flags; and, beyond, the houses of the bazaar were bright in the sun—light blue and yellow and white. In the narrow streets the crowds were promenading, chaffering, and admiring all day. In the cloth shops country folk were buying finery for Ramlila time—bright cottons, and tinsel for the children. All the booths were full of merchandise placed on little wooden platforms just raised above the ground, and the sellers squatted by their goods. Red, golden, and white grain was piled in heaps before the shops of the grain merchants; farther on, a pyramid of oranges; and beyond—in the street of the workers in brass—a great pile of brazen vessels flaunted the sun. The Dancing Fakir doubtless, saw all these things, as he sat at the street corner listening to the talk of two Sadhus with shaven heads and orange-coloured garb. He gathered that there was a good deal of ill-feeling under all the bustle and chatter. The Deputy Commissioner had forbidden the procession to pass down the Bara Bazaar on account of Mohammedan scruples about their mosque in that street. The procession was immemorial: curse that mosque; curse the Sircar, who ordered these things! There were extra police about too, who had arrived by rail—an officer and thirty men. There were to be speeches at the mela that afternoon; Babu Gopi Nath, the great speaker, was himself coming. He was the friend of Mahatma Gandhi Ji. The Sircar was afraid of Gopi Nath. He was no mere windbag either, for he had led the riot at Khaspur, when many men had been killed. So ran the talk; the Dancing Fakier was well used to it. Hatred of the English and their ways had become a common enough theme in the bazaar, and he generally disregarded it. This time he heard more than usual. There was a whisper about looting the liquor shops, and the arrival of two hundred wild men from Khaspur. The Dancing Fakir wandered on. He did not care.

That year the crowd at the mela beat all records, and the Bijapur maidan was filled to overflowing. On the outskirts, children rode on rough merry-go-rounds at two pies a time. There were conjurers who spent most of their time drum-beating to an audience always on the move. There were snake-charmers from Khaspur; a man who had crawled on all-fours from Hyderabad, and who now lay on the ground yelling strangely; a travelling show from Benaras, the actors wearing red masks; three bands of one sort and another; and a Dancing Fakir who never changed his face. But the main attraction was a rough platform in the centre of the open meadow, where Gopi Nath was speaking. He was not much to look at—a little dark man with a moustache, glasses, and a small round black cap on his head. But when he held up his hand and began to speak of wrongs, there was a subtle change in the crowd. Hitherto there had been idle bustle. Now there was a silence—then a restlessness; an atmosphere of expectation; something vaguely menacing. Gopi Nath did not rant; at first he spoke slowly; then took advantage of the lull to grip his hearers, following with an appeal of swift eloquence. He had caught that crowd: eyes stared; breathing quickened; men pressed forward without knowing it. One by one the side-shows ceased. The Dancing Fakir was still, listening on the outskirts. No one moved, except the police in their khaki coats and red turbans quietly patrolling the crowd. Then there was a rustle—a murmur, like the sea. Gopi Nath was urging the crowd to loot the liquor shops, sources of the Sircar's wealth. Then later—one could not miss the words; they were like a clarion call—'Hotel'—'Club'—'Blood of the English dogs!' There came that unmistakable low growl of an angry mob, for one moment before the rush—then pandemonium.

Babu Gopi Nath had won them. The mob was beyond control; respectable people were fleeing from the ground to lock themselves in their houses. The rest were as one man—and that man was mad and would soon be drunk as well. Bijapur was only a Civil Station; it had no garrison beyond fifty police; Government was credited with trusting to luck in these matters; the English ladies were at the Club, playing tennis.

Babu Gopi Nath slipped off quietly to the car placed at his disposal by the All-India Non-cooperation Society, and was soon far away. After all, he was not a man of action.

Then came the awakening of the Dancing Fakir. He did not consider explanations; he had never cared an anna for the Government, and had been long estranged from his own kind. But he thought of the Club—half a mile away, at the bottom of the straight, broad road from the maidan. He had passed it the day before. It lay straight ahead, beyond the cross-roads, where you turned to the right for the Collector's Court and the Treasury, and to the left for the bazaar and the river. The crowd would keep straight on; it had one idea only: the Club was the goal suggested. At this thought, a little spark which had almost died in the Dancing Fakir glowed up and fired him. He became not Jackson, but Alfred Henry Jackson. He saw only the tennis players.

He would have to act very quickly; the police had been overpowered; the crowd were beating their dead bodies with lathis. Just as well—they would hardly move seriously for a few minutes. There was a struggling mass of humanity outside the liquor shop in the little street abutting on the maidan. The Dancing Fakir suddenly grew active. He ran, leaping and shouting, to the liquor shop, passing a group of men who were beating two bunnias. The shop was already alight; bottles and pipas were broken, and the contents were streaming into the road. The Dancing Fakir knelt down, with others, in the dust, and lapped and lapped at the liquor. The spirit, to which he had lately been a stranger, fired his brain and gave him great strength. He could lead now—lead ten thousand men. He must lead them to the right at those cross-roads, towards the Treasury. He had seen a strong armed guard on the Treasury. But there was no time to lose: the crowd had begun to move; they were leaving the bodies.

Suddenly, the Dancing Fakir leapt to his feet, caught a sword from a man near him, and danced madly through the crowd, yelling. He danced up to the nearest dead policeman, with leaps like those of a charging animal, and wildly hacked off his head; he snatched a long lathi, and impaled the head, tying it firm with the red turban. Then he raised it on high. People noticed the wild Fakir dancing through the crowd; two or three followed him; then more and more. Faster he went, and faster—the head aloft—waving his wild hair, singing. And, the crowd followed him with an ugly sound, filling the wide road with a mass of running, pushing figures. The Dancing Fakir had only one thought—"Would they turn to the right?" Now, they were at the cross-roads; he brandished the head and danced facing them, adjuring them, screaming at them. And, they followed him. For a crowd is one man, and the Dancing Fakir had hit upon an old secret of leading rabbles. They will follow something on high—and a head on a pole is the best leader of all. He was covered in dust; blood was on his face and body—and something unearthly in his eyes; but in his heart he triumphed as he had never triumphed before. He led them right down the road to the Treasury; the police reinforcements cut off their rear and barricaded the cross-roads behind them. The police guard on the Treasury held their fire till the crowd came very near, and then fired volley after volley.

The Dancing Fakir sprang high in the air at the first volley, and fell—quite dead.

# Maza: A Vignette

By *'Ganpat'*

Maza lay in the warm glow of the afternoon sun, a mud-built village upon a mound in the lee of low hills, the outliers of the ranges which climbed away northward, ever higher and higher, towards the forest-clad slopes forming the outer wall of Asmaka which nineteen hundred years later a German philologist called Dardistan.

The sky was cloudless and the air still and wine-like, the air of the northern Indian spring. The emerald of the young crops showed in the wide expanse of the fields about and a dozen little water channels ran glinting silver among the green from where, higher up, the stony bed of a torrent debouched from the hills. In the fields around men and women were working, and here and there grazed cattle and a herd or two of goats.

On the highest mud tower of the village stood a watchman with an ancient spear, who leaned against the parapet looking out towards the north. He was not very alert for the day was warm and although it was his duty to watch for raiders, of late years things had been so quiet, nothing eventful ever happened now.

Moreover, he was an oldish man and his eyes not so keen as they had once been in his youth. Besides, there was nothing really for him to do, for peace lay upon the land, the wars of his youth were things of the past, indeed, men now seemed to think that there would never be any more war. The land was full of talk, full of new edicts and laws from far away rulers and nearer priests and lawmakers. The last few months, however, there had been many rumours from the outer countries, talk of restless people moving southward seeking new lands to conquer, of the Sakoi in particular, but all the wise men explained that this was empty babble, nothing like war or invasion could ever happen again. Had not Buddha shown the way of peace five hundred years earlier and had not the whole world—at least all of it that mattered, one did not worry about the outer barbarians who could not even write—now absorbed his teaching thoroughly? Witness the great shrines growing up everywhere in India.

In the old watchman's youth things, of course, had been different, men had frequently made war, raid and counter-raid had been the normal business along the frontier, and every man who laid claim to the title of his manhood was a fighting man at need, trained to fight and skilled with his weapons. Thus, the land had flourished and the little Græco-Bactrian colonies, first founded by Alexander of Macedon, had thriven and grown into states where men might reap what each has sown, each household secure in the linked strength of the villages and of the state which saw to the defence of all.

There were not so many men as usual in the fields today, for many of them were absent at Bazira whither they had gone for the big fair two days previously. In the watchman's youth they had also gone there but then it had been for other things, for weapon showings and trials of skill at arms and manly contests.

It seemed that this year there was to be another of these disputations by men from the south, great teachers, skilled in warfare of words, swift in the splitting of hairs whereby they gained great honour and, still more important, place which spelt riches. This year there was one in particular whom all the countryside had gathered to hear, he had new explanations of old truths, and his silver tongue could disprove the very existence of all those things which hitherto men had considered as the most palpable facts inseparable from man's very nature.

The watchman who belonged to a fast disappearing generation felt sometimes that it was all very much above his head, and today as he looked out occasionally into the dazzling sunshine he wished in an incoherent way that times were simpler. Then, he rubbed his eyes a little and stared at what seemed to be rather an unusual sight at that early hour of the afternoon—a herd of goats coming down the steep track which led out under some clay cliffs. It was very early for the goats to return and he wondered why they were coming back, wondered still more when he saw that the two youths in charge of them were evidently hurrying their flock.

Suddenly, one of the youth shot on ahead down the steep incline, and a moment later a horseman appeared behind the goats, then another, then three more, all moving fast. The old man stared for few horsemen ever came by that road. Then, he understood as he saw the horsemen increase their pace, observed the startled goats scatter from the hurrying hoofs, and then saw the frantic dash of the second youth as he tried to escape the spear point, which in another moment had driven in under his shoulder blades and flung him forward on to his face. The horses swept on and at the foot of the track the scene was repeated while higher up a score more horsemen came into sight.

The old man grasped his spear and called with high quavering voice the call he had known so well in his earlier years, the call to arms. "The Sakoi! Sakoi! Sakoi! A raid! A raid! Men to their arms. The women within the walls! The Sakoi! A raid!"

But Maza of late was unaccustomed to quick action—there had been peace too long on the northern border, and a generation had grown up which knew not war, so that it was some long time before his cry was repeated elsewhere and he saw men and women hurrying back from the fields. A grey bearded village elder, steel cap hurriedly pulled onto his sparse locks, an old sword gripped in his hand, came panting up the stairs to enquire what was afoot. Behind him followed a sleek clean-shaven man in flowing garments with a somewhat fleshy and sensual but very intellectual face, to whom both the old men seemed to pay considerable deference. He was an official of Bazira although he hailed from much further south as could be seen by his features.

The watchman pointed to where, not three hundred yards away, a dozen wild horsemen were rounding up some women in the fields, then to a little way beyond them where fully fifty armed men on ponies were pouring down the track. Behind these again a swirl of dust above the clay cliffs showed more arriving. The watchman and the elder turned to the clean-shaven man for orders—in their younger days both had seen raids, heard also upon such occasions men above them issuing swift orders. But now, instead, they saw the official girding up his garments and slipping down the stairs. Ten minutes later they caught a last sight of him lashing a fast pony down the track to Bazira. He considered it his urgent duty to report the matter at once, for he felt, quite rightly, that he was utterly incompetent to deal with such a situation. Talk, however plausible, would serve no purpose with the savages yonder, and neither he nor any of his ancestors had ever handled steel or faced anything so uncivilised as a fighting man with drawn sword in his hand.

The village elder was as old as the watchman, moreover, he limped badly from a wound got many years before when he had been a leader under one of the Græco-Bactrian chiefs, a noted fighter. Like the watchman he felt a little out of his depth in this modern world of talk—he had never had a fluent tongue. He called out some orders to those assembling below and he spat very deliberately over the edge of the parapet as he saw the clean shaven one mounting his horse. There had never been any love lost between those two whose views on life were poles apart.

The raiders were now close on the village, and men slammed to the heavy iron-studded wooden gates and, hurriedly armed or half-armed with axes and spears, took post on the mud walls while a couple of bowmen climbed into perches above the entrance. Maza was not a big village and though it contained, perhaps, two hundred men of fair fighting age, many of these were away at Bazira. Nevertheless, half-armed and quite untrained as they were, the grey beards and the boys and the few men of fighting age fought well enough, for they were folk of the soil, uneducated and not at all vocal, conversant only with the hard facts of life, and lacking all knowledge of speculative theories. But they checked the raiders for a time.

Behind them the women gathered, talking in low hushed tones at this sudden unexpected materialisation of what they had come to regard as unthinkable attack by men with weapons in their hands, men who would kill and loot and rape, outland men of no civilisation to whom the cultured few referred as savages, as from one point of view the Scythian hordes, the forerunners of the fighting people who later settled in the northern Punjab, indeed were, since they believed in deeds and not in words, and what they wanted they took, unless they found the owners stronger than themselves.

Presently, however, the shouts from the south side of the village betokened ill, and shortly afterwards a panting wounded man came bearing news that the enemy were in at the south gate and driving up the narrow street. There were not less than four hundred of them to judge by the mass of rough haired ponies tethered out of arrowshot of the walls, and they were all hardbitten fighting men under a shrewd and cunning leader. On the low hills to southward another hundred had taken up a position covering the track from Bazira to deal with any attempt at help. As the fierce faced Sakoi leader, however, had remarked to his second in command when he sent that party there, there would be nothing for them to do since the nominal rulers of Bazira would merely talk, they had done nothing else for years.

That day Maza learnt the price of unpreparedness, learned it to the full as the Sakoi drove up through the little twisted alleys, killing all before them, men, women, and children. They were tall men and gaunt, many of them clad in skin cloaks of wild beasts, and they laughed sometimes as their blades or spear points went home, laughed immoderately over the death struggles of grey-bearded householders killed, while trying to save their women-folk from worse than death.

Then a house was fired, its defence was good and the Sakoi had paid more in blood than they wanted to, so they fired it and it blazed, and the ring of spear points stood ready to catch the inmates should they run, as two of them did, to be pitchforked back into the blazing mass. They fired more houses after that for sheer *joie-de-vivre,* it was good sport turning spears into toasting forks with writhing bodies on the points. Only here and there sometimes women, the young and well-favoured, were not thrust back, but after their jewellery and any rich clothes had been torn off them, were huddled together in custody for distribution after the fight was over. Wailing women who knew what was to come and some of whose clothes were splashed with the blood of husbands and brothers and fathers, and even of babes at breast.

And so, the fight raged on, less and less of fighting, and more and more of slaughter, until the sole place holding out was the high tower whence the watchman had first seen the Sakoi. There were desperate men holding that and they held it bitterly.

It was practically dark now and the only light was the red leaping flames from the burning houses round that lit up steel cap and red stained blade and wolfish faces of men who passed from shadow to shadow to avoid the arrows from above. At one point opposite the tower, in the leaping glare from a burning house, a group of the raiders were parcelling out some women, they felt they had done their share of the work, others could deal with that obstinate tower ahead. They laughed and talked together in rough uncouth voices as they looked over the shrinking women, tearing still further their already torn clothing. On some of the men glittered gold and silver ornaments in striking contrast to their rough leather and homespun clothes, their tarnished steel helmets and battered shields, necklaces and bracelets, nose and ear ornaments torn from other women. They settled the distribution, more or less amicably, took hold of their prizes, and disappeared with them into the shadows.

In the upper storey of the tower half a dozen women waited for the end. One fine looking woman, older than the rest, strove to comfort a young girl who clung to her, and she nursed a dagger in the folds of her dress. She had seen that play in the light of the flames yonder, and a dagger kiss was better than an outland embrace. She felt that hope was very faint, the times were evil, men had been bewitched by a froth of words, even she had sometimes been swayed by the magic speech of those men who said that war was dead, that arms were useless waste of substance and indeed, provocative of evil, but that if danger should ever arise they would meet and dispel it. She was a daughter of fighting line and she realised now that it had all been wrong, that in sober truth it is the well-led and disciplined soldier who alone stands between women and ultimate slavery and shame.

As they listened to the shouts and cries outside, the whistle of arrows, the thud of blows upon the door below which was heavily barricaded, they waited for the acrid reek of smoke to creep up the narrow staircase and tell them that the end was at hand. It came at last, and although the flames delayed, the heat mounted and the crackling of blazing wood below showed that the door was likely to give before long.

The older woman rose to her feet and, supporting the girl, made her way up to the open roof of the tower, to stand there among the handful of men who were firing their last arrows into the Sakoi below. She stood hesitating a while, looking out into the night, screening her eyes from the leaping flames that licked up the inside of the tower.

The still starlit night showed nothing, no answering welcome blaze gleamed upon the low hills nor in the plains to tell her that help was at hand. Nor, indeed, could there be any since at that moment the clean-shaven official was talking volubly with other of his kin in Bazira. There was nothing to be done since there were no trained troops to send nor any men to lead such fighting men as might be found. They called upon certain headmen of the district to gather their young men and rescue Maza, and the headmen openly laughed at them—they had their own homes to think of. Furthermore, the headmen were sullen and angry for they felt they had been tricked. There had been real danger after all, and the glib tongued ones had hidden it. Herein, they misjudged the talkers for had these honestly thought danger threatened them they would have secured armies at all costs. They had merely made the elemental mistake of thinking mere words can rule a world of men.

A hundred miles to westward lived an old-fashioned chief who was as openly contemptuous of those who nominally governed Bazira as they were secretly frightened of him. But he had a following of fighting men whom he trained and led in some archaic fashion—it was a boast of his house that some of Alexander's blood ran in his veins, quite a likely story, for more than one Bactrian Queen's son had laid claim to kingship as body heir of Alexander, and been openly supported therein by his mother. They could send to him for aid. It was a bitter pill but they swallowed it, and in the end he came with his unlettered following of spearmen and archers. But when he came, he stopped, and thereafter the late rulers of Bazira disappeared and no man worried to ask how or whither, though it was common talk that the old chief had filled Bazira's rather empty treasury from their hoarded personal wealth. The self-styled descendant of the Macedonian understood human nature thoroughly. He kept Bazira contented for many years though when any disobeyed his orders or his lightest wishes he dealt them swift and heavy-handed justice which made them respect and like him.

But his coming did not affect the fate of Maza that night as the woman looked out from the tower. Below her the clamour increased as the heavy crash and sudden uplift of dancing sparks showed that the now burning door had given way. Then came the sound of blows and outland voices, shrieks and oaths, and the trample of feet on the wooded floor below as men fought about it hand to hand, men without hope fighting desperately in a last effort to save the women huddled behind them.

Then presently, they were dead and the Sakoi checked to bind up wounds and get their breath for the last assault up that further flight of stairs in front, which was narrow and menacing, and where two or three men might hold up five times their number. The grim-faced Sakoi leader himself was there now, he did not lack courage and with him were many equally hard fighters, swordsmen, and spearmen, and men with curved axes.

In the far corner two of his men stood guard over the half a dozen women, there was one who was particularly beautiful and the Sakoi chief intended her for his own pleasure presently. He grinned affably in her direction and the wilted at his look and the sight of his mouth.

The woman on the roof listened as the men about her passed back into the dark staircase to sell their lives as dearly as possible. Among them came the grey-bearded elder, her brother, and he limped badly as he went, his old face gaunt in the light of the blazing house beyond, his sword firmly gripped in his knotted veined old hand. He hoped to kill a man before the finish came.

"It is the end, Unna, we die" he said quietly to her as he passed, and she nodded in silence, showing the dagger she held. In the room below a woman's voice rose in a sobbing wail that was drowned again in an instant by a chorus of coarse laughs. Then, once more broke out the grating sound of steel on steel, the trample of feet, and the noise of a body rolling down the stairs.

The remnants of the defenders fought well in the stairway and held it for some little time, since the enemy could come but two at a time and even your keenest fighter will sometimes hesitate to tackle the man who has made up his mind that there is nothing left but death. Moreover, like most of the northern Indian peasantry in all ages, the villagers of Maza were a fighting folk, and with proper leadership would have been more than a match for the Sakoi. As the elder did his best with his ancient sword, he had succeeded in slaying not merely one man but two already, though he was sorely wounded, and his sole remaining companion, a well-built bobbed-haired youth was also wounded in three places, the thought of that lack of leadership was peculiarly bitter. His youth had been passed under leaders of courage who understood men and life as it is and not merely manuscripts.

Then, he gripped his sword again to meet a new rush, went down with a spear point in his chest, and coughed out his life while men beat at him with swords and axes as they dragged him away from the stairway which his maimed old body cumbered.

The woman on the tower drew the terror-stricken girl closer to her and gave one last long look out to the silent hills whence aid might have come. Life was very dear but other things were dearer. Her blade shimmered in the starlight and the girl gave a little gasp as with a choking sob she crumpled in the older woman's arms. Unna laid the limp form down gently, raised the wet blade once more, and, sheathing it in her own breast, sank slowly down across the girl's lifeless body. It was the end.

# This "Familiar" of Mine

By *Hilmer Rey*

> "....*and who is now shadowing thee on behalf of the war in perpetuity that thy family wages on his family? ... as far as is known to me and my kinsfolk it is a fool who goes by the name of Safarchat: it is he that is my familiar for the moment.*
> "....*What? Safarchat, thy familiar? Lookout, and look oft brother, that man is no fool, he is a thrice accursed dog.*"
>
> (Part of a conversation at any time and anywhere in a village on the North-West Frontier).

It was years ago that I first came across this *"familiar"* of mine, how long ago I just do not care to remember—I loathed him at sight (this much I can recollect, also that each successive visit to me was in the nature of a nightmare, with all its attendant horrors); I still loathe him but the bitter, aching hate of our first few encounters is now a little dulled.

I suppose familiarity with one's own *"familiar"* does breed a contempt—that should be only natural—but with me things are now too far gone for me to retrieve myself and I sometimes long for an end to things and then again sometimes I long to live with a desperation that is pitiful.

But what are these *"things"* that I speak of and who is this "familiar" that I dread so much yet with whom I am so familiar that I hold him in contempt? The Risaldar had said long ago that he was a cravenhearted knave; no, he said he would send a cravenhearted fool....

*But listen!*

The valley on the Frontier which supplies salt in such quantity and with which I had been connected for so many years was not in anyway conducive to gaiety or amusement; my job was a one-man job and except for a stray missionary I saw no other company but my own. Of course, there were Pathans all around me and of course, I knew them intimately, but then the Pathan is very much of a rough diamond at times and one can have too much of him.

I had a hobby. Most men have hobbles for collecting something, with some it is wives while others make a hobby of losing them, some gather stamps while others collect coins, but with me my grand passion lay in the gathering together of chips of quartz and crystal, precious and semi-precious stones and I guarded them lovingly with all the care and affection of the true lapidary.

It is not generally known that the mountains of the North-West Frontier of India can, if "tapped" carefully, produce a variety of precious and semi-precious stones sufficient to supply the world for many years to come with all its requirements of tourmalines, emeralds, sapphires, topazes, garnets, beryls and half a dozen other forms of gems yet to be named.

And, there are occasional opals to be had.

Here, if one is lucky (and show me the Pathan who does not believe in chance though he will solemnly avow his faith is against it) one might pick up, buy, steal or otherwise acquire gems worth a fortune, and I was the only European in the country! Just think of the opportunities I had; I eagerly devoured all the latest literature on the subject, purchased the right types of lenses and a microscope, bought myself a pair of mathematically exact troy scales and settled down to my hobby with a grim earnestness which bordered on passion.

I developed a "sixth" sense as it were and very smart had to be the man who could deceive me in the matter of precious stones, oh! very smart, indeed. I adjudged the "precious" stones from the rest by virtue of that combination of essential qualities which, in my opinion, went to the fashioning of these the finest of God's works; these qualities being hardness, brilliancy, beauty, lustre, durability and rareness while the semi-precious I judged for their beauty alone with of course, a fair percentage of rareness.

The best stone I came across in all my forty years of roving around the North-West during my service or since my retirement was Shah Wali's opal. I have it now and I love it with the same keen and deep affection that I first gave it when I lost my heart to it long years ago.

But it has been my undoing.

*Listen, please.*

Riding my Kabul mare down a gully one morning in late December while the frost lay undisturbed on the grass I found myself on the skirts of a village which passed in those days on the, as yet incomplete, maps as *Makaikili* or village or maize; it was a prosperous enough sort of place and had in common with other villages its square flat-roofed houses, watch towers, spy holes and powder magazine.

The presiding genius of the place was Shah Wali, a jovial old villain and a true host whose hospitality knew no bounds. He was possessed of an opal which for size and beauty has never been equalled.

That it was loot I was certain of and that originally it had come down to our valley by way of Kandahar I was equally certain of, for Shah Wali was "a man of many hands" as they have it in Pushto and had wandered far afield in his youth as the many scars on his neck and shoulders from the rigours of many a mountain battle in the service of the Amir Badshah Saheb (whose army is said to keep fit by indulging in frequent shamfights which begin in the morning in jest and end at sundown in tragedy when some youthful sepoy forgets to charge his sniper with blank and slips in a ball!) could well testify to.

I had long coveted this jewel. My heart was centered on it and I meant to get it but the manner of obtaining it was not clear to me; my hunger was whetted by the knowledge that he had placed it somewhere for safe custody ever since the day that one of the young Khans of a neighbouring *khel,* or tribe, had set men on to waylay him and rob him of his treasure.

'Twas here that I was overtaken by a funeral procession moving at a swift amble—for the morning was cold—towards the village *kabristan* or graveyard. We met in a defile and at the moment of passing each other I observed the comparative richness of the bier, the number of mourners and the colour of the shroud indicating, first that the deceased was of position, secondly popular in the place and lastly, that *he,* or it, had been a man.

I turned over in my mind the number of likely people that my clues were applicable to and I brought my list down to three.

There was old Pir Baksh the *Darogha,* a martyr to sciatica, and Gholam Sarwar the pensioned *lambardar*, who, report said, consumed "*charas*" on the sly, and there was Elahee Baksh the retired butcher but what his particular malady was I just cannot bring to mind.

However, I was wholly unprepared for the shock that awaited me when I hailed an urchin in the wake of the procession with:

> "Say, *halak,* who dies? Tell me that I too may know sorrow for the memory of the dead."
>
> "'Tis Shah Wali, the vendor of many wares. He dies of a pain received in the night but from whence none dare yet say. He was old but had no enemies and his family mourn crying, *How is this? How is this?* His son has been called from Peshawar but men say he will not remain, for he is in the service of the Sarkar and is enhungered for honour. Still, who knows the minds of the big men. Salaam, I go…!"

Shah Wali! Good God, but how could this be, I had seen the man but yesterday and he was hale and hearty. It was only yesterday that we had bargained (as we had done for so many years) for this priceless opal of his and we had parted with his standing jest "*A min ta sarah,* Saheb Bahadur, thou shalt receive it as a gift from me ere I die, if I die in peace!"

Clearly, the boy had meant that the man had been murdered when he had spoken of *this pain in the night* but whether he had meant poison or a stab in the dark was not quite clear; as far as I was aware he had been free of any of those desperately long drawnout blood feuds that just then were playing havoc with some of the best families I knew. So, still puzzling over it, I turned the mare's nose to the village and dismounted as became a mourner and I approached the house of my friend.

My condolences to the women of the house by an old hag of a maid-servant were not at all well-received; but I dismissed the momentary feeling of discomfiture I experienced with the thought that this calamity that had befallen their house was perhaps, too heavy for them and they would respond suitably later on.

But I did not bargain for the terrible blow I was to receive later on in the week when a particularly smart Risaldar clicked his heels and saluted me at my bungalows. He refused the proffered chair with ill-concealed embarrassment.

"*Stare mashe*, lad" said I, "How is this, sit yourself down and tell me the tale of your wanderings since last we met". "*Khwar mashe*", he responded reluctantly and slid into a chair. He buried his face in the bend of his arm and groaned miserably. "Tell me, *Sahib*, that it is not true what these swines, and less than swine, say of you. Oh, my God, you that were as a small father to me, you that gave me my first rifle, you that helped me into the Service, tell me *Sahib*, that this is not true."

I was, indeed, puzzled and sat back frowning into space; what on earth could the fellow mean, what was this that I was being asked about? I leaned forward and touched him gently on the shoulder.

"Say, boy, would it not be better to tell me all, is it of your father that you would have us talk?"

He sniffed disconsolately and nodded, then looked away. "Forgive me that it should be I that utter these words but I come in the face of great opposition, *Sahib*. I come,

*Sahib,* as you and I have been comrades of old and we have broken bread together. Even now as I speak it is known that I come for perhaps the last time, for after this visit is over outwardly we must appear as sworn enemies whatever our hearts may feel one for the other."

What on earth could the Risaldar mean, the mystery was growing deeper and deeper for me, besides I was feeling impatient at all this cheap melodrama and its talk of sworn enemies and last visits.

"Have done," cried I angrily, "Have done! What talk is this between men who have been as father and son. Speak your mind my son, and tell me what troubles you, that I may show you a road to travel by."

And then, I drew the story from him bit by bit. It was sorry enough as a tale goes but the awful horror of the affair as the reason for his visit took possession of me slowly. *I,* (Yes, *I*!) was accused of having connived at the old man's death to enable me to gain the much coveted stone I was known to be after. It was generally known that I was on the point of retirement so that the time left for me to negotiate with Shah Wali was daily growing shorter, it was also known that I had said (though in jest) that I would gladly sell my soul for five minutes' ownership of the gem, for had not the women of the house, moving mysteriously behind the partitions while their lord and master sat and discoursed with me on the topics of the day over a glass of sherbet, heard me say this very thing to the owner!

Merciful Heaven, was all this to be held against me now?

"Boy," said I sternly, "Such talk is the talk of fools, I admit I wanted the bauble but I valued your father's friendship

above all things. Tell me what you intend doing."
"*Sahib,* we are as men that are related by blood, such talk is as you say the talk of fools, it is the women who have bound this load to your back and though they are as cattle and have the minds of cattle it is through them and by them that a man preserves the honour of his homestead. You, with your many years in this country know that I speak truth when I speak thus. *Sahib*, I have a plan, but first take this...."

And, he handed me the opal!

To say that I was dumbfounded is to put it mildly, very mildly indeed: everything faded into complete insignificance as I gazed upon the *darling* in my hand. The reverent awe I felt for this perfectly priceless gem that now lay in my hand and which the son of my dead friend said I could have, was overwhelming.

The cunning little lights that winked comprehendingly up at me from between my fingers as I hollowed my hands and allowed it to nestle in closer, and ever closer, touched my very soul with a mysterious power that seemed to gain energy, and more energy, from a Divine source.

I was enraptured, I was transported with delight, and seized and wrung his hand in my frenzy, "Oh, thank you, thank you, thank you," I cried, and then once again, "Thank you!"

The ominous frown that was darkening his face recalled me to myself and the reaction that set in now bit deep into me. I begged his pardon as humbly as I could at forgetting his sorrow in the far less (to him) important matter touching the acquisition to my collection of the opal.

"Yes, perhaps it would be as well to listen to me, for time is fleeting and once I leave your gates we cannot meet again. "Keep the gem," he said with a slightly contemptuous note to his voice, "since you appreciate it so highly, and anyway my father (*Peace be on his soul!*) always intended you should have it and charged me to deliver it to none but you, for he knew you love these things for their own sake and not for their money's worth; yes, keep it. Now listen to my plan."

He proceeded to explain that though he personally did not believe the accusation against me, and when he had come to think of it away from his own home where it seems everyone was obsessed with the idea that I alone was the culprit, he was nevertheless, bound by custom to make some attempt at retaliation to wipe out the stain on his honour. He considered it his bounded duty to hound me from place to place and at an appointed time to assassinate me. *BUT,* since old associations were strong, and he desired to keep faith with his father's friend, he would see to it that the "*familiar*" or "shadow" detailed to be my ultimate undoing should be a man, who the Risaldar personally knew to be so craven-hearted a fool that he would always come up to fighting pitch and would then fade away like the frightened cur he was at heart.

The Risaldar would be following his movements closely and to make assurance doubly sure that I would not come to grief he would warn me by means of telegrams, letters, codes, Oh! by a hundred different means so that I should be prepared. He advised me strongly not to shoot in self-defence or have the man locked up because then the women of the house might send another assassin who would perhaps be bolder than the first.

It was early morning by the time our discussion came to an end, the evening and night had slipped by unnoticed and our plans were complete. I had agreed to pay a contribution of five hundred rupees each year towards the expenses of my *"familiar"* since the Risaldar's Army pay was not large enough to bear this imposition and he could hardly arrange this from the funds running with his father's business since there were younger sons and shareholders to be considered.

I appreciated his frankness and even at his request agreed to reside somewhere on the frontier within reach so that the task or protecting me should not be made any harder...!

I would have agreed to anything just then; for, consider my position, everyone in the district knew that the Risaldar had called on me with an ultimatum, I was a marked man from the moment he left my threshold. Out of respect to the Risaldar, the feud would not begin at once as the Sarkar might think it funny that I had been murdered so soon after he had visited me and while he was still in the district. So, he was to spend his leave to the fullest possible extent in the village and give me time to send in my papers and arrange for my pension.

We shook hands on it and then he left the house; I gazed after him and saw him ride slowly down to the gate with his head bowed in sorrow. "A good fellow," thought I, "Oh, a very good fellow, indeed," and then I fell to considering my opal and forgot my troubles as I schemed the hundred and one delights that I was to draw from the possession of this most priceless of gems.

"Five hundred rupees a year? You dear little thing, you are worth ten times that amount every year..." and so I maundered on.

I sent in my papers that day and packed up. Urgent private affairs was the reason I pleaded for the sudden haste of the application and I am sure none of the many departments concerned with my documents ever guessed the real reasons that led me to write *"for urgent private affairs"*.

Was ever a stranger pact entered into between two men?

Here was I, on the one hand, to pay a man for Heaven knows how many years to come, a sum of money to help him in making abortive attempts on my life. *This was to save the honour of his house!*

He, on the other hand, *still to preserve the honour of his house,* was to persist in failure after failure in attempts on my life!

Who would tire of it first? I could not say.

I know I was tired of it in the first six weeks. It began with the poisoning of my two dogs. I hurried off to Nowshera; a month later I received a telegram from Peshawar concerning a basket of fruit which I *might* expect on a certain Wednesday night; I am not quite a fool so I read the message again and Wednesday night found me clinging like a leech to some friends of mine in Rawalpindi. They must have wondered at the sudden enthusiasm I had developed for their society! And so, it goes painfully on.

One day, the messages will miscarry; I know they will for I feel it in my very bones. And then, I shall die a ghastly death, split from ear to ear or carved in slices with the care and precision of a master chef. I am tired of it all, dead tired, and I wish I could end it once and for all.

Of course, I could get the police in but my friend's honour is at stake, and if the police wanted to exhume the corpse... I shudder to think of the awful consequences to the Risaldar on his next visit to his home, it would be too awful for words.

I am comparatively safe as it is but there are times when the familiarity I have complained of makes me slow to act on the warnings with the desired alacrity I evinced years ago when I was fresh to this cat and mouse game. I know I shall wake up one night to find him poised over me for the final stroke.

There are times when I feel compelled to write my friend to get it over quickly. To hurry, hurry, hurry, for the love of God, *hurry*. But when the desperation reaches its worst I slip my hand into a little chamois leather bag concealed in my vest pocket, and I extract a splendid globule of radiant, startled sunshine....

Why, it is *then* that I say, *"To HELL with my familiar."*

# The Werewolf

By C.A. *Kincaid*

It was a terribly hot afternoon in July some fifty years ago in Upper Sind. In the Deccan cooling showers had turned the hard earth, baked by the summer winds, into a perfect paradise. The soil there was bright with long green grass. The hills rose emerald to the sky, although their summits were often veiled by the monsoon mists; and delightful breezes, swept over the glad earth to the great joy of foreign sojourners in the Indian plateau. Even in the Punjab and the Gangetic valley heavy rain had fallen and if the air seemed stuffy to the traveller from southern India, his eyes rejoiced in the rich foliage and endless maize fields, while his ears listened joyfully to the murmuring sound of new-born streams, as they tinkled and splashed on their way to join the brimming rivers.

In Upper Sind the landscape was quite different. Rain hardly ever falls there except in the cold weather and while more favoured parts of India revel in the monsoon, none of it reaches that strange land. Irrigated by canals from the Indus, the fields are in winter gay with young wheat and he who visits Upper Sind in January may well think that he has reached some heavenly spot. But let him go there in July or August and he will soon change his opinion. All day long the hot wind roars driving the mercury up to 120° in the shade; nor is there much relief at night. The hot wind drops, but the thermometer still marks over a hundred; the sandflies and mosquitoes buzz all night and moonbeams like the rays of a powerful electric headlight pour down on the would-be sleeper's face making slumbering exceedingly difficult.

In the middle of this sunsplashed region is Sehwan, formerly an important town, but now greatly sunk in importance. One thing it still claims with justice that it is one of the hottest places on earth. A Persian poet once in the bitterness of his heart asked the Almighty why, after making Sehwan and Sibi, he thought it worth while to make Hell. The afternoon on which this story opens was well worthy of Sehwan's ancient reputation. The train steamed slowly into Sehwan station from Sukkur. The railway on the left bank of the Indus had not then been built, so the railtrack passed through Sehwan on its way to Karachi and the seacoast. The last carriage on the train was the saloon of the Traffic Superintendent. It was far roomier than the ordinary first class carriages, as befitted the quarters of a senior railway official; but nothing could keep out the heat or make the interior cool. The shutters were closed. A railway coolie pulled a diminutive punka fixed on the roof, but he merely stirred into motion the heavy, hot air. There were two occupants of the saloon; one was the Traffic Superintendent, Frank Bollinger; the other was a Major Sinclair, whom he had known for some years. He had invited his friend to share the saloon instead of sweltering in the first class compartment and sharing it with two missionaries, their wives and baby.

"I shall be devoutly thankful," said Bollinger, "when we get out of this Hell into the monsoon area."

"When will that be?"

"Once we pass the Lakhi gorge it will be better. They say the monsoon dies there and so they call the gorge the gate of Hell. It is true that once past that frightful mass of heated limestone, one does begin to feel a breath of cooler air. It gradually grows in strength; so we ought to get a good night on our way to Karachi."

"I am very glad to hear that. I could not sleep a wink in this part of the world, could you?"

"Oh! I have had such a long experience of hot nights that I might; but thank God! there will be no need to make the experiment."

Just then, the train drew up in Sehwan station. The station master, Isarmal, who had known Bollinger in earlier days, came running up to pay his respects. His face beamed all over with the pleasure that an Indian almost always feels at meeting a former English friend. Bollinger remembered well the little station master and was also very glad to see him and have a chat over old times.

To let the two old acquaintances have their talk out, Major Sinclair got out of the carriage and strolled about on the platform. After Bollinger and Isarmal had been gossiping together for about a quarter of an hour, the former said suddenly:

"I say, Mr Isarmal, why are we staying here so long? I never remember waiting more than five minutes at Sehwan before."

"I am afraid, Sir—I am very sorry, Sir—the river has breached the line some four miles down and the train cannot go on until tomorrow morning."

"Do you mean to say that we shall have to stay all night in this inferno? I am afraid, the Major Sahib will not like that at all. He was grumbling at the heat when the train was moving; what he'll say when he hears that we will have to pass the night in a stationary train, I can't think. He will swear horribly."

"Yes indeed, Sir," said Mr Isarmal, anxious to agree to everything his English friend said, "the Major Sahib will swear horribly."

Just then all doubts were settled by the arrival of Sinclair in a frightful temper. After so varied an outburst of blasphemy that it filled Bollinger with respectful awe, he shouted:

"Damn it all, Bollinger, have you heard that we have to spend the night in this hellhole?"

"Yes; I'm awfully sorry, old chap; but it cannot be helped. The Indus is in flood and it is just as capricious as a spoilt harlot. Still, it will only be for one night and you'll be able to wipe out your arrears of sleep, when we near Karachi."

"My dear chap, I'm not going to sleep in your saloon. I have just been talking to the khansama of the rest-house. He says it is up on the top of a hill and all night one gets a cool breeze from the river. He'll give us dinner and he'll call us at six a.m. so that we shan't miss the train. He'll put our beds out in the open and he swears that we'll be able to sleep like tops."

Just then the khansama himself came up. He was a powerfully built Panjabi Musulman with a long black beard and very strange yellow eyes. His face in repose had a villainous expression. He had a smile that rarely came off, but it was a very unpleasant one; it was rather like the smile of a savage Alsatian fawning on its master. He could speak a little broken English, which in the case of poor linguists like Major Sinclair was a great attraction. On reaching the saloon he stood at the door and addressing Bollinger very deferentially, said:

"The Major Sahib, he coming to resthouse. Sahib, please come, too, and have good night in cool breeze. I give good dinner and you get good sleep and I wake you six a.m. Madras time. Down here too dammed hot, you get no sleep at all, Sahib."

Bollinger could not help thinking of the old nursery rhyme "Won't you walk into my parlour said the spider to the fly" and anyway he had no wish to leave his comfortable saloon and a dinner served by his own servants for a hard bed and a doubtful meal at a rest-house half a mile away. He politely thanked the khansama.

"No, Khansama; I shall be quite all right here. It may be hot, but I doubt whether it will be any cooler on the top of your Himalayan peak. After all, I have been there and it is only about thirty feet high and my dinner will be better than any you can give me."

The khansama's yellow eyes flashed disagreeably, but he continued as before to smile in his canine way and to repeat mechanically:

"Sahib, I give you very good dinner. A cool breeze will blow all night. You get good sleep and to-morrow I call you at six a.m. Madras time."

At last, Bollinger said impatiently: "It's no use going on jabbering like that. I'm just not going to your rest-house. I'm going to stay here and there's an end of it."

Suddenly, Sinclair broke in: "Well, I'm not. I'm damned if I'm going to spend the night in your sardine box." Turning to his butler, he said: "Here, boy, get my luggage out of the saloon and put it in a tonga and tell the man to drive to the rest-house. You can come with the khansama in another."

Bollinger, taken aback, replied with stiff courtesy: "My dear Sinclair, you must, of course, please yourself. I shall stay in the old sardine box and you'll have a good dinner and a capital night. Goodnight!"

The Major, without troubling to answer, walked off with the khansama and Bollinger resumed his talk with Mr Isarmal the station master.

When the khansama and Sinclair had passed out of sight Isarmal suddenly said in a low earnest voice: "Thank God, you did not go, Sahib, with that terrible man. If you had you would be as good as dead already. The Major Sahib will not be alive tomorrow."

"What on earth are you talking about, Isarmal?"

"It is that khansama, sir. He is not really a man, but a—a—a—I have forgotten the English word; we call it in Sindi a *lakhibaghar*."

"A hyena, you mean," said Bollinger, who knew some Sindi.

"Yes, Sahib, he turns himself every night into a hyena and eats anyone whom he finds sleeping alone on a cot in the open. We say that he is the reincarnation of a horrible man called Anu Kasai."

"Oh, you mean that fellow who ate up Bodlo Bahar?"

"Yes, I see the Sahib knows the story. Bodlo Bahar was the disciple of our great Sehwan saint Lal Shabaz. One day he disappeared. The following morning one of the saint's disciples saw that the bits of mutton that he was cooking for his dinner were jumping about strangely in his pot. Other disciples had the same tale to tell. So, Lal Shahbaz said: 'It must be our Bodlo Bahar,' and went to the Governor of Sehwan. He asked from whom they had bought the mutton. They all said 'From the butcher Anu Kasai.' Now, this wicked man had once been very prosperous, but he had fallen on evil days; and having no money to buy sheep he used to murder strangers and sell their flesh as mutton. The Governor arrested Anu Kasai and searched his shop and house. They were full of human bones. He had for months escaped punishment, but he was caught when he killed a saint like Bodlo Bahar."

"How did the Governor punish him?"

"He walled him up in the battlements of Sehwan fort, that is the hill on which the resthouse now stands. As you pass it you can see a sort of hollow in the side of it. That is where they walled up Anu the butcher."

"But what is this talk of the khansama being his reincarnation?"

"Well, Sahib, he has only been here three or four months and yet several people in the town have disappeared. Whenever they have done so, a large hyena has been seen galloping through Sehwan. Not only that, but two Chota Sahibs (subordinate Europeans) who went to the resthouse also have disappeared. The khansama said the same in both cases. They dined and slept outside the resthouse, but when he brought the tea next morning they had vanished. We say the khansama turns himself into a hyena and eats them during the night. You will never see the Major Sahib again, I am afraid; but thank God you are here! Still, at night close the doors and windows of your saloon, otherwise that khansama may attack you even here. We always shut ourselves in at night, although it is so hot."

Bollinger was far too wise to laugh at the station master's story. He did not believe that the khansama and the hyena were the same: but remembering his villainous expression he did think it possible that he was a murderer; and after Isarmal had left he began to wonder what he should do.

At last, he determined to go to the resthouse and share the danger, if any, with Sinclair. He had no gun, but he had a long heavy hunting knife that, had it been a bit sharper, would have been a very efficient weapon. He did not bother to take his servant as he did not wish to have him on his hands, too. In the glare of the setting sun he walked alone along the dusty limestone road and then up the steep side of the old fort, now the rest-house. He noticed as he walked a depression in the fort wall and said to himself that that must be the place where they walled up Anu Kasai. At last, he reached the top of the old fort. It formed a plateau and in the centre was the rest-house. He arrived just as Sinclair was sitting down to dinner outside the building. It certainly was far cooler than in the station siding, for a cool breeze blew from the river.

"Come along, Bollinger, I am so glad you have come," said Sinclair cordially. "You must dine with me. We can get a good night here in the breeze. I say, I'm awfully sorry for having been so grumpy just now. I cannot make out what came over me."

"Oh, that's all right!" said Bollinger cheerily, wondering secretly what Sinclair would think of Isarmal's tale. The khansama also welcomed Bollinger and made ready a place for him. He then served an excellent dinner and after dinner began to put the two officers' cots outside.

"Oh, don't do that, we shall sleep inside."

"It will be damned hot, almost as hot as in your saloon below."

"Oh no, we shall leave the windows open and so get a through draught. The station master tells me that the place is alive with scorpions and that one may well get stung if one sleeps outside."

Sinclair looked towards the khansama, but he made no objection, so Sinclair said, "Very well; but it will be so hot that we shall not get a wink of sleep."

"Oh well, no matter, we'll play picquet until midnight. After that it will cool down sufficiently for us to sleep indoors."

"Right-o!" said Sinclair gloomily, wishing Bollinger in the infernal regions.

From nine on the two men played cards and Bollinger deliberately played badly so that Sinclair might win and remain interested in the game. The simple device succeeded and Sinclair was so pleased that at 11 p.m. he was still absorbed in the picquet. Just then, someone tried the door, but Bollinger had bolted it. A few seconds later, the khansama appeared at the window in front of which had been fixed wire netting to keep the numerous pigeons from soiling the rooms.

"I have brought iced lemonade for the Sahibs," said the khansama with an obsequious grin. Bollinger thought that he had never seen any man with such an odious expression and his yellow eyes were twinkling as if with some horrible anticipation.

"All right," said Sinclair. "I'll open the door." He rose, and before Bollinger could stop him he had drawn the bolt. Bollinger pushed him aside and flung his weight against the door. It was too late. A huge paw and the muzzle of a monstrous hyena forced their way through the opening. Bollinger brought his knife down with all his strength on the paw. It was too blunt to cut deeply through the hair, but the blow was a heavy one and numbed the brute's limb. A bloodcurdling growl followed and the paw and snout were withdrawn. Bollinger slammed the door and shot the bolt.

"Thank God, we got the better of that brute. I fancy we're rid of it for the night!"

Hearing a noise he looked round and cried "By God! we're not!" Through a gap in the netting of one of the windows the hyena had forced its head and in a few seconds would have been in the room. This time, Bollinger decided to use the point and not the edge of his knife. He made a thrust at the brute's throat. It swung its head aside in time to avoid a fatal stab; nevertheless, the knife scored a deep cut in its neck. It gave another bloodcurdling growl, dragged out its head and, with blood streaming from its wound, it raced off laughing in the diabolical way that hyenas do when hurt.

"By Jove! What an escape!" said Sinclair thankfully; "but I suppose you fight that sort of brute everyday."

"No, thank Heaven, I don't, " and then Bollinger told Sinclair the station master's story and how, on hearing it, he had come to the rest-house to see if his help was needed.

Sinclair went up to Bollinger and shook him cordially by the hand: "Then, my dear chap, I owe you my life. I cannot say how grateful I feel. I shall never forget your help."

The other smiled and said: "Oh, nonsense! You'd have done the same for me. But, I say, didn't you bring your boy with you?"

"Yes, I did. I wonder where he is. I hope to goodness the khansama has not killed him."

"Well, we had better go and look but we must be very wary, for if the hyena killed your boy he'll come back."

"All right, come along. You've got a knife, haven't you? I'am afraid I've got nothing."

The two men went to the back of the resthouse and there they found below a slight slope the dead body of Sinclair's Goanese servant. His throat was completely torn open. The hyena must have crept up noiselessly to the servant's bed and torn out his throat, killing him instantly. Then, it must have again become the khansama and tried to enter the resthouse with the iced lemonade.

Sinclair stood sorrowfully by the dead man, who had been many years in his service and to whom he was greatly attached.

"I say, we can't do anything for the poor chap," said Bollinger, "so we had better go straight back to the resthouse. I have a horrid feeling that the brute is somewhere near, coming back to its kill. By God! there it is!"

He pointed to where a huge striped form was galloping straight for them. The two men ran for the resthouse as fast as they could; they only reached it in time through Bollinger throwing his coat at the brute's head and thus gaining a moment's respite.

"I wonder what it will do now," said Sinclair, but it did nothing. It went slowly back to the body of the Goanese and began to crunch it up, every now and then breaking into screams of diabolical laughter when its neck hurt it.

"I wish to God I had a gun", said Bollinger, "but as we haven't, let's try to get some sleep. One will sit up and watch while the other lies down. I'll sit up first."

"All right," said Sinclair, and lying down on one of the cots fell dead asleep in spite of the heat and his servant's death.

Bollinger sat in a chair and tried as best he could to keep awake. Still, he must have dropped off for a minute or so, for waking up with a start he saw in the bright moonlight the baleful glare of the hyena's eyes as it stared at him through the wire netting. He drew his knife and ran with a shout towards the netting but the hyena with a growl of fury jumped back and galloped off.

Sinclair woke and hearing what had happened said: "We must both sit up, otherwise the brute will return and get us."

The two friends sat and smoked and talked through the weary hours until about 5:30 a.m. when their troubles came to an end. A crowd of Sindis, led by Isarmal, came to the resthouse to see what had happened to the two Englishmen.

"God be praised!" exclaimed Isarmal earnestly. "Nothing has happened and you are both safe!"

"We are safe, but look at this," and Bollinger led the crowd of Sindis to the half-eaten remains of the unfortunate Goanese: "The khansama killed him!"

Isarmal's face grew grim and turning to the rest of the crowd he cried: "Brothers, we are Sindis. The khansama is a Panjabi and therefore, of a race that we hate. He is clearly the reincarnation of Anu Kasai. When the train has gone we must deal with him."

The two Englishmen walked back with Isarmal to the station, where the train was standing; as they walked, Bollinger related the events of the night. Afterwards, Isarmal repeated the story in Sindi to the men following him. On reaching the saloon nothing more was said. The two weary travellers got in and Isarmal, as he waved on the train, turned to the Sindis, who were mostly Musulmans, and cried: "The Sahibs are safe, *Alhamdalilla* (God be praised)!"

After a hot, slow journey the Englishmen reached Karachi. On the way Bollinger said: "I fancy the khansama has had a bad quarter of an hour. He is a Panjabi and as Isarmal said of a race hated by the Sindis."

"But why do the Sindis hate the Panjabis? I like them."

"I really do not quite know. Perhaps, like French and Germans Sindis and Panjabis live too near together. The Panjabis, too, are bigger men as a rule than the Sindis and they throw their weight about. The Sindis seem very much afraid of them. Indeed I remember hearing a Sindi proverb that says: 'If one Panjabi comes, sit still and say nothing. If two come, then pack up your kit at once, abandon your house and clear out." Anyway, Panjabis are not liked in these parts."

"They don't seem to be!"

Two mornings after their arrival Davidson, the District Superintendent of Police, burst unceremoniously into Bollinger's bungalow and onto the verandah, where he was having his *chota hazri* or morning tea.

"I'm sorry, Bollinger, but I must see you. I have just received an official report from the Chief Constable of Sehwan to the effect that the villagers, led by the station master, broke into the khansama's house, dragged him out although he was very ill and walled him into the battlements of the old fort. He hints that you know something about it. In the meantime, he has arrested the station master, Isarmal I think he calls him."

"Half a mo,' Davidson! I fancy I have a letter from the station master in my morning post. I'll open it." Tearing open the envelope, Bollinger read aloud the following note, very short and quaintly expressed:

> "Honoured Sir,
>
> The Chief Constable of Sehwan, who is a Panjabi, is troubling us 'because of the death of that Anu Kasai, the khansama. After Your Honour's departure we went to his house and found him very ill from a severe wound in the throat. We found in his house the property of the two missing Chota Sahibs; seeing this he became very obstinate and refused to answer our questions. Very soon he died. When dead, we put him where Anu Kasai was walled up. The Sahib knows the facts and will kindly do the needful."

"Well, Bollinger, he says you know the facts, for goodness sake let me have them."

Bollinger told the full story of the adventure and Sinclair supported him in every detail. Still, as told in an Englishman's house in Karachi, it did not sound very convincing.

"Hang it all, Bollinger! You can't expect me to believe this tale of a werewolf.

"Well, Isarmal says that they found in the khansama's house the property of those two missing subordinates. That raises a presumption that he is a murderer, anyway."

"The Chief Constable says nothing about that."

"He is a brother Panjabi and can scarcely be expected to. Look here, instead of arguing, let's go off and call on the Commissioner. He is Inspector-General of Police, as well as of everything else and we'll abide by his orders."

"Right-o!" said the District Superintendent and at 11 a.m. all three men met to call on Government House.

The Commissioner was a big genial man who combined with a very cordial manner a vast amount of commonsense. He greeted all three men pleasantly. Then, he turned to the D.S.P. who was in uniform:

"Well, Davidson, what's the trouble?"

"I think, Sir, Bollinger had better tell you his yarn first and then I'll supplement it with my information."

"Capital! Go ahead, Bollinger."

The railwayman repeated his story and Sinclair confirmed it. Then, Davidson shewed the Commissioner his Chief Constable's report and Bollinger produced Isarmal's letter.

The Commissioner's keen intellect grasped immediately all the facts and came at once to a decision.

"Look here, Bollinger, you can't expect me to accept as gospel your story of the werewolf or werehyena; but the khansama seems to have been a murderer all right. The discovery in his house of the property of the two subordinates points to that. I have often been worried as to what became of them. Again, I do not see why we should not believe Isarmal's statement that they did not wall in the khansama until he was dead. Anyway, it will be impossible to disprove it; for all the eye-witnesses will support Isarmal. In any case, if you go into the witness box, Bollinger, and tell your adventure with the khansama-cum-hyena, my administration will be the laughing stock of all India. Think how the young lions of the *Pioneer* will sharpen their wit at our expense. No! No, we must stop the prosecution at all costs. Look here, Davidson, you wire to the Chief Constable to drop the case and release Isarmal and any others he may have arrested. I shall myself transfer to some other district the Chief Constable; for he seems to have been very slack over the disappearance of the two subordinates. Well, good morning."

Isarmal was duly released and resumed his duties as station master. But Bollinger did not forget him. Using his influence with the railway chiefs, he got Isarmal first promoted to be station master of Radhan and then of Sukkur, a very important post. This Isarmal retained until his retirement. He lived for many years on an ample pension and nothing gave him greater pleasure than to tell the story of the Panjabi who could turn himself into a hyena and how he nearly ate up the two Sahibs. He gave ample credit to Bollinger Sahib for his courage and resource; but the person for whom he reserved the fullest commendation was none other than Mr Isarmal, late station master of Sukkur.

# Susanna's Seven Husbands

By *Ruskin Bond*

Locally, the tomb was known as "the grave of the seven-times married one".

You'd be forgiven for thinking it was Bluebeard's grave; he was reputed to have killed several wives in turn because they showed undue curiosity about a locked room. But this was the tomb of Susanna Anna-Maria Yeates, and the inscription (most of it in Latin) stated that she was mourned by all who had benefited from her generosity, her beneficiaries having included various schools, orphanages, and the church across the road. There was no sign of any other graves in the vicinity and presumably, her husbands had been interred in the old Rajpur graveyard, below the Delhi Ridge.

I was still in my teens when I first saw the ruins of what had once been a spacious and handsome mansion. Desolate and silent, its well-laid paths were overgrown with weeds, its flower-beds had disappeared under a growth of thorny jungle. The two-storeyed house had looked across the Grand Trunk Road. Now abandoned, feared and shunned, it stood encircled in mystery, reputedly the home of evil spirits.

Outside the gate, along the Grand Trunk Road, thousands of vehicles sped by—cars, trucks, buses, tractors, bullock-carts—but few noticed the old mansion or its mausoleum, set back as they were from the main road, hidden by mango, neem and peepul trees. One old and massive peepul tree grew out of the ruins of the house, strangling it much as its owner was said to have strangled one of her dispensable paramours.

As a much married person with a quaint habit of disposing of her husbands whenever she tired of them, Susanna's malignant spirit was said to haunt the deserted garden. I had examined the tomb, I had gazed upon the ruins, I had scrambled through shrubbery and overgrown rose-bushes, but I had not encountered the spirit of this mysterious woman. Perhaps, at the time, I was too pure and innocent to be targeted by malignant spirits. For, malignant she must have been, if the stories about her were true.

No one had been down into the vaults of the ruined mansion. They were said to be occupied by a family of cobras, traditional guardians of buried treasure. Had she really been a woman of great wealth, and could treasure still be buried there? I put these questions to Naushad, the furniture-maker, who had lived in the vicinity all his life, and whose father had made the furniture and fittings for this and other great houses in Old Delhi.

"Lady Susanna, as she was known, was much sought after for her wealth," recalled Naushad. She was no miser, either. She spent freely, reigning in state in her palatial home, with many horses and carriages at her disposal. You see the stables there, behind the ruins? Now, they are occupied by bats and jackals. Every evening she rode through the Roshanara Gardens, the cynosure of all eyes, for she was beautiful as well as wealthy. Yes, all men sought her favours, and she could choose from the best of them. Many were fortune-hunters. She did not discourage them. Some found favour for a time, but she soon tired of them. None of her husbands enjoyed her wealth for very long!

"Today, no one enters those ruins, where once there was mirth and laughter. She was the Zamindari lady, the owner of much land, and she administered her estate with a strong hand. She was kind if rents were paid when they fell due, but terrible if someone failed to pay."

"Well, over fifty years have gone by since she was laid to rest, but still men speak of her with awe. Her spirit is restless, and it is said that she often visits the scenes of her former splendour. She has been seen walking through this gate, or riding in the gardens, or driving in her phaeton down the Rajpur road."

"And, what happened to all those husbands?" I asked.

"Most of them died mysterious deaths. Even the doctors were baffled. Tomkins Sahib drank too much. The lady soon tired of him. A drunken husband is a burdensome creature, she was heard to say. He would have drunk himself to death, but she was an impatient woman and was anxious to replace him. You see those *datura* bushes growing wild in the grounds? They have always done well here."

"Belladonna?" I suggested.

"That's right, *huzoor.* Introduced in the whisky-soda, they put him to sleep for ever."

"She was quite humane in her way."

"Oh, very humane, sir. She hated to see anyone suffer. One sahib, I don't know his name, drowned in the tank behind the house, where the water-lilies grew. But she made sure he was half-dead before he fell in. She had large, powerful hands, they said."

"Why did she bother to marry them? Couldn't she just have had men friends?"

"Not in those days, dear sir. Respectable society would not have tolerated it. Neither in India nor in the West would it have been permitted."

"She was born out of her time," I remarked.

"True, sir. And remember, most of them were fortune-hunters. So, we need not waste too much pity on them."

"*She* did not waste any."

"She was without pity. Especially when she found out what they were really after. The snakes had a better chance of survival."

"How did the other husbands take their leave of this world?"

"Well, the Colonel-sahib shot himself while cleaning his rifle. Purely an accident, *huzoor*. Although some say she had loaded his gun without his knowledge. Such was her reputation by now that she was suspected even when innocent. But she bought her way out of trouble. It was easy enough, if you were wealthy."

"And, the fourth husband?"

"Oh, he died a natural death. There was a cholera epidemic that year, and he was carried off by the *haija*. Although, again, there were some who said that a good dose of arsenic produced the same symptoms! Anyway, it was cholera on the death certificate. And, the doctor who signed it was the next to marry her."

"Being a doctor, he was probably quite careful about what he ate and drank.

"He lasted about a year."

"What happened?"

"He was bitten by a cobra."

"Well, that was just bad luck, wasn't it? You could hardly blame it on Susanna."

"No, *huzoor*, but the cobra was in his bedroom. It was coiled around the bed-post. And, when he undressed for the night, it struck! He was dead when Susanna came into the room an hour later. She had a way with snakes. She did not harm them and they never attacked her."

"And, there were no antidotes in those days. Exit the doctor. Who was the sixth husband?"

"A handsome man. An indigo planter. He had gone bankrupt when the indigo trade came to an end. He was hoping to recover his fortune with the good lady's help. But our Susanna-*mem*, she did not believe in sharing her fortune with anyone."

"How did she remove the indigo planter?"

"It was said that she lavished strong drink upon him, and when he lay helpless, she assisted him on the road we all have to take by pouring molten lead in his ears."

"A painless death, I'm told."

"But a terrible price to pay *huzoor,* simply because one is no longer needed...."

We walked along the dusty highway, enjoying the evening breeze, and some time later we entered the Roshanara Gardens, in those days Delhi's most popular and fashionable meeting place.

"You have told me how six of her husbands died, Naushad. I thought there were seven?"

"Ah, a gallant young magistrate, who perished right here, *huzoor.* They were driving through the park after dark when the lady's carriage was attacked by brigands. In defending her, the gallant young man received a fatal sword wound."

"Not the lady's fault, Naushad."

"No, my friend. But he was a magistrate, remember, and the assailants, one of whose relatives had been convicted by him, were out for revenge. Oddly enough, though, two of the men were given employment by the lady Susanna at a later date. You may draw your own conclusions."

"And, were there others?"

"Not husbands. But an adventurer, a soldier of fortune came along. He found her treasure, they say. He lies buried with it, in the cellars of the ruined house. His bones lie scattered there, among gold and silver and precious jewels. The cobras guard them still! But how he perished was a mystery, and remains so till this day."

"What happened to Susanna?"

"She lived to a good old age, as you know. If she paid for her crimes, it wasn't in this life! As you know, she had no children. But she started an orphanage and gave generously to the poor and to various schools and institutions, including a home for widows. She died peacefully in her sleep."

"A merry widow,' I remarked. "The Black Widow spider!"

Don't go looking for Susanna's tomb. It vanished some years ago, along with the ruins of her mansion. A smart new housing estate came up on the site, but not after several workmen and a contractor succumbed to snake bite! Occasionally, residents complain of a malignant ghost in their midst, who is given to flagging down cars, especially those driven by single men. There have been one or two mysterious disappearances. Ask anyone living along this stretch of the Delhi Ridge, and they'll tell you that's it's true.

And, after dusk, an old-fashioned horse and carriage can sometimes be seen driving through the Roshanara Gardens. Ignore it, my friend. Don't stop to answer any questions from the beautiful fair lady who smiles at you from behind lace curtains. She's still looking for her a suitable husband.

# When Glister Walked

By *Oscar Cook*

Dennis, district officer of the Labuk district in British North Borneo, had been spending a few days' "local leave" on Tingling Estate, for, Walkely, the manger, and he were great friends. The night before his departure the two men had sat together in the latter's mosquito-room, fitted up like a "den", and with pipes well lit had roamed in desultory manner over many fields of conversation.

For the last ten minutes or so there had been silence between them—the silence of friends in complete accord. Dennis broke it.

"Throw me a match, Walley," he said.

Walkely moved as though to comply, then stopped as his "boy" entered, carrying a tray containing whisky and soda, which he placed on a table near his master. He was about to depart when Walkely spoke.

"The *Tuan* is leaving to-morrow before breakfast, Amat. Tell Cookie to make some sandwiches and see the thermos flask is filled with hot tea."

*"Tuan."*

"And, hand these to the *Tuan*." Walkely pointed to the matches.

Amat obeyed and went out.

Walkely rose from his long chair, mixed the drinks and held out a glass to Dennis.

"To our next meeting," he said, and raised his glass. Dennis followed suit.

Then, yawning, Dennis rose, and stretching his arms well above his head, looked sleepily in the direction of his bedroom.

Walkely nodded assent and held open the mosquito-door.

A few minutes later the house was in darkness, save for the lights that shone through the open windows of the two bedrooms.

The rooms were on either side of a large dining-room, which in turn opened out from the main verandah, off one side of which was built the mosquito-room. At the far end of the dining-room were two folding doors that led to a passage and pantry, and thence down some steps to the kitchen and "boys'" quarters at the rear of the house.

As Dennis undressed he sleepily hummed the latest foxtrot record received from England. Then, dimming the light, he got into bed.

From where he lay he could hear Walkely moving about his room, and could see the reflection his light cast on the exposed *attap* roof of the house. As he idly watched, speculating dreamily on Walley's success as a manager, Walkely's lamp in turn was lowered. Followed the creaking noise of a body turning on a spring mattress—then silence.

Dennis rolled from his left to right side preparatory to sleep.

"Nighty-night, Old Thing," he grunted.

"Night," came back the sleepy reply.

Then, all was quiet save for the gentle rustling of the rubber trees and the occasional hoot of an owl.

Presently, Dennis awoke to full alertness. He was not strung up; no sound nor fear nor nightmare had aroused him. He was simply and quietly awake. Turning on his side he looked at his watch. The hands pointed to 2 a.m. He closed his eyes, but sleep would not be wooed.

For a long time Dennis lay in the nearly darkened room, watching the waving branch of a rubber tree outside the window, that moved gently to the sighing of the breeze.

Suddenly, he heard the sound of feet ascending the steps that led from garden to verandah doors.

But half-awake, he listened.

Slowly, the footsteps mounted the stairs; then came the lifting of the latch that fastened the low wooden gates, and the creaking of moving hinges. The footsteps entered, continued the full length of the verandah, to pass into the dining-room beyond. Here, for a moment they halted. Then they moved again, shuffling uncertainly—forward, backward, sideways—as those of a person trying to locate something in the dark.

Again, they moved with steady tread and reached the intervening doors that shut off the passage.

Dennis listened and waited. What the devil is old Walley doing? he sleepily wondered.

A sudden rush of cool air struck on him over the top of the bedroom wall, billowing out his mosquito net.

Creak—creak—creak—the doors were opening. The footsteps went along the passage and came to a standstill at the end.

"Boy!"

The call was clear and decisive, but Dennis failed to quite recognise the voice, though he realised it was a European's.

There came no answer.

"Boy!"

This time the call was sharper, and impatience was in its tone. Still, no reply.

In the silence Dennis, wondering greatly, waited, for he was still uncertain whether the voice was Walkely's or another's.

The footsteps sounded again as they descended the stairs that led to the servants' quarters. On the bottom step they halted.

"Boy!"

The call was long, loud, and angry. Yet still, no answer came.

Up the stairs the footsteps returned. They strode along the passage, paused as the doors were closed and the latch clicked, then swiftly moved through the dining-room out on to the wide verandah. Here, for a moment they rested.

Sounded the fumbling for a latch, the squeak of a faulty hinge, and from the sharp banging of a door Dennis knew the footsteps had entered the mosquito-room.

He sprang out of bed, and, sitting on its edge, hurriedly pushed his feet into slippers. Then, as he was about to move, the lamp in the room went out.

"Damn!" he muttered, and fumbled for his matches, but before he found them he was listening to the opening and shutting of drawers.

He struck a match, and by its light crossed to the lamp, the wick of which, however, refused to burn, though he wasted many matches upon it.

In the gathering darkness, for the moon was setting, he moved toward the door, but, with his hand upon the knob, stood still, for the footsteps were shuffling again and the sharp banging to of the mosquito-door made him jump.

Through the verandah the footsteps went, gaining sureness with every stride. The gates creaked and the latch fell to. Down the stairs the footsteps clumped, the sound growing fainter till it became lost in the night.

Three deep-toned notes from the officer gong boomed on the air. Dennis shivered, kicked off his slippers and returned to bed. The air was cold, so he drew his blanket well around him.

"Old Walley's walking in his sleep or else indulging in a midnight prowl," he muttered. Half a minute later, he was sound asleep.

As Dennis's eyes opened to the beauties of a tropic dawn, the clink of silver spoons against china reached his ears and the scent of a cigarette crept into the room. He plunged his head into a basin of cold water, brushed his hair, and still in his *sarong* and *kabaiab*, went out on to the verandah, where Walkely paused in the act of conveying a cup to his mouth.

" 'Morning, Dennis," he grunted, and continued drinking his tea.

He was never very talkative the first thing in the morning.

Dennis answered and busied himself with the teapot. Then, under cover of meticulously choosing a piece of toast, he studied Walkely, who showed no signs of having spent a sleepless night.

Suddenly, Walkely looked up and caught Dennis's eye upon him.

"Well," he asked, "What is it?"

"Nothing," Dennis curtly replied.

"Then, why look at me like that?"

"Sorry, Old Thing," Dennis stammered. "I was only wondering——"

"Yes?"

"What the devil were you up to last night—walking all over the house and shouting for your boy?"

"Then you heard it, too?" Walkely asked the question with relief.

"It! What's *it?*" Dennis retorted. "Didn't I hear *you* come up the verandah steps, open the gates and walk to the back? You called 'Boy' three times, but got no answer. Then, you walked back through the house and down the steps. What was wrong, Walley?"

Walkely looked Dennis full in the eyes as he slowly answered:

"Nothing! Nothing was wrong, and I never moved from my room till this morning."

"But—then who the——?"

"I never moved," Walkely repeated. "What you heard was Glister."

"Glister! What on earth do you mean? Who's Glister?"

"You know. The chap who was manager here before Bellamy. He shot himself. Died in your room—on your bed. He's buried in the garden at the foot of the hill below your window. Great pity, but—drink and a native woman—nice chap, too."

Walkely ceased as the light of recollection shone on Dennis's face.

"Yes, I remember," he spoke almost to himself. "I met him once at a Jesselton Race Meeting. A tall, good-looking fellow?"

Walkely nodded, and Dennis continued:

"He was awfully keen on a beautiful native woman—a Dusun named Jebee."

"Yes. She was lured away from Glister by another man. It was a dirty thing to do."

"The swine! I only hope——"

"You needn't worry," Walkely interrupted. "He rues the day all right, I'll bet, for she's got him body and soul—doped to the eyes—and her temper is that of a fiend incarnate. She is priestess, too, of the *Gusi,* and he daren't call his soul his own."

"So, poor old Glister's loss was really his gain, if only he'd known!" Dennis's words were gently spoken.

"Yes. But he felt her absence, and in the loneliness that followed, the drink got him again."

For nearly a minute there was silence between the two. It was as if their memories had recalled Glister's spirit to his old home, almost as if he were sitting at the table with them, while the tinkling of Jebee's anklets sounded from an adjoining room. ...

Dennis broke the silence.

"And, you mean that—that was he, last night?" he asked.

"Yes." The word seemed drawn reluctantly from Walkely's lips.

"But, good lord, man!—you don't mean?—you can't—it's preposterous."

"I know." Walkely spoke slowly. "It sounds absurd, doesn't it? But Old Bellamy went through it, saw him and spoke to him, and once even shot at him."

"Bellamy! Bellamy shot him?"

"Yes. And, there isn't much mysticism about him—he's as much imagination as a turnip."

"But——"

"All the 'buts' in the world won't alter matters. Bellamy's seen him. I've seen him, and you've heard him. He's there—and it happens, and it's always the same—only——"

"What?" The word was wrung from Dennis.

"He's never entered the mosquito-room before."

"You think——"

"I don't know! How can I? I'm only wondering why he went there—what he was searching for."

"Drink, perhaps?"

Walkely shook his head.

"No," he said. "The room wasn't built in his days. No; there's something worrying him, something that's caused this variation of his usual walk."

His eyes met Dennis's and he gave a short, half-ashamed laugh. Then:

"Get on with your tea. When you've finished we'll go and look at his grave. I always inspect it twice a month and put a coolie on cleaning it up and looking after the flowers. We'll have a look to-day."

As Dennis dressed with unusual slowness his mind was full of the tragedy so strangely recalled. "Poor old Glister!" he muttered. "What an end!"

An impatient call roused Dennis from his reverie and he hastened to the verandah, to find Walkely already on the garden steps conversing with Gaga, the head *mandor* of many years' standing.

The three at once set off. Down well-laid cement steps, along a broad path that wound among a profusion of bright-coloured flowers they went. Overhead a flaming sun rode in an azure sky, and a faint breeze fanned their faces with its cooling breath, perfumed with the scent of dew and the fragrant, elusive blossoms of the rubber trees.

At the foot of the hill they turned and went in single file along a narrow path that followed the winding contour of the hill.

The three walked in silence, for speech was difficult along that narrow track. Suddenly the path, dipping down, turned sharply, and Walkely, who was leading, became for an instant lost to view. Dennis, humming a Dusun love song, followed close behind, but as he reached the turn the tune died abruptly on his lips and he stood stone-still.

"Good lord! What can it mean?"

The words were gasped by Walkely, who stood transfixed, staring with horror-struck eyes straight before him.

Instinctively, Walkely turned to Dennis, who, like himself, stood with gaze fixed and staring eyes.

"What can it mean?" he gasped a second time.

For, they had reached the grave, and *it was open*. Heaped under the railings surrounding it, which were intact, were piles of fresh-dug earth, and all round lay the scattered flowers, withered and trampled into twisted shapes.

The eyes of Dennis and Walkely met. In each there lurked a question that neither dared to ask. Each heard again the shuffling footsteps of the previous night, and the opening and shutting of the drawers in the mosquito-room.

A shadow fell across them as they stood. There came a startled cry, the quick pattering of bare feet, and Gaga flung himself upon his knees, burying his hands in the earth.

"Gaga!"

The word was a sharp command of outraged wrath. But the man did not heed, and his hands continued fumbling, fingering, searching.

Walkely stooped down to seize the kneeling *mandor* by the shoulder, then straightened up as the latter rose and, turning, showed a face pallid under the yellow of his skin, from which stark horror shone.

"The *pandang, Tuan*," he gasped. "The *pandang*! It has gone!"

Walkely looked at him in stupefaction.

"Gaga——" he began, but got no further, for the man, heedless of Walkely's upraised hand, broke in:

"The *pandang, Tuan,* the silver *pandang* that Jebee used to wear as token of her priesthood of the *Gusi*, has gone. The silver *pandang* is no more!"

He ceased, and for a moment there was silence among the three.

On Walkely's face there showed a blank amazement, but Dennis's brows had gathered in a frown and his lips had closed in a deep, straight line. He was the first to speak.

"Walkely," he said, "may I ask Gaga questions?"

Walkely nodded his assent, and Dennis turned to Gaga.

"Gaga, tell me, what makes you say the silver *pandang* is no more?"

"Because," Gaga stammered in his emotion, "because—when Tuan Glister was buried the *pandang* was buried, too—and—now..."

His gaze sought for the coffin for a moment, and he fingered a charm of monkeys' teeth that hung around his neck.

"Tell me, Gaga," Dennis's voice was very gentle, "all you know. Begin at the beginning."

Gaga looked relieved, for a native resents questioning and loves to tell a story in his own way.

"The *Tuans* know," he began, "that *Tuan* Glister had a *myai* named Jebee. She came to him when she was very young, but vowed by the oaths of her parents to the priesthood of the *Gusi*, the sacred jars we Dusuns worship, which only our womenkind may tend. But she was young and beautiful and full of life. Her beauty was unmatched in all this land of Sabah; her form was lithe, her footsteps light; her waist was small; yet she was vowed in wifehood to a jar, the sacred *Gusi*! Her lips and eyes, though warring with her blood, were innocent of love till *Tuan* Glister visited the village in search of coolies for the estate.

"Then"—Gaga paused, seeming for a moment at a loss to find his words—"then—the *Tuan* was tall and handsome, and possessed golden hair. He had a laughing, winning way and eyes that darted here and there and made the warm blood race within your veins when once his glance had rested on you. His eyes discovered Jebee, and——"

Gaga looked nervously from Dennis and Walkely as he shuffled his feet, frightened of saying too much concerning a white man before others of his race.

Dennis read the meaning of his glance.

"Yes, Gaga. You may speak," he said, "for the *Tuan Besar* and I are friends and we would give *Tuan* Glister's wandering spirit peace. Say all that is in your heart. We understand."

"*Tuan*!" Gaga's tone conveyed a depth of grateful meaning. "That night there was dancing and feasting in the village, and pitcher after pitcher of *tapai* was consumed. The Tuan drank, too, but none could stand against him, and one by one they sank into a heavy sleep. Only the *Tuan* remained. He left the headman's house, and going through the village reached Jebee's home.

"It was that darkest hour before dawn when the chill wind blows, yet she was seated on the topmost step. The light of the dying moon seemed focused on the silver buckle that she wore, hung from a rotan girdle around her waist.

"Their eyes met. No word was said. The *Tuan* stretched out his arms and Jebee went to him, and the Tuan's arms enfolded her."

Gaga ceased. The silence lengthened till the office gong, booming eight deep notes, shattered the spell.

"How do you know all this, Gaga?" Walkely asked at length. "You never mentioned it before!"

A look of surprise flitted over the *mandor's* face, then he quietly replied:

"The *Tuan* never asked me my story before, nor is it customary for the white man to discuss others of his race with natives. How do I know? Why, *Tuan Besar*, was I not present on that night, and is not Jebee my sister, though of a different mother?"

"The *Tuan* had saved my life, and Jebee was young. The warm blood danced in her veins, and her heart cried out for a mate. And so ... The river, *Tuan*, flowed far from the village. The *Tuan's* boat was there. All in the village slept. The *Tuan* led her to the boat, while I stole up the steps, entered the house and made a bundle of her clothes. Then, to the waiting boat I followed. The *Tuan* had covered Jebee with his coat and she was sleeping, but the silver buckle hung round his neck. And, from that day it never left him. We three were alone in the boat. The *Tuan* and I picked up the paddles, and as their blades in silence touched the water the moon slipped beneath the earth and the *Burong bantu* hooted thrice. An evil omen, which the *Tuan* heeded not and Jebee did not hear.

"Till the sun was high we paddled and by noon were far beyond pursuit, for the river flowed very swiftly and one does not wake early from such a sleep as those in the village were sleeping."

Gaga paused, then he added:

"The rest of the story the *Tuans* know. For a little while the *Tuan* and Jebee were happy. But the omen of the *Burong bantu* and the dying moon would not be denied.

"And, the shadow of the *Gusi* lay between them. So, though the *Tuan* loved her he drank too deeply, and she found favour in another's sight and went away. But the *Tuans* know the rest. I buried him—there was no white man on the estate—and as he died he made me promise to bury the buckle with him, hanging round his neck. It was the only thing of Jebee's that he kept."

"And, now?"

Dennis put the question sharply, and his eyes held Gaga's gaze.

"I am afraid, *Tuan*—sore afraid."

"Of what?"

"I do not know; and the silver *pandang* has been stolen, though its hiding-place was unknown. To none has it value, save to my people, and for years now they have let it rest. But, *Tuan*, they never forget, and the *Gusi* is most sacred. In the great blue jar that Jebee used to tend, and should have wedded, Maboga, the bad Spirit, dwells. Of late evil has befallen my people: the buffaloes bring forth no young, and the crops refuse to ripen; so, *Tuan*, I am afraid."

Gaga ceased, and once again a silence fell upon the three.

Suddenly, it was broken by the hurrying footsteps and laboured breathing of a man who ran, and round the bend appeared an *opas*.

All three looked up at his approach and saw stark fear upon his face.

"*Tuan! Tuan*!" he gasped. "*Tuan* Glister cannot be found. His house is empty, and his bedroom disarranged, and on the floor is a pool of blood——"

His eyes caught sight of the open grave. The words faltered on his tongue, then ceased, and he stood silent, trembling like a leaf.

At the mention of that name Dennis started, but before he could speak Walkely answered the question hovering on his lips.

"Young Glister's my new assistant, Dennis," he spoke in a queer, strained voice; "he came only last month; you haven't met him yet."

"But——"

"He's a younger brother of ..." Walkely looked toward the grave. "It's horrible!" he muttered.

In a flash the meaning of the rifled grave and Glister's disappearance grew plain, and the frown on Dennis's face grew deeper and his lips grew more compressed. Heedless of Walkely's questionings of the jibbering *opas* he turned to Gaga.

"Gaga," he said, "I see the hand of Maboga stretching out, seeking revenge for the insult of years ago. His arm is long. It stretches from the *Tuan's* grave to a village in the hills. Is it not so?"

"*Tuan*?" Gaga answered.

"It stretches," Dennis continued, "from the village to the new *Tuan's* house as well, for what the white man took must be repaid with interest. What think you, Gaga?"

"That the *Tuan* is wise and reads the Dusun as a book."

"Dennis!" Walkely had dismissed the *opas*, and putting out his hand, grasped Dennis's arm. "Dennis," he cried, "what do you mean? Glister has disappeared, there's blood upon his floor and we stand here while heaven knows what devil's work is being done! What do you mean—with interest?"

"Listen, Walley." Dennis weighed his words and spoke with slow conviction. "I'm in the dark almost as much as you—but I know the Dusuns and the fetish of their *Gusi* worship. When Glister took Jebee from her people, she broke their vows and outraged the sacred jars; but while the years were plentiful and their calves were strong they did not worry; when, as now, the inevitable lean year comes they seek a reason for their troubles."

"You men...?" asked Walkely, still perplexed.

"That reason is Maboga. They think he will not be appeased unless..."

Dennis did not finish, but his glance wandered to the open grave and back to Walkely's strained white face, on which the dawning light of comprehension showed.

"Good heavens!" he muttered. "You really thing...?"

Dennis nodded, then turned to Gaga.

"Gaga," he said, "tell me exactly what happens at the Feast."

"The silver buckles of the priestesses, *Tuan*, are hung upon the *Gusis'* lips. Then, when the dying moon is half-way set, the mateless wives say prayers and wash the sacred jars, and call upon the spirits to come forth and give their judgment on the village for the year. This year I think Maboga's jar will once again be decked. But who will cleanse the sacred lips I cannot think, for while Jebee lives the *pandang* may be worn by no one else. *Tuan* Glister dared, and paid the price."

"And, Maboga?" Dennis's voice was low, almost a whisper.

For a moment Gaga hesitated, then he replied: "The *Tuan* himself has said: 'What the white man took must be repaid—with interest.'"

He paused; then he added: "A white man's head has never yet hung in a Dusuan house, but three days hence Maboga will decide."

The eyes of Dennis and Walkely met. Both seemed to hear again the shufflings in the night, the opening and the shutting of the drawers. Both understood the object of that search.

"I'll borrow Glister's revolver, Walley, for we'll go alone with only Gaga as our guide, and attend this Feast," said Dennis.

For hours the booming of gongs had been borne upon the breeze, yet though the three had been steadily ascending, the deep-toned notes still sounded far away.

On the crest of a hill Dennis and his companion halted for a brief rest, and then onward and upward the trio climbed, while the track grew narrower and stonier and the jungle pressed closer on every side, and long trailing thorn-edged creepers, hanging from the trees, whipped their faces and tore their clothes.

The leading beast stopped and Gaga raised his hand. Without a word the two white men drew level, for the path had widened out and they stood upon the border of a glade, dissected by a muddy stream, whose banks were scored with a myriad hoof-marks.

Gaga slipped from his animal and softly spoke.

"We are nearly there, *Tuan*. This is their grazing-ground, but all the animals are at the village, for all have ridden to the Feast."

Dennis nodded and proceeded, like the others, to tether his beast.

Then, on foot the three moved forward, but with a quicker pace, for the gongs were loudly booming with a beat that would not be denied. Even as they crossed the muddy stream, the swaying, rhythmic time, rising and falling with the cadence of a dance, gave place to an insistent note that rose and rose, till only one intense vibration, one single throbbing note, beat on the heavy air with a malignant strength sapping all kindly thoughts and fanning to flame the primal lusts of hate and vengeance.

A little farther and the path rose with a sudden precipitousness that forced them to mount the well-worn stones as though they climbed a stair. They reached the top, to stand upon a tiny plain, on which the shadows of the encircling trees were slowly lengthening.

Even as they rested to regain their breath that one insistent note ceased, and for an instant silence reigned.

Then, from the glade's farther end arose a cry, faint at first, then slowly louder, harsher, stronger, swelling to a might pæan, to a tumultuous cry: "Maboga; Maboga! *Aki* Maboga!" And, stillness once again, save for the hurried padding of running feet as the three raced across the shadow-flecked glade.

Panting, they reached a wall of jungle, pierced by a sunken path that twined its short length through the heart of a moss-clad hill, whose riven sides were lit with weird, fantastic lights, thrown from countless torches that burned upon a plateau at its end.

In the shadow of a belt of trees they paused to take stock of their surroundings.

The plateau formed a horseshoe, and at its apex stood a native house built eight feet off the ground, whose length stretched three hundred feet. At either end, leading to the only doors, were rough-hewn steps, carved from solid logs of timber, and from these steps arose two poles, six feet in height, between which was stretched a length of knotted rotan. From this, like a gruesome necklace, hung two rows of ghastly human heads—blackened and dried from the smoke of years—save at each end. And, there hung two heads with staring, sightless eyes, and bared lips exposing whitened teeth; and from them the red blood dripped.

Upon the ground, placed in a semi-circle, stood the jars—the sacred *Gusi*—ranged in accordance with their height and rank. From either end they tapered up toward the central spot, where, side by side, rose two of flaming blue that reached the height of a man's shoulder.

The rim, or lip, of each was of a different hue—one black, one white—while from the neck of those whose lip was black grew four large ears, and in the lobes of each was placed a human skull.

Behind each jar, save one, a woman stood; her thick black hair piled high upon her head, framing her lime-washed face from which her dark eyes shone; her figure swathed from chin to toe in shrouded black, girt at the waist with a girdle of mice and monkeys' teeth.

A silver *pandang* hung under the lip of every jar but one, and resting on its swelling shoulder shimmered and winked in the torches' fantastic light.

Facing the jars, the Dusuns sat in rows, immobile and intent. There shone upon the face of everyone a strained expectancy, showing in the taut muscles of the back and the restless, twining fingers of the hands. Thus, they waited—in that strange, uncanny silence—for the answer to their cry, "Maboga, Maboga, *Aki* Maboga!"

Almost forgetful of the purpose of their errand, Dennis and Walkely watched, fascinated by the scene before them, lit by the waning moon and the lurid, flickering torches. Something of its primæval instincts and the tension of the squatting natives crept into their veins and held them spellbound as they gazed upon the coloured jars, with their glittering, shining buckles, each with its dumb, attendant white-faced woman, backed by the long, unbroken shadow of the palm-roofed house.

While the moon sank slowly in the west, until its lower rim began to kiss the topmost ridge of the roof, the silence lengthened, till it seemed as if nature slept and those rows of squatting natives were graven images devoid of breath.

But all at once there came a creaking sound, and the tension snapped. A long, rippling murmur, half-sigh, half-gasp, filled the air, and Gaga's hand gripped Dennis's arm.

"Look, *Tuan*, look!" he whispered, and pointed to a hut which stood alone and almost hidden in the shade of a mighty billian tree.

The two men obeyed, following the line of Gaga's pointing finger.

The hut door opened slowly as the noise increased. But though no light burned within, a shadowy form was faintly visible moving toward the glade. Slowly, silently, though still half-hidden by the shade, the form drew near. Then, as all eyes were turned upon it a glinting speck of light winked in the gloom. And, as the figure moved the winking light moved, too.

Slowly, steadily from the shade into the flickering fringe of torches; from the fringe into the full lurid glare moved the figure and the light.

A quick intake of many breaths; a long, loud gasp of terrified surprise. Then silence—and a woman, with a silver buckle hanging from a girdle round her waist, stood before the great blue sacred jar, from under whose deep black lip no silver buckle hung.

Over the silence, that like a living spirit lay upon the glade, Gaga's excited whisper just reached Dennis's and Walkely's ears.

"*Tuan*, it is Jebee, and she wears the silver *pandang* that I buried in *Tuan* Glister's grave! *Tuan, Tuan*, I am afraid!"

Even as he spoke the woman raised her rounded arms, on which no gleaming bangles shone, and with a single gesture unloosed the coils of her high-wound hair. The long, thick tresses fell around her like a black cloak.

Again, she raised her arms, this time in supplication, and her low, clear voice went chanting through the glade.

"*Aki* Maboga of the Sacred *Gusi*, Spirit of Evil who dwelleth in the great blue jar, hear now thy erring daughter, thy forsworn priestess, and forgive. Here, in my shame I stand before thee and the assembled people, bearing the silver *pandang*, symbol of thy might and power, which in my youth and wilful love I disgraced.

"Thou, who for long has been neglected, till thy just wrath burst into flame, so that the crops no longer ripen and the herds cease to bring forth young, lift, I beseech thee, *Aki* Maboga, the shadow of thy anger from off my race.

"Through me and for my sin my people have been punished; through me, O *Aki*, pronounce the penance thou dost claim."

She ceased, and as a wailing cry rose from the assembled natives, slipped slowly to her knees, and flinging her arms round the greet jar's neck, rested her lips upon its blackened rim.

Walkely stirred, but Dennis's warning hand bade him keep still. Gaga, speechless and with bulging eyes, stared at the kneeling figure.

A wind was stirring in the trees. The moon had sunk completely out of sight, and here and there a flickering torch gutted and burnt out.

Thus, in the creeping darkness they waited, while the moments grew to minutes burdened with suspense—waited for Maboga's answer that his deep black lips would whisper in Jebee's listening ear.

At length, with infinite grace, she rose, and stood clothed in her long black hair behind the great blue jar; for on its swelling shoulders, glinting against its deep black lip, the silver *pandang* lay.

The wind was sighing in the trees. The rustling leaves made soft accompaniment to her voice, which trembled with emotion.

"My lips have kissed the sacred *Gusi*—my tears have washed its deep black lip. The silver *pandang* has returned to deck the shrine of the Great Spirit, who has spoken, for my ears have caught his whispering breath."

A murmur rose, then faded, and she continued:

"Rejoice, O people, for I see the crops on all the hillsides ripening and herds with their young. But for his clemency Maboga asks a price."

She paused; then stretching out her arms cried in a ringing voice: "What will you give, my people, to allay your desperate plight?"

Quick as the summer lightning, swift as an adder's tongue came the answer from those rows of waiting natives.

"What the white man took, let him repay with interest. The head of the white man's brother we will give as a make-peace to Maboga, and as thy wedding gift."

She raised her hand, and there was silence.

"Thy words are good; thy offering acceptable unto——"

Her words were drowned in a great shout of fear, as a lighted torch fell from its bamboo socket on to the palm-roofed house.

Like running water fanned by the rising breeze, the flames spread rapidly, till in the twinkling of an eye the wooden house was nothing but three hundred feet of sheeted flame.

Then, pandemonium reigned and terror stalked the glade.

But to the watching three the fire was providential, for the burning house lit up a hut, till now hidden in the gloom, and at its single window they beheld young Glister's bloodstained face.

Under the shadow of the trees, skirting the edge of the tiny plain, they raced. A few more yards and they would reach the door; another second—out of the shadows by the hut a naked figure sprang, her long black hair streaming in the breeze, a glittering, sharp-edged sword in her hand.

With an oath, Walkely forged ahead, but, missing his footing on a twisted root, stumbled and fell.

The sudden, instinctive tightening of his fingers, a flare and a sharp report; a cry of pain, a sagging, drooping form—and Jebee lay a crumpled figure across the threshold of the hut.

# Si Urag of the Tail

By *Oscar Cook*

Dennis sat on the verandah of his bungalow and gazed meditatively around him. He could not look at the view, because there was none to speak of, since the house was built on an island in the middle of the Luago River. On all sides of the island grew the tall, rank elephant-grass and nipapalm. Here and there a stunted, beetle-ridden coconut tree just topped the dense vegetation, a relic of some clearing and plantation commenced by a native, then left to desolation and the ever-encroaching jungle.

Dennis was bored. He was two years overdue for leave; also the day was unusually hot. The hour was about four, but though the sun was beginning to slant there was no abatement in the fierceness of its rays. After lunch he had followed the immemorial custom and undressed for a short siesta, but sleep was denied him. The mechanical action of undressing had quickened his brain. The room seemed stifling; the bed felt warm. He bathed, dressed and betook himself to the verandah. Here, he smoked and thought.

And, his thoughts were none too pleasant, for there was much that was troubling him. Throughout the morning he had been listening to the endless intricacies of a native land case—a dispute over boundaries and ownership. He had reserved his judgment till the morrow, for the evidence had been involved and contradictory. He had meant to go over the salient points during the afternoon, and instead, here he was seated on his verandah smoking and thinking of an entirely different matter. Try as he would, his mind would not keep on the subject of the land, but roamed ever and ever over the mystery that was fast setting its seal of terror and fear on the district.

From a village in the *ulu* of the river, strange rumours had come floating downstream. At first, they were as light and airy as thistledown—just a passing whisper—a fairy story over which to smile; then they passed, but came again, more substantial and insistent, stronger and sterner and not to be denied. Their very number compelled a hearing; their very sameness breathed a truth. Inhabitants from the village had gone forth and never returned; never a trace of them had been found. First, a young girl, then her father. She had been absent six days, and he had gone to look for her. But he looked in vain, and in his turn disappeared. Then, a young boy, and next an aged woman. Then, after a longer period a tame ape, and finally the headman's favourite wife.

Fear settled on the village; its inhabitants scarce dared leave their houses, save in batches to collect water and food. But fear travels fast, and the rumours reached Klagan and came to Dennis's ears. In the end the mystery caught him in its toils, weaved itself into his every waking moment and excited his interest beyond control.

An idle native story: the tale of a neighbouring village with an axe of its own to grind. He was a fool to worry over it. Such mare's nests were of almost daily occurrence, thus Dennis argued;

and then from two other villages came similar tales. Two little girls had gone to bathe in the height of the noonday sun. At moonrise they had not returned. Nor, in the days that passed were they ever seen again. Two lovers met one moonlit night and waded to a boulder in midstream of the river. Here, they sat oblivious of the world around them. They were seen by a couple of natives passing downstream in their boat and then—never again.

Down the river crept the cold, insidious Fear like a plague, taking toll of every village in its path. In their houses huddled the natives, while crops were unsown and pigs uprooted the plantations; while crocodiles devoured untended buffaloes, and squirrels and monkeys rifled the fruit trees. From source to mouth the Fear crept down and in the end forced Dennis's hand, compelling him to action.

Thus, as he sat on his verandah and cursed the heat of the sun and the humidity of the tropics, unbidden and unsought the mystery filled his thoughts; and he began to wonder as to if and when his native sergeant and three police would return. For, he had sent them to the *ulu* to probe and solve the meaning of the rumours. They had been gone three weeks, and throughout this time no word had been heard of or come from them.

In the office a clock struck five. Its notes came booming across to Dennis. Then silence—not complete and utter stillness; such is never possible in the tropics, but the silence of that hour when the toilers—man and animal—by day realise that night is approaching; when the toilers by night have not yet awakened.

Lower and lower sank the sun. In the sky a moon was faintly visible. Dennis rose, about to call for tea, then checked the desire. From afar upstream came the chug, chug, chug of a motor-boat. Its beat just reached his ears. He looked at his wrist-watch. In ten minutes he would go down to the floating wharf. That would give him plenty of time to watch the boat round the last bend of the river. In the meanwhile …

But he went at once to the wharf after all, for mystery gripped him, causing him feverishly to pace up and down the tiny floating square. Chug, chug, chug, louder and louder came the noise; then fainter and fainter, and then was lost altogether as the dense jungle cut off the sound as the boat traversed another bend of the river. Chug, chug, chug, faintly, then louder and stronger. A long-drawn note from the horn of a buffalo smote the air, and the boat swung round the final bend. Only a quarter of a mile separate it now from Dennis.

As the boat drew nearer he saw that she was empty save for the *serang* and boatmen. Then, the Fear gripped him too, and he quickly returned to the house. With shaking hand he poured out a whisky-and-soda, flung himself into a chair and shouted for his "boy".

"*Tuan*!" The word, though quietly spoken, made him flinch, for the "boy" had approached him silently, as all well-trained servants do. Quickly, too, he had obeyed the summons, but in that brief space of time Dennis's mind had escaped his body and immediate wants to roam the vast untrodden fields of speculation and fear.

With an effort he pulled himself together.

"The motor-boat is returning. Tell the *serang* to come to me as soon as he has tied her up. See that no one is within earshot."

"*Tuan*!" And, the boy departed.

Scarcely had the boy left than the *serang* stood in front of Dennis. His story was brief, though harrowing, but it threw no light upon the mystery. For two days, till they reached the rapids, they had used the motor-boat. Then, they transhipped into a native dug-out, leaving the motor in charge of a village headman. For three days they had paddled and poled upstream till they came to the mouth of the Buis River. Here, the sergeant and police left them, telling them to wait for their return, and struck inland along a native track. For sixteen days they waited, though their food had given out and they had taken turns to search the jungle for edible roots. Then, on the sixteenth day it happened—the horrible coming of Nuin.

The boatmen had gone to look for roots. The *serang* was dozing in the dug-out. Suddenly it shook and rocked. Something clutched the *serang's* arm. It was Nuin's hand. Startled into wakefulness, the *serang* sat up; then he screamed and covered his eyes with his hands. When he dared look again Nuin was lying on the river bank. His clothes were in rags. Round his chest and back ran a livid weal four inches wide. His left leg hung broken and twisted. His right arm was entirely missing. His face was caked in congealed blood.

As the *serang* looked, Nuin opened his lips to speak, but his voice was only a whisper. Tremblingly, haltingly, the *serang* went to him and put his ear to his mouth. "Sergeant—others—dead—three days—west—man—with—big—big—others." The whisper faded away; Nuin gave a shudder and was dead.

They buried him near the river and then left, paddling night and day till they reached the rapids. A night they spent in the village, for they were racked with sleeplessness and they left the next morning, reaching Klagan the same day.

Such was the *serang's* report.

The Fear spread farther down the river till it reached the sea and spread along the coast.

In the barracks that night were two women who would never see their men again; was born a baby who would never know his father; wept a maiden for the lover whose lips she would never kiss again.

As the earliest streaks of dawn came stealing across the sky, the chugging of a motor-boat broke the stillness of the night. Dennis himself was at the wheel, for the *serang* was suffering with fever. With him were nine police and a corporal. They carried stores for twenty days.

The journey was a replica of the *serang's,* save that at the village by the rapids no friendly headman or villagers took charge of the motor-boat. The village had fled before the Fear. On the fifth day Buis was reached as the setting sun shot the sky with blood-red streamers.

On the banks of the rive the earth was uprooted; among the loosened earth were human bones and the marks of pigs' feet. Among the bones was a broken tusk, sure sign of some fierce conflict that had raged over Nuin's remains.

Dennis shuddered as he saw the scene; his Murut police, pagans from the interior of North Borneo, fingered their charms of monkeys' teeth and dried snake-skins that hung around their necks or were attached to the rotan belts around their waists, that carried their heavy *parangs*.

Occasionally, throughout the night the droning noise of myriad insects was broken by the shrill bark of deer or kijang. Sometimes the sentry, gazing into the vast blackness of the jungle, saw the beady eyes of a pig, lit up for a moment by the flames of the campfire. Sometimes a snake, attracted by the glare, glided through the undergrowth, then passed on. Once or twice a nightjar cried and an owl hooted—eerie sounds in the pitch-black night. Otherwise a heavy brooding stillness, like an autumn mist, crept over the jungle and enveloped the camp. Hardly a policeman slept; but dozed and waked and dozed again, only to wake once more and feel the Fear grow ever stronger. Dennis, on his camp-bed under a *kajang* awning, tossed and tossed the long night through.

Dawn broke to a clap of thunder. Rain heralded in the new day.

"Three days—west." This was all Dennis knew; all he had to guide him. For this and the next two days the party followed a track that led steadily in a westerly direction. On the evening of the third day it came out into a glade. Here, Dennis pitched his camp. The tiny space of open sky and glittering stars breathed a cooler air and purer fragrance than the camps roofed in by the canopy of mighty trees. Thus, the tired and haunted police slept, and Dennis ceased his tossing. Only the sentry was awake—or should have been. Perhaps, he too dozed or fell fast asleep, for a few unconscious moments. If so he paid a heavy penalty.

Dennis awoke the next morning at a quarter to six to see only the smouldering remains of the campfire.

"Sentry!" he called. But no answer was vouchsafed. "Sentry!" he cried again, but no one came. Aroused by his voice, the sleeping camp stirred to wide and startled awakeness.

The corporal came across to Dennis, saluted, then stood at attention, waiting.

"The fire's nearly out; where's the sentry?" Dennis queried.

The corporal looked around him, gazed at the smouldering fire, counted his men, then looked at Dennis with fear-stricken eyes.

"*Tuan*!" he gasped. "He is not—there are only eight men!"

"Is not? What d'you mean? Where's he gone?" As Dennis snapped his question cold fear gripped his heart. He knew; some inner sense told him that the man had disappeared in the same mysterious fashion as those early victims. Here, in the midst of his camp, the terrible, unseen thing had power!

"Where's he gone?" Dennis repeated his question fiercely to quench his rising fear. "What d'you mean?"

For answer the corporal only stood and trembled. His open, twitching mouth produced no sound.

With an oath Dennis flung himself from his bed. "Search the glade, you fool," he cried, "and find his tracks! He can't be far away. No, stay," he added as the corporal was departing. "Who is it?"

"Bensaian, *Tuan,*" gasped the terrified man.

Dennis's eyes narrowed and a frown spread over his face.

"Bensaian!" he repeated. "He was Number Three. His watch was from twelve till two."

"Tuan!"

"Then he's never been rèlieved. From two o'clock at least he's been missing!"

"*Tuan*! I must have slept. I saw Auraner relieve Si Tuah, but I was tired and——"

"Search for his tracks," Dennis cried, breaking in on his protestations, "but see no man enters the jungle."

In that tiny glade the search was no prolonged affair, but no traces of the missing man were found—save one. A brass button, torn from his tunic, lay at the foot of a mighty billian tree. But where and how he had gone remained a mystery. Only the regular footprints as he had walked to and fro on his beat were just discernible, and these crossed and recrossed each other in hopeless confusion.

Over the tops of the trees the sun came stealing, bathing the glade in its warming light, but Dennis heeded it not.

"Three days—west." The words kept hammering in his brain as he sat on the edge of his bed and smoked cigarette after cigarette. Up and down the glade a sentry walked. Round the fire the police were crouched cooking their rice; over another Dennis's boy prepared his *Tuan's* breakfast.

At length, when ready, he brought it over to him, poured out his coffee and departed to join the whispering police. But though the coffee grew cold and flies settled on the food, Dennis sat on, unmoved, deep in his distraction.

This was the fourth day! For three days they had journeyed west, following Nuin's almost last conscious words. The glade was hemmed in by the impenetrable jungle; no path led out of it save that along which they had come. It formed a cul-de-sac, indeed. And, Bensaian was missing!

As Dennis sat and pondered, this one great fact became predominant. Bensaian was missing. Then what did it mean? Only that here the thing had happened, lived or breathed or moved about. Here, then, would be found the answer to the riddle! In this little glade of sunlight must they watch and wait. Into the trackless jungle he dared not enter, even if his men could hack a path. To return the way they had come would make his errand worse than fruitless. Watching and waiting only remained.

So they waited. Day turned to evening and evening into night; the dawn of another day displaced the night; the sun again rode over the tops of the jungle. But nothing happened. Only the policemen grew more frightened; only Dennis's nerves grew more frayed. Then, once again the night descended, but no one in the camp dared really sleep.

Up and down walked the sentry, resting every now and then, as he turned against the billian tree. A gentle breeze stirred the branches of the encircling trees, bearing on the air a faint aromantic smell that soothed the nervous senses of the resting camp as a narcotic dispels pain. One by one the police ceased whispering and gently dozed, calmed by the sweet fragrance. Dennis ceased his endless smoking; stretched himself at ease upon his bed. The sense of mystery seemed forgotten by all; a sense of peace seemed brooding over them.

Midnight came and the wakeful sentry was relieved. His relief, but half-awake, railed at his fate—the half-unconscious dozing was so pleasant, and this marching up and down the glade while others rested so utterly to his distaste.

As for the fortieth time he turned about at the base of the great billian tree, he lowered his rifle, rested for a few seconds with his hands upon its barrel, then leaned against the dark-ridged stem; just for a moment he would rest, his rifle in his hands—just for a moment only, then once again take up his beat.

Take wind in the trees was gradually increasing; the fragrance on the air became more pronounced. The camp was almost wrapt in slumber. On his bed Dennis sleepily wondered whence came the pleasing, soothing odour that seemed to breathe so wondrous a peace. Against the billian tree the sentry still was leaning; his rifle slipped from the faint grasp of his hands, but he heeded not the rattle as it struck the ground.

Peace in the glade from whence came so much mystery! Peace while the dread, though unknown, agent drew near apace!

Down from the top of the billian tree it slowly descended, branch by branch; slowly, carefully, silently, till it rested on the lowest branch still thirty feet above the sentry.

The bark of a deer broke the stillness of the night. From afar came an answering note. Somehow the sound awakened the sentry. He looked around him, saw the fire was burning bright, picked up his fallen rifle and commenced to walk about.

Down the far side of the tree a bark rope descended till its weighted end just rested on the ground. Down the rope a man, naked save for a bark-made loin-cloth, descended till he too reached the earth. Then, pressed flatly to the great tree's trunk, he waited.

Across the glade the sentry turned about. With listless, heavy steps he was returning. Nearer and nearer he approached. At the foot of the billian tree he halted, turned and leaned against its trunk. The tension of his limbs relaxed. The rifle slipped from his grasp, but hung suspended by the strap that had become entangled over his arm. A light unconsciousness, hardly to be designated sleep, stole over him. From the camp there was no sign of wakefulness.

Slowly, a figure crept noiselessly round the tree and stood gazing at the policeman. Naked indeed, he was save for the *chawat* of bark; his thick black hair hung over his neck and reached beyond his shoulders, framing a face out of which gleamed two fanatical shining eyes. His body to the waist was covered with tattoo. From each of his breasts the designs started, spreading to waist-line and round to the back. The nipple of each breast gleamed a fiery, burnished gold, while from their fringe spread outward, like a full-blown flower, five oval petals of wondrous purple hue. From the golden centre of each flower ten long pistils spread, curving downward and round his body. At their source they too were of a purple hue, but as they reached the petals their colour turned to gleaming gold, which slowly changed to glistening silver as their ridged ends were reached. These ridged ends were circular, and their silver rims framed brilliant scarlet mouths shaped like the sucking orifice with which the huge and slimy horse-leech gluts its loathsome thirst for blood.

The man's arms were unusually long; his finger-nails had never been clipped; the splay of his toes, especially between the big and the next one, uncommonly wide.

One hand still clutched the bark rope; the other hung loosely at his side. Though he was tall, standing five feet ten inches, and heavily built, he moved as lightly as a cat.

Lightly he let go the rope and extended his two long arms toward his unconscious prey. The cry of a nightjar sounded close at hand. The somnolent sentry stirred as the sound just reached his brain. With a spring the man was upon him. One hand upon his mouth, one arm around his chest pinioning his arms to his side. With a swiftness incredible he reached the far side of the tree, let go his grasp upon the sentry's mouth, and using the rope as a rail, commenced to climb step over step with an amazing agility.

"*Tolong*!" The cry, laden with overwhelming fear, rent the stillness of the night. "*Tol*——"

All further sound ended in a gurgle as the relentless pressure round the sentry's chest squeezed out all breath from his body. The camp at that sudden cry of human agony and fear awoke to life. Instinctively the police seized their rifles; the corporal blew fiercely on his whistle; Dennis hurriedly pulled on his mosquito boots and picked up his revolver from under his pillow.

"Corporal!"

"*Tuan*!"

"*Siapa itu*?"

The cries rent the air simultaneously. Then came silence for the fraction of a second, as everyone stared hopelessly at one another as they realised the glade was empty of the sentry.

"Si Tuah! Tuah!" Dennis's voice rose in a long cry, breaking the sudden silence that followed the camp's awakening. "Tu-ah," he called again.

Somewhere from among the trees came a sound—a kind of muffled sob—a choking, gurgling cry of fear. To the edge of the jungle close to the billian tree Dennis and the corporal darted.

"Look, *Tuan*, a rope!" the latter gasped.

"My God!" Dennis whispered. "What does it mean?"

"It's made of bark and——" began the corporal; but the rest of his words were drowned by a loud report.

"*Jaga! Tuan, Jaga*!" he cried, as a jumbled shape came hurtling down from the branches of the tree and the frayed ends of the rope came writhing about them. The snapping of a twig overhead, and a smoking rifle fell at their feet.

As the shape reached the ground with a sickening bump, two figures fell apart and then lay still.

"Seize that man and bind him!" Dennis cried, pointing to the naked form, as he bent over the prostrate figure of Si Tuah. "Gently, men, gently," he added, as four police picked him up and carried him over to their *kajang* shelter.

His left arm hung loosely by his side, two ribs were also broken, but his heart still faintly beat. Dennis poured a little brandy down his throat. Slowly Ti Tuah came to. He tried to rise to sitting posture, but fell back with a groan of pain.

"He came upon me from behind the tree—I must have dozed," he muttered. "He picked me up—the pressure of his grasp was awful—and then commenced to climb the tree, holding the rope as a rail and walking up step by step. I struggled—just as we neared the branches his grip slackened—I could not cry—I had no breath—I only groaned; I struggled once again—my foot kicked the butt of my rifle—my toe found the trigger and I pressed and pressed—there came a report—we fell—and——"

Si Tuah had fainted again. Dennis's eyes met those of the corporal. "The shot must have severed the rope," he whispered.

"*Tuan*, his *nasib* was good," the corporal answered, and they crossed to where the human vulture lay, one leg twisted under him, his *chawat* all awry. As the policemen rolled him over on his face to knot the ropes—they showed but little pity for his unconscious state—the *chawat* came undone and slipped from his waist.

"Look, *Tuan*, look!" the corporal gasped, and pointed with shaking finger. "Look, he has a tail—it's not a man—it has a tail!" And, feverishly he fingered the charms that hung around his neck.

Dennis looked, following the pointing finger, then bending down, looked long and closely. It was as the corporal said. The man possessed a tail—a long, hard protuberance that projected from his spine for about four inches.

"Bring him to the camp," he ordered. "Place two sentries; one over him, one on the camp. He is only stunned; there are no bones broken. In the morning when Tuah's better we'll learn some more."

Dennis walked across to his bed. The Fear was gone, but the mystery was still unexplained. The campfire burnt brightly, giving out a smell of pungent wood-smoke. The soothing aromatic scent of an hour ago was no more. From the police came intermittent whisperings; from the man with the tail naught but heavy breathing. On his bed Dennis tossed and wondered.

As the early dawn first faintly flooded the sky, shriek upon shriek rent the air. Si Tuah had become delirious. The man with the tail awoke and listened. From a group of police squatting over a fire their voices reached him. His eyes blinked in perplexity. Quietly as he lay, he dug with his nails a small round hole in the earth about five inches deep. Then gingerly he moved, and in spite of his bonds sat up. From his bed Dennis watched him. Into the hole he fitted his tail, then looked at his bonds and the group of police. He opened his mouth, but no sound came forth. His tied hands he stretched out to them. His face expressed a yearning. It was as if their voices brought a comfort or recalled a past. Then, tear after tear rolled down his cheeks.

Calling the corporal, Dennis crossed to the weeping man. At Dennis's approach he looked up, then with a cry buried his face in his bound hands and rocked his body to and fro. He was afraid—afraid of a white man, the like of which he had never seen before.

"Peace, fool," the corporal said roughly, speaking unconsciously in Murut; "stop your wailing, the *Tuan* is no ghost but a man, albeit all-powerful."

Slowly, the tailed being ceased his weeping and looked up. "A man!" he muttered. "A man and the colour of the gods!" He spoke a bastard Murut and Malay that caused Dennis to start and the corporal to frown in perplexity, for his meaning was clear, though many of the words, akin to either language, were yet unlike either. But they understood him.

"And, your name?" Dennis asked in Malay; but the being only shook his head in fear, extending his hands in supplication.

"Loosen his bonds," Dennis commanded. "Ask him his name and tribe and village."

The corporal obeyed, and then translated.

The man's name was Si Urag. He came of a Murut race that years ago had captured some Malay traders. All had been killed except the women. These had been made to marry the headmen. Then came a plague, and nearly all died. The remnants, according to custom, moved their village. For days and days they walked in the trackless jungle. Then, from the trees they were attacked by a race of dwarfs who lived in houses in the branches. All save him were killed. He lay stunned; when he recovered consciousness he saw that the dwarfs had tails and that they were disembowelling the dead and dying and hanging their entrails round their necks. Fear seized him. He tried to rise and run away. He staggered to his feet, tottered a yard or two and then collapsed. Terrified, face downward, he waited for his foes. With a rush of feet they came. He waited for the blow. It never fell. Suddenly, he felt a gentle pull upon his tail—the tail over which all his life he had been ridiculed; then came a muttering of voices. From the face of the moon a cloud passed by. He was in a glade and lying near a pool. Over the air a heavy scent was hanging. Suddenly, the waters stirred. Out of their depths a flaming gold-and-purple flower arose. Ten tentacles spread out with gaping, wide open, blood-red mouths. Shriek upon shriek of utter agony rent the air. Into the flaming golden centre of each tentacle, curving inward, dropped a dwarf. Into the depths of the pool the flower sank down. All was still. Si Urag was alone.

That night he slept in a house among the branches of a tree. The surviving dwarfs had fled.

In the morning he collected the corpses of his friends and placed them near the lake. That night from his tree-house he watched. The moon was one day off the full. When at its highest point in the sky, the waters of the pool became disturbed. Again, the golden-purple flower arose from its depths and the soothing scent spread over the jungle. Again, the red-mouthed tentacles spread over the shore and sucked up the corpses, curved themselves in toward the golden centre, dropped in its bell-shaped mouth the stiffened bodies. Once again, the human-feeding flower sank beneath the waters. Once again, all was still. Gradually, the narcotic smell grew less; slowly the moon sank in the west. All was dark and silent.

On the next and two following nights the flower appeared. Each night the hungry tentacles sought for food—human or animal. Then, with the waning of the moon the flower rose up no more. Still, in his tree-house Si Urag watched and lived. Where else was he to go? His tribe was killed; the dwarfs had fled, and of them he was afraid. On account of his tail he was shy to intermingle with other humans, even if he knew where to find them. Here, was his house, safe from wild beasts that roamed at night; in the pool were many fish, in the jungle many roots and fruit. Here, was the wondrous flower that fed on men, that spread its wondrous scent, to whom he felt he owed his life. Here, then, he would live and consecrate his life in a kind of priesthood to the flaming gold-and-purple orchid.

The corporal ceased and his eyes met those of Dennis. There was no need to answer the unspoken question in them. The mystery of those disappearances was explained.

"And, that?" Dennis pointed to the tattooing on the prisoner's body.

Si Urag understood the gesture, if not the words.

"Is the picture of the flower I serve," he answered, looking at the corporal. "Two nights ago I fed it with a man clothed like that"—and he pointed to the police. "A night ago I caught a pig and deer; last night I caught a man"—he pointed to where Si Tuah lay in his delirium—"but a magic spoke from out a tube that flashed fire and the rope was severed and ..." He shrugged his shoulders with a world of meaning, then, "I am hungry; give me some rice," he begged.

For a while he ate his fill. Then, when the sun rose high over the little glade Dennis questioned him further, and from his answers formed a great resolve.

The glade of the golden-purple flower was but a few miles away. A little cutting of the jungle, and a hidden path—Si Urag's path—would be found. That night the moon would be but two days past its zenith, the wondrous flower would rise for the last time for a month—or rise never to rise again, hoped Dennis.

Si Urag was complacent. Was it fear or cunning? Who could tell? His face was like a mask as he agreed to lead the little party to the pool where dwelt the sacred flower.

The hour was after midnight. In the camp three police watched the delirious Si Tuah. Along a narrow track that led from the jungle to a pool, silently stole eight men. In the west a clipped moon was slowly sinking. Out of the jungle crept the men, into a glade silvered by the light of the moon.

"To the right ten paces ex——" Dennis's whispered orders faded away, giving place to a breathless gasp of surprise. There in the middle of the pool was the great golden-purple flower, its centre flaming gold, its petals deepest purple, its ten pistils curling and waving about—curling and waving toward the little group of men as they emerged from the track, the blood-red, silver-rimmed mouths opening and shutting in hungry expectation. Over the glade lay the heavy aromatic scent.

Speechless, spellbound, the little party looked at the wondrous, beautiful sight. The deadening spell of that narcotic scent was spreading through their veins. Lower and lower slowly sank the moon.

Si Urag fell upon his knees, covered his face with his hands and commenced to mumble a prayer. His action jerked the rope with which he was attached to Dennis and the corporal. With a start the former awoke as from a trance. All the waving pistils were pointing and stretching toward the huddled group. The moon was nearly touching the farther edge of the sky. Soon—soon ...

"To the right ten paces extend!" Like pistol shots Dennis's words broke in upon the night. Unconsciously, automatically, the police obeyed. Si Urag remained in prayer. "Load!" The one word cut the stillness like a knife. The waving pistils changed their curves—followed the extending men, stretched and strained their blood-red mouths.

"At point-blank—fire!" Six tongues of flame; one loud and slightly jagged report. Four pistils writhed and twisted in an agony of death. In the flaming golden centre, a jagged hole. The heavy aromatic scent came stealing stronger and stronger from the maimed and riddled centre. The moon just touched the far horizon. Slowly, the wondrous flower began to sink, the waters became disturbed, the pistils seemed to shrink.

Si Urag rose from his knees and prayers; uncovered his ears, over which he had placed his hand at the sound of the report. From Dennis to the corporal he looked in mute and utter supplication. From head to foot he trembled.

Slowly, the moon and flower were sinking. One pistil, bigger, stronger, fuller-mouthed than the rest, seemed reluctant to retreat, but pointed and waved at the silent three.

Into his *chawat* Si Urag dived his hand. Quick as lightning he withdrew it. A slash to the right, another to the left, and he was free. A mighty spring, a piercing cry, and he hurled himself, as a devotee, into the great, ravenous, blood-red mouth. Slowly, the pistil curved inward. Over the golden bell-shaped centre it poised. Then, it bent its head; its silver rim distended and then closed. Si Urag was no more.

The moon sank down out of sight; the wondrous flower with its maddened, fanatical victim slipped beneath the waters of the pool. The stillness of the jungle remained; the scent of dew-laden earth arose. Darkness—and a memory—surrounded the group of seven.

The tropic sleepiness of three p.m. hung over Klagan. Suddenly, the chugging of a motor boat was heard coming from afar upstream. Down to the tiny floating wharf the populace descended, headed by the *serang*. Round the last bend swung the motor-boat, drew alongside the wharf and came to rest. Out of it silently stepped Dennis and the weary police. One of them carried two rifles, which told the wondering people of a death. Two of them supported Si Tuah, which told them a struggle had taken place. Over his features spread a smile as his hands met those of his wife. " 'Twas a near thing, Miang," he murmured, "and it happened at the dead of night. A man with a tail and a golden-purple orchid which he worshipped."

From the people rose a gasp of wonder and cries of disbelief. Then, Dennis raised his hand.

"Si Tuah speaks the truth," he said, "but Si Urag of the Tail no longer lives, and the flower no more can blossom. The Fear is dead."

Then, unsteadily he walked to his house.

# A Kathi Robin Hood

By C.A. *Kincaid*

In Kathiawar, as indeed in other parts of India, officials love to pass their ten December and January holidays in Christmas camps. Many years ago the District Superintendent of the Kathiawar Agency Police had among others invited my friend B——, the Agency Judge, to join him in a Christmas camp at Than, a small territory belonging to the Lakhtar State. This has always been a favourite spot for Christmas camps. It is near the railway and possesses half a dozen excellent jheels or marshes, abundant partridge and sandgrouse and an unlimited quantity of black-buck. The latter is a valuable consideration when a camp of six or seven persons has to be fed.

The Police Superintendent had gone to Than on the 23rd December to see that everything was in order. His guests dropped in at various times on the 24th. The first combined shoot was to take place on the day after, namely on Christmas Day. When the guests were half-way through dinner, the Policeman pulled out of his pocket two or three vernacular letters and handed them to my friend B——and said:

"You can read Gujarati, B——, see what you can make of them."

B—— took the letters, read and re-read them carefully and then exclaimed: "What damned impudence!"

The curiosity of the guests had been steadily growing. At last, a Major Willoughby could no longer control his impatience: "What are you two fellows conspiring about? For God's sake tell us what the letters contain."

"Well," replied B——, "they amount to a series of threats from a certain Lakha Wala. He calls himself an outlaw and he warns us to go home because he and his gang do not mean to let us shoot. I shall translate the first one for you:

" '*In the service of the Superintendent Sahib of Police; You and your friends should go away. You will get no shooting. I and my Kathis will see to that.*

*Lakha Wala, Outlaw,*"

"Pooh!" cried Major Willoughly, "the blighter is only bluffing. How is he going to stop us from shooting?"

"Who is this Lakha Wala, anyway?" asked a young merchant from Bombay.

"He is a Kathi Landholder from the Junagadh State," replied the Policeman. "He has been an outlaw for the last three years. He had a considerable estate on the outskirts of the Gir forest until the Junagadh State claimed from him a small marriage tax. It only came to six rupees a year; but Lakha Wala thought somehow that his honour required that he should refuse to pay it. Instead of seeking Agency intervention, which he might well have obtained, he wrote a violent letter to the State, denying its sovereign jurisdiction. Naturally, the State Administration seized the village, as it was held on feudal tenure. Lakha Wala and his relatives then became outlaws, just as the Earl of Huntingdon did when he became Robin Hood. Since then, the villain has been robbing right and left and has given me no end of trouble. However, I shall send a man to Rajkot to get some of my mounted police here as secretly as possible. In the meantime, we shall see whether Lakha Wala really means business."

Next morning after the usual Christmas salutation and more than the usual early breakfast, the Policeman and his guests—in all five guns—started in tongas or on horseback to a jheel three and a half miles away. It was a reed-grown lake with narrow winding reaches that stretched out of the main water. On the banks of the reaches were excellent stands for guns. The duck flying up the centre of the water were never more than twenty-five or thirty yards from the edge and therefore well within range. The biggest bags were usually taken off this jheel and it was as a rule shot before the others. The Policeman and his friends reached the jheel in about half an hour, got out their guns and drew for places. There did not seem to be many duck about; but Willoughby hopefully tried to explain this by saying: "It is a cold morning and the duck, I expect, are all hiding in the reeds. Directly the first shot is fired the sky will be black with them."

It took the gun, who had drawn the farthest place, about a quarter of an hour to reach his stand. Having reached it, he fired a cartridge into the air as a signal. Then, he waited for the sky to blacken with the flying duck, but nothing happened. One or two teal raced about aimlessly; a spotbill rose and at once disappeared; a dozen shovellers, their long necks and shovel-shaped beaks outstretched, flew up and down the lake. Of the huge flights of mallard, gadwell and pochard that usually offered themselves as a prey to sportsmen, there was nothing to be seen.

At 11 a.m. the guns, after waiting more and more hopelessly for sport, decided to meet, discuss the situation and have their second breakfast.

"I am awfully sorry, you chaps," said the Policeman apologetically, "I do not understand it. Usually, this is our best jheel and we expect to get at least a hundred head for five guns. Let us see what we have got."

At his orders the shikari laid out the game and it made a poor display. One marble teal, one common teal, five shovellers were the tale of duck. Besides these there were a brace of painted partridge, a couple of quail and three snipe that had been shot by the guns as they came back from their stands.

"Well, fourteen head for a Christmas Day's shoot is pretty rotten," grumbled Willoughby. "It looks as if Lakha Wala has carried out his threat."

Just then a piece of paper, stuck in a cleft stick, caught B2—'s eye. He went and took it. On it were written in Gujarati the following words:

*"Welcome, gentlemen, welcome; think kindly of me,*
*Lakha Wala, Outlaw."*

The absence of game was now sufficiently accounted for. Lakha Wala and his Kathis had skilfully driven every bird off the little lake. Willoughby said; "Well, it doesn't matter much, let us go out after blackbuck. It will be nice to add a little venison to our larder." The Policeman sent for carts from the neighbouring village and while the guns breakfasted, the shikaris 'camouflaged' the carts with jowari stalks, so as to make the blackbuck think that they were cultivators' carts engaged in ordinary agricultural work. After breakfast each gun took a cart and started out in different directions.

At five o'clock they all met again for tea and all had the same story to tell. They had never got near a buck. The most that anyone had seen was a frightened herd on the skyline; but directly the cart came within half a mile, the herd set off at full gallop. Lakha Wala's gang had, no doubt, been at work and had chased the buck until they were too terrified to stand. It was a disgruntled party that returned to camp. There, the policeman tried to console his guests by saying that he would change his programme and go next day to a jheel different from the one originally fixed. The change in the programme did not have the desired effect. The shoot on Boxing Day was a repetition of that on Christmas Day. There were no duck and the blackbuck were as wild as hawks and Lakha Wala had left a similar note with the same mocking words. The third and fourth day yielded no better results, although the Policeman changed his plans repeatedly. It was clear that one of the servants who knew English was giving information to Lakha Wala.

On the evening of the fourth day the Policeman took his guests out of the hearing of the servants and said:

"My mounted police have arrived. They are half a mile from the camp. They railed from Rajkot to Morvi and then marched by night. I do not think that Lakha Wala knows about their coming. What I propose is that we mention at table the time and place of tomorrow's shoot. Lakha Wala will go early to the spot. We shall start several hours before we are expected, accompanied by the mounted police, and shall catch the dacoits at their dirty work. What do you say? We shall have a man hunt instead of a duck shoot. Are you agreeable?"

The proposal was acclaimed with enthusiasm. At dinner, the Policeman announced that they would try the first jheel again; but that in view of the uncertainty of the sport they would start about 10 a.m. Next morning at 4 a.m. the five guns in riding kit and carrying rifles stole quietly out of their tents. Led by the Policeman they walked the half mile to the mounted men's camp. There he took five mounts for himself and his guests. They had left their own horses behind so as not to give the alarm. Then, with the remaining twenty mounted police, the guns rode to the jheel. It was still pitch dark as they approached it; but they could hear shots fired along the banks. Lakha Wala and his Kathis were busy frightening the duck.

Guided by the sound and the flashes, the Englishmen and the mounted police rode round the lake and succeeded in arresting Lakha Wala's men one after the other; but Lakha Wala himself they did not arrest. One of the outlaws pointed out where their horses were tethered and these, too, were secured. Among them was Lakha Wala's own mount, a splendid Kathi mare, shaped exactly like the horses on the Parthenon frieze. Her ears were bent inwards; she had noble shoulders and perfect quarters. Her only defect seemed to be her legs. Below the knees she seemed 'underpinned'; but to anyone acquainted with the Kathi breed the defect was not a real one. The solidity of the bone made up for its slimness. The Kathi mare was indeed, such an animal as a brigand chief should have. She was fast enough to catch anything on four legs and enduring enough to shake off any pursuit.

"Lakha Wala cannot be far off," said the Policeman and he asked several questions of the prisoners. They, however, resolutely refused to answer.

"There is a cultivator over there," said Willoughby, "let us ask him."

The Englishmen and the mounted men got off their horses and went up to the cultivator and the policemen asked him whether he had seen Lakha Wala. At first, the man seemed frightened and pretended not to understand. At last, after repeated questions, he bent forward and whispered into the Policeman's ear.

"For God's sake, Sahib, do not let Lakha Wala know that I gave you the information. He would torture me to death. I did see him half an hour ago; he was crawling through the reeds towards the southern end of the lake. If you ride there now you will certainly catch him."

The Policeman repeated the information in Gujarati and in English and all were about to remount. Suddenly, his Musulman risaldar or troop sergeant major exclaimed in Hindustani:

"Sahib, that man is no cultivator. He is wearing a gold anklet. It must be Lakha Wala himself!"

The words had hardly left the risaldar's mouth when the so-called cultivator sprang forward like a tiger. There was a flash and a groan. The risaldar sank to the ground with a silver-handled dagger in his heart. The cultivator dropped into the reeds close by and vanished. The Policeman went to the risaldar and tried to help him, but it was useless. He was stone dead. For several hours the party searched the reeds all round the lake, but without result. They never saw Lakha Wala again.

The death of the risaldar cast a gloom over the camp. The Policeman had greatly esteemed his brave and resourceful subordinate and his guests felt that in view of what had happened they could not shoot anymore. They took the dead risaldar into Rajkot, where he was buried with military honours. My friend B—had the satisfaction of trying Lakha Wala's gang and giving them swinging sentences.

The policeman could not catch Lakha Wala, although he sought for him everywhere. He, however, revenged himself by entering Lakha Wala's Kathi mare under his own name for the Rajkot sky races; she swept the board.

It was not until more than twenty years afterwards that I heard the sequel to B—'s story. I was then Judicial Commissioner in Sind; but I had always kept up old Kathiawar friendships. One day an old Nagar Brahman called on me. I was very pleased to see him as I had often met him in Rajkot. We talked for a long time about people and places in Kathiawar, that I had known in old days. Suddenly, B—'s story came into my mind and I asked my visitor if he had ever heard what had happened to Lakha Wala.

"Has your Honour not heard? I thought that you knew everything that had happened in Kathiawar."

I was forced to admit that in spite of my omniscience I had never heard the fate of Lakha Wala.

"Then I shall tell you," replied the Nagar, "for, I was then in the service of the Thakor of X. Since that time His Highness has not treated me well. Still, it is not for that reason that I tell your Honour, but because I know that you will not let the matter go any further." The Nagar then began his story with infinite gusto.

"I was private secretary to His Highness when Lakha Wala came to X and asked for shelter. His Highness was greatly troubled about the man. The chiefs of Kathiawar, as you know, hate to give up an outlaw who has thrown himself on their mercy. At the same time His Highness was unwilling to have difficulties with the English police. He kept excellent order in his own territories and he did not want it thought that he deliberately harboured gang robbers. He called together his chief officials and told them to advise him after due reflection what should be done with the man. In the meantime, he gave orders for Lakha Wala's detention in the State jail.

"That evening we all met in the Thakor Sahib's diwankhana or state room, where all the official business was discussed and transacted. Our chief took his seat at one end. The lights were brought in: we stood up and salaamed to them, as is our custom. His Highness then asked us our opinion. I advised that we should neglect old tradition and surrender Lakha Wala to the Agency police; for, I had by that time learnt that the man had murdered the risaldar. I added, too, that he had no longer followers, land or horse. He had lost his prestige, so why should we shield him?

"My saying that Lakha Wala had lost his horse carried great weight; for, as you know, a Kathi outlaw without a horse is like a Rajput without a sword or a Brahman without learning. Still, the Bhats (State bards) and Charans (State minstrels) in the hall would not hear of our surrendering an outlaw. We spent a long time talking over the matter. At last, the oldest bard present rose."

"'Protector of the Poor,' he began, 'you will remember that three years ago a Brahman beggar committed suicide just outside the town and since then we have had no rain. Why not sacrifice this Lakha Wala to the earth goddess to wipe out the stain of the Brahman's blood?'"

"Had a Brahman committed suicide?" I asked.

"Yes; but the Thakor Sahib was in no way to blame. The beggar was no better than a robber. He stole things right and left and extorted money from all the shopkeepers in the town; so at last, our chief told his police to drive him out of the State. But the Brahman, who was half-mad with opium and drink, stabbed himself in a rage and dying, invoked all sorts of curses on the State. The worst of it was that we did not have proper rain afterwards."

"Our chief was impressed by the old bard's suggestions; but he said that he would pass no orders without hearing Lakha Wala." He sent for the Kathi and said:

"'I dare not give you shelter, Lakha Wala. Which would you

sooner I did? I can either hand you over to the British police, who will certainly have you hanged; or, I can sacrifice you to the earth goddess, after duly honouring you for a fortnight, as an atonement for the death of the Brahman who, as you know, killed himself and cursed the State three years ago?'

"Lakha Wala thought for a moment: 'I do not want to be handed over to the British police; they would cause me to be hanged by a paria. If the Protector of the Poor will give me a month's honour and behead instead of hanging me, I shall agree to be sacrificed to the earth goddess."

"Eventually, it was agreed that Lakha Wala should be honoured for the weeks and beheaded, not hanged. Once the terms were settled Lakha Wala was released on parole, decked with garlands by the State dancing girls and feasted sumptuously at the State expense."

"But," I asked, "could not Lakha Wala have escaped, as he was allowed to go free?"

"Of course, Sahib, and an ordinary criminal would have done so, but Lakha Wala was not an ordinary criminal. He was a Kathi noble and he never thought of breaking his word. Moreover, he really enjoyed all the honour that he received as the sacrificial victim. Every morning, he was decked with fresh garlands by the dancing girls; in the streets all salaamed to him and he had never been so well fed in his life. Indeed, on the day before his execution His Highness had him weighed and found that he had gained more than a stone in weight."

"And, what about the day of execution; was Lakha Wala as brave then?"

"Yes, indeed," said my Nagar friend enthusiastically "he could not have borne himself more bravely. He might have been one of our epic heroes come back to life. He walked by himself, unbound and unguarded, to the very spot where the Brahman had committed suicide and there knelt down. A Kathi in the State service struck his neck with a sword and it was all over in a moment."

"Well, I hope that the sacrifice brought good rain?"

"Sahib, I cannot, of course, say whether the rain was brought by the sacrifice or not; but it is a fact that in the following monsoon our State had rain, such as it had not had for thirty years. We had a bumper crop. His Highness paid off all his debts and three years' arrears of tribute to the British government and still had a very large sum over."

"Did the government not hear of the matter?"

"No, Sahib; Colonel Chaser, the Political Agent, did; but he kept the matter quiet. After all, His Highness had paid his tribute up to date, so why should Colonel Chaser make a fuss?"

"Oh! come," I said. "I do not suppose the Colonel was influenced by money considerations. It is surely more likely that so wise a man took the view that since Lakha Wala had been executed, it did not much matter whether he had been punished by an Indian chief or the British court, or whether he had been beheaded or hanged."

"It may be as you say," conceded my Nagar friend, "for indeed, the Colonel Sahib was a very wise man."

# HAUNTED HOUSES

# Introduction

No matter how modern or advanced a man may claim to be, some taint of superstition lingers in his blood, inherited from ancestors who had a strong affinity with the supernatural. Ask anyone to spend a night alone in an empty old house, and he will hesitate to do so. And if he does, he will have a hard time falling asleep. Every little sound—a branch tapping on a window-pane, a rat scuttling about in the attic, the wind coming down the chimney—will serve to accentuate his isolation. And even if he does not see a "real" ghost, the ghosts of the past (his own past included) will come crowding round him and there will be no one to turn to for security or companionship.

Every old house has a character of its own. The older the house, the stronger the emanations from the past. People have lived and loved and died within its walls. The furniture has stories to tell. The mirrors have reflected the faces of people long gone. Hundreds of feet have crossed the threshold.

Haunted houses are the most favoured locations for writers of ghost stories. In India, old houses in hill-stations often have spooky reputations. In the plains it could be an old *dak*-bungalow, forest rest-house, ancient fort or palace. And many old schools have their ghostly lore.

My old school, Bishop Cotton's in Simla, was proud of its 'Lefroy ghost', Lefroy being the House to which the ghost had once belonged. He was a boy killed in a train accident on his way back to school from some distant part of the country. But on the day school opened he was seen in the corridors, in chapel, and in the Lefroy dormitory. Every year, on opening day, he showed up to give his attendance. I don't know if he still does so. He'd be a very Old Boy by now!

Other old schools have their ghostly legends, and I have heard of hauntings at Barnes, Deolali; St. Peter's, Agra; and Mayo, Ajmer. My father told me that Lovedale, in the Nilgiris (where he did his teacher's training, *circa* 1916) was often visited by the ghost of a former Headmaster. La Martiniere, Lucknow, where my mother studied, was sometimes inspected by the wrath of its Founder, who was buried in the basement. I don't know if he visits the Martiniere in Calcutta. Ghosts don't travel too well.

There is a school ghost in this collection, but it's the houses that provide the hauntings and the inspiration for some of the world's greatest writers of supernatural fiction: M.R. James, Algernon Blackwood, Bram Stoker, Hugh Walpole, Mrs Belloc Lowndes.

I like to do my late-night reading in an old rocking-chair that I picked up at an antique shop a few months ago. It had once belonged to a former Maharani, I was told. It creaks rather loudly when in motion, but I've got used to that.

The other night, after I'd gone to bed and switched off the lights, I heard the old chair creaking. Turning on the light, I saw that the chair was quite empty although it was rocking backwards and forwards as though it had an occupant. Presently it was still.

This is something that has happened several times during the past few weeks. Perhaps the rocking-chair's former owner wishes to use it from time to time. I don't mind her rocking and rolling in the chair, just so long as she doesn't appear in person, reading *The Rupa Book of Haunted Houses*. I leave that to you, dear reader.

# The Ghost

By *Walter de la Mare*

'Who knocks?' 'I, who was beautiful,
Beyond all dreams to restore,
I, from the roots of the dark thorn am hither.
And knock on the door.'

'Who speaks?' 'I—once was my speech
Sweet as the bird's on the air,
When echo lurks by the waters to heed;
'Tis I speak thee fair.'

'Dark is the hour!' 'Ay, and cold.'
'Lone is my house.' 'Ah, but mine?'
'Sight, touch, lips, eyes yearned in vain.'
'Long dead these to thine...'

Silence. Still faint on the porch
Brake the flames of the stars.
In gloom groped a hope-wearied hand
Over keys, bolts, and bars.

A face peered. All the grey night
    In chaos of vacancy shone;
Naught but vast sorrow was there—
    The sweet cheat gone.

# A Pair of Hands

By *Sir Arthur Quiller-Couch*

'Yes' said Miss Le Petyt, gazing into the deep fireplace and letting her hands and her knitting lie for the moment idle in her lap. 'Oh, yes, I have seen a ghost. In fact, I have lived in a house with one for quite a long time.'

'How you *could*—!' began one of my host's daughters; and '*You*, Aunt Emily?' cried the other at the same moment.

Miss Le Petyt, gentle soul, withdrew her eyes from the fireplace and protested with a gay little smile. 'Well, my dears, I am not quite the coward you take me for. And, as it happens, mine was the most harmless ghost in the world. In fact'—and here she looked at the fire again—'I was quite sorry to lose her.'

'It was a woman, then? Now *I* think,' said Miss Blanche, 'that female ghosts are the horridest of all. They wear little shoes with high red heels, and go about *tap, tap*, wringing their hands.'

'This one wrung her hands, certainly. But I don't know about the high red heels, for I never saw her feet. Perhaps she was like the Queen of Spain, and hadn't any. And as for the hands, it all depends *how* you wring them. There's an elderly shopwalker at Knightsbridge, for instance—'

'Don't be prosy, dear, when you know that we're just dying to hear the story.'

Miss Le Petyt turned to me with a small deprecating laugh. 'It's such a little one.'

'The story, or the ghost?'

'Both.'

And this was Miss le Petyt's story:

'It happened when I lived down in Cornwall, at Tresillack on the south coast. Tresillack was the name of the house, which stood quite alone at the head of a coombe, within sound of the sea but without sight of it; for though the coombe led down to a wide open beach, it wound and twisted half a dozen times on its way, and its overlapping sides closed the view from the house, which was advertised as "secluded". I was very poor in those days. Your father and all of us were poor then, as I trust, my dears, you will never be; but I was young enough to be romantic and wise enough to like independence, and this word "secluded" took my fancy.

'The misfortune was that it had taken the fancy, or just suited the requirements, of several previous tenants. You know, I dare say, the kind of person who rents a secluded house in the country? Well, yes, there are several kinds; but they seem to agree in being odious. No one knows where they come from, though they soon remove all doubt about where they're "going to", as the children say. "Shady" is the word, is it not? Well, the previous tenants of Tresillack (from first to last a bewildering series) had been shady with a vengeance.

'I knew nothing of this when I first made application to the landlord, a solid yeoman inhabiting a farm at the foot of the coombe, on a cliff overlooking the beach. To him I presented myself fearlessly as a spinster of decent family and small but assured income, intending a rural life of combined seemliness and economy. He met my advances politely enough, but with an air of suspicion which offended me. I began by disliking him for it: afterwards I set it down as an unpleasant feature in the local character. I was doubly mistaken. Farmer Hosking was slow-witted, but as honest a man as ever stood up against hard times; and a more open and hospitable race than the people on that coast I never wish to meet. It was the caution of a child who had burnt his fingers, not once but many times. Had I known what I afterwards learned of Farmer Hosking's tribulations as landlord of a "secluded country residence", I should have approached him with the bashfulness proper to my suit and faltered as I undertook to prove the bright exception in a long line of painful experiences. He had bought the Tresillack estate twenty years before—on mortgage, I fancy—because the land adjoined his own and would pay him for tillage. But the house was a nuisance, an incubus, and had been so from the beginning,

'"Well, miss," he said, "you're welcome to look over it; a pretty enough place, inside and out. There's no trouble about keys, because I've put in a housekeeper, a widow-woman, and she'll show you round. With your leave I'll step up the coombe so far with you, and put you in your way." As I thanked him he paused and rubbed his chin. "There's one thing I must tell you, though. Whoever takes the house must take Mrs Carkeek along with it."

'"Mrs Carkeek?" I echoed dolefully. "Is that the housekeeper?"

'"Yes: she was wife to my late hind. I'm sorry, miss," he added, my face telling him no doubt what sort of woman I expected Mrs Carkeek to be; "but I had to make it a rule after—

after some things that happened. And I dare say you won't find her so bad. Mary Carkeek's a sensible comfortable woman, and knows the place. She was in service there to Squire Kendall when he sold up and went: her first place it was."

'"I may as well see the house, anyhow," said I dejectedly. So we started to walk up the coombe. The path, which ran beside a little chattering stream, was narrow for the most part, and Farmer Hosking, with an apology, strode on ahead to beat aside the brambles. But whenever its width allowed us to walk side by side I caught him from time to time stealing a shy inquisitive glance under his rough eyebrows. Courteously though he bore himself, it was clear that he could not sum me up to his satisfaction or bring me square with his notion of a tenant for his "secluded country residence".

'I don't know what foolish fancy prompted it, but about halfway up the coombe I stopped short and asked:

'"There are no ghosts, I suppose?"

'It struck me, a moment after I had uttered it, as a supremely silly question; but he took it quite seriously. "No; I never heard tell of any *ghosts.*" He laid a queer sort of stress on the word. "There's always been trouble with servants, and maids' tongues will be runin'. But Mary Carkeek lives up there alone, and she seems comfortable enough."

'We walked on. By and by he pointed with his stick. "It don't look like a place for ghosts, now, do it?"

'Certainly it did not. Above an untrimmed orchard rose a terrace of turf scattered with thorn-bushes, and above this a terrace of stone, upon which stood the prettiest cottage I had ever seen. It was long and low and thatched; a deep verandah ran from end to end. Clematis, Banksia roses and honeysuckle climbed the posts of this verandah, and big blooms of the Maréchal

Niel were clustered along its roof, beneath the lattices of the bedroom windows. The house was small enough to be called a cottage, and rare enough in features and in situation to confer distinction on any tenant. It suggested what in those days we should have called "elegant" living. And I could have clapped my hands for joy.

'My spirits mounted still higher when Mrs Carkeek opened the door to us. I had looked for a Mrs Gummidge, and I found a healthy middle-aged woman with a thoughtful but contented face, and a smile which, without a trace of obsequiousness, quite bore out the farmer's description of her. She was a comfortable woman; and while we walked through the rooms together (for Mr Hosking waited outside) I "took to" Mrs Carkeek. Her speech was direct and practical; the rooms, in spite of their faded furniture, were bright and exquisitely clean; and somehow the very atmosphere of the house gave me a sense of well-being, of feeling at home and cared for; yes, *of being loved*. Don't laugh, my dears; for when I've done you may not think this fancy altogether foolish.

'I stepped out into the verandah, and Farmer Hosking pocketed the pruning-knife which he had been using on a bush of jasmine.

'"This is better than anything I had dreamed of," said I.

'"Well, miss, that's not a wise way of beginning a bargain, if you'll excuse me."

'He took no advantage, however, of my admission; and we struck the bargain as we returned down the coombe to his farm, where the hired chaise waited to convey me back to the market-town. I had meant to engage a maid of my own, but now it occurred to me that I might do very well with Mrs Carkeek. This, too, was settled in the course of the next day or two, and within the week I had moved into my new home.

'I can hardly describe to you the happiness of my first month at Tresillack; because (as I now believe) if I take the reasons which I had for being happy, one by one, there remains over something which I cannot account for. I was moderately young, entirely healthy; I felt myself independent and adventurous; the season was high summer, the weather glorious, the garden in all the pomp of June, yet sufficiently unkempt to keep me busy, give me a sharp appetite for meals, and send me to bed in that drowsy stupor which comes of the odours of earth. I spent the most of my time out-of-doors, winding up the day's work as a rule with a walk down the cool valley, along the beach and back.

'I soon found that all housework could be safely left to Mrs Carkeek. She did not talk much; indeed her only fault (a rare one in housekeepers) was that she talked too little, and even when I addressed her seemed at times unable to give me her attention. It was as though her mind strayed off to some small job she had forgotten, and her eyes wore a listening look, as though she waited for the neglected task to speak and remind her. But as a matter of fact she forgot nothing. Indeed, my dears, I was never so well attended to in my life.

'Well, that is what I'm coming to. That, so to say, is just *it*. The woman not only had the rooms swept and dusted, and my meals prepared to the moment. In a hundred odd little ways this orderliness, these preparations, seemed to read my desires. Did I wish the roses renewed in a bowl upon the dining-table, sure enough at the next meal they would be replaced by fresh ones. Mrs Carkeek (I told myself) must have surprised and interpreted a glance of mine. And yet I could not remember having glanced at the bowl in her presence. And now on earth had she guessed the very roses, the very shapes and colours I had lightly wished for? This is only an instance, you understand. Every day, and from morning to night, I happened on others, each slight enough, but all together bearing witness to a ministering intelligence as subtle as it was untiring.

'I am a light sleeper, as you know, with an uncomfortable knack of waking with the sun and roaming early. No matter how early I rose at Tresillack, Mrs Carkeek seemed to have prevented me. Finally I had to conclude that she arose and dusted and tidied as soon as she judged me safely a-bed. For once, finding the drawing-room (where I had been sitting late) "redded up" at four in the morning, and no trace of a plate of raspberries which I had carried thither after dinner and left overnight, I determined to test her, and walked through to the kitchen, calling her by name. I found the kitchen as clean as a pin, and the fire laid, but no trace of Mrs Carkeek. I walked upstairs and knocked at her door. At the second knock a sleepy voice cried out, and presently the good woman stood before me in her nightgown, looking (I thought) very badly scared.

'"No," I said, "it's not a burglar. But I've found out what I wanted, that you do your morning's work over-night. But you mustn't wait for me when I choose to sit up. And now go back to your bed like a good soul, whilst I take a run down to the beach."

'She stood blinking in the dawn. Her face was still white.

'"Oh, miss," she gasped, "I made sure you must have seen something!"

'"And so I have," I answered, "but it was neither burglars nor ghosts."

'"Thank God!" I heard her say as she turned her back to me in her grey bedroom—which faced the north. And I took this for a carelessly pious expression and ran downstairs, thinking no more of it.

'A few days later I began to understand.

'The plan of Tresillack house (I must explain) was simplicity itself. To the left of the hall as you entered was the dining-room; to the right the drawing-room, with a boudoir beyond. The foot of the stairs faced the front door, and beside it, passing a glazed inner door, you found two others right and left, the left opening on the kitchen, the right on a passage which ran by a store-cupboard under the bend of the stairs to a neat pantry with the usual shelves and linen-press, and under the window (which faced north) a porcelain basin and brass tap. On the first morning of my tenancy I had visited this pantry and turned the tap; but no water ran. I supposed this to be accidental. Mrs Carkeek had to wash up glassware and crockery, and no doubt Mrs Carkeek would complain of any failure in the water-supply.

'But the day after my surprise visit (as I called it) I had picked a basketful of roses, and carried them into the pantry as a handy place to arrange them in. I chose a china bowl and went to fill it at the tap. Again the water would not run.

'I called Mrs Carkeek. "What is wrong with this tap?" I asked. "The rest of the house is well enough supplied."

'"I don't know, miss. I never use it."

'"But there must be a reason; and you must find it a great nuisance washing up the plate and glasses in the kitchen. Come around to the back with me, and we'll have a look at the cisterns."

'"The cisterns'll be all right, miss. I assure you I don't find it a trouble."

'But I was not to be put off. The back of the house stood but ten feet from a wall which was really but a stone face built against the cliff cut away by the architect. Above the cliff rose the kitchen-garden, and from its lower path we looked over the wall's parapet upon the cisterns. There were two—a very large one, supplying the kitchen and the bathroom above the kitchen;

and a small one, obviously fed by the other, and as obviously leading, by a pipe which I could trace, to the pantry. Now the big cistern stood almost full, and yet the small one, though on a lower level, was empty.

'"It's as plain as daylight," said I. "The pipe between the two is choked." And I clambered onto the parapet.

'"I wouldn't miss. The pantry tap is only cold water, and no use to me. From the kitchen boiler I gets it hot, you see."

'"But I want the pantry water for my flowers." I bent over and groped. "I thought as much!" said I, as I wrenched out a thick plug of cork and immediately the water began to flow. I turned triumphantly on Mrs Carkeek, who had grown suddenly red in the face. Her eyes were fixed on the cork in my hand. To keep it more firmly wedged in its place somebody had wrapped it round with a rag of calico print; and, discoloured though the rag was, I seemed to recall the pattern (a lilac sprig). Then, as our eyes met, it occurred to me that only two mornings before Mrs Carkeek had worn a print gown of that same sprigged pattern.

'I had the presence of mind to hide this very small discovery, sliding over it with some quite trivial remark; and presently Mrs Carkeek regained her composure. But I own I felt disappointed in her. It seemed such a paltry thing to be disingenuous over. She had deliberately acted a fib before me; and why? Merely because she preferred the kitchen to the pantry tap. It was childish. "But servants are all the same," I told myself. "I must take Mrs Carkeek as she is; and, after all, she is a treasure."

'On the second night after this, and between eleven and twelve o'clock, I was lying in bed and reading myself sleepy over a novel of Lord Lytton's, when a small sound disturbed me. I listened. The sound was clearly that of water trickling; and I set it down to rain. A shower (I told myself) had filled the water-pipes which drained the roof. Somehow I could not fix the sound. There was a water-pipe against the wall just outside my window. I rose and drew up the blind.

'To my astonishment no rain was falling; no rain had fallen. I felt the slate window-sill; some dew had gathered there—no more. There was no wind, no cloud: only a still moon high over the eastern slope of the coombe, the distant plash of waves, and the fragrance of many roses. I went back to bed and listened again. Yes, the trickling sound continued, quite distinct in the silence of the house, not to be confused for a moment with the dull murmur of the beach. After a while it began to grate on my nerves. I caught up my candle, flung my dressing-gown about me, and stole softly downstairs.

'Then it was simple. I traced the sound to the pantry. "Mrs Carkeek has left the tap running," said I, and, sure enough, I found it so—a thin trickle steadily running to waste in the porcelain basin. I turned of the tap, went contentedly back to my bed, and slept.

'—for some hours. I opened my eyes in darkness, and at once knew what had awakened me. The tap was running again. Now it had shut easily in my hand, but not so easily that I could believe it had slipped open again of its own accord. "This is Mrs Carkeek's doing," said I; and am afraid I added "Bother Mrs Carkeek!"

'Well, there was no help for it: so I struck a light, looked at my watch, saw that the hour was just three o'clock, and descended the stairs again. At the pantry door I paused. I was not afraid—not one little bit. In fact, the notion that anything might be wrong had never crossed my mind. But I remember thinking, with my hand on the door, that if Mrs Carkeek were in the pantry I might happen to give her a severe fright.

'I pushed the door open briskly. Mrs Carkeek was not there. But something *was* there, by the porcelain basin—something which might have sent me scurrying upstairs two steps at a time, but which as a matter of fact held me to the spot. My heart seemed to stand still—so still! And in the stillness I remember setting down the brass candlestick on a tall nest of drawers beside me.

'Over the porcelain basin and beneath the water trickling from the tap I saw two hands.

'That was all—two small hands, a child's hands. I cannot tell you how they ended.

'No: they were not cut off. I saw them quite distinctly: just a pair of small hands and the wrists, and after that—nothing. They were moving briskly—washing themselves clean. I saw the water trickle and splash over them—not *through* them—but just as it would on real hands. They were the hands of a little girl, too. Oh, yes, I was sure of that at once. Boys and girls wash their hands differently. I can't just tell you what the difference is, but it's unmistakable.

'I saw all this before my candle slipped and fell with a crash. I had set it down without looking—for my eyes were fixed on the basin—and had balanced it on the edge of the nest of drawers. After the crash, in the darkness there, with the water running, I suffered some bad moments. Oddly enough, the thought uppermost with me was that I *must* shut off that tap before escaping. I *had* to. And after a while I picked up all my courage, so to say, between my teeth, and with a little sob thrust out my hand and did it. Then I fled.

'The dawn was close upon me: and as soon as the sky reddened I took my bath, dressed and went downstairs. And there at the pantry door I found Mrs Carkeek, also dressed, with my candlestick in her hand.

'"Ah!" said I, "you picked it up."

'Our eyes met. Clearly Mrs Carkeek wished me to begin, and I determined at once to have it out with her.

'"And you knew all about it. That's what accounts for your plugging up the cistern."

'"You saw...?" she began.

'"Yes, yes. And you must tell me all about it—never mind how bad. Is——is it—murder?"

'"Law bless you, miss, whatever put such horrors in your head?"

'"She was washing her hands."

'"Ah, so she does, poor dear! But—murder! And dear little Miss Margaret, that wouldn't go to hurt a fly!"

'"Miss Margaret?"

'"Eh, she died at seven years. Squire Kendan's only daughter; and that's over twenty years ago. I was her nurse, miss, and I know—diphtheria it was; she took it down in the village."

'"But how do you know it is Margaret?"

'"Those hands—why, how could I mistake, that used to the her nurse?"

'"But why does she wash them?"

'"Well, miss, being always a dainty child—and the housework, you see——"

'I took a long breath. "Do you mean to tell me that all this tidying and dusting——" I broke off. "Is it *she* who has been taking this care of me?"

'Mrs Carkeek met my look steadily.

'"Who else, miss?"

'"Poor little soul!"

'"Well now"—Mrs Carkeek rubbed my candlestick with the edge of her apron—"I'm so glad you take it like this. For there isn't really nothing to be afraid of—is there?" She eyed me wistfully. "It's my belief she loves you, miss. But only to think what a time she must have had with the others!"

'"The others?" I echoed.

'"The other tenants, miss: the ones afore you."

'"Were they bad?"

'"They was awful. Didn't Farmer Hosking tell you? They carried on fearful—one after another, and each one worse than the last."

'"What was the matter with them? Drink?"

'"Drink, miss, with some of 'em. There was the Major—he used to go mad with it, and run about the coombe in his night-shirt. Oh, scandalous! And his wife drank too—that is, if she ever *was* his wife. Just think of that tender child washing up after their nasty doings!"

'I shivered.

'"But that wasn't the worst, miss—not by a long way. There was a pair here—from the colonies, or so they gave out—with two children, a boy and gel, the eldest scarce six. Poor mites!"

'"Why, what happened?"

'"They beat those children, miss—your blood would boil!—*and* starved, *and* tortured 'em, it's my belief. You could hear their screams, I've been told, away back in the high road, and that's the best part of half a mile. Sometimes they was locked up without food for days together. But it's my belief that little Miss Margaret managed to feed them somehow. Oh, I can see her, creeping to the door and comforting!"

'"But perhaps she never showed herself when these awful people were here, but took to flight until they left."

'"You didn't never know her, miss. The brave she was! She'd have stood up to lions. She's been here all the while:

and only to think what her innocent eyes and ears must have took in! There was another couple——" Mrs Carkeek sunk her voice.

'"Oh, hush!" said I, "if I'm to have any peace of mind in this house!"

'"But you won't go, miss? She loves you, I know she do. And think what you might be leaving her to—what sort of tenant might come next. For she can't go. She's been here ever since her father sold the place. He died soon after. You mustn't go!"

'Now I had resolved to go, but all of a sudden I felt how mean this resolution was.

'"After all," said I, "there's nothing to be afraid of."

'"That's it, miss; nothing at all. I don't even believe it's so very uncommon. Why, I've heard my mother tell of farmhouses where the rooms were swept every night as regular as clock work, and the floors sanded, and the pots and pans scoured, and all while the maids slept. They put it down to the piskies; but we know better, miss, and now we've got the secret between us we can lie easy in our beds, and if we hear anything, say 'God bless the child!' and go to sleep."

'"Mrs Carkeek," said I, "there's only one condition I have to make."

'"What's that?"

'"Why, that you let me kiss you."

'"Oh, you dear!" said Mrs Carkeek as we embraced: and this was as close to familiarity as she allowed herself to go in the whole course of my aquaintance with her.

'I spent three years at Tresillack, and all that while Mrs Carkeek lived with me and shared the secret. Few women, I dare to say, were ever so completely wrapped around with love as we were during those three years. It ran through my waking life like a song: it smoothed my pillow, touched and made my table comely, in summer lifted the heads of the flowers as I passed, and in winter watched the fire with me and kept it bright.

'Why did I ever leave Tresillack? Because one day, at the end of five years, Farmer Hosking brought me word that he had sold the house—or was about to sell it; I forget which. There was no avoiding it, at any rate; the purchaser being a Colonel Kendall, a brother of the old Squire.

'"A married man?" I asked.

'"Yes, miss; with a family of eight. As pretty children as ever you see, and the mother a good lady. It's the old home to Colonel Kendall."

'"I see. And that is why you feel bound to sell."

'"It's a good price, too, that he offers. You mustn't think but I'm sorry enough——"

'"To turn me out? I thank you, Mr Hosking; but you are doing the right thing."

'Since Mrs Carkeek was to stay, the arrangement lacked nothing of absolute perfection—except, perhaps, that it found no room for me.

'"*She*—Margaret—will be happy," I said; "with her cousins, you know."

'"Oh yes, miss, she will be happy, sure enough," Mrs Carkeek agreed.

'So when the time came I packed up my boxes, and tried to be cheerful. But on the last morning, when they stood corded in the hall, I sent Mrs Carkeek upstairs upon some poor excuse, and stepped alone into the pantry.

'"Margaret!" I whispered.

'There was no answer at all. I had scarcely dared to hope for one. Yet I tried again, and, shutting my eyes this time, stretched out both hands and whispered:

'"Margaret!"

'And I will swear to my dying day that two little hands stole and rested—for a moment only—in mine.'

# A School Story

By *M.R. James*

Two men in a smoking-room were talking of their private-school days. 'At *our* school,' said A., 'we had a ghost's footmark on the staircase. What was it like? Oh, very unconvincing. Just the shape of a shoe, with a square toe, if I remember right. The staircase was a stone one. I never heard any story about the thing. That seems odd, when you come to think of it. Why didn't somebody invent one, I wonder?'

'You never can tell with little boys. They have a mythology of their own. There's a subject for you, by the way—"The Folklore of Private Schools".'

'Yes; the crop is rather scanty, though. I imagine, if you were to investigate the cycle of ghost stories, for instance, which the boys at private schools tell each other, they would all turn out to be highly-compressed versions of stories out of books.'

'Nowadays the *Strand* and *Pearson's*, and so on, would be extensively drawn upon.'

'No doubt: they weren't born or thought of in *my* time. Let's see. I wonder if I can remember the staple ones that I was told.

First, there was the house with a room in which a series of people insisted on passing a night; and each of them in the morning was found kneeling in a corner, and had just time to say, "I've seen it," and died.'

'Wasn't that the house in Berkeley Square?'

'I dare say it was. Then there was the man who heard a noise in the passage at night, opened his door, and saw someone crawling towards him on all fours with his eye hanging out on his cheek. There was besides, let me think—Yes! the room where a man was found dead in bed with a horseshoe mark on his forehead, and the floor under the bed was covered with marks of horseshoes also; I don't know why. Also, there was the lady who, on locking her bedroom door in a strange house, heard a thin voice among the bed-curtains say, "Now we're shut in for the night." None of those had any explanation or sequel. I wonder if they go on still, those stories.'

'Oh, likely enough—with additions from the magazines, as I said. You never heard, did you, of a real ghost at a private school? I thought not; nobody has that ever I came across.'

'From the way in which you said that, I gather that *you* have.'

'I really don't know; but this is what was in my mind. It happened at my private school thirty odd years ago, and I haven't any explanation of it.

'The school I mean was near London. It was established in a large and fairly old house—a great white building with very fine grounds about it; there were large cedars in the garden, as there are in so many of the older gardens in the Thames valley, and ancient elms in the three or four fields which we used for our games. I think probably it was quite an attractive place, but boys seldom allow that their schools possess any tolerable features.

'I came to the school in a September, soon after the year

1870; and among the boys who arrived on the same day was one whom I took to: a Highland boy, whom I will call McLeod. I needn't spend time in describing him: the main thing is that I got to know him very well. He was not an exceptional boy in any way—not particularly good at books or games—but he suited me.

'The school was a large one: there must have been from 120 to 130 boys there as a rule, and so a considerable staff of masters was required, and there were rather frequent changes among them.

'One term—perhaps it was my third or fourth—a new master made his appearance. His name was Sampson. He was a tallish, stoutish, pale, black-bearded man. I think we liked him: he had travelled a good deal, and had stories which amused us on our school walks, so that there was some competition among us to get within earshot of him. I remember too—dear me, I have hardly thought of it since then!—that he had a charm on his watch-chain that attracted my attention one day, and he let me examine it. It was, I now suppose, a gold Byzantine coin; there was an effigy of some absurd emperor on one side; the other side had been worn practically smooth, and he had had cut on it—rather barbarously—his own initials, G.W.S., and a date, 24 July 1865. Yes, I can see it now: he told me he had picked it up in Constantinople: it was about the size of a florin, perhaps rather smaller.

'Well, the first odd thing that happened was this. Sampson was doing Latin grammar with us. One of his favourite methods—perhaps it is rather a good one—was to make us construct sentences out of our own heads to illustrate the rules he was trying to make us learn. Of course, that is a thing which gives a silly boy a chance of being impertinent: there are lots of school stories in which that happens—or anyhow there might be. But Sampson was too good a disciplinarian for us to think of trying that on with him. Now, on this occasion he was telling us how to express *remembering* in Latin: and he ordered us each to make a sentence bringing in the verb *memini*, "I remember." Well, most of us made up some ordinary sentence such as "I remember my father," or "He remembers his book," or something equally uninteresting: and I dare say a good many put down *memino librum meum*, and so forth: but the boy I mentioned—McLeod—was evidently thinking of something more elaborate than that. The rest of us wanted to have our sentences passed, and get on to something else, so some kicked him under the desk, and I, who was next to him, poked him and whispered to him to look sharp. But he didn't seem to attend. I looked at his paper and saw he had put down nothing at all. So I jogged him again harder than before and upbraided him sharply for keeping us all waiting. That did have some effect. He started and seemed to wake up, and then very quickly he scribbled about a couple of lines on his paper, and showed it up with the rest. As it was the last, or nearly the last, to come in, and as Sampson had a good deal to say to the boys who had written *meminiscimus patri meo* and the rest of it, it turned out that the clock struck twelve before he had got to McLeod, and McLeod had to wait afterwards to have his sentence corrected. There was nothing much going on outside when I got out, so I waited for him to come. He came very slowly when he did arrive, and I guessed there had been some sort of trouble. "Well," I said, "what did you get?" "Oh, I don't know," said McLeod, "nothing much: but I think Sampson's rather sick with me." "Why, did you show him up some rot?" "No fear," he said. "It was all right as far as I could see: it was like this: *Memento*—that's right enough for remember, and it takes a genitive,—*memento putei inter quatuor taxos*." "What silly rot!" I said. "What made you shove that down? What does it mean?"

"That's the funny part," said McLeod. "I'm not quite sure what it does mean. All I know is, it just came into my head and I corked it down. I know what I *think* it means, because just before I wrote it down I had a sort of picture of it in my head: I believe it means 'Remember the well among the four'—what are those dark sort of trees that have red berries on them?" "Mountain ashes, I s'pose you mean." "I never heard of them," said McLeod; "no, *I'll* tell you—yews." "Well, and what did Sampson say?" "Why, he was jolly odd about it. When he read it he got up and went to the mantelpiece and stopped quite a long time without saying anything, with his back to me. And then he said, without turning round, and rather quiet, 'What do you suppose that means?' I told him what I thought; only I couldn't remember the name of the silly tree: and then he wanted to know why I put it down, and I had to say something or other. And after that he left off talking about it, and asked me how long I'd been here, and where my people lived, and things like that: and then I came away: but he wasn't looking a bit well."

'I don't remember any more that was said by either of us about this. Next day McLeod took to his bed with a chill or something of the kind, and it was a week or more before he was in school again. And as much as a month went by without anything happening that was noticeable. Whether or not Mr Sampson was really startled, as McLeod had thought, he didn't show it. I am pretty sure, of course, now, that there was something very curious in his past history, but I'm not going to pretend that we boys were sharp enough to guess any such thing.

'There was one other incident of the same kind as the last which I told you. Several times since that day we had had to make up examples in school to illustrate different rules, but there had never been any row except when we did them wrong. At last, there came a day when we were going through those dismal things which people call Conditional Sentences, and we were told to make a conditional sentence, expressing a future consequence. We did it, right or wrong, and showed up our bits of paper, and Sampson began looking through them. All at once he got up, made some odd sort of noise in his throat, and rushed out by a door that was just by his desk. We sat there for a minute or two, and then—I suppose it was incorrect—but we went up, I and one or two others, to look at the papers on his desk. Of course, I thought someone must have put down some nonsense or other, and Sampson had gone off to report him. All the same, I noticed that he hadn't taken any of the papers with him when he ran out. Well, the top paper on the desk was written in red ink—which no one used—and it wasn't in anyone's hand who was in the class. They all looked at it—McLeod and all—and took their dying oaths that it wasn't theirs. Then I thought of counting the bits of paper. And of this I made quite certain: that there were seventeen bits of paper on the desk, and sixteen boys in the form. Well, I bagged the extra paper, and kept it, and I believe I have it now. And now you will want to know what was written on it. It was simple enough, and harmless enough, I should have said.

'"*Si tu non veneris ad me, ego veniam ad te,*"

which means, I suppose, "If you don't come to me, I'll come to you."'

'Could you show me the paper?' interrupted the listener.

'Yes, I could: but there's another odd thing about it. That same afternoon I took it out of my locker—I know for certain it was the same bit, for I made a finger-mark on it—and no single trace of writing of any kind was there on it. I kept it, as I said, and since that time I have tried various experiments to see whether sympathetic ink had been used, but absolutely without result.

'So much for that. After about half an hour Sampson looked in again: said he had felt very unwell, and told us we might go. He came rather gingerly to his desk and gave just one look at the uppermost paper: and I suppose he thought he must have been dreaming: anyhow, he asked no questions.

'That day was a half-holiday, and next day Sampson was in school again, much as usual. That night the third and last incident in my story happened.

'We—McLeod and I—slept in a dormitory at right angles to the main building. Sampson slept in the main building on the first floor. There was a very bright full moon. At an hour which I can't tell exactly, but some time between one and two, I was woken up by somebody shaking me. It was McLeod; and a nice state of mind he seemed to be in. "Come," he said, —"come! there's a burglar getting in through Sampson's window." As soon as I could speak, I said, "Well, why not call out and wake everybody up?" "No, no," he said, "I'm not sure who it is: don't make a row: come and look." Naturally I came and looked, and naturally there was no one there. I was cross enough, and should have called McLeod plenty of names: only—I couldn't tell why—it seemed to me that there *was* something wrong—something that made me very glad I wasn't alone to face it. We were still at the window looking out, and as soon as I could, I asked him what he had heard or seen. "I didn't *hear* anything at all," he said, "but about five minutes before I woke you, I found myself looking out of this window here, and there was a man sitting or kneeling on Sampson's window-sill, and looking in, and I thought he was beckoning." "What sort of man?" McLeod wriggled. "I don't know," he said, "but I can tell you one thing—he was beastly thin:

and he looked as if he was wet all over: and," he said, looking round and whispering as if he hardly liked to hear himself, "I'm not at all sure that he was alive."

'We went on talking in whispers some time longer, and eventually crept back to bed. No one else in the room woke or stirred the whole time. I believe we did sleep a bit afterwards, but we were very cheap next day.

'And next day Mr Sampson was gone: not to be found: and I believe no trace of him has ever come to light since. In thinking it over, one of the oddest things about it all has seemed to me to be the fact that neither McLeod nor I ever mentioned what we had seen to any third person whatever. Of course, no questions were asked on the subject, and if they had been, I am inclined to believe that we could not have made any answer: we seemed unable to speak about it.

'That is my story,' said the narrator. 'The only approach to a ghost story connected with a school that I know, but still, I think, an approach to such a thing.'

The sequel to this may perhaps be reckoned highly conventional; but a sequel there is, and so it must be produced. There had been more than one listener to the story, and, in the latter part of that same year, or of the next, one such listener was staying at a country house in Ireland.

One evening his host was turning over a drawer full of odds and ends in the smoking-room. Suddenly he put his hand upon a little box. "Now,' he said, 'you know about old things; tell me what that is.' My friend opened the little box, and found in it a thin gold chain with an object attached to it. He glanced at the object and then took off his spectacles to examine it more narrowly. 'What's the history of this?' he asked. 'Odd enough,' was the answer. 'You know the yew thicket in the shrubbery: well, a year or two back we were cleaning out the old well that used to be in the clearing there, and what do you suppose we found?'

'Is it possible that you found a body?' said the visitor, with an odd feeling of nervousness.

'We did that: but what's more, in every sense of the word, we found two.'

'Good Heavens! Two? Was there anything to show how they got there? Was this thing found with them?'

'It was. Amongst the rags of the clothes that were on one of the bodies. A bad business, whatever the story of it may have been. One body had the arms tight round the other. They must have been there thirty years or more—long enough before we came to this place. You may judge we filled the well up fast enough. Do you make anything of what's cut on that gold coin you have there?'

'I think I can,' said my friend, holding it to the light (but he read it without much difficulty); 'it seems to be G.W.S. 24 July 1865.'

# The Room

By *Eleanor Scott*

"You all agree, then?" asked Massingham, looking round at his guests.

"Quite, quite," said young Grindley of Brasenose.

"I am ready to fall in," said the Parson.

Vernon merely grunted. Really, after a dinner like that, it was a beastly shame to chatter.

'I'll do it, of course," said Reece, the tubby little curate whom Massingham had invited more out of cussedness than anything.

"All right, then. Mind, I don't guarantee that there is a ghost. I'm only going on local gossip and the fact that it's so damned hard to get any servants. And the house-agents, of course."

'You don't mean to say that *they* admit there's a ghost?" asked Ladislaw.

"No," grinned Massingham; "I'm going by what they didn't say ... By the way, are you coming in, Mac?"

Ladislaw flushed.

"I—of course I will, if that's part of the bargain," he said a little doubtfully.

"My dear chap," drawled Grindley, "surely—I mean, I know people who think there's something in it and that, but *surely*—?"

"I don't know," blurted Ladislaw. "Oh well, of course no one believes in the white-sheet-and-clanking-chains ghost; but—no, perhaps there aren't any in England," he ended abruptly.

They shouted with laughter. Ladislaw had in him the blood of generations of Highlanders, fanatical in their isolation and pride. Ladislaw grinned shamefacedly. He knew—well, perhaps he knew more than the others.

"Well, since we're all agreed," said Massingham briskly, "the next thing to do is to draw lots as to the order we go in. And look here," he added, reddening a little, "If anyone feels, when it comes to the point, that—that he'd rather drop it, you know, we'd—well, nobody's think the worse of him." He looked round a little shamefacedly. "I don't want any nervous wrecks on my conscience," he added with a half-laugh.

Everybody smiled in his own individual fashion—Grindley just a trite superior, Ladislaw sympathetic, the Parson very kind and indulgent, Vernon bored, and Reece with the spontaneity of a child. Massingham, his duty done, looked relieved.

"Let's draw, then," he said. "I'll put all our names in this" —he tipped out the cigars from the box— "and numbers from one to—let's see—six, in this." he took a clean tumbler off the tray. Then he drew out his pocket-book and tore out two leaves which he again tore, each into six pieces. On one set he wrote numbers, on the other names. Then, folding up the scraps, he dropped one set into the box and the other into the tumbler.

"Now, let's see—Reece, you're the most transparently honest. You draw."

Reece jogged his chair up, his face beaming like a small boy at a conjuring show.

"What do I do?" he asked eagerly.

"You take one paper out of the box and another out of the glass and open them."

Reece obeyed.

"Amory," he said, opening one—"three."

The Parson smiled, still indulgent. "So two of you experience the ghost before I do," he said.

Reece went on with the drawing.

"Ladislaw—four," he said. "Grindley—one."

"Good old Grindley!" "Do down the spook, Grinders!" "Leave some for me!" vociferated the crowd, now thoroughly aroused.

"Reece—six. Oh, I did hope I'd be fairly early! Never mind. Vernon—two. Massingham—five. That's all." Reece beamed round on the company, polishing his circular steel-rimmed spectacles, rosy with excitement.

"Then I take it the order is Grindley, Vernon, myself, Ladislaw, Massingham, Reece," said the Parson. "Upon my word, I hope something will come of it. I rather envy you, Grindley—and you, Reece." Then he drew Reece a little aside. "I mean to exorcise anything I see," he said in a low voice. "Did you think of doing that? I'm quite willing to come last if—if the others really want to find out if they can see anything."

"Just as you like," said Reece. "But won't your exorcism have a better chance of proof if you try it on somewhere in the middle? I mean, say Grindley and Vernon—er—see something, and I Ladislaw and Massingham and I don't——"

"Yes, you're right," said Amory, with more animation than usual. "It's best as it is. It's a clearer proof of the truth. Yes, Reece, you're quite right. Thank you."

His eyes had a curious gleam—the light of the fanatic, eager, bright and hard—in them.

"Lord! I pity the poor ghost when Amory once gets going," said Vernon with a short laugh. "I shouldn't like to be up against you when you were really mad, old man."

"Oh, come!" said Amory, flushing a little, with a rather shamefaced laugh. "It's only when I'm sure that I'm face to face with something really evil that I get angry. Then, I admit, I'm—er—"

"Implacable," put in Grindley. "It's most extraordinary," he went on, "how people seem to take a pride in certain of their—well, faults. Look at Massingham, now: he's got an absolute devil of a temper—I wouldn't answer for the safety of anyone who roused him—but I don't mind betting that he'll not only own to it, but be quite proud of it."

"Eh, what's that?" asked Massingham from the side-board. "What's that about me?"

"Isn't it true that you're rather hot-tempered?" drawled Grindley.

"Got a brute of a temper," answered Massingham cheerfully. "'Fact, when I do get going, I absolutely see red." He turned back to the syphon.

Grindley smiled faintly.

"I believe anger and pride are deadly sins, aren't they, Amory?—and no one minds owning to 'em; in fact, most people rather like being accused of 'em. But if I were to say that Vernon was a greedy sensualist, or that you, Amory, were the most damnably narrow, uncharitable brute I'd ever met, you'd be quite annoyed. Here's an example now," went on the youthful moralist. "You know that pretty maid Lily who used to wait at dinner? What's become of her?"

"Left," growled Massingham. "She—er—well, *you* know. Pity, too, for I don't think she was a real bad 'un. Pretty girls don't stand much chance in country villages."

"Exactly," said Grindley. "It wasn't, probably, her fault at all, if you can call it a fault to follow the dictates of Nature: yet she gets kicked downhill by the likes of us."

"Really, Grindley," said Amory, his thin face pale, "I know it's the fashion to be cynical about these things, but I consider it most immoral to take any but the strongest views on such a subject. If I had my way I should so deal with these cases as to prevent effectually their ever occurring again."

"Oh, come now, Amory!" broke in Vernon. "The cart-tail and whipping-post, eh? Damn it all, man, it's nature! Why, even in the Bible isn't there a woman—a real bad lot, too—who—er—got let off, don't you know?"

"If you mean the eighth chapter of St John's Gospel," said Amory coldly, "most critics agree that it's not authentic. I believe the Romans admit it to be an interpolation. And in any case, there was no condoning of the crime: the woman was told to 'sin no more,' not that it was 'natural' and therefore not worthy of blame."

"Oh, well," yawned Vernon, "we all know that it's you Christians who go in for whips and tortures and burnings alive. Poor degraded sensualists like myself believe in the motto 'Live and let live.'"

Amory opened his mouth for an indignant reply, but Massingham cut in.

"I suppose we all show up on a question of that kind," he said, philosophically. "Amory'd do anything—anything at all—to punish transgressors—eh, Amory?" The Parson nodded. "Old Vernon says 'Let' em, if they want to. It don't hurt anyone else.' (Please stop me if I'm misjudging anyone.) Grindley says 'It's below me, of course, vulgar and that: but I believe it's natural, like over-eating or getting-drunk.' I—well, I dislike the whole thing thoroughly, but I can't help thinking it's a necessary evil.

As for Ladislaw, I don't believe he even knows it exists, or if he does he's so disgusted he shuts it out of his existence. Reece—I'm blessed if I know what Reece thinks."

"I think," said Reece, very pink and hot, and stammering in his confusion, "that it's a horrible thing, like d-deformity, that we are responsible for, just as we are for c-consumption or drink. It's b-beastly, but it's our f-fault, and we've got to s-stop it. And I'm af-fraid I don't quite agree with you, Amory, that p-punishment stops it. It's d-decency in people's lives that *p-prevents* it. And we've got to see that they have a chance to—well, to live c-clean. I say, I'm sorry. I didn't mean to jaw like that." He collapsed into a deep arm-chair.

Grindley yawned.

"I'd no idea I'd uncork such deep vials of emotion and opinion," he said in his most irritating voice. "Shall we chuck it?" He lit a cigarette. "By-the-way, Masser. I suppose the—er—experiment begins to-night?"

"Just as you like," said Massingham. "It's your look-out, since you're the first on the list."

"Oh, well, I'll begin at once," said Grindley, rising. "I only hope they've made me up a decent bed. I believe that's really why people can't sleep in haunted rooms—maids won't take any trouble with the beds. Good-night, you men."

"'Night, old chap." "Mind you have a good yarn for us to-morrow night." "Don't sleep right through the show, lazy swine," "Call out if you're frightened."

And so young Oxford went up to encounter the spirits of all time.

"If it wasn't that I'd promised," said Grindley next evening, with an abruptness strange to him, "I'd never say a word. And, mind, it isn't what you expect, any of you. I didn't see a thing."

His eyes, flickering and dark in his white face, glanced nervously round the group of men. He passed his tongue rapidly over his lips.

"But—something happened?" asked Vernon.

"Yes—oh yes! Something happened all right. But what it was I don't know—a dream, or a vision, or—an incarnation."

They looked at him intently. Could this nervous boy be the calm and slightly superior Grindley who had talked so fluently and well of the power of the trained intellect?

"P'raps once I tell you I'll get over it a bit," he broke out at last. "I think—I'm—possessed … No, I mean it absolutely literally. I never guessed before what it meant….

"I didn't take long over going to bed. It's a pleasant enough room, you know, and I was a bit sleepy after the warmth and the talking and that, and I never for a moment thought I'd be disturbed. If I'd known, nothing in this world—or the next—would ever have persuaded me to sleep in that cursed—yes, I mean it, *cursed*—room."

He paused a moment, trying to recover some of his wonted calm.

"Well, I went to bed, and, I suppose, to sleep. I never before quite understood what Hamblet meant about the dreams that might come when you're lying in the grave, dead. I thought I did, but I didn't. And he only guessed what the dreams of death might be. I *know*….

"I don't mean you to think that I just had a bad dream. I quite literally *became someone else*—in every nerve of my body, in every thought of my mind—yes, and in every secret wish of my heart. I knew myself intimately. I was myself in another incarnation, older, stronger, freer, nearer to elemental things, but still myself. … I wish I could make you understand!"

He broke off abruptly, and as abruptly resumed:

"Of course, you all know the story of Dr Faustus. It's a fine, dramatic story, you think, and Marlowe made a glorious, marvellous poem of it. You don't know—thank God every day of your lives that you don't know—what a fearful story it is. I do know. Last night—and God only knows how long before—I *was* that man."

He gulped.

"I-I'd done it, you know. I'd abandoned all goodness: I'd made my intellect, *mine*, my God, and worshipped it. I'd blasphemed, and—I had sold my soul.

"I can't attempt to tell you what it was like. You couldn't ever imagine it if you hadn't felt it. I was terrified at what I'd done. I was the living home of everything evil—I tell you, I was evil through and through, as if some fearful vapour had surrounded and soaked me. And—I was *afraid*. I tried to pray, and I knew it was hopeless. How could I hope to be heard? Oh, it's easy to talk of Despair—you don't know, you can never guess, what it is! I fought and struggled. I began broken prayers, and abandoned them at the first word, knowing I couldn't pray....

"I can't tell you how long it lasted. I lived a whole spiritual life through. No words can tell you what it was—it was a living hell, and it's—it's heaven to be awake."

"Grindley, old chap," said Reece softly, "it—it wasn't *you*, you know. It was some evil outside of you. It wasn't the real you."

Grindley turned a haggard face.

"It was—a possible me. I might have been—I nearly was—just that, blasphemous, hopeless. But—I know in time .... I'm going out," he added abruptly. "Reece, will you come?"

Reece rose—Reece, on whom Grindley had often exercised a pretty wit; Reece the plain, the stupid, the comical and the kindly; and, without a word, they set out together.

The others lit pipes and cigarettes, poked the fire, mixed drinks; they breathed more freely.

"'Pon my word," said Vernon between puffs, "I'd no idea Grindley was such a kid. 'Xpect he was horribly jumpy the whole time. Poor kid, he's beastly upset! And all about a dream!"

"Well, but it must have been a horribly vivid and peculiarly beastly dream," said Massingham. "He looks quite changed. Poor old Grindley!"

"Why 'poor'?" asked Ladislaw. "I call him lucky."

"*Lucky!*" exclaimed two or three of the others. And "How d'you make that out?" asked Vernon.

"Well—he knows in time. He's warned. It *was* in him, you know—that ambition and pride of intellect. Well—he's cured."

"Want to back out, Vernon?" asked Massingham, grinning. "Your shot to-night, you know. Don't think there's much chance of your letting your ambition and intellect sell *your* soul to the devil, you lazy swine. You'll sell it another way."

Vernon grinned blandly.

"If the bed's warm and comfortable I'll be all right, thanks," he yawned. "Don't mind how soon I get off, either. Say good-night to the others for me, will you?"

He rose, stretching his arms, a fine figure of a man, verging on the corpulent, a little spoilt by good living, but handsome still.

It was very late when Grindley and Reece returned. They went upstairs, still together.

Everyone noticed how odd Vernon looked at breakfast. He did not look terrified and—yes, possessed—like Grindley; he looked like a man who has been brought face to face with some disgusting sight—white and shaken and sick. He ate nothing; he sat and crumbled bread with trembling fingers, and every now and then he would lift his eyes and look at one or another of them in a queer appealing way, as if he were guilty of some sin, and sorry for it, and his friends were his judges.

Everybody was a little uncomfortable and ill at ease: it was so odd to see Vernon, the debonair and confident Vernon, so piteously shaken. Breakfast was a hasty meal, for everyone was anxious to get it over and escape from those troubled questioning eyes.

But as chairs were pushed back and pipes lighted, Vernon suddenly spoke,

"I'm not going to make any story for you chaps to-night," he said abruptly. "There isn't one—for you. Yes. I've seen something. And I shan't forget what I've seen, as long as I live." Sweat started out on his forehead. "I'm not going to try and tell you what it was," he went on jerkily. "I'd as soon try to describe the most loathsome surgical operation or the most indecent physical illness. And if I wanted to, I couldn't. Thank Heaven, we haven't made the words for what I saw."

Eyes met startled eyes over the untidy table. It was mad, the whole business—a ghost hinted at while the remains of breakfast still littered the table; Vernon, of all people, confused ashamed, disgusted, and—yes—penitent.

"Grindley was right," said Vernon heavily; "that place *is* cursed. And he's right, too, when he says that no one who hasn't tried can even guess what evil it puts into your mind, and how it brings out the vile things you have in your own soul. Only I'd rather have had his—dream, or incarnation, or whatever it was, than——"

There was silence in the room. Suddenly Vernon stood up. Involuntarily everyone looked at him—at the handsome face, now tormented with a kind of passion of disgust and remorse, at the haunted eyes that used to be so gay.

"I'm—I'm not so bad as that yet!" he cried with a sound like a sob, and left them sitting there.

Grindley rose, and soon was seen passing the window, making for the stables. Ladislaw sat with bowed head, contemplating his plate. Reece and Amory murmured together, and Massingham caught the words "holy water." He got up and went across to them.

"I say, you men, shall we drop it?" he asked. He was quite pale. "Grindley's collapse didn't altogether surprise me, but when poor old Vernon gets bowled over like this it's too much of a good thing. He looks ghastly. I didn't think he had it in him to feel like that."

The others glanced at one another.

"There must be some—well, influence or something—in that room," Massingham continued. "Something pretty awful, too. And I don't want anybody to go in there just out of bravado and get—well, damaged."

"I agree," said the Parson gravely, "that there must be something evil in that room. It's not contrary to dogma to believe that some places are soaked, as it were, in evil influence. But that's all the more reason, Massingham, for me to spend the night there. If exorcism and prayer can lay your ghost, I promise you it shall be laid."

"I know you're not afraid," said Massingham. "I'll admit that in a way it's your job. But, Amory, you know that young Grindley wasn't just a frightened kid last night. Something *had* happened to him—something pretty awful. And God only knows what it can have been that poor old Vernon saw. He's horrified—and I should have said that no god or devil could horrify Vernon."

"Whatever it is," said Amory steadily— "and I don't think we can deny that there is something—it's not stronger, nor half as strong, as the Powers that will be on my side. I am going into that room to-night, Massingham, convinced that there is in it some shocking evil, and equally convinced that I shall overcome it. It cannot withstand the minister of God."

Massingham flushed, as some men do when asked to talk familiarly of God. He preferred to speak of Providence.

"Well, Amory, you know best," he said. "Do as you think right. Only, for heaven's sake, if you feel the smallest reluctance when it comes to the point, do chuck it! Swear you will."

"I am going to lay that spirit," said the Parson, steadily as ever, with a set mouth and a light in his eyes that warned Massingham that remonstrance was useless. He shrugged his shoulders.

"It's a pity you weren't born in the days of martyrs, Amory," he remarked. "You'd have enjoyed going to the stake for your principles."

Amory said nothing. Perhaps it was as well.

There was an unusual silence in the smoking-room that night. Grindley had been out in the wind and rain all day, and looked more his normal self, though there was an odd hesitation in his manner and dread still lurked in his eyes. He glanced over his shoulder often, like a man who fears a horrible presence at his elbow; and he kept close to Reece. Vernon sat, his head sunk between his shoulders, staring sombrely at the fire. No one knew where he had been all that long and dreary day. The Parson sat apart, reading with moving lips, a look of exaltation on his face. Ladislaw and Massingham made an idle pretence at talk.

Suddenly Amory rose.

"Good-night, all of you," he said. "It will be all right in the morning."

Massingham got slowly to his feet.

"Amory," he began doubtfully; but the Parson's eyes were bright and his face transfigured.

"Hush, Massingham," he said. "Nothing you can say shall stop me. This is my duty, and I shall do it. I will crush this evil thing down into the everlasting fire of punishment——"

A quick cry broke in on him.

"Don't! Don't talk of everlasting punishment! You don't know what it means. God wouldn't—He *couldn't*——"

Amory smiled.

"Grindley, God is, before all, just. Evil must receive its reward. By God's grace, I hope to be His minister in dealing out that punishment."

Massingham looked at him heavily.

"Well—good luck," he said. Amory smiled, an odd smile of confidence, pity, and triumph. The door closed softly behind him.

For a few minutes there was silence. Then Grindley whispered:

"He can't *really* believe there's a God like that?"

No one answered; then Vernon, speaking for the first time that evening, muttered:

"Some evil deserves—anything."

He rose heavily and went out. A little later Grindley caught Reece's eye: the little curate laid down his book, and without a word the odd pair left the room together. Massingham and Ladislaw sat on and on in silence, Massingham smoking sombrely, Ladislaw nervously touching up the fire.

At last, the Scotsman dropped the poker with a clatter.

"Massingham," he said in a queer strained voice, "I can't bear this. What do you imagine is going on in there?"

Massingham stirred.

"God only knows!" he said. Then he added suddenly:

"I'm going to listen. Don't you come, Mac. I'd rather you didn't."

He went out, and Ladislaw heard his steps mounting the stairs, going along the corridor, fading into silence. In the smoking-room the fire sank lower and the ashes fell softly.

In a few minutes Massingham returned, paler, and looking a little apprehensive.

"Well?" asked Ladislaw.

"There's—something awful going on in there," said Massingham jerkily. "I don't know what. I heard Amory's voice—and hard breathing, and a kind of ghastly muffled moaning noise—"

Ladislaw sprang up.

"Moaning? Amory?"

Massingham shook his head.

"Amory's voice was steady enough," he said. "It was like steel—ice—I don't know. ... *He* wasn't the—thing—that moaned."

Ladislaw shuddered.

"Could you hear what he said?"

"Not entirely," said Massingham reluctantly. He wiped his forehead, and Ladislaw saw that his hand shook.

The two men stared into each other's eyes.

"There was a smell like scorching," added Massingham suddenly, "and a horrible sound, like something cracking very slowly—or crushing, p'r'aps."

Again they stood in silence, straining their ears.

"Oh, for God's sake, let's go and stop it!" cried Ladislaw abruptly; and both men turned on an impulse and ran up the shallow wooden stairs.

At the top they came face to face with Amory himself. He stood staring blindly before him, his skin stretched and white over the bones of his face, his eyes wide and blank and horrified.

"Amory! Thank God you're here!" cried Massingham.

Amory stared on silently. Then suddenly he spoke.

"*The tears ran down over my hands*," he said in an odd, strained voice. He held his hands, thin and dry and rigid, a little before him. Massingham and Ladislaw looked at them instinctively. Then Ladislaw touched Amory gently on the shoulder.

"Come away, man," he said in his soft Highland voice.

The lids blinked rapidly once over Amory's blank staring eyes. Otherwise he did not move. Ladislaw slipped his hand through the rigid arm. Together he and Massingham got Amory down the stairs.

The clock struck three as they passed through the hall, and the sound seemed to rouse Amory from his stupor of horror. He passed a hand rapidly over his face, and then looked in an odd bewildered way at the concerned faces of his two friends. He shuddered a little.

"Massingham—" he said in a troubled voice.

"Yes, Amory; all right, old chap," said Massingham.

"Massingham—oh, Massingham, the tears ran down over my hands. I went on, and the tears ran down over my hands."

They sat with him till day came, a watery yellow rim between the wet earth and the weeping sky. They could hear the little sound as he passed his tongue over his dry lips.

The next day was Sunday. When Massingham's guests first came, there had been some talk of Amory's preaching in the village church to relieve the vicar, an old man in feeble health; but Massingham hardly liked to broach the subject to a man so utterly broken as Amory. But it seemed that he himself had not forgotten.

He appeared at the breakfast-table, exhausted and livid, but composed; and at the end of the meal through which he sat, silent and nervous, looking like a man who has passed through an agony—he spoke.

"What time is the service, Massingham?"

"Eleven. But, I say, Amory, you're not fit to preach."

"I know. I'm utterly unfit. But I must preach to-day, if I never enter a pulpit again."

"But, Amory, you're ill—done in. You ought to rest."

"*Rest!*" said Amory, raising his head for the first time; and at the look in his tortured eyes Massingham dropped his own.

It was an odd sermon, prefaced not by a single text, but by a reading from St Paul's Epistle to the Corinthians—that famous passage that deals with charity. And Amory spoke in a voice strained to the point of quivering of the guilt of those who condemn their brothers. His usual beautiful style was gone. His sentences were harsh, abrupt, and broken. There was one strange passage, which he delivered as if under appalling physical stress, his white-knuckled hands clutching the pulpit, sweat beading his brow and lips.

"Years *ago*," he said, "men tried to convert their opponents by torture. They showed them the human version of hell. They ground their bones, scorched their flesh, tore their eyes." (Here he turned ashy white to the lips.) "The tears of their victims wetted their hands, and they lifted those hands, wet with tears and blood, to God, the merciful God, to ask His blessing and His help. We torture souls in the same Name. We condemn them to a lingering death of torture by despair. I have tortured a soul to death—crushed it, broken—" He stopped, gasped audibly, opened his mouth once or twice, and then added abruptly," Be merciful. You don't know—you can't judge other souls. Have mercy, always." He paused again, and then, in the astonished silence of the country church, abruptly left the puplit.

That was the only reference he made to the appalling happenings of that night.

In the afternoon Ladislaw, Massingham and Vernon sat together at one end of the long library. Reece and Grindley, at the far end, talked together; Amory alone was absent.

"I say," said Massingham a little awkwardly, "don't you chaps think we've gone far enough? I mean, there's not much point in crocking ourselves over this confounded business, is there? Look at Reece, for instance; we don't want to push a simple-minded kid like that into this hell-hole. What do you think?"

"Reece won't hurt." Said Vernon heavily.

"Oh, I don't know," said Massingham. "He's more sensitive than you'd think. Look what he's done for poor old Grindley. What do you say, Mac?"

"No one ought to go near that room," cried Ladislaw fiercely. "You're right, Massingham—hell-hole's the word for it."

Vernon opened his mouth and closed it without speaking.

"*I'm* not going!" said Ladislaw. "It's my turn to-night, isn't it? Well, I've got pluck enough not to go."

Vernon looked up at him with an odd questioning glance, and their eyes met.

"You know?" asked Vernon.

Ladislaw nodded. "Enough," he said. "I've seen things—at home. I know what might—anyway, I'm not going."

He rose and went towards the door; then he turned back.

"What about you, Massingham? Will you be wise in time and chuck it too?"

Massingham flushed a little.

"No, I don't think I'll chuck it," he said slowly. "Oh, I'm in a funk all right! But I can't exactly ask people here, and make them face—whatever's in that room—and not go myself, can I?"

Vernon suddenly broke in.

"Massingham—don't," he said, laying his hand on the other mans' arm. "We, who've been—we'll understand. And Ladislaw will."

Massingham looked at him intently.

"I think I must go, Vernon," he said very quietly. "Besides, if Reece, why not me?"

Vernon got rather red.

"Look here," he said, "I've been, and I know what I'm talking about. Reece will be all right; but you——! Don't ask why, Dick, but don't—don't go into that damned place."

Massingham looked gravely at Vernon's pleading face, and shook his head.

"I'm sorry, Bill," he said. Vernon stared with a kind of hopeless entreaty into his face, then turned away with a half-groan.

At eleven that night Massingham went to face his ordeal.

Massingham said nothing of his experiences when he joined his friends next day. Like those who had already met Fate in that room of his, he was very pale, and his eyes had that same piteous look—the look of one who has sinned past hope of forgiveness, and yet hopes, however faintly, that his friends may not cast him out. He spoke very little, and not at all of the subject that lay uppermost in all their minds. Only, when dusk was falling, and they all sat together in the long library, he said suddenly, breaking into the conversation with the manner of a man who has been totally abstracted:

"Reece, I want to ask something of you."

"Yes?" said Reece in his commonplace tone of cheerful willingness.

"Don't go into that ghastly room to-night."

The other voices had all died away, as does ordinary talk when the speakers hear the voice of a dying man. But Massingham's request was like the releasing of a spring—as if they had been waiting for a signal.

Amory spoke first.

"Reece, he's right," he said in a very gentle voice. "It's not necessary, and it's——" He gulped.

"Yes, Reece," chimed in Ladislaw, "don't go. Let me have a companion in my cowardice!" he added, with a half-laugh.

Grindley said nothing, but he looked at the little curate with a glance oddly compounded of confidence and entreaty, admiration and fear.

Reece looked at Vernon.

"What do you think, Vernon?" he asked.

Vernon hesitated: then:

"Go, if you like, I say," he said. "It's not as if you were—like the rest of us."

"*Vernon!*" broke in Massingham sharply. He knew that the two were utterly opposed, but really....! "Don't listen to him, Reece. Don't go. I tell you it's ghastly. No one can imagine it." He became very pale. "Don't go," he urged again.

Reece was still looking steadily into Vernon's eyes; neither wavered. Then the little curate turned to Massingham.

"I'm sorry, Massingham," he said, "but if you don't mind, I'd like to go. All the rest of you have been."

"Oh, if that's the way you look at it!" exclaimed Massingham bitterly. Then his voice dropped and sounded weary. "Have it your own way," he muttered. "I suppose it's your own look-out. You've been warned." He walked away.

The others glanced at each other. Was it of any use to say any more? Then they gave it up. After all, simple as he was, Reece was not a child.

Still, they all felt horribly uncomfortable when, shortly before eleven, Reece laid down the copy of *Punch* over which he had been chuckling for nearly an hour, and rose.

"Good-night, you chaps," he said. "See you in the morning."

Grindley half rose; Reece caught his eye and grinned.

"'Night," he said again and, went out.

The others with one accord drew together round the fire. For a few minutes no one spoke.

"Good lord!" said Massingham suddenly. "I think this is the most horrible thing that's happened yet. He's such an utter kid to go into that pit of evil. He doesn't know—anything."

"If you come to that," said Amory, "I don't think any of us really knew what evil was. There's something in that room—God only knows what—some loathsome spirit of evil—that fills you until you become evil incarnate."

"There is—you're right!" cried Grindley excitedly. "You are—cut off. It's appalling——"

"It is appalling," said Massingham slowly, "to know that one is cut off oneself from hope of mercy or forgiveness. It is worse to cut off someone else."

They looked at him attentively.

"When one lets go the reins—allows blind fury to possess one utterly," said Massingham, still in that slow, almost detached voice, "one does not only kill one's own soul. There's the other soul. It's let out of the dead, heavy body—a damned soul, reproaching you for its damnation. And you can do nothing—

nothing! It's—oh, I can't tell you! There aren't human words for a thing like that, which is inhuman."

The others remained silent.

"Have you ever thought," added Massingham abruptly, "how terrible it must be to be God? To know things like that, and let them be, because they're just?"

"God is merciful first and just afterwards," said Amory. "I know I used to say the reverse, but now I know better."

"You may be right," said Massingham. 'There must be an amazing amount of goodness somewhere when there is such a quantity of unspeakable evil in men like us, who thought ourselves decent fellows enough."

Grindley moved impatiently.

"There is," he said: "I know there is. But I can't bear to think of that horror of evil which we all know of, let loose on Reece. He knows all I could tell him, but you can't *tell* about——"

"No, you can't," agreed Amory.

"What I can't understand," said Massingham, "was why you were so—well, so callous—about it, Vernon. You had as ghastly a time as any of us, and yet, when you could have dissuaded that kid—(for you could have dissuaded him, only you could)—you let him go on."

"It's like this," said Vernon, and the others were astonished at the gentleness of his voice. "Some—that night—I've felt the most tremendous reverence for innocence—purity of mind and thought. It seems to me that evil can't touch it, but it might touch evil. Do you see what I mean?—You do, Amory."

"Y-Yes, I do," admitted the Parson; "but—oh, Vernon, it's the ghastly risk! None of us ever guessed what would happen to the others, and we were more or less intimate with them. Now we know—(a little: we shall never know really)—what each has gone through; we can see how it worked. That room is so evil that when a man goes into it all the worst in him is drawn out. He is himself still, but filled and soaked with evil passions. He becomes vice incarnate——"

"Yes!" cried Vernon; "that's it!"

"What evil is in Reece?" asked Ladislaw.

They were silent a little, and then Grindley said apologetically:

"You see, one knows him so little. As Amory said, we aren't intimate with him, any of us. We've only been in close contact with him just lately, when we're all abnormal. I don't know—I hate to think of him alone up there, unsuspecting——"

They tell silent again, like men who anxiously await news. Suddenly Ladislaw rose and went and opened the door. They all listened intently. The house was utterly still.

Ladislaw came back, but he left the door open. "Just in case," he murmured, half-apologetically.

The night wore on. Somehow no one cared to go to bed. With the others it had been different—they could look after themselves: but they all felt a queer responsibility for Reece. He was such a kid, they kept saying, and the danger was so horrible. The dead silence of the house, dark and brooding beyond the open door of the warm and well-lit smoking-room, was terrible. Reece was out there, alone....

Dawn showed grey at last, and slowly the night lifted. The five men had been silent for the last hour or more. Now they looked dully, almost hopelessly, at each other's faces, grey in the early light, and silently they rose. It was over. Whatever had happened was ended.

They all felt a shock of surprise, relief—yes, and delight—when Reece came into the dining-room. He looked round at their drawn faces with concern.

"I say—is anything wrong?" he asked.

"No," said Massingham, with a half-laugh. "No; not if you're all right."

"Oh, *I'm* all right," said the little curate cheerfully. "Never slept better in my life, and that's saying a lot."

"Then, you saw——?" began Grindley.

"I didn't see a thing," said Reece half-regretfully. "Something missing in my make-up, I expect. It *is* a pity! However, I've had my chance."

And he fell hungrily on his breakfast.

# Nobody's House

By *A.M. Burrage*

They faced each other across the threshold of the great door in the dimness of two meagre lights. It was just dusk on a windy autumn evening, and Mrs Park, the caretaker, had brought a candle with her to answer the summons at the door. Behind the stranger the last grey light of the day filtered through veils of dingy, low-flying clouds. Between them the candle flame fluttered in the draught like a yellow pennon, the cavernous darkness of the hall advancing and retreating like some monster at once curious and shy.

The man was tall and broad and seemingly in the early fifties. He wore a grey moustache and beard, both closely trimmed, and his black velour hat was pulled low down over a high forehead. His overcoat was cut to an old-fashioned pattern, having, a cape to it and it was perhaps this which lent him an air of—even at his years—having outlived his age.

He was fumbling in an inside pocket when the door was opened, and he said nothing until he had produced an envelope.

"I have no order from Messrs Flake and Limepenny to see

the house." Here he offered Mrs Park the envelope. "I am afraid I have called at an inopportune time, but I missed one train and the next arrived late. Perhaps, however, you won't mind showing me over?"

He spoke slowly and a little nervously, as if he were repeating a speech which he had previously prepared. His voice was very low and mellowed and gentle. Mrs Park stood back from the threshold.

"Will you come in, sir?" she said. "I am afraid you won't be seeing the house at its best. I shall have to show you over by candle; there is no gas or electric light."

He stepped inside and scrutinized her. She was a tall, gaunt, middle-aged woman of the kind which is generally described as "superior". Nature had intended her to become matron of an institute. Fate and widowhood had forced her a rung or two down the ladder. She looked what she was—honest, hard-working, and almost devoid of sympathy.

"I'm afraid," she added in her hard, toneless voice, "you'll find everything just anyhow. I wasn't expecting anybody. Very few people come here nowadays. And a place of this size takes more than one pair of hands to keep it clean."

"It has been empty a long time, then?" he hazarded.

"Ever since——" She checked herself suddenly. "For more than twenty years, I should think." She turned her shoulder upon him, lifting the candle above her head. "This is supposed to be a fine hall, and everybody admires the staircase. If the house doesn't find a tenant or a purchaser soon, I hear they intend removing the staircase and selling it separately. There is a lot of fine oak panelling, too. The library——"

Turning to see if he were listening, she saw him start and shiver and rub his long, thin hands together.

"Excuse me," he said. "I have been a long time in the train and I am very cold. I wonder if it would be troubling you too much to get me a cup of tea."

"Yes, I could do that," she answered. "The kettle is on, for I intended having one myself. Will you come this way? Perhaps you would like a warm by the fire?"

She led the way across the hall and through a baize-covered door at the end. Turning once to see if she were giving him sufficient light, Mrs Park noticed that he walked with a slight limp.

He followed her down a short passage, through a great kitchen ruddy with firelight, down another passage, and into a small room intended to be used as a housekeeper's parlour. Here there was warmth, even stuffiness. A paraffin lamp stood burning on a flaming red table-cloth.

The room was full of hideous modern cottage furniture, and decorated largely with the portraits of people who ought to have known better than to be photographed. But a fire burned brightly in the grate and a kettle on a brass trivet murmured and rattled its lid. This commonplace room lighted and hot and over-furnished, was at least a relief from the dark passage and the draughty, gloom-ridden hall.

"I'll give you your tea in here, sir, and take mine in the kitchen," the caretaker said.

"Nonsense. Why should you? Besides, I want to talk. Oh, here's the order to view. You see … Mr Stephen Royds—that's my name … to view…."

He was running this thumbnail along the sheet of heavily headed office note-paper. Mrs Park glanced perfunctorily at the typewriting. So far as she was concerned, an order to view was a superfluous formality. She was more interested in this Mr Royds, who, having removed his hat, disclosed a head of sparse iron-grey hair. He spoke like a gentleman but there was nothing opulent in his appearance. He looked an unlikely purchaser or tenant; but for that matter she had never been able to visualize the sort of person whom the house would suit.

"I'll remove my greatcoat if you don't mind," he said while Mrs Park went to a cupboard for another cup and saucer. "The room is warm." He laid the coast across the back of a chair. "Do you live here entirely alone?"

"Yes."

"Aren't you—nervous?"

She looked up sharply.

"Nervous? What is there to be nervous about?"

"I didn't know. Some people cannot bear loneliness. Can you tell me why the house has been on the market all these years?"

Mrs Park smiled grimly.

"That's easy enough," she said. "It's nobody's house."

"What do you mean—nobody's house?"

"People who can afford to keep up a great house like this generally want land along with it. There isn't any land. People who don't' want land can't afford to keep up a house like this. The estate was sold to Major Skirting. He's a house of his own. He's let the land and he's been trying to let or sell the house ever since. I've shown hundreds over but nobody's ever thought twice about taking it."

"Strange. It's a good house. But the land ... yes, I quite follow you. Whom used it to belong to?"

Mrs Park set the cup and saucer down upon the table with a rattle.

"A gentleman named Harboys," she said; and became rigid, her head a little on one side.

"Do you hear anything?" he asked sharply.

"No, I'll make the tea."

"I suppose you sometimes fancy you hear things?"

She bent over the kettle, giving him no answer. He waited until the teapot was full and then gently repeated the question.

"Hear things?" she repeated with some show of asperity. "No. Why should I?"

"I didn't know. These empty old houses...."

"I'm not one of the fanciful sort, sir.... Will you help yourself to milk and sugar?"

She let him see that the talk had veered in a direction contrary to her liking. There was veiled fear in her eyes, and, watching her intently, he could see that she was not impervious to loneliness. Here was a woman who suffered more than she knew. She could bluff her nerves by sheer will-power, but this will-power was steadily losing in the long battle. Mrs Park was afraid of something, and always, in her inner consciousness, fighting against that fear.

"Thank you," the strange said, taking the cup and saucer. "Who was this Harboys? Is he still alive?"

"I couldn't say."

"Isn't there some story about the house?"

"I don't know."

"Forgive me. I think you do."

"There are stories. ... You don't need to listen...."

She spoke jerkily. Once more he remarked that look in her eyes.

"Tell me," he said gently.

"I can't sir. If Major Skirting knew I told people I should lose my job. He'd think I was trying to prevent people from taking the house."

"It wouldn't prevent me. Wasn't this Harboys supposed to have shot——"

"Ah!"— She set cup and saucer down with a rattle. "Then you've heard something already, sir!"

"A little. You had better tell me all. It will not affect me as a prospective purchaser."

Mrs Park passed a hand across her forehead.

"I don't like talking about it, sir. You see, I live here all alone...."

She checked herself suddenly, finding herself about to admit to a second person something which she never confessed even to herself.

"Just so," Royds said sympathetically. "And you sometimes hear noises? What noises?"

"Oh, it's imagination," she said. "Or the wind. Sometimes the wind sounds like footsteps and voices, and sometimes I seem to hear. ... It may be a loose door somewhere that bangs."

He leaned forward, his eyes shining with the excitement of some strange fascination.

"You mean you hear a shot fired?" he asked, scarcely above a whisper.

Her one hand resting on the tablecloth contracted nervously.

"I've known it sound like a shot. Oh, I don't believe...."

"They say the house is haunted?" he asked eagerly.

"They say. ... Oh, when there's been a tragedy happen in a house people will always——"

"Never mind what people say. What do *you* say?" The timbre of his voice had changed; under excitement it had hardened, grown louder. "*Is* the house haunted?"

There was something compelling in Royds's gaze, in the new tone of his voice. She answered him sullenly, helplessly.

"I don't know. I've heard things. I tell myself they're nothing." She groped for a handkerchief. "I've *got* to tell myself they're nothing."

"You haven't—*seen* anything?" he asked, in a low, strained, voice.

"No, thank God! I never go near the library after dark."

"The library? So it was there. Tell me."

Mrs Park gulped some tea and replenished her cup with a shaking hand.

"It must have been about twenty years ago," she said in a low and curiously unwilling tone. "The place belonged to a Mr Gerald Harboys. He was quite young—not much more than thirty, and very well liked. Some said he was a bit queer, but there was a strain of queerness in all the Harboys. Mad on hunting, he was, and one of the best riders in these parts. You'll be surprised at the size of the stables when you see them. He had them built.

"He'd married a young wife, one of the Miss Greys from Hornfield Manor, and some say he thought more of her than he did of his horses. She used to ride, too, and the pair of them, and Mr Peter Marsh from Brinkchurch, were always together.

"Harboys and Marsh had known each other since they were in the cradle. Whether there was really anything between Marsh and Mrs Harboys I don't know. There's been arguments about that for years, but they're both dead and gone now, and nobody will ever know.

"About one Christmas-time Harboys took a fall in the hunting field and broke his leg and it was during his convalescence that he got into one of his queer moods. I dare say it was being kept out of the hunting field, which brought it on. His leg mended slowly, and right at the end of January he could only just get about with a stick.

"Mrs Harboys followed the hounds every time there was a meet in the neighbourhood, and, with her husband unable to get about, she saw more of Peter Marsh than usual. But nobody seemed to know that Mr Harboys was jealous or that he suspected anything wrong.

"Well, one day, at the end of January, Mrs Harboys went out hunting, and her husband brooded all day over the library fire. During the afternoon he amused himself by cleaning a revolver, which he afterwards laid aside on the mantelpiece within reach.

"Mrs Harboys came in just after dark. Peter Marsh had been piloting her, and she brought him with her. While she was ordering tea and poached eggs to be sent up to the morning-room, she sent Peter Marsh into the library to get himself a whisky, and tell Mr Harboys about the day's hunting. He had not been in the library a minute, when angry voices were heard and then a shot.

"The butler then burst into the room and found Peter Marsh lying dead, and Mr Harboys, still in his chair before the fire, staring wildly at the body, with the revolver in his hand."

She paused, and in the silence she heard Royds breathing heavily. His head was bent and his gaze lowered to the near edge of the table, so that she could scarcely see his face.

"Mr Harboys," she resumed, "pleaded not guilty at the trial and said that his mind was a blank at the time when the shot was fired. He couldn't remember anything that had happened between Marsh coming into the room and then the butler bending over the dead body. His counsel put in a plea for insanity, but the jury would not have it. They found him guilty and added a recommendation to mercy. The death penalty was changed to penal servitude for life."

She broke off and began to muse, knitting her brows.

"That must be twenty years ago. ... They let them out after twenty years. He out already, or soon will be, if he's alive."

Slowly Royds lifted his head and turned burning eyes upon her face.

"And do you think Harboys did it?" he demanded.

The question took Mrs Park aback.

"Of course! Why! How else could it have happened? There was only those two in the room. It couldn't have happened any other way."

Royds got upon his legs. His pale face shining with little drops of moisture, his eyes aflame with a strange passion.

"I swear to you," he cried, "that I don't believe Harboys did it. I knew the men——"

Mrs Park's stare intensified and she uttered a smothered exclamation.

"——I knew him well as child and boy and man. I was at school with Harboys. I tell you he was incapable of murder! All the circumstantial evidence in the world would not weigh atom with me against my knowledge of his character. They say he had fits of madness. Another lie! But mad or sane he couldn't have done it. He loved his wife—and old Peter Marsh. He knew that they were two of God's best and whitest people. I tell you——"

He broke off suddenly and lowered his voice.

"I'm frightening you," he said. "I didn't mean to. Oh, but think! There's Harbooys been rotting in prison these twenty years, remembering nothing of those few dreadful moments. To this day doesn't know if he's innocent or guilty. Think of it."

Mrs Park lifted her white face and twitching lips. One hand had stolen to the region of her heart. Each rapid stroke of her pulses seemed to shake her.

"Why have you come here?" she cried cried in a voice which rose high and querulous with a nameless dread. "You don't want the house! You never intended—"

"No," said Royds, "I came here to find out."

"What?"

"They say strange things happen in the library. I have heard stories. You tell me you have heard footfalls, voices, the sound of a shot. Don't you understand, woman? What happened in the library that evening twenty years ago is known only to God! The man who lives remembers nothing. If it be true that Peter Marsh returns. ... Oh, don't you understand? It is the only way of learning ... the only way...."

Mrs Park stood up; her slim body made a barrier between him and the door.

"I can't let you go to the library," she cried sharply.

"I must. I'm going to spend the night there. I'm going to wait until Peter——"

"I can't let you," she said again.

"But you must. Don't you understand? This means life or death to a man."

She backed almost to the door.

"It's madness!" she cried. "Nobody has ever endured that room after nightfall."

"I will!"

"I shall be sent away if it is found out."

"It won't be found out. I'll recompense you if it is. Here, I came prepared to pay for the privilege." He tugged a bundle of bank notes roughly out of his breast pocket and flung them on the table. "How much do you want? Five pounds? Ten? Twenty?"

Mrs Park's gaze lingered on the roll of notes. She knew the value of money. Besides, she was alone in the great house with a man it might be dangerous to thwart.

"Come," said Royds, "here are five five-pound notes. Take them and act like a sensible woman. Then I shall go to the library, and you will make me a fire. Is there any furniture there?"

"No," muttered the woman, her gaze still on the roll of bank notes.

"Then, if you will permit me, I will take a chair."

He picked up the notes again and transferred all of them but five to his breast pocket. With these five he advanced and pressed them into the woman's hand. Her fingers closed over them.

"I'm doing wrong," she muttered.

"You're doing right. I'll get the truth to-night if I have to summon the devil himself. Now, come and help me make a fire in the library."

She turned heavily away without a word and went to a cupboard, from the bottom of which she took a bundle of firewood and an old sheet of newspaper, which she dropped on top of the contents of the half-filled scuttle. Then she lit a candle in a brass stick and motioned him towards the door. He picked up a chair as he followed her.

The house was very still as they passed through the kitchen and passages leading to the hall. Their footfalls on the uncarpeted floors rang out sonorously through the hollow shell of the house.

To the woman this shattering of a silence which seemed almost sacred was a new weapon put into the hands of Terror. Her overstrained nerves cried out in protest at each of the man's heavy steps. Around her, in the shifting penumbra beyond reach of the candle light, above her in the empty upper chambers of the house, all manner of sleeping horrors, shapeless abominations of the night-world, seemed to waken and listen and draw near. The silent house seemed full of stealthy movement, and each blotch of darkness was an ambush peopled by the lewd phantasms of her mind. The man walking behind her seemed to be without nerves, or he had so stimulated them as to bring them entirely under his control.

Evidently he knew the house, for he passed her in the hall taking the lead in the procession of two, and went straight to the library door, which he flung open and passed on the crest of the following candle light.

The library was a long room in an angle of the house. A long row of windows fronted the hearth, and two more faced the door. The walls were of oak panels stained a mahogany colour, but in that dim light they looked black, as if they were hung with funereal trappings.

The man lingered between the door and the first of the windows, while Mrs Park, half-closing her eyes, hurried across to the fireplace with the scuttle. He seemed to be searching for something. Presently he found it.

"There's a hole in one of these panels," he announced.

Mrs Park's heart gave a leap.

"Yes," she stammered. "It's a—a bullet hole. The shot lodged there after—after——"

"Yes," he said, quietly, "I understand." He crossed the room with the chair and set it down at that corner of the hearth which faced the door and the damaged panel. "And that afternoon, over twenty years ago, I was sitting here——"

There was a crash as the scuttle fell from the woman's hands. All her horror and amazement expressed itself in one thin, muffled scream.

"*You* were sitting there! *You*! Gerald Harboys! Gerald Harboys, the murderer!"

He answered quietly: "Gerald Harboys or Stephen Royds—God help me, what does it matter? Murderer or not—only God knows! But I shall learn to-night. Light that fire, woman, and leave me."

She left him, and stumbled blindly back to the little vulgar room behind the kitchen. But a fascination stronger than terror drew her back to the outside of the library door, there trembling to wait and to listen. ...

Harboys, to give him his real name at the last, settled himself on the chair and at first busied himself with the building up of the fire. Then he took a revolver from his coat pocket, and placed it upon the mantelpiece within his reach. This done he looked out across the room with a steady gaze.

The firelight wrought strange patterns among the shadows, but in the swiftly changing measures of this shadow-dance he found nothing of what he sought. Presently he began to speak aloud, quietly but very distinctly, so that the shivering woman outside the door brought her hands to her tightening throat.

"Peter, Peter." The tone was almost wheedling. "Can you hear me? I'm sitting in just the same place that I sat that evening, with my bad leg resting on a stool. Here am I, and here's that damned revolver. Now, Peter, won't you come? They say you're always here—that you can't rest because your best friend shot you. Did I shoot you, Peter? My mind's a blank—a blank! For twenty years I have been trying to remember. I have not known peace day and night for twenty years, Peter. Oh, come and tell me! I want to know—to *know*. There's something wrong, Peter. I couldn't have done it. How could I have shot you, boy?"

He relapsed into silence, his gaze never leaving the space between the door and the first window. After a long minute his voice broke out again, choked and almost tearful.

"Is it because you hate me that you won't show yourself,

Peter? Was I mad? And did I do it after all? Don't hate me, Peter. I've suffered! Have pity! One way or another I want to end this agony to-night. Oh, God, make him merciful to me! Peter, we'd been friends so long. School ... don't you remember Wryvern, and those long talks under the lime-trees in the Close on summer nights? And study teas? And going up to Lords'?"

He babbled on, while kaleidoscopic pictures passed before the eyes of his memory. Cool, dewy morning, and the cricket eleven tumbling out of houses for fielding practice; rows of languid boys in dim classrooms and a scratching of pens; bright sunlight, and white shapes moving on a green sward; crowded touch-lines, and the scrum forming, and goal-posts standing up stark against a grey November sky. In each and all of them he caught a wavering, vanishing glimpse of Peter Marsh.

"Peter!" he cried out again. "Can't you hear me? Won't you come to me? You *do* come back. They all say so. That woman hears you. You—in your scarlet coat, as you came in that evening. I remember ... when I saw you lying there ... the blood scarcely showed. I was sitting here waiting for Muriel. I heard you both come up the drive. Muriel was laughing at something. You were both talking to the groom outside. Then I heard you in the hall, and Muriel ordered tea and went upstairs. And I thought: 'She doesn't come in to see me. I'm nothing to her now I'm crocked. It's all Peter, Peter, Peter. By God!' I said, "I've been blind as well as lame. The things I've seen which they pretended were nothing ... The things I haven't seen, but heard of in whispers and hints.' All in a moment my brain caught fire. 'Damn you!' I said, 'I'll teach you to make a cuckold of a lame man!' Then ... you came in."

The trembling woman outside heard him utter a hoarse cry.

"Peter! Peter! Oh, God, I'm beginning to remember! You stood where you're standing now, touching the handle of the door. That's right! And you said—I remember now—'Give us a peg, Jerry. I'm frozen. There's a devil of an east wind.' Peter! Peter! Don't look like that! I'm remembering ... remembering. Oh, God, have mercy ... have mercy!"

A hoarse scream echoed through the room, a chair reeled over with a crash, and then followed a frenzied shouting.

*"I remembr ... I remember ... damn you! when you turned your back on me ... like that...."*

A shot rang out; then another. Then silence enfolded Nobody's House and its one living inmate, a swooning woman, who clung to the oak balustrade.

It was half an hour later when Mrs Park forced herself into the library. The red glow of the fire was still dancing on the walls and floor. For a moment one ruddy gleam seemed to take a fantastic shape—like the prostrate figure of a man in hunting pink.

Harboys lay crumpled and face downwards across the hearth, the revolver still in his hand, the ugly wound in his temple mercifully hidden. To that end had he remembered.

Where there had been a bullet hole in one of the panels the police next morning found two. They were side by side and scarcely an inch apart.

# The Judge's House

## *from Dracula's Guest*

By *Bram Stoker*

When the time for his examination drew near Malcolm Malcolmson made up his mind to go somewhere to read by himself. He feared the attractions of the seaside, and also he feared completely rural isolation, for of old he knew its charms, and so he determined to find some unpretentious little town where there would be nothing to distract him. He refrained from asking suggestions from any of his friends, for he argued that each would recommend some place of which he had knowledge, and where he had already acquaintances. As Malcolmson wished to avoid friends he had no wish to encumber himself with the attention of friends' friends, and so he determined to look out for a place for himself. He packed a portmanteau with some clothes and all the books he required, and then took ticket for the first name on the local time-table which he did not know.

When at the end of three hours' journey he alighted at Benchurch, he felt satisfied that he had so far obliterated his tracks as to be sure of having a peaceful opportunity of pursuing his studies. He went straight to the one in which the sleepy little place contained, and put up for the night. Benchurch was a market-town, and once in three weeks was crowded to excess, but for the remainder of the twenty-one days it was as attractive as a desert. Malcolmson looked around the day after his arrival to try to find quarters more isolated than even so quiet an inn as "The Good Traveller" afforded. There was only one place which took his fancy, and it certainly satisfied his wildest ideas regarding quiet; in fact, quiet was not the proper word to apply to it—desolation was the only term conveying any suitable idea of its isolation. It was an old rambling, heavy-built house of the Jacobean style, with heavy gables and windows, unusually small, and set higher than was customary in such houses, and was surrounded with a high brick wall massively built. Indeed, on examination, it looked more like a fortified house than an ordinary dwelling. But all these things pleased Malcolmson. "Here," he thought, "is the very spot I have been looking for, and if I can only get opportunity of using it I shall be happy.' His joy was increased when he realised beyond doubt that it was not at present inhabited.

From the post-office he got the name of the agent, who was rarely surprised at the application to rent a part of the old house. Mr Carnford, the local lawyer and agent, was a genial old gentleman, and frankly confessed his delight at anyone being willing to live in the house.

"To tell you the truth," said he, "I should be only too happy, on behalf of the owners, to let anyone have the house rent free for a term of years if only to accustom the people here to see it inhabited. It has been so long empty that some kind of absurd prejudice has grown up about it, and this can be best put down by its occupation—if only," he added with a sly glance at Malcomson, "by a scholar like yourself, who wants its quiet for a time."

Malcolmson thought it needless to ask the agent about the "absurd prejudice"; he knew he would get more information, if he should require it, on that subject from other quarters. He paid his three months' rent, got a receipt, and the name of an old woman who would probably undertake to "do" for him, and came away with the keys in his pocket. He then went to the landlady of the inn, who was a cheerful and most kindly person, and asked her advice as to such stores and provisions as he would be likely to require. She threw up her hands in amazement when he told her where he was going to settle himself.

"Not in the Judge's House!" she said, and grew pale as she spoke. He explained the locality of the house, saying that he did not know its name. When he had finished she answered:

"Aye, sure enough—sure enough the very place! It is the Judge's House sure enough." He asked her to tell him about the place, why so called, and what there was against it. She told him that it was so called locally because it had been many years before—how long she could not say, as she was herself from another part of the country, but she thought it must have been a hundred years or more—the abode of a judge who was held in great terror on account of his harsh sentences and his hostility to prisoners at Assizes. As to what there was against the house itself she could not tell. She had often asked, but no one could inform her; but there was a general feeling that there was *something*, and for her own part she would not take all the money in Drinkwarter's Bank and stay in the house an hour by herself. Then she apologised to Malcolmson for her disturbing talk.

"It is too bad of me, sir, and you—and a young gentleman,

too—if you will pardon me saying it, going to live there all alone. If you were my boy—and you'll excuse me for saying it—you wouldn't sleep there a night, not if I had to go there myself and pull the big alarm bell that's on the roof!" The good creature was so manifestly in earnest, and was so kindly in her intentions, that Malcolmson, although amused, was touched. He told her kindly how much he appreciated her interest in him, and added:

"But, my dear Mrs Witham, indeed you need not be concerned about me! A man who is reading for the Mathematical Tripos has too much to think of to be disturbed by any of these mysterious 'somethings,' and his work is of too exact and prosaic a kind to allow of his having any corner in his mind for mysteries of any kind. Harmonical Progression, Permutations and Combinations, and Elliptic Functions have sufficient mysteries for me!" Mrs Witham kindly undertook to see after his commissions, and he went himself to look for the old woman who had been recommended to him. When he returned to the Judge's House with her, after an interval of a couple of hours, he found Mrs Witham herself waning with several men and boys carrying parcels, and an upholsterer's man with a bed in a cart, for she said, though tables and chairs might be all very well, a bed that hadn't been aired for mayhap fifty years was not proper for young bones to lie on. She was evidently curious to see the inside of the house; and though manifestly so afraid of the 'somethings' that at the slightest sound she clutched on to Malcolmson, whom she never left for a moment, went over the whole place.

After his examination of the house, Malcolmson decided to take up his abode in the great dining-room, which was big enough to serve for all his requirements; and Mrs Witham, with the aid of the charwoman, Mrs Dempster, proceeded to arrange matters. When the hampers were brought in and unpacked, Malcolmson saw that with much kind forethought she had sent from her own kitchen sufficient provisions to last for a few days. Before going she expressed all sorts of kind wishes; and at the door turned and said:

"And perhaps, air, as the room is big and draughty it might be well to have one of those big screens put round your bed at night—tough, truth to tell, I would die myself if I were to be so shut in with all kinds of—of 'things,' that put their heads round the sides, or over the top, and look on me!" The image which she had called up was too much for her nerves, and she fled incontinently.

Mrs Dempster sniffed in a superior manner as the landlady disappeared, and remarked that for her own part she wasn't afraid of all the bogies in the kingdom.

"I'll tell you what it is, sir," she said; "bogies is all kinds and sorts of things—except bogies! Rats and mice, and beetles; and creaky doors, and loose slates, and broken panes, and stiff drawer handles, that stay out when you pull them and then fall down in the middle of the night. Look at the wainscot of the room! It is old—hundreds of years old! Do you think there's no rats and beetles there! And do you imagine, sir, that you won't see none of them! Rats is bogies, I tell you and bogies is rats; and don't you get to think anything else!"

"Mrs Dempster," said Malcolmson gravely, making her a polite bow, "you know more than a Senior Wrangler! And let me say, that, as a mark of esteem for your indubitable soundness of head and heart, I shall, when I go, give you possession of this house, and let you stay here by yourself for the last two months of my tenancy, for four weeks will serve my purpose."

"Thank you kindly, sir!" she answered, "but I couldn't sleep away from home a night. I am in Greenhow's Charity, and if I slept a night away from my rooms I should lose all I have got to live on. The rules is very strict; and there's too many watching for a vacancy for me to run any risks in the matter. Only for that, sir, I'd gladly come here and attend on you altogether during your stay."

"My good woman," said Malcolmson hastily, "I have come here on purpose to obtain solitude; and believe me that I am grateful to the late Greenhow for having so organised his admirable charity—whatever it is—that I am perforce denied the opportunity of suffering from such a form of temptation! Saint Anthony himself could not be more rigid on the point!"

The old woman laughed harshly. "Ah, you young gentlemen," she said, "you don't fear for naught; and belike you'll get all the solitude you want here." She set to work with her cleaning; and by nightfall, when Malcolmson returned from his walk—he always had one of his books to study as he walked—he found the room swept and tidied, a fire burning in the old hearth, the lamp lit, and the table spread for supper with Mrs Witham's excellent fare. "This is comfort, indeed," he said, as he rubbed his hands.

When he had finished his supper, and lifted the tray to the other end of the great oak dining-table, he got out his books again, put fresh wood on the fire, trimmed his lamp, and set himself down to a spell of real hard work. He went on without pause till about eleven o'clock, when he knocked off for a bit to fix his fire and lamp, and to make himself a cup of tea. He had always been a tea-drinker, and during his college life had sat late at work and had taken tea late. The rest was a great luxury to him, and he enjoyed it with a sense of delicious, voluptuous ease. The renewed fire leaped and sparkled, and threw quaint shadows through the great old room; and as he sipped his hot tea he revelled in the sense of isolation from his kind. Then it was that he began to notice for the first time what a noise the rats were making.

"Surely," he thought, "they cannot have been at it all the time I was reading. Had they been, I must have noticed it!" Presently, when the noise increased, he satisfied himself that it was really new. It was evident that at first the rats had been frightened at the presence of a stranger, and the light of fire and lamp; but that as the time went on they had grown bolder and were now disporting themselves as was their wont.

How busy they were! And hark to the strange noises! Up and down behind the old wainscot, over the ceiling and under the floor they raced, and gnawed, and scratched! Malcolmson smiled to himself as he recalled to mind the saying of Mrs Dempster, "Bogies is rats, and rats is bogies!" The tea began to have its effect of intellectual and nervous stimulus, he saw with joy another long spell of work to be done before the night was past, and in the sense of security which it gave him, he allowed himself the luxury of a good look round the room. He took his lamp in one hand, and went all around, wondering that so quaint and beautiful an old house had been so long neglected. The carving of the oak on the panels of the wainscot was fine, and on and round the doors and windows it was beautiful and of rare merit. There were some old pictures on the walls, but they were coated so thick with dust and dirt that he could not distinguish any detail of them, though he held his lamp as high as he could over his head. Here and there as he went round he saw some crack or hole blocked for a moment by the face of a rat with its bright eyes glittering in the light, but in an instant it was gone, and a squeak and a scamper followed.

The thing that most struck him, however, was the rope of the great alarm bell on the roof, which hung down in a corner of the room on the right-hand side of the fireplace. He pulled up close to the hearth a great high-backed carved oak chair, and sat down to his last cup of tea. When this was done he made up the fire, and went back to his work, sitting at the corner of the table, having the fire to his left. For a while the rats disturbed him somewhat with their perpetual scampering, but he got accustomed to the noise as one does to the ticking of a clock or to the roar of moving water; and he became so immersed in his work that everything in the world, except the problem which he was trying to solve, passed away from him.

He suddenly looked up, his problem was still unsolved and there was in the air that sense of the hour before the dawn, which is so dread to doubtful life. The noise of the rats had ceased. Indeed it seemed to him that it must have ceased but lately and that it was the sudden cessation which had disturbed him. The fire had fallen low, but still it threw out a deep red glow. As he looked he started in spite of his *sang froid*.

There on the great high-backed carved oak chair by the right side of the fireplace sat an enormous rat, steadily glaring at him with baleful eyes. He made a motion to it as though to hunt its away, but it did not stir. Then he made the motion of throwing something. Still it did not stir, but showed its great white teeth angrily, and its cruel eyes shone in the lamplight with an added vindictiveness.

Malcolmson felt amazed, and seizing the poker from the hearth ran at it to kill it. Before, however, he could strike it, the rat, with a squeak that sounded like the concentration of hate, jumped upon the floor, and, running up the rope of the alarm bell, disappeared in the darkness beyond the range of the green-shaded lamp. Instantly, strange to say, the noisy scampering of the rats in the wainscot began again.

By this time Malcolmson's mind was quite off the problem; and as a shrill cock-crow outside told him of the approach of morning, he went to bed and to sleep.

He slept so sound that he was not even waked by Mrs Dempster coming in to make up his room. It was only when she had tidied up the place and got his breakfast ready and tapped on the screen which closed in his bed that he woke. He was a little tired still after his night's hard work, but a strong cup of tea soon freshened him up, and, taking his book, he went out for his morning walk, bringing with him a few sandwiches lest he should not care to return till dinner time. He found a quiet walk between high elms some way outside the town, and here he spent the greater part of the day studying his Laplace. On his return he looked in to see Mrs Witham and to thank her for her kindness. When she saw him coming through the diamond-paned bay-window of her sanctum she came out to meet him and asked him in. She looked at him searchingly and shook her head as she said:

"You must not overdo it, sir. You are paler this morning than you should be. Too late hours and too hard work on the brain isn't good for any man! But tell me, sir, how did you pass the night? Well, I hope? But, my heart! sir, I was glad when Mrs Dempster told me this morning that you were all right and sleeping sound when she went in."

"Oh, I was all right," he answered, smiling, "the 'somethings' didn't worry me, as yet. Only the rats; and they had a circus, I tell you, all over the place. There was one wicked looking old devil that sat up on my own chair by the fire, and wouldn't go till I took the poker to him, and then he ran up the rope of the alarm bell and got to somewhere up the wall or the ceiling—I couldn't see where, it was so dark."

"Mercy on us," said Mrs Witham, "an old devil, and sitting

on a chair by the fireside! Take care, sir! Take care! There's many a true word spoken in jest."

"How do you mean? 'Pon my word I don't understand."

"An old devil! The old devil, perhaps. There! sir, you needn't laugh," for Malcolmson had broken into a hearty peal. "You young folks thinks it easy to laugh at things that makes older ones shudder. Never mind, sir,! Never mind! Please God, you'll laugh all the time. It's what I wish you myself!" and the good lady beamed all over in sympathy with his enjoyment, her fears gone for a moment.

"Oh, forgive me!" said Malcolmson presently. "Don't think me rude; but the idea was too much for me—that the old devil himself was on the chair last night!" And at the thought he laughed again. Then he went home to dinner.

This evening the scampering of the rats began earlier; indeed it had been going on before his arrival, and only ceased whilst his presence by its freshness disturbed them. After dinner he sat by the fire for a while and had a smoke; and then, having cleared his table, began to work as before. To-night the rats disturbed him more than they had done on the previous night. How they scampered up and down and under and over! How they squeaked, and scratched, and gnawed! How they, getting bolder by degrees, came to the mouths of their holes and to the chinks and cracks and crannies in the wainscoting till their eyes shone like tiny lamps as the firelight rose and fell. But to him, now doubtless accustomed to them, their eyes were not wicked; only their playfulness touched him. Sometimes the boldest of them made sallies out on the floor or along the mouldings of the wainscot. Now and again as they disturbed him Malcolmson made a sound to frighten them, smiting the table with his hand or giving a fierce "Hsh, hsh," so that they fled straightway to their holes.

And so the early part of the night wore on; and despite the noise Malcolmson got more and more immersed in his work.

All at once he stopped, as on the previous night, being overcome by a sudden sense of silence. There was not the faintest sound of gnaw, or scratch, or squeak. The silence was as of the grave. He remembered the odd occurrence of the previous night, and instinctively he looked at the chair standing close by the fireside. And then a very odd sensation thrilled through him.

There, on the great old high-backed carved oak chair beside the fireplace sat the same enormous rat, steadily glaring at him with baleful eyes.

Instinctively he took the nearest thing to his hand, a book of logarithms, and flung it at it. The book was badly aimed and the rat did not stir, so again the poker performance of the previous night was repeated; and again the rat, being closely pursued, fled up the rope of the alarm bell. Strangely too, the departure of this rat was instantly followed by the renewal of the noise made by the general rat community. On this occasion, as on the previous one, Malcolmson could not see at what part of the room the rat disappeared, for the green shade of his lamp left the upper part of the room in darkness, and the fire had burned low.

On looking at his watch he found it was close on midnight; and, not sorry for the *divertissement*, he made up his fire and made himself his nightly pot of tea. He had got through a good spell of work, and thought himself entitled to a cigarette; and so he sat on the great carved oak chair before the fire and enjoyed it. Whilst smoking he began to think that he would like to know where the rat disappeared to, for he had certain ideas of the morrow not entirely disconnected with a rat-trap. Accordingly he lit another lamp and placed it so that it would shine well into the right-hand corner of the wall by the fireplace. Then he got all the books he had with him, and placed them handy to throw at the vermin. Finally he lifted the rope of the alarm bell and placed the end of it on the table, fixing the extreme end under the lamp. As he handled it he could not help noticing how pliable it was, especially for so strong a rope, and one not in use. "You could hang a man with it," he thought to himself. When his preparations were made he looked around, and said complacently:

"There now, my friend, I think we shall learn something of you this time!" He began his work again, and though as before somewhat disturbed at first by the noise of the rats, soon lost himself in his propositions and problems.

Again, he was called to his immediate surroundings suddenly. This time it might not have been the sudden silence only which took his attention; there was a slight movement of the rope, and the lamp moved. Without stirring, he looked to see if his pile of books was within range, and then cast his eye along the rope. As he looked he saw the great rat drop from the rope on the oak armchair and sit there glaring at him. He raised a book in his right hand, and taking careful aim, flung it at the rat. The latter, with a quick movement, sprang aside and dodged the missile. He then took another book, and a third, and flung them one after another at the rat, but each time unsuccessfully. At last, as he stood with a book poised in his hand to throw, the rat squeaked and seemed afraid. This made Malcolmson more than ever eager to strike, and the book flew and struck the rat a resounding blow. It gave a terrified squeak, and turning on its pursuer a look of terrible malevolence, ran up the chair-back and made a great jump to the rope of the alarm bell and ran up it like lightning. The lamp rocked under the sudden strain, but it was a heavy one and did not topple over. Malcolmson kept his eyes on the rat, and saw it by the light of the second lamp leap to a moulding of the wainscot and disappear through a hole in one of the great pictures which hung on the wall, obscured and invisible through its coating of dirt and dust.

"I shall look up my friends' habitation in the morning," said the student, as he went over to collect his books. "The third picture from the fireplace; I shall not forget." He picked up the books one by one, commenting on them as he lifted them. "*Conic Sections* he does not mind, nor *Cycloidal Oscillations,* nor the *Principia,* nor *Quaternions*, nor *Thermodynamics*. Now for the book that fetched him!" Malcolmson took it up and looked at it. As he did so he started, and a sudden pallor overspread his face. He looked round uneasily and shivered slightly, as he murmured to himself:

"The Bible my mother gave me! What an odd coincidence." He sat down to work again, and the rats in the wainscot renewed their gambols. They did not disturb him, however; somehow their presence gave him a sense of companionship. But he could not attend to his work, and after striving to master the subject on which he was engaged gave it up in despair, and went to bed as the first streak of dawn stole in through the eastern window.

He slept heavily but uneasily, and dreamed much; and when Mrs Dempster woke him late in the morning he seemed ill at ease, and for a few minutes did not seem to realise exactly where he was. His first request rather surprised the servant.

"Mrs Dempster, when I am out to-day I wish you would get the steps and dust or wash those pictures—especially that one the third from the fireplace—I want to see what they are."

Late in the afternoon Malcolmson worked at his books in the shaded walk, and the cheerfulness of the previous day came back to him as the day wore on, and he found that his reading was progressing well. He had worked out to a satisfactory conclusion all the problems which had as yet baffled him, and it was in a state of jubilation that he paid a visit to Mrs Witham at "The Good Traveller." He found a stranger in the cosy sitting-room with the landlady, who was introduced to him as Dr Thornhill. She was not quite at ease, and this, combined with the Doctor's plunging at once into a series of questions, made Malcolmson come to the conclusion that his presence was not an accident, so without preliminary he said:

"Dr Thornhill, I shall with pleasure answer you any question you may choose to ask me if you will answer me one question first."

The Doctor seemed surprised, but he smiled and answered at once. "Done! What is it?"

"Did Mrs Witham ask you to come here and see me and advise me?"

Dr Thornhill for a moment was taken aback, and Mrs Witham got fiery red and turned away; but the doctor was a frank and ready man, and he answered at once and openly:

"She did: but she didn't intend you to know it. I suppose it was my clumsy haste that made you suspect. She told me that she did not like the idea of your being in that house all by yourself, and that she thought you took too much strong tea. In fact, she wants me to advise you if possible to give up the tea and the very late hours. I was a keen student in my time, so I suppose I may take the liberty of a college man, and without offence, advise you not quite as a stranger."

Malcolmson with a bright smile held out his hand. "Shake! as they say in America," he said. "I must thank you for your kindness and Mrs Witham too, and your kindness deserves a return on my part. I promise to take no more strong tea—no tea at all till you let me—and I shall go to bed to-night at one o'clock at latest. Will that do?"

"Capital," said the Doctor. "Now tell us all that you noticed in the old house," and so Malcolmson then and there told in minute detail all that had happened in the last two nights. He was interrupted every now and then by some exclamation from Mrs Witham, till finally when he told of the episode of the Bible the landlady's pent-up emotions found vent in a shriek; and it was not till a stiff glass of brandy and water had been administered that she grew composed again. Dr Thornhill listened with a face of growing gravity, and when the narrative was complete and Mrs Witham had been restored he asked:

"The rat always went up the rope of the alarm bell?"

"Always."

"I suppose you know," said the Doctor after a pause, "what the rope is?"

"No!"

"It is," said the Doctor slowly, "the very rope which the hangman used for all the victims of the Judge's judicial rancour!" Here he was interrupted by another scream from Mrs Witham, and steps had to be taken for her recovery. Malcolmson having looked at his watch, and found that it was close to his dinner hour, had gone home before her complete recovery.

When Mrs Witham was herself again she almost assailed the Doctor with angry questions as to what he meant by putting such horrible ideas into the poor young man's mind. "He has quite enough there already to upset him," she added. Dr Thornhill replied:

"My dear madam, I had a distinct purpose in it! I wanted to draw his attention to the bell rope, and to fix it there. It may be that he is in a highly overwrought state, and has been studying too much, although I am bound to say that he seems as sound and healthy a young man, mentally and bodily, as ever I saw—but then the rats—and that suggestion of the devil." The doctor shook his head and went on. "I would have offered to go and stay the first night with him but that I felt sure it would have been a cause of offence. He may get in the night some strange fright or hallucination; and if he does I want him to pull that rope. All alone as he is it will give us warning, and we may reach him in time to be of service. I shall be sitting up pretty late to-night and shall keep my ears open. Do not be alarmed if Benchurch gets a surprise before morning."

"Oh, Doctor, what do you mean? What do you mean?"

"I mean this; that possibly—nay, more probably—we shall hear the great alarm bell from the Judge's House to-night," and the Doctor made about as effective an exit as could be thought of.

When Malcolmson arrived home he found that it was a little after his usual time, and Mrs Dempster had gone away—the rule of Greenhow's Charity were not to be neglected. He was glad to see that the place was bright and tidy with a cheerful fire and a well-trimmed lamp. The evening was colder than might have been expected in April, and a heavy wind was blowing with such rapidly-increasing strength that there was every promise of a storm during the night. For a few minutes after his entrance the noise of the rats ceased; but so soon as they became accustomed to his presence they began again. He was glad to hear them, for he felt once more the feeling of companionship in their noise, and his mind ran back to the strange fact that they only ceased to manifest themselves when that other—the great rat with the baleful eyes—came upon the scene. The reading-lamp only was lit and its green shade kept the ceiling and the upper part of the room in darkness, so that the cheerful light from the hearth spreading over the floor and shining on the white cloth laid over the end of the table was warm and cheery. Malcolmson sat down to his dinner with a good appetite and a buoyant spirit. After his dinner and a cigarette he sat steadily down to work, determined not to let anything disturb him, for he remembered his promise to the doctor, and made up his mind to make the best of the time at his disposal.

For an hour or so he worked all right, and then his thoughts began to wander from his books. The actual circumstances around him, the calls on his physical attention, and his nervous susceptibility were not to be denied. By this time the wind had become a gale, and the gale a storm. The old house, solid though it was, seemed to shake to its foundations, and the storm roared and raged through its many chimneys and its queer old gables, producing strange, unearthly sounds in the empty rooms and corridors. Even the great alarm bell on the roof must have felt the force of the wind, for the rope rose and fell slightly, as though the bell were moved a little from time to time, and the limber rope fell on the oak floor with a hard and hollow sound.

As Malcolmson listened to it he bethought himself of the doctor's words, "It is the rope which the hangman used for the victims of the Judge's judicial rancour," and he went over to the corner of the fireplace and took it in his hand to look at it. There seemed a sort of deadly interest in it, and as he stood there he lost himself for a moment in speculation as to who these victims were, and the grim wish of the Judge to have such a ghastly relic ever under his eyes. As he stood there the swaying of the bell on the roof still lifted the rope now and again; but presently there came a new sensation—a sort of tremor in the rope, as though something was moving along it.

Looking up instinctively Malcolmson saw the great rat coming slowly down towards him, glaring at him steadily. He dropped the rope and started back with a muttered curse, and the rat turning ran up the rope again and disappeared, and at the same instant Malcolmson became conscious that the noise of the rats, which had ceased for a while, began again.

All this set him thinking, and it occurred to him that he had not investigated the lair of the rat or looked at the pictures, as he had intended. He lit the other lamp without the shade, and, holding it up, went and stood opposite the third picture from the fireplace on the right-hand side where he had seen the rat disappear on the previous night.

At the first glance he started back so suddenly that he almost dropped the lamp, and a deadly pallor overspread his face. His knees shook, and heavy drops of sweat came on his forehead, and he trembled like an aspen. But he was young and plucky, and pulled himself together, and after the pause of a few seconds stepped forward again, raised the lamp, and examined the picture which had been dusted and washed, and now stood out clearly.

It was of a judge dressed in his robes of scarlet and ermine. His face was strong and merciless, evil, crafty, and vindictive, with a sensual mouth, hooked nose of ruddy colour, and shaped like the beak of a bird of prey. The rest of the face was of a cadaverous colour. The eyes were of peculiar brilliance and with a terribly malignant expression. As he looked at them, Malcolmson grew cold, for he saw there the very counterpart of the eyes of the great rat. The lamp almost fell from his hand, he saw the rat with its baleful eyes peering out through the hole in the corner of the picture, and noted the sudden cessation of the noise of the other rats. However, he pulled himself together, and went on with his examination of the picture.

The Judge was seated in a great high-backed carved oak chair, on the right-hand side of a great stone fireplace where, in the corner, a rope hung down from the ceiling, its end lying coiled on the floor. With a feeling of something like horror, Malcolmson recognised the scene of the room as it stood, and gazed around him in an awe-struck manner as though he expected to find some strange presence behind him. Then he looked over to the corner of the fireplace—and with a loud cry he let the lamp fall from his hand.

There, in the Judge's arm-chair, with the rope hanging behind, sat the rat with the Judge's baleful eyes, now intensified and with a fiendish leer. Save for the howling of the storm without there was silence.

The fallen lamp recalled Malcolmson to himself. Fortunately it was of metal, and so the oil was not spilt. However, the practical need of attending to it settled at once his nervous apprehensions. When he had turned it out, he wiped his brow and thought for a moment.

"This will not do," he said to himself. "If I go on like this I shall become a crazy fool. This must stop! I promised the Doctor I would not take tea. Faith, he was pretty right! My nerves must have been getting into a queer state. Funny I did not notice it. I never felt better in my life. However, it is all right now, and I shall not be such a fool again."

Then he mixed himself a good stiff glass of brandy and water and resolutely sat down to his work.

It was nearly an hour when he looked up from his book, disturbed by the sudden stillness. Without, the wind howled and roared louder than ever, and the rain drove in sheets against the windows, beating like hail on the glass; but within there was no sound whatever save the echo of the wind as it roared in the great chimney, and now and then a hiss as a few raindrops found their way down the chimney in a lull of the storm. The fire had fallen low and had ceased to flame, though it threw out a red glow. Malcolmson listened attentively, and presently heard a thin, squeaking noise, very faint. It came from the corner of the room where the rope hung down, and he thought it was the creaking of the rope on the floor as the swaying of the bell raised and lowered it. Looking up, however, he saw in the dim light the great rat clinging to the rope and gnawing it. The rope was already nearly gnawed through—he could see the lighter colour where the strands were laid bare. As he looked the job was completed, and the severed end of the rope fell clattering on the oaken floor, whilst for an instant the great rat remained like a knob or tassel at the end of the rope, which now began to sway to and fro. Malcolmson felt for a moment another pang of terror as he thought that now the possibility of calling the outer world to his assistance was cut off, but an intense anger took its place, and seizing the book he was reading he hurled it at the rat. The blow was well aimed, but before the missile could reach it the rat dropped off and struck the floor with a soft thud. Malcolmson instantly rushed over towards it, but it darted away and disappeared in the darkness of the shadows of the room. Malcolmson felt that his work was over for the night, and determined then and there to vary the monotony of the proceedings by a hunt for the rat, and took off the green shade of the lamp so as to insure a wider spreading light. As he did so the gloom of the upper part of the room was relieved, and in the new flood of light, great by comparison with the previous darkness, the pictures on the wall stood out boldly. From where he stood, Malcolmson saw right opposite to him the third picture on the wall from the right of the fireplace. He rubbed his eyes in surprise, and then a great fear began to come upon him.

In the centre of the picture was a great irregular patch of brown canvas, as fresh as when it was stretched on the frame. The background was as before, with chair and chimney-corner and rope, but the figure of the Judge had disappeared.

Malcolmson, almost in a chill of horror, turned slowly round, and then he began to shake and tremble like a man in a palsy. His strength seemed to have left him, and he was incapable of action or movement, hardly even of thought. He could only see and hear.

There, on the great high-backed carved oak chair sat the Judge in his robes of scarlet and ermine, with his baleful eyes glaring vindictively, and a smile of triumph on the resolute, cruel mouth, as he lifted with his hands a *black cap*. Malcolmson felt as if the blood was running from his heart, as one does in moments of prolonged suspense. There was a singing in his ears. Without, he could hear the roar and howl of the tempest, and through it, swept on the storm, came the striking of midnight by the great chimes in the marketplace. He stood for a space of time that seemed to him endless, still as a statue and with wide-open, horror-struck eyes, breathless. As the clock struck, so the smile of triumph on the Judge's face intensified, and at the last stroke of midnight he placed the black cap on his head.

Slowly and deliberately the Judge rose from his chair and picked up the piece of the rope of the alarm bell which lay on the floor, drew it through his hands as if he enjoyed its touch, and then deliberately began to knot one end of it, fashioning it into a noose. This he tightened and tested with his foot, pulling hard at it till he was satisfied and then making a running noose of it, which he held in his hand. Then he began to move along the table on the opposite side to Malcolmson, keeping his eyes on him until he had passed him, when with a quick movement he stood in front of the door. Malcolmson then began to feel that he was trapped, and tried to think of what he should do. There was some fascination in the Judge's eyes, which he never took off him, and he had, perforce, to look. He saw the Judge approach—still keeping between him and the door—and raise the noose and throw it towards him as if to entangle him. With a great effort he made a quick movement to one side, and saw the rope fall beside him, and heard it strike the oaken floor. Again the Judge raised the noose and tried to ensnare him, ever keeping his baleful eyes fixed on him, and each time by a mighty effort the student just managed to evade it. So this went on for many times, the Judge seeming never discouraged nor discomposed at failure, but playing as a cat does with a mouse. At last in despair, which had reached its climax, Malcolmson cast a quick glance round him. The lamp seemed to have blazed up, and there was a fairly good light in the room. At the many rat-holes and in the chinks and crannies of the wainscot he saw the rats' eyes; and this aspect, that was purely physical, gave him a gleam of comfort. He looked around and saw that the rope of the great alarm bell was laden with rats. Every inch of it was covered with them, and more and more were pouring through the small circular hole in the ceiling whence it emerged, so that with their weight the bell was beginning to sway.

Hark! it had swayed till the clapper had touched the bell. The sound was but a tiny one but the bell was only beginning to sway, and it would increase.

At the sound the Judge, who had been keeping his eyes fixed on Malcolmson, looked up, and a scowl of diabolical anger overspread his face. His eyes fairly glowed like hot coals, and he stamped his foot with a sound that seemed to make the house shake. A dreadful peal of thunder broke overhead as he raised the rope again, whilst the rats kept running up and down the rope as though working against time. This time, instead of throwing it, he drew close to his victim, and held open the noose as he approached. As he came closer there seemed something paralysing in his very presence, and Malcolmson stood rigid as a corpse. He felt the Judge's icy fingers touch his throat as he adjusted the rope. The noose tightened—tightened. Then the Judge, taking the rigid form of the student in his arms, carried him over and placed him standing in the oak chair, and stepping up beside him, put his hand up and caught the end of the swaying rope of the alarm bell. As he raised his hand the rats fled squeaking, and disappeared through the hole in the ceiling. Taking the end of the noose which was round Malcolmson's neck he tied it to the hanging bell-rope, and then descending pulled away the chair.

When the alarm bell of the Judge's House began to sound a crowd soon assembled. Lights and torches of various kinds appeared, and soon a silent crowd was hurrying to the spot. They knocked loudly at the door, but there was no reply. Then they burst in the door, and poured into the great dining-room, the doctor at the head.

There at the end of the rope of the great alarm bell hung the body of the student, and on the face of the Judge in the picture was a malignant smile.

# In the Crowd at the Station

By *Ruskin Bond*

In the crowd at the station,
A tall man turned and smiled at me.
Although I couldn't be quite sure,
I felt I'd seen his face before.

Two days later, I saw him again,
Getting off the Agra train.
He smiled once more, and this time
I returned the compliment,
Before he was lost in the crowd.

And *then* I remembered.
Of course!
This was one of the dead men
We'd had for dissection.
I'd been Demonstrator then.
I remember saying:
"Here's a fine-looking corpse."

And then we peeled his skin away,
And cut him up, a little every day.

Now I don't go near the Agra train.
I wonder:
Will he smile when I see him again?

# The Decoy

By *Algernon Blackwood*

It belonged to the category of unlovely houses about which an ugly superstition clings, one reason being, perhaps, its inability to inspire interest in itself without assistance. It seemed too ordinary to possess individuality, much less to exert an influence. Solid and ungainly, its huge bulk dwarfing the park timber, its best claim to notice was a negative one—it was unpretentious.

From the little hill its expressionless windows stared across the Kentish Weald, indifferent to weather, dreary in winter, bleak in spring, unblessed in summer. Some colossal hand had tossed it down, then let it starve to death, a country mansion that might well strain the adjectives of advertisers and find inheritors with difficulty. Its soul had fled, said some; it had committed suicide, thought others; and it was an inheritor, before he killed himself in the library, who thought this latter, yielding, apparently, to a hereditary taint in the family. For two other inheritors followed suit, with an interval of twenty years between them, and there was no clear reason to explain the three disasters. Only the first owner, indeed, lived permanently in the house, the others using it in the summer months and then deserting it with relief. Hence, when John Burley, present inheritor, assumed possession, he entered a house about which clung an ugly superstition, based, nevertheless, upon a series of undeniably ugly facts.

This century deals harshly with superstitious folk, deeming them fools or charlatans; but John Burley, robust, contemptuous of half lights, did not deal harshly with them, because he did not deal with them at all. He was hardly aware of their existence. He ignored them as he ignored, say, the Esquimaux, poets, and other human aspects that did not touch his scheme of life. A successful business man, he concentrated on what was real; he dealt with business people. His philanthropy, on a big scale, was also real; yet, though he would have denied it vehemently, he had his superstition as well. No man exists without some taint of superstition in his blood; the racial heritage is too rich to be escaped entirely. Burley's took this form—that unless he gave his tithe to the poor he would not prosper. This ugly mansion, he decided, would make an ideal Convalescent Home.

'Only cowards or lunatics kill themselves,' he declared flatly, when his use of the house was criticised. 'I'm neither one nor t'other.' He let out his gusty, boisterous laugh. In his invigorating atmosphere such weakness seemed contemptible, just as superstition in his presence seemed feeblest ignorance. Even its picturesqueness faded. 'I can't conceive,' he boomed, 'can't even imagine to myself,' he added emphatically, 'the state of mind in which a man can *think* of suicide, much less do it.' He threw his chest out with a challenging air. 'I tell you, Nancy, it's either cowardice or mania. And I've no use for either.'

Yet he was easy-going and good-humoured in his denunciation. He admitted his limitations with a hearty laugh his wife called noisy. Thus he made allowances for the fairy fears of sailorfolk,

a. d had even been known to mention haunted ships his Companies owned. But he did so in the terms of tonnage and £ s.d. His scope was big; details were made for clerks.

His consent to pass a night in the mansion was the consent of a practical businessman and philanthropist who dealt condescendingly with foolish human nature. It was based on the commonsense of tonnage and £ s.d. The local newspapers had revived the silly story of the suicides, calling attention to the effect of the superstition upon the fortunes of the house, and so, possibly, upon the fortunes of its present owner. But the mansion, otherwise a white elephant, was precisely ideal for his purpose, and so trivial a matter as spending a night in it should not stand in the way. 'We must take people as we find them, Nancy.'

His young wife had her motive, of course, in making the proposal, and, if she was amused by what she called 'spook-hunting', he saw no reason to refuse her the indulgence. He loved her, and took her as he found her—late in life. To allay the superstitions of prospective staff and patients and supporters, all, in fact, whose goodwill was necessary to success, he faced this boredom of a night in the building before its opening was announced. "You see, John, if you, the owner, do this, it will nip damaging talk in the bud. If anything went wrong later it would only be put down to this suicide idea, this haunting influence. The Home will have a bad name from the start. There'll be endless trouble. It will be a failure.'

'You think my spending a night there will stop the nonsense?' he enquired.

'According to the old legend it breaks the spell,' she replied. 'That's the condition, anyhow.'

'But somebody's sure to die there sooner or later,' he objected. 'We can't prevent that.'

'We can prevent people whispering that they died unnaturally.' She explained the working of the public mind.

'I see,' he replied, his lip curling, yet quick to gauge the truth of what she told him about collective instinct.

'Unless *you* take poison in the hall,' she added laughingly, 'or elect to hang yourself with your braces from the hat peg.'

'I'll do it,' he agreed, after a moment's thought. 'I'll sit up with you. It will be like a honeymoon over again, you and I on the spree—eh?' He was even interested now; the boyish side of him was touched perhaps; but his enthusiasm was less when she explained that three was a better number than two on such an expedition.

'I've often done it before, John. We were always three.'

'Who?' he asked bluntly. He looked wonderingly at her, but she answered that if anything went wrong a party of three provided a better margin for help. It was sufficiently obvious. He listened and agreed. 'I'll get young Mortimer,' he suggested. 'Will he do?'

She hesitated. 'Well—he's cheery; he'll be interested, too. Yes, he's as good as another.' She seemed indifferent.

'And he'll make the time pass with his stories,' added her husband.

So Captain Mortimer, late officer on a T.B.D., a 'cheery lad', afraid of nothing, cousin of Mrs Burley, and now filling a good post in the company's London offices, was engaged as third hand in the expedition. But Captain Mortimer was young and ardent, and Mrs Burley was young and pretty and ill-mated, and John Burley was a neglectful and self-satisfied husband.

Fate laid the trap with cunning, and John Burley, blind-eyed, careless of detail, floundered into it. He also floundered out again, though in a fashion none could have expected of him.

The night agreed upon eventually was as near to the shortest in the year as John Burley could contrive—June 18th—when the sun set at 8.18 and rose about a quarter to four. There would be barely three hours of true darkness. 'You're the expert,' he admitted, as she explained that sitting through the actual darkness only was required, not necessarily from sunset to sunrise. 'We'll do the thing properly. Mortimer's not very keen, he had a dance or something,' he added, noticing the look of annoyance that flashed swiftly in her eyes; 'but he got out of it. He's coming.' The pouting expression of the spoilt woman amused him. 'Oh, no, he didn't need much persuading really,' he assured her. 'Some girl or other, of course. He's young, remember.' To which no comment was forthcoming, though the implied comparison made her flush.

They motored from South Audley Street after an early tea, in due course passing Sevenoaks and entering the Kentish Weald; and, in order that the necessary advertisement should be given, the chauffeur, warned strictly to keep their purpose quiet, was to put up at the country inn and fetch them an hour after sunrise; they would breakfast in London. 'He'll tell everybody,' said his practical and cynical master; 'the local newspaper will have it all next day. A few hours' discomfort is worthwhile if it ends the nonsense. We'll read and smoke, and Mortimer shall tell us yarns about the sea.' He went with the driver into the house to superintend the arrangement of the room, the lights, the hampers of food, and so forth, leaving the pair upon the lawn.

'Four hours isn't much, but it's something,' whispered Mortimer, alone with her for the first time since they started. 'It's simply ripping of you to have got me in. You look divine to-night. You're the most wonderful woman in the world.' His blue eyes shone with the hungry desire he mistook for love. He looked as if he had blown in from the sea, for his skin was tanned and his light hair bleached a little by the sun. He took her hand, drawing her out of the slanting sunlight towards the rhododendrons.

'I didn't, you silly boy. It was John suggested your coming.' She released her hand with an affected effort. 'Besides, you overdid it—pretending you had a dance.'

'You could have objected,' he said eagerly, 'and didn't. Oh, you're too lovely, you're delicious!' He kissed her suddenly with passion. There was a tiny struggle, in which she yielded too easily, he thought.

'Harry, you're an idiot!' she cried breathlessly, when he let her go. 'I really don't know how you dare! And John's your friend. Besides, you know'—she glanced round quickly— 'it isn't safe here.' Her eyes shone happily, her cheeks were flaming. She looked what she was, a pretty, young, lustful animal, false to ideals, true to selfish passion only. 'Luckily,' she added, 'he trusts me too fully to think anything.'

The young man, worship in his eyes, laughed gaily. 'There's no harm in a kiss,' he said. 'You're a child to him, he never thinks of you as a woman. Anyhow, his head's full of ships and kings and scaling-wax,' he comforted her, while respecting her sudden instinct which warned him not to touch her again, 'and he never sees anything. Why, even at ten yards——'

From twenty yards away a big voice interrupted him, as John Burley came round a corner of the house and across the lawn towards them. The chauffeur, he announced, had left the hampers in the room on the first floor and gone back to the inn. 'Let's take a walk round,' he added, joining them, 'and see the garden. Five minutes before sunset we'll go in and feed.' He laughed. 'We must do the thing faithfully, you know, mustn't we, Nancy? Dark to dark, remember. Come on, Mortimer'—he took the young man's arm—'a last look round before we go in and hang ourselves from adjoining hooks in the matron's room!' He reached out his free hand towards his wife.

'Oh, hush, John!' she said quickly. 'I don't like—especially now the dusk is coming.' She shivered, as though it were a genuine little shiver, pursing her lips deliciously as she did so; whereupon he drew her forcibly to him, saying he was sorry, and kissed her exactly where she had been kissed two minutes before, while young Mortimer looked on. 'We'll take care of you between us,' he said. Behind a broad back the pair exchanged a swift but meaning glance, for there was that in his tone which enjoined wariness, and perhaps after all he was not so blind as he appeared. They had their code, these two. 'All's well,' was signalled; 'but another time be more careful!'

There still remained some minutes' sunlight before the huge red ball of fire would sink behind the wooded hills, and the trio, talking idly, a flutter of excitement to two hearts certainly, walked among the roses. It was a perfect evening, windless, perfumed, warm. Headless shadows preceded them gigantically across the lawn as they moved, and one side of the great building lay already dark; bats were flitting, moths darted to and fro above the azalea and rhododendron clumps. The talk turned chiefly on the uses of the mansion as a Convalescent Home, its probable running cost, suitable staff, and so forth.

'Come along,' John Burley said presently, breaking off and turning abruptly, 'we must be inside, actually inside, before the sun's gone. We must fulfil the conditions faithfully,' he repeated as though fond of the phrase. He was in earnest over everything in life, big or little, once he set his hand to it.

They entered, this incongruous trio of ghost-hunters, no one of them really intent upon the business in hand, and went slowly upstairs to the great room where the hampers lay. Already in the hall it was dark enough for three electric torches to flash usefully and help their steps as they moved with caution, lighting one corner after another. The air inside was chill and damp. 'Like an unused museum,' said Mortimer. 'I can smell the specimens.' They looked about them, sniffing. 'That's humanity,' declared his host, employer, friend, 'with cement and whitewash to flavour it'; and all three laughed as Mrs Burley said she wished they had picked some roses and brought them in. Her husband was again in front on the broad staircase. Mortimer just behind him, when she called out. 'I don't like being last,' she exclaimed. 'It's so black behind me in the hall. I'll come between you two,' and the sailor took her outstretched hand, squeezing it, as he passed her up. 'There's a figure, remember,' she said hurriedly turning to gain her husband's attention, as when she touched wood at home. 'A figure is seen; that's part of the story. The figure of a man.' She gave a tiny shiver of pleasure, half-imagined alarm as she took his arm.

'I hope we shall see it,' he mentioned prosaically.

'I hope we shan't,' she replied with emphasis. 'It's only seen before—something happens.' Her husband said nothing, while Mortimer remarked facetiously that it would be a pity if they had their trouble for nothing. 'Something can hardly happen to all three of us,' he said lightly, as they entered a large room where the paper-hangers had conveniently left a rough table of bare planks. Mrs Burley, busy with her own thoughts, began to unpack the sandwiches and wine. Her husband strolled over to the window. He seemed restless.

'So this'—his deep voice startled her—'is where one of us'—he looked round him—'is to——'

'John!' She stopped him sharply, with impatience. 'Several times already I've begged you.' Her voice rang rather shrill and querulous in the empty room, a new note in it. She was beginning to feel the atmosphere of the place, perhaps. On the sunny lawn it had not touched her, but now, with the fall of night, she was aware of it, as shadow called to shadow and the kingdom of darkness gathered power. Like a great whispering gallery, the whole house listened.

'Upon my word, Nancy,' he said with contrition, as he came and sat down beside her, 'I quite forgot again. Only I cannot take it seriously. It's utterly unthinkable to me that a man——'.

'But why evoke the idea at all?' she insisted in a lowered voice, that snapped despite its faintness. 'Men, after all, don't do such things for nothing.'

'We don't know everything in the universe, do we?' Mortimer put in, trying clumsily to support her. 'All I know just now is that I'm famished and this veal and ham pie is delicious.' He was very busy with his knife and fork. His foot rested lightly on her own beneath the table; he could not keep his eyes off her face; he was continually passing new edibles to her.

'No,' agreed John Burley, 'not everything. You're right there.'

She kicked the younger man gently, flashing a warning with her eyes as well, while her husband, emptying his glass, his head thrown back, looked straight at them over the rim, apparently seeing nothing. They smoked their cigarettes round the table, Burley lighting a big cigar. 'Tell us about the figure, Nancy?' he inquired. 'At least there's no harm in that. It's new to me. I hadn't heard about a figure.' And she did so willingly, turning her chair sideways from the dangerous, reckless feet. Mortimer could now no longer touch her. 'I know very little,' she confessed; 'only what the paper said. It's a man … And he changes.'

'How changes?' asked her husband. 'Clothes, you mean, or what?'

Mrs Burley laughed, as though she was glad to laugh. Then she answered: 'According to the story he shows himself each time to the man——'

'The man who——?'

'Yes, yes, of course. He appears to the man who dies—as himself.'

'H'm,' grunted her husband, naturally puzzled. He stared at her.

'Each time the chap saw his own double'—Mortimer came this time usefully to the rescue—'before he did it.'

Considerable explanation followed, involving much psychic jargon from Mrs Burley, which fascinated and impressed the sailor, who thought her as wonderful as she was lovely, showing it in his eyes for all to see. John Burley's attention wandered. He moved over to the window, leaving them to finish the discussion between them; he took no part in it, made no comment even, merely listening idly and watching them with an air of absent-mindedness through the cloud of cigar smoke round his head. He moved from window to window, ensconcing himself in turn in each deep embrasure, examining the fastenings measuring the thickness of the stonework with his handkerchief. He seemed restless, bored, obviously out of place in this ridiculous expedition. On his big massive face lay a quiet, resigned expression his wife had never seen before. She noticed it now as, the discussion ended, the pair tidied away the *debris* of dinner, lit the spirit lamp for coffee and laid out a supper which would be very welcome with the dawn. A draught passed through the room, making the papers flutter on the table. Mortimer turned down the smoking lamps with care.

'Wind's getting up a bit—from the south,' observed Burley from his niche, closing one-half of the casement window as he said it. To do this, he turned his back a moment, fumbling for several seconds with the latch, while Mortimer, noting it, seized his sudden opportunity with the foolish abandon of his age and temperament. Neither he nor his victim perceived that, against the outside darkness, the interior of the room was plainly reflected in the window-pane. One reckless, the other terrified, they snatched the fearful joy, which might, after all, have been lengthened by another full half-minute, for the head they feared, followed by the shoulders, pushed through the side of the casement still open, and remained outside, taking in the night.

'A grand air,' said his deep voice, as the head drew in again. 'I'd like to be at sea a night like this.' He left the casement open and came across the room towards them. 'Now,' he said cheerfully, arranging a seat for himself, 'let's get comfortable for the night. Mortimer, we expect stories from you without ceasing, until dawn or the ghost arrives. Horrible stories of chains and headless men, remember. Make it a night we shan't forget in a hurry.' He produced his gust of laughter.

They arranged their chairs, with other chairs to put their feet on, and Mortimer contrived a footstool by means of a hamper for the smallest feet; the air grew thick with tobacco smoke; eyes flashed and answered, watched perhaps as well; ears listened and perhaps grew wise; occasionally, as a window shook, they started and looked round; there were sounds about the house from time to time, when the entering wind, using broken or open windows, set loose objects rattling.

But Mrs Burley vetoed horrible stories with decision. A big, empty mansion, lonely in the country, and even with the comfort of John Burley and a lover in it, has its atmosphere. Furnished rooms are far less ghostly. This atmosphere now came creeping everywhere, through spacious halls and sighing corridors, silent, invisible, but all-pervading, John Burley alone impervious to it, unaware of its soft attack upon the nerves. It entered possibly with the summer night wind, but possibly it was always there ... And Mrs Burley looked often at her husband, sitting near her at an angle; the light fell on his fine strong face; she felt that, though apparently so calm and quiet, he was really very restless; something about him was a little different; she could not define it; his mouth seemed set as with an effort; he looked, she thought curiously to herself, patient and very dignified; he was rather a dear after all. Why did she think the face inscrutable? Her thoughts wandered vaguely, unease, discomfort among them somewhere, while the heated blood—she had taken her share of wine—seethed in her.

Burley turned to the sailor for more stories. 'Sea and wind in them,' he asked. 'No horrors, remember!' And Mortimer told a tale about the shortage of rooms at a Welsh seaside place where spare rooms fetched fabulous prices, and one man alone refused to let—a retired captain of South Seas trader, very poor, a bit crazy apparently. He had two furnished rooms in his house worth twenty guineas a week. The rooms faced south; he kept them full of flowers; but he would not let. An explanation of his unworldly obstinacy was not forthcoming until Mortimer—they fished together—gained his confidence. 'The South Wind lives in them,' the old fellow told him. 'I keep them free for her.'

'For *her?*'

'It was on the South Wind my love came to me,' said the other softly; 'and it was on the South Wind that she left——'

It was an odd tale to tell in such company, but he told it well.

'Beautiful,' thought Mrs Burley. Aloud she said a quiet, 'Thank you. By "left" I suppose he meant she died or ran away?'

John Burley looked up with a certain surprise. 'We ask for a story,' he said, 'and you give us a poem.' He laughed. 'You're in love, Mortimer,' he informed him, 'and with my wife, probably.'

'Of course I am, sir,' replied the young man gallantly. 'A sailor's heart, you know,' while the face of the woman turned pink, then white. She knew her husband more intimately than Mortimer did, and there was something in his tone, his eyes, his words, she did not like. Harry was an idiot to choose such a tale. An irritated annoyance stirred in her, close upon dislike. 'Anyhow, it's better than horrors,' she said hurriedly.

'Well,' put in her husband, letting forth a minor gust of laughter, 'it's possible, at any rate. Though one's as crazy as the other.' His meaning was not wholly clear. 'If a man really loved,' he added in his blunt fashion, 'and was tricked by her, I could almost conceive his——'

'Oh, don't preach, John, for Heaven's sake. You're so dull in the pulpit.' But the interruption only served to emphasise the sentence which, otherwise, might have been passed over.

'Could conceive his finding life so worthless,' persisted the other, 'that——' He hesitated. 'But there, now, I promised I wouldn't,' he went on, laughing good-humouredly. Then, suddenly, as though in spite of himself, driven it seemed: 'Still, under such conditions, he might show his contempt for human nature and for life by——'

It was a tiny stifled scream that stopped him this time.

'John, I hate, I loathe you, when you talk like that. And you've broken your word again.' She was more than petulant; a nervous anger sounded in her voice. It was the way he had said it, looking from them towards the window, that made her quiver. She felt him suddenly as a man; she felt afraid of him.

Her husband made no reply; he rose and looked at his watch leaning sideways towards the lamp, so that the expression of his face was shaded. 'Two o'clock,' he remarked. 'I think I'll take a turn through the house. I may find a workman asleep or something. Anyhow, the light will soon come now.' He laughed; the expression of his face, his tone of voice, relieved her momentarily. He went out. They heard his heavy tread echoing down the carpetless long corridor.

Mortimer began at once. 'Did he mean anything?' he asked breathlessly. 'He doesn't love you the least little bit, anyhow. He never did. I do. You're wasted on him. You belong to me. The words poured out. He covered her face with kisses. Oh, I didn't mean *that,*' he caught between the kisses.

The sailor released her, staring. 'What then?' he whispered. 'Do you think he saw us on the lawn?' he paused a moment, as she made no reply. The steps were audible in the distance still. 'I know!' he exclaimed suddenly. 'It's the blessed house he feels. That's what it is. He doesn't like it.'

A wind sighed through the room, making the papers flutter; something rattled; and Mrs Burley started. A loose end of rope swinging from the paperhanger's ladder caught her eye. She shivered slightly.

'He's different,' she replied in a low voice, nestling very close again, 'and so restless. Didn't you notice what he said just now—that under certain conditions he could understand a man'—she hesitated—'doing it,' she concluded, a sudden drop in her voice. 'Harry,' she looked full into his eyes, 'that's not like him. He didn't say that for nothing.'

'Nonsense! He's bored to tears, that's all. And the house is getting on your nerves, too.' He kissed her tenderly. Then, as she responded, he drew her nearer still and held her passionately, mumbling incoherent words, among which 'nothing to be afraid of' was distinguishable. Meanwhile, the steps were coming nearer. She pushed him away. 'You must behave yourself. I insist. You shall, Harry.' Then buried herself in his arms, her face hidden against his neck—only to disentangle herself the next instant and stand clear of him. 'I hate you, Harry,' she exclaimed sharply, a look of angry annoyance flashing across her face. 'And I *hate* myself. Why do you treat me——?' She broke off as the steps came closer, patted her hair straight, and stalked over to the open window.

'I believe after all you're only playing with me,' he said viciously. He stared in surprised disappointment, watching her. 'It's him you really love,' he added jealously. He looked and spoke like a petulant spoilt boy.

She did not turn her head. 'He's always been fair to me, kind and generous. He never blames me for anything. Give me a cigarette, and don't play the stage hero. My nerves are on edge, to tell you the truth.' Her voice jarred harshly, and as he lit her cigarette he noticed that her lips were trembling; his own hand trembled too. He was still holding the match, standing beside her at the window-sill, when the steps crossed the threshold and John Burley came into the room. He went straight up to the table and turned the lamp down. 'It was smoking,' he remarked. 'Didn't you see?'

'I'm sorry, sir.' And Mortimer sprang forward too late to help him. 'It was the draught as you pushed the door open.' The big man said, 'Ah!' and drew a chair over, facing them. 'It's just *the* very house,' he told them. 'I've been through every room on this floor. It will make a splendid Home, with very little alteration, too.' He turned round in his creaking wicker chair and looked up at his wife, who sat swinging her legs and smoking in the window embrasure. 'Lives will be saved inside these old walls. It's a good investment,' he went on, talking rather to himself it seemed. 'People will die here, too——'

'Hark!' Mrs Burley interrupted him. 'That noise—what is it?' A faint thudding sound in the corridor or in the adjoining room was audible, making all three look round quickly, listening for a repetition, which did not come. The papers fluttered on the table, the lamps smoked an instant.

'Wind,' observed Burley calmly, 'our little friend, the South Wind. Something blown over again, that's all.' But, curiously, the three of them stood up. 'I'll go and see,' he continued. 'Doors and windows are all open to let the paint dry.' Yet he did not move; he stood there watching a white moth that dashed round and round the lamp, flopping heavily now and again upon the bare deal table.

'Let me go, sir,' put in Mortimer eagerly. He was glad of the chance; for the first time he, too, felt uncomfortable. But there was another, who, apparently, suffered a discomfort greater than his own and was accordingly even more glad to get away. 'I'll go,' Mrs Burley announced, with decision. 'I'd like to. I haven't been out of this room since we came. I'm not an atom afraid.'

It was strange that for a moment she did not make a move either; it seemed as if she waited for something. For perhaps fifteen seconds no one stirred or spoke. She knew by the look in her lover's eyes that he had now become aware of the slight, indefinite change in her husband's manner, and was alarmed by it. The fear in him woke her contempt; she suddenly despised the youth, and was conscious of a new, strange yearning towards her husband; against her worked nameless pressure, troubling her being. There was an alteration in the room, she thought; something had come in. The trio stood listening to the gentle wind outside, waiting for the sound to be repeated; two careless, passionate young lovers and a man stood waiting, listening, watching in that room; yet it seemed there were five persons altogether and not three, for two guilty consciences stood apart and separate from their owners. John Burley broke the silence.

'Yes, you go, Nancy. Nothing to be afraid of—there. It's only wind.' He spoke as though he meant it.

Mortimer bit his lips. 'I'll come with you,' he said instantly. He was confused. 'Let's all three go. I don't think we ought to be separated.' But Mrs Burley was already at the door. 'I insist,' she said, with a forced laugh. 'I'll call if I'm frightened,' while her husband, saying nothing, watched her from the table.

'Take this,' said the sailor, flashing his electric torch as he went over to her. 'Two are better than one.' He saw her figure exquisitely silhouetted against the black corridor beyond; it was clear she wanted to go; any nervousness in her was mastered by a stronger emotion still; she was glad to be out of their presence for a bit. He had hoped to snatch a word of explanation in the corridor, but her manner stopped him. Something else stopped him, too.

'First door on the left,' he called out, his voice echoing down the empty length. 'That's the room where the noise came from. Shout if you want us.'

He watched her moving away, the light held steadily in front of her, but she made no answer, and he turned back to see John Burley lighting his cigar at the lamp chimney, his face thrust forward as he did so. He stood a second, watching him, as the lips sucked hard at the cigar to make it draw; the strength of the features was emphasised to sternness. He had meant to stand by the door and listen for the least sound from the adjoining room, but now found his whole attention focussed on the face above the lamp. In that minute he realised that Burley had wished—had meant—his wife to go. In that minute also he forgot his love, his shameless, selfish little mistress, his worthless, caddish little self. For John Burley looked up. He straightened slowly, puffing hard and quickly to make sure his cigar was lit, and faced him. Mortimer moved forward into the room, self-conscious, embarrassed, cold.

'Of course, it was only wind,' he said lightly, his one desire being to fill the interval while they were alone with commonplaces. He did not wish the other to speak. 'Dawn wind, probably.' He glanced at his wrist-watch. 'It's half-past two already and the sun gets up at a quarter to four. It's light by now, I expect. The shortest night is never quite dark.' He rambled on confusedly, for the other's steady, silent stare embarrassed him. A faint sound of Mrs Burley moving in the next room made him stop a moment. He turned instinctively to the door, eager for an excuse to go.

'That's nothing,' said Burley, speaking at last and in a firm quiet voice. 'Only my wife, glad to be alone—my young and pretty wife. She's all right. I know her better than you do. Come in and shut the door.'

Mortimer obeyed. He closed the door and came close to the table, facing the other, who at once continued.

'If I thought,' he said, in that quiet deep voice, 'that you two were serious'—he uttered his words very slowly, with emphasis, with intense severity—'do you know what I should do? I will tell you, Mortimer. I should like one of us two—you or myself—to remain in this house, dead.'

His teeth gripped his cigar tightly; his hands were clenched; he went on through a half-closed mouth. His eyes blazed steadily.

'I trust her so absolutely—understand me?—that my belief in women, in human beings, would go. And with it the desire to live. Understand me?'

Each word to the young careless fool was a blow in the face, yet it was the softest blow, the flash of a big deep heart, that hurt the most. A dozen answers—denial, explanation, confession, taking all guilt upon himself—crowded his mind, only to be dismissed. He stood motionless and silent, staring hard into the other's eyes. No word passed his lips; there was no time in any case. It was in this position that Mrs Burley, entering at that moment, found them. She saw her husband's face; the other man stood with his back to her. She came in with a little nervous laugh. 'A bell-rope swinging in the wind and hitting a sheet of metal before the fireplace,' she informed them. And all three laughed together then, though each laugh had a different sound. 'But I hate this house,' she added. 'I wish we had never come.'

'The moment there's light in the sky,' remarked her husband quietly, 'we can leave. That's the contract; let's see it through. Another half-hour will do it. Sit down, Nancy, and have a bit of something.' He got up and placed a chair for her. 'I think I'll take another look round.' He moved slowly to the door. 'I may go out on to the lawn a bit, and see what the sky is doing.'

It did not take half a minute to say the words, yet to Mortimer it seemed as though the voice would never end. His mind was confused and troubled. He loathed himself, he loathed the woman through whom he had got into this awkward mess.

The situation had suddenly become extremely painful; he had never imagined such a thing; the man he had thought blind had after all seen everything—known it all along, watched them, waited. And the woman, he was now certain, loved her husband; she had fooled him, Mortimer, all along, amusing herself.

'I'll come with you, sir. Do let me,' he said suddenly. Mrs Burley stood pale and uncertain between them. She looked scared. What has happened, she was clearly wondering.

'No, no, Harry'—he called him 'Harry' for the first time—'I'll be back in five minutes at most. My wife mustn't be alone either.' And he went out.

The young man waited till the footsteps sounded some distance down the corridor, then turned, but he did not move forward; for the first time he let pass unused what he called 'an opportunity'. His passion had left him; his love, as he once thought it, was gone. He looked at the pretty woman near him, wondering blankly what he had ever seen there to attract him so wildly. He wished to Heaven he was out of it all. He wished he were dead. John Burley's words suddenly appalled him.

One thing he saw plainly—she was frightened. This opened his lips.

'What's the matter?' he asked, and his hushed voice shirked the familiar Christian name. 'Did you see anything?' He nodded his head in the direction of the adjoining room. It was the sound of his own voice addressing her coldly that made him abruptly see himself as he really was, but it was her reply, honestly given, in a faint even voice, that told him she saw her own self too with similar clarity. God, he thought, how revealing a tone, a single word can be!

'I saw—nothing. Only I feel uneasy—dear.' That 'dear' was a call for help.

'Look here,' he cried, so loud that she held up a warning finger, 'I'm—I've been a damned fool, a cad! I'm most frightfully ashamed. I'll do anything—*anything* to get it right.' He felt cold, naked, his worthlessness laid bare; she felt, he knew, the same. Each revolted suddenly from the other. Yet, he knew not quite how or wherefore this great change had thus abruptly come about, especially on her side. He felt that a bigger, deeper emotion than he could understand was working on them, making mere physical relationships seem empty, trivial, cheap and vulgar. His cold increased in face of this utter ignorance.

'Uneasy?' he repeated, perhaps hardly knowing exactly why he said it. 'Good Lord, but he can take care of himself——'

'Oh, *he* is a man,' she interrupted; 'yes.'

Steps were heard, firm, heavy steps, coming back along the corridor. It seemed to Mortimer that he had listened to this sound of steps all night, and would listen to them till he died. He crossed to the lamp and lit a cigarette, carefully this time, turning the wick down afterwards. Mrs Burley also rose, moving over towards the door, away from him. They listened a moment to these firm and heavy steps, the tread of a man, John Burley. A man ... and a philanderer, flashed across Mortimer's brain like fire, contrasting the two with fierce contempt for himself. The tread became less audible. There was distance in it. It had turned in somewhere.

'There!' she exclaimed in a hushed tone. 'He's gone in.'

'Nonsense! It passed us. He's going out on to the lawn.'

The pair listened breathlessly for a moment, when the sound of steps came distinctly from the adjoining room, walking across the boards, apparently towards the window.

'There!' she repeated. 'He did go in.'

Silence of perhaps a minute followed, in which they heard each other's breathing. 'I don't like being alone—in there,' Mrs Burley said in a thin faltering voice, and moved as though to go out. Her hand was already on the knob of the door, when Mortimer stopped her with a violent gesture.

'Don't! For God's sake, don't!' he cried, before she could turn it. He darted forward. As he laid a hand upon her arm a thud was audible through the wall. It was a heavy sound, and this time there was no wind to cause it.

It's only that loose swinging thing,' he whispered thickly, a dreadful confusion blotting out clear thought and speech.

'There was no loose swaying thing at all,' she said in a failing voice, then reeled and swayed against him. 'I invented that. There was nothing.' As he caught her, staring helplessly it seemed to him that a face with lifted lids rushed up at him. He saw two terrified eyes in a patch of ghastly white. Her whisper followed, as she sank into his arms. 'It's John, he's——'

At which instant, with terror at its climax, the sound of steps suddenly became audible once more—the firm and heavy tread of John Burley coming out again into the corridor. Such was their amazement and relief that they neither moved nor spoke. The steps drew nearer. The pair seemed petrified; Mortimer did not remove his arms, nor did Mrs Burley attempt to release herself. They stared at the door and waited. It was pushed wider the next second, and John Burley stood beside them. He was so close he almost touched them—there in each other's arms.

'Jack, dear!' cried his wife, with a searching tenderness that made her voice seem strange.

He gazed a second at each in turn. 'I'm going out on to the lawn for a moment,' he said quietly. There was no expression on his face; he did not smile, he did not frown; he showed no feeling, no emotion—just looked into their eyes, and then withdrew round the edge of the door before either could utter a word in answer. The door swung to behind him. He was gone.

'He's going to the lawn. He said so.' It was Mortimer speaking, but his voice shook and stammered. Mrs Burley had released herself. She stood now by the table, silent, gazing with fixed eyes at nothing, her lips parted, her expression vacant. Again, she was aware of an alteration in the room: something had gone out. … He watched her a second, uncertain what to say or do. It was the face of a drowned person, occurred to him. Something intangible, yet almost visible stood between them in that narrow space. Something had ended, there before his eyes, definitely ended. The barrier between them rose higher, denser. Through this barrier her words came to him with an odd whispering remoteness.

'Harry. ... You saw? You noticed?'

'What d'you mean?' he said gruffly. He tried to feel angry, contemptuous, but his breath caught absurdly.

'Harry—he was different. The eyes, the hair, the'—her face grew like death—'the twist in his face——'

'What on earth are you saying? Pull yourself together.' He saw that she was trembling down the whole length of her body, as she leaned against the table for support. His own legs shook. He stared hard at her.

'Altered, Harry ... altered.' Her horrified whisper came at him like a knife. For it was true. He, too, had noticed something about the husband's appearance that was not quite normal. Yet, even while they talked, they heard him going down the carpetless stairs; the sounds ceased as he crossed the hall; then came the noise of the front door banging, the reverberation even shaking the room a little where they stood.

Mortimer went over to her side. He walked unevenly.

'My dear! For God's sake—this is sheer nonsense. Don't let yourself go like this. I'll put it straight with him—it's all my fault.' He saw by her face that she did not understand his words; he was saying the wrong thing altogether; her mind was utterly elsewhere. 'He's all right,' he went on hurriedly. 'He's not on the lawn now——'

He broke off at sight of her. The horror that fastened on her brain plastered her face with deathly whiteness.

'That was not John at all,' she cried, a wail of misery and terror in her voice. She rushed to the window and he followed.

To his immense relief a figure moving below was plainly visible. It was John Burley. They saw him in the faint grey of the dawn, as he crossed the lawn, going away from the house. He disappeared.

'There you are! See?' whispered Mortimer reassuringly. 'He'll be back in——' when a sound in the adjoining room, heavier, louder than before, cut appallingly across his words, and Mrs Burley, with that wailing scream, fell back into his arms. He caught her only just in time, for he stiffened into ice, daft with the uncomprehended terror of it all, and helpless as a child.

'Darling, my darling—oh, God!' He bent, kissing her face wildly. He was utterly distraught.

'Harry! Jack—oh, oh!' she wailed in her anguish. 'It took on his likeness. It deceived us ... to give him time. He's done it.'

She sat up suddenly. 'Go,' she said, pointing to the room beyond, then sank fainting, a dead weight in his arms.

He carried her unconscious body to a chair, then entering the adjoining room he flashed his torch upon the body of her husband hanging from a bracket in the wall. He cut it down five minutes too late.

# The Story of Yand Manor House

By *E. and H. Heron*

Looking through the notes of Mr Flaxman Low, one sometimes catches through the steel-blue hardness of facts, the pink flush of romance, or more often the black corner of a horror unnameable. The following story may serve as an instance of the latter. Mr Low not only unravelled the mystery at Yand, but at the same time justified his life-work to M. Thierry, the well-known French critic and philosopher.

At the end of a long conversation, M. Thierry, arguing from his own standpoint as a materialist, had said:

"The factor in the human economy which you call 'soul' cannot be placed."

"I admit that," replied Low. "Yet, when a man dies, is there not one factor unaccounted for in the change that comes upon him? Yes! For though his body still exists, it rapidly falls to pieces, which proves that that has gone which held it together."

The Frenchman laughed, and shifted his ground.

"Well, for my part, I don't believe in ghosts! Spirit manifestations, occult phenomena—is not this the ashbin into which a certain clique shoot everything they cannot understand, or for which they fail to account?"

"Then what should you say to me, Monsieur, if I told you that I have passed a good portion of my life in investigating this particular ashbin, and have been lucky enough to sort a small part of its contents with tolerable success?" replied Flaxman Low.

"The subject is doubtless interesting—but I should like to have some personal experience in the matter," said Thierry dubiously.

"I am at present investigating a most singular case," said Low. "Have you a day or two to spare?"

Thierry thought for a minute or more.

"I am grateful," he replied. "But, forgive me, is it a convincing ghost?"

"Come with me to Yand and see. I have been there once already, and came away for the purpose of procuring information from MSS, to which I have the privilege of access, for I confess that the phenomena at Yand lie altogether outside any former experience of mine."

Low sank back into his chair with his hands clasped behind his head—a favourite position of his—and the smoke of his long pipe curled up lazily into the golden face of an Isis, which stood behind him on a bracket. Thierry, glancing across, was struck by the strange likeness between the faces of the Egyptian goddess and this scientist of the nineteenth century. On both rested the calm, mysterious abstraction of some unfathomable thought. As he looked, he decided.

"I have three days to place at your disposal."

"I thank you heartily," replied Low. "To be associated with so brilliant a logician as yourself in an inquiry of this nature is more than I could have hoped for! The material with which I have to deal is so elusive, the whole subject is wrapped in such obscurity and hampered by so much prejudice, that I can find few really qualified persons who care to approach these investigations seriously. I go down to Yand this evening, and hope not to leave without clearing up the mystery. You will accompany me?"

"Most certainly. Meanwhile, pray tell me something of the affair."

"Briefly the story is as follows. Some weeks ago I went to Yand Manor House at the request of the owner, Sir George Blackburton, to see what I could make of the events which took place there. All they complain of is the impossibility of remaining in one room—the dining-room."

"What then is he like, this M. le Spook?" asked the Frenchman, laughing.

"No one has ever seen him, or for that matter heard him."

"Then how——"

"You can't see him, nor hear him, nor smell him," went on Low, "but you can feel him and—taste him!"

"*Mon Dieu!* But this is singular! Is he then of so bad a flavour?"

"You shall taste for yourself," answered Flaxman Low smiling. "After a certain hour no one can remain in the room, they are simply crowded out."

"But who crowds them out?" asked Thierry.

"That is just what I hope we may discover to-night or to-morrow."

The last train that night dropped Mr Flaxman Low and his companion at a little station near Yand. It was late, but a trap in waiting soon carried them to the Manor House. The big bulk of the building stood up in absolute blackness before them.

"Blackburton was to have met us, but I suppose he has not yet arrived," said Low. "Hullo! The door is open," he added as he stepped into the hall.

Beyond a dividing curtain they now perceived a light. Passing behind this curtain they found themselves at the end of the long hall, the wide staircase opening up in front of them.

"But who is this?" exclaimed Thierry.

Swaying and stumbling at every step, there tottered slowly down the stairs the figure of a man. He looked as if he had been drinking, his face was livid, and his eyes sunk into his head.

"Thank Heaven you've come! I heard you outside," he said in a weak voice.

"It's Sir George Blackburton," said Low, as the man lurched forward and pitched into his arms.

They laid him down on the rugs and tried to restore consciousness.

"He has the air of being drunk, but it is not so," remarked Thierry. "Monsieur has had a bad shock of the nerves. See the pulses drumming in his throat."

In a few minutes Blackburton opened his eyes and staggered to his feet.

"Come. I could not remain there alone. Come quickly."

They went rapidly across the hall, Blackburton leading the way down a wide passage to a double-leaved door, which, after a perceptible pause, he threw open, and they all entered together.

On the great table in the centre stood an extinguished lamp, some scattered food, and a big, lighted candle. But the eyes of all three men passed at once to a dark recess beside the heavy, carved chimneypiece, where a rigid shape sat perched on the back of a huge, oak chair.

Flaxman Low snatched up the candle and crossed the room towards it.

On the top of the chair, with his feet upon the arms, sat a powerfully-built young man huddled up. His mouth was open, and his eyes twisted upwards. Nothing further could be seen from below but the ghastly pallor of cheek and throat.

"Who is this?" cried Low. Then he laid his hand gently on the man's knee.

At the touch the figure collapsed in a heap upon the floor, the gaping, set, terrified face turned up to theirs.

"He's dead!" said Low after a hasty examination. "I should say he's been dead some hours."

"Oh, Lord! Poor Batty!" groaned Sir George, who was entirely unnerved. "I'm glad you've come."

"Who is he?" said Thierry, "and what was he doing here?"

"He's a gamekeeper of mine. He was always anxious to try conclusions with the ghost, and last night he begged me to lock him in here with food for twenty-four hours. I refused at first, but then I thought if anything happened while he was in here alone, it would interest you. Who could imagine it would end like this?"

"When did you find him?" asked Low.

"I only got here from my mother's half an hour ago. I turned on the light in the hall and came in here with a candle. As I entered the room, the candle went out, and—and—I think I must be going mad."

"Tell us everything you saw," urged Low.

"You will think I am beside myself; but as the light went out and I sank almost paralysed into an armchair, I saw two barred eyes looking at me!"

"Barred eyes? What do you mean?"

"Eyes that looked at me through thin vertical bars, like the bars of a cage. What's that?"

With a smothered yell Sir George sprang back. He had approached the dead man and declared something had brushed his face.

"You were standing on this spot under the overmantel. I will remain here. Meantime, my dear Thierry, I feel sure you will help Sir George to carry this poor fellow to some more suitable place," said Flaxman Low.

When the dead body of the young gamekeeper had been carried out, Low passed slowly round and about the room. At length he stood under the old carved overmantel, which reached to the ceiling and projected bodily forward in quaint heads of satyrs and animals. One of these on the side nearest the recess represented a griffin with a flanged mouth. Sir George had been standing directly below this at the moment when he felt the touch on his face. Now alone in the dim, wide room, Flaxman Low stood on the same spot and waited. The candle threw its dully yellow rays on the shadows which seemed to gather closer and wait also. Presently a distant door banged, and Low, leaning forward to listen, distinctly felt something on the back of his neck!

He swung round. There was nothing! He searched carefully on all sides, then put his hand up to the griffin's head. Again came the same soft touch, this time upon his hand, as if something had floated past on the air.

This was definite. The griffin's head located it. Taking the candle to examine more closely, Low found four long black hairs depending from the jagged fangs. He was detaching them when Thierry reappeared.

"We must get Sir George away as soon as possible," he said.

"Yes, we must take him away, I fear," agreed Low. "Our investigation must be put off till to-morrow."

On the following day they returned to Yand. It was a large country-house, pretty and old-fashioned, with lattice windows and deep gables, that looked out between tall shrubs and across lawns set with beaupots, where peacocks sunned themselves on the velvet turf. The church spire peered over the trees on one side; and an old wall covered with ivy and creeping plants, and pierced at intervals with arches, alone separated the gardens from the churchyard.

The haunted room lay at the back of the house. It was square and handsome, and furnished in the style of the last century. The oak overmantel reached to the ceiling, and a wide window, which almost filled one side of the room, gave a view of the west door of the church.

Low stood for a moment at the open window looking out at the level sunlight which flooded the lawns and parterres.

"See that door sunk in the church wall to the left?" said Sir George's voice at his elbow. "That is the door of the family vault. Cheerful outlook, isn't it?"

"I should like to walk across there presently," remarked Low.

"What! Into the vault?" asked Sir George, with a harsh laugh. "I'll take you if you like. Anything else I can show you or tell you?"

"Yes. Last night I found this hanging from the griffin's head," said Low, producing the thin wisp of black hair. "It must have touched your cheek as you stood below. Do you know to whom it can belong?"

"It's a woman's hair! No, the only woman who has been in this room to my knowledge for months is an old servant with grey hair, who cleans it," returned Blackburton. "I'm sure it was not here when I locked Batty in."

"It is human hair, exceedingly coarse and long uncut," said Low; "but it is not necessarily a woman's."

"It is not mine at any rate, for I'm sandy; and poor Batty was fair. Good-night; I'll come round for you in the morning."

Presently, when the night closed in, Thierry and Low settled down in the haunted room to await developments. They smoked and talked deep into the night. A big lamp burned brightly on the table, and the surroundings looked homely and desirable.

Thierry made a remark to that effect, adding that perhaps the ghost might see fit to omit his usual visit.

"Experience goes to prove that ghosts have a cunning habit of choosing persons either credulous or excitable to experiment upon," he added.

To M. Thierry's surprise, Flaxman Low agreed with him.

"They certainly choose suitable persons," he said, "that is, not credulous persons, but those whose senses are sufficiently keen to detect the presence of a spirit. In my own investigations, I try to eliminate what you would call the supernatural element. I deal with these mysterious affairs as far as possible on material lines."

"Then what do you say of Batty's death? He died of fright—simply."

"I hardly think so. The manner of his death agrees in a peculiar manner with what we know of the terrible history of this room. He died of fright and pressure combined. Did you hear the doctor's remark? It was significant. He said: 'The indications are precisely those I have observed in persons who have been crushed and killed in a crowd!'"

"That is sufficiently curious, I allow. I see that it is already past two o'clock. I am thirsty; I will have a little seltzer." Thierry rose from his chair, and, going to the side-board, drew a tumblerful from the syphon. "Pah! What an abominable taste!"

"What? The seltzer?"

"Not at all?" returned the Frenchman irritably. "I have not touched it yet. Some horrible fly has flown into my mouth, I suppose. Pah! Disgusting!"

"What is it like?" asked Flaxman Low, who was at the moment wiping his own mouth with his handkerchief.

"Like? As if some repulsive fungus had burst in the mouth."

"Exactly. I perceive it also. I hope you are about to be convinced."

"What?" exclaimed Thierry, turning his big figure round and staring at Low. "You don't mean——"

As he spoke the lamp suddenly went out.

"Why, then, have you put the lamp out at such a moment?" cried Thierry.

"I have not put it out. Light the candle beside you on the table."

Low heard the Frenchman's grunt of satisfaction as he found the candle, then the scratch of a match. It sputtered and went out. Another match and another behaved in the same manner, while Thierry swore freely under his breath.

"Let me have your matches, Monsieur Flaxman; mine are, no doubt damp," he said at last.

Low rose to feel his way across the room. The darkness was dense.

"It is the darkness of Egypt—it may be felt. Where then are you, my dear friend?" he heard Thierry saying, but the voice seemed a long way off.

"I am coming," he answered, "but it's so hard to get along."

After Low had spoken the words, their meaning struck him. He paused and tried to realise in what part of the room he was. The silence was profound, and the growing sense of oppression seemed like a nightmare. Thierry's voice sounded again, faint and receding.

"I am suffocating, Monsieur Flaxman, where are you? I am near the door. Ach!"

A strangling bellow of pain and fear followed, that scarcely reached Low through the thickening atmosphere.

"Thierry, what is the matter with you?" he shouted. "Open the door."

But there was no answer. What had become of Thierry in that hideous, clogging gloom! Was he also dead, crushed in some ghastly fashion against the wall? What was this?

The air had become palpable to the touch, heavy, repulsive, with the sensation of cold humid flesh!

Low pushed out his hands with a mad longing to touch a table, a chair, anything but this clammy, swelling softness that thrust itself upon him from every side, baffling him and filling his grasp.

He knew now that he was absolutely alone—struggling against what?

His feet were slipping in his wild efforts to feel the floor—the dank flesh was creeping upon his neck, his cheek—his breath came short and labouring as the pressure swung him gently to and fro, helpless, nauseated!

The clammy flesh crowded upon him like the bulk of some fat, horrible creature; then came a stinging pain on the cheek. Low clutched at something—there was a crash and a rush of air—

The next sensation of which Mr Flaxman Low was conscious was one of deathly sickness. He was lying on wet grass, the wind blowing over him, and all the clean, wholesome smells of the open air in his nostrils.

He sat up and looked about him. Dawn was breaking windily in the east, and by its light he saw that he was on the lawn of

Yand Manor House. The latticed window of the haunted room above him was open. He tried to remember what had happened. He took stock of himself, in fact, and slowly felt that he still held something clutched in his right hand—something dark-coloured, slender, and twisted. It might have been a long shred of bark or the cast skin of an adder—it was impossible to see in the dim light.

After an interval the recollection of Thierry recurred to him. Scrambling to his feet, he raised himself to the window-sill and looked in. Contrary to his expectation, there was no upsetting of furniture; everything remained in position as when the lamp went out. His own chair and the one Thierry had occupied were just as when they had arisen from them. But there was no sign of Thierry.

Low jumped in by the window. There was the tumbler full of seltzer, and the litter of matches about it. He took up Thierry's box of matches and struck a light. It flared, and he lit the candle with ease. In fact, everything about the room was perfectly normal; all the horrible conditions prevailing but a couple of hours ago had disappeared.

But where was Thierry? Carrying the lighted candle, he passed out of the door, and searched in the adjoining rooms. In one of them, to his relief, he found the Frenchman sleeping profoundly in an armchair.

Low touched his arm. Thierry leapt to his feet, fending off an imaginary blow with his arm. Then he turned his scared face on Low.

"What! You, Monsieur Flaxman! How have you escaped?"

"I should rather ask you how you escaped," said Low, smiling at the havoc the night's experiences had worked on his friend's looks and spirits.

"I was crowded out of the room against the door. That infernal thing—what was it?—with its damp, swelling flesh, inclosed me!" A shudder of disgust stopped him. "I was a fly in an aspic. I could not move. I sank into the stifling pulp. The air grew thick. I called to you, but your answers became inaudible. Then I was suddenly thrust against the door by a huge hand—it felt like one, at least. I had a struggle for my life, I was all but crushed, and then, I do not know how, I found myself outside the door. I shouted to you in vain. Therefore, as I could not help you, I came here, and—I will confess it, my dear friend—I locked and bolted the door. After some time I went again into the hall and listened; but, as I heard nothing, I resolved to wait until daylight and the return of Sir George."

"That's all right," said Low. "It was an experience worth having."

"But, no! Not for me! I do not envy you your researches into mysteries of this abominable description. I now comprehend perfectly that Sir George has lost his nerve if he has had to do with this horror. Besides, it is entirely impossible to explain these things."

At this moment they heard Sir George's arrival, and went out to meet him.

"I could not sleep all night for thinking of you!" exclaimed Blackburton on seeing them; "and I came along as soon as it was light. Something has happened."

"But certainly something has happened," cried M. Thierry shaking his head solemnly; "something of the most bizarre, of the most horrible! Monsieur Flaxman, you shall tell Sir George this story. You have been in that accursed room all night, and remain alive to tell the tale!"

As Low came to the conclusion of the story Sir George suddenly exclaimed:

"You have met with some injury to your face, Mr Low."

Low turned to the mirror. In the now strong light three parallel weals from eyes to mouth could be seen.

"I remember a stinging pain like a lash on my cheek. What would you say these marks were caused by, Thierry?" asked Low.

Thierry looked at them and shook his head.

"No one in their senses would venture to offer any explanation of the occurrences of last night," he replied.

"Something of this sort, do you think?" asked Low again, putting down the object he held in his hand on the table.

Thierry took it up and described it aloud.

"A long and thin object of a brown and yellow colour and twisted like a sabre-bladed corkscrew," then he started slightly and glanced at Low.

"It's a human nail, I imagine," suggested Low.

"But no human being has talons of this kind—except, perhaps, a Chinaman of high rank."

"There are no Chinamen about here, nor ever have been, to my knowledge," said Blackburton shortly. "I'm very much afraid that, in spite of all you have so bravely faced, we are no nearer to any rational explanation."

"On the contrary, I fancy I begin to see my way. I believe, after all, that I may be able to convert you. Thierry," said Flaxman Low.

"Convert me?"

"To a belief in the definite aim of my work. But you shall judge for yourself. What do you make of it so far? I claim that you know as much of the matter as I do."

"My dear good friend, I make nothing of it," returned Thierry, shrugging his shoulders and spreading out his hands. "Here we have a tissue of unprecedented incidents that can be explained on no theory whatever."

"But this is definite," and Flaxman Low held up the blackened nail.

"And how do you propose to connect that nail with the black hairs—with the eyes that looked through the bars of a cage—the fate of Batty, with its symptoms of death by pressure and suffocation—our experience of swelling flesh, that something which filled and filled the room to the exclusion of all else? How are you going to account for these things by any kind of connected hypothesis?" asked Thierry, with a shade of irony.

"I mean to try," replied Low.

At lunch time Thierry inquired how the theory was getting on.

"It progresses," answered Low. "By the way, Sir George, who lived in this house for some time prior to, say, 1840? He was a man—it may have been a woman, but, from the nature of his studies, I am inclined to think it was a man—who was deeply read in ancient necromancy, Eastern magic, mesmerism, and subjects of a kindred nature. And was he not buried in the vault you pointed out?"

"Do you know anything more about him?" asked Sir George in surprise.

"He was I imagine," went on Flaxman Low reflectively, "hirsute and swarthy, probably a recluse, and suffered from a morbid and extravagant fear of death."

"How do you know all this?"

"I only asked about it. Am I right?"

"You have described my cousin, Sir Gilbert Blackburton, in every particular. I can show you his portrait in another room."

As they stood looking at the painting of Sir Gilbert

Blackburton, with his long, melancholy, olive face and thick, black beard, Sir George went on. "My grandfather succeeded him at Yand. I have often heard my father speak of Sir Gilbert, and his strange studies and extraordinary fear of death. Oddly enough, in the end he died rather suddenly, while he was still hale and strong. He predicted his own approaching death, and had a doctor in attendance for a week or two before he died. He was placed in a coffin he had had made on some plan of his own and buried in the vault. His death occurred in 1842 or 1843. If you care to see them I can show you some of his papers, which may interest you."

Mr Flaxman Low spent the afternoon over the papers. When evening came, he rose from his work with a sigh of content, stretched himself, and joined Thierry and Sir George in the garden.

They dined at Lady Blackburton's, and it was late before Sir George found himself alone with Mr Flaxman Low and his friend.

"Have you formed any opinion about the thing which haunts the Manor House?" he asked anxiously.

Thierry elaborated a cigarette, crossed his legs, and added:

"If you have in truth come to any definite conclusion, pray let us hear it, my dear Monsieur Flaxman."

"I have reached a very definite and satisfactory conclusion," replied Low. "The Manor House is haunted by Sir Gilbert Blackburton, who died, or, rather, who seemed to die, on the 15th of August, 1842."

"Nonsense! The nail fifteen inches long at the least—how do you connect it with Sir Gilbert?" asked Blackburton testily.

"I am convinced that it belonged to Sir Gilbert," Low answered.

"But the long black hair like a woman's?"

"Dissolution in the case of Sir Gilbert was not complete—

not consummated, so to speak—as I hope to show you later. Even in the case of dead persons the hair and nails have been known to grow. By a rough calculation as to the growth of nails in such cases, I was enabled to indicate approximately the date of Sir Gilbert's death. The hair too grew on his head."

"But the barred eyes? I saw them myself!" exclaimed the young man.

"The eyelashes grow also. You follow me?"

"You have, I presume, some theory in connection with this?" observed Thierry. "It must be a very curious one."

"Sir Gilbert in his fear of death appears to have mastered and elaborated a strange and ancient formula by which the grosser factors of the body being eliminated, the more ethereal portions continue to retain the spirit, and the body is thus preserved from absolute disintegration. In this manner true death may be indefinitely deferred. Secure from the ordinary chances and changes of existence, this spiritualised body could retain a modified life practically for ever."

"This is a most extraordinary idea, my dear fellow," remarked Thierry.

"But why should Sir Gilbert haunt the Manor House, and one special room?"

"The tendency of spirits to return to the old haunts of bodily life is almost universal. We cannot yet explain the reason of this attraction of environment."

"But the expansion—the crowding substance which we ourselves felt? You cannot meet that difficulty," said Thierry persistently.

"Not as fully as I could wish, perhaps. But the power of expanding and contracting to a degree far beyond our comprehension is a well-known attribute of spiritualised matter."

"Wait one little moment, my dear Monsieur Flaxman," broke in Thierry's voice after an interval; "this is very clever and ingenious indeed. As a theory I give it my sincere admiration. But proof—proof is what we now demand."

Flaxman Low looked steadily at the two incredulous faces.

"This," he said slowly, "is the hair of Sir Gilbert Blackburton, and this nail is from the little finger of his left hand. You can prove my assertion by opening the coffin."

Sir George, who was pacing up and down the room impatiently, drew up.

"I don't like it at all, Mr Low, I tell you frankly. I don't like it at all. I see no object in violating the coffin. I am not concerned to verify this unpleasant theory of yours. I have only one desire; I want to get rid of this haunting presence, whatever it is."

"If I am right," replied Low, "the opening of the coffin and exposure of the remains to strong sunshine for a short time will free you for ever from this presence."

In the early morning, when the summer sun struck warmly on the lawns of Yand, the three men carried the coffin from the vault to a quiet spot among the shrubs where, secure from observation, they raised the lid.

Within the coffin lay the semblance of Gilbert Blackburton, maned to the ears with long and coarse black hair. Matted eyelashes swept the fallen cheeks, and beside the body stretched the bony hands, each with its dependent sheaf of switch-like nails. Low bent over and raised the left hand gingerly.

The little finger was without a nail!

Two hours later they came back and looked again. The sun had in the meantime done its work; nothing remained but a fleshless skeleton and a few half-rotten shreds of clothing.

The ghost of Yank Manor House has never since been heard of.

When Thierry bade Flaxman Low good-bye, he said:

"In time, my dear Monsieur Flaxman, you will add another to our sciences. You establish your facts too well for my peace of mind."

# The Story of the Spaniards, Hammersmith

By *E. and H. Heron*

Lieutenant Roderick Houston, of H.M.S. *Sphinx*, had practically nothing beyond his pay, and he was beginning to be very tired of the West African station, when he received the pleasant intelligence that a relative had left him a legacy. This consisted of a satisfactory sum in ready money and a house in Hammersmith, which was rated at over £200 a year, and was said in addition to be comfortably furnished. Houston, therefore, counted on its rental to bring his income up to a fairly desirable figure. Further information from home, however, showed him that he had been rather premature in his expectations, whereupon, being a man of action, he applied for two months' leave, and came home to look after his affairs himself.

When he had been a week in London he arrived at the conclusion that he could not possibly hope single-handed to tackle the difficulties which presented themselves. He accordingly wrote the following letter to his friend, Flaxman Low:

"The Spaniards, Hammersmith, 23-3-1892

"DEAR LOW,—Since we parted some three years ago, I have heard very little of you. It was only yesterday that I met our mutual friend, Sammy Smith ('Silkworm' of our schooldays), who told me that your studies have developed in a new direction, and that you are now a good deal interested in psychical subjects. If this be so, I hope to induce you to come and stay with me here for a few days by promising to introduce you to a problem in your own line. I am just now living at 'The Spaniards,' a house that has lately been left to me, and which in the first instance was built by an old fellow named Van Nuysen, who married a great-aunt of mine. It is a good house, but there is said to be 'something wrong' with it. It lets easily, but unluckily the tenants cannot be persuaded to remain above a week or two. They complain that the place is haunted by something—presumably a ghost—because its vagaries bear just that brand of inconsequence which stamps the common run of manifestations.

"It occurs to me that you may care to investigate the matter with me. If so, send me a wire when to expect you.

"Yours ever,

"RODERICK HOUSTON."

Houston waited in some anxiety for an answer. Low was the sort of man one could rely on in almost any emergency. Sammy Smith had told him a characteristic anecdote of Low's career at Oxford, where, although his intellectual triumphs may be forgotten, he will always be remembered by the story that when Sands, of Queen's, fell ill on the day before the'Varsity sports, a telegram was sent to Low's rooms: "Sands ill. You must do the hammer for us." Low's reply was pithy: "I'll be there." Thereupon he finished the treatise upon which he was engaged, and next day his strong, lean figure was to be seen swinging the hammer amidst vociferous cheering, for that was the occasion on which he not only won the event, but beat the record.

On the fifth day Low's answer came from Vienna. As he read it, Houston recalled the high forehead, long neck—with its accompanying low collar—and thin moustache of his scholarly, athletic friend and smiled. There was so much more in Flaxman Low than anyone gave him credit for.

> "MY DEAR HOUSTON,—Very glad to hear of you again. In response to your kind invitation, I thank you for the opportunity of meeting the ghost, and still more for the pleasure of your companionship. I came here to inquire into a somewhat similar affair. I hope, however, to be able to leave to-morrow, and will be with you some time on Friday evening.
>
> "Very sincerely yours,
> "FLAXMAN LOW."

"P.S.—By the way, will it be convenient to give your servants a holiday during the term of my visit, as, if my investigations are to be of any value, not a grain of dust must be disturbed in your house, excepting by ourselves? —F.L."

"The Spaniards" was within some fifteen minutes' walk of Hammersmith Bridge. Set in the midst of a fairly respectable neighbourhood, it presented an odd contrast to the commonplace dullness of the narrow streets crowded about it. As Flaxman Low drove up in the evening light, he reflected that the house might have come from the back of beyond—it gave an impression of something old-world and something exotic.

It was surrounded by a ten-foot wall, above which the upper storey was visible, and Low decided that this intensely English house still gave some curious suggestion of the tropics. The interior of the house carried out the same idea, with its sense of space and air, cool tints and wide, matted passages.

"So you have seen something yourself since you came?" Low said, as they sat at dinner, for Houston had arranged that meals should be sent in for them from a hotel.

"I've heard tapping up and down the passage upstairs. It is an uncarpeted landing which runs the whole length of the house. One night, when I was quicker than usual, I saw what looked like a bladder disappear into one of the bedrooms—your room it is to be, by the way—and the door closed behind it," replied Houston discontentedly. "The usual meaningless antics of a ghost."

"What had the tenants who lived here to say about it?" went on Low.

"Most of the people saw and heard just what I have told you, and promptly went away. The only one who stood out for a little while was old Filderg—you know the man? Twenty years ago he made an effort to cross the Australian deserts—he stopped for eight weeks. When he left he saw the house-agent, and said he was afraid he had done a little shooting practice in the upper passage, and he hoped it wouldn't count against him in the bill, as it was done in defence of his life. He said something had jumped on to the bed and tried to strangle him. He described it as cold and glutinous, and he pursued it down the passage, firing at it. He advised the owner to have the house pulled down; but, of course, my cousin did nothing of the kind. It's a very good house, and he did not see the sense of spoiling his property."

"That's very true," replied Flaxman Low, looking round. "Mr Van Nuysen had been in the West Indies, and kept his liking for spacious rooms."

"Where did you hear anything about him?" asked Houston in surprise.

"I have heard nothing beyond what you told me in your letter; but I see a couple of bottles of Gulf weed and a lace-plant ornament, such as people used to bring from the West Indies in former days."

"Perhaps I should tell you the history of the old man," said Houston doubtfully; "but we aren't proud of it!"

Flaxman Low considered a moment.

"When was the ghost seen for the first time?"

"When the first tenant took the house. It was let after old Van Nuysen's time."

"Then it may clear the way if you will tell me something of him."

"He owned sugar plantations in Trinidad, where he passed the greater part of his life, while his wife mostly remained in England—incompatibility of temper it was said. When he came home for good and built this house they still lived apart, my aunt declaring that nothing on earth would persuade her to return to him. In course of time he became a confirmed invalid, and he then insisted on my aunt joining him. She lived here for perhaps a year, when she was found dead in bed one morning—in your room."

"What caused her death?"

"She had been in the habit of taking narcotics, and it was supposed that she smothered herself while under their influence."

"That doesn't sound very satisfactory," remarked Flaxman Low.

"Her husband was satisfied with it anyhow, and it was no one else's business. The family were only too glad to have the affair hushed up."

"And what became of Mr Van Nuysen?"

"That I can't tell you. He disappeared a short time after. Search was made for him in the usual way, but nobody knows to this day what became of him."

"Ah, that was strange, as he was such an invalid," said Low, and straightway fell into a long fit of abstraction, from which he was roused by hearing Houston curse the incurable foolishness and imbecility of ghostly behaviour. Flaxman woke up at this. He broke a walnut thoughtfully and began in a gentle voice:

"My dear fellow, we are apt to be hasty in our condemnation of the general behaviour of ghosts. It may appear incalculably foolish in our eyes, and I admit there often seems to be a total absense of any apparent object or intelligent action. But remember that what appears to us to be foolishness may be wisdom in the spirit world, since our unready senses can only catch broken glimpses of what is, I have not the slightest doubt, a coherent whole, if we could trace the connection."

"There may be something in that," replied Houston indifferently. "People naturally say that this ghost is the ghost of old Van Nuysen. But what connection can possibly exist between what I have told you of him and the manifestations—a tapping up and down the passage and the drawing about of a bladder like a child at play? It sounds idiotic!"

"Certainly. Yet, it need not necessarily be so. There are isolated facts, we must look for the links which lie between. Suppose a saddle and a horse-shoe were to be shown to a man who had never seen a horse, I doubt whether he, however intelligent, could evolve the connecting idea! The ways of spirits are strange to us simply because we need further data to help us to interpret them."

"It's a new point of view," returned Houston, "but upon my word, you know, Low, I think you're wasting your time!"

Flaxman Low smiled slowly; his grave, melancholy face brightened.

"I have," said he, "gone somewhat deeply into the subject. In other sciences one reasons by analogy. Psychology is unfortunately a science with a future but without a past, or more probably it is a lost science of the ancients. However that may be, we stand to-day on the frontier of an unknown world, and progress is the result of individual effort; each solution of difficult phenomena forms a step towards the solution of the next problem. In this case, for example, the bladder-like object may be the key to the mystery."

Houston yawned.

"It all seems pretty senseless, but perhaps you may be able to read reason into it. If it were anything tangible, anything a man could meet with his fists, it would be easier."

"I entirely agree with you. But suppose we deal with this affair as it stands, on similar lines, I mean on prosaic, rational lines, as we should deal with a purely human mystery."

"My dear fellow," returned Houston, pushing his chair back from the table wearily, "you shall do just as you like, only get rid of the ghost!"

For some time after Low's arrival nothing very special happened. The tappings continued, and more than once Low had been in time to see the bladder disappear into the closing door of his bedroom, though, unluckily, he never chanced to be inside the room on these occasions, and however quickly he followed the bladder, he never succeeded in seeing anything further. He made a thorough examination of the house, and left no space unaccounted for in his careful measurement. There were no cellars, and the foundation of the house consisted of a thick layer of concrete.

At length, on the sixth night, an event took place, which, as Flaxman Low remarked, came very near to putting an end to the investigations as far as he was concerned. For the preceding two nights he and Houston had kept watch in the hope of getting a glimpse of the person or thing which tapped so persistently up and down the passage. But they were disappointed, for there were no manifestations. On the third evening, therefore, Low went off to his room a little earlier than usual, and fell asleep almost immediately.

He says he was awakened by feeling a heavy weight upon his feet, something that seemed inert and motionless. He recollected that he had left the gas burning, but the room was now in darkness.

Next, he was aware that the thing on the bed had slowly shifted, and was gradually travelling up towards his chest. How it came on the bed he had no idea. Had it leaped or climbed? The sensation he experienced as it moved was of some ponderous, pulpy body, not crawling or creeping, but spreading! It was horrible! He tried to move his lower limbs, but could not because of the deadening weight. A feeling of drowsiness began to overpower him, and a deadly cold, such as he said he had before felt at sea when in the neighbourhood of icebergs, chilled upon the air.

With a violent struggle he managed to free his arms, but the thing grew more irresistible as it spread upwards. Then he became conscious of a pair of glassy eyes, with livid, everted lids, looking into his own. Whether they were human eyes or beast eyes, he could not tell, but they were watery, like the eyes of a dead fish, and gleamed with a pale, internal lustre.

Then he owns he grew afraid. But he was still cool enough to notice one peculiarity about this ghastly visitant—although the head was within a few inches of his own, he could detect no breathing. It dawned upon him that he was about to be suffocated, for, by the same method of extension, the thing was now coming over his face! It felt cold and clammy, like a mass of mucilage or a monstrous snail. And every instant the weight became greater. He is a powerful man, and he struck with his fists again and again at the head. Some substance yielded under the blows with a sickening sensation of bruised flesh.

With a lucky twist he raised himself in the bed and battered away with all the force he was capable of in his cramped position. The only effect was an occasional shudder or quake that ran through the mass as his half-arm blows rained upon it. At last, by chance, his hand knocked against the candle beside him. In a moment he recollected the matches. He seized the box, and struck a light.

As he did so, the lump slid to the floor. He sprang out of bed, and lit the candle. He felt a cold touch upon his leg, but when he looked down there was nothing to be seen. The door, which he had locked overnight, was now open, and he rushed out into the passage. All was still and silent with the throbbing vacancy of night time.

After searching round, he returned to his room. The bed still gave ample proof of the struggle that had taken place, and by his watch he saw the hour to be between two and three.

As there seemed nothing more to be done, he put on his dressing-gown, lit his pipe, and sat down to write an account of the experience he had just passed through for the Psychical

Research Society—from which paper the above is an abstract.

He is a man of strong nerves, but he could not disguise from himself that he had been at handgrips with some grotesque form of death. What might be the nature of his assailant he could not determine, but his experience was supported by the attack which had been made on Filderg, and also—it was impossible to avoid the conclusion—by the manner of Mrs Van Nuysen's death.

He thought the whole situation over carefully in connection with the tapping and the disappearing bladder, but, turn these events how he would, he could make nothing of them. They were entirely incongruous. A little later he went and made a shakedown in Houston's room.

"What was the thing!" asked Houston, when Low had ended his story of the encounter.

Low shrugged his shoulders.

"At least, it proves that Filderg did not dream," he said.

"But this is monstrous! We are more in the dark than ever. There's nothing for it but to have the house pulled down. Let us leave-to-day."

"Don't be in a hurry, my dear fellow. You would rob me of a very great pleasure; besides, we may be on the verge of some valuable discovery. This series of manifestations is even more interesting than the Vienna mystery I was telling you of."

"Discovery or not," replied the other, "I don't like it."

The first thing next morning Low went out for a quarter of an hour. Before breakfast a man with a barrowful of sand came into the garden. Low looked up from his paper, leant out of the window, and gave some order.

When Houston came down a few minutes later he saw the yellowish heap on the lawn with some surprise.

"Hullo! What's this?" he asked.

"I ordered it," replied Low.

"All right. What's it for?"

"To help us in our investigations. Our visitor is capable of being felt, and he or it felt a very distinct impression on the bed. Hence I gather it can also leave an impression on sand. It would be an immense advance if we could arrive at any correct notion of what sort of feet the ghost walks on. I propose to spread a layer of this sand in the upper passage, and the result should be footmarks if the tapping comes to-night."

That evening the two men made a fire in Houston's bedroom, and sat there smoking and talking, to leave the ghost "a free run for once," as Houston phrased it. The tapping was heard at the usual hour, and presently the accustomed pause at the other end of the passage and the quiet closing of the door.

Low heaved a long sigh of satisfaction as he listened.

"That's my bedroom door," he said: "I know the sound of it perfectly. In the morning, and with the help of daylight, we shall see what we shall see."

As soon as there was light enough for the purpose of examining the footprints, Low roused Houston.

Houston was as full of excitement as a boy, but his spirits fell by the time he had passed from end to end of the passage.

"There are marks," he said, "but they are as perplexing as everything else about this haunting brute, whatever it is. I suppose you think this is the print left by the thing which attacked you the night before last?"

"I fancy it is," said Low, who was still bending over the floor eagerly. "What do you make of it, Houston?"

"The brute has only one leg, to start with," replied Houston, "and that leaves the mark of a large, clawless pad! It's some animal—some ghoulish monster!"

"On the contrary," said Low, "I think we have now every reason to conclude that it is a man?"

"A man? What man ever left footmarks like these?"

"Look at these hollows and streaks at the sides; they are the traces of the sticks we have heard tapping."

"You don't convince me," returned Houston doggedly.

"Let us wait another twenty-four hours, and to-morrow night, if nothing further occurs, I will give you my conclusions. Think it over. The tapping, the bladder, and the fact that Mr Van Nuysen had lived in Trinidad. Add to these things this single pad-like print. Does noting strike you by way of a solution?"

Houston shook his head.

"Nothing. And I fail to connect any of these things with what happened both to you and Filderg."

"Ah! now," said Flaxman Low, his face clouding a little, "I confess you lead me into a somewhat different region, though to me the connection is perfect."

Houston raised his eyebrows and laughed.

"If you can unravel this tangle of hints and events and diagnose the ghost, I shall be extremely astonished," he said. "What can you make of the footless impression?"

"Something, I hope. In fact, that mark may be a clue—an outrageous one, perhaps, but still a clue."

That evening the weather broke, and by night the storm had risen to a gale, accompanied by sharp bursts of rain.

"It's a noisy night," remarked Houston; "I don't suppose we'll hear the ghost, supposing it does turn up."

This was after dinner, as they were about to go into the smoking-room. Houston, finding the gas low in the hall, stopped to turn it higher; at the same time asking Low to see if the jet on the upper landing was also alight.

Flaxman Low glanced up and uttered a slight exclamation, which brought Houston to his side.

Looking down at them from over the banisters was a face—a blotched, yellowish face, flanked by two swollen, protruding ears, the whole aspect being strangely leonine. It was but a glimpse, a clash of meeting glances, as it were, a glare of defiance, and the face was quickly withdrawn as the two men literally leapt up the stairs.

"There's nothing here," exclaimed Houston, after a search had been carried out through every room above.

"I didn't suppose we'd find anything," returned Low.

"This fairly knots up the thread," said Houston. "You can't pretend to unravel it now."

"Come down," said Low briefly; "I'm ready to give you my opinion, such as it is."

Once in the smoking-room, Houston busied himself in turning on all the light he could procure, then he saw to securing the windows, and piled up an immense fire, while Flaxman Low, who, as usual, had a cigarette in his mouth, sat on the edge of the table and watched him with some amusement.

"You saw that abominable face?" cried Houston, as he threw himself into a chair. "It was as material as yours or mine. But where did he go to? He must be somewhere about."

"We saw him clearly. That is sufficient for our purpose."

"You are very good at enumerating points, Low. Now just listen to my list. The difficulties grow with every fresh discovery. We're at a deadlock now, I take it? The sticks and the tapping point to an old man, the playing with a bladder to a child; the footmark might be the pad of a tiger minus claws, yet the thing that attacked you at night was cold and pulpy. And, lastly, by way of a wind-up, we see a lion-like, human face! If you can make all these items square with each other, I'll be happy to hear what you have got to say."

"You must first allow me to ask you a question. I understood you to say that no blood relationship existed between you and old Mr Van Nuysen?"

"Certainly not. He was quite an outsider," answered Houston brusquely.

"In that case you are welcome to my conclusions. All the things you have mentioned point to one explanation. This house is haunted by the ghost of Mr Van Nuysen, and he was a leper."

Houston stood up and stared at his companion.

"What a horrible notion! I must say I fail to see how you have arrived at such a conclusion."

"Take the chain of evidence in rather different order," said Low. "Why should a man tap with a stick?"

"Generally because he's blind."

"In cases of blindness, one stick is used for guidance. Here we have two for support."

"A man who has lost the use of his feet."

"Exactly; a man who has from some cause partially lost the use of his feet."

"But the bladder and the lion-like face?" went on Houston.

"The bladder, or what seemed to us to resemble a bladder, was one of his feet, contorted by the disease and probably swathed in linen, which foot he dragged rather than used; consequently, in passing through a door, for example, he would be in the habit of drawing it in after him. Now, as regards the single footmark we saw. In one form of leprosy, the smaller bones of the extremities frequently fall away. The pad-like impression was, as I believe, the mark of the other foot—a toeless foot which he used, because in a more advanced stage of the disease the maimed hand or foot heals and becomes callous."

"Go on," said Houston; "it sounds as if it might be true. And the lion-like face I can account for myself. I have been in China, and have seen it before in lepers."

"Mr Van Nuysen had been in Trinidad for many years, as we know, and while there he probably contracted the disease."

"I suppose so. After his return," added Houston, "he shut himself up almost entirely, and gave out that he was a martyr to rheumatic gout, this awful thing being the true explanation."

"It also accounts for Mrs Van Nuysen's determination not to return to her husband."

Houston appeared much disturbed.

"We can't drop it here, Low," he said, in a constrained voice. "There is a good deal more to be cleared up yet. Can you tell me more?"

"From this point I find myself on less certain ground," replied Low unwillingly. "I merely offer a suggestion, remember—I don't ask you to accept it. I believe Mrs Van Nuysen was murdered!"

"What?" exclaimed Houston. "By her husband?"

"Indications tend that way."

"But, my good fellow—"

"He suffocated her and then made away with himself. It is a pity that his body was not recovered. The condition of the remains would be the only really satisfactory test of my theory. If the skeleton could even now be found, the fact that he was a leper would be finally settled."

There was a prolonged pause until Houston put another question.

"Wait a minute, Low," he said. "Ghosts are admittedly immaterial. In this instance our spook has an extremely palpable body. Surely this is rather unusual? You have made everything else more or less plain. Can you tell me why this dead leper should have tried to murder you and old Filderg? And also how he came to have the actual physical power to do so?"

Low removed his cigarette to look thoughtfully at the end of it. "Now I lapse into the purely theoretical," he answered. "Cases have been known where the assumption of diabolical agency is apparently justifiable."

"Diabolical agency?—I don't follow you."

"I will try to make myself clear, though the subject is still in a stage of vagueness and immaturity. Van Nuysen committed a murder of exceptional atrocity, and afterwards killed himself. Now, bodies of suicides are known to be peculiarly susceptible to spiritual influences, even to the point of arrested corruption. Add to this our knowledge that the highest aim of an evil spirit is to gain possession of a material body. If I carried out my theory to its logical conclusion, I should say that Van Nuysen's body is hidden somewhere on these premises—that this body is intermittently animated by some spirit, which at certain periods is forced to re-enact the gruesome tragedy of the Van Nuysens. Should any living person chance to occupy the position of the first victim, so much the worse for him!"

For some minutes Houston made no remark on this singular expression of opinion.

"But have you ever met with anything of the sort before?" he said at last.

"I can recall," replied Flaxman Low thoughtfully, "quite a number of cases which would seem to bear out this hypothesis. Among them a curious problem of haunting exhaustively examined by Busner in the early part of 1888, at which I was myself lucky enough to assist. Indeed, I may add that the affair which I have recently been engaged upon in Vienna offers some rather similar features. There, however we had to stop short of excavation, by which alone any specific results might have been attained."

"Then you are of opinion," said Houston, "that pulling the house to pieces might cast some further light upon this affair?"

"I cannot see any better course," said Mr Low.

Then Houston closed the discussion by a very definite declaration.

"This house shall come down!"

So "The Spaniards" was pulled down.

The work of demolition, begun at the earliest possible moment, did not occupy very long, and during its early stages, under the boarding at an angle of the landing was found a skeleton. Several of the phalanges were missing, and other indications also established beyond a doubt the fact that the remains were the remains of a leper.

The skeleton is now in the museum of one of our city hospitals. It bears a scientific ticket, and is the only evidence extant of the correctness of Mr Flaxman Low's methods and the possible truth of his extraordinary theories.

# The Haunted Doll's House

By *M.R. James*

'I suppose you get stuff of that kind through your hands pretty often?' said Mr Dillet, as he pointed with his stick to an object which shall be described when the time comes: and when he said it, he lied in his throat, and knew that he lied. Not once in twenty years—perhaps not once in a lifetime—could Mr Chittenden, skilled as he was in ferreting out the forgotten treasures of half-a-dozen counties, expect to handle such a specimen. It was collectors' palaver, and Mr Chittenden recognized it as such.

'Stuff of that kind, Mr Dillet! It's a museum piece, that is.'

'Well, I suppose there are museums that'll take anything.'

'I've seen one, not as good as that, years back,' said Mr Chittenden, thoughtfully. 'But that's not likely to come into the market: and I'm told they 'ave some fine ones of the period over the water. No: I'm only telling you the truth, Mr Dillet, when I say that if you was to place an unlimited order with me for the very best that could be got—and you know I 'ave facilities for getting to know of such things, and a reputation to maintain—

well, all I can say is, I should lead you straight up to that one and say. "I can't do no better for you than that, Sir."'

'Hear, hear!' said Mr Dillet, applauding ironically with the end of his stick on the floor of the shop. 'How much are you sticking the innocent American buyer for it, eh?'

'Oh, I shan't be over hard on the buyer, American or otherwise. You see, it stands this way, Mr Dillet—if I knew just a bit more about the pedigree——'

'Or just a bit less,' Mr Dillet put in.

'Ha, ha! You will have your joke, Sir. No, but as I was saying, if I knew just a little more than what I do about the piece—though anyone can see for themselves it's a genuine thing, every last corner of it, and there's not been one of my men allowed to so much as touch it since it came into the shop—there'd be another figure in the price I'm asking.'

'And what's that: five and twenty?'

"Multiply that by three and you've got it, Sir. Seventy-five's my price.

'And fifty's mine,' said Mr Dillet.

The point of agreement was, of course, somewhere between the two, it does not matter exactly where—I think sixty guineas. But half an hour later the object was being packed, and within an hour Mr Dillet had called for it in his car and driven away. Mr Chittenden, holding the cheque in his hand, saw him off from the door with smiles, and returned, still smiling, into the parlour where his wife was making the tea. He stopped at the door.

'It's gone,' he said.

'Thank God for that!' said Mrs Chittenden, putting down the teapot. 'Mr Dillet, was it?'

'Yes, it was.'

'Well, I'd sooner it was him than another.'

'Oh, I don't know, he ain't a bad feller, my dear.'

'Maybe not, but in my opinion he'd be none the worse for a bit of a shake up.'

'Well, if that's your opinion, it's my opinion he's put himself into the way of getting one. Anyhow, we shan't have no more of it, and that's something to be thankful for.'

And so Mr and Mrs Chittenden sat down to tea.

And what of Mr Dillet and of his new acquisition? What it was, the title of this story will have told you. What it was like, I shall have to indicate as well as I can.

There was only just room enough for it in the car, and Mr Dillet had to sit with the driver: he had also to go slow, for though the rooms of the Doll's House had all been stuffed carefully with soft cotton-wool, jolting was to be avoided, in view of the immense number of small objects which thronged them; and the ten-mile drive was an anxious time for him, in spite of all the precautions he insisted upon. At last his front door was reached, and Collins, the butler, came out.

'Look here, Collins, you must help me with this thing—it's a delicate job. We must get it out upright, see? It's full of little things that mustn't be displaced more than we can help. Let's see, where shall we have it?' (After a pause for consideration.) 'Really, I think I shall have to put it in my own room, to begin with at any rate. On the big table—that's it.'

It was conveyed—with much talking—to Mr Dillet's spacious room on the first floor, looking out on the drive. The sheeting was unwound from it, and the front thrown open, and for the next hour or two Mr Dillet was fully occupied in extracting the padding and setting in order the contents of the rooms.

When this thoroughly congenial task was finished, I must say that it would have been difficult to find a more perfect and attractive specimen of a Doll's House in Strawberry Hill Gothic than that which now stood on Mr Dillet's large kneehole table, lighted up by the evening sun which came slanting through three tall sash-windows.

It was quite six feet long, including the chapel or oratory which flanked the front on the left as you faced it, and the stable on the right. The main block of the house was, as I have said, in the Gothic manner: that is to say, the windows had pointed arches and were surmounted by what are called ogival hoods, with crockets and finials such as we see on the canopies of tombs built into church walls. At the angles were absurd turrets covered with arched panels. The chapel had pinnacles and buttresses and a bell in the turret and coloured glass in the windows. When the front of the house was open you saw four large rooms, bedroom, dining-room, drawing-room and kitchen, each with its appropriate furniture in a very complete state.

The stable on the right was in two storeys, with its proper complement of horses, coaches and grooms, and with its clock and Gothic cupola for the clock bell.

Pages, of course, might be written on the outfit of the mansion—how many frying pans, how many gilt chairs, what pictures, carpets, chandeliers, four-posters, table linen, glass, crockery and plate it possessed; but all this must be left to the imagination. I will only say that the base or plinth on which the house stood (for it was fitted with one of some depth which allowed of a flight of steps to the front door and a terrace, partly balustraded) contained a shallow drawer or drawers in which were neatly stored sets of embroidered curtains, changes of raiment for the inmates, and, in short, all the materials for an infinite series of variations and refittings of the most absorbing and delightful kind.

'Quintessence of Horace Walpole, that's what it is: he must have had something to do with the making of it.' Such was Mr Dillet's murmured reflection as he knelt before it in a reverent ecstasy. 'Simply wonderful; this is my day and no mistake. Five hundred pound coming in this morning for that cabinet which I never cared about, and now this tumbling into my hands for a tenth, at the very most, of what it would fetch in town. Well, well! It almost makes one afraid something'll happen to counter it. Let's have a look at the population, anyhow.'

Accordingly, he set them before him in a row. Again, here is an opportunity, which some would snatch at, of making an inventory of costume: I am incapable of it.

There were a gentleman and lady, in blue satin and brocade respectively. There were two children, a boy and a girl. There was a cook, a nurse, a footman, and there were the stable servants, two postillions, a coachman, two grooms.

'Anyone else? Yes, possibly.'

The curtains of the four-poster in the bedroom were closely drawn round four sides of it, and he put his finger in between them and felt in the bed. He drew the finger back hastily, for it almost seemed to him as if something had—not stirred, perhaps, but yielded—in an odd live way as he pressed it. Then he put back the curtains, which ran on rods in the proper manner, and extracted from the bed a white-haired old gentleman in a long linen nightdress and cap, and laid him down by the rest. The tale was complete.

Dinner time was now near, so Mr Dillet spent but five minutes in putting the lady and children into the drawing-room, the gentleman into the dining-room, the servants into the kitchen and stables, and the old man back into his bed. He retired into his dressing room next door, and we see and hear no more of him until something like eleven o'clock at night.

His whim was to sleep surrounded by some of the gems of his collection. The big room in which we have seen him contained his bed: bath, wardrobe, and all the appliances of dressing were in a commodious room adjoining: but his four-poster, which itself was a valued treasure, stood in the large room where he sometimes wrote, and often sat, and even received visitors. To-night he repaired to it in a highly complacent frame of mind.

There was no striking clock within earshot—none on the staircase, none in the stable, none in the distant church tower. Yet, it is indubitable that Mr Dillet was startled out of a very pleasant slumber by a bell tolling One.

He was so much startled that he did not merely lie breathless with wide-open eyes, but actually sat up in his bed.

He never asked himself, till the morning hours, how it was that, though there was no light at all in the room, the Doll's House on the kneehole table stood out with complete clearness. But it was so. The effect was that of a bright harvest moon shining full on the front of a big white stone mansion—a quarter of a mile away it might be, and yet every detail was photographically sharp. There were trees about it, too—trees rising behind the chapel and the house. He seemed to be conscious of the scent of a cool still September night. He thought he could hear an occasional stamp and clink from the stables, as of horses stirring. And with another shock he realized that, above the house, he was looking, not at the wall of his room with its pictures, but into the profound blue of a night sky.

There were lights, more than one, in the windows, and he quickly saw that this was no four-roomed house with a movable front, but one of many rooms, and staircases—a real house, but seen as if through the wrong end of a telescope. 'You mean to show me something,' he muttered to himself, and he gazed earnestly on the lighted windows. They would in real life have been shuttered or curtained, no doubt, he thought; but, as it was, there was nothing to intercept his view of what was being transacted inside the rooms.

Two rooms were lighted—one on the ground floor to the right of the door, one upstairs, on the left—the first brightly enough, the other rather dimly. The lower room was the dining-room: a table was laid, but the meal was over, and only wine and glasses were left on the table. The man of the blue satin and the woman of the brocade were alone in the room, and they were talking very earnestly, seated close together at the table, their elbows on it: every now and again stopping to listen, as it seemed. Once *he* rose, came to the window and opened it and put his head out and his hand to his ear. There was a lighted taper in a silver candlestick on a sideboard. When the man left the window he seemed to leave the room also; and the lady, taper in hand, remained standing and listening. The expression on her face was that of one striving her utmost to keep down a fear that threatened to master her—and succeeding. It was a hateful face, too; broad, flat and sly. Now the man came back and she took some small thing from him and hurried out of the room. He, too, disappeared, but only for a moment or two. The front door slowly opened and he stepped out and stood on the top of the *perron*, looking this way and that; then turned towards the upper window that was lighted, and shook his fist.

It was time to look at that upper window. Through it was seen a four-post bed: a nurse or other servant in an arm-chair, evidently sound asleep; in the bed an old man lying: awake, and, one would say, anxious, from the way in which he shifted about and moved his fingers, beating tunes on the coverlet. Beyond the bed a door opened. Light was seen on the ceiling, and the lady came in: she set down her candle on a table, came to the fireside and roused the nurse. In her hand she had an old-fashioned wine bottle, ready uncorked. The nurse took it, poured some of the contents into a little silver sauce-pan, added some spice and sugar from casters on the table, and set it to warm on the fire. Meanwhile, the old man in the bed beckoned feebly to the lady, who came to him smiling, took his wrist as if to feel his pulse, and bit her lip as if in consternation. He looked at her anxiously, and then pointed to the window, and spoke. She nodded, and did as the man below had done; opened the casement and listened—perhaps rather ostentatiously: then drew in her head and shook it, looking at the old man, who seemed to sigh.

By this time the posset on the fire was steaming, and the nurse poured it into a small two-handled silver bowl and brought it to the bedside. The old man seemed disinclined for it and was waving it away, but the lady and the nurse together bent over him and evidently pressed it upon him. He must have yielded, for they supported him into a sitting position, and put it to his lips. He drank most of it, in several draughts, and they laid him down. The lady left the room, smiling good-night to him, and took the bowl, the bottle and the silver sauce-pan with her. The nurse returned to the chair, and there was an interval of complete quiet.

Suddenly the old man started up in his bed—and he must have uttered some cry, for the nurse started out of her chair and made but one step of it to the bedside. He was a sad and terrible sight—flushed in the face, almost to blackness, the eyes glaring whitely, both hands clutching at his heart, foam at his lips.

For a moment the nurse left him, ran to the door, flung it wide open, and, one supposes, screamed aloud for help, then darted back to the bed and seemed to try feverishly to soothe him—to lay him down—anything. But as the lady, her husband, and several servants, rushed into the room with horrified faces, the old man collapsed under the nurse's hands and lay back, and the features, contorted with agony and rage, relaxed slowly into calm.

A few moments later, lights showed out to the left of the house, and a coach with flambeaux drove up to the door. A white-wigged man in black got nimbly out and ran up the steps, carrying a small leather trunk-shaped box. He was met in the doorway by the man and his wife, she with her handkerchief clutched between her hands, he with a tragic face, but retaining his self-control. They led the newcomer into the dining-room, where he set his box of papers on the table, and, turning to them, listened with a face of consternation at what they had to tell. He nodded his head again and again, threw out his hands slightly, declined, it seemed, offers of refreshment and lodging for the night, and within a few minutes came slowly down the steps entering the coach and driving off the way he had come. As the man in blue watched him from the top of the steps, a smile not pleasant to see stole slowly over his fat white face. Darkness fell over the whole scene as the lights of the coach disappeared.

But Mr Dillet remained sitting up in the bed: he had rightly guessed that there would be a sequel. The house front glimmered out again before long. But now there was a difference. The lights were in other windows, one at the top of the house, the other illuminating the range of coloured windows of the chapel. How he saw through these is not quite obvious, but he did. The interior was as carefully furnished as the rest of the establishment, with its minute red cushions on the desks, its Gothic stall-canopies, and its western gallery and pinnacled organ with gold pipes. On the centre of the black and white pavement was a bier: four tall candles burned at the corners. On the bier was a coffin covered with a pall of black velvet.

As he looked the folds of the pall stirred. It seemed to rise at one end: it slid downwards: it fell away, exposing the black coffin with its silver handles and name-plate. One of the tall candlesticks swayed and toppled over. Ask no more, but turn, as Mr Dillet hastily did, and look in at the lighted window at the top of the house, where a boy and girl lay in two truckle-beds, and a four-poster for the nurse rose above them. The nurse was not visible for the moment; but the father and mother were there, dressed now in mourning, but with very little sign of mourning in their demeanour. Indeed, they were laughing and talking with a good deal of animation, sometimes to each other, and sometimes throwing a remark to one or other of the children, and again laughing at the answers. Then the father was seen to go on tiptoe out of the room, taking with him as he went a white garment that hung on a peg near the door. He shut the door after him. A minute or two later it was slowly opened again, and a muffled head poked round it. A bent form of sinister shape stepped across to the truckle-beds, and suddenly stopped, threw up its arms and revealed, of course, the father, laughing. The children were in agonies of terror, the boy with the bed clothes over his head, the girl throwing herself out of bed into her mother's arms. Attempts at consolation followed—the parents took the children on their laps, patted them, picked up the white gown and showed there was no harm in it, and so forth; and at last putting the children back into bed, left the room with encouraging waves of the hand. As they left it, the nurse came in, and soon the light died down.

Still, Mr Dillet watched immovable.

A new sort of light—not of lamp or candle—a pale ugly light, began to dawn around the door-case at the back of the room. The door was opening again. The seer does not like to dwell upon what he saw entering the room: he says it might be described as a frog—the size of a man—but it had scanty white hair about its head. It was busy about the truckle-beds, but not for long. The sound of cries—faint, as if coming out of a vast distance—but, even so, infinitely appalling, reached the ear.

There were signs of a hideous commotion all over the house: lights passed along and up, and doors opened and shut, and running figures passed within the windows. The clock in the stable turret tolled one, and darkness fell again.

It was only dispelled once more, to show the house front. At the bottom of the steps dark figures were drawn up in two lines, holding flaming torches. More dark figures came down the steps, bearing, first one, then another small coffin. And the lines of torch-bearers with the coffins between them moved silently onward to the left.

The hours of night passed on—never so slowly, Mr Dillet thought. Gradually he sank down from sitting to lying in his bed—but he did not close an eye: and early next morning he sent for the doctor.

The doctor found him in a disquieting state of nerves, and recommended sea-air. To a quiet place on the East Coast he accordingly repaired by easy stages in his car.

One of the first people he met on the sea front was Mr Chittenden, who, it appeared, had likewise been advised to take his wife away for a bit of a change.

Mr Chittenden looked somewhat askance upon him when they met: and not without cause.

'Well, I don't wonder at you being a bit upset, Mr Dillet. What? yes, well, I might say 'orrible upset, to be sure, seeing what me and my poor wife went through ourselves. But I put it to you, Mr Dillet, one of two things: was I going to scrap a lovely piece like that on the one 'and, or was I going to tell customers: "I'm selling you a regular picture-palace-dramar in reel life of the olden time, billed to perform regular at one o'clock a.m."? Why, what would you 'ave said yourself? And next thing you know, two Justices of the Peace in the back parlour, and pore Mr and Mrs Chittenden off in a spring cart to the County Asylum and everyone in the street saying, "Ah, I thought it 'ud come to that. Look at the way the man drank!"—and me next door, or next door but one, to a total abstainer, as you know. Well, there was my position. What? Me'ave it back in the shop? Well, what do *you* think? No, but I'll tell you what I will do. You shall have your money back, bar the ten pound I paid for it, and you make what you can.'

Later in the day, in what is offensively called the 'smoke-room' of the hotel, a murmured conversation between the two went on for some time.

'How much do you really know about that thing, and where it came from?'

'Honest, Mr Dillet, I don't know the 'ouse. Of course, it came out of the lumber room of a country 'ouse—that anyone could guess. But I'll go as far as say this, that I believe it's not a hundred miles from this place. Which direction and how far I've no notion. I'm only judging by guess-work. The man as I actually paid the cheque to ain't one of my regular men, and I've lost sight of him; but I 'ave the idea that this part of the country was hi, beat, and that's every word I can tell you. But now, Mr Dillets there's one thing that rather physicks me—that old chap—I suppose you saw him drive up to the door—I thought so: now, would he have been the medical man, do you take it? My wife would have it so, but I stuck to it that was the lawyer, because he had papers with him, and one he took out was folded up.'

'I agree,' said Mr Dillet. 'Thinking it over, I came to the conclusion that was the old man's will, ready to be signed.'

'Just what I thought,' said Mr Chittenden, 'and I took it that will would have cut out the young people, eh? Well, well! It's been a lesson to me, I know that. I shan't buy no more dolls' houses, nor waste no more money on the pictures—and as to this business of poisonin' grandpa, well, if I know myself, I never 'ad much of a turn for that. Live and let live: that's bin my motto throughout life, and I ain't found it a bad one.'

Filled with these elevated sentiments, Mr Chittenden retired to his lodgings. Mr Dillet next day repaired to the local Institute, where he hoped to find some clue to the riddle that absorbed him. He gazed in despair at a long file of the Canterbury and York Society's publications of the Parish Registers of the district. No print resembling the house of his nightmare was among those that hung on the staircase and in the passages. Disconsolate, he found himself at last in a derelict room, staring at a dusty model of a church in a dusty glass case: *Model of St Stephen's Church, Coxham. Presented by J. Merewether, Esq., of Ilbridge House, 1877. The work of his ancestor James Merewether, d. 1786.* There was something in the fashion of it that reminded him dimly of his horror. He retraced his steps to a wall map he had noticed, and made out that Ilbridge House was in Coxham Parish. Coxham was, as it happened, one of the parishes of which he had retained the name when he glanced over the file of printed registers, and it was not long before he found in them the record of the burial of Roger Milford, aged 76, on the $11^{th}$ of September, 1757, and of Roger and Elizabeth Merewether, aged 9 and 7, on the $19^{th}$ of the same month. It seemed worth while to follow up this clue, frail as it was; and in the afternoon he drove out to Coxham. The east end of the north aisle of the church is a Milford chapel, and on its north wall are tablets to the same persons; Roger, the elder, it seems, was distinguished by all the qualities which adorn 'the Father, the Magistrate, and the Man': the memorial was erected by his attached daughter Elizabeth, 'who did not long survive the loss of a parent ever solicitous for her welfare, and of two amiable children.' The last sentence was plainly an addition to the original inscription.

A yet late slab told of James Merewether, husband of Elizabeth, 'who in the dawn of life practised, not without success, those arts which, had he continued their exercise, might in the opinion of the most competent judges have earned for him the name of the British Vitruvius: but who, overwhelmed by the visitation which deprived him of an affectionate partner and a blooming offspring, passed his Prime and Age in a secluded yet elegant Retirement: his grateful Nephew and Heir indulges a pious sorrow by this too brief recital of his excellences.'

The children were more simply commemorated. Both died on the night of the 12th of September.

Mr Dillet felt sure that in Ilbridge House he had found the scene of his drama. In some old sketch-book, possibly in some old print, he may yet find convincing evidence that he is right. But the Ilbridge House of to-day is not that which he sought; it is an Elizabethan erection of the forties, in red brick with stone quoins and dressings. A quarter of a mile from it, in a low part of the park, backed by ancient, stag-horned, ivy-strangled trees and thick undergrowth, are marks of a terraced platform overgrown with rough grass. A few stone balusters lie here and there, and a heap or two, covered with nettles and ivy, of wrought stones with badly carved crockets. This, someone told Mr. Dillet, was the site of an older house.

As he drove out of the village, the hall clock struck four, and

Mr Dillet started up and clapped his hands to his ears. It was not the first time he had heard that bell.

Awaiting an offer from the other side of the Atlantic, the doll's house still reposes, carefully sheeted, in a loft over Mr Dillet's stables, whither Collins conveyed it on the day when Mr Dillet started for the sea coast.

# The Gardener

By *E.F. Benson*

Two friends of mine, Hugh Grainger and his wife, had taken for a month of Christmas holiday the house in which we were to witness such strange manifestations, and when I received an invitation from them to spend a fortnight there I returned them an enthusiastic affirmative. Well already did I know that pleasant heathery countryside, and most intimate was my acquaintance with the subtle hazards of its most charming golf-links. Golf, I was given to understand, was to occupy the solid day for Hugh and me, so that Margaret should never be obliged to set her hand to the implements with which the game, so detestable to her, was conducted....

I arrived there while yet the daylight lingered, and as my hosts were out, I took a ramble round the place. The house and garden stood on a plateau facing south; below it were a couple of acres of pasture that sloped down to a vagrant stream crossed by a footbridge, by the side of which stood a thatched cottage with a vegetable patch surrounding it. A path ran close past this across the pasture from a wicket-gate in the garden, conducted you over the foot-bridge, and, so my remembered sense of geography told me, must constitute a short-cut to the links that lay not half a mile beyond. The cottage itself was clearly on the land of the little estate, and I at once supposed it to be the gardener's house. What went against so obvious and simple a theory was that it appeared to be untenanted. No wreath of smoke, though the evening was chilly, curled from its chimneys, and, coming closer, I fancied it had that air of "waiting" about it which we so often conjure into unused habitations. There it stood, with no sign of life whatever about it, though ready, as its apparently perfect state of repair seemed to warrant, for fresh tenants to put the breath of life into it again. Its little garden, too, though the palings were neat and newly painted, told the same tale; the beds were untended and unweeded, and in the flower-border by the front door was a row of chrysanthemums which had withered on their stems. But all this was but the impression of a moment, and I did not pause as I passed it, but crossed the foot-bridge and went on up the heathery slope that lay beyond. My geography was not at fault, for presently I saw the club-house just in front of me. Hugh no doubt would be just about coming in from his afternoon round, and so we would walk back together. On reaching the club-house, however, the steward told me that not five minutes before Mrs Grainger had called in her car for her husband, and I therefore retraced my steps by the path along which I had already come. But I made a detour, as a golfer will, to walk up the fairway of the seventeenth and eighteenth holes just for the pleasure of recognition, and looked respectfully at the yawning sandpit which so inexorably guards the eighteenth green, wondering in what circumstances I should visit it next, whether with a step complacent and superior, knowing that my ball reposed safely on the green beyond, or with the heavy footfall of one who knows that laborious delving lies before him.

The light of the winter evening had faded fast, and when I crossed the foot-bridge on my return the dusk had gathered. To my right, just beside the path, lay the cottage, the whitewashed walls of which gleamed whitely in the gloaming; and as I turned my glance back from it to the rather narrow plank which bridged the stream I thought I caught out of the tail of my eye some light from one of its windows, which thus disproved my theory that it was untenanted. But when I looked directly at it again I saw that I was mistaken: some reflection in the glass of the red lines of sunset in the west must have deceived me, for in the inclement twilight it looked more desolate than ever. Yet, I lingered by the wicket gate in its low palings, for though all exterior evidence bore witness to its emptiness, some inexplicable feeling assured me, quite irrationally, that this was not so, and that there was somebody there. Certainly there was nobody visible, but, so this absurd idea informed me, he might be at the back of the cottage concealed from me by the intervening structure, and, still oddly, still unreasonably, it became a matter of importance to my mind to ascertain whether this was so or not, so clearly had my perceptions told me that the place was empty, and so firmly had some conviction assured me that it was tenanted. To cover my inquisitiveness, in case there was some one there, I could inquire whether this path was a short cut to the house at which I was staying, and, rather rebelling at what I was doing. I went through the small garden, and rapped at the door. There was no answer, and, after waiting for a response to a second summons, and having tried the door and found it locked. I made the circuit of the house. Of course, there was no one there, and I told myself that I was just like a man who looks under his bed for a burglar and would be beyond measure astonished if he found one.

My hosts were at the house when I arrived, and we spent a cheerful two hours before dinner in such desultory and eager conversation as is proper between friends who have not met for some time. Between Hugh Grainger and his wife it is always impossible to light on a subject which does not vividly interest one or other of them, and golf, politics, the needs of Russia, cooking, ghosts, the possible victory over Mount Everest, and the income tax were among the topics which we passionately discussed. With all these plates spinning, it was easy to whip up any one of them, and the subject of spooks generally was lighted upon again and again.

"Margaret is on the high road to madness," remarked Hugh on one of these occasions, "for she has begun using planchette. If you use planchette for six months, I am told, most careful doctors will conscientiously certify you as insane. She's got five months more before she goes to Bedlam."

"Does it work?" I asked.

"Yes, it says most interesting things," said Margaret. "It says things that never entered my head. We'll try it to-night."

"Oh, not to-night," said Hugh. "Let's have an evening off."

Margaret disregarded this.

"It's no use asking planchette questions," she went on, "because there is in your mind some sort of answer to them. If I ask whether it will be fine to-morrow, for instance, it is probably I—though indeed I don't mean to push—who makes the pencil say 'yes.'"

"And then it usually rains," remarked Hugh.

"Not always: don't interrupt. The interesting thing is to let the pencil write what it chooses. Very often it only makes loops and curves—though they may mean something—and every now and then a word comes, of the significance of which I have no idea whatever, so I clearly couldn't have suggested it. Yesterday evening, for instance, it wrote 'gardener' over and over again. Now what did that mean? The gardener here is a Methodist with a chin-beard. Could it have meant him? Oh, it's time to dress. Please don't be late, my cook is so sensitive about soup."

We rose, and some connection of ideas about "gardener" linked itself up in my mind.

"By the way, what's that cottage in the field by the footbridge?" I asked. "Is that the gardener's cottage?"

"It used to be," said Hugh. "But the chin-beard doesn't live there: in fact nobody lives there. It's empty. If I was owner here, I should put the chin-beard into it, and take the rent off his wages. Some people have no idea of economy. Why did you ask?"

I saw Margaret was looking at me rather attentively.

"Curiosity," I said. "Idle curiosity."

"I don't believe it was," said she.

"But it was," I said. "It was idle curiosity to know whether the house was inhabited. As I passed it, going down to the club-house, I felt sure it was empty, but coming back I felt so sure that there was some one there that I rapped at the door, and indeed walked round it."

Hugh had preceded us upstairs, as she lingered a little.

"And there was no one there?" she asked. "It's odd: I had just the same feeling as you about it."

"That explains planchette writing 'gardener' over and over again," said I. "You had the gardener's cottage on your mind."

"How ingenious!" said Margaret. "Hurry up and dress."

A gleam of strong moonlight between my drawn curtains when I went up to bed that night led me to look out. My room faced the garden and the fields which I had traversed that afternoon, and all was vividly illuminated by the full moon. The thatched cottage with its white walls close by the stream was very distinct, and once more, I suppose, the reflection of the light on the glass of one of its windows made it appear that the room was lit within. It struck me as odd that twice that day this illusion should have been presented to me, but now a yet odder thing happened. Even as I looked the light was extinguished.

The morning did not at all bear out the fine promise of the clear night, for when I woke the wind was squealing, and sheets of rain from the south-west were dashed against my panes. Golf was wholly out of the question, and, though the violence of the storm abated a little in the afternoon, the rain dripped with a steady sullenness. But I wearied of indoors, and, since the two others entirely refused to set foot outside, I went forth mackintoshed to get a breath of air. By way of an object in my tramp, I took the road to the links in preference to the muddy short-cut through the fields, with the intention of engaging a couple of caddies for Hugh and myself next morning, and lingered awhile over illustrated papers in the smoking-room. I must have read for longer than I knew, for a sudden beam of sunset light suddenly illuminated my page, and looking up, I saw that the rain had ceased, and that evening was fast coming on. So instead of taking the long detour by the road again, I set forth homewards by the path across the fields. That gleam of sunset was the last of the day, and one again, just as twenty-four hours ago, I crossed the foot-bridge in the gloaming. Till that moment, as far as I was aware, I had not thought at all about the cottage there, but now in a flash the light I had seen there last night, suddenly extinguished, recalled itself to my mind, and at the same moment I felt that invincible conviction that the cottage was tenanted.

Simultaneously in these swift processes of thought I looked towards it, and saw standing by the door the figure of a man. In the dusk I could distinguish nothing of his face, if indeed it was turned to me, and only got the impression of a tallish fellow, thickly built. He opened the door, from which there came a dim light as of a lamp, entered, and shut it after him.

So then my conviction was right. Yet, I had been distinctly told that the cottage was empty: who, then, was he that entered as if returning home? One more, this time with a certain qualm of fear, I rapped on the door, intending to put some trivial question; and rapped again, this time more drastically, so that there could be no question that my summons was unheard. But still I got no reply, and finally I tried the handle of the door. It was locked. Then, with difficulty mastering an increasing terror, I made the circuit of the cottage, peering into each unshuttered window. All was dark within, though but two minutes ago I had seen the gleam of light escape from the opened door.

Just because some chain of conjecture was beginning to form itself in my mind, I made no allusion to this odd adventure, and after dinner Margaret, amid protests from Hugh, got out the planchette which had persisted in writing "gardener." My surmise was, of course, utterly fantastic, but I wanted to convey no suggestion of any sort to Margaret. ... For a long time the pencil skated over her paper making loops and curves and peaks like a temperature chart, and she had begun to yawn and weary over her experiment before any coherent word emerged. And then, in the oddest way, her head nodded forward and she seemed to have fallen asleep.

Hugh looked up from his book and spoke in a whisper to me.

"She fell asleep the other night over it," he said.

Margaret's eyes were closed, and she breathed the long, quiet breaths of slumber, and then her hand began to move with a curious firmness. Right across the big sheet of paper went a level line of writing, and at the end her hand stopped with a jerk, and she woke.

She looked at the paper.

"Hallo," she said. "Ah, one of you has been playing a trick on me!"

We assured her that this was not so, and she read what she had written.

'Gardener, gardener," it ran. "I am the gardener. I want to come in. I can't find her here."

"O Lord, that gardener again!" said Hugh.

Looking up from the paper, I saw Margaret's eyes fixed on mine, and even before she spoke I know what her thought was.

"Did you come home by the empty cottage?" she asked.

"Yes: why?"

"Still empty?" she said in a low voice. "Or—or anything else?"

I did not want to tell her just what I had seen—or what, at any rate, I thought I had seen. If there was going to be anything odd, anything worth observation, it was far better that our respective impressions should not fortify each other.

"I tapped again, and there was no answer," I said.

Presently there was a move to bed: Margaret initiated it, and after she had gone upstairs Hugh and I went to the front door to interrogate the weather. Once more the moon shone in a clear sky, and we strolled out along the flagged path that fronted the house. Suddenly Hugh turned quickly and pointed to the angle of the house.

"Who on earth is that?" he said. "Look! There! He has gone round the corner."

I had but the glimpse of a tallish man of heavy build.

"Didn't you see him?" asked Hugh. "I'll just go round the house, and find him; I don't want any one prowling round us at night. Wait here, will you, and if he comes round the other corner ask him what his business is."

Hugh had left me, in our stroll, close by the front door which was open, and there I waited until he should have made his circuit. He had hardly disappeared when I heard, quite distinctly, a rather quick but heavy footfall coming along the paved walk towards me from the opposite direction. But there was absolutely no one to be seen who made this sound of rapid walking. Closer and closer to me came the steps of the invisible one, and then with a shudder of horror I felt somebody unseen push by me as I stood on the threshold. That shudder was not merely of the spirit, for the touch of him was that of ice on my hand. I tried to seize this impalpable intruder, but he slipped from me, and the next moment I heard his steps on the parquet of the floor inside. Some door within opened and shut, and I heard no more of him. Next moment Hugh came running round the corner of the house from which the sound of steps had approached.

"But where is he?" he asked. "He was not twenty yards in front of me—a big, tall fellow."

"I saw nobody," I said. "I heard his step along the walk, but there was nothing to be seen."

"And then?" asked Hugh.

"Whatever it was seemed to brush by me, and go into the house," said I.

There had certainly been no sound of steps on the bare oak stairs, and we searched room after room through the ground floor of the house. The dining-room door and that of the smoking-room were locked, that into the drawing-room was open, and the only other door which could have furnished the impression of an opening and a shutting was that into the kitchen and servants' quarters. Here again our quest was fruitless; through pantry and scullery and boot-room and servants' hall we searched, but all was empty and quiet. Finally we came to the kitchen, which too was empty. But by the fire there was set a rocking-chair, and this was oscillating to and fro as if some one, lately sitting there, had just quitted it. There it stood gently rocking, and this seemed to convey the sense of a presence, invisible now, more than even the sight of him who surely had been sitting there could have done. I remember wanting to steady it and stop it, and yet my hand refused to go forth to it.

When we had seen, and in especial what we had not seen, would have been sufficient to furnish most people with a broken night, and assuredly I was not among the strong-minded exceptions. Long I lay wide-eyed and open-eared, and when at last I dozed I was plucked from the border-land of sleep by the sound, muffled but unmistakable, of some one moving about the house. It occurred to me that the steps might be those of Hugh conducting a lonely exploration, but even while I wondered a tap came at the door of communication between our rooms, and, in answer to my response, it appeared that he had come to see whether it was I thus uneasily wandering. Even as we spoke the step passed my door, and the stairs leading to the floor above creaked to its ascent. Next moment it sounded directly above our heads in some attics in the roof.

"Those are not the servants' bedrooms," said Hugh. "No one sleeps there. Let us look once more: it must he somebody."

With lit candles we made our stealthy way upstairs, and just when we were at the top of the flight, Hugh, a step ahead of me, uttered a sharp exclamation.

"But something is passing by me!" he said, and he clutched at the empty air. Even as he spoke, I experienced the same sensation, and the moment afterwards the stairs below us creaked again, as the unseen passed down.

All night long that sound of steps moved about the passages, as if some one was searching the house, and as I lay and listened that message which had come through the pencil of the planchette to Margaret's fingers occurred to me. "I want to come in. I cannot find her here." ... Indeed some one had come in, and was sedulous in his search. He was the gardener, it would seem. But what gardener was this invisible seeker, and for whom did he seek?

Even as when some bodily pain ceases it is difficult to recall with any vividness what the pain was like, so next morning, as I dressed, I found myself vainly trying to recapture the horror of the spirit which had accompanied these nocturnal adventures. I remembered that something within me had sickened as I watched the movements of the rocking-chair the night before and as I heard the steps along the paved way outside, and by that invisible pressure against me knew that some one had entered the house. But now in the sane and tranquil morning, and all day under the serene winter sun, I could not realise what it had been. The presence, like the bodily pain, had to be there for the realisation of it, and all day it was absent. Hugh felt the same; he was even disposed to be humorous on the subject.

"Well, he's had a good look," he said, "whoever he is, and whomever he was looking for. By the way, not a word to Margaret, please. She heard nothing of these perambulations, nor of the entry of—of whatever it was. Not gardener, anyhow: who ever heard of a gardener spending his time walking about the house? If there were steps all over the potato-patch, I might have been with you."

Margaret had arranged to drive over to have tea with some friends of hers that afternoon, and in consequence Hugh and I refreshed ourselves at the club-house after our game, and it was already dusk when for the third day in succession I passed homewards by the whitewashed cottage. But to-night I had no sense of it being subtly occupied; it stood mournfully desolate, as is the way of untenanted houses, and no light nor semblance of such gleamed from its windows. Hugh, to whom I had told the odd impressions I had received there, gave them a reception as flippant as that which he had accorded to the memories of the night, and he was still being humorous about them when we came to the door of the house.

"A psychic disturbance, old boy," he said. "Like a cold in the head. Hallo, the door's locked."

He rang and rapped, and from inside came the noise of a turned key and withdrawn bolts.

"What's the door locked for?" he asked his servant who opened it.

The man shifted from one foot to the other.

"The bell rang half an hour ago, sir," he said, "and when I came to answer it there was a man standing outside, and——"

"Well?" asked Hugh.

"I didn't like the looks of him, sir," he said, "and I asked him his business. He didn't say anything, and then he must have gone pretty smartly away, for I never saw him go."

"Where did he seem to go?" asked Hugh, glancing at me.

"I can't rightly say, sir. He didn't seem to go at all. Something seemed to brush by me."

"That'll do," said Hugh rather sharply.

Margaret had not come in from her visit, but when soon after the crunch of the motor wheels was heard Hugh reiterated his wish that nothing should be said to her about the impression which now, apparently, a third person shared with us. She came in with a flush of excitement on her face.

"Never laugh at my planchette again," she said. "I've heard the most extraordinary story from Maud Ashfield—horrible, but so frightfully interesting."

"Out with it." said Hugh.

"Well, there was a gardener here," she said. "He used to live at that little cottage by the foot-bridge, and when the family were up in London he and his wife used to be caretakers and live here."

Hugh's glance and mine met: then he turned away. I knew, as certainly as if I was in his mind, that his thoughts were identical with my own.

"He married a wife much younger than himself," continued Margaret, "and gradually he became frightfully jealous of her. And one day in a fit of passion he strangled her with his own hands. A little while after some one came to the cottage, and found him sobbing over her, trying to restore her. They went for the police, but before they came he had cut his own throat. Isn't it all horrible? But surely it's rather curious that the planchette said 'Gardener. I am the gardener. I want to come in. I can't find her here." You see I knew nothing about it. I shall do planchette again to-night. Oh dear me, the post goes in half an hour, and I have a whole budget to send. But respect my planchette for the future, Hughie."

We talked the situation out when she had gone, but Hugh, unwillingly convinced and yet unwilling to admit that something more than coincidence lay behind that "planchette nonsense," still insisted that Margaret should be told nothing of what we had heard and seen in the house last night, and of the strange visitor who again this evening, so we must conclude, had made his entry.

"She'll be frightened," he said, "and she'll begin imagining things. As for the planchette, as likely as not it will do nothing but scribble and make loops. What's that? Yes: come in!"

There had come from somewhere in the room one sharp, peremptory rap. I did not think it came from the door, but Hugh, when no response replied to his words of admittance, jumped up and opened it. He took a few steps into the hall outside, and returned.

"Didn't you hear it?" he asked.

"Certainly. No one there?"

"Not a soul."

Hugh came back to the fireplace and rather irritably threw a cigarette which he had just lit into the fender.

"That was rather a nasty jar," he observed; "and if you ask me whether I feel comfortable, I can tell you I never felt less comfortable in my life. I'm frightened, if you want to know, and I believe you are, too."

I hadn't the smallest intention of denying this, and he went on.

"We've got to keep a hand on ourselves," he said. "There's nothing so infectious as fear, and Margaret mustn't catch it from us. But there's something more than our fear, you know. Something has got into the house and we're up against it. I never believed in such things before. Let's face it for a minute. *What* is it anyhow?"

"If you want to know what I think it is," said I, "I believe it to be the spirit of the man who strangled his wife and then cut his throat. But I don't see how it can hurt us. We're afraid of our own fear really."

"But we're up against it," said Hugh. "And what will it do? Good Lord, if I only knew what it would do I shouldn't mind. It's the not knowing. … Well, it's time to dress."

Margaret was in her highest spirits at dinner. Knowing nothing of the manifestations of that presence which had taken place in the last twenty-four hours, she thought it absorbingly interesting that her planchette should have "guessed" (so ran her phrase) about the gardener, and from that topic she flitted to an equally interesting form of patience for three which her friend had shown her, promising to initiate us into it after dinner. This she did, and, not knowing that we both above all things wanted to keep planchette at a distance, she was delighted with the success of her game. But suddenly she observed that the evening was burning rapidly away, and swept the cards together at the conclusion of a hand.

"Now just half an hour of planchette," she said.

"Oh, mayn't we play one more hand?" asked Hugh. "It's the best game I've seen for years. Planchette will be dismally slow after this."

"Darling, if the gardener will only communicate again, it won't be slow," said she.

"But it is such drivel," said Hugh.

"How rude you are! Read your book, then."

Margaret had already got out her machine and a sheet of paper, when Hugh rose.

"Please don't do it to-night, Margaret," he said.

"But why? You needn't attend."

"Well, I ask you not to, anyhow," said he.

Margaret looked at him closely.

"Hughie, you've got something on your mind," she said. "Out with it. I believe you're nervous. You think there is something queer about. What is it?"

I could see Hugh hesitating as to whether to tell her or not, and I gathered that he chose the chance of her planchette inanely scribbling.

"Go on then," he said.

Margaret hesitated: she clearly did not want to vex Hugh, but his insistence must have seemed to her most unreasonable.

"Well, just ten minutes," she said, "and I promise not to think of gardeners."

She had hardly laid her hand on the board when her head fell forward, and the machine began moving. I was sitting close to her, and as it rolled steadily along the paper the writing became visible.

"I have come in," it ran, "but still I can't find her. Are you hiding her? I will search the room where you are."

What else was written but still concealed underneath the planchette I did not know, for at that moment a current of icy air swept round the room, and at the door, this time unmistakably, came a loud peremptory knock. Hugh sprang to his feet.

"Margaret, wake up," he said, "something is coming!"

The door opened, and there moved in the figure of a man. He stood just within the door, his head bent forward, and he turned it from side to side, peering, it would seem, with eyes staring and infinitely sad, into every corner of the room.

"Margaret, Margaret," cried Hugh again.

But Margaret's eyes were open, too; they were fixed on this dreadful visitor.

"Be quiet, Hughie," she said below her breath, rising as she spoke. The ghost was now looking directly at her. Once the lips above the thick, rust-coloured beard moved, but no sound came forth, the mouth only moved and slavered. He raised his head, and, horror upon horror, I saw that one side of his neck was laid open in a red, glistening gash....

For how long that pause continued, when we all three stood stiff and frozen in some deadly inhibition to move or speak, I have no idea: I suppose that at the utmost it was a dozen seconds. Then the spectre turned, and went out as it had come. We heard his steps pass along the parqueted floor; there was the sound of bolts withdrawn from the front door, and with a crash that shook the house it slammed to.

"It's all over," said Margaret. "God have mercy on him!"

# The Staircase

By *Hugh Walpole*

It doesn't matter in the least where this old house is. There were once many houses like it. Now there are very few.

It was born in 1540 (you can see the date of its birth over the lintel of the porch, cut into the stone). It is E-shaped with central porch and wings at each end. Its stone is now, in its present age, weathered to a beautiful colour of pearl-grey, purple-shadowed. This stone makes the house seem old, but it is not old; its heart and veins are strong and vigorous, only its clothes now are shabby.

It is a small house as Tudor manor-houses go, but its masonry is very solid, and it was created by a spirit who cared that it should have every grace of proportion and strength. The wings have angle buttresses, and the porch rises to twisted terminals; there are twisted terminals with cupola tops also upon the gables, and the chimneys too are twisted. The mullioned windows have arched heads, and the porch has a Tudor arch. The arch is an entrance to a little quadrangle, and there are rooms above and gables on either side. Here and there is rich carving very fancifully designed.

It is set upon a little hill, and the lawn runs down to a small formal garden with box-hedges mounted by animals fancifully cut, a sun-dial, a little stone temple. Fields spread on either side of it and are bordered completely by a green tangled wood. The trees climb skywards on every side, but they are not too close about the house. They are too friendly to it to hurt it in any way. Over the arched porch a very amiable gargoyle hangs his head. He has one eye closed and a protruding chin from which the rain drips on a wet day, and in the winter icicles hang from it.

All the country about the house is very English, and the villages have names like Croxton, Little Pudding, Big Pudding, Engleheart and Applewain. A stream runs at the end of the lower field, runs through the wood, under the road, by other fields, so far as Bonnet where it becomes a river and broadens under bridges at Peckwit, the country town.

The house is called Candil Place and is very proud of its name. Its history for the last hundred years has been very private and personal. No one save myself and the house knows the real carises of its history, just as no one knows the real crisis of your history save yourself. You have doubtless been often surprised that neighbours think that such and such events have been the dramatic changing moments in your life—as when you lost your wife or your money or had scarlet fever—when in reality it was the blowing of a window curtain, the buying of a ship in silver, or the cry of a child on the stair.

So it has been with this house which has had its heart wrung by the breaking of a bough in the wind, a spark flying from the chimney, or a mouse scratching in the wainscot. From its birth it has had its own pride, its own reserve, its own consequence. Everything that has happened in it, every person who has come to it or gone from it, every song that has been sung in it, every oath sworn in it, every shout, every cry, every prayer, every yawn has found a place in its history.

Its heart has been always kindly, hospitable, generous; it has had as many intentions as we have all had, towards noble ends and fine charities. But life is not so easy as that.

Its first days were full of light and colour. Of course it was always a small house; Sir Mortimer Candil, who helped to create it, loved it, and the house gave him its heart. The house knew that he did for it what he could with his means; the house suffered with him when his first wife died of the plague, rejoiced with him when he married again so beautiful a lady, suffered with him once more when the beautiful lady ran away to Spain with a rascal.

There is a little room, the Priest's Room, where Sir Mortimer shut himself in and cried, one long summer day, his heart away. When he came out of there he had no heart any more, and the house, the only witness of that scene, put its arms about him, loved him more dearly than it had ever done, and mourned him most bitterly when he died.

Sir Edmund had a sister Henrietta, who was the cause of all the later trouble. The house never from the beginning liked Henrietta.

The house was willing to grant that Henrietta loved her brother, but in a mean, grasping, greedy manner, and jealousy was her other name.

They were children of a late marriage and their parents died of the smallpox when Edmund was nineteen and Henrietta twenty-one. After that Henrietta ruled the house because Edmund was scarcely ever there, and the house disliked exceedingly her rule. This house was, as I have said, a loyal and faithful friend and servant of the Candil family. Some houses are always hostile to their owners, having a great unreasoning pride of their own and considering the persons who inhabit them altogether unworthy of their good fortune. But partly for the sake of Sir Mortimer, who had created and loved it, and partly because it was by nature kindly, and partly because it always hoped for the best, the house had always chosen only the finest traits in the Candil character and refused to look at any other.

But, if there is one thing that a house resents, it is to be shabbily and meanly treated. When a carpet is worn, a window rattling in the breeze, a pipe in rebellion, a chair on the wobble, the house does everything towards drawing the attention of its master. This house had been always wonderfully considerate of expense and the costliness of all repair. It knew that its masters were not men of great wealth and must go warily with their purposes, but, until Henrietta, the Candils had been generous within their powers. They had had a pride in the house which made them glad to be generous. Henrietta had no such pride. She persisted in what she called an 'adequate economy,' declaring that it was her duty to her brother who drove her, but as the house (who was never deceived about anything) very well knew, this so-called 'economy' became her god and to save money her sensual passion.

She grew into a long bony woman with a faint moustache on her upper lip and a strange, heavy, flat-footed way of walking. The Staircase, a little conceited perhaps because of its lovely banisters that were as delicate as lace, hated her tread and declared that she was so common that she could not be a Candil. Several times the Staircase tripped her up out of sheer maliciousness. The Store-room hated her more than did any other part of the house. Every morning she was there, skimping and cheese-paring, making this last and doing without that, wondering whether this were not too expensive and that too 'outrageous.' Of course, her maidservants would not stay with her. She found it cheapest to engage little charity-girls, and when she had them she starved them. It is true that she also starved herself, but that was no virtue; the house would see the little charity-girls crying from sheer hunger in their beds, and its heart would ache for them.

This was of course to some degree different when Edmund came home from his travels, but not very different, because he was always considerably under his sister's influence. He was soft-hearted and she was hard, and, as the house very well knew, the hard ones always win.

Henrietta loved her brother, but she was also afraid of him. She was very proud of him but yet more proud of her domination over him. When he was thirty and she thirty-two she was convinced that he would never marry. It had been once her terror that he should, and she would lie awake thinking one moment of the household accounts and the next of wicked girls who might entrap her brother. But it seemed that he was never in love; he returned from every travel as virgin as before.

She said to him one morning, smiling her rather grim smile: 'Well, brother, you are a bachelor for life, I think.'

It was then that he told her that he was shortly to marry Miss Dorothy Preston of Cathwick Hall.

He spoke very quietly, but, as the armchair in the Adam Room noticed, he was not quite at his ease. They were speaking in the Adam Room at the time, and this armchair had only recently been purchased by Edmund Candil. The room was not known then as the Adam Room (it had that title later) but it was the room of Edmund's heart. The fireplace was in the Adam style and so were the ceiling, and the furniture, the chairs, the table, the sofa, the commode Edmund had had made for him in London.

Very lovely they were, of satin-wood and mahogany, with their general effect of straight line but modified by lovely curves, delicate and shining. In the centre of the commode was a painted vase of flowers, on the ceiling a heavenly tracing of shell-like circles. Everywhere grace and strength and the harmony of perfect workmanship.

This room was for Edmund the heart of England, and he would stand in it, his dark eyes glowing, fingering his stock, slapping his tight thigh with his riding-whip, a glory at his heart. Many things he had brought with him from foreign countries. There was the Chinese room, and the little dining-room was decorated with Italian pictures. In his own room that he called the Library there was an ink-horn that had been (they said) Mirabeau's, a letter of Marie Antoinette's, a yellow lock cut from the hair of a mermaid and some of the feathers from the head-dress of an African chieftain. Many more treasures than these. But it was the Parlour with the fine furniture bought by him in London that was England, and it was of this room that he thought when he was tossing on the Bay of Biscay or studying pictures in Florence or watching the ablutions of natives in the Sacred River.

It was in this room that he told his sister that he intended marriage.

She made no protest. She knew well enough when her brother's mind was made up. But it was a sunny morning when he told her, and as the sun, having embraced merrily the box-hedge peacocks and griffins, looked in to wish good-morning to the sofa and the round shining satin-wood table that balanced itself so beautifully on its slim delicate legs, it could tell that the table and chairs were delighted about something.

'What is it?' said the sun, rubbing its chin on the window-sill.

'There's a new mistress coming,' said the table and chairs.

And, when she came, they all fell at once in love with her. Was there ever anyone so charming and delicate in her primrose-coloured gown, her pretty straw bonnet and the grey silk scarf about her shoulders? Was there ever anyone so charming?

Of course, Henrietta did not think so. This is an old story, this one of the family relations greeting so suspiciously the new young bride, but it is always actual enough in its tragedy and heart-break however often it may have happened before.

Is it sentimental to be sorry because the new Lady Candil was sad and lonely and cried softly for hours at night while her husband slept beside her? At that time at least the house did not think so. Possibly by now it has grown more cynical. It cannot, any more than the humans who inhabit it, altogether be unaware of the feeling and colour of its time.

In any case the house loved Dorothy Candil and was deeply grieved at her trouble. That trouble was, one must realise, partly of her own making.

Her husband loved her, nay, he adored her with all the tenderness and tenacity that were part of his character. He adored her and was bored by her: as everyone knows, this is a most aggravating state of feeling. He thought her beautiful, good, amiable and honest, but he had nothing at all to say to her. For many a man she would have been exactly fitting, for it was not so much that she was stupid as that she had no education and no experience. He gave her none of these things as he should have done. Nor did he realise that this life, in the depths of English country, removed from all the enterprise and movement of the town, removed also by the weather from any outside intercourse for weeks at a time, was for someone without any great resources in herself depressing and enervating.

And then she was frightened of him. How well the house understood this! It too was, at times, afraid of him, of his silences, his obstinacy and easy capacity of semi-liveliness, a sensitiveness that his reticence forbade him to express.

How often in the months that followed the marriage did the house long to advise her as to her treatment of him. The sofa in the parlour was especially wise in such cases. Long before it had been covered with its gay cherry-coloured silk it had been famous among friends and neighbours for its delicacy in human tactics.

There came a morning when Lady Candil sat on a corner of it, her lovely little hand (she was delicate, slim, fragile, her body had the consistency of egg-shell china) clenching the shining wood of its strong arm for support, and a word from her would have put everything right. The sofa could feel the throbbing of her heart, and looking across to the thick, stiff, obstinate body of her husband, longed to throw her into his arms. But she could not say the word, and the mischanced moment became history for both of them. Had they not loved so truly it might have been easier for them; as it was, shyness and obstinacy built the barrier.

And of course Henrietta assisted. How grimly was she pleased as she sat in her ugly old russet gown, pretending to read Lord Clarendon's History (for she made a great pretence of improving her mind), but in reality listening to the unhappy silences between them and watching for the occasion when a word from her to her brother would skilfully widen the breach. For she hated poor Dorothy. She must in any case have done so out of jealousy and disappointment, but Dorothy was also precisely the example in woman whom she most despised. A weak, feckless, helpless thing whose pretty looks were an insult!

Then Dorothy felt her peril and rose to meet it. The house may have whispered in her ear!

Yes, she rose to meet it, but, as life only too emphatically teaches us, it is no good crying for the moon—and it is no good, however urgent we may be, begging for qualities that we have not got. She had a terrible habit of being affectionate at the wrong time. A kind of fate pursued her in this. He would return from his afternoon's ride, pleasantly weary, eager for his wife and happy in the thought of a little romantic dalliance, and she, fancying that he would not be disturbed, would leave him to snore beside the fire. Or, a neighbour squire would visit him and he be off with him for the afternoon and she feel neglected. Or, he would be absorbed in a newsletter with a lively account of French affairs and she choose that moment to sit on his knee and tug his hair.

Dorothy was in truth one of those unfortunate persons—and they are among the most unfortunate in the world—who are insensitive to the moods and atmospheres of others. These err not through egotism nor stupidity, but rather through a sort of colour-blindness so that they see their friend red when he is yellow and green when he is blue. Neither Dorothy nor Edmund had any gift of words.

So, a year and a half after his marriage, Edmund, with an ache in his heart, although he would own this to nobody, went once again to foreign parts. The house implored him not to go: he almost heard its protests.

On one of his last evenings there—a windy spring evening—he came in from a dark twilight walk, splashed with the mud of the country paths, the sense of the pale hedgerow primroses yet in his eye, the chatter of birds in his ear, and standing in the hall heard the William and Mary clock with the moon and stars, the banisters of the staircase, the curtains of the long hall window whisper to him:

'Don't' go! Don't go! Don't go!'

He stood there and thought: 'By Gemini, I'll not leave this!' Dorothy came down the stairs to greet him and, seeing him lost in thought, stole upstairs again. In any case he had taken his seat in the coach, and his place in the packet-boat was got for him by a friend in London.

'Don't go!' said the portrait of old Uncle Candil.

He strode upstairs and Dorothy was reading *Grandison* by the fire, and although her heart was beating with love for him, was too timid to say so.

So to foreign parts he went again and, loving her so dearly, wrote letters to her which he tore up without sending lest she should think him foolish—such being the British temperament.

How the house suffered then, that Dorothy should be left to the harsh economies of sister Henrietta. Henrietta was not a bad woman, but she was mean, selfish, proud and stupid. She was also jealous. Very quickly and with little show of rebellion Dorothy submitted to her ways. If true love is in question absence does indeed make the heart grow fonder, and Dorothy thought of her husband night, morning, and night again.

She was snubbed, starved, and given a thorough sense of her insufficiencies. It is surprising how completely one human being can convince another of incompetence, ignorance and silly vanity if they be often alone together and one of them a woman. Women are more whole-hearted than men in what they do, whether for good or ill, and Henrietta was very whole-hearted indeed in this affair.

She convinced Dorothy before her husband's return that she was quite unworthy of his love, that he found her dull and unresponsive, that he was deeply disappointed in the issue of his marriage, and that she had deceived him most basely. You may say that she was a poor-spirited little thing, but she was very lonely, half-starved, and her love made her defenceless.

The appetite grows with what it feeds on, and Henrietta found that 'educating Dorothy,' as she called it, was a very worthy and soul-satisfying occupation. Dorothy began to be frightened, not only of herself and of Henrietta but of everything around her, the house, the gardens, the surrounding country.

The house did its utmost to reassure her. When she lay awake in her bed at night the house would hush any noise that might disturb her, the furniture of her room, the hangings above her bed, the old chest of Cromwell's time, the Queen Anne wardrobe, the warming-pan, the fire-irons that had the heads of grinning dogs, the yellow rug from Turkey, the Italian lamp beside her bed, they all crowded about her to tell her that they loved her. After a while she was conscious of their affection. Her bedroom and the parlour were for her the happiest places in the house, the only places indeed where she was not afraid.

She did not know that they were saying anything to her—she had not that kind of perception—but she felt reassured by them, and she would lock herself into her bedroom and sit there for hours thinking of her husband and wondering where he might be.

She became so painfully aware of Henrietta that she saw her when she wasn't there. She saw her always just around a corner, behind a tree, on the other side of the rose-garden well, peering over the sun-dial, hiding behind the curtain. She became a slave to her, doing all that she was told, going where she was bid. The house considered it a disgusting business.

One evening she broke into a flash of rebellion.

'Edmund loves me!' she cried, her little breasts panting, her small hands clenched. 'And you hate me! Why do you hate me? I have never done you any harm.'

'Hate! Hate! I have other things to do—and if he loves you, why does he stay so long away?'

Ah! why indeed? The house echoed the question, the very floors trembling with agitation. The stupid fool! Could he not see the treasure that he had? Did he think that such glories were to be picked up anywhere, any day, for the asking? The fire spat a piece of coal on to the hearthrug in contempt of human blindness.

When the time arrived at last for Edmund's return, Dorothy was in a fitting condition of miserable humility. Edmund did not love her. He was bored with her too dreadfully. But indeed how could he love her? How could anybody love her, poor incompetent stupid thing that she was! And yet in her heart she knew that she was not so stupid. Did Edmund love her only a little she could jump all the barriers and be really rather brilliant—much more brilliant than Henrietta, who was certainly not brilliant at all. It was this terrible shyness that held her back, that and Henrietta's assurance that Edmund did not love her. And indeed he did not seem to. It was but too likely that Henrietta was right.

As the time approached for Edmund's return Henrietta was in a fine bustle and the house was in one, too. The house smiled contemptuously at Henrietta's parsimonious attempts to freshen it up. As though the house could not do that a great deal better than Henrietta ever could! Bees-waxing the floors, rubbing the furniture, shining up the silver—what were these little superficialities compared with the inner spiritual shake that the house gave itself when it wanted to? A sort of glow stole over windows, stairs and hall; a silver shine, a richer colour crept into the amber curtains, the cherry-coloured sofa; the faces in the portraits smiled, the fire-irons glittered, the mahogany shone again. Edmund had been away too long; the house would not let him go so easily next time.

The night before his return Dorothy did not sleep, but lay there, here eyes burning, her heart thickly beating, determining on the bold demonstrative person she would be. She would show Henrietta whether he loved her or no. But at the thought of Henrietta she shivered and drew the bed-clothes closely about her. She seemed to be standing beside the bed, illumined in the darkness by her own malignant fires, her yellow skin drawn tightly across the supercilious bones, her hands curving over some fresh mean economy, her ridiculous head-dress wagging like a mocking spirit above her small red-rimmed eyes. Yes, if only Henrietta were not there...

And the old chest murmured softly: 'If only Henrietta were not there...'

The post-chaise came up to the door darkly like a ghost, for it had been snowing all day and the house was wrapped in silence. The animals on the box-tree hedge stood out fantastically against the silver-grey of the evening sky, and the snow fell like the scattering feathers of a heavenly geese-flock.

Edmund stepped into the hall and had Dorothy in his arms. At that moment they knew how truly they loved one another. He wondered as he flung his mind back in an instant's retrospect over a phantasmagoria of Indian Moguls, Chinese rivers and the flaming sunsets of Arabia how it could be that he had not known that his life was here, here with his beloved house above him, his adored wife in his arms. His head up like a conqueror's, he mounted the stairs, almost running into his wonderful parlour, to see once again the vase of flowers on the commode, the slender beautiful legs of his chair, the charming circles of his delicate ceiling. 'How could I have stayed away?' he thought. 'I will never leave this again!'

And that night, clasped in one another's arms, they discovered one another again: shyness fled and heart was open to heart.

Nevertheless, there remained Henrietta. Would you believe that one yellow-faced old maid could direct and dominate two normal healthy creatures? You know that she can, and is doing it somewhere or other at this very moment. And all for their good. No one ever did anything mean to anyone else yet save for their good, and so it will be until the end of this frail planet.

She told Edmund that she had been 'educating Dorothy.' He would find her greatly improved; she feared that her worst fault was Hardness of Heart. Hardness of Heart! A sad defect!

During those snowy days Henrietta tried to show her brother that no one in the world truly loved him but herself. She had shown him this before and found the task easy; now it was more difficult. Dorothy's shyness had been melted by this renewed contact; he could not doubt the evidence of his eyes and the many little unconscious things that spoke for her when she had no idea that they were speaking. Now they rode and walked together and he explained to her how *he* was, how that at a time his thoughts would be far, far away in Cairo or Ispahan and that she must not think that he did not care for her because he was dreaming, and she told him that when he had frightened her she had been stupid, but that now that he frightened her no longer she would soon be brilliant. ... So Henrietta's task was difficult.

And then in the spring, when the daffodils blew among the long grasses and the white violets were shining in the copse, a chance word of hers showed her the way. She hated Dorothy now because she suspected that Dorothy was planning to be rid of her. The fear that she would be turned out of the house never left her, and so, as fear always does, it drove her to baser things than belonged truly to her nature. She hinted that in Edmund's absence Dorothy had found a neighbouring squire 'good company.'

And there had been perhaps another or two … men … At that word every frustrated instinct in Henrietta's body turned in rebellion. She had not spoken before she believed it true. She had this imaginative gift, common to lonely persons. She was herself amazed at the effect of her words on Edmund. If she had ever doubted Edmund's love for his wife (and she had not really doubted it) she was certain of the truth at last. Dorothy … Dorothy … His stout body trembled; his eyes were wounded; he turned from his sister as though he were ashamed both of her and of himself. After that there was no peace.

It was now that the house wondered most deeply at these strange human beings. The little things that upset them, the odd things that, at a moment, they would believe! Here, for instance, was their Edmund, whom they so truly admired, loving his Dorothy and entirely trusting her. Now, at a moment's word from a sour-faced virgin, there is a fire of torment in his heart. He looks on every male with an eager restless suspicion. While attempting to appear natural he watches Dorothy at every corner and counters in his mind her lightest word.

'Why,' said the Italian lamp (which from its nationality knew everything about jealousy) to the Cromwellian chest, 'I have never known so foolish a suspicion,' to which the Cromwellian chest replied in its best Roundhead manner: 'Woman … the devil's bait … always has been … always will be.'

He attacked his sister again and again. 'With whom has she been? Has she ever stayed from the house a night? What friends has she made?'

To which Henrietta would indignantly reply: 'Brother, brother. What are you about? This jealousy is most unbecoming. I have suggested no impropriety … only a little foolishness born of idleness.'

But it did not need time for Dorothy to discover that something was once again terribly amiss.

This strange husband of hers, so unable to express himself—she had but just won him back to her and now he was away again! With the courage born of their new relationship she asked him what was the trouble. And he told her: 'Nothing. ... Nothing! Nothing at all! Why should there be trouble? You are for ever imagining...' And then looked at her so strangely that she blushed and turned away as though she were indeed guilty. Guilty of what? She had not the least idea. But what she did know was that it was dear sister Henrietta who was responsible, and now, as May came with a flourish of birds and blossom and star-lit nights, she began to hate Henrietta with an intensity quite new to her gentle nature.

So, with jealousy and hatred, alive and burning, the house grew very sad. It hated these evil passions and had said long ago that they ruined with their silly bitterness every good house in the world. The little Chinese cabinet with the purple dragons on its doors said that in China everything was much simpler—you did not drag a situation to infinity as these sluggish English do, but simply called Death in to make a settlement—a much simpler way. In any case the house began to watch and to listen with the certainty that the moment was approaching when it must interfere.

Jealousy always heightens love, and so, if Edmund had loved Dorothy at the first, that cool, placid anticipation was nothing to the fevered passion which he now felt. When he was away from her he longed to have her in his arms, covering her with kisses and assuring her that he had never doubted her, and when he was with her he suspected her every look, her every word. And she, miserable now and angry and ill, could not tell what possessed him, her virtue being so secure that she could not conceive that anyone should suspect it. Only she was well aware that Henrietta was to blame.

These were also days of national anxiety and unrest; the days when Napoleon jumping from Elba alighted in France and for a moment promised to stay there. Warm, stuffy, breathless days, when everyone was waiting, the house with the rest.

On the staircase one summer evening Dorothy told Henrietta something of her mind. 'If I had my way,' she ended in a shaking rage, 'you would not be here plotting against us!'

So that was it! At last Henrietta's suspicions were confirmed. In a short while Dorothy would have her out of the house; and then where would she go? The thought of her desolation, loneliness, loss of power, gripped her heart like a cat's claws. The two little charity-girls had a time of it during those weeks and cried themselves to sleep in their attic that smelt of mice and apples, dreaming afterwards of strong lovers who beat their mistress into a pulp.

'Give me proof!' said Edmund, so bitterly tormented. 'If it is true, give me proof!'

And Henrietta answered, sulkily: 'I have never said anything,' and a window-sash fell on his fingers and bruised them just to teach him not to be so damnable a fool.

Nevertheless, Henrietta had her proof. She had been cherishing it for a year at least. This was a letter written by a young Naval Lieutenant, cousin of a neighbouring squire, after he had danced with Dorothy at a Christmas ball. It was only a happy careless boy's letter, he in love with Dorothy's freshness, and because he was never more than a moment in any one place, careless of consequences. He said in his letter that she was the most beautiful of God's creatures, that he would dream of her at sea, and the rest. Dorothy kept it. Henrietta stole it....

The day came when the coach brought the news of the Waterloo victory. On that summer evening rockets were breaking into the pale sky above the dark soft shelter of the wood; on Bendon Hill they were waiting for dark to light the bonfire. You could hear the shouting and singing from the high-road. The happiness at the victory and the sense that England was delivered blew some of the cobwebs from Edmund's brain; he took Dorothy into the garden and there, behind the sun-dial, put his arms around her and kissed her.

Henrietta, watching the rockets strike the sky from her window, saw them, and fear, malice, loneliness, greed, hurt pride and jealousy all rose in her together. She turned over the letter in her drawer and vowed that her brother should not go to bed that night before he had heard of it.

'Look out! Look out!' cried her room to the rest of the house. 'She will make mischief with the letter. We must prevent her...'

'She has done mischief enough,' chattered the clock from the hall. 'She must be prevented...' whistled the chimneys. Something must be done and at once. But how? By whom?

She is coming. She stands outside her door, glancing about the dim sunset passage. The picture of Ranelagh above her head wonders—shall it fall on her? The chairs along the passage watch her anxiously as she passes them. But what can they do? Each must obey his own laws.

Stop her! Stop her! Stop her! Edmund and Dorothy are coming in from the garden. The sun is sinking, the shadows lengthening across the lawn. One touch on his arm: 'Brother, may I have a word?' and all the harm is done—misery and distress, unhappiness in the house, separation and loneliness. Stop her! Stop her!

All the house is quivering with agitation. The curtains are blowing, the chimneys are twisting, the tables and chairs are creaking: Stop her! Stop her! Stop her!

The order has gone out. She is standing now at the head of the staircase leading to the hall. She waits, her head bent a little, listening. Something seems to warn her. Edmund and Dorothy are coming in from the garden. The fireworks are beginning beyond the wood, and their gold and crimson showers are rivalling the stars.

Henrietta, nodding her head as though in certainty, has taken her step, some roughness in the wood has caught her heel (was it there a moment ago?), she stumbles, she clutches at the balustrade, but it is slippery and refuses to aid her. She is falling; her feet are away in air, her head strikes the board; she screams, once and then again; a rush, a flash of huddled colour, and her head has struck the stone of the hall floor.

How odd a silence followed! Dorothy and Edmund were still a moment lingering by the door looking back to the shower of golden stars, hearing the happy voices singing in the road. Henrietta was dead and so made no sound.

But all through the house there was a strange humming as though everything from top to bottom were whispering.

Everything in the house is moving save the woman at the bottom of the stairs.

# Thurnley Abbey

By *Perceval Landon*

Three years ago I was on my way out to the East, and as an extra day in London was of some importance, I took the Friday evening mail-train to Brindisi instead of the usual Thursday morning Marseilles express. Many people shrink from the long forty-eight-hour train journey through Europe, and the subsequent rush across the Mediterranean on the nineteen-knot *Isis* or *Osiris*; but there is really very little discomfort on either the train or the mail-boat, and unless there is actually nothing for me to do, I always like to save the extra day and a half in London before I say good-bye to her for one of my longer tramps. This time—it was early, I remember, in the shipping season, probably about the beginning of September—there were few passengers, and I had a compartment in the P&O. Indian express to myself all the way from Calais. All Sunday I watched the blue waves dimpling the Adriatic, and the pale rosemary along the cuttings; the plain white towns, with their flat roofs and their bold "duomos," and the grey-green gnarled olive orchards of Apulia. The journey was just like any other. We ate in the dining-car as often and as long as we decently could. We slept after luncheon; we dawdled the afternoon away with yellow-backed novels; sometimes we exchanged platitudes in the smoking-room, and it was there that I met Alastair Colvin.

Colvin was a man of middle height, with a resolute, well-cut jaw; his hair was turning grey; his moustache was sun-whitened, otherwise he was clean-shaven—obviously a gentleman, and obviously also a pre-occupied man. He had no great wit. When spoken to, he made the usual remarks in the right way, and I dare say he refrained from banalities only because he spoke less than the rest of us; most of the time he buried himself in the Wagon-lit Company's time-table, but seemed unable to concentrate his attention on any one page of it. He found that I had been over the Siberian railway, and for a quarter of an hour he discussed it with me. Then he lost interest in it, and rose to go to his compartment. But he came back again very soon, and seemed glad to pick up the conversation again.

Of course, this did not seem to me to be of any importance. Most travellers by train become a trifle infirm of purpose after thirty-six hours' rattling. But Colvin's restless way I noticed in somewhat marked contrast with the man's personal importance and dignity; especially ill-suited was it to his finely made large hand with strong, broad, regular nails and its few lines. As I looked at his hand I noticed a long, deep, and recent scar of ragged shape. However, it is absurd to pretend that I thought anything was unusual. I went off at five o'clock on Sunday afternoon to sleep away the hour or two that had still to be got through before we arrived at Brindisi.

Once there, we few passengers transhipped our hand baggage, verified our berths—there were only a score of us in all—and then, after an aimless ramble of half an hour in Brindisi, we returned to dinner at the Hôtel International, not wholly surprised that the town had been the death of Virgil. If I remember rightly, there is a gaily painted hall at the International—I do not wish to advertise anything, but there is no other place in Brindisi at which to await the coming of the mails—and after dinner I was looking with awe at a trellis overgrown with blue vines, when Colvin moved across the room to my table. He picked up *Il Secolo*, but almost immediately gave up the pretence of reading it. He turned squarely to me and said:

"Would you do me a favour?"

One doesn't do favours to stray acquaintances on Continental expresses without knowing something more of them than I knew of Colvin. But I smiled in a noncommittal way, and asked him what he wanted. I wasn't wrong in part of my estimate of him; he said bluntly:

"Will you let me sleep in your cabin on the *Osiris*?" And he coloured a little as he said it.

Now, there is nothing more tiresome than having to put up with a stable-companion at sea, and I asked him rather pointedly:

"Surely, there is room for all of us?" I thought that perhaps he had been partnered off with some mangy Levantine, and wanted to escape from him at all hazards.

Colvin, still somewhat confused, said: "Yes; I am in a cabin by myself. But you would do me the greatest favour if you would allow me to share yours."

This was all very well, but, besides the fact that I always sleep better when alone, there had been some recent thefts on board English liners, and I hesitated, frank and honest and self-conscious as Colvin was. Just then the mail-train came in with a clatter and a rush of escaping steam, and I asked him to see me again about it on the boat when we started. He answered me curtly—I suppose he saw the mistrust in my manner? "I am a member of White's." I smiled to myself as he said it, but I remembered in a moment that the man—if he were really what he claimed to be, and I make no doubt that he was—must have been sorely put to it before he urged the fact as a guarantee of his respectability to a total stranger at a Brindisi hotel.

That evening, as we cleared the red and green harbour-lights of Brindisi, Colvin explained. This is his story in his own words.

"When I was travelling in India some years ago, I made the acquaintance of a youngish man in the Forests Service. We camped out together for a week, and I found him a pleasant companion. John Broughton was a light-hearted soul when off duty, but a steady and capable man in any of the small emergencies that continually arise in that department. He was liked and trusted by Indians and though a trifle over-pleased with himself when he escaped to civilisation at Simla or Calcutta, Broughton's future was well assured in Government service, when a fair-sized estate was unexpectedly left to him, and he joyfully shook the dust to the Indian plains from his feet and returned to England. For five years he drifted about London. I saw him now and then. We dined together about every eighteen months, and I could trace pretty exactly the gradual sickening of Broughton with a merely idle life. He then set out on a couple of long voyages, returned as restless as before, and at last told me that he had decided to marry and settle down at his place, Thurnley Abbey, which had long been empty. He spoke about looking after the property and standing for his constituency in the usual way. Vivien Wilde, his *fiancée*, had, I suppose, begun to take him in hand. She was a pretty girl with a deal of fair hair and rather an exclusive manner; deeply religious in a narrow school, she was still kindly and high-spirited, and I thought that Broughton was in luck. He was quite happy and full of information about his future.

"Among other things, I asked him about Thurnley Abbey. He confessed that he hardly knew the place. The last tenant, a man called Clarke, had lived in one wing for fifteen years and seen no one. He had been a miser and a hermit. It was the rarest thing for a light to be seen at the Abbey after dark. Only the barest necessities of life were ordered, and the tenant himself received them at the side-door. His one half-caste manservant, after a month's stay in the house, had abruptly left without warning, and had returned to the Southern States. One thing Broughton complained bitterly about: Clarke had wilfully spread the rumour among the villagers that the Abbey was haunted, and had even condescended to play childish tricks with spirit-lamps and salt in order to scare trespassers away at night. He had been detected in the act of this tomfoolery, but the story spread, and no one, said Broughton, would venture near the house except in broad daylight. The hauntedness of Thurnley Abbey was now, he said with a grin, part of the gospel of the countryside, but he and his young wife were going to change all that. Would I propose myself any time I liked? I, of course, said I would, and equally, of course, intended to do nothing of the sort without a definite invitation.

"The house was put in thorough repair, though not a stick of the old furniture and tapestry were removed. Floors and ceilings were relaid: the roof was made watertight again, and the dust of half a century was scoured out. He showed me some photographs of the place. It was called an Abbey, though as a matter of fact it had been only the infirmary of the long-vanished Abbey of Closter some five miles away. The larger part of this building remained as it had been in pre-Reformation days, but a wing had been added in Jacobean times, and that part of the house had been kept in something like repair by Mr Clarke. He had in both the ground and first floors set a heavy timber door, strongly barred with iron, in the passage between the earlier and the Jacobean parts of the house, and had entirely neglected the former. So there had been a good deal of work to be done.

"Broughton, whom I saw in London two or three times about this period, made a deal of fun over the positive refusal of the workmen to remain after sundown. Even after the electric light had been put into every room, nothing would induce them to remain, though, as Broughton observed, electric light was death on ghosts. The legend of the Abbey's ghosts had gone far and wide, and the men would take no risks. They went home in batches of five and six, and even during the daylight hours there was an inordinate amount of talking between one and another, if either happened to be out of sight of his companion. On the whole, though nothing of any sort or kind had been conjured up even by their heated imaginations during their five months' work upon the Abbey, the belief in the ghosts was rather strengthened than otherwise in Thurnley because of the men's confessed nervousness, and local tradition declared itself in favour of the ghost of an immured num."

"'Good old nun!' said Broughton.

"I asked him whether in general he believed in the possibility of ghosts, and, rather to my surprise, he said that he couldn't say he entirely disbelieved in them. A man in India had told him one morning in camp that he believed that his mother was dead in England, as her vision had come to his tent the night before. He had not been alarmed, but had said nothing, and the figure vanished again. As a matter of fact, the next possible dak-walla brought on a telegram announcing the mother's death. 'There the thing was,' said Broughton. But at Thurnley he was practical enough. He roundly cursed the idiotic selfishness of Clarke, whose silly antics had caused all the inconvenience. At the same time, he couldn't refuse to sympathise to some extent with the ignorant workmen. 'My own idea,' said he, 'is that if a ghost ever does come in one's way, one ought to speak to it.'

"I agreed. Little as I knew of the ghost world and its conventions, I had always remembered that a spook was in honour bound to wait to be spoken to. It didn't seem much to do, and I felt that the sound of one's own voice would at any rate reassure oneself as to one's wakefulness. But there are few ghosts outside Europe—few, that is, that a white man can see—and I had never been troubled with any. However, as I have said, I told Broughton that I agreed.

"So the wedding took place, and I went to it in a tall hat which I bought for the occasion, and the new Mrs Broughton smiled very nicely at me afterwards. As it had to happen, I took the Orient Express that evening and was not in England again for nearly six months. Just before I came back I got a letter from Broughton. He asked if I could see him in London or come to Thurnley, as he thought I should be better able to help him than anyone else he knew. His wife sent a nice message to me at the end, so I was reassured about at lest one thing. I wrote from Budapest that I would come and see him at Thurnley two days after my arrival in London, and as I sauntered out of the Pannonia into the Kerepesi Utcza to post my letters, I wondered of what earthly service I could be to Broughton. I had been out with him after tiger on foot, and I could imagine few men better able at a pinch to manage their own business. However, I had nothing to do, so after dealing with some small accumulations of business during my absence, I packed a kit-bag and departed to Euston.

"I was met by Broughton's great limousine at Thurnley Road station, and after a drive of nearly seven miles we echoed through the sleepy streets of Thurnley village, into which the main gates of the park thrust themselves, splendid with pillars and spread-eagles and tom-cats rampant atop of them. I never was a herald, but I know that the Broughtons have the right to supporters—Heaven knows why! From the gates a quadruple avenue of beech-trees led inwards for a quarter of a mile. Beneath them a neat strip of fine turf edged the road and ran back until the poison of the dead beech-leaves killed it under the trees. There were many wheel-tracks on the road, and a comfortable little pony trap jogged past me laden with a country parson and his wife and daughter. Evidently there was some garden party going on at the Abbey. The road dropped away to the right at the end of the avenue, and I could see the Abbey across a wide pasturage and a broad lawn thickly dotted with guests.

"The end of the building was plain. It must have been almost mercilessly austere when it was first built, but time had crumbled the edges and toned the stone down to an orange-lichened grey wherever it showed behind its curtain of magnolia, jasmine, and ivy. Farther on was the three-storeyed Jacobean house, tall and handsome. There had not been the slightest attempt to adapt the one to the other, but the kindly ivy had glossed over the touching-point. There was a tall flèche in the middle of the building, surmounting a small bell tower. Behind the house there rose the mountainous verdure of Spanish chestnuts all the way up the hill.

"Broughton had seen me coming from afar, and walked across from his other guests to welcome me before turning me over to the butler's care. This man was sandy-haired and rather inclined to be talkative. He could, however, answer hardly any questions about the house; he had, he said, only been there three weeks.

Mindful of what Broughton had told me, I made no inquiries about ghosts, though the room into which I was shown might have justified anything. It was a very large low room with oak beams projecting from the white ceiling. Every inch of the walls, including the doors, was covered with tapestry, and a remarkably fine Italian fourpost bedstead, heavily draped, added to the darkness and dignity of the place. All the furniture was old, well made, and dark. Underfoot there was a plain green pile carpet, the only new thing about the room except the electric light fittings and the jugs and basins. Even the looking-glass on the dressing-table was an old pyramidal Venetian glass set in heavy repoussé frame of tarnished silver.

"After a few minutes' cleaning up, I went downstairs and out upon the lawn, where I greeted my hostess. The people gathered there were of the usual country type, all anxious to be pleased and roundly curious as to the new master of the Abbey. Rather to my surprise, and quite to my pleasure, I rediscovered Glenham, whom I had known well in old days in Barotseland: he lived quite close, as, he remarked with a grin, I ought to have known. 'But,' he added, 'I don't live in a place like this.' He swept his hand to the long, low lines of the Abbey in obvious admiration, and then, to my intense interest, muttered beneath his breath, 'Thank God!' He saw that I had overheard him, and turning to me said decidedly, 'Yes, "thank God"' I said, and I meant it. I wouldn't live at the Abbey for all Broughton's money.'

" 'But surely,' I demurred, 'you know that old Clarke was discovered in the very act of setting light to his bug-a-boos?

"Glenham shrugged his shoulders. 'Yes, I know about that. But there is something wrong with the place still. All I can say is that Broughton is a different man since he has lived here. I don't believe that he will remain much longer. But—you're staying here?—well, you'll hear all about it to-night. There's a big dinner, I understand.' The conversation turned off to old reminiscences, and Glenham soon after had to go.

"Before I went to dress that evening I had twenty minutes' talk with Broughton in his library. There was no doubt that the man was altered, gravely altered. He was nervous and fidgety, and I found him looking at me only when my eye was off him. I naturally asked him what he wanted of me. I told him I would do anything I could, but that I couldn't conceive what he lacked that I could provide. He said with a lustreless smile that there was, however, something, and that he would tell me the following morning. It struck me that he was somehow ashamed of himself. And perhaps ashamed of the part he was asking me to play. However, I dismissed the subject from my mind and went up to dress in my palatial room. As I shut the door a draught blew out the Queen of Sheba from the wall, and I noticed that the tapestries were not fastened to the wall at the bottom. I have always held very practical views about spooks, and it has often seemed to me that the slow waving in firelight of loose tapestry upon a wall would account for ninety-nine per cent of the stories one hears. Certainly, the dignified undulation of this lady with her attendants and huntsmen—one of whom was untidily cutting the throat of a fallow deer upon the very steps on which King Solomon, a grey-faced Flemish nobleman with the order of the Golden Fleece, awaited his fair visitor—gave colour to my hypothesis.

"Nothing much happened at dinner. The people were very much like those of the garden party. A young woman next me seemed anxious to know what was being read in London. As she was far more familiar than I with the most recent magazines and literary supplements, I found salvation in being myself instructed in the tendencies of modern fiction. All true art, she said, was shot through and through with melancholy. How vulgar were the attempts at wit that marked so many modern books! From the beginning of literature it had always been tragedy that embodied the highest attainment of every age. To call such works morbid merely begged the question. No thoughtful man—she looked sternly at me through the steel rim of her glasses—could fail to agree with me. Of course, as one would, I immediately and properly said that I slept with Pett Ridge and Jacobs under my pillow at night, and that if *Jorrocks* weren't quite so large and cornery, I would add him to the company. She hadn't read any of them, so I was saved—for a time. But I remember grimly that she said that the dearest wish of her life was to be in some awful and soul-freezing situation of horror, and I remember that she dealt hardly with the hero of Nat Paynter's vampire story, between nibbles at her brown-bread ice. She was a cheerless soul, and I couldn't help thinking that if there were many such in the neighbourhood, it was not surprising that old Glenham had been stuffed with some nonsense or other about the Abbey. Yet, nothing could well have been less creepy than the glitter of silver and glass, and the subdued lights and cackle of conversation all round the dinner-table.

"After the ladies had gone I found myself talking to the rural dean. He was a thin, earnest man, who at once turned the conversation to old Clarke's buffooneries. But, he said, Mr Broughton had introduced such a new and cheerful spirit, not only into the Abbey, but, he might say, into the whole neighbourhood, that he had great hopes that the ignorant superstitions of the past were from henceforth destined to oblivion. Thereupon his other neighbour, a portly gentleman of independent means and position, audibly remarked 'Amen,' which damped the rural dean, and we talked of partridges past, partridges present, and pheasants to come. At the other end of the table Broughton sat with a couple of his friends, red-faced hunting men. Once I noticed that they were discussing me, but I paid no attention to it at the time. I remembered it a few hours later.

"By eleven all the guests were gone, and Broughton, his wife, and I were alone together under the fine plaster ceiling of the Jacobean drawing-room. Mrs Broughton talked about one or two of the neighbours, and then, with a smile, said that she knew I would excuse her, shook hands with me, and went off to bed. I am not very good at analysing things, but I felt that she talked a little uncomfortably and with a suspicion of effort, smiled rather conventionally, and was obviously glad to go. These things seem trifling enough to repeat, but I had throughout the faint feeling that everything was not square. Under the circumstances, this was enough to set me wondering what on earth the service could be that I was to render—wondering also whether the whole business were not some ill-advised jest in order to make me come down from London for a mere shooting-party.

"Broughton said little after she had gone. But he was evidently labouring to bring the conversation round to the so-called haunting of the Abbey. As soon as I saw this, of course I asked him directly about it. He then seemed at once to lose interest in the matter. There was no doubt about it: Broughton was somehow a changed man, and to my mind he had changed in no way for the better. Mrs Broughton seemed no sufficient cause. He was clearly very fond of her, and she of him. I reminded him that he was going to tell me what I could do for him in the morning, pleaded my journey, lighted a candle, and went upstairs with him. At the end of the passage leading into the old house he grinned weakly and said, 'Mind, if you see a ghost, do talk to it; you said you would.' He stood irresolutely a moment and then turned away. At the door of his dressing-room he paused once more: 'I'm here,' he called out, 'if you should want anything. Good night,' and he shut his door.

"I went along the passage to my room, undressed, switched on a lamp beside my bed, read a few pages of *The Jungle Book*, and then, more than ready for sleep, turned the light off and went fast asleep.

"Three hours later I woke up. There was not a breath of wind outside. There was not even a flicker of light from the fireplace. As I lay there, an ash tinkled slightly as it cooled, but there was hardly a gleam of the dullest red in the grate. An owl cried among the silent Spanish chestnuts on the slope outside. I idly reviewed the events of the day, hoping that I should fall off to sleep again before I reached dinner. But at the end I seemed as wakeful as ever. There was no help for it. I must read my *Jungle Book* again till I felt ready to go off, so I fumbled for the pear at the end of the cord that hung down inside the bed, and I switched on the bedside lamp. The sudden glory dazzled me for a moment. I felt under my pillow for my book with half-shut eyes. Then, growing used to the light, I happened to look down to the foot of my bed.

"I can never tell you really what happened then. Nothing I could ever confess in the most abject words could even faintly picture to you what I felt. I know that my heart stopped dead, and my throat shut automatically. In one instinctive movement I crouched back up against the head-boards of the bed, staring at the horror. The movement set my heart going again, and the sweat dripped from every pore. I am not a particularly religious man, but I had always believed that God would never allow any supernatural appearance to present itself to man in such a guise and in such circumstances that harm, either bodily or mental, could result to him. I can only tell you that at that moment both my life and my reason rocked unsteadily on their seats."

The other *Osiris* passengers had gone to bed. Only he and I remained leaning over the starboard railing, which rattled uneasily now and then under the fierce vibration of the over-engined mail-boat. Far over, there were the lights of a few fishing-smacks riding out the night, and a great rush of white combing and seething water fell out and away from us overside.

At last Colvin went on:

"Leaning over the foot of my bed, looking at me, was a figure swathed in a rotten and tattered veiling. This shroud passed over the head, but left both eyes and the right side of the face bare. It then followed the line of the arm down to where the hand grasped the bed-end. The face was not entirely that of a skull, though the eyes and the flesh of the face were totally gone. There was a thin, dry skin drawn tightly over the features, and there was some skin left on the hand. One wisp of hair crossed the forehead. It was perfectly still. I looked at it, and it looked at me, and my brains turned dry and hot in my head. I had still got the pear of the electric lamp in my hand, and I played idly with it; only I dared not turn the light out again. I shut my eyes, only to open them in a hideous terror the same second. The thing had not moved. My heart was thumping, and the sweat cooled me as it evaporated. Another cinder tinkled in the grate, and a panel creaked in the wall.

"My reason failed me. For twenty minutes, or twenty seconds, I was able to think of nothing else but this awful figure, till there came, hurtling through the empty channels of my senses, the remembrance that Broughton and his friends had discussed me furtively at dinner. The dim possibility of its being a hoax stole gratefully into my unhappy mind, and once there, one's pluck came creeping back along a thousand tiny veins. My first sensation was one of blind unreasoning thankfulness that my brain was going to stand the trial. I am not a timid man, but the best of us needs some human handle to steady him in time to extremity, and in this faint but growing hope that after all it might be only a brutal hoax, I found the fulcrum that I needed. At last I moved.

"How I managed to do it I cannot tell you, but with one spring towards the foot of the bed I got within arm's-length and struck out one fearful blow with my fist at the thing. It crumbled under it, and my hand was cut to the bone. With a sickening revulsion after my terror, I dropped half-fainting across the end of the bed. So it was merely a foul trick after all. No doubt the trick had been played many a time before: no doubt Broughton and his friends had had some large bet among themselves as to what I should do when I discovered the gruesome thing. From my state of abject terror I found myself transported into an insensate anger. I shouted curses upon Broughton. I dived rather than climbed over the bed-end on to the sofa. I tore at the robed skeleton—how well the whole thing had been carried out, I thought—I broke the skull against the floor, and stamped upon its dry bones. I flung the head away under the bed, and rent the brittle bones of the trunk in pieces. I snapped the thin thigh-bones across my knee, and flung them in different directions. The shin-bones I set up against a stool and broke with my heel. I raged like a Berserker against the loathly thing, and stripped the ribs from the backbone and slung the breastbone against the cupboard. My fury increased as the work of destruction went on. I tore the frail rotten veil into twenty pieces, and the dust went up over everything, over the clean blotting-paper and the silver inkstand.

At last my work was done. There was but a raffle of broken bones and strips of parchment and crumbling wool. Then, picking up a piece of the skull—it was the cheek and temple bone of the right side, I remember—I opened the door and went down the passage to Broughton's dressing-room. I remember still how my sweat-dripping pyjamas clung to me as I walked. At the door I kicked and entered.

"Broughton was in bed. He had already turned the light on and seemed shrunken and horrified. For a moment he could hardly pull himself together. Then I spoke. I don't know what I said. Only I know that from a heart full and over-full with hatred and contempt, spurred on by shame of my own recent cowardice, I let my tongue run on. He answered nothing. I was amazed at my own fluency. My hair still clung lankily to my wet temples, my hand was bleeding profusely, and I must have looked a strange sight. Broughton huddled himself up at the head of the bed just as I had. Still he made no answer, no answer, no defence. He seemed pre-occupied with something besides my reproaches, and once or twice moistened his lips with his tongue. But he could say nothing though he moved his hands now and then, just as a baby who cannot speak moves its hands.

"At last the door into Mrs Broughton's room opened and she came in, white and terrified. 'What is it? What is it? Oh, in God's name! What is it?' she cried again and again, and then she went up to her husband and sat on the bed in her night-dress, and the two faced me. I told her what the matter was. I spared her husband not a word for her presence there. Yet, he seemed hardly to understand. I told the pair that I had spoiled their cowardly joke for them. Broughton looked up.

" 'I have smashed the foul thing into a hundred pieces,' I said, Broughton licked his lips again and his mouth worked.' By

God!' I shouted, 'it would serve you right if I thrashed you within an inch of your life. I will take care that not a decent man or woman of my acquaintance ever speaks to you again. 'And there,' I added, throwing the broken piece of the skull upon the floor beside his bed, 'there is a souvenir for you, of your damned work to-night!'

"Broughton saw the bone, and in a moment it was his turn to frighten me. He squealed like a hare caught in a trap. He screamed and screamed till Mrs Broughton, almost as bewildered as myself held on to him and coaxed him like a child to be quiet. But Broughton—and as he moved I thought that ten minutes ago I perhaps looked as terribly ill as he did—thrust her from him, and scrambled out of the bed on to the floor, and still screaming put out his hand to the bone. It had blood on it from my hand. He paid no attention to me whatever. In truth I said nothing. This was a new turn indeed to the horrors of the evening. He rose from the floor with the bone in his hand and stood silent. He seemed to be listening. 'Time, time, perhaps,' he muttered, and almost at the same moment fell at full length on the carpet, cutting his head against the fender. The bone flew from his hand and came to rest near the door. I picked Broughton up, haggard and broken, with blood over face. He whispered hoarsely and quickly, 'Listen, listen!' We listened.

"After ten seconds' utter quiet, I seemed to hear something. I could not be sure, but at last there was no doubt. There was a quiet sound as of one moving along the passage. Little regular steps came towards us over the hard oak flooring. Broughton moved to where his wife sat, white and speechless, on the bed, and pressed her face into his shoulder.

"Then, the last thing that I could see as he turned the light out, he fell forward with his own head pressed into the pillow of the bed. Something in their company, something in their cowardice, helped me, and I faced the open doorway of the room, which was outlined fairly clearly against the dimly lighted passage. I put out one hand and touched Mrs Broughton's shoulder in the darkness. But at the last moment I too failed. I sank on my knees and put my face in the bed. Only we all heard. The footsteps came to the door, and there they stopped. The piece of bone was lying a yard inside the door. There was a rustle of moving stuff, and the thing was in the room. Mrs Broughton was silent: I could hear Broughton's voice praying, muffled in the pillow: I was cursing my own cowardice. Then the steps moved out again on the oak boards of the passage, and I heard the sounds dying away. In a flash of remorse I went to the door and looked out. At the end of the corridor I thought I saw something that moved away. A moment later the passage was empty. I stood with my forehead against the jamb of the door almost physically sick.

"'You can turn the light on,' I said, and there was an answering flare. There was no bone at my feet. Mrs Broughton had fainted. Broughton was almost useless, and it took me ten minutes to bring her to. Broughton only said one thing worth remembering. For the most part he went on muttering prayers. But I was glad afterwards to recollect that he had said that thing. He said in a colourless voice, half as a question, half as a reproach, 'You didn't speak to her.'

"We spent the remainder of the night together. Mrs Broughton actually fell off into a kind of sleep before dawn, but she suffered so horribly in her dreams that I shook her into consciousness again. Never was dawn so long in coming. Three or four times Broughton spoke to himself. Mrs Broughton would then just tighten her hold on his arm, but she could say nothing. As for me, I can honestly say that I grew worse as the hours passed and the light strengthened. The two violent reactions had battered down my steadiness of view, and I felt that the foundations of my life had been built upon the sand. I said nothing, and after binding up my hand with a towel, I did not move. It was better so. They helped me and I helped them, and we all three knew that our reason had gone very near to ruin that night. At last, when the light came in pretty strongly, and the birds outside were chattering and singing, we felt that we must do something. Yet we never moved. You might have thought that we should particularly dislike being found as we were by the servants: yet nothing of that kind mattered a straw, and an overpowering listlessness bound us as we sat, until Chapman, Broughton's man, actually knocked and opened the door. None of us moved. Broughton, speaking hardly and stiffly, said, 'Chapman, you can come back in five minutes.' Chapman, was a discreet man, but it would have made no difference to us if he had carried his news to the 'room' at once.

"We looked at each other and I said I must go back. I meant to wait outside till Chapman returned. I simply dared not re-enter my bedroom alone. Broughton roused himself and said that he would come with me. Mrs Broughton agreed to remain in her own room for five minutes if the blinds were drawn up and all the doors left open.

"So Broughton and I, leaning stiffly one against the other, went down to my room. By the morning light that filtered past the blinds we could see our way, and I released the blinds. There was nothing wrong in the room from end to end, except smears of my own blood on the end of the bed, on the sofa, and on the carpet where I had torn the thing to pieces."

Colvin had finished his story. There was nothing to say. Seven bells stuttered out from the fo'c'sle, and the answering cry wailed through the darkness. I took him downstairs.

"Of course, I am much better now, but it is a kindness of you to let me sleep in your cabin."

# The Unbolted Door

By *Mrs Belloc Lowndes*

"Leave that door alone, young feller; and remember once for all that it's never to be locked or bolted. Not that there's any fear of its being locked, as the master always has the key on him."

Mrs Torquil heard the muffled words. Cote, their seventy-year-old butler, instructing the new footman in slow, impressive tones, as is the way of butlers when addressing their humble subordinates.

But this subordinate belonged to the new dispensation, so he answered back.

"That's a funny idea—that is."

"It may seem funny to you, seeing you're a stranger, Henry, but 'tis only a sad one to me."

"Sad? Why that, Mr Cote?"

From where Anne Torquil had stayed her steps at the door of her bedchamber she heard the now quavering, long familiar, old voice, answer—"'Twas this way it happened. Mr John—and a rare nice young chap he was—was not just put down 'killed' by his Colonel, when he didn't come back from what was then styled 'a raid in the henemy lines.' He was just reported 'missing.' Cruel I called it then, and cruel I calls it now—for 'twas bound to encourage false hopes."

"It must 'a done, Mr Cote," —the young voice had become grave.

"Mrs Torquil knew well enough what 'missing' meant. But the master, he just couldn't bring hisself to believe his son—his heir, too, mind you—had gone, so to speak for ever. I mind well how a few days after the Armistice Mr Torquil came along one night just as I was locking up, and he says, says he, 'Just leave the door of the small hall as it is, Cote. Master John always came into the house that way, because of the short-cut from the gate. Many soldiers are coming back now from Germany who was put down as "missing," so my son may walk through that door any day.' That's what he said then, poor gentleman; and that door, Henry, has never been locked or bolted, since."

The men's footsteps died away, and something stirred in Anne Torquil's unhappy atrophied heart. How very strange that she should not have known till to-night, of her husband's order? It was true that, at all ages past babyhood, the boy had been wont to burst through the outer door of what was called "the small hall" with a cry of "Mother! Where are you? Upstairs?" And yet, dearly as he loved her, close as they were to one another, she had always known that John had cared most for his inarticulate father.

She was so moved, now, that something of the frightful anguish of six years ago came back and restlessly she began to walk up and down the beautiful bedroom many of her friends envied her. How piteous that to her it should be a room of intolerable memories.

In the wide Jacobean bed, where she now spent her often wakeful nights, had been born the son whose coming had seemed inevitable. Convinced that as to this matter she would be as lucky as in all else, she had laughed at the thought that her baby could be a girl. How often, in the last six years, she had wished she had died on the glorious day her boy was born.

Her good friend then, and still her good friend, Dr Maynard, the old village doctor, had taken it on himself, more than once, during the perfect years which had followed John's birth, to hint that it was a pity the child had no brother, no sister to share his delightful nursery. But she, Anne Torquil, had been wilfully deaf to such advice. Always, during the whole of her happy spoilt young life, she had done what she wanted; and never had she done anything she had not definitely wished to do. She had given her Jack a splendid son, what good old Cote called an heir; that, surely, was quite enough?

Suddenly now, she stopped in her pacing opposite a carved wood mirror. She had been standing just here during her last happy moment of life. It was in the autumn of 1918; her husband was home, convalescing from what had been a severe wound; there were rumours of Peace, and they were confidently expecting their boy home on his first leave. At exactly three o'clock, on a fine early October day, there had come what had been, then, a very familiar knuckle knock on her door. Even when she was a bride of seventeen, and the two were more like a pair of happy children than an married couple, Jack had always knocked before he came into his wife's, Anne's, room.

Blithely she had called out, "Come in!"

And he had come in, with a telegram open in his hand.

It was as if she could hear now, to-night, six years later, the sound of his hoarse voice uttering her name—and then, when she had put up her arm with an instinctive violent movement to ward off the blow, the further words, "Thank God not killed, my darling! Only missing."

Only missing? And John's father had gone on not only hoping against hope, but firmly convinced that, from the depths of some German prison, or even from some German mental home, the boy would come back.

She, from the first, in dry-eyed despair, had felt no hope at all. And her husband's obstinate—what to herself she more than once harshly called his idiotic—optimism, had pained, exasperated, sometimes maddened, her.

She stared now, as if hypnotized, at her own reflection in the dark glass of the mirror. Though she would be forty-five on her next birthday, it was true, as tiresome people so often told her, that she still, at times, looked like a girl. Time had scarcely touched her lovely face and slender rounded figure with his rude finger; but Jack Torquil, not yet fifty, might have been ten years older than his age. For the first time in her life, to-night, Anne asked herself, with a touch of unease, if her husband was as unhappy as she was herself.

This evening she had watched him sitting hunched up in an easy chair, a book in his hand, on the other side of the fire. Suddenly he had taken up a pencil—it was a thing Jack Torquil was given to do, and it always irritated his wife—and marked a passage in the book he was reading. Looking up, he had thrown her a queer, shamed, pleading look; and when he had risen and left the library, to go through his usual ritual of taking a turn out of doors with the three dogs, she had walked across the room to see what it was he had marked in his book. And then she had been at once annoyed, diverted, and, maybe, a little touched; for what her husband had marked had been two lines, the first ridiculously familiar, the second, till this moment, unknown to her:

"It is the little rift within the lute
That by and by will make the music mute."

And now, while slowly undressing, the remembered the two lines Jack had marked. What he, no doubt, still thought of as "a little rift" between them was, in actual fact, a chasm which was ever yawing wider and wider. Yet once, only once, in their now long joint life, had she spoken bitter words to him.

It had been years ago, at a time when he was still full of hope, and she, alas! starkly hopeless, as to their son's possible return. The lover in him had awakened, and when his lips had sought hers she had said fiercely, "Never, Jack. Never again." So literally had he accepted her decree, that not once, since then, had he even knocked on the door of the room they had shared so blissfully for twenty-one years.

To-day, the eve of Armistice Day, had been an intolerable day, and Anne told herself that next year they would have people here for the first fortnight of November. They were rich, hospitable—both, in their quite different ways, popular. But the real reason why they were never alone, excepting for the Christmas holidays, and part of November of each year, was that a dual solitude becomes intolerable when shared by a man and woman who were once ardent, exultingly happy, lovers.

As Anne Torquil got into her great bed, the stable clock began to strike twelve, ushering in another Armistice Day; and, as she lay back, smarting, difficult tears rose to her still undimmed eyes.

The thought of her boy was very near to her to-night, so near, indeed, that an overwhelming wish to gaze on his pictured face came over her.

Slipping out of bed, she went over to painted cabinet where she kept certain sacred, secret things. Among them was her husband's adoring letters, each beginning *My darling little love*, written during their short engagement; also all her son's photographs from babyhood.

She had had a sketch of him done by Sargent when he was at Sandhurst. That now hung in his father's bedroom. There was no portrait of him in any other part of the house which knew him no more. Some of their later friends did not know they had ever had a child.

Unlocking the drawer in which lay all the photographs of John, she took out the last one, taken of him just after he had received his commission, and wearing his first uniform. While she gazed into the boyish face, he seemed to be smiling proudly, confidently, merrily, up at her.

As she put it back in the drawer, she remembered a clumsy attempt, most kindly meant, of sympathy on the part of their Vicar. He had met her during one of the long lonely walks she had taken that first year of woe, in between her still strenuous war work, for, after the Armistice, Torquilton House had gone on for a long time being a soldiers' convalescent hospital. And, "Who being dead, yet liveth," the Vicar had said in a low voice.

Throwing her head back, she had exclaimed: "You know, my husband is still quite convinced that John was not killed? He thinks he may come back any day."

With a startled look, and making no attempt to answer her, the would-be comforter had gone his way.

To-day, at almost the same place, oddly enough, she had had such an encounter with old Dr Maynard which had not hurt, so much as angered, her. He had retired in 1919, and she never saw him alone, now. But this time his only son—a son the war had spared—had dropped him from their car, so that he might have a little walk.

The old man had taken her hand in his, and said feelingly, "I should like to think you happy, dear Mrs Torquil." And, as she had shaken her head—she couldn't pretend to him—he had gone on, with a touch of real admiration in his feeble voice, "You're wonderful! You won't mind my saying so? But how young you keep! Why, this afternoon, you might be twenty-five instead of——"

"Nearly forty-five? Yes, and I do still feel young, worse luck. I'd give a good deal to feel old, Dr Maynard."

And then he had said a word about her husband which brought the colour rushing up into her face. The doctor had always been chary of his words, but every word had always told. "Can't you bring yourself to be kind to him?" he had said, looking straight into her still lovely face. She had answered at once, and very coldly, "Not in the way you mean."

Shaking his white head sadly he had taken her hand in his again, "You must forgive an old friend—eh?"

She had nodded quickly. But she had felt then, and she felt now, that she could not forgive that—yes, impertinent—question.

The twelfth stroke of the clock fell on the still air, and all at once she heard the electric light being turned out in the hall below, followed by the sound of her husband's footsteps coming up the stairs. There came over her an odd, unexpected impulse. Just to go out and bid him good night. But she restrained that impulse. All the same, she walked across to the door, and, turning off the light, noiselessly opened it a little way.

Jack Torquil was making his way up the easy stairs with the steps of an old man, though, as she and Dr Maynard both knew, he was still young at heart, however deeply grief and hope deferred had scarred his face. And, still feeling moved by what their old manservant had unconsciously revealed, she waited to hear those slow footsteps make their way into the room which was no longer called "Mr Torquil's dressing-room."

And then it was as if her heart stood still, for the handle of the unbolted door in the hall below turned in the darkness, and there came an upward rush of cold air, followed by her husband's startled shout, "What goes there?"

There was a moment's pause, and after that pause, as if from infinitely far away, there rang out two words in a voice she had never thought to hear again, even in another life, for Anne Torquil had come not to believe the promise the Vicar had repeated, thinking to comfort her.

And the words uttered in her son's voice pierced her innermost soul, for "Poor father," was all her beloved had come back to say.

Then she heard Jack Torquil's eager, joyful— "John? My dear, dear boy!" and the sound of his feet pounding down the stairs.

As she rushed out to the circular gallery, she heard the handle turn again in the darkness. The lights below were put full on and, looking over the balustrade, she saw her husband standing in the empty hall, staring, with bewildered eyes, at the closed door.

At last he turned, and, looking up, saw her pale face and wide-open eyes gazing down.

"You heard him, too, Anne?"

Straightening herself, she ran round the gallery and so downstairs. There, with what had become a way of forgotten tenderness, she took his hand. "Of course, I heard him, too! The door opened, and he came in with the wind. Having said what was in his dear mind he went back—but where, Jack, where?"

Later that night, as Anne lay in his arms, John's father muttered, "He came back for you, my darling; to comfort you. That was quite right."

"For me, Jack? Oh, no!"

"But he did, little love. Surely you heard what he said?" And she felt the surprise in his voice.

She whispered, "What did he say—to you?"

"Only what you heard—only the two words, Anne, 'Dear mother.'"

He waited a moment, and then he said humbly, for he was a very simple kind of man, "Just to let you know, dearest, and perhaps to let me know, too, that all is well with the child."

# Gone Fishing

By *Ruskin Bond*

The house was called 'Undercliff', because that's where it stood—under a cliff. The man who went away—the owner of the house—was Robert Astley. And the man who stayed behind—the old family retainer—was Prem Bahadur.

Astley had been gone many years. He was still a bachelor in his late thirties when he'd suddenly decided that he wanted adventure, romance, faraway places; and he'd given the keys of the house to Prem Bahadur—who'd served the family for thirty years—and had set off on his travels.

Someone saw him in Sri Lanka. He'd been heard of in Burma, around the ruby mines at Mogok. Then he turned up in Java, seeking a passage through the Sunda Straits. After that the trail petered out. Years passed. The house in the hill-station remained empty.

But Prem Bahadur was still there, living in an outhouse.

Every day he opened up Undercliff, dusted the furniture in all the rooms, made sure that the bedsheets and pillowcases were clean, and set out Astley's dressing-gown and slippers.

In the old days, whenever Astley had come home after a journey or a long tramp in the hills, he had liked to bathe and change into his gown and slippers, no matter what the hour. Prem Bahadur still kept them ready. He was convinced that Robert would return one day.

Astley himself had said so.

'Keep everything ready for me, Prem, old chap. I may be back after a year, or two years, or even longer, but I'll be back, I promise you. On the first of every month I want you to got to my lawyer, Mr Kapoor. He'll give you your salary and any money that's needed for the rates and repairs. I want you to keep the house tip-top!'

'Will you bring back a wife, Sahib?'

'Lord, no! Whatever put that idea in your head?'

'I thought, perhaps—because you wanted the house kept ready….'

'Ready for me, Prem. I don't want to come home and find the old place falling down.'

And so Prem had taken care of the house—although there was no news from Astley. What had happened to him? The mystery provided a talking-point whenever local people met on the Mall. And in the bazaar the shopkeepers missed Astley because he was a man who spent freely.

His relatives still believed him to be alive. Only a few months back a brother had turned up—a brother who had a farm in Canada and could not stay in India for long. He had deposited a further sum with the lawyer and told Prem to carry on as before. The salary provided Prem with his few needs. Moreover, he was convinced that Robert would return.

Another man might have neglected the house and grounds, but not Prem Bahadur. He had a genuine regard for the absent owner. Prem was much older—now almost sixty and none too strong, suffering from pleurisy and other chest troubles—but he remembered Robert as both a boy and a young man. They had been together on numerous hunting and fishing trips in the mountains. They had slept out under the stars, bathed in icy mountain streams, and eaten from the same cooking-pot. Once, when crossing a small river, they had been swept downstream by a flash-flood, a wall of water that came thundering down the gorges without any warning during the rainy season. Together they had struggled back to safety. Back in the hill-station, Astley told everyone that Prem had saved his life; while Prem was equally insistent that he owed his life to Robert.

This year the monsoon had begun early and ended late. It dragged on through most of September, and Prem Bahadur's cough grew worse and his breathing more difficult.

He lay on his charpai on the veranda, staring out at the garden, which was beginning to get out of hand, a tangle of dahlias, snake-lilies and convolvulus. The sun finally came out. The wind shifted from the south-west to the north-west, and swept the clouds away.

Prem Bahadur had taken his charpai into the garden, and was lying in the sun, puffing at his small hookah, when he saw Robert Astley at the gate.

He tried to get up but his legs would not oblige him. The hookah slipped from his hand.

Astley came walking down the garden path and stopped in front of the old retainer, smiling down at him. He did not look a day older than when Prem Bahadur had last seen him.

'So you have come at last,' said Prem.

'I told you I'd return.'

'It has been many years. But you have not changed.'

'Nor have you, old chap.'

'I have grown old and sick and feeble.'

'You'll be fine now. That's why I've come.'

'I'll open the house,' said Prem, and this time he found himself getting up quite easily.

'It isn't necessary,' said Astley.

'But all is ready for you!'

'I know. I have heard of how well you have looked after everything. Come then, let's take a last look round. We cannot stay, you know.'

Prem was a little mystified but he opened the front door and took Robert through the drawing-room and up the stairs to the bedroom. Robert saw the dressing-gown and the slippers, and he placed his hand gently on the old man's shoulder.

When they returned downstairs and emerged into the sunlight, Prem was surprised to see himself—or rather his skinny body—stretched out on the charpai. The hookah lay on the ground, where it had fallen.

Prem looked at Astley in bewilderment.

'But who is that—lying there?'

'It was you. Only the husk now, the empty shell. This is the real you, standing here beside me.'

'You came for me?'

'I couldn't come until you were ready. As for me, I left *my* shell a long time ago. But you were determined to hang on, keeping this house together. Are you ready now?'

'And the house?'

'Others will live in it. Nothing is lost for ever, everything begins again. ... But come, it's time to go fishing....'

Astley took Prem by the arm, and they walked through the dappled sunlight under the deodars and finally left that place for another.

# Nothing

By *Walter de la Mare*

*Whsst*, and away, and over the green,
Scampered a shape that never was seen.
It ran without sound, it ran without shadow,
Never a grass-blade in unmown meadow,
Stooped at the thistledown fall of its foot.
I watched it vanish, yet saw it not—
A moment past, it had gazed at me;
Now nought but myself and the spindle tree.
A nothing!—Of air? Of earth? Of sun?—
From emptiness come, into vacancy gone!....
*Whsst*, and away, and over the green,
Scampered a shape that never was seen.

# SCARY STORIES

# Introduction

If there's one thing I've learnt in the course of a long writing life, it's that young readers love getting a scare. I do, too, provided it's only on the printed page.

Offer a fourteen-year old a choice between reading a book of love stories or a collection of ghost stories, and nine times out of ten the ghost stories will win hands down. Lovers are inclined to be predictable. Ghosts, never!

Occasionally a reader comes up to me with the complaint: "Sir, your ghosts aren't frightening enough. They're so friendly!" Young readers don't want friendly ghosts, they want scary ghosts—or werewolves, vampires, witches, maniacs, and monsters of all kinds! And so, to compensate for all the harmless ghosts I've created or presented over the years, I have chosen a set of stories guaranteed to make the reader (regardless of his or her age) shiver, shudder, and look under the bed before sleeping with the lights on.

Not all the stories in this collection are about the supernatural. There are no ghosts in "Henry" or "Boomerang", but they are among the most frightening stories I have ever read. Terror comes from the unexpected, the uninvited, the unexplained. The stories by Saki and W.W. Jacobs carry the horrific little twist that we have come to associate with these writers.

Nevertheless, the supernatural element is a strong one. Algernon Blackwood was a master of the genre, and "The Empty House" is a classic on the theme of....well, empty houses and whatever lurks within them.

Rudyard Kipling wrote a number of successful ghost stories, most of them set in India. I first heard the story of "The Phantom Rickshaw" from my father, who took me up to Simla in 1943, to admit me to a boarding-school. One of Kipling's best. And his eerie little tale, "At the Pit's Mouth", though not really a ghost story, sent a shiver down my spine. As did another Simla apparition in my own brief contribution, "A Face in the Night".

Three stories set in Simla! Have I deserted Mussoorie, you might well ask. Not so. It's just a supernatural coincidence.

The East End of London, which I explored as a young man, provided the background for Thomas Burke's powerful stories. One of his best, "The Hollow Man", is presented here. Arthur Morrison was another fine writer who went to the poorer parts of London and Paris for his haunting tales. Oscar Cook spent many years in North Borneo, and a number of his chilling tales are set in that mysterious region.

Let me just add that most of the stories in this collection are great short stories in their own right. Beautifully crafted, stylish, and written with a fluency and clarity that is rare in modern writers. That they are scary or entertaining adds to their readability; but you can enjoy them as literature too.

## *The Empty House*

BY ALGERNON BLACKWOOD

Certain houses, like certain persons, manage somehow to proclaim at once their character for evil. In the case of the latter, no particular feature need betray them; they may boast an open countenance and an ingenuous smile; and yet a little of their company leaves the unalterable conviction that there is something radically amiss with their being: that they are evil. Willy nilly, they seem to communicate an atmosphere of secret and wicked thoughts which makes those in their immediate neighbourhood shrink from them as from a thing diseased.

And, perhaps, with houses the same principle is operative, and it is the aroma of evil deeds committed under a particular roof, long after the actual doers have passed away, that makes the gooseflesh come and the hair rise. Something of the original passion of the evil-doer, and of the horror felt by his victim, enters the heart of the innocent watcher, and he becomes suddenly conscious of tingling nerves, creeping skin, and a chilling of the blood. He is terror-stricken without apparent cause.

There was manifestly nothing in the external appearance of this particular house to bear out the tales of the horror that was said to reign within. It was neither lonely nor unkempt. It stood, crowded into a corner of the square, and looked exactly like the houses on either side of it. It had the same number of windows as its neighbours; the same balcony overlooking the gardens; the same white steps leading up to the heavy black front door; and, in the rear, there was the same narrow strip of green, with neat box borders, running up to the wall that divided it from the backs of the adjoining houses. Apparently, too, the number of chimney pots on the roof was the same; the breadth and angle of the eaves; and even the height of the dirty area railings.

And yet this house in the square, that seemed precisely similar to its fifty ugly neighbours, was as a matter of fact entirely different—horribly different.

Wherein lay this marked, invisible difference is impossible to say. It cannot be ascribed wholly to the imagination, because persons who had spent some time in the house, knowing nothing of the facts, had declared positively that certain rooms were so disagreeable they would rather die than enter them again, and that the atmosphere of the whole house produced in them symptoms of a genuine terror; while the series of innocent tenants who had tried to live in it and been forced to decamp at the shortest possible notice, was indeed little less than a scandal in the town.

When Shorthouse arrived to pay a "week-end" visit to his Aunt Julia in her little house on the sea-front at the other end of the town, he found her charged to the brim with mystery and excitement. He had only received her telegram that morning, and he had come anticipating boredom; but the moment he touched her hand and kissed her apple-skin wrinkled cheek, he caught the first waves of her electrical condition. The impression deepened when he learned that there were to be no other visitors, and that he had been telegraphed for with a very special object.

Something was in the wind, and the "something" would doubtless bear fruit; for this elderly spinster aunt, with a mania for psychical research, had brains as well as will power, and by hook or by crook she usually managed to accomplish her ends. The revelation was made soon after tea, when she sidled close up to him as they paced slowly along the sea-front in the dusk.

"I've got the keys," she announced in a delighted, yet half awesome voice. "Got them till Monday!"

"The keys of the bathing-machine, or—?" he asked innocently, looking from the sea to the town. Nothing brought her so quickly to the point as feigning stupidity.

"Neither," she whispered. "I've got the keys of the haunted house in the square—and I'm going there to-night."

Shorthouse was conscious of the slightest possible tremor down his back. He dropped his teasing tone. Something in her voice and manner thrilled him. She was in earnest.

"But you can't go alone—" he began.

"That's why I wired for you," she said with decision.

He turned to look at her. The ugly, lined, enigmatical face was alive with excitement. There was the glow of genuine enthusiasm round it like a halo. The eyes shone. He caught another wave of her excitement, and a second tremor, more marked than the first, accompanied it.

"Thanks, Aunt Julia," he said politely; "thanks awfully."

"I should not dare to go quite alone," she went on, raising her voice; "But with you I should enjoy it immensely. You're afraid of nothing, I know."

"Thanks *so* much," he said again. "Er—is anything likely to happen?"

"A great deal *has* happened," she whispered, "though it's been most cleverly hushed up. Three tenants have come and gone in the last few months, and the house is said to be empty for good now."

In spite of himself Shorthouse became interested. His aunt was so very much in earnest.

"The house is very old indeed," she went on, "and the story—an unpleasant one—dates a long way back. It has to do with a murder committed by a jealous stableman who had some affair with a servant in the house. One night he managed to secrete himself in the cellar, and when everyone was asleep, he crept upstairs to the servants' quarters, chased the girl down to the next landing, and before anyone could come to the rescue threw her bodily over the banisters into the hall below."

"And the stableman——?"

'Was caught, I believe, and hanged for murder; but it all happened a century ago, and I've not been able to get more details of the story."

Shorthouse now felt his interest thoroughly aroused but, though he was not particularly nervous for himself, he hesitated a little on his aunt's account.

'On one condition," he said at length.

'Nothing will prevent my going," she said firmly; "but I may as well hear your condition."

"That you guarantee your power of self-control if anything really horrible happens. I mean—that you are sure you won't get too frightened."

"Jim," she said scornfully, "I'm not young, I know, nor are my nerves; but *with you* I should be afraid of nothing in the world!"

This, of course, settled it, for Shorthouse had no pretensions to being other than a very ordinary young man, and an appeal to his vanity was irresistible. He agreed to go.

Instinctively, by a sort of sub-conscious preparation, he kept himself and his forces well in hand the whole evening, compelling an accumulative reserve of control by that nameless inward process of gradually putting all the emotions away and turning the key upon them—a process difficult to describe, but wonderfully effective, as all men who have lived through severe trials of the inner man well understand. Later, it stood him in good stead.

But it was not until half-past ten, when they stood in the hall, well in the glare of friendly lamps and still surrounded by comforting human influences, that he had to make the first call upon this store of collected strength. For, once the door was closed, and he saw the deserted silent street stretching away white in the moonlight before them, it came to him clearly that the real test that night would be in dealing with *two fears* instead of one. He would have to carry his aunt's fear as well as his own. And, as he glanced down at her sphinx-like countenance and realised that it might assume no pleasant aspect in a rush of real terror, he felt satisfied with only one thing in the whole adventure—that he had confidence in his own will and power to stand against any shock that might come.

Slowly they walked along the empty streets of the town; a bright autumn moon silvered the roofs, casting deep shadows; there was no breath of wind; and the trees in the formal gardens by the sea-front watched them silently as they passed along. To his aunt's occasional remarks Shorthouse made no reply, realising that she was simply surrounding herself with mental buffers—saying ordinary things to prevent herself thinking of extraordinary things. Few windows showed lights, and from scarcely a single chimney came smoke or sparks. Shorthouse had already begun to notice everything, even the smallest details. Presently they stopped at the street corner and looked up at the name on the side of the house full in the moonlight, and with one accord, but without remark, turned into the square and crossed over to the side of it that lay in shadow.

"The number of the house is thirteen," whispered a voice at his side; and neither of them made the obvious reference, but passed across the broad sheet of moonlight and began to march up the pavement in silence.

It was about half-way up the square that Shorthouse felt an arm slipped quietly but significantly into his own, and knew then that their adventure had begun in earnest, and that his companion was already yielding imperceptibly to the influences against them. She needed support.

A few minutes later they stopped before a tall, narrow house that rose before them into the night, ugly in shape and painted a dingy white. Shutterless windows, without blinds, stared down upon them, shining here and there in the moonlight. There were weather streaks in the wall and cracks in the paint, and the balcony bulged out from the first floor a little unnaturally. But, beyond this generally forlorn appearance of an unoccupied house, there was nothing at first sight to single out this particular mansion for the evil character it had most certainly acquired.

Taking a look over their shoulders to make sure they had not been followed, they went boldly up the steps and stood against the huge black door that fronted them forbiddingly. But the first wave of nervousness was now upon them, and Shorthouse fumbled a long time with the key before he could fit it into the lock at all. For a moment, if truth were told, they both hoped it would not open, for they were a prey to various unpleasant emotions as they stood there on the threshold of their ghostly adventure. Shorthouse, shuffling with the key and hampered by the steady weight on his arm, certainly felt the solemnity of the moment. It was as if the whole world—for all experience seemed at that instant concentrated in his own consciousness—were listening to the grating noise of that key. A stray puff of wind wandering down the empty street woke a momentary rustling in the trees behind them, but otherwise this rattling of the key was the only sound audible; and at last it turned in the lock and the heavy door swung open and revealed a yawning gulf of darkness beyond.

With a last glance at the moonlit square, they passed quickly in, and the door slammed behind them with a roar that echoed prodigiously through empty halls and passages. But, instantly, with the echoes, another sound made itself heard, and Aunt Julia leaned suddenly so heavily upon him that he had to take a step backwards to save himself from falling.

A man had coughed close beside them—so close that it seemed they must have been actually by his side in the darkness.

With the possibility of practical jokes in his mind, Shorthouse at once swung his heavy stick in the direction of the sound; but it met nothing more solid than air. He heard his aunt give a little gasp beside him.

"There's someone here," she whispered: "I heard him."

"Be quiet!" he said sternly. "It was nothing but the noise of the front door."

"Oh! get a light—quick!" she added, as her nephew, fumbling with a box of matches, opened it upside down and let them all fall with a rattle on to the stone floor.

The sound, however, was not repeated; and there was no evidence of retreating footsteps. In another minute they had a candle burning, using an empty end of a cigar case as a holder; and when the first flare had died down he held the impromptu lamp aloft and surveyed the scene. And it was dreary enough in all conscience, for there is nothing more desolate in all the abodes of men than an unfurnished house dimly lit, silent, and forsaken, and yet tenanted by rumour with the memories of evil and violent histories.

They were standing in a wide hall-way; on their left was the open door of a spacious dining-room, and in front the hall ran, ever narrowing, into a long, dark passage that led apparently to the top of the kitchen stairs. The broad uncarpeted staircase rose in a sweep before them, everywhere draped in shadows, except for a single spot about half-way up where the moonlight came in through the window and fell on a bright patch on the boards. This shaft of light shed a faint radiance above and below it, lending to the objects within its reach a misty outline that was infinitely more suggestive and ghostly than complete darkness. Filtered moonlight always seems to paint faces on the surrounding gloom, and as Shorthouse peered up into the well of darkness and thought of the countless empty rooms and passages in the upper part of the old house, he caught himself longing again for the safety of the moonlit square, or the cosy, bright drawing-room they had left an hour before. Then realising that these thoughts were dangerous, he thrust them away again and summoned all his energy for concentration on the present.

"Aunt Julia," he said aloud, severely, "we must now go through the house from top to bottom and make a thorough search."

The echoes of his voice died away slowly all over the building, and in the intense silence that followed he turned to look at her. In the candlelight he saw that her face was already ghastly pale; but she dropped his arm for a moment and said in a whisper, stepping close in front of him—

"I agree. We must be sure there's no one hiding. That's the first thing."

She spoke with evident effort, and he looked at her with admiration.

"You feel quite sure of yourself? It's not too late——"

"I think so," she whispered, her eyes shifting nervously toward the shadows behind. "Quite sure, only one thing——"

"What's that?"

"You must never leave me alone for an instant."

"As long as you understand that any sound or appearance must be investigated at once, for to hesitate means to admit fear. That is fatal."

"Agreed," she said, a little shakily, after a moment's hesitation. "I'll try——"

Arm in arm, Shorthouse holding the dripping candle and the stick, while his aunt carried the cloak over her shoulders, figures of utter comedy to all but themselves, they began a systematic search.

Stealthily, walking on tip-toe and shading the candle lest it should betray their presence through the shutterless windows, they went first into the big dining-room. There was not a stick of furniture to be seen. Bare walls, ugly mantel-pieces and empty grates stared at them. Everything, they felt, resented their intrusion, watching them, as it were, with veiled eyes; whispers followed them; shadows flitted noiselessly to right and left; something seemed ever at their back, watching, waiting an opportunity to do them injury. There was the inevitable sense that operations which went on when the room was empty had been temporarily suspended till they were well out of the way again. The whole dark interior of the old building seemed to become a malignant Presence that rose up, warning them to desist and mind their own business; every moment the strain on the nerves increased.

Out of the gloomy dining-room they passed through large folding doors into a sort of library or smoking-room, wrapt equally in silence, darkness, and dust; and from this they regained the hall near the top of the back stairs.

Here a pitch black tunnel opened before them into the lower regions, and—it must be confessed—they hesitated. But only for a minute. With the worst of the night still to come it was essential to turn from nothing. Aunt Julia stumbled at the top step of the dark descent, ill lit by the flickering candle, and even Shorthouse felt at least half the decision go out of his legs.

"Come on!" he said peremptorily, and his voice ran on and lost itself in the dark, empty spaces below.

"I'm coming," she faltered, catching his arm with unnecessary violence.

They went a little unsteadily down the stone steps, a cold, damp air meeting them in the face, close and malodorous. The kitchen, into which the stairs led along a narrow passage, was large, with a lofty ceiling. Several doors opened out of it—some into cupboards with empty jars still standing on the shelves, and others into horrible little ghostly back offices, each colder and less inviting than the last. Black beetles scurried over the floor, and once, when they knocked against a deal table standing in a corner, something about the size of a cat jumped down with a rush and fled, scampering across the stone floor into the darkness. Everywhere there was a sense of recent occupation, an impression of sadness and gloom.

Leaving the main kitchen, they next went towards the scullery. The door was standing ajar, and as they pushed it open to its full extent Aunt Julia uttered a piercing scream, which she instantly tried to stifle by placing her hand over her mouth. For a second Shorthouse stood stock-still, catching his breath. He felt as if his spine had suddenly become hollow and someone had filled it with particles of ice.

Facing them, directly in their way between the doorposts, stood the figure of a woman. She had dishevelled hair and wildly staring eyes, and her face was terrified and white as death.

She stood there motionless for the space of a single second. Then the candle flickered and she was gone—gone utterly—and the door framed nothing but empty darkness.

"Only the beastly jumping candle-light," he said quickly, in a voice that sounded like someone else's and was only half under control. "Come on, aunt. There's nothing there."

He dragged her forward. With a clattering of feet and a great appearance of boldness they went on, but over his body the skin moved as if crawling ants covered it, and he knew by the weight on his arm that he was supplying the force of locomotion for two. The scullery was cold, bare, and empty; more like a large prison cell than anything else. They went round it, tried the door into the yard, and the windows, but found them all fastened securely. His aunt moved beside him like a person in a dream. Her eyes were tightly shut, and she seemed merely to follow the pressure of his arm. Her courage filled him with amazement. At the same time he noticed that a certain odd change had come over her face, a change which somehow evaded his power of analysis.

"There's nothing here, aunty," he repeated aloud quickly. "Let's go upstairs and see the rest of the house. Then we'll choose a room to wait up in."

She followed him obediently, keeping close to his side, and they locked the kitchen door behind them. It was a relief to get up again. In the hall there was more light than before, for the moon had travelled a little further down the stairs. Cautiously they began to go up into the dark vault of the upper house, the boards creaking under their weight.

On the first floor they found the large double drawing-rooms, a search of which revealed nothing. Here also was no sign of furniture or recent occupancy; nothing but dust and neglect and shadows. They opened the big folding doors between front and back drawing-rooms and then came out again to the landing and went on upstairs.

They had not gone up more than a dozen steps when they both simultaneously stopped to listen, looking into each other's eyes with a new apprehension across the flickering candle flame. From the room they had left hardly ten seconds before came the sound of doors quietly closing. It was beyond all question; they heard the booming noise that accompanies the shutting of heavy doors, followed by the sharp catching of the latch.

"We must go back and see," said Shorthouse briefly, in a low tone, and turning to go downstairs again.

Somehow she managed to drag after him, her feet catching in her dress, her face livid.

When they entered the front drawing-room it was plain that the folding doors had been closed—half a minute before. Without hesitation Shorthouse opened them. He almost expected to see someone facing him in the back room; but only darkness and cold air met him. They went through both rooms, finding nothing unusual. They tried in every way to make the doors close of themselves, but there was not wind enough even to set the candle flame flickering. The doors would not move without strong pressure. All was silent as the grave. Undeniably the rooms were utterly empty, and the house utterly still.

"It's beginning." Whispered a voice at his elbow which he hardly recognised as his aunt's.

He nodded acquiescence, taking out his watch to note the time. It was fifteen minutes before midnight; he made the entry of exactly what had occurred in his notebook, setting the candle in its case upon the floor in order to do so. It took a moment or two to balance it safely against the wall.

Aunt Julia always declared that at this moment she was not actually watching him, but had turned her head towards the inner room, where she fancied she heard something moving; but, at any rate, both positively agreed that there came a sound of rushing feet, heavy and very swift—and the next instant the candle was out!

But to Shorthouse himself had come more than this, and he has always thanked his fortunate stars that it came to him alone and not to his aunt too. For, as he rose from the stooping position of balancing the candle, and before it was actually extinguished, a face thrust itself forward so close to his own that he could almost have touched it with his lips. It was a face working with passion; a man's face, dark, with thick features, and angry, savage eyes. It belonged to a common man, and it was evil in its ordinary normal expression, no doubt, but as he saw it, alive with intense, aggressive emotion it was a malignant and terrible human countenance.

There was no movement of the air; nothing but the sound of rushing feet—stockinged or muffed feet; the apparition of the face; and the almost simultaneous extinguishing of the candle.

In spite of himself, Shorthouse uttered a little cry, nearly losing his balance as his aunt clung to him with her whole weight in one moment of real, uncontrollable terror. She made no sound, but simply seized him bodily. Fortunately, however, she had seen nothing, but had only heard the rushing feet, for her control returned almost at once, and he was able to disentangle himself and strike a match.

The shadows ran away on all sides before the glare, and his aunt stooped down and groped for the cigar case with the precious candle. Then they discovered that the candle had not been *blown* out at all; it had been *crushed* out. The wick was pressed down into the wax, which was flattened as if by some smooth, heavy instrument.

How his companion so quickly overcame her terror, Shorthouse never properly understood; but his admiration for her self-control increased tenfold, and at the same time served to feed his own dying flame—for which he was undeniably grateful. Equally inexplicable to him was the evidence of physical force they had just witnessed. He at once suppressed the memory of stories he had heard of "physical mediums" and their dangerous phenomena; for if these were true, and either his aunt or himself was unwittingly a physical medium, it meant that they were simply aiding to focus the forces of a haunted house already charged to the brim. It was like walking with unprotected lamps among uncovered stores of gunpowder.

So, with as little reflection as possible, he simply re-lit the candle and went up to the next floor. The arm in his trembled, it is true, and his own tread was often uncertain, but they went on with thoroughness, and after a search revealing nothing they climbed the last flight of stairs to the top floor of all.

Here they found a perfect nest of small servants' rooms, with broken pieces of furniture, dirty cane-bottomed chairs, chests of drawers, cracked mirrors, and decrepit bedsteads. The rooms had low sloping ceilings already hung here and there with cobwebs, small windows, and badly plastered walls—a depressing and dismal region which they were glad to leave behind.

It was on the stroke of midnight when they entered a small room on the third floor, close to the top of the stairs, and arranged to make themselves comfortable for the remainder of their adventure. It was absolutely bare, and was said to be the room—then used as a clothes closet—into which the infuriated groom had chased his victim and finally caught her. Outside, across the narrow landing, began the stairs leading up to the floor above, and the servants' quarters where they had just searched.

In spite of the chilliness of the night there was something in the air of this room that cried for an open window. But there was more than this. Shorthouse could only describe it by saying that he felt less master of himself here than in any other part of the house. There was something that acted directly on the nerves, tiring the resolution, enfeebling the will. He was conscious of this result before he had been in the room five minutes, and it was in the short time they stayed there that he suffered the wholesale depletion of his vital forces, which was, for himself, the chief horror of the whole experience.

They put the candle on the floor of the cupboard, leaving the door a few inches ajar, so that there was no glare to confuse the eyes, and no shadow to shift about on walls and ceiling. Then they spread the cloak on the floor and sat down to wait, with their backs against the wall.

Shorthouse was within two feet of the door on to the landing; his position commanded a good view of the main staircase leading down into the darkness, and also of the beginning of the servants' stairs going to the floor above; the heavy stick lay beside him within easy reach.

The moon was now high above the house. Through the open window they could see the comforting stars like friendly eyes watching in the sky. One by one the clocks of the town struck midnight, and when the sounds died away the deep silence of a windless night fell again over everything. Only the boom of the sea, far away and lugubrious, filled the air with hollow murmurs.

Inside the house the silence became awful; awful, he thought, because any minute now it might be broken by sounds portending terror. The strain of waiting told more and more severely on the nerves; they talked in whispers when they talked at all, for their voices aloud sounded queer and unnatural. A chilliness, not altogether due to the night air, invaded the room, and made them cold. The influences against them, whatever these might be, were slowly robbing them of self-confidence, and the power of decisive action: their forces were on the wane, and the possibility of real fear took on a new and terrible meaning. He began to tremble for the elderly woman by his side, whose pluck could hardly save her beyond a certain extent.

He heard the blood singing in his veins. It sometimes seemed so loud that he fancied it prevented his hearing properly certain other sounds that were beginning very faintly to make themselves audible in the depths of the house. Every time he fastened his attention on these sounds, they instantly ceased. They certainly came no nearer. Yet he could not rid himself of the idea that movement was going on somewhere in the lower regions of the house. The drawing-room floor, where the door had been so strangely closed, seemed too near; the sounds were further off than that. He thought of the great kitchen, with the scurrying black-beetles, and of the dismal little scullery; but, somehow or other, they did not seem to come from there either. Surely they were not *outside* the house!

Then, suddenly, the truth flashed into his mind, and for the space of a minute he felt as if his blood had stopped flowing and turned to ice.

The sounds were not downstairs at all; they were *upstairs*—upstairs, somewhere among those horrid gloomy little servants' rooms with their bits of broken furniture, low ceilings, and cramped windows—upstairs where the victim had first been disturbed and stalked to her death.

And the moment he discovered where the sounds were, he began to hear them more clearly. It was the sound of feet, moving stealthily along the passage overhead, in and out among the rooms, and past the furniture.

He turned quickly to steal a glance at the motionless figure seated beside him, to note whether she had shared his discovery. The faint candlelight coming through the crack in the cupboard door, threw her strongly-marked face into vivid relief against the white of the wall. But it was something else that made him catch his breath and stare again. An extraordinary something had come into her face and seemed to spread over her features like a mask; it smoothed out the deep lines and drew the skin everywhere a little tighter so that the wrinkles disappeared; it brought into the face—with the sole exception of the old eyes—an appearance of youth and almost of childhood.

He stared in speechless amazement—amazement that was dangerously near to horror. It was his aunt's face indeed, but it was her face of forty years ago, the vacant innocent face of a girl. He had heard stories of that strange effect of terror which could wipe a human countenance clean of other emotions, obliterating all previous expression; but he had never realised that it could be literally true, or could mean anything so simply horrible as what he now saw. For the dreadful signature of overmastering fear was written plainly in that utter vacancy of the girlish face beside him; and when, feeling his intense gaze, she turned to look at him, he instinctively closed his eyes tightly to shut out the sight.

Yet, when he turned a minute later, his feelings well in hand, he saw to his intense relief another expression; his aunt was smiling, and though the face was deathly white, the awful veil had lifted and the normal look was returning.

"Anything wrong?" was all he could think of to say at the moment. And the answer was eloquent, coming from such a woman.

"I feel cold—and a little frightened," she whispered.

He offered to close the window, but she seized hold of him and begged him not to leave her side even for an instant.

'It's upstairs, I know," she whispered, with an odd half laugh; "but I can't possibly go up."

But Shorthouse thought otherwise, knowing that in action lay their best hope of self-control.

He took the brandy flash and poured out a glass of neat spirit, stiff enough to help anybody over anything. She swallowed it with a little shiver. His only idea now was to get out of the house before her collapse became inevitable; but this could not safely be done by turning tail and running from the enemy. Inaction was no longer possible; every minute he was growing less master of himself, and desperate, aggressive measures were imperative without further delay. Moreover, the action must be taken *towards* the enemy, not away from it; the climax, if necessary and unavoidable, would have to be faced boldly. He could do it now; but in ten minutes he might not have the force left to act for himself, much less for both!

Upstairs, the sounds were meanwhile becoming louder and closer, accompanied by occasional creaking of the boards. Someone was moving stealthily about, stumbling now and then awkwardly against the furniture.

Waiting a few moments to allow the tremendous dose of spirits to produce its effect, and knowing this would last but a short time under the circumstances, Shorthouse then quietly got on his feet, saying in a determined voice—

"Now, Aunt Julia, we'll go upstairs and find out what all this noise is about. You must come too. It's what we agreed."

He picked up his stick and went to the cupboard for the candle. A limp form rose shakily beside him breathing hard, and he heard a voice say very faintly something about being "ready to come." The woman's courage amazed him; it was so much greater than his own; and, as they advanced, holding aloft the dripping candle, some subtle force exhaled from this trembling, white-faced old woman at his side that was the true source of his inspiration. It held something really great that shamed him and gave him the support without which he would have proved far less equal to the occasion.

They crossed the dark landing, avoiding with their eyes the deep black space over the banisters. Then they began to mount the narrow staircase to meet the sounds which, minute by minute, grew louder and nearer. About half-way up the stairs Aunt Julia stumbled and Shorthouse turned to catch her by the arm, and just at that moment there came a terrific crash in the servants' corridor overhead. It was instantly followed by a shrill, agonised scream that was a cry of terror and a cry for help melted into one.

Before they could move aside, or go down a single step, someone came rushing along the passage overhead, blundering horribly, racing madly, at full speed, three steps at a time, down the very staircase where they stood. The steps were light and uncertain; but close behind them sounded the heavier tread of another person, and the staircase seemed to shake.

Shorthouse and his companion just had time to flatten themselves against the wall when the jumble of flying steps was upon them, and two persons, with the slightest possible interval between them, dashed past at full speed. It was a perfect whirlwind of sound breaking in upon the midnight silence of the empty building.

The two runners, pursuer and pursued, had passed clean through them where they stood, and already with a thud the boards below had received first one, then the other. Yet they had seen absolutely nothing—not a hand, or arm, or face, or even a shred of flying clothing.

There came a second's pause. Then the first one, the lighter of the two, obviously the pursued one, ran with uncertain footsteps into the little room which Shorthouse and his aunt had just left. The heavier one followed. There was a sound of scuffling, gasping, and smothered screaming; and then out on to the landing came the step—of a single person *treading weightily*.

A dead silence followed for the space of half a minute, and then was heard a rushing sound through the air. It was followed by a dull, crashing thud in the depths of the house below—on the stone floor of the hall.

Utter silence reigned after. Nothing moved. The flame of the candle was steady. It had been steady the whole time, and the air had been undisturbed by any movement whatsoever. Palsied with terror, Aunt Julia, without waiting for her companion, began fumbling her way downstairs; she was crying gently to herself, and when Shorthouse put his arm round her and half carried her he felt that she was trembling like a leaf. He went into the little room and picked up the cloak from the floor, and, arm in arm, walking very slowly, without speaking a word or looking once behind them, they marched down the three flights into the hall.

In the hall they saw nothing, but the whole way down the stairs they were conscious that someone followed them; step by step; when they went faster IT was left behind, and when they went more slowly IT caught them up. But never once did they look behind to see; and at each turning of the staircase they lowered their eyes for fear of the following horror they might see upon the stairs above.

With trembling hands Shorthouse opened the front door, and they walked out into the moonlight and drew a deep breath of the cool night air blowing in from the sea.

# *The Phantom 'Rickshaw*

BY RUDYARD KIPLING

> May no ill dreams disturb my rest,
> Nor Powers of Darkness me molest.
>
> Evening Hymn

One of the few advantages that India has over England is a great Knowability. After five years' service a man is directly or indirectly acquainted with the two or three hundred Civilians in his Province, all the Messes of ten or twelve Regiments and Batteries, and some fifteen hundred other people of the non-official caste. In ten years his knowledge should be doubled, and at the end of twenty he knows, or knows something about, every Englishman in the Empire, and may travel anywhere and everywhere without paying hotel-bills.

Globe-trotters who expect entertainment as a right, have, even within my memory, blunted this open-heartedness, but nonetheless to-day, if you belong to the Inner Circle and are neither a Bear nor a Black Sheep, all houses are open to you, and our small world is very, very kind and helpful.

Rickett of Kamartha stayed with Polder of Kumaon some fifteen years ago. He meant to stay two nights, but was knocked down by rheumatic fever, and for six weeks disorganised Polder's establishment, stopped Polder's work, and nearly died in Polder's bedroom. Polder behaves as though he had been placed under eternal obligation by Rickett, and yearly sends the little Ricketts a box of presents and toys. It is the same everywhere. The men who do not take the trouble to conceal from you their opinion that you are an incompetent ass, and the women who blacken your character and misunderstand your wife's amusements, will work themselves to the bone in your behalf if you fall sick or into serious trouble.

Heatherlegh, the Doctor, kept, in addition to his regular practice, a hospital on his private account—an arrangement of loose boxes for Incurables, his friend called it—but it was really a sort of fitting-up shed for craft that had been damaged by stress of weather. The weather in India is often sultry, and since the tale of bricks is always a fixed quantity, and the only liberty allowed is permission to work overtime and get no thanks, men occasionally break down and become as mixed as the metaphors in this sentence.

Heatherlegh is the dearest doctor that ever was, and his invariable prescription to all his patients is, 'Lie low, go slow, and keep cool.' He says that more men are killed by overwork than the importance of this world justifies. He maintains that overwork slew Pansay, who died under his hands about three years ago. He has, of course, the right to speak authoritatively, and he laughs at my theory that there was a crack in Pansay's head and a little bit of the Dark World came through and pressed him to death. 'Pansay went off the handle,' says Heatherlegh, 'after the stimulus of long leave at Home. He may or he may not have behaved like a blackguard to Mrs. Keith-Wessington. My notion is that the work of the Katabundi Settlement ran him off his legs, and that he took to brooding and making much of an ordinary P. & O. flirtation. He certainly was engaged to Miss Mannering, and she certainly broke off the engagement. Then he took a feverish chill and all that nonsense about ghosts developed. Overwork started his illness, kept it alight, and killed him, poor devil. Write him off to the System that uses one man to do the work of two and a half men.'

I do not believe this. I use to sit up with Pansay sometimes when Heatherlegh was called out to patients and I happened to be within claim. The man would make me most unhappy by describing in a low, even voice, the procession that was always passing at the bottom of the bed. He had a sick man's command of language. When he recovered I suggested that he should write out the whole affair from beginning to end, knowing that ink might assist him to ease his mind.

He was in a high fever while he was writing, and the blood-and-thunder Magazine diction he adopted did not calm him. Two months afterwards he was reported fit for duty, but, in spite of the fact that he was urgently needed to help an undermanned Commission stagger through a deficit, he preferred to die; vowing at the last that he was hag-ridden. I got his manuscript before he died, and this is his version of the affair, dated 1885, exactly as he wrote it:—

My doctor tells me that I need rest and change of air. It is not improbable that I shall get both ere long—rest that neither the red-coated messenger nor the mid-day gun can break, and change of air far beyond that which any homeward-bound steamer can give me. In the meantime I am resolved to stay where I am; and, in flat defiance of my doctor's orders, to take all the world into my confidence. You shall learn for yourselves the precise nature of my malady, and shall, too, judge for yourselves whether any man born of woman on this weary earth was ever so tormented as I.

Speaking now as a condemned criminal might speak ere the drop-bolts are drawn, my story, wild and hideously improbable as it may appear, demands at least attention. That it will ever receive credence I utterly disbelieve. Two months ago I should have scouted as mad or drunk the man who had dared tell me the like. Two months ago I was the happiest man in India. To-day, from Peshawar to the sea, there is no one more wretched. My doctor and I are the only two who know this. His explanation is, that my brain, digestion, and eyesight are all slightly affected; giving rise to my frequent and persistent 'delusions.' Delusions, indeed I call him a fool; but he attends me still with the same unwearied smile, the same bland professional manner, the same neatly-trimmed red whiskers, till I begin to suspect that I am an ungrateful, evil-tempered invalid. But you shall judge for yourselves.

Three years ago it was my fortune—my great misfortune—to sail from Gravesend to Bombay, on return from long leave, with one Agnes Keith-Wessington, wife of an officer on the Bombay side. It does not in the least concern you to know what manner of woman she was. Be content with the knowledge that, ere the voyage had ended, both she and I were desperately and unreasoningly in love with one another. Heaven knows that I can make the admission now without one particle of vanity. In matters of this sort there is always one who gives and another who accepts. From the first day of our ill-omened attachment, I was conscious that Agnes's passion was a stronger, a more dominant, and—if I may use the expression—a purer sentiment than mine. Whether she recognised the fact then, I do not know. Afterwards it was bitterly plain to both of us.

Arrived at Bombay in the spring of the year, we went our respective ways, to meet no more for the next three or four months, when my leave and her love took us both to Simla. There we spent the season together; and there my fire of straw burnt itself out to a pitiful end with the closing year. I attempt no excuse. I make no apology. Mrs. Wessington had given up much for my sake, and was prepared to give up all. From my own lips, in August 1882, she learnt that I was sick of her presence, tired of her company, and weary of the sound of her voice. Ninety-nine women out of a hundred would have wearied of me as I wearied of them; seventy-five of that number would have promptly avenged themselves by active and obtrusive flirtation with other men. Mrs. Wessington was the hundredth. On her neither my openly-expressed aversion nor the cutting brutalities with which I garnished our interviews had the least effect.

'Jack, darling!' was her one eternal cuckoo cry: 'I'm sure it's all a mistake—a hideous mistake; and we'll be good friends again some day. *Please* forgive me, Jack, dear.'

I was the offender, and I knew it. That knowledge transformed my pity into passive endurance, and, eventually, into blind hate—the same instinct, I suppose, which prompts a man to savagely stamp on the spider he has but half killed. And with this hate in my bosom the season of 1882 came to an end.

Next year we met again at Simla—she with her monotonous face and timid attempts at reconciliation, and I with loathing of her in every fibre of my frame. Several times I could not avoid meeting her alone; and on each occasion her words were identically the same. Still the unreasoning wail that it was all a 'mistake'; and still the hope of eventually 'making friends.' I might have seen, had I cared to look, that that hope only was keeping her alive. She grew more wan and thin month by month. You will agree with me, at least, that such conduct would have driven any one to despair. It was uncalled for; childish; unwomanly. I maintain that she was much to blame. And again, sometimes, in the black, fever-stricken night-watches, I have begun to think that I might have been a little kinder to her. But that really *is* a 'delusion.' I could not have continued pretending to love her when I didn't; could I? It would have been unfair to us both.

Last year we met again—on the same terms as before. The same weary appeals, and the same curt answers from my lips. At least I would make her see how wholly wrong and hopeless were her attempts at resuming the old relationship. As the season wore on, we fell apart—that is to say, she found it difficult to meet me, for I had other and more absorbing interests to attend to. When I think it over quietly in my sickroom, the season of 1884 seems a confused nightmare wherein light and shade were fantastically intermingled—my courtship of little Kitty Mannering; my hopes, doubts, and fears; our long rides together; my trembling avowal of attachment; her reply; and now and again a vision of a white face flitting by in the 'rickshaw with the black and white liveries I once watched for so earnestly; the wave of Mrs. Wessington's gloved hand; and, when she met me alone, which was but seldom, the irksome monotony of her appeal. I loved Kitty Mannering; honestly, heartily loved her, and with my love for her grew my hatred for Agnes. In August Kitty and I were engaged. The next day I met those accursed 'magpie' *jhampanies* at the back of Jakko, and, moved by some passing sentiment of pity, stopped to tell Mrs. Wessington everything. She knew it already.

'So I hear you're engaged, jack dear.' Then, without a moment's pause: 'I'm sure it's all a mistake—a hideous mistake. We shall be as good friends some day, Jack, as we ever were.'

My answer might have made even a man wince. It cut the dying woman before me like the blow of a whip. 'Please forgive me, Jack; I didn't mean to make you angry; but it's true, it's true!'

And Mrs. Wessington broke down completely. I turned away and left her to finish her journey in peace, feeling, but only for a moment or two, that I had been an unutterably mean hound. I looked back, and saw that she had turned her 'rickshaw with the idea, I suppose, of overtaking me.

The scene and its surroundings were photographed on my memory. The rain-swept sky (we were at the end of the wet weather), the sodden, dingy pines, the muddy road, and the black powder-riven cliffs formed a gloomy background against which the black and white liveries of the *jhampanies*, the yellow-panelled 'rickshaw and Mrs. Wessington's down-bowed golden head stood out clearly. She was holding her handkerchief in her left hand and was leaning back exhausted against the 'rickshaw cushions. I turned my horse up a bypath near the Sanjowlie Reservoir and literally ran away. Once I fancied I heard a faint call of 'Jack!' This may have been imagination. I never stopped to verify it. Ten minutes later I came across Kitty on horseback; and, in the delight of a long ride with her, forgot all about the interview.

A week later Mrs. Wessington died, and the inexpressible burden of her existence was removed from my life. I went Plainsward perfectly happy. Before three months were over I had forgotten all about her, except that at times the discovery of some of her old letters reminded me unpleasantly of our bygone relationship. By January I had disinterred what was left of our correspondence from among my scattered belongings and had burnt it. At the beginning of April of this year, 1885, I was at Simla—semi-deserted Simla—once more, and was deep in lover's talks and walks with Kitty. It was decided that we should be married at the end of June. You will understand, therefore, that, loving Kitty as I did, I am not saying too much when I pronounce myself to have been, at that time, the happiest man in India.

Fourteen delightful days passed almost before I noticed their flight. Then, aroused to the sense of what was proper among mortals circumstanced as we were, I pointed out to Kitty that an engagement ring was the outward and visible sign of her dignity as an engaged girl; and that she must forthwith come to Hamilton's to be measured for one. Up to that moment, I give you my word, we had completely forgotten so trivial a matter. To Hamilton's we accordingly went on the 15th of April 1885. Remember that—whatever my doctor may say to the contrary—I was then in perfect health, enjoying a well-balanced mind and an *absolutely* tranquil spirit. Kitty and I entered Hamilton's shop together, and there, regardless of the order of affairs, I measured Kitty for the ring in the presence of the amused assistant. The ring was a sapphire with two diamonds. We then rode out down the slope that leads to the Combermere Bridge and Peliti's shop.

While my Waler was cautiously feeling his way over the loose shale, and Kitty was laughing and chattering at my side—while all Simla, that is to say as much of it as had then come from the Plains, was grouped round the Reading-room and Peliti's veranda,—I was aware that some one, apparently at a vast distance, was calling me by my Christian name. It struck me that I had heard the voice before, but when and where I could not at once determine. In the short space it took to cover the road between the path from Hamilton's shop and the first plank of the Combermere Bridge I had thought over half a dozen people who might have committed such a solecism, and had eventually decided that it must have been some singing in my ears. Immediately opposite Peliti's shop my eye was arrested by the sight of four *jhampanies* in 'magpie' livery, pulling a yellow-panelled, cheap, bazar 'rickshaw. In a moment my mind flew back to the previous season and Mrs. Wessington with a sense of irritation and disgust. Was it not enough that the woman was dead and done with, without her black and white servitors reappearing to spoil the day's happiness? Whoever employed them now I thought I would call upon, and ask as a personal favour to change her *jhampanies'* livery. I would hire the men myself, and, if necessary, buy their coats from off their backs. It is impossible to say here what a flood of undesirable memories their presence evoked.

'Kitty,' I cried, 'there are poor Mrs. Wessington's *jhampanies* turned up again! I wonder who has them now?'

Kitty had known Mrs. Wessington slightly last season, and had always been interested in the sickly woman.

'What? Where?' she asked. 'I can't see them anywhere."

Even as she spoke, her horse, swerving from a laden mule, threw himself directly in front of the advancing 'rickshaw. I had scarcely time to utter a word of warning when to my unutterable horror, horse and rider passed *through* men and carriage as if they had been thin air.

'What's the matter?' cried Kitty; 'what made you call out so foolishly, Jack? If I *am* engaged I don't want all creation to know about it. There was lots of space between the mule and the veranda; and, if you think I can't ride—— There!'

Whereupon wilful Kitty set off, her dainty little head in the air, at a hand-gallop in the direction of the Band-stand; fully expecting, as she herself afterwards told me, that I should follow her. What was the matter? Nothing indeed. Either that I was mad or drunk, or that Simla was haunted with devils. I reined in my impatient cob, and turned round. The 'rickshaw had turned too, and now stood immediately facing me, near the left railing of the Combermere Bridge.

'Jack! Jack, darling!' (There was no mistake about the words this time: they rang through my brain as if they had been shouted in my ear.) 'It's some hideous mistake, I'm sure. *Please* forgive me, Jack, and lets' be friends again.'

The 'rickshaw-hood had fallen back, and inside, as I hope and pray daily for the death I dread by night, sat Mrs. Keith-Wessington, handkerchief in hand, and golden head bowed on her breast.

How long I stared motionless I do not know. Finally, I was aroused by my syce taking the Waler's bridle and asking whether I was ill. From the horrible to the commonplace is but a step. I tumbled off my horse and dashed, half fainting, into Peliti's for a glass of cherry-brandy. There two or three couples were gathered round the coffee-tables discussing the gossip of the day. Their trivialities were more comforting to me just then than the consolations of religion could have been. I plunged into the midst of the conversation at once; chatted, laughed, and jested with a face (when I caught a glimpse of it in a mirror) as white and drawn as that of a corpse. Three or four men noticed my condition; and, evidently setting it down to the results of over-many pegs, charitably endeavoured to draw me apart from the rest of the loungers. But I refused to be led away. I wanted the company of my kind—as a child rushes into the midst of the dinner-party after a fright in the dark. I must have talked for about ten minutes or so, though it seemed an eternity to me, when I heard Kitty's clear voice outside enquiring for me. In another minute she had entered the shop, prepared to upbraid me for failing so signally in my duties. Something in my face stopped her.

'Why, Jack,' she cried, 'what *have* you been doing? What *has* happened? Are you ill?' Thus driven into a direct lie, I said that the sun had been a little too much for me. it was close upon five o'clock of a cloudy April afternoon, and the sun had been hidden all day. I saw my mistake as soon as the words were out of my mouth: attempted to recover it; blundered hopelessly and followed Kitty, in a regal rage, out of doors, amid the smiles of my acquaintances. I made some excuse (I have forgotten what) on the score of my feeling faint; and cantered away to my hotel, leaving Kitty to finish the ride by herself.

In my room I sat down and tried calmly to reason out the matter. Here was I, Theobald Jack Pansay, a well-educated Bengal Civilian in the year of grace 1885, presumably sane, certainly healthy, driven in terror from my sweetheart's side by the apparition of a woman who had been dead and buried eight months ago. These were facts that I could not blink. Nothing was further from my thought than any memory of Mrs. Wessington when Kitty and I left Hamilton's shop. Nothing was more utterly commonplace than the stretch of wall opposite Peliti's. It was broad daylight. The road was full of people; and yet here, look you, in defiance of every law of probability, in direct outrage of Nature's ordinance, there had appeared to me a face from the grave.

Kitty's Arab had gone *through* the 'rickshaw: so that my first hope that some woman marvellously like Mrs. Wessington had hired the carriage and the coolies with their old livery was lost. Again and again I went round this treadmill of thought; and again and again gave up baffled and in despair. The voice was as inexplicable as the apparition. I had originally some wild notion of confiding it all to Kitty; of begging her to marry me at once; and in her arms defying the ghostly occupant of the 'rickshaw. 'After all,' I argued, 'the presence of the 'rickshaw is in itself enough to prove the existence of a spectral illusion. One may see ghosts of men and women, but surely never coolies and carriages. The whole thing is absurd. Fancy the ghost of a hillman!'

Next morning I sent a penitent note to Kitty, imploring her to overlook my strange conduct of the previous afternoon. My Divinity was still very wroth, and a personal apology was necessary. I explained, with a fluency born of night-long pondering over a falsehood, that I had been attacked with a sudden palpitation of the heart—the result of indigestion. This eminently practical solution had its effect: and Kitty and I rode out that afternoon with the shadow of my first lie dividing us.

Nothing would please her save a canter round Jakko. With my nerves still unstrung from the previous night I feebly protested against the notion, suggesting Observatory Hill, Jutogh, the Boileaugunge road—anything rather than the Jakko round. Kitty was angry and a little hurt; so I yielded from fear of provoking further misunderstanding, and we set out together towards Chota Simla. We walked a greater part of the way, and, according to our custom, cantered from a mile or so below the Convent to the stretch of level road by the Sanjowlie Reservoir. The wretched horses appeared to fly, and my heart beat quicker and quicker as we neared the crest of the ascent. My mind had been full of Mrs. Wessington all the afternoon; and every inch of the Jakko road bore witness to our old-time walks and talks. The bowlders were full of it; the pines sang it aloud overhead; the rain-fed torrents giggled and chuckled unseen over the shameful story; and the wind in my ears chanted the iniquity aloud.

As a fitting climax, in the middle of the level men call the Ladies' Mile the Horror was awaiting me. No other 'rickshaw was in sight—only the four black and white *jhampanies*, the yellow-panelled carriage, and the golden head of the woman within—all apparently just as I had left them eight months and one fortnight ago! For an instant I fancied that Kitty *must* see what I saw—we were so marvellously sympathetic in all things. Her next words undeceived me—'Not a soul in sight! Come along, Jack, and I'll race you to the Reservoir buildings!' Her wiry little Arab was off like a bird, my Waler following close behind, and in this order we dashed under the cliffs. Half a minute brought us within fifty yards of the 'rickshaw. I pulled my Waler and fell back a little. The 'rickshaw was directly in the middle of the road; and once more the Arab passed through it, my horse following. 'Jack! Jack dear! *Please* forgive me,' rang with a wail in my ears, and, after an interval: 'It's all a mistake, a hideous mistake!'

I spurred my horse like a man possessed. When I turned my head at the Reservoir works, the black and white liveries were still waiting—patiently waiting—under the gray hillside, and the wind brought me a mocking echo of the words I had just heard. Kitty bantered me a good deal on my silence throughout the remainder of the ride. I had been talking up till then wildly and at random. To save my life I could not speak afterwards naturally, and from Sanjowlie to the Church wisely held my tongue.

I was to dine with the Mannerings that night, and had barely time to canter home to dress. On the road to Elysium Hill I overheard two men talking together in the dusk.—'It's a curious thing,' said one, 'how completely all trace of it disappeared. You know my wife was insanely fond of the woman (never could see anything in her myself), and wanted me to pick up her old 'rickshaw and coolies if they were to be got for love or money. Morbid sort of fancy I call it; but I've got to do what the *Memsahib* tells me. Would you believe that the man she hired it from tells me that all four of the men—they were brothers—died of cholera on the way to Hardwar, poor devils; and the 'rickshaw has been broken up by the man himself. 'Told me he never used a dead *Memsahib's* 'rickshaw. 'Spoilt his luck. Queer notion, wasn't it? Fancy poor little Mrs. Wessington spoiling any one's luck except her own!' I laughed aloud at this point; and my laugh jarred on me as I uttered it. So there *were* ghosts of 'rickshaws after all, and ghostly employments in the other world! How much did Mrs. Wessington give her men? What were their hours? Where did they go?

And for visible answer to my last question I saw the infernal Thing blocking my path in the twilight. The dead travel fast, and by short cuts unknown to ordinary coolies. I laughed aloud a second time and checked my laughter suddenly, for I was afraid I was going mad. Mad to a certain extent I must have been, for I recollect that I reined in my horse at the head of the 'rickshaw, and politely wished Mrs. Wessington 'Good-evening.' Her answer was one I knew only too well. I listened to the end; and replied that I had heard it all before, but should be delighted if she had anything further to say.; Some malignant devil stronger than I must have entered into me that evening, for I have a dim recollection of talking the commonplaces of the day for five minutes to the Thing in front of me.

'Mad as a hatter, poor devil—or drunk. Max, try and get him to come home.'

Surely *that* was not Mrs. Wessington's voice! The two men had overheard me speaking to the empty air, and had returned to look after me. They were very kind and considerate, and from their words evidently gathered that I was extremely drunk. I thanked them confusedly and cantered away to my hotel, there changed, and arrived at the Mannerings' ten minutes late. I pleaded the darkness of the night as an excuse; was rebuked by Kitty for my unlover-like tardiness; and sat down.

The conversation had already become general; and under cover of it, I was addressing some tender small talk to my sweetheart when I was aware that at the further end of the table a short red-whiskered man was describing, with much broidery, his encounter with a mad unknown that evening.

A few sentences convinced me that he was repeating the incident of half an hour ago. In the middle of the story he looked round for applause, as professional story-tellers do, caught my eye, and straightway collapsed. There was a moment's awkward silence, and the red-whiskered man muttered something to the effect that he had 'forgotten the rest,' thereby sacrificing a reputation as a good story-teller which he had built up for six seasons past. I blessed him from the bottom of my heart, and—went on with my fish.

In the fulness of time that dinner came to an end; and with genuine regret I tore myself away from Kitty—as certain as I was of my own existence that it would be waiting for me outside the door. The red-whiskered man, who had been introduced to me as Dr. Heatherlegh of Simla, volunteered to bear me company as far as our roads lay together. I accepted his offer with gratitude.

My instinct had not deceived me. It lay in readiness in the Mall, and, in what seemed devilish mockery of our ways, with a lighted head lamp. The red-whiskered man went to the point at once, in a manner that showed he had been thinking over it all dinner-time.

'I say, Pansay, what the deuce was the matter with you this evening on the Elysium Road?' The suddenness of the question wrenched an answer from me before I was aware.

'That!' said I, pointing to it.

'*That* may be either D.T. or Eyes for aught I know. Now you don't liquor. I saw as much at dinner, so it can't be D.T. There's nothing whatever where you're pointing, though you're sweating and trembling with fright, like a scared pony. Therefore, I conclude that it's Eyes. And I ought to understand all about them. Come along home with me. I'm on the Blessington lower road.'

To my intense delight the 'rickshaw instead of waiting for us kept about twenty yards ahead—and this, too, whether we walked, trotted, or cantered. In the course of that long night ride I had told my companion almost as much as I have told you here.

'Well, you've spoilt one of the best tales I've ever laid tongue to,' said he, 'but I'll forgive you for the sake of what you've gone through. Now come home and do what I tell you; and when I've cured you, young man, let this be a lesson to you to steer clear of women and indigestible food till the day of your death.'

The 'rickshaw kept steady in front; and my red-whiskered friend seemed to derive great pleasure from my account of its exact whereabouts.

'Eyes, Pansay—all Eyes, Brain, and Stomach. And the greatest of these three is Stomach. You've too much conceited Brain, too little Stomach, and thoroughly unhealthy Eyes. Get your Stomach straight and the rest follows. And all that's French for a liver pill. I'll take sole medical charge of you from this hour! For you're too interesting a phenomenon to be passed over.'

By this time we were deep in the shadow of the Blessington lower road and the 'rickshaw came to a dead stop under a pine-clad, overhanging shale cliff. Instinctively I halted too, giving my reason. Heatherlegh rapped out an oath.

'Now, if you think I'm going to spend a cold night on the hillside for the sake of a Stomach-*cum*-Brain-*cum*-Eye illusion—— Lord, ha' mercy! What's that?'

There was a muffled report, a blinding smother of dust just in front of us, a crack, the noise of rent boughs, and about ten yards of the cliff-side—pines, undergrowth, and all—slid down into the road below, completely blocking it up. The uprooted trees swayed and tottered for a moment like drunken giants in the gloom, and then fell prone among their fellows with a thunderous crash. Our two horses stood motionless and sweating with fear. As soon as the rattle of falling earth and stone had subsided, my companion muttered: 'Man, if we'd gone forward we should have been ten feet deep in our graves by now. "There are more things in heaven and earth" … Come home, Pansay, and thank God. I want a peg badly.'

We retraced our way over the Church Ridge, and I arrived at Dr. Heatherlegh's house shortly after midnight.

His attempts towards my cure commenced almost immediately, and for a week I never left his sight. Many a time in the course of that week did I bless the good-fortune which had thrown me in contact with Simla's best and kindest doctor. Day by day my spirits grew lighter and more equable. Day by day, too, I became more and more inclined to fall in with Heatherlegh's 'spectral illusion' theory, implicating eyes, brain, and stomach. I wrote to Kitty, telling her that a slight sprain caused by a fall from my horse kept me indoors for a few days; and that I should be recovered before she had time to regret my absence.

Heatherlegh's treatment was simple to a degree. It consisted of liver pills, cold-water baths, and strong exercise, taken in the dusk or at early dawn—for, as he sagely observed: 'A man with a sprained ankle doesn't walk a dozen miles a day, and your young woman might be wondering if she saw you.'

At the end of the week, after much examination of pupil and pulse, and strict injunctions as to diet and pedestrianism, Heatherlegh dismissed me as brusquely as he had taken charge of me. Here is his parting benediction: 'Man, I certify to your mental cure, and that's as much as to say I've cured most of your bodily ailments. Now, get your traps out of this as soon as you can; and be off to make love to Miss Kitty.'

I was endeavouring to express my thanks for his kindness. He cut me short.

'Don't think I did this because I like you. I gather that you've behaved like a blackguard all through. But, all the same, you're a phenomenon, and as queer a phenomenon as you are a blackguard. No!'—checking me a second time— 'not a rupee, please. Go out and see if you can find the eyes-brain-and-stomach business again. I'll give you a lakh for each time you see it.'

Half an hour later I was in the Mannerings' drawing-room with Kitty—drunk with the intoxication of present happiness and the foreknowledge that I should never more be troubled with its hideous presence. Strong in the sense of my new-found security, I proposed a ride at once; and, by preference, a canter round Jakko.

Never had I felt so well, so overladen with vitality and mere animal spirits, as I did on the afternoon of the 30th of April. Kitty was delighted at the change in my appearance, and complimented me on it in her delightfully frank and outspoken manner. We left the Mannerings' house together, laughing and talking, and cantered along the Chota Simla road as of old.

I was in haste to reach the Sanjowlie Reservoir and there make my assurance doubly sure. The horses did their best, but seemed all too slow to my impatient mind. Kitty was astonished at my boisterousness. 'Why, Jack!' she cried at last, 'you are behaving like a child. What are you doing?'

We were just below the Convent, and from sheer wantonness I was making my Waler plunge and curvet across the road as I tickled it with the loop of my riding-whip.

'Doing?' I answered; 'nothing, dear. That's just it. If you'd been doing nothing for a week except lie up, you'd be as riotous as I.

> 'Singing and murmuring in your feastful mirth,
> Joying to feel yourself alive;
> Lord over Nature, Lord of the visible Earth,
> Lord of the senses five.'

My quotation was hardly out of my lips before we had rounded the corner above the Convent; and a few yards further on could see across to Sanjowlie. In the centre of the level road stood the black and white liveries, the yellow-panelled 'rickshaw, and Mrs. Keith-Wessington. I pulled up, looked, rubbed my eyes, and, I believe, must have said something. The next thing I knew was that I was lying face downward on the road, with Kitty kneeling above me in tears.

'Has it gone, child?' I gasped. Kitty only wept more bitterly.

'Has what gone, Jack dear? What does it all mean? There must be a mistake somewhere, Jack. A hideous mistake.' Her last words brought me to my feet—mad—raving for the time being.

'Yes, there *is* a mistake somewhere,' I repeated, 'a hideous mistake. Come and look at It.'

I have an indistinct idea that I dragged Kitty by the wrist along the road up to where It stood, and implored her for pity's sake to speak to It; to tell It that we were betrothed; that neither Death nor Hell could break the tie between us: and Kitty only knows how much more to the same effect. Now and again I appealed passionately to the Terror in the 'rickshaw to bear witness to all I had said, and to release me from a torture that was killing me. As I talked I suppose I must have told Kitty of my old relations with Mrs. Wessington, for I saw her listen intently with white face and blazing eyes.

'Thank you, Mr. Pansay,' she said, 'that's *quite enough. Syce ghora lao.'*

The syces, impassive as Orientals always are, had come up with the recaptured horses; and as Kitty sprang into her saddle I caught hold of her bridle, entreating her to hear me out and forgive. My answer was the cut of her riding-whip across my face from mouth to eye, and a word or two of farewell that even now I cannot write down. So I judged and judged rightly, that Kitty knew all; and I staggered back to the side of the 'rickshaw. My face was cut and bleeding, and the blow of the riding-whip had raised a livid blue wheal on it. I had no self-respect. Just then, Heatherlegh, who must have been following Kitty and me at a distance, cantered up.

'Doctor,' I said, pointing to my face, 'here's Miss Mannering's signature to my order of dismissal and—— I'll thank you for that lakh as soon as convenient.'

Heatherlegh's face, even in my abject misery, moved me to laughter.

'I'll stake my professional reputation——' he began.

'Don't be a fool,' I whispered. 'I've lost my life's happiness and you'd better take me home.'

As I spoke the 'rickshaw was gone. Then I lost all knowledge of what was passing. The crest of Jakko seemed to heave and roll like the crest of a cloud and fall in upon me.

Seven days later (on the 7th of May, that is to say) I was aware that I was lying in Heatherlegh's room as weak as a little child. Heatherlegh was watching me intently from behind the papers on his writing-table. His first words were not encouraging; but I was too far spent to be much moved by them.

'Here's Miss Kitty has sent back your letters. You corresponded a good deal, you young people. Here's a packet that looks like a ring and a cheerful sort of a note from Mannering Papa, which I've taken the liberty of reading and burning. The old gentleman's not pleased with you.'

'And Kitty?' I asked dully.

'Rather more drawn than her father from what she says. By the same token you must have been letting out any number of queer reminiscences just before I met you. 'Says that a man who would have behaved to a woman as you did to Mrs. Wessington ought to kill himself out of sheer pity for his kind. She's a hot-headed little virago, your mash. 'Will have it too that you were suffering from *D.T.* when that row on the Jakko road turned up. 'Says she'll die before she ever speaks to you again.'

I groaned and turned over on the other side.

'Now you've got your choice, my friend. This engagement has to be broken off; and the Mannerings don't want to be too hard on you. Was it broken through *D.T.* or epileptic fits? Sorry I can't offer you a better exchange unless you'd prefer hereditary insanity. Say the word and I'll tell 'em it's fits. All Simla knows about that scene on the Ladies' Mile. Come! I'll give you five minutes to think over it.'

During those five minutes I believe that I explored thoroughly the lowest circles of the Inferno which it is permitted man to tread on earth. And at the same time I myself was watching myself faltering through the dark labyrinths of doubt, misery, and utter despair. I wondered, as Heatherlegh in his chair might have wondered, which dreadful alternative I should adopt. Presently I heard myself answering in a voice that I hardly recognised—

'They're confoundedly particular about morality in these parts. Give 'em fits, Heatherlegh, and my love. Now let me sleep a bit longer.'

Then my two selves joined, and it was only I (half crazed, devil-driven I) that tossed in my bed tracing step by step the history of the past month.

'But I am in Simla,' I kept repeating to myself. 'I, Jack Pansay, am in Simla, and there are no ghosts here. It's unreasonable of that woman to pretend there are. Why couldn't Agnes have left me alone? I never did her any harm. It might just as well have been me as Agnes. Only I'd never have come back on purpose to kill *her*. Why can't I be left alone—left alone and happy?'

It was high noon when I first awoke: and the sun was low in the sky before I slept—slept as the tortured criminal sleeps on his rack, too worn to feel further pain.

Next day I could not leave my bed. Heatherlegh told me in the morning that he had received an answer from Mr. Mannering, and that, thanks to his (Heatherlegh's) friendly offices, the story of my affliction had travelled through the length and breadth of Simla, where I was on all sides much pitied.

'And that's rather more than you deserve,' he concluded pleasantly, 'though the Lord knows you've been going through a pretty severe mill. Never mind; we'll cure you yet, you perverse phenomenon.'

I declined firmly to be cured. 'You've been much too good to me already, old man,' said I; 'but I don't think I need trouble you further.'

In my heart I knew that nothing Heatherlegh could do would lighten the burden that had been laid upon me.

With that knowledge came also a sense of hopeless, impotent rebellion against the unreasonableness of it all. There were scores of men no better than I whose punishments had at least been reserved for another world; and I felt that it was bitterly, cruelly unfair that I alone should have been singled out for so hideous a fate. This mood would in time give place to another where it seemed that the 'rickshaw and I were the only realities in a world of shadows; that Kitty was a ghost; that Mannering. Heatherlegh, and all the other men and women I knew were all ghosts; and the great, gray hills themselves but vain shadows devised to torture me. From mood to mood I tossed backwards and forwards for seven weary days; my body growing daily stronger and stronger, until the bedroom looking-glass told me that I had returned to every-day life, and was as other men once more. Curiously enough my face showed no signs of the struggle I had gone through. It was pale indeed, but as expressionless and commonplace as ever. I had expected some permanent alteration—visible evidence of the disease that was eating me away. I found nothing.

On the 15th of May I left Heatherlegh's house at eleven o'clock in the morning; and the instinct of the bachelor drove me to the Club. There I found that every man knew my story as told by Heatherlegh, and was, in clumsy fashion, abnormally kind and attentive. Nevertheless, I recognised that for the rest of my natural life I should be among but not of my fellows; and I envied very bitterly indeed the laughing coolies on the Mall below. I lunched at the Club, and at four o'clock wandered aimlessly down the Mall in the vague hope of meeting Kitty. Close to the Band-stand the black and white liveries joined me; and I heard Mrs. Wessington's old appeal at my side. I had been expecting this ever since I came out; and was only surprised at her delay. The phantom 'rickshaw and I went side by side along the Chota Simla road in silence. Close to the bazar, Kitty and a man on horseback overtook and passed us. For any sign she gave I might have been a dog in the road. She did not even pay me the compliment of quickening her pace; though the rainy afternoon had served for an excuse.

So Kitty and her companion, and I and my ghostly Light-o'-Love, crept round Jakko in couples. The road was streaming with water; the pines dripped like roof-pipes on the rocks below, and the air was full of fine, driving rain. Two or three times I found myself saying to myself almost aloud: 'I'm Jack Pansay on leave at Simla—*at Simla!* Every-day, ordinary Simla. I mustn't forger that—I mustn't forget that.' Then I would try to recollect some of the gossip I had heard at the Club: the prices of So-and-So's horses—anything, in fact, that related to the work-a-day Anglo-Indian world I knew so well. I even repeated the multiplication-table rapidly to myself, to make quite sure that I was not taking leave of my senses. It gave me much comfort; and must have prevented my hearing Mrs. Wessington for a time.

Once more I wearily climbed the Convent slope and entered the level road. Here Kitty and the man started off at a canter, and I was left alone with Mrs. Wessington. 'Agnes,' said I, 'will you put back your hood and tell me what it all means?' The hood dropped noiselessly, and I was face to face with my dead and buried mistress. She was wearing the dress in which I had last seen her alive; carried the same tiny handkerchief in her right hand; and the same card-case in her left. (A woman eight months dead with a card-case!) I had to pin myself down to the multiplication-table, and to set both hands on the stone parapet of the road, to assure myself that that at least was real.

'Agnes,' I repeated, 'for pity's sake tell me what it all means.' Mrs. Wessington leaned forward, with that odd, quick turn of the head I used to know so well, and spoke.

If my story had not already so madly overleaped the bounds of all human belief I should apologise to you now. As I know that no one—no, not even Kitty, for whom it is written as some sort of justification of my conduct—will believe me, I will go on. Mrs. Wessington spoke and I walked with her from the Sanjowlie road to the turning below the Commander-in-Chief's house as I might walk by the side of any living woman's 'rickshaw, deep in conversation. The second and most tormenting of my moods of sickness had suddenly laid hold upon me, and like the prince in Tennyson's poem, 'I seemed to move amid a world of ghosts.' There had been a garden-party at the Commander-in-Chief's, and we two joined the crowd of homeward-bound folk. As I saw them it seemed that *they* were the shadows—impalpable fantastic shadows—that divided for Mrs. Wessington's 'rickshaw to pass through. What we said during the course of that weird interview I cannot—indeed, I dare not—tell. Heatherlegh's comment would have been a short laugh and a remark that I had been 'mashing a brain-eye-and-stomach chimera.' It was a ghastly and yet in some indefinable way a marvellously dear experience. Could it be possible, I wondered, that

I was in this life to woo a second time the woman I had killed by my own neglect and cruelty?

I met Kitty on the homeward road—a shadow among shadows.

If I were to describe all the incidents of the next fortnight in their order, my story would never come to an end; and your patience would be exhausted. Morning after morning and evening after evening the ghostly 'rickshaw and I used to wander through Simla together. Wherever I went the four black and white liveries followed me and bore me company to and from my hotel. At the Theatre I found them amid the crowd of yelling *jhampanies;* outside the Club veranda, after a long evening of whist; at the Birthday Ball, waiting patinetly for my reappearance; and in broad daylight when I went calling. Save that it cast no shadow, the 'rickshaw was in every respect as real to look upon as one of wood and iron. More than once, indeed, I have had to check myself from warning some hard-riding friend against cantering over it. More than once I have walked down the Mall deep in conversation with Mrs. Wessington to the unspeakable amazement of the passers-by.

Before I had been out and about a week I learned that the 'fit' theory had been discarded in favour of insanity. However, I made no change in my mode of life. I called, rode, and dined out as freely as ever. I had a passion for the society of my kind which I had never felt before; I hungered to be among the realities of life; and at the same time I felt vaguely unhappy when I had been separated too long from my ghostly companion. It would be almost impossible to describe my varying moods from the 15th of May up to-day.

The presence of the 'rickshaw filled me by turns with horror, blind fear, a dim sort of pleasure, and utter despair. I dared not leave Simla; and I knew that my stay there was killing me. I knew, moreover, that it was my destiny to die slowly and a little every day. My only anxiety was to get the penance over as quietly as might be. Alternately I hungered for a sight of Kitty and watched her outrageous flirtations with my successor—to speak more accurately, my successors—with amused interest. She was as much out of my life as I was out of hers. By day I wandered with Mrs. Wessington almost content. By night I implored Heaven to let me return to the world as I used to know it. Above all these varying moods lay the sensation of dull, numbing wonder that the seen and the Unseen should mingle so strangely on this earth to hound one poor soul to its grave.

★

*August 27.*—Heatherlegh has been indefatigable in his attendance on me; and only yesterday told me that I ought to send in an application for sick leave. An application to escape the company of a phantom! A request that the Government would graciously permit me to get rid of five ghosts and an airy 'rickshaw by going to England! Heatherlegh's proposition moved me to almost hysterical laughter. I told him that I should await the end quietly at Simla; and I am sure that the end is not far off. Believe me that I dread its advent more than any word can say; and I torture myself nightly with a thousand speculations as to the manner of my death.

Shall I die in my bed decently and as an English gentleman should die; or, in one last walk on the Mall, will my soul be wrenched from me to take its place for ever and ever b the side of that ghastly phantasm? Shall I return to my old lost allegiance in the next world, or shall I meet Agnes loathing her and bound to her side through all eternity? Shall we two hover over the scene of our lives till the end of Time? As the day of my death draws nearer, the intense horror that all living flesh feels toward escaped spirits from beyond the grave grows more and more powerful. It is an awful thing to go down quick among the dead with scarcely one-half of our life completed. It is a thousand times more awful to wait as I do in your midst, for I know not what unimaginable terror. Pity me, at least on the score of my 'delusion,' for I know you will never believe what I have written here. Yet as surely as ever a man was done to death by the Powers of Darkness, I am that man.

In justice, too, pity her. For as surely as ever woman was killed by man, I killed Mrs. Wessington. And the last portion of my punishment is even now upon me.

# *Boomerang*

BY OSCAR COOK

Warwick threw himself into a chair beside me, hitched up his trousers, and, leaning across, tapped me on the knee. "You remember the story about Mendingham which you told me?" he asked.

I nodded. I was not likely to forget that affair.

"Well," he went on, "I've got as good a one to tell you. Had it straight from the filly's mouth, so to speak—and it's red-hot."

I edged away in my chair, for there was something positively ghoulish in his delight, in the coarse way which he referred to a woman, and one who, if my inference were correct, must have known tragedy. But there is no stopping Warwick: he knows or admits no finer feelings or shame when his thirst for "copy" is aroused. Like the little boy in the well-known picture, "he won't be happy till he's 'quenched' it".

I ordered drinks, and when they had been served and we were alone, bade him get on with his sordid story.

"It's a wild tale," he began, "of two planter fellows in the interior of Borneo—and, as usual, there's a woman."

"*The* woman?" I could not refrain from asking, thinking of his earlier remark.

'The same," he replied. "A veritable golden-haired filly, only her mane is streaked with grey and there's a great livid scar or weal right round her neck. She's the wife of Leopold Thring. The other end of the triangle is Clifford Macy."

"And where do you come in?" I inquired.

Warwick closed one eye and pursed his lips.

"As a spinner of yarns," he answered sententiously. Then, with a return to his usual cynicism, "The filly is down and out, but for some silly religious scruples feels she must live. I bought the story, therefore, after verifying the facts. Shall I go on?"

I nodded, for I must admit I was genuinely interested. The eternal triangle always intrigues: set in the wilds of Borneo it promised a variation of incident unusually refreshing in these sophisticated days. Besides, that scar was eloquent.

Warwick chuckled.

"The two men were partners," he went on, "on a small experimental estate far up in the interior. They had been at it for six years and were just about to reap the fruits of their labours very handsomely. Incidentally, Macy had been out in the Colony the full six years—and the strain was beginning to tell. Thring had been home eighteen months before, and on coming back had brought his bride, Rhona.

"That was the beginning of the trouble. It split up the partnership: brought in a new element: meant the building of a new bungalow."

"For Macy?" I asked.

"Yes. And he didn't take kindly to it. He had got set. And then there was the loneliness of night after night alone, while the others—you understand?"

I nodded.

"Well," Warwick continued, "the expected happened. Macy flirted, philandered, and then fell violently in love. He was one of those fellows who never do things by halves. If he drank, he'd get fighting drunk: if he loved, he went all out on it: if he hated—well, hell was let loose."

"And—Mrs. Thring?" I queried, for it seemed to me that she might have a point of view.

"Fell between two stools—as so many women of a certain type do. She began by being just friendly and kind—you know the sort of thing—cheering the lonely man up, drifted into woman's eternal game of flirting, and then began to grow a little afraid of the fire she'd kindled. Too late she realized that she couldn't put the fire out—either hers or Macy's—and all the while she clung to some hereditary religious scruples.

"Thring was in many ways easygoing, but at the same time possessed of a curiously intense strain of jealous possessiveness. He was generous, too. If asked, he would share or give away his last shirt or crust. But let him think or feel that his rights or dues were being curtailed or taken and—well, he was a tough customer of rather primitive ideas.

"Rhona—that's the easiest way to think of the filly—soon found she was playing a game beyond her powers. Hers was no poker face, and Thring began to sense that something was wrong. She couldn't dissemble, and Macy made no attempt to hide his feelings. He didn't make it easy for her, and I guess from what the girl told me, life about this time was for her a sort of glorified hell—a suspicious husband on one hand, and an impetuous, devil-may-care lover on the other. She was living on a volcano."

"Which might explode any minute." I quietly said.

Warwick nodded.

"Exactly; or whenever Thring chose to spring the mine. He held the key to the situation, or, should I say, the time-fuse? The old story, but set in a primitive land full of possibilities. You've got me?"

For answer I offered Warwick a cigarette, and, taking one myself, lighted both.

"So far," I said, "with all your journalistic skill you've not got off the beaten track. Can't you improve?"

He chuckled, blew a cloud of smoke, and once again tapped my knee in his irritating manner.

"Your cynicism," he countered, "is but a poor cloak for your curiosity. In reality you're jumping mad to know the end, eh?"

I made no reply, and he went on.

"Well, matters went on from day to day till Rhona became worn to the proverbial shadow. Thring wanted to send her home, but she wouldn't go. She owed a duty to her husband: she couldn't bear to be parted from her lover, and she didn't dare leave the two men alone. She was terribly, horribly afraid.

"Macy grew more and more openly amorous and less restrained. Thring watched whenever possible with the cunning of an iguana. Then came a rainy, damp spell that tried nerves to the uttermost and the inevitable stupid little disagreements between Rhona and Thring—mere trifles, but enough to let the lid off. He challenged her——"

"And she?" I could not help asking, for Warwick has, I must admit, the knack of keeping one on edge.

"Like a blithering but sublime little idiot admitted that it was all true."

For nearly a minute I was speechless. Somehow, although underneath I had expected Rhona to behave so, it seemed such a senseless, unbelievable thing to do. Then at last I found my voice.

"And Thring?" I said simply.

Warwick emptied his glass at a gulp.

"That's the most curious thing in the whole yarn," he answered slowly. "Thring took it as quietly as a lamb."

"Stunned?" I suggested.

"That's what Rhona thought: what Macy believed when Rhona told him what had happened. In reality he must have been burning mad, a mass of white-hot revenge controlled by a devilish, cunning brain: he waited. A scene or a fight—and Macy was a big, man—would have done no good. He would get his own back in his own time and in his own way. Meanwhile, there was the lull before the storm.

"Then, as so often happens, Fate played a hand. Macy went sick with malaria—really ill—and even Thring had to admit the necessity for Rhona to nurse him practically night and day. Macy owned his eventual recovery to her care, but even so his convalescence was a long job. In the end Rhona too crocked up through overwork, and Thring had them both on his hands. This was an opportunity better than he could have planned—it separated the lovers and gave him complete control.

"Obviously the time was ripe, ripe for Thring to score his revenge.

"The rains were over, the jungle had ceased wintering, and spring was in the air. The young grass and vegetation were shooting into new life: concurrently all the creepy, crawly insect life of the jungle and estate was young and vigorous and hungry too. These facts gave Thring the germ of an idea which he was not slow to perfect—an idea as devilish as man could devise."

Warwick paused to press out the stub of his cigarette, and noticing that even he seemed affected by his recital, I prepared myself as best I could for a really gruesome horror. All I said, however, was, "Go on."

"It seems," he continued, "that in Borneo there is a kind of mammoth earwig—a thing almost as fine and gossamer as a spider's web, as long as a good-sized caterpillar, that lives on waxy secretions. These are integral parts of some flowers and trees, and lie buried deep in their recesses. It is one of the terrors of these particular tropics, for it moves and rests so lightly on a human being that one is practically unconscious of it, while, like its English relation, it has a decided liking for the human ear: on account of man's carnivorous diet the wax in this has a strong and very succulent taste."

As Warwick gave me those details, he sat upright on the edge of his easy-chair. He spoke slowly, emphasizing each point by hitting the palm of his left hand with the clenched fist of his right. It was impossible not to see the drift and inference of his remarks.

"You mean——?" I began.

"Exactly," he broke in quickly, blowing a cloud of smoke from a fresh cigarette which he had nervously lighted. "Exactly. It was a devilish idea. To put the giant earwig on Macy's hair just above the ear."

"And then…?" I knew the fatuousness of the question, but speech relieved the growing sense of ticklish horror that was creeping over me.

"Do nothing. But rely on the filthy insect running true to type. Once in Macy's ear, it was a thousand-to-one chance against it ever coming out the same way: it would not be able to turn: to back out would be almost an impossibility, and so, feeding as it went, it would crawl right across inside his head, with the result that——"

The picture Warwick was drawing was more than I could bear: even my imagination, dulled by years of legal dry-as-dust affairs, saw and sickened at the possibilities. I put out a hand and gripped Warwick's arm.

"Stop, man!" I cried hoarsely. "For God's sake, don't say any more. I understand. My God, but the man Thring must be a fiend!"

Warwick looked at me, and I saw that even his face had paled.

"*Was*," he said meaningly. "Perhaps you're right, perhaps he *was* a fiend. Yet, remember, Macy stole his wife."

"But a torture like that! The deliberate creation of a living torment that would grow into madness. Warwick, you can't condone that!"

He looked at me for a moment and then slowly spread out his hands.

"Perhaps you're right," he admitted. "It was a bit thick, I know. But there's more to come."

I closed my eyes and wondered if I could think of an excuse for leaving Warwick; but in spite of my real horror, my curiosity won the day.

"Get on with it," I muttered, and leant back, eyes still shut, hands clenched. With teeth gritted together as if I myself were actually suffering the pain of that earwig slowly, daily creeping farther into and eating my brain, I waited.

Warwick was not slow to obey.

"I have told you," he said, "that Rhona had to nurse Macy, and even when he was better, though still weak, Thring insisted on her looking after him, though now he himself came more often.

"One afternoon Rhona was in Macy's bungalow alone with him: the house-boy was out. Rhona was on the veranda: Macy was asleep in the bedroom. Dusk was just falling: bats were flying about: the flying foxes, heavy with fruit, were returning home: the inevitable house rats were scurrying about the floors: the lamps had not been lit. An eerie, devastating hour. Rhona dropped some needlework and fought back tears. Then from the bedroom came a shriek. "My head! My ear! Oh, God! My ear! Oh, God! The pain!"

"That was the beginning. The earwig had got well inside. Rhona rushed in and did all she could. Of course, there was nothing to see. Then for a little while Macy would be quiet because the earwig was quiet, sleeping or gorged. Then the vile thing would move or feed again, and Macy once more would shriek with the pain.

"And so it went on, day by day. Alternate quiet and alternate pain, each day for Macy, for Rhona a hell of nerve-rending expectancy. Waiting, always waiting for the pain that crept and crawled and twisted and writhed and moved slowly, ever slowly, through and across Macy's brain."

Warwick paused so long that I was compelled to open my eyes. His face was ghastly. Fortunately I could not see my own.

"And Thring?" I asked.

"Came often each day. Pretended sorrow and served out spurious dope—Rhona found the coloured water afterwards. He cleverly urged that Macy should be carried down to the coast for medical treatment, knowing full well that he was too ill and worn to bear the smallest strain. Then when Macy was an utter wreck, broken completely in mind and body, with hollow, hunted eyes, with ever-twitching fingers, with a body no part of which he could properly control or keep still, the earwig came out—at the other ear.

"As it happened, both Thring and Rhona were present. Macy must have suffered an excruciating pain, followed as usual by a period of quiescence: then, feeling a slight ticklish sensation on his cheek, put up his hand to rub or scratch. His fingers came in contact with the earwig and its fine gossamer hairs. Instinct did the rest. You follow?"

My tongue was still too dry to enable me to speak. Instead I nodded, and Warwick went on.

"He naturally was curious and looked to see what he was holding. In an instant he realized. Even Rhona could not be in doubt. The hairs were faintly but unmistakably covered here and there with blood, with wax and with grey matter.

"For a moment there was absolute silence between the three. At last Macy spoke.

" 'My God!' he just whispered. 'Oh, my God! What an escape!'

"Rhona burst into tears. Only Thring kept silent, and that was his mistake. The silence worried Macy, weak though he was. He looked from Rhona to Thring, and at the critical moment Thring could not meet his gaze. The truth was out. With an oath Macy threw the insect, now dead from the pressure of his fingers, straight into Thring's face. Then he crumpled up in his chair and sobbed and sobbed till even the chair shook."

Again Warwick paused till I thought he would never go on. I had heard enough, I'll admit, and yet it seemed to me that at least there should be an epilogue.

"Is that all?" I tentatively asked.

Warwick shook his head.

"Nearly, but not quite," he said. "Rhona had ceased weeping and kept her eyes fixed on Thring—she dared not go and comfort Macy now. She saw him examine the dead earwig, having picked it up from the floor to which it had fallen, turn it this way and that, then produce from a pocket a magnifying-glass which he used daily for the inspection and detection of leaf disease on certain of the plants. As she watched, she saw the fear and disappointment leave his face, to be replaced by a look of cunning and evil satisfaction. Then for the first time he spoke.

" 'Macy!' he called, in a sharp, loud voice.

Macy looked up.

"Thring held up the earwig. 'This is dead now,' he said—'dead. As dead as my friendship for you, you swine of a thief, as dead as my love for that whore who was my wife. It's dead, I tell you, dead, but it's a female. D'you get me? A female, and a female lays eggs, and before it died it——'

"He never finished. His baiting at last roused Macy, endowing him with the strength of madness and despair. With one spring he was at Thring's throat, bearing him down to the ground. Over and over they rolled on the floor, struggling for possession of the great hunting-knife stuck in Thring's belt. One moment Macy was on top, the next, Thring. Their breath and oaths came in great trembling gasps. They kicked and bit and scratched. And all the while Rhona watched, fascinated and terrified. Then Thring got definitely on top. He had one hand on Macy's throat, both knees on his chest, and with his free hand he was feeling for the knife. In that instant Rhona's religious scruples went by the board. She realized she only loved Macy, that her husband didn't count. She rushed to Macy's help. Thring saw her coming and let drive a blow at her head which almost stunned her. She fell on top of him just as he was whipping out the knife. Its edge caught her neck. The sudden spurt of blood shot into Thring's eyes, and blinded him. It was Macy's last chance. He knew it, and he took it.

"When Rhona came back to consciousness, Thring was dead. Macy was standing beside the body, which was gradually swelling to huge proportions as he worked, weakly but steadily, at the white ant exterminator pump, the nozzle of which was pushed down the dead man's throat."

Warwick ceased. This last had been a long, unbroken recital, and mechanically he picked up his empty glass as if to drain it. The action brought me back to nearly normal. I rang for the waiter—the knob of the electric bell luckily being just over my head. While waiting, I had time to speak.

"I've heard enough," I said hurriedly, "to last me a lifetime. You've made me feel positively sick. But there's just one point. What happened to Macy? Did he live?"

Warwick nodded.

"That's another strange fact. He still lives. He was tried for the murder of Thring, but there was no real evidence. On the other hand, his story was too tall to be believed, with the result—well, you can guess."

"A lunatic asylum—for life?" I asked.

Warwick nodded again. Then I followed his glance. A waiter was standing by my chair.

"Two double whisky-and-sodas," I ordered tersely, and then, with shaking fingers, lighted a cigarette.

# *Mrs. Raeburn's Waxwork*

BY LADY ELEANOR SMITH

The rain, which had poured with a pitiless ferocity for so long upon the chimneys and roofs of the great manufacturing city, seemed at length to enclose the whole town within towering prison-walls of burnished steel. It was now afternoon; the short winter day was nearly over, and it had rained thus from dawn, would probably continue to rain throughout the night. A dark, wet dusk began to envelop the city like a sable blanket; the street-lamps sprang into life, looming ahead like the ghosts of drowned and weary daffodils, casting watery and trembling reflections upon the shining rivers that were pavements. There were few people walking the mournful streets, and those that were had to struggle and batter their way through sharp gusts of wind, bent double beneath dripping and top-heavy umbrellas.

Such a one was Patrick Lamb, and so great was his hurry that more than once as he stumbled over an unperceived kerb he ran the risk of entangling both himself and his umbrella in the foaming, muddy torrents of the gutters beneath his feet. He had every reason to hurry; he was on his way to apply for a job, and he feared that unless he hastened he would be too late to secure this vacancy which meant so much to him.

Turning at last into a dark and narrow street, he saw opposite to him a ramshackle building of yellow brick, from the roof of which swelled forth a glass dome encrusted with the dirt and soot of ages. A flight of shallow steps led to a swing door. This was his destination.

He flung open the door and was immediately confronted by a turnstile, near which sat a seedy-looking man in an ill-fitting uniform not unlike that of a fireman.

"Sixpence, please," said the man, and whistled through his teeth.

Patrick Lamb shook his head.

"No.... I'm not a visitor. I have an appointment with Mr. Mugivan, the manager."

"Ah—ha," said the attendant knowingly, and showed him into a tiny slice of a room filled with papers, files, account-books and dust. Here sat Mr. Mugivan, a fat, podgy man with thick legs and a face like a tomato.

"Good afternoon," said Patrick Lamb hesitatingly, "I hear that you have a vacancy here for an—an attendant."

Mr. Mugivan stared for a moment at the young man's sallow, rather long face, at his deep-set grey eyes and slender, puny body.

"Who told you so?"

"My landlady, in Bury Street. She knew the last man you had here."

"And what made you come?"

"Necessity. I'm in need of work. I was stranded here a week ago with a theatrical company."

There was a silence. Mr. Mugivan suddenly laughed, looking at his visitor rather defiantly with little red-rimmed eyes that were not unlike the eyes of a pig.

"Rather a come-down, isn't it, for an actor to find himself minding Mugivan's Waxworks?"

"That doesn't matter—sir. And, if you'll only let me, I'll mind them damn well."

"It's long hours," said the proprietor, still speaking contemptuously. "Nine in the morning till seven at night. An hour for lunch and an hour for tea. Two pounds a week—and the attendant has to wear a uniform. *An actor* wouldn't fancy that, would he?"

"Maybe I'm not an actor," said Patrick Lamb.

Mr. Mugivan spat upon the floor.

"I'll give you a trial, anyhow. What's your name?"

Patrick told him.

"Well, Lamb," and the proprietor creaked himself out of his chair, revealing incidentally that he wore carpet slippers and had bunions, "come with me and I'll show you Mugivan's Beauties before you go. You can start to-morrow morning."

Obediently Patrick followed his new employer through the turnstile, which was swung round obligingly by the other attendant, down a narrow white-washed tunnel into a large apartment.

"Ever seen figures before?" inquired Mr. Mugivan.

"Waxworks? Not since I was a kid."

"Hall of Monarchs," said Mr. Mugivan, sucking his teeth with a deprecating sound.

The room in which they found themselves was bare and vault-like; here, too, the walls were white-washed; the floor was covered with a red drugget, and in the middle of the room was placed a sofa upholstered in shabby crimson plush. Yet although bare the room was not empty, but crowded, crowded with a pale throng of mute and stiff and silent figures. They stood in groups, a dais to each group, and were protected from the public by a red cord which imprisoned them, like sheep in a pen, so that had they wished they could not have strayed, but must for ever remain captive. There they stood and would no doubt stand throughout the ages, these tinsel kings and queens, Plantagenets and Stuarts, Tudors and Hanoverians, calm and blank and dreadfully remote, pallid of cheek and glassy of eye, indifferent to all who passed by to gape at them—a host of waxen princes, all dead, many of them forgotten, terribly isolated in their garish splendour, uncannily galvanised into a crude semblance of life that yet denied them even the elements of life, leaving them fixed, frozen and staring, while the dust thickened upon their cheap and fusty robes of purple and sham ermine.

Opposite the door through which they had come was another door leading to yet another chamber. Mr. Mugivan led the way.

"Curiosities and Horrors," he explained carelessly. They passed through the second door.

Here was another room, replica of the first, but more dimly lit, more melancholy than even the Hall of Monarchs, since the illumination that winked upon this dreary scene was greenish, ghastly, such a light as might have been expected to proceed from a sconce of corpse candles. Here were more massed ranks of still, impassive figures, paler these than the monarchs in the dim grotto of their melancholy chamber, and more repellent perhaps because their stiff, indifferent bodies were clothed in the garments of everyday and borrowed no majesty from princes' robes, however sham. A skeleton gleamed white in one corner of the room, there was a stuffed ox with six legs, a tiny waxen midget and a giant of local fame. Save for these the room was peopled only with men who had killed and who had paid the penalty for killing.

A throng staring before them, expressionless, rigid, mask-like, brooding perhaps upon their crimes.

Mr. Mugivan seemed more at home in the second room. He became almost conversational.

"Here's Hopkins, the Norwich strangler … Tracey, who shot a policeman … John Joseph Gilmore, cut the throats of his wife and two children…"

They moved across the room. Then, near the slit of a window, crossed by iron bars, Patrick saw her for the first time. She stood on a little dais by herself, a young woman, or, rather, the effigy of a young woman, dressed neatly in dark clothes that were already old-fashioned in cut. She carried herself proudly, like a queen, and whereas the other waxworks were completely expressionless of countenance, this one alone, with proudly curling lips and short, imperious nose, seemed, he thought, actually to live, perhaps because she was disdain incarnate. She stood there easily, gracefully, long, pale hands folded upon her breast, and Patrick, gazing, felt the cool, amused stare of her grey eyes. For a moment his heart leaped sharply, startling him, and he had a sudden impulse to move forward and look more closely at her; then this sensation was succeeded by a creeping feeling of curious discomfort. He was embarrassed; he had to avert his eyes.

"Who's that woman?" he asked impetuously, and then wished that he had not spoken.

Mr. Mugivan answered him casually, with his back turned to the effigy.

"That's Mrs. Raeburn, the poisoner … and that's the lot, so come on."

"Mrs. Raeburn? I seem to know the name."

"No doubt, no doubt. It was well enough known at one time."

They walked away, towards the Hall of Monarchs, and Patrick was acutely conscious of the supercilious grey eyes that must be gazing after them. The sham eyes of a sham woman, a waxen effigy! He felt acutely ridiculous.

Mr. Mugivan said no more until they found themselves once again in the little office. Then, offering Patrick a cigarette, he asked suddenly:

"You're not a fanciful sort of chap by any chance?"

"Fanciful? You mean nervous? No, I can't say that I am. Why?"

"No place for fancies, this," confided Mr Mugivan, waving his hand in the direction of the exhibition; "it's a lonely sort of a job most of the time, and once you start thinking the figures are looking at you, well, you're done, that's all. Last chap we had here took to having fancies. That's why you've got his job."

Patrick felt suddenly rebellious.

"I can safely say I shan't have fancies," he said, laughing. "I may not be particularly brave—in fact I'm not—but I must say it would take more than a parcel of wax dolls to scare me."

"Figures aren't dolls," Mr. Mugivan corrected, shocked.

"Figures, then," and he thought: "Talking of figures, that woman Mrs. Raeburn's got a good one."

But neither he nor Mr. Mugivan mentioned the name of the woman poisoner aloud.

"Nine o'clock to-morrow, then," said Mr. Mugivan.

"Nine o'clock to-morrow."

And so they parted.

He discovered, the next day, two things about his new job. One was that his long and often lonely vigil with the waxworks gave him at times the curious and eerie sensation of being buried alive in a vault filled with the dead, the other that, with the morning, Mrs. Raeburn, poisoner, had become once more a waxen effigy, and was no longer a living, breathing woman. This was comforting, yet in some strange way disappointing, for it was idle to deny that he had thought of her very frequently during the course of the night, and that the prospect of meeting once more the direct gaze of her rather mocking eyes had undoubtedly stimulated him and sent him forth into the cheerless streets kindled with an eager, sparkling excitement which he rather half-heartedly strove to suppress.

As the morning dragged by he studied a catalogue of the exhibition, trying to memorise the many dossiers of princes and murderers. He was accustomed to learn by heart, and in three hours his task was almost complete, yet with one exception. A curious revulsion prevented him from reading, even to himself, the brief account in the catalogue of Mrs. Raeburn's crime, of discovering, through the medium of one cheap, smudged paragraph, that she had been an infamous woman, a monster of vice and cruelty. Taking a pen-knife from his pocket he cut away from his catalogue all record of her dark deeds. Yet she remained throughout the morning a lifeless effigy, and after glancing at her once, he gladly looked away.

He went out to lunch and returned for the long vigil of the afternoon. Few people came to visit the exhibition: a pair of school-children in charge of a maiden aunt, two girls, who giggled and eyed him coyly, an old man, and an amorous couple who plainly regarded his presence as a nuisance.

It was foggy outside; dusk fell early. For the first time that day, as he paced the Hall of Monarchs, he became sensible of the loneliness of his position. Once again the feeling of being buried among the dead returned to him, intensified this time by a bored and brooding melancholy, whereas in the morning there had also been a sense of adventure. The very tread of his feet, the only sound in the still apartment, smote lugubriously upon his ears. He would have liked to smoke, but this was, of course, forbidden.

At length he turned, and obeying an impulse which was becoming every second stronger, he moved towards the farther chamber, the Hall of Curiosities and Horrors. Here the twilight struck gloomily upon the wan and glimmering faces of the murderers, upturned to greet the first dark, smoky greyness of night: greenish they were once more, and dismal; and very hopeless in the blank resignation of their weary vigil in this dim room that was filled with the very breath of genteel decay.

He went straight towards the figure of Mrs. Raeburn, standing tall and quiet and erect on her dais below the barred window. He had never been so near to her before; their eyes met, and once more she had recaptured that spark of life which had so curiously impressed him on the previous day. He gazed for some moments at her pale, clear-cut face, at her direct, ironic eyes. She appeared to return his scrutiny gravely, earnestly, scornfully, yet with a glint of interest and humour in her regard. She seemed, he thought, a woman well used to curious eyes, well able to defend herself against the stares of the inquisitive. Suddenly, to his immense astonishment, he spoke to her, and his voice rang out strangely enough in that silent room.

"I wonder what you have done?" he asked her abruptly. "For God's sake, what can you have done that you should be here?"

There was a long pause, during the course of which he continued to examine her closely. Was it his imagination, or did her lips really curve, was there an answering twinkle in her eye? And then he turned sharply, for he had caught, or thought that he had caught, a soft, eager rustling sound from the throng of effigies behind his back. And suddenly he was saved, for two little boys came pattering in to visit the curiosities and horrors.

The next day saw him resolutely keeping to the Hall of Monarchs. Here, with the lifeless dummies of long dead kings, he was safe. In that other room he realised that he was in peril. And the day after, although he hungered for a glimpse of Mrs. Raeburn's pale face, he still remained aloof. The next day was Saturday, with a steady stream of patrons who would have made the dankest vault seem homely and prosaic. Then Sunday, a holiday.

On Monday he returned to the exhibition ready to laugh at himself for a morbid fool. The rain had stopped; a feeble ray of primrose sunshine, filtering through the barred window of the second chamber, made even Mrs. Raeburn seem little more than a cunningly fashioned doll of life size. And he had spoken to her, as though she were alive and could hear and understand him! He was disgusted with himself.

Yet, with the swiftly flowing dusk the murderers changed once more; assumed as was their wont with the shades of night the vivid and evil personalities they must have worn during their lifetime; seemed to stretch themselves as though released from some long spell of immobility; nodded, perhaps, to one another—even winked; perhaps brushed the dust from their shabby garments, smothered yawns, and waited, quietly expectant, for the closing of the exhibition. So Patrick thought, but it was difficult to see, for the shadows were thick in this lost and forgotten room.

He went towards the effigy of Mrs. Raeburn and was not surprised to find that her eyes, alive and brilliant, almost feverish in their eager intensity, remained fixed direct upon him as though she waited to see whether he would, after his three days' absence, speak once more to her.

He was, however silent. He stared at her proud and beautiful mouth, at her long, pale hands, at the white stem of her throat, and admitted to himself that he desired her. Yet he had no immediate wish to touch her, but only longed passionately for the stiff, waxen body of this effigy to melt and transform itself into warm living flesh and blood. Somewhere, somehow, this miracle must be accomplished, for if he was unable to possess her he thought that, such was the spell she had cast upon him, he must inevitably pine and sicken, for she was La Belle Dame Sans Merci, and he was in her thrall. At last he spoke to her, softly, scarcely knowing that he spoke.

"You are a witch," he said, "and you possess me body and soul. You ought to be burnt, and since you are made of wax it should not be difficult to destroy you....I have a good mind to try."

This time there was no mistake; a gleam of sardonic laughter came to her eyes, a strange and elfin smile to her curling lips. She defied him. And as before, the row of murderers behind seemed to move simultaneously with the rustling murmur of excitement. As before, too, he was saved by a footstep from the outer world. He turned sharply. A woman came into the room.

Patrick stiffened, became once more the respectful and vigilant attendant. The woman hesitated for a moment, then approached him slowly, for she was bent and squat and elderly, and walked with the help of a stick. He noticed vaguely that she was dressed in dingy black, with a frowsy bonnet askew upon her head and a film of veil that partially concealed her face. He bent down politely.

"Yes, madam? Is there anything I can do?"

"There is," said the old woman. Her voice was clear and decisive, the voice of one who is accustomed to command. "I have stupidly neglected to buy a catalogue at the door, and as I am old, and not so good a walker as I was, I wonder if you would save my going back by being kind enough to tell me something about the waxworks. These are murderers, are they not?"

Patrick, only too pleased to occupy his mind in this accustomed fashion, began mechanically:

"Yes, madam. There on my right is Richard Sayers, the Scottish body-snatcher, who shot two men before he was arrested, and protested his innocence to the last.... Next to Sayers is Mugivan's conception of Jack the Ripper, the criminal who was never captured....this figure is modelled according to the description of his appearance given to the police by those persons who protested that they had seen him before or after his appalling crimes.... Next to Jack the Ripper we have Landru...."

But while his voice droned on he was dreading the moment when they must face Mrs. Raeburn, when he would look once more upon her pale, remote face and meet once again her steady, contemptuous gaze. He lingered beside the midget, the freakish ox, the local giant. The old woman listened to him attentively, beady eyes darting from beneath her heavy veil. Once or twice she asked him a question, but otherwise was silent, seeming pleasantly absorbed in his monotonous catalogue of grim and fiendish crimes. At last the moment dreaded by Patrick could be postponed no longer; at last they faced the figure of Mrs. Raeburn, standing slim and straight and self-possessed beneath the grating window. Suddenly Patrick remembered that he knew nothing of this murderess save that she had killed by poison; here he was speechless and could recite no bloodthirsty dossier, nor did he even know her victim; only that she was young and fair and that she had cast a spell upon him, and these things could not be told to his companion. There was a pause during the course of which the old woman examined the wax figure attentively and in silence. At length he mumbled:

"This is Mrs. Raeburn ... the poisoner."

As he spoke he shot a sharp glance at the effigy and observed that she was blank and mask-like once more; indifferent both to him and his companion. His witch had again become a waxwork.

The old lady shuffled closer to the figure, peered with a certain attentive inquisitiveness, then turned to him and remarked critically:

"The likeness is not very good."

He was startled, and gaped, unable quite to grasp the purport of her words.

He asked: "You knew her?"

She did not answer him, but said, still peering: "She was taller, she had more dignity, more of an air. And I think she was wilder. But it's long ago," and her face changed all the time.

He asked again, trembling, his hands clammy cold, his voice unconsciously menacing: "You knew her?"

For the first time the old creature turned to look at him, seeming to observe him closely. She chuckled, and at first he thought that one of the waxworks had laughed, so ghostly, so unexpected, was this little bubbling sound in the quietness of the dim hall.

She said, still chuckling: "I am Mrs. Raeburn."

And as he did not answer she pulled back her veil. She was younger than he had at first supposed. She revealed a fat, gross, heavy-jowled face, sallow, unhealthy, with high Mongolian cheek-bones. Her nose was squat and thick, her cheeks carved with two deep-cut lines running from her nostrils to the corners of her mouth. Her little sharp grey eyes were almost buried in folds of flesh. Beneath the shoddy bonnet a strand of hair hung untidily; it was dyed a bright orange tint. The face, which leered forth so boldly at Patrick, was seamed and stamped with the marks of every foul and obscene vice; brazen, debauched, so brutal as to be three parts animal, it seemed to hang in the air, this gargoyle face, to gloat triumphantly upon his horror and confusion. Then, swiftly, the woman whisked back her veil and said crisply, in her clear and resonant voice:

"It didn't do me justice, your image," Then in a moment she was gone, while behind her the effigy of Mrs. Raeburn, poisoner, remained standing cool and pale and remote upon her dais, all the paler, all the cooler, for being now the centre of a flood of cold and frozen moonlight.

Patrick fled after the old woman, not because he wished to see her again, but because of the two of them the waxen image had become the more repulsive, yet, when he reached the Hall of Monarchs, she had already disappeared.

He waited, sick and shivering, until the clock struck seven and the show shut down, then he went in search of Mr. Mugivan, whom he found in his office, reading an evening paper, with his feet on his desk.

"Good evening," said Patrick. "I want to tell you something."

Mr. Mugivan put down his paper.

"My word, young fellow, you look cheap. What is it now?'

Patrick, gulping, said: "Do you know who's been here this afternoon?"

"I do not," said Mr. Mugivan. "I'm proprietor of a waxwork show, not a magician. Who has been here?"

"Mrs. Raeburn. The real Mrs. Raeburn. She came to see her waxwork. She's just gone."

As Mr. Mugivan gaped, his red face became curiously mottled—white and purple in patches, Patrick noticed dispassionately.

"Mrs. Raeburn?"

"Yes."

Mr. Mugivan climbed laboriously from his chair.

"Mrs. Raeburn, eh? Somebody's been pulling your leg. You don't know your catalogue, either. Mrs. Raeburn indeed?"

And he pulled a document from the untidy desk, licked his thumb, and flipped over a page.

"Mrs. Raeburn," he said, speaking very loud and not looking at Patrick, "was scragged—hanged, you understand—hanged by the neck for the murder of her husband more than twenty years ago. That being so, you could hardly have seen her here just now. And that's enough of your funny stuff for one day."

Patrick said nothing. There was really nothing to say. Nor did Mr. Mugivan break the silence, but waddled to and fro about the little room, changing his carpet slippers for boots, struggling into his overcoat, cramming a check cap upon his head. In a moment he had gone.

Patrick switched off the office light, then went forth, as was his custom, to extinguish the gas jets in the exhibition before locking up for the night. His comrade of the turnstile had already gone home; he was alone, entirely alone, with more than a hundred waxen effigies. It was now quite dark outside, for the moon had fled behind a screen of clouds, and there was a rushing sound of strong wind, which swept in gusts past the shuttered windows.

He paused to light a forbidden cigarette, and then it was that he realised with an odd detachment that what he had seen during the afternoon was not a ghost, but something even more monstrous—a disembodied soul. The foul and evil soul of this wretched woman whose lovely image had bewitched him. The hideous reflection of a hideous mind. Behind her seeming purity and beauty had always been this horror, dormant, waiting to leap forth and devour. The wind rose, moaning, battering at the panes.

On such a night, he mused, as he tramped towards the monarchs, ghouls would surely stalk abroad and witches soar through the air clutching their broomsticks and screaming aloud their lust for Satan. Vampires, sorcerers, fiends. A nightmare pack of horrors.... He stretched on tip-toe to lower the gas above the wan, impassive face of King Richard II.... And in the old days witches were burnt alive like the guys now consumed by flames each Fifth of November.... And after burning he supposed that these evil women could do no more harm, but were destroyed for ever, they and their spells. A good job, too. He entered the second chamber.

★

That night the inhabitants of the city were surprised to perceive a crimson flush sweeping the sky above the roof-tops of a distant street. Then came a clanging of bells, a roar of motor-engines, and, hot-foot, in pursuit of the fire brigade, a yelling, excited rabble. Mugivan's Waxwork Exhibition was on fire. No one wanted to miss the show, doubly welcome because it was free.

The wind was strong that night, and licked the flames eagerly, strengthening them until the efforts of the men armed with hose-pipes became pathetic in their futility. At length the roof crashed in, and a wall of roaring flame rose as though to leap into the sky. They were triumphant, these pillars of fire, as though they knew that they were purifying, destroying a witch.

By morning Mugivan's Waxwork Show was a drenched and sooty ruin. Many of the figures were entirely destroyed, the monarchs having been on the whole unluckier than the murderers. Down in the Hall of Curiosities and Horrors there were a few survivors. Some were quite untouched. Mrs. Raeburn, for instance, appeared to have emerged unscathed from the ordeal, and stood upon her dais proudly and gracefully, pale hands folded demurely upon her breast. And yet, on closer inspection, Mrs. Raeburn proved not to be entirely unharmed. Her waxen face had melted, and running, the stuff had twisted upon her features a strange and devilish sneer. Save for her pride of carriage she was unrecognisable, distorted. And then the firemen made a further discovery.

Lying near by, where the flames had crackled most fiercely, was a charred and sodden bundle of clothing. They bent to examine it. It was, they found, a human body, the body of a young man.

# *A Face in the Night*

BY RUSKIN BOND

It may give you some idea of rural humour if I begin this tale with an anecdote that concerns me. I was walking alone through a village at night when I met an old man carrying a lantern. I found, to my surprise, that the man was blind. 'Old man,' I asked, 'if you cannot see, why do you carry a lamp?'

'I carry this,' he replied, 'so that fools do not stumble against me in the dark.'

This incident has only a slight connection with the story that follows, but I think it provides the right sort of tone and setting. Mr. Oliver, an Anglo-Indian teacher, was returning to his school late one night, on the outskirts of the hill station of Simla. The school was conducted on English public school lines and the boys, most of them from well-to-do Indian families, wore blazers, caps, and ties. *Life* magazine, in a feature on India had once called this school the 'Eton of the East'.

Individuality was not encouraged; they were all destined to become 'leaders of men'.

Mr. Oliver had been teaching in the school for several years. Sometimes it seemed like an eternity; for one day followed upon another with the same monotonous routine. The Simla bazaar, with its cinemas and restaurants, was about two miles from the school; and Mr. Oliver, a bachelor, usually strolled into the town in the evening, returning after dark, when he would take a short cut through a pine forest.

When there was a strong wind, the pine trees made sad, eerie sounds that kept most people to the main road. But Mr. Oliver was not a nervous or imaginative man. He carried a torch and, on the night I write of, its pale gleam—the batteries were running down—moved fitfully over the narrow forest path. When its flickering light fell on the figure of a boy, who was sitting alone on a rock, Mr. Oliver stopped. Boys were not supposed to be out of school after 7 p.m., and it was now well past nine.

'What are you doing out here, boy?' asked Mr. Oliver sharply, moving closer so that he could recognize the miscreant. But even as he approached the boy, Mr. Oliver sensed that something was wrong. The boy appeared to be crying. His head hung down, he held his face in his hands, and his body shook convulsively. It was a strange, soundless weeping, and Mr. Oliver felt distinctly uneasy.

'Well—what's the matter?' he asked, his anger giving way to concern. 'What are you crying for?' The boy would not answer or look up. His body continued to be racked with silent sobbing.

'Come on, boy, you shouldn't be out here at this hour. Tell me the trouble. Look up!'

The boy looked up. He took his hands from his face and looked up at his teacher. The light from Mr. Oliver's torch fell on the boy's face—if you could call it a face.

He had no eyes, ears, nose, or mouth. It was just a round smooth head—with a school cap on top of it. And that's where the story should end—as indeed it has for several people who have had similar experiences and dropped dead of inexplicable heart attacks. But for Mr. Oliver it did not end there.

The torch fell from his trembling hand. He turned and scrambled down the path, running blindly through the trees and calling for help. He was still running towards the school buildings when he saw a lantern swinging in the middle of the path. Mr. Oliver had never before been so pleased to see the night-watchman. He stumbled up to the watchman, gasping for breath and speaking incoherently.

'What is it, Sir?' asked the watchman. 'Has there been an accident? Why are you running?'

'I saw something—something horrible—a boy weeping in the forest—and he had no face!'

'No face, Sir?'

'No eyes, nose, mouth—nothing.'

'Do you mean it was like this, Sir?' asked the watchman, and raised the lamp to his own face. The watchman had no eyes, no ears, no features at all—not even an eyebrow!

The wind blew the lamp out, and Mr. Oliver had his heart attack.

## *Henry*

BY PHYLLIS BOTTOME

For four hours every morning and for twenty minutes before a large audience at night Fletcher was locked up with murder. It glared at him from twelve pairs of amber eyes; it clawed the air close to him, it spat naked hate at him, and watched with uninterrupted intensity to catch him for one moment off his guard.

Fletcher had only his will and his eyes to keep death at bay.

Of course, outside the cage into which Fletcher shut himself nightly with his twelve tigers were the keepers, standing at intervals around it with concealed pistols; but they were outside it. The idea was that if anything happened to Fletcher they would be able by prompt action to get him out alive; but they had his private instructions to do nothing of the kind, to shoot straight at his heart, and pick off the guilty tiger afterwards to cover their intention. Fletcher knew better than to try to preserve anything the tigers left of him, if once they had started in.

The lion-tamer in the next cage was better off than Fletcher, he was intoxicated by a rowdy vanity which dimmed fear. He stripped himself half naked every night, covered himself with ribbons, and thought so much of himself that he hardly noticed his lions. Besides, his lions had all been born in captivity, were slightly doped, and were only lions.

Fletcher's tigers weren't doped because dope dulled their fears of the whip and didn't dull their ferocity; captivity softened nothing in them, and they hated man.

Fletcher had taught tigers since he was a child; his father had started him on baby tigers, who were charming. They hurt you as much as they could with an absent-minded roguishness difficult to resist; what was death to you was play to them; but as they couldn't kill him, all the baby a loud, contented, pleasant noise. Henry was purring!

Fletcher's voice changed from the sharp brief order like the crack of a whip into a persuasive companionable drawl. Henry's eyes reopened; he rose, stood rigid for a moment, and then slowly the rigidity melted out of his powerful form. Once more that answering look came into the tiger's eyes. He stared straight at Fletcher without blinking and jumped on his tub. He sat on it impassively, his tail waving, his great jaws closed. He eyed Fletcher attentively and without hate. Then Fletcher knew that this tiger was not as other tigers, not as any other tiger.

He threw down his whip, Henry never moved; he approached; Henry lifted his lip to snarl, thought better of it, and permitted the approach. Fletcher took his life in his hand and touched Henry.

Henry snarled mildly, but his great claws remained closed; his eyes expressed nothing but a gentle warning; they simply said: "You know I don't like being touched; be careful, I might have to claw you!"

Fletcher gave a brief nod; he knew the margin of safety was slight, but he had a margin. He could do something with Henry.

Hour after hour every day he taught Henry, but he taught him without a pistol or whip. It was unnecessary to use anything beyond his voice and his eyes. Henry read his eyes eagerly. When he failed to catch Fletcher's meaning, Fletcher's voice helped him out. Henry did not always understand even Fletcher's voice, but where he differed from the other tigers was that he wished to understand; nor had he from the first the slightest inclination to kill Fletcher.

He used to sit for hours at the back of his cage waiting for Fletcher. When he heard far off—unbelievably far off—the sound of Fletcher's step, he moved forward to the front of his cage and prowled restlessly to and fro till Fletcher unlocked the door and entered. Then Henry would crouch back a little, politely, from no desire to avoid his friend, but as a mere tribute to the superior power he felt in Fletcher. Directly Fletcher spoke, he came forward proudly and exchanged their wordless eye language.

Henry like doing his tricks alone with Fletcher. He jumped on and off his tub following the mere wave of Fletcher's hand. He soon went further, jumped on a high stool and leapt through a large white paper disc held up by Fletcher. Although the disc looked as if he couldn't possibly get through it, yet the clean white sheet always yielded to his impact; he did get through it, blinking a little, but feeling a curious pride that he had faced the odious thing—and pleased Fletcher.

He let Fletcher sit on his back, though the mere touch of an alien creature was repulsive to him. But he stood perfectly still, his hair rising a little, his teeth bared, a growl half suffocated in his throat. He told himself it was Fletcher. He must control his impulse to fling him off and tear him up.

In all the rehearsals and performances in the huge arena, full of strange noises, blocked with alien human beings, Henry led the other tigers; and though Fletcher's influence over him was weakened, he still recognised it. Fletcher seemed farther away from him at these times, less sympathetic and godlike, but Henry tried hard to follow the intense persuasive eyes and the brief emphatic voice; he would not lose touch even with this attenuated ghost of Fletcher.

It was with Henry and Henry alone that Fletcher dared his nightly stunt, dropped the whip and stick at his feet and let Henry do his tricks as he did them in his cage alone, with nothing beyond Fletcher's eyes and voice to control him. The other eleven tigers, beaten, glaring and snarling on to their tubs, sat impassively despising Henry's unnatural docility. He had the chance they had always wanted, and he didn't take it—what kind of tiger was he?

But Henry ignored the other tigers. Reluctantly standing with all four feet together on his tub, he contemplated a further triumph. Fletcher stood before him, holding a stick between his hands and above his head, intimately, compellingly, through the language of his eyes Fletcher told Henry to jump from his tub over his head. What Fletcher said was: "Come on, old thing! Jump! Come on! I'll duck in time. You won't hurt me! It's my stunt! Stretch your old paws together and jump!"

And Henry jumped. He hated the dazzling lights, loathed the hard, unexpected, senseless sounds which followed his leap, and he was secretly terrified that he would land on Fletcher. But it was very satisfactory when, after his rush through the air, he found he hadn't touched Fletcher, but had landed on another tub carefully prepared for him; and Fletcher said to him as plainly as possible before he did the drawer trick with the other tigers: "Well! You are a one-er, and no mistake!"

The drawer trick was the worst of Fletcher's stunts. He had to put a table in the middle of the cage and whip each tiger up to it. When he had them placed each on his tub around the table he had to feed them with a piece of raw meat deftly thrown at the exact angle to reach the special tiger for which it was intended, and to avoid contract with eleven other tigers ripe to dispute his intention. Fletcher couldn't afford the slightest mistake or a fraction of delay.

Each tiger had to have in turn his piece of raw meat, and the drawer shut after it—opened—the next morsel thrown exactly into the grasp of the next tiger, and so on until the twelve were fed.

Fletcher always placed Henry at his back. Henry snatched in turn his piece of raw meat, but he made no attempt, as the other tigers always did, to take anyone else's; and Fletcher felt the safer for knowing that Henry was at his back. He counted on Henry's power to protect him more than he counted on the four keepers standing outside the cage with their pistols. More than once, when one of the other tigers turned restive, Fletcher had found Henry rigid, but very light on his toes, close to his side, between him and danger.

The circus manager spoke to Fletcher warningly about his foolish infatuation for Henry.

"Mark my words, Fletcher," he said, "the tiger doesn't live that wouldn't do you in if it could. You give Henry too many chances—one day he'll take one of them." But Fletcher only laughed. He knew Henry; he had seen the soul of the great tiger leap to his eyes and shine there in answer to his own eyes. A man does not kill his god; at least not willingly. It is said that two thousand years ago he did some such thing, through ignorance, but Fletcher forgot this incident. Besides, on the whole, he believed more in Henry than he did in his fellow-men.

This was not surprising, because Fletcher had very little time for human fellowship. When he was not teaching tigers not to kill him, he rested from the exhaustion of the nerves which comes from a prolonged companionship with eager, potential murders; and the rest of the time Fletcher boasted of Henry to the lion-tamer, and taught Henry new tricks.

Macormack, the lion-tamer, had a very good stunt lion, and he was extravagantly jealous of Henry. He could not make his lion go out backwards before him from the arena cage into the passage as Henry had learned to do before Fletcher, and when he had tried Ajax had, not seriously, but with an intention rather more than playful, flung him against the bars of the cage.

Macormack brooded deeply on this slight from his pet, and determined to take it out of Fletcher's.

"Pooh!" he said. "You call yourself damned plucky for laying your ole 'oof on 'Enry's scruff, and e' don't 'alf look wicked while you're doin' it. Why don't ye put yer 'ead in 'is mouf and be done with it? That 'ud be talking, that would!"

"I wouldn't mind doing it," said Fletcher reflectively, after a brief pause, "once I get him used to the idea. 'Is jaw aint so big as a lion's, still I could get the top of me 'ead in."

The lion-tamer swaggered off jeering, and Fletcher thought out how best to lay this new trick before Henry for his approval.

But from the first Henry didn't approve of it. He showed quite plainly that he didn't want his head touched. He didn't like his mouth held forcibly open, and wouldn't have anything put between his teeth without crunching. Fletcher wasted several loaves of bread over the effort—and only succeeded once or twice gingerly and very ungracefully in getting portions of his own head in and out in safety. Henry roared long and loudly at him, clawed the air, and flashed all the language he could from his flaming eyes into Fletcher's, to explain that this thing wasn't done between tigers! It was hitting below the belt! An infringement of an instinct too deep for him to master: and Fletcher knew that he was outraging Henry's instinct, and decided to refrain.

"It ain't fair to my tiger!" he said to himself regretfully; and he soothed Henry with raw meat and endearments, promising to refrain from his unnatural venture.

But when the hour for the performance came, Fletcher forgot his promise. He was enraged at Macormack's stunt lion for getting more than his share of the applause. He had the middle cage, and what with the way Macormack swaggered half naked in his scarlet ribbons, and the lion roared—the pulverising, deep-toned, desert roar—and yet did all his tricks one after the other like a little gentleman, it did seem as if Henry barely got a round of his due applause.

Henry jumped through his white disc—so did the stunt lion! He took his leap over Fletcher's head—the stunt lion did something flashy with a drum, not half as dangerous, and the blind and ignorant populace ignored Henry and preferred the drum.

"I don't care!" said Fletcher to himself, "Henry's got to take my head in his mouth whether he likes it or not—that'll startle 'em!"

He got rid of all the other tigers. Henry was used to that, he liked it; now he would do his own final stunt—walk out backwards into the passage which led to the cages, and Fletcher would hurry out through the arena and back to Henry's cage, give him a light extra supper, and tell him what a fine tiger he was.

But Fletcher called him into the middle of the state instead and made him take that terrible attitude he had taught him for the new trick. His eyes said: "You'll do this once for me, old man, won't you?"

Henry's eyes said: "Don't ask it! I'm tired! I'm hungry! I want to get out!"

But Fletcher wouldn't read Henry's eyes any more. He tried to force his head sideways into the terrible open jaws, and Henry's teeth, instinctive, reluctant, compelled, closed on Fletcher's neck.

What Henry minded after the momentary relief of his instinctive action was the awful stillness of Fletcher. It wasn't the stillness of the arena—that was nothing, a mere deep indrawn breath. Fletcher lay limp between his paws, as if the trick were over, as if all tricks were over. He wouldn't get up, he didn't look at Henry. Henry's eyes gazed down unblinkingly into the blank eyes of Fletcher. All Henry's soul was in his eyes, watching for Fletcher's soul to rise to meet them. And for an age nothing happened, until at last Henry realised that nothing ever would.

Before the nearest keeper shot Henry, Henry knew that he had killed his god. He lifted up his heavy painted head and roared out through the still arena, a loud despairing cry.

His heart was pierced before they reached his heart.

# *The Interlopers*

BY SAKI (H.H. MUNRO)

In a forest of mixed growth somewhere on the eastern spurs of the Carpathians, a man stood one winter night watching and listening, as though he waited for some beast of the woods to come within the range of his vision, and, later, of his rifle. But the game for whose presence he kept so keen an outlook was none that figured in the sportsman's calendar as lawful and proper for the chase. Ulrich von Gradwitz patrolled the dark forest in quest of a human enemy.

The forest lands of Gradwitz were of wide extent and well stocked with game, the narrow strip of precipitous woodland that lay on its outskirt was not remarkable for the game it harboured or the shooting it afforded, but it was the most jealously guarded of all its owner's territorial possessions. A famous lawsuit, in the days of his grandfather, had wrested it from the illegal possession of a neighbouring family of petty landowners, the dispossessed party had never acquiesced in the judgment of the Courts, and along series of poaching affrays and similar scandals had embittered the relationships between the families for three generations. The neighbour feud had grown into a personal one since Ulrich had come to be head of his family; if there was a man in the world whom he detested and wished ill to it was Georg Znaeym, the inheritor of the quarrel and the tireless game-snatcher and raider of the disputed border-forest. The feud might, perhaps, have died down or been compromised if the personal ill-will of the two men had not stood in the way; as boys they had thirsted for one another's blood, as men each prayed that misfortune might fall on the other, and this wind-scourged winter night Ulrich had banded together his foresters to watch the dark forest, not in quest of four-footed quarry, but to keep a look-out for the prowling thieves whom he suspected of being afoot from across the land boundary. The roebuck, which usually kept in the sheltered hollows during a storm-wind, were running like driven things tonight, and there was movement and unrest among the creatures that were wont to sleep through the dark hours. Assuredly there was a disturbing element in the forest, and Ulrich could guess the quarter from whence it came.

He strayed away by himself from the watchers whom he had placed in ambush on the crest of the hill, and wandered far down the steep slopes amid the wild tangle of undergrowth, peering through the tree-trunks and listening through the whistling and skirling of the wind and the restless beating of the branches for sight or sound of the marauders. If only on this wild night, in this dark, lone spot, he might come across Georg Znaeym, man to man, with none to witness—that was the wish that was uppermost in his thoughts. And as he stepped round the trunk of a huge beech he came face to face with the man he sought.

The two enemies stood glaring at one another for a long silent moment. Each had a rifle in his hand, each had hate in his heart and murder uppermost in his mind. The chance had come to give full play in the passions of a lifetime. But a man who has been brought up under the code of a restraining civilization cannot easily nerve himself to shoot down his neighbour in cold blood and without word spoken, except for an offence against his hearth and honour. And before the moment of hesitation had given way to action a deed of Nature's own violence overwhelmed them both. A fierce shriek of the storm had been answered by a splitting crash over their heads, and ere they could leap aside a mass of falling beech tree had thundered down on them. Ulrich von Gradwitz found himself stretched on the ground, one arm numb beneath him and the other held almost as helplessly in a tight tangle of forked branches, while both legs were pinned beneath the fallen mass. His heavy shooting-boots had saved his feet from being crushed to pieces, but if his fractures were not as serious as they might have been, at least it was evident that he could not move from his present position till someone came to release him. The descending twigs had slashed the skin of his face, and he had to wink away some drops of blood from his eyelashes before he could take in a general view of the disaster. At his side, so near that under ordinary circumstances he could almost have touched him, lay Georg Znaeym, alive and struggling, but obviously as helplessly pinioned down as himself. All round them lay a thick-strewn wreckage of splintered braches and broken twigs.

Relief at being alive and exasperation at his captive plight brought a strange medley of pious thank-offerings and sharp curses to Ulrich's lips. Georg, who was nearly blinded with the blood which trickled across his eyes, stopped his struggling for a moment to listen, and then gave a short, snarling laugh.

'So you're not killed, as you ought to be, but you're caught, anyway,' he cried: 'caught fast. Ho, what a jest. Ulrich von Gradwitz snared in his stolen forest. There's real justice for you!'

And he laughed again, mockingly and savagely.

'I'm caught in my own forest-land,' retorted Ulrich. 'When my men come to release us you will wish, perhaps, that you were in a better plight than caught poaching on a neighbour's land, shame on you.'

Georg was silent for a moment, then he answered quietly.

'Are you sure that your men will find much to release? I have men, too, in the forest tonight, close behind me, and *they* will be here first and do the releasing. When they drag me out from under these damned branches it won't need much clumsiness on their part to roll this mass of trunk right over on the top of you. Your men will find you dead under a fallen beech tree. For form's sake I shall send my condolences to your family.'

'It is a useful hint.' Said Ulrich fiercely. 'My men had orders to follow in ten minutes' time, seven of which must have gone by already, and when they get me out—I will remember the hint. Only as you will have met your death poaching on my lands I don't think I can decently send any message of condolence to your family.'

'Good,' snarled Georg. 'good. We fight this quarrel out to the death, you and I and our foresters, with no cursed interlopers to come between us. Death and damnation to you, Ulrich von Gradwitz.

'The same to you. Georg Znaeym, forest thief, game-snatcher.'

Both men spoke with the bitterness of possible defeat before them, for each knew that it might be long before his men would seek him out or find him; it was a bare matter of chance which party would arrive first on the scene.

Both had now given up the useless struggle to free themselves from the mass of wood that held them down; Ulrich limited his endeavours to an effort to bring his one partially free arm near enough to his outer coat-pocket to draw out his wine-flask. Even when he had accomplished that operation it was long before he could manage the unscrewing of the stopper or get any of the liquid down his throat. But what a Heaven-sent draught it seemed! It was an open winter, and little snow had fallen as yet, hence the captives suffered less from the cold than might have been the case at that season of the year; nevertheless, the wine was warming and reviving to the wounded man, and he looked across with something like a throb of pity to where his enemy lay, keeping the groans of pain and weariness from crossing his lips.

'Could you reach this flask if I threw it over to you?' asked Ulrich suddenly: 'there is good wine in it, and one may as well be as comfortable as one can. Let us drink, even if tonight one of us dies.'

'No, I can scarcely see anything, there is so much blood caked round my eyes,' said Georg, 'and in any case I don't drink wine with an enemy.'

Ulrich was silent for a few minutes, and lay listening to the weary screeching of the wind. An idea was slowly forming and growing in his brain, an idea that gained strength every time that he looked across at the man who was fighting so grimly against pain and exhaustion. In the pain and languor that Ulrich himself was feeling the old fierce hatred seemed to be dying down.

'Neighbour,' he said presently, 'do as you please if your men come first. It was a fair compact. But as for me, I've changed my mind. If my men are the first to come you shall be the first to be helped, as though you were my guest. We have quarrelled like devils all our lives over this stupid strip of forest, where the trees can't even stand upright in a breath of wind. Lying here tonight, thinking. I've come to think we've been rather fools; there are better things in life than getting the better of a boundary dispute. Neighbour, if you will help me to bury the old quarrel I—I will ask you to be my friend.'

Georg Znaeym was silent for so long that Ulrich thought, perhaps, he had fainted with the pain of his injuries. Then he spoke slowly and in jerks.

'How the whole region would stare and gabble if we rode into the market-square together. No one living can remember seeing a Znaeym and a von Gradwitz talking to one another in friendship. And what peace there would be among the forester folk if we ended our feud tonight. And if we choose to make peace among our people there is none other to interfere, no interlopers from outside... You would come and keep the Sylvester night beneath my roof, and I would come and feast on some high day at your castle...I would never fire a shot on your land, save when you invited me as a guest; and you should come and shoot with me down in the marshes where the wildfowl are. In all the countryside there are none that could hinder if we willed to make peace. I never thought to have wanted to do other than hate you all my life, but I think I have changed my mind about things too, this last half-hour. And you offered me your wine-flask... Ulrich von Gradwitz, I will be your friend.'

For a space both men were silent, turning over in their minds the wonderful changes that this dramatic reconciliation would bring about. In the cold, gloomy forest, with the wind tearing in fitful gusts through the naked branches and whistling round the tree-trunks, they lay and waited for the help that would now bring release and succour to both parties. And each prayed a private prayer that his men might be the first to arrive, so that he might be the first to show honourable attention to the enemy that had become a friend.

Presently, as the wind dropped for a moment, Ulrich broke silence.

'Let's shout for help,' he said; 'in this lull our voices may carry a little way.'

'They won't carry far through the trees and undergrowth, said Georg, 'but we can try. Together then.'

The two raised their voices in a prolonged hunting call.

Together again, 'said Ulrich a few minutes later, after listening in vain for an answering halloo.

'I heard something that time, I think, said Ulrich.

'I heard nothing but the pestilential wind,' said Georg hoarsely.

There was silence again for some minutes, and then Ulrich gave a joyful cry.

'I can see figures coming through the wood. They are following in the way I came down the hillside.'

Both men raised their voices in as loud a shout as they could muster.

They hear us! They've stopped. Now they see us. They're running down the hill towards us,' cried Ulrich.

'How many of them are there?' asked Georg.

'I can't see distinctly,' said Ulrich; 'nine or ten.'

'Then they are yours,' said Georg; 'I had only seven out with me.'

They are making all the speed they can, brave lads,' said Ulrich gladly.

'Are they your men?' asked Georg. 'Are they your men?' he repeated impatiently as Ulrich did not answer.

'No,' said Ulrich with a laugh, the idiotic chattering laugh of a man unstrung with hideous fear.

'Who are they?' asked Georg quickly, straining his eyes to see what the other would gladly not have seen.

'*Wolves*.'

# *The Story of Medhans Lea*

By E. and H. Heron

The following story has been put together from the account of the affair given by Nare-Jones, sometime house-surgeon at Bart's, of his strange terror and experiences both in Medhans Lea and the pallid avenue between the beeches; of the narrative of Savelsan, of what he saw and heard in the billiard room and afterwards; of the silent and indisputable witness of big, bullnecked Harland himself; and, lastly of the conversation which subsequently took place between these three men and Mr. Flaxman Low, the noted psychologist.

It was by the merest chance that Harland and his two guests spent that memorable evening of the 18th of January, 1899, in the house of Medhans Lea. The house stands on the slope of a partially-wooded ridge in one of the Midland Counties. It faces south, and overlooks a wide valley bounded by the blue outlines of the Bredon hills. The place is secluded, the nearest dwelling being a small public-house at the cross roads some mile and a half from the lodge gates.

Medhans Lea is famous for its long straight avenue of beeches, and for other things. Harland, when he signed the lease, was thinking of the avenue of beeches; not of the other things, of which he knew nothing till later.

Harland had made his money by running tea plantations in Assam, and he owned all the virtues and faults of a man who has spent most of his life abroad. The first time he visited the house he weighed seventeen stone and ended most of his sentences with "don't yer know?" His ideas could hardly be said to travel on the higher planes of thought, and his chief aim in life was to keep himself down to the seventeen stone. He had a red neck and a blue eye, and was a muscular, inoffensive, good-natured man, with courage to spare, and an excellent voice for accompanying the banjo.

After singing the lease, he found that Medhans Lea needed an immense amount of putting in order and decorating. While this was being done, he came backwards and forwards to the nearest provincial town, where he stopped at a hotel, driving out almost daily to superintend the arrangements of his new habitation. Thus he had been away for the Christmas and New Year, but about the $15^{th}$ January he returned to the Red Lion, accompanied by his friends Nare-Jones and Savelsan, who proposed to move with him into his new house during the course of the ensuing week.

The immediate cause of their visit to Medhans Lea on the evening of the $18^{th}$ inst. was the fact that the billiard table at the Red Lion was not fit, as Harland remarked, to play shinty on, while there was an excellent table just put in at Medhans Lea, where the big billiard-room in the left wing had a wide window with a view down a portion of the beech avenue.

"Hang it!" said Harland, "I wish they would hurry up with the house. The painters aren't out of it yet, and the people don't come to the Lodge till Monday."

"It's a pity, too," remarked Savelsan regretfully, "when you think of that table."

Savelsan was an enthusiast in billiards, who spent all the time he could spare from his business, which happened to be teabroking, at the game. He was the more sorry for the delay, since Harland was one of the few men he knew to whom it was not necessary to give points.

"It's a ripping table," returned Harland. "Tell you what," he added, struck by a happy idea, "I'll send out Thomas to make things straight for us tomorrow, and we'll put a case of syphons and a bottle of whisky under the seat of the trap, and drive over for a game after dinner."

The other two agreed to this arrangement, but in the morning Nare-Jones found himself obliged to run up to London to see about securing a berth as ship's doctor. It was settled, however, that on his return he was to follow Harland and Savelsan to Medhans Lea.

He got back by the 8.30, entirely delighted, because he had booked a steamer bound for the Persian Gulf and Karachi, and had gained the cheering intelligence that a virulent type of cholera was lying in wait for the advent of the Mecca pilgrims in at any rate two of the chief ports of call, which would give him precisely the experience he desired.

Having dined, and the night being fine, he ordered a dogcart to take him out to Medhans Lea. The moon had just risen by the time he reached the entrance to the avenue, and as he was beginning to feel cold he pulled up, intending to walk to the house. Then he dismissed the boy and cart, a carriage having been ordered to come for the whole party after midnight. Nare-Jones stopped to light a cigar before entering the avenue, then he walked past the empty lodge. He moved briskly in the best possible temper with himself and all the world. The night was still, and his collar up, his feet fell silently on the dry carriage road, while his mind was away on blue water forecasting his voyage on the *S.S. Sumatra*.

He says he was quite halfway up the avenue before he became conscious of anything unusual. Looking up at the sky, he noticed what a bright, clear night it was, and how sharply defined the outline of the beeches stood out against the vault of heaven. The moon was yet low, and threw netted shadows of bare twigs and branches on the road which ran between black lines of trees in an almost straight vista up to the dead grey face of the house now barely two hundred yards away. Altogether it struck him as forming a pallid picture, etched in like a steel engraving in black, and grey, and white.

He was thinking of this when he was aware of words spoken rapidly in his ear, and he turned half expecting to see someone behind him. No one was visible. He had not caught the words, nor could he define the voice; but a vague conviction of some horrible meaning fixed itself in his consciousness.

The night was very still, ahead of him the house glimmered grey and shuttered in the moonlight. He shook himself, and walked on oppressed by a novel sensation compounded of disgust and childish fear; and still, from behind his shoulder, came the evil, voiceless murmuring.

He admits that he passed the end of the avenue at an amble, and was abreast of a semi-circle of shrubbery, when a small object was thrust out from the shadow of the bushes, and lay in the open light. Though the night was peculiarly still, it fluttered and balanced a moment, as if windblown, then came in skimming flights to his feet. He picked it up and made for the door, which yielded to his hand, and he flung it to and bolted it behind him.

Once in the warmly-lit hall his senses returned, and he waited to recover breath and composure before facing the two men whose voices and laughter came from the room on his right. But the door of the room was thrown open, and the burly figure of Harland in his shirt-sleeves appeared on the threshold.

"Hullo, Jones, that you? Come along!" he said genially.

"Bless me!" exclaimed Nare-Jones irritably, "there's not a light in any of the windows. It might be a house of the dead!"

Harland stared at him, but all he said was: "Have a whisky-and-soda?"

Savelsan, who was leaning over the billiard table, trying side-strokes with his back to Nare-Jones, added:

"Did you expect us to illuminate the place for you? There's not a soul in the house but ourselves."

"Say when," said Harland, poising the bottle over a glass.

Nare-Jones laid down what he held in his hand on the corner of the billiard table, and took up his glass.

"What in creation's this?" asked Savelsan.

"I don't know; the wind blew it to my feet just outside," replied Nare-Jones, between two long pulls at the whisky-and-soda.

"*Blown* to your feet?" repeated Savelsan, taking up the thing and weighing it in his hand. "It must be blowing a hurricane then."

"It isn't blowing at all," returned Nare-Jones blankly. "The night is dead calm."

For the object that had fluttered and rolled so lightly across the turf and gravel was a small battered, metal calf, made of some heavy brass amalgam.

Savelsan looked incredulously into Nare-Jones' face, and laughed.

"What's wrong with you? You look queer."

Nare-Jones laughed too; he was already ashamed of the last ten minutes.

Harland was meantime examining the metal calf.

"It's a Bengali image," he said, "It's been knocked about a good bit, by Jove! You say it blew out of the shrubbery?"

"Like a bit of paper, I give you my word, though there was not a breath of wind going," admitted Nare-Jones.

"Seems odd, don't yet know?" remarked Harland carelessly, "Now you two fellows had better begin; I'll mark."

Nare-Jones happened to be in form that night, and Savelsan became absorbed in the delightful difficulty of giving him a sound thrashing.

Suddenly Savelsan paused in his stroke.

"What's the sin's that?" he asked.

They stood listening. A thin, broken crying could be heard.

"Sounds like green plover," remarked Nare-Jones chalking his cue.

"It's a kitten they've shut up somewhere," said Harland.

"That's a child, and in the deuce of a fright, too," said Savelsan. "You'd better go and tuck it up in its little bed, Harland," he added, with a laugh.

Harland opened the door. There could no longer be any doubt about the sounds; the stifled shrieks and thin whimpering told of a child in the extremity of pain and fear.

"It's upstairs," said Harland. "I'm going to see."

Nare-Jones picked up a lamp and followed him.

"I stay here," said Savelsan sitting down by the fire.

In the hall the two men stopped and listened again. It is hard to locate a noise, but this seemed to come from the upper landing.

"Poor little beggar!" exclaimed Harland, as he bounded up the staircase. The bedroom doors opening on the square central landing above were all locked, the keys being on the outside. But the crying led them into a side passage which ended in a single room.

"It's in here, and the door's locked," said Nare-Jones. "Call out and see who's there."

But Harland was set on business. He flung his weight against the panel, and the door burst open, the lock ricochetting noisily into a corner. As they passed in, the crying ceased abruptly.

Harland stood in the centre of the room, while Nare-Jones held up the light to look round.

"The dickens!" exclaimed Harland exhaustively.

The room was entirely empty.

Not so much as a cupboard broke the smooth surface of the walls, only the two low windows and the door by which they had entered.

"This is the room above the billiard-room, isn't it?" said Nare-Jones at last.

"Yes. This is the only one I have not had furnished yet. I thought I might—?

He stopped short, for behind them burst out a peal of harsh, mocking laughter, that rang and echoed between the bare walls.

Both men swung round simultaneously, and both caught a glimpse of a tall, thin figure in black, rocking with laughter in the doorway, but when they turned it was gone. They dashed out into the passage and landing. No one was to be seen. The doors were locked as before, and the staircase and hall were vacant.

After making a prolonged search through every corner of the house, they went back to Savelsan in the billiard-room.

"What were you laughing about? What is it anyway?" began Savelsan at once.

"It's nothing. And we didn't laugh," replied Nare-Jones definitely.

"But I heard you," insisted Savelsan. "And where's the child?"

"I wish you'd go up and find it," returned Harland grimly, "We heard the laughing and saw, or thought we saw, a man in black—"

"Something like a priest in a cassock," put in Nare-Jones.

"Yes, like a priest," assented Harland, "but as we turned he disappeared."

Savelsan sat down and gazed from one to the other of his companions.

"The house behaves as if it was haunted," he remarked; "only there is no such thing as an authenticated ghost outside the experiences of the Psychical Research Society. I'd ask the Society down if I were you, Harland. You never can tell what you may find in these old houses."

"It's not an old house," replied Harland. "It was built somewhere about '40. I certainly saw that man; and, look to it, Savelsan, I'll find out who or what he is. That I swear! The English law makes no allowance for ghosts—nor will I."

"You'll have your hands full, or I'm mistaken," exclaimed Savelsan, grinning. "A ghost that laughs and cries in a breath, and rolls battered images about your front door, is not to be trifled with. The night is young yet—not much past eleven. I vote for a peg all round and then I'll finish off Jones."

Harland, sunk in a fit of sullen abstraction, sat on a settee, and watched them. On a sudden he said:

"It's turned beastly cold."

"There's a beastly smell, you mean," corrected Savelsan crossly, as he went round the table. He had made a break of forty and did not want to be interrupted. "The draught is from the window."

"I've not noticed it before this evening," said Harland, as he opened the shutters to make sure.

As he did so the night air rushed in heavy with the smell as of an old well that has not been uncovered for years, a smell of slime and unwholesome wetness. The lower part of the window was wide open and Harland banged it down.

"It's abomible!" he said, with an angry sniff. "Enough to give us all typhoid."

"Only dead leaves," remarked Nare-Jones. "There are the rotten leaves of twenty winters under the trees and outside this window. I noticed them when we came over on Tuesday."

"I'll have them cleared away to-morrow. I wonder how Thomas came to leave this window open," grumbled Harland, as he closed and bolted the shutter. "What do you say—forty-five?" and he went over to mark it up.

The game went on for some time, and Nare-Jones was lying across the table with the cue poised, when he heard a slight sound behind him. Looking round he saw Harland, his face flushed and angry, passing softly—wonderfully softly for so big a man, Nare-Jones remembers thinking—along the angle of the wall towards the window.

All three men unite in declaring that they were watching the shutter, which opened inwards as if thrust by some furtive hand from outside. At the moment Nare-Jones and Savelsan were standing directly opposite to it on the further side of the table, while Harland crouched behind the shutter intent on giving the intruder a lesson.

As the shutter unfolded to its utmost the two men opposite saw a face pressed against the glass, a furrowed evil face, with a wide laugh perched upon its sinister features.

There was a second of absolute stillness, and Nare-Jone's eyes met those other eyes with the fascinated horror of a mutual understanding, as all the foul fancies that had pursued him in the avenue poured back into his mind.

With an uncontrollable impulse of resentment, he snatched a billiard ball from the table and flung it with all his strength at the face.

The ball crashed through the glass and through the face beyond it! The glass fell shattered, but the face remained for an instant peering and grinning at the aperture, then as Harland sprang forward it was gone.

"The ball went clean through it!" said Savelsan with a gasp.

They crowded to the window, and throwing up the sash, leant out. The dank smell clung about the air, a boat-shaped moon glimmered between the bare branches, and on the white drive beyond the shrubbery the billiard ball could be seen a shining spot under the moon. Noting more.

"What was it?" asked Harland.

" 'Only a face at the window,' " quoted Savelsan with an awkward attempt at making light of his own scare. "Devilish queer face too, eh, Jones?"

"I wish I'd got him!" returned Harland frowning. "I'm not going to put up with any tricks about the place, don't yer know?"

"You'd bottle any tramp loafing around," said Nare-Jones.

Harland looked down at his immense arms outlined in his shirt-sleeves.

"I could that," he answered. "But this chap—did you hit him?'

"Clean through the face! Or, at any rate, it looked like it" replied Savelsan, as Nare-Jones stood silent.

Harland shut the shutter and poked up the fire.

"It's a cursed creepy affair!" he said, "I hope the servants won't get hold of this nonsense. Ghosts play the very mischief with a house. Though I don't believe in them myself," he concluded.

Then Savelsan broke out in an unexpected place.

"Nor do I—as a rule," he said slowly. "Still, you know it is a sickening idea to think of a spirit condemned to haunt the scene of its crime waiting for the world to die."

Harland and Nare-Jones looked at him.

"Have a whisky neat," suggested Harland, soothingly. "I never knew you taken that way before."

Nare-Jones laughed out. He says he does not know why he laughed nor why he said what follows.

"It's this way," he said. "The moment of foul satisfaction is gone for ever, yet for all time the guilty spirit must perpetuate its sin—the sin that brought no lasting reward, only a momentary reward experienced, it may be, centuries ago, but to which still clings the punishment of eternally rehearsing in loneliness, and cold, and gloom, the sin of other days. No punishment can be conceived more horrible. Savelsan is right."

"I think we've had enough about ghosts," said Harland, cheerfully, "let's go on. Hurry up, Savelsan."

"There's the billiard ball," said Nare-Jones. "Who'll go fetch?"

"Not I," replied Savelsan promptly. "When that—was at the window, I felt sick."

Nare-Jones nodded. "And I wanted to bolt!" he said emphatically.

Harland faced about from the fire.

"And I, though I saw nothing but the shutter, I—hang it!—don't yet know—so did I! There was panic in the air for a minute. But I'm shot if I'm afraid now," he concluded doggedly, "I'll go."

His heavy animal face was lit with courage and resolution.

"I've spent close upon five thousand pounds over this blessed house first and last, and I'm not going to be done out of it by any infernal spiritualism!" he added, as he took down his coat and pulled it on.

"It's all in view from the window except those few yards through the shrubbery," said Savelsan. "Take a stick and go. Though, on second thoughts, I bet you a fiver you don't."

"I don't want a stick," answered Harland. "I'm not afraid—not now—and I'd meet most men with my hands."

Nare-Jones opened the shutters again; the sash was low and he pushed the window up, and leant far out.

"It's not much of a drop," he said, and slung his legs out over the lintel; but the night was full of the smell, and something else. He leapt back into the room. "Don't go, Harland!"

Harland gave him a look that set his blood burning.

"What is there, after all, to be afraid of in a ghost?" he asked heavily.

Nare-Jones, sick with the sense of his own newly-born cowardice, yet entirely unable to master it, answered feebly:

"I can't say, but don't go."

The words seemed inevitable, though he could have kicked himself for hanging back.

There was a forced laugh from Savelsan.

"Give it up and stop at home, little man," he said.

Harland merely snorted in reply, and laid his great leg over the window ledge. The other two watched his big, tweed-clad figure as it crossed the grass and disappeared into the shrubbery.

"You and I are in a preposterous funk," said Savelsan, with unpleasant explicitness, as Harland, whistling loudly, passed into the shadow.

But this was a point on which Nare-Jones could not bring himself to speak at the moment. Then they sat on the sill and waited. The moon shone out clearly above the avenue, which now lay white and undimmed between its crowding trees.

"And he's whistling because he's afraid," continued Savelsan.

"He's not often afraid," replied Nare-Jones shortly; "besides, he's doing what neither of us were very keen on."

The whistling stopped suddenly. Savelsan said afterwards that he fancied he saw Harland's huge, grey-clad shoulders, with uplifted arms, rise for a second above the bushes.

Then out of the silence came peal upon peal of that infernal laughter, and, following it, the thin pitiful crying of the child. That too ceased, and an absolute stillness seemed to fall upon the place.

They leant out and listened intently. The minutes passed slowly. In the middle of the avenue the billiard ball glinted on the gravel, but there was no sign of Harland emerging from the shrubbery path.

"He should be there by now," said Nare-Jones anxiously.

They listened again; everything was quiet. The ticking of Harland's big watch on the mantelpiece was distinctly audible.

"This is too much," said Nare-Jones. "I'm going to see where he is."

He swung himself out on the grass, and Savelsan called to him to wait, as he was coming also. While Nare-Jones stood waiting, there was a sound as of a pig grunting and rooting among the dead leaves in the shrubbery.

They ran forward into the darkness, and found the shrubbery path. A minute later they came upon something that tossed and snorted and rolled under the shrubs.

"Great Heavens!" cried Nare-Jones, "it's Harland!"

"He's breaking somebody's neck," added Savelsan, peering into the gloom.

Nare-Jones was himself again. The powerful instinct of his profession—the help-giving instinct, possessed him to the exclusion of every other feeling.

"He's in a fit—just a fit," he said in matter of fact tones, as he bent over the struggling form; "that's all."

With the assistance of Savelsan, he managed to carry Harland out into the open drive. Harland's eyes were fearful, and froth hung about his blue puffing lips as they laid him down upon the ground. He rolled over, and lay still, while from the shadows broke another shout of laughter.

"It's apoplexy. We must get him away from here," said Nare-Jones. "But, first, I'm going to see what is in those bushes."

He dashed through the shrubbery, backwards and forwards. He seemed to feel the strength of ten men as he wrenched and tore and trampled the branches, letting in the light of the moon to its darkness. At last he paused, exhausted.

"Of course, there's nothing," said Savelsan wearily. "What did you expect after the incident of the billiard ball?"

Together, with awful toil, they bore the big man down the narrow avenue, and at the lodge gates they met the carriage.

Some time later the subject of their common experiences at Medhans Lea was discussed amongst the three men. Indeed, for many weeks Harland had not been in a state to discuss any subject at all, but as soon as he was allowed to do so, he invited Nare-Jones and Savelsan to meet Mr. Flaxman Low, the scientist, whose works on psychology and kindred matters are so well known at the Metropole, to thresh out the matter.

Flaxman Low listened with his usual air of gentle abstraction, from time to time making notes on the back of an envelope. He looked at each narrator in turn as he took up the thread of the story. He understood perfectly that the man who stood furthest from the mystery must inevitably have been the self-centred Savelsan; next in order came Nare-Jones, with sympathetic possibilities, but a crowded brain; closest of all would be big, kindly Harland, with more than one strong animal instinct about him, and whose bulk of matter was evidently permeated by a receptive spirit.

When they had ended, Savelsan turned to Flaxman Low.

"There you have the events, Mr. Low. Now, the question is how to deal with them."

"Classify them," replied Flaxman Low.

"The crying would seem to indicate a child," began Savelsan, ticking off the list on his fingers; "the black figure, the face at the window, and the laughter are naturally connected. So far I can go alone. I conclude that we saw the apparition of a man, possibly a priest, who had during his lifetime illtreated a child, and whose punishment it is to haunt the scene of his crime."

"Precisely—the punishment being worked out under conditions which admit of human observation," returned Flaxman Low. "As for the child the sound of crying was merely part of the *mise-en-scène*. The child was not there."

"But that explanation stops short of several points. Now about the suggestive thoughts experienced by my friend, Nare-Jones; what brought on the fit in the case of Mr. Harland, who assures us that he was not suffering from fright or other violent emotion; and what connection can be traced between all these things and the Bengali image?" Savelsan ended.

"Let us take the Bengali figure first," said Low. "it is just one of those discrepant particulars which, at first sight, seem wholly irreconcilable with the rest of the phenomena, yet these often form a test point, by which our theories are proved or otherwise." Flaxman Low took up the metal calf from the table as he spoke. "I should be inclined to connect this with the child. Observe it. It has not been roughly used; it is rubbed and dinted as a plaything usually is. I should say the child may have had Anglo-Indian relations."

At this, Nare-Jones bent forward, and in his turn examined the figure, while Savelsan smiled his thin, incredulous smile.

"These are ingenious theories," he said; "but we are really no nearer to facts, I am afraid."

"The only proof would be an inquiry into the former history of Medhans Lea; if events had happened there which would go to support this theory, why, then—But I cannot supply that information since I never heard of Medhans Lea or the ghost until I entered this room."

"I know something of Medhans Lea," put in Nare-Jones. "I found out a good deal about it before I left the place. And I must congratulate Mr. Low on his methods, for his theory tallies in a wonderful manner with the facts of the case. The house was long known to be haunted. It seems that many years ago a lady, the widow of an Indian officer, lived there with her only child, a boy, for whom she engaged a tutor, a dark-looking man, who wore a long black coat like a cassock, and was called 'the Jesuit' by the country people.

"One evening the man took the boy out into the shrubbery. Screams were heard, and when the child was brought in he was found to have lost his reason. He used to cry and shriek incessantly, but was never able to tell what had been done to him as long as he lived. As for this metal calf, the mother probably brought it with her from India, and the child used it as a toy, perhaps, because he was allowed no others. Hullo!" In handling the calf, Nare-Jones had touched some hidden spring, the head opened, disclosing a small cavity, from which dropped a little ring of blue beads, such as children make. He held it up. "This affords good proof."

"Yes," admitted Savelsan grudgingly. "But how about your sensations and Harland's seizure? You must know what was done to the child, Harland—what did you see in the shrubbery?"

Harland's florid face assumed a queer pallor.

"I saw something," replied he hesitatingly, "but I can't recall what it was. I only remember being possessed by a blind terror, and then nothing more until I recovered consciousness at the hotel next day."

"Can you account for this, Mr. Low?" asked Nare-Jones, "and there was also my strange notion of the whispering in the avenue."

"I think so," replied Flaxman Low. "I believe that the theory of atmospheric influences, which includes the power of environment to reproduce certain scenes and also thoughts, would throw light upon your sensations as well as Mr. Harland's. Such influences play a far larger part in our everyday experience than we have as yet any idea of."

There was a silence of a few moments; then Harland spoke:

"I fancy that we have said all that there is to be said upon the matter. We are much obliged to you, Mr. Low. I don't know how it strikes you other fellows, but, speaking for myself, I have seen enough of ghosts to last me for a very long time."

"And now," ended Harland wearily," if you have no objections, we will pass on to pleasanter subjects."

# *At The Pit's Mouth*

BY RUDYARD KIPLING

Once upon a time there was a Man and his Wife and a Tertium Quid.

All three were unwise, but the Wife was the unwisest. The Man should have looked after his Wife, who should have avoided the Tertium Quid, who, again, should have married a wife of his own, after clean and open flirtations, to which nobody can possibly object, round Jakko or Observatory Hill. When you see a young man with his pony in a white lather, and his hat on the back of his head flying down-hill at fifteen miles an hour to meet a girl who will be properly surprised to meet him, you naturally approve of that young man, and wish him Staff appointments, and take an interest in his welfare, and, as the proper time comes, give them sugar-tongs or side-saddles according to your means and generosity.

The Tertium Quid flew down-hill on horseback, but it was to meet the Man's Wife; and when he flew up-hill it was for the same end. The Man was in the Plains, earning money for the Wife to spend on dresses and four-hundred-rupee bracelets, and inexpensive luxuries of that kind. He worked very hard, and sent her a letter or a post-card daily. She also wrote to him daily, and said that she was longing for him to come up to Simla. The Tertium Quid used to lean over her shoulder and laugh as she wrote the notes. Then the two would ride to the Post-office together.

Now, Simla is a strange place and its customs are peculiar; nor is any man who has not spent at least ten seasons there qualified to pass judgment on circumstantial evidence, which is the most untrustworthy in the Courts. For these reasons, and for others which need not appear, I decline to state positively whether there was anything irretrievably wrong in the relations between the Man's Wife and the Tertium Quid. If there was, and hereon you must form your own opinion, it was the Man's Wife's fault. She was kittenish in her manners, wearing generally an air of soft and fluffy innocence. But she was deadlily learned and evil-instructed; and, now and again, when the mask dropped, men saw this, shuddered and—almost drew back. Men are occasionally particular, and the least particular men are always the most exacting.

Simla is eccentric in its fashion of treating friendships. Certain attachments which have set and crystallised through half a dozen seasons acquire almost the sanctity of the marriage bond, and are revered as such. Again, certain attachments equally old, and, to all appearance, equally venerable, never seem to win any recognised official status; while a chance-sprung acquaintance, not two months born, steps into the place which by right belongs to the senior. There is no law reducible to print which regulates these affairs.

Some people have a gift which secures them infinite toleration, and others have not. The Man's Wife had not. If she looked over the garden wall, for instance, women taxed her with stealing their husbands. She complained pathetically that she was not allowed to choose her own friends. When she put up her big white muff to her lips, and gazed over it and under her eyebrows at you as she said this thing, you felt that she had been infamously misjudged, and that all the other women's instincts were all wrong; which was absurd. She was not allowed to own the Tertium Quid in peace; and was so strangely constructed that she would not have enjoyed peace had she been so permitted. She preferred some semblance of intrigue to cloak even her most commonplace actions.

After two months of riding, first round Jakko, then Elysium, then Summer Hill, then Observatory Hill, then under Jutogh, and lastly up and down the Cart Road as far as the Tara Devi gap in the dusk, she said to the Tertium Quid, 'Frank, people say we are too much together, and people are so horrid.'

The Tertium Quid pulled his moustache, and replied that horrid people were unworthy of the consideration of nice people.

'But they have done more than talk—they have written—written to my hubby—I'm sure of it,' said the Man's Wife, and she pulled a letter from her husband out of her saddle-pocket and gave it to the Tertium Quid.

It was an honest letter, written by an honest man, then stewing in the Plains on two hundred rupees a month (for he allowed his wife eight hundred and fifty), and in a silk banian and cotton trousers. It is said that, perhaps, she had not thought of the unwisdom of allowing her name to be so generally coupled with the Tertium Quid's; that she was too much of a child to understand the dangers of that sort of thing; that he, her husband, was the last man in the world to interfere jealously with her little amusements and interests, but that it would be better were she to drop the Tertium Quid quietly and for her husband's sake. The letter was sweetened with many pretty little pet names, and it amused the Tertium Quid considerably. He and She laughed over it, so that you, fifty yards away, could see their shoulders shaking while the horses slouched along side by side.

Their conversation was not worth reporting. The upshot of it was that, next day, no one saw the Man's Wife and the Tertium Quid together. They had both gone down to the Cemetery, which, as a rule, is only visited officially by the inhabitants of Simla.

A Simla funeral with the clergyman riding, the mourners riding, and the coffin creaking as it swings between the bearers, is one of the most depressing things on this earth, particularly when the procession passes under the wet, dank dip beneath the Rockcliffe Hotel, where the sun is shut out, and all the hill streams are wailing and weeping together as they go down the valleys.

Occasionally, folk tend the graves, but we in India shift and are transferred so often that, at the end of the second year, the Dead have no friends—only acquaintances who are far too busy amusing themselves up the hill to attend to old partners. The idea of using a Cemetery as a rendezvous is distinctly a feminine one. A man would have said simply, 'Let people talk. We'll go down the Mall.' A woman is made differently, especially if she be such a woman as the Man's Wife. She and the Tertium Quid enjoyed each other's society among the graves of men and women whom they had known and danced with aforetime.

They used to take a big horse-blanket and sit on the grass a little to the left of the lower end, where there is a dip in the ground, and where the occupied graves stop short and the ready-made ones are not ready. Each well-regulated Indian Cemetery keeps half a dozen graves permanently open for contingencies and incidental wear and tear. In the Hills these are more usually baby's size, because children who come up weakened and sick from the Plains often succumb to the effects of the Rains in the Hills or get pneumonia from their *ayahs* taking them through damp pine-woods after the sun has set. In Cantonments, of course, the man's size is more in request; these arrangements varying with the climate and population.

One day when the Man's Wife and the Tertium Quid had just arrived in the Cemetery, they saw some coolies breaking ground. They had marked out a full-size grave, and the Tertium Quid asked them whether any *Sahib* was sick. They said that they did not know; but it was an order that they should dig a *Sahib's* grave.

'Work away,' said the Tertium Quid, 'and let's see how it's done.'

The coolies worked away, and the Man's Wife and the Tertium Quid watched and talked for a couple of hours while the grave was being deepened. Then a coolie, taking the earth in baskets as it was thrown up, jumped over the grave.

'That's queer,' said the Tertium Quid. 'Where's my ulster?'

'What's queer?' said the Man's Wife.

'I have got a chill down my back—just as if a goose had walked over my grave.'

'Why do you look at the thing, then?' said the Man's Wife. 'Let us go.'

The Tertium Quid stood at the head of the grave, and stared without answering for a space. Then he said, dropping a pebble down, 'It is nasty—and cold: horribly cold. I don't think I shall come to the Cemetery any more. I don't think grave-digging is cheerful.'

The two talked and agreed that the Cemetery was depressing. They also arranged for a ride next day out from the Cemetery through the Mashobra Tunnel up to Fagoo and back, because al the world was going to a garden-party at Viceregal Lodge, and all the people of Mashobra would go too.

Coming up the Cemetery road, the Tertium Quid's horse tried to bolt up-hill, being tired with standing so long, and managed to strain a back sinew.

'I shall have to take the mare to-morrow,' said the Tertium Quid, 'and she will stand nothing heavier than a snaffle.'

They made their arrangements to meet in the Cemetery, after allowing all the Mashobra people time to pass into Simla. That night it rained heavily, and, next day, when the Tertium Quid came to the trysting-place, he saw that the new grave had a foot of water in it, the ground being a tough and sour clay.

'Jove! That looks beastly,' said the Tertium Quid. 'Fancy being boarded up and dropped into that well!'

They then started off to Fagoo, the mare playing with the snaffle and picking her way as though she were shod with satin, and the sun shining divinely. The road below Mashobra to Fagoo is officially styled the Himalayan-Thibet Road; but in spite of its name it is not much more than six feet wide in most places, and the drop into the valley below may be anything between one and two thousand feet.

'Now we're going to Thibet,' said the Man's Wife merrily, as the horses drew near to Fagoo. She was riding on the cliff-side.

'Into Thibet,' said the Tertium Quid, 'ever so far from people who say horrid things, and hubbies who write stupid letters. With you—to the end of the world!'

A coolie carrying a log of wood came round a corner, and the mare went wide to avoid him—forefeet in and haunches out, as a sensible mare should go.

'To the world's end,' said the Man's Wife, and looked unspeakable things over her near shoulder at the Tertium Quid.

He was smiling, but, while she looked, the smile froze stiff as it were on his face, and changed to a nervous grin—the sort of grin men wear when they are not quite easy in their saddles. The mare seemed to be sinking by the stern, and her nostrils cracked while she was trying to realise what was happening. The rain of the night before had rotted the drop-side of the Himalayan-Thibet Road, and it was giving way under her. 'What are you doing?' said the man's Wife. The Tertium Quid gave no answer. He grinned nervously and set his spurs into the mare, who rapped with her forefeet on the road, and the struggle began. The Man's Wife screamed, 'Oh, Frank, get off!'

But the Tertium Quid was glued to the saddle—his face blue and white—and he looked into the Man's Wife's eyes. Then the Man's Wife clutched at the mare's head and caught her by the nose instead of the bridle. The brute threw up her head and went down with a scream, the Tertium Quid upon her, and the nervous grin still set on his face.

The Man's Wife heard the tinkle-tinkle of little stones and loose earth falling off the roadway, and the sliding roar of the man and horse going down. Then everything was quiet, and she called on Frank to leave his mare and walk up. But Frank did not answer. He was underneath the mare, nine hundred feet below, spoiling a patch of Indian corn.

As the revellers came back from Viceregal Lodge in the mists of the evening, they met a temporarily insane woman, on a temporarily mad horse, swinging round the corners, with her eyes and her mouth open, and her head like the head of a Medusa. She was stopped by a man at the risk of his life, and taken out of the saddle, a limp heap, and put on the bank to explain herself. This wasted twenty minutes, and then she was sent home in a lady's rickshaw, still with her mouth open and her hands picking at her riding-gloves.

She was in bed through the following three days, which were rainy; so she missed attending the funeral of the Tertium Quid, who was lowered into eighteen inches of water, instead of the twelve to which he had first objected.

# *The Dead Man of Varley Grange*

## A Victorian Ghost Story ... Author Unknown

"Hallo, jack! Where are you off to? Going down to the governor's place for Christmas?"

Jack Darent, who was in my old regiment, stood drawing on his dogskin gloves upon the 23rd of December the year before last. He was equipped in a long Ulster and top hat, and a hansom, already loaded with a gun-case and portmanteau, stood awaiting him. He had a tall, strong figure, a fair, fresh-looking face, and the merriest blue eyes in the world. He held a cigarette between his lips, and late as was the season of the year there was a flower in his buttonhole. When did I ever see handsome Jack Darent and he did not look well dressed and well fed and jaunty? As I ran up the steps of the Club he turned round and laughed merrily.

"My dear fellow, do I look the sort of man to be victimized at a family Christmas meeting? Do you know the kind of business they have at home? Three maiden aunts and a bachelor uncle, my eldest brother and his insipid wife, and all my sister's six noisy children at dinner. Church twice a day, and snap-dragon between the services! No, thank you! I have a great affection for my old parents, but you don't catch me going in for that sort of national festival!"

"You irreverent ruffian!" I replied, laughing. "Ah, if you were a married man——"

"Ah, if I were a married man!" replied Captain Darent with something that was almost a sigh, and then, lowering his voice, he said hurriedly, "How is Miss Lester, Fred?"

"My sister is quite well, thank you," I answered with becoming gravity; and it was not without a spice of malice that I added, "She has been going out to a great many balls and enjoying herself very much."

Captain Darent looked profoundly miserable.

"I don't see how a poor fellow in a marching regiment, a younger son too, with nothing in the future to look to, is ever to marry nowadays," he said almost savagely; "when girls, too, are used to so much luxury and extravagance that they can't live without it. Matrimony is at a deadlock in this century, Fred, chiefly owing to the price of butchers' meat and bonnets. In fifty years' time it will become extinct and the country be depopulated. But I must be off, old man, or I shall miss my train."

"You have never told me where you are going to, Jack."

"Oh, I am going to stay with old Henderson, in Westernshire; he has taken a furnished house, with some first-rate pheasant shooting, for a year. There are seven of us going—all bachelors, and all kindred spirits. We shall shoot all day and smoke half the night. Think what you have lost, old fellow, by becoming a Benedick!"

"In Westernshire, is it?" I inquired. "Whereabouts is this place, and what is the name of it? For I am a Westernshire man by birth myself, and I know every place in the county."

"Oh, it's a tumbledown sort of old house, I believe," answered Jack carelessly. "Gables and twisted chimneys outside, and uncomfortable spindle-legged furniture inside—you know the sort of thing; but the shooting is capital, Henderson says, and we must put up with our quarters. He has taken his French cook down, and plenty of liquor, so I've no doubt we shan't starve."

"Well, but what is the name of it?" I persisted, with a growing interest in the subject.

"Let me see," referring to a letter he pulled out of his pocket. "Oh, here it is—Varley Grange."

"Varley Grange!" I repeated, aghast. "Why, it has not been inhabited for years."

"I believe not," answered Jack unconcernedly. "The shooting has been let separately; but Henderson took a fancy to the house too and thought it would do for him, furniture and all, just as it is. My dear Fred, what are you looking so solemnly at me for?"

"Jack, let me entreat of you not to go to this place," I said, laying my hand on his arm.

"Not go! Why, Lester, you must be mad! Why on earth shouldn't I go there?"

"There are stories—uncomfortable things said of that house." I had not the moral courage to say, "It is haunted," and I felt myself how weak and childish was my attempt to deter him from his intended visit; only—I knew all about Varley Grange.

I think handsome Jack Darent thought privately that I was slightly out of my senses, for I am sure I looked unaccountably upset and dismayed by the mention of the name of the house that Mr. Henderson had taken.

"I daresay it's cold and draughty and infested with rats and mice," he said laughingly; "and I have no doubt the creature-comforts will not be equal to Queen's Gate; but I stand pledged to go now, and I must be off this very minute, so have no time, old fellow, to inquire into the meaning of your sensational warning. Good-bye, and—and remember me to the ladies."

He ran down the steps and jumped into the hansom.

"Write to me if you have time!" I cried out after him; but I don't think he heard me in the rattle of the departing cab. He nodded and smiled at me and was swiftly whirled out of sight.

As for me, I walked slowly back to my comfortable house in Queen's Gate. There was my wife presiding at the little five o'clock tea-table, our two fat, pink and white little children tumbling about upon the hearthrug amongst dolls and bricks, and two utterly spoilt and overfed pugs; and my sister Bella—who, between ourselves, was the prettiest as well as dearest girl in all London—sitting on the floor in her handsome brown velvet gown, resigning herself gracefully to be trampled upon by the dogs, and to have her hair pulled by the babies.

"Why, Fred, you look as if you had heard bad news," said my wife, looking up anxiously as I entered.

"I don't know that I have heard of anything very bad; I have just seen Jack Darent off for Christmas," I said, turning instinctively towards my sister. He was a poor man and a younger son, and of course a very bad match for the beautiful Miss Lester; but for all that I had an inkling that Bella was not quite indifferent to her brother's friend.

"Oh!" says that hypocrite. "Shall I give you a cup of tea, Fred?"

It is wonderful how women can control their faces and pretend not to care a straw when they hear the name of their lover mentioned. I think Bella overdid it, she looked so supremely indifferent.

"Where on earth do you suppose he is going to stay, Bella?"

"Who? Oh, Captain Darent! How should I possibly know where he is going? Archie, pet, please don't poke the doll's head quite down Ponto's throat; I know he will bite it off if you do."

This last observation was addressed to my son and heir.

"Well, I think you will be surprised when you hear: he is going to Westernshire, to stay at Varley Grange."

"*What!*" No doubt about her interest in the subject now! Miss Lester turned as white as her collar and sprang to her feet impetuously, scattering dogs, babies and toys in all directions away from her skirts as she rose.

"You cannot mean it, Fred! Varley Grange, why, it has not been inhabited for ten years; and the last time—— Oh, do you remember those poor people who took it? What a terrible story it has!" She shuddered.

"Well, it is taken now," I said, "by a man I know, called Henderson—a bachelor; he has asked down a party of men for a week's shooting, and Jack Darent is one of them."

"For Heaven's sake prevent him from going!" cried Bella, clasping her hands.

"My dear, he is gone!"

"Oh, then write to him—telegraph—tell him to come back!" she urged breathlessly.

"I am afraid it is no use," I said gravely. "He would not come back; he would not believe me; he would think I was mad."

"Did you tell him anything?" she asked faintly.

"No, I had no time. I did say a word or two, but he began to laugh."

"Yes, that is how it always is!" she said distractedly. "People laugh and pooh-pooh the whole thing, and then they go there and see for themselves, and it is too late!"

She was so thoroughly upset that she left the room. My wife turned to me in astonishment; not being a Westernshire woman, she was not well up in the traditions of that venerable county.

"What on earth does it all mean, Fred?" she asked me in amazement. 'What is the matter with Bella, and why is she so distressed that Captain Darent is going to stay at that particular house?"

"It is said to be haunted, and——"

"You don't mean to say you believe in such rubbish, Fred?" interrupted my wife sternly, with a side-glance of apprehension at our first-born who, needless to say, stood by, all eyes and ears, drinking in every word of the conversation of his elders.

"I never know what I believe or what I don't believe," I answered gravely. "All I can say is that there are very singular traditions about that house, and that a great many credible witnesses have seen a very strange thing there, and that a great many disasters have happened to the persons who have seen it."

"What has been seen, Fred? Pray tell me the story! Wait, I think I will send the children away."

My wife rang the bell for the nurse, and as soon as the little ones had been taken from the room she turned to me again.

"I don't believe in ghosts or any such rubbish one bit, but I should like to hear your story."

"The story is vague enough," I answered.

"In the old days Varley Grange belonged to the ancient family of Varley, now completely extinct. There was, some hundred years ago, a daughter, famed for her beauty and her fascination. She wanted to marry a poor, penniless squire, who loved her devotedly. Her brother,

Dennis Varley, the new owner of Varley Grange, refused his consent and shut his sister up in the nunnery that used to stand outside his park gates—there are a few ruins of it left still. The poor nun broke her vows and ran away in the night with her lover. But her brother pursued her and brought her back with him. The lover escaped, but the lord of Varley murdered his sister under his own roof, swearing that no scion of his race should live to disgrace and dishonour his ancient name.

"Ever since that day Dennis Varley's spirit cannot rest in its grave—he wanders about the old house at night-time, and those who have seen him are numberless. Now and then the pale, shadowy form of a nun flits across the old hall, or along the gloomy passages, and when both strange shapes are seen thus together misfortune and illness, and even death, is sure to pursue the luckless man who has seen them, with remorseless cruelty."

"I wonder you believe in such rubbish," says my wife at the conclusion of my tale.

I shrug my shoulders and answer nothing, for who are so obstinate as those who persist in disbelieving everything that they cannot understand?

It was little more than a week later that, walking by myself along Pall Mall one afternoon, I suddenly came upon Jack Darent walking towards me.

"Hallo, jack! Back again? Why, man, how odd you look!"

There was a change in the man that I was instantly aware of. His frank, careless face looked clouded and anxious, and the merry smile was missing from his handsome countenance.

"Come into the Club, Fred," he said, taking me by the arm. "I have something to say to you."

He drew me into a corner of the Club smoking-room.

"You were quite right. I wish to Heaven I had never gone to that house."

"You mean—have you seen anything?" I inquired eagerly.

"I have seen *everything*," he answered with a shudder. "They say one dies within a year——"

"My dear fellow, don't be so upset about it," I interrupted; I was quite distressed to see how thoroughly the man had altered.

"Let me tell you about it, Fred."

He drew his chair close to mine and told me his story, pretty nearly in the following words:

"You remember the day I went down you had kept me talking at the Club door; I had a race to catch the train; however, I just did it. I found the other fellows all waiting for me. There was Charlie Wells, the two Harfords, old Colonel Riddell, who is such a crack shot, two fellows in the Guards, both pretty fair, a man called Thompson, a barrister, Henderson and myself—eight of us in all. We had a remarkably lively journey down, as you may imagine, and reached Varley Grange in the highest possible spirits. We all slept like tops that night.

"The next day we were out from eleven till dusk among the coverts, and a better day's shooting I never enjoyed in the whole course of my life, the birds literally swarmed. We bagged a hundred and thirty brace. We were all pretty well tired when we got home, and did full justice to a very good dinner and first-class Perrier-Jouet. After dinner we adjourned to the hall to smoke. This hall is quite the feature of the house. It is large and bright, panelled half-way up with sombre old oak, and vaulted with heavy carved oaken rafters. At the farther end runs a gallery, into which opened the door of my bedroom, and shut off from the rest of the passages by a swing door at either end.

"Well, all we fellows sat up there smoking and drinking brandy and soda, and jawing, you know—as men always do when they are together—about sport of all kinds, hunting and shooting and salmon-fishing; and I assure you not one of us had a thought in our heads beyond relating some wonderful incident of a long shot or big fence by which he would each cap the last speaker's experiences. We were just, I recollect, listening to a long story of the old Colonel's, about his experiences among bisons in Cachemire, when suddenly one of us—I can't remember who it was—gave a sort of shout and started to his feet, pointing up to the gallery behind us. We all turned round, and there—I give you my word of honour, Lester—stood a man leaning over the rail of the gallery, staring down upon us.

"We all saw him. Every one of us. Eight of us, remember. He stood there full ten seconds, looking down with horrible glittering eyes at us. He had a long tawny beard, and his hands, that were crossed together before him, were nothing but skin and bone. But it was his face that was so unspeakably dreadful. It was livid—the face of a dead man!"

"How was he dressed?"

"I could not see; he wore some kind of a black cloak over his shoulders, I think, but the lower part of his figure was hidden behind the railings. Well, we all stood perfectly speechless for, as I said, about ten seconds; and then the figure moved, backing slowly into the door of the room behind him, which stood open. It was the door of my bedroom! As soon as he had disappeared our senses seemed to return to us. There was a general rush for the staircase, and, as you may imagine, there was not a corner of the house that was left unsearched; my bedroom especially was ransacked in every part of it. But all in vain; there was not the slightest trace to be found of any living being. You may suppose that not one of us slept that night. We lighted every candle and lamp we could lay hands upon and sat up till daylight, but nothing more was seen.

"The next morning, at breakfast, Henderson, who seemed very much annoyed by the whole thing, begged us not to speak of it any more. He said that he had been told, before he had taken the house, that it was supposed to be haunted; but, not being a believer in such childish follies, he had paid but little attention to the rumour. He did not, however, want it talked about, because of the servants, who would be so easily frightened. He was quite certain, he said, that the figure we had seen last night must be somebody dressed up to practise a trick upon us, and he recommended us all to bring our guns down loaded after dinner, but meanwhile to forget the startling apparition as far as we could.

"We, of course, readily agreed to do as he wished, although I do not think that one of us imagined for a moment that any amount of dressing-up would be able to simulate the awful countenance that we had all of us seen too plainly. It would have taken a Hare or an Arthur Cecil, with all the theatrical appliances known only to those two talented actors, to have 'made-up' the face, that was literally that of a corpse. Such a person could not be amongst us—actually in the house—without our knowledge.

"We had another good day's shooting, and by degrees the fresh air and exercise and the excitement of the sport obliterated the impression of what we had seen in some measure from the minds of most of us. That evening we all appeared in the hall after dinner with our loaded guns besides us; but, although we sat up till the small hours and looked frequently up at the gallery at the end of the hall, nothing at all disturbed us that night.

"Two nights thus went by and nothing further was seen of the gentleman with the tawny beard. What with the good company, the good cheer and the pheasants, we had pretty well forgotten all about him.

"We were sitting as usual upon the third night, with our pipes and our cigars; pleasant glow from the bright wood fire in the great chimney lighted up the old hall, and shed a genial warmth about us; when suddenly it seemed to me as if there came a breath of cold, chill air behind me, such as one feels when going down into some damp, cold vault or cellar.

"A strong shiver shook me from head to foot. Before even I saw it I *knew* that It was there.

"It leant over the railing of the gallery and looked down at us all just as it had done before. There was no change in the attitude, no alteration in the fixed, malignant glare in those stony, lifeless eyes; no movement in the white and bloodless features. Below, amongst the eight of us gathered there, there arose a panic of terror. Eight strong, healthy, well-educated nineteenth-century Englishmen, and yet I am not ashamed to say that we were paralysed with fear. Then one, more quickly recovering his senses than the rest, caught at his gun, that leant against the wide chimney-corner, and fired.

"The hall was filled with smoke, but as it cleared away every one of us could see the figure of our supernatural visitant slowly backing, as he had done on the previous occasion, into the chamber behind him, with something like a sardonic smile of scornful derision upon his horrible, death-like face.

"The next morning it is a singular and remarkable fact that four out of the eight of us received by the morning post—so they stated—letters of importance which called them up to town by the very first train! One man's mother was ill, another had to consult his lawyer, whilst pressing engagements, to which they could assign no definite name, called away the other two.

"There were left in the house that day but four of us—Wells, Bob Harford, our host, and myself. A sort of dogged determination not to be worsted by a scare of this kind kept us still there. The morning light brought a return of common sense and of natural courage to us. We could manage to laugh over last night's terrors whilst discussing our bacon and kidneys and hot coffee over the late breakfast in the pleasant morning-room, with the sunshine streaming cheerily in through the diamond-paned windows.

" 'It *must* be a delusion of our brains,' said one.

" 'Our host's champagne,' suggested another.

" 'A well-organised hoax,' opined a third.

" 'I will tell you what we will do,' said our host. 'Now that those other fellows have all gone—and I suppose we don't any of us believe much in those elaborate family reasons which have so unaccountably summoned them away—we four will sit up regularly night after night and watch for this thing, whatever it may be. I do not believe in ghosts. However, this morning I have taken the trouble to go out before breakfast to see the Rector of the parish, an old gentleman who is well up in all the traditions of the neighbourhood, and I have learnt from him the whole of the supposed story of our friend of the tawny beard, which, if you like, I will relate to you.'

"Henderson then proceeded to tell us the tradition concerning the Dennis Varley who murdered his sister, the nun—a story which I will not repeat to you, Lester, as I see you know it already.

"The clergyman had furthermore told him that the figure of the murdered nun was also sometimes seen in the same gallery, but that this as a very rate occurrence. When both murderer and his victim are seen together terrible misfortunes are sure to assail the unfortunate living man who sees them; and if the nun's face is revealed death within the year is the doom of the ill-fated person who has seen it.

" 'Of course,' concluded our host, 'I consider all these stories to be absolutely childish. At the same time I cannot help thinking that some human agency—probably a gang of thieves or housebreakers—is at work, and that we shall probably be able to unearth an organized system of villainy by which the rogues, presuming on the credulity of the persons who have inhabited the place, have been able to plant themselves securely among some secret passages and hidden rooms in the house, and have carried on their depredations undiscovered and unsuspected. Now, will all of you help me to unravel this mystery?'

"We all promised readily to do so. It is astonishing how brave we felt at eleven o'clock in the morning; what an amount of pluck and courage each man professed himself to be endued with; how lightly we jested about the 'old boy with the beard,' and what jokes we cracked about the murdered nun!

" 'She would show her face oftener if she was good-looking. No fear of her looking at Bob Harford, he was too ugly. It was Jack Darent who was the showman of the party; she'd be sure to make straight for him if she could, he was always run after by the women,' and so on, till we were all laughing loudly and heartily over our own witticisms. That was eleven o'clock in the morning.

"At eleven o'clock at night we could have given a very different report of ourselves.

"At eleven o'clock at night each man took up his appointed post in solemn and somewhat depressed silence.

"The plan of our campaign had been carefully organized by our host. Each man was posted separately with about thirty yards between them, so that no optical delusion, such as an effect of firelight upon the oak panelling, nor any reflection from the circular mirror over the chimney-piece, should be able to deceive more than one of us. Our host fixed himself in the very centre of the hall, facing the gallery at the end; Wells took up his position half-way up the short, straight flight of steps; Harford was at the top of the stairs upon the gallery itself; I was opposite to him at the further end. In this manner, whenever the figure—ghost or burglar—should appear, it must necessarily be between two of us, and be seen from both the right and the left side. We were prepared to believe that one amongst us might be deceived by his senses or by his imagination, but it was clear that two persons could not see the same object from a different point of view and be simultaneously deluded by any effect of light or any optical hallucination.

"Each man was provided with a loaded revolver, a brandy and soda and a sufficient stock of pipes or cigars to last him through the night. We took up our position at eleven o'clock exactly, and waited.

"At first we were all four very silent and, as I have said before, slightly depressed; but as the hour wore away and nothing was seen or heard we began to talk to each other. Talking, however, was rather a difficulty. To begin with, we had to shout—at least we in the gallery had to shout to Henderson, down in the hall; and though Harford and Wells could converse quite comfortably, I, not being able to see the latter at all from my end of the gallery, had to pass my remarks to him second-hand through Harford, who amused himself in misstating every intelligent remark that I entrusted him with; added to which natural impediments to the 'flow of the soul,' the elements thought fit to create such a hullabaloo without that conversation was rendered still further work of difficulty.

"I never remember such a night in all my life. The rain came down in torrents; the wind howled and shrieked wildly amongst the tall chimneys and the bare elm-trees without. Every now and then there was a lull, and then, again and again, a long sobbing moan came swirling round and round the house, for all the world like the cry of a human being in agony. It was a night to make one shudder, and thank Heaven for a roof over one's head.

"We all sat on at our separate posts hour after hour, listening to the wind and talking at intervals; but as the time wore on insensibly we became less and less talkative, and a sort of depression crept over us.

"At last we relapsed into a profound silence; then suddenly there came upon us all that chill blast of air, like a breath from a charnel-house, that we had experienced before, and almost simultaneously a hoarse cry broke from Henderson in the body of the hall below, and from Wells half-way up the stairs.

"Harford and I sprang to our feet, and we too saw it.

"The dead man was slowly coming up the stairs. He passed silently up with a sort of still, gliding motion, within a few inches of poor Wells, who shrank back, white with terror, against the wall. Henderson rushed wildly up the staircase in pursuit, whilst Harford and I, up on the gallery, fell instinctively back at his approach.

"He passed between us.

"We saw the glitter of his sightless eyes—the shrivelled skin upon his withered face—the mouth that fell away, like the mouth of a corpse, beneath his tawny beard. We felt the cold death-like blast that came with him, and the sickening horror of his terrible presence. Ah! can I ever forget it?"

With a strong shudder Jack Darent buried his face in his hands, and seemed too much overcome for some minutes to be able to proceed.

"My dear fellow, are you *sure*?" I said in an awestruck whisper.

He lifted his head.

"Forgive me, Lester; the whole business has shaken my nerves so thoroughly that I have not yet been able to get over it. But I have not yet told you the worst."

"Good heavens—is there worse?' I ejaculated.

He nodded.

"No sooner," he continued, "had this awful creature passed us than Harford clutched at my arm and pointed to the farther end of the gallery.

" 'Look!' he cried hoarsely, 'the nun!'

"There, coming towards us from the opposite direction, was the veiled figure of a nun.

"There were the long, flowing black and white garments—the gleam of the crucifix at her neck—the jangle of her rosary-beads from her waist; but her face was hidden.

"A sort of desperation seized me. With a violent effort over myself, I went towards this fresh apparition.

" 'It *must* be a hoax,' I said to myself, and there was a half-formed intention in my mind of wrenching aside the flowing draperies and of seeing for myself who and what it was. I strode towards the figure—I stood within half a yard of it. The nun raised her head slowly—and, Lester—*I saw her face!*"

There was a moment's silence.

"What was it like, Jack?" I asked him presently.

He shook his head.

"That I can never tell to any living creature."

"Was it so horrible?"

He nodded assent, shuddering.

"And what happened next?"

"I believe I fainted. At all events I remembered nothing further. They made me go to the vicarage the next day. I was so knocked over by it all—I was quite ill. I could not have stayed in the house. I stopped there all yesterday, and I got up to town this morning. I wish to Heaven I had taken your advice, old man, and had never gone to that horrible house."

"I wish you had, Jack," I answered fervently.

"Do you know that I shall die within the year?" he asked me presently.

I tried to pooh-pooh it.

"My dear fellow, don't take the thing so seriously as all that. Whatever may be the meaning of these horrible apparitions, there can be nothing but an old wife's fable in *that* saying. Why on earth should you die—you of all people, a great strong fellow with a constitution of iron? You don't look much like dying!"

"For all that I shall die. I cannot tell you why I am so certain—but I know that it will be so," he answered in a low voice. "And some terrible misfortune will happen to Harford—the other two never saw her—it is he and I who are doomed."

★

A year has passed away. Last summer fashionable society rang for a week or more with the tale of poor Bob Harford's misfortune. The girl whom he was engaged to, and to whom he was devotedly attached—young, beautiful and wealthy—ran away on the eve of her wedding-day with a drinking, swindling villain who had been turned out of ever so many clubs and tabooed for ages by every respectable man in town, and who had nothing but a handsome face and a fascinating manner to recommend him, and who by dint of these had succeeded in gaining a complete ascendancy over the fickle heart of poor Bob's lovely fiancée. As to Harford, he sold out and went off to the backwoods of Canada, and has never been heard of since.

And what of Jack Darent? Poor, handsome Jack, with his tall figure and his bright, happy face, and the merry blue eyes that had wiled Bella Lester's heart away! Alas! far away in Southern Africa, poor Jack

Darent lies in an unknown grave—slain by a Zulu assegai on the fatal plain of Isandula!

And Bella goes about clad in sable garments, heavy-eyed and stricken with sore grief. A widow in heart, if not in name.

## *The Hollow Man*

BY THOMAS BURKE

He came up one of the narrow streets which lead from the docks, and turned into a road whose farther end was gay with the light of London. At the end of this road he went deep into the lights of London, and sometimes into its shadows, farther and farther away from the river; and did not pause until he had reached a poor quarter near the centre.

He was a tall, spare figure, wearing a black mackintosh. Below this could be seen brown dungaree trousers. A peaked cap hid most of his face; the little that was exposed was white and sharp. In the autumn mist that filled the lighted streets as well as the dark he seemed a wraith, and some of those who passed him looked again, not sure whether they had indeed seen a living man. One or two of them moved their shoulders, as though shrinking from something.

His legs were long, but he walked with the short, deliberate steps of a blind man, though he was not blind. His eyes were open, and he stared straight ahead; but he seemed to see nothing and hear nothing.

Neither the mournful hooting of sirens across the black water of the river, nor the genial windows of the shops in the big streets near the centre drew his head to right or left. He walked as though he had no destination in mind, yet constantly, at this corner or that, he turned. It seemed that an unseen hand was guiding him to a given point of whose location he was himself ignorant.

He was searching for a friend of fifteen years ago, and the unseen hand, or some dog-instinct, had led him from Africa to London, and was now leading him, along the last mile of his search, to a certain little eating-house. He did not know that he was going to the eating-house of his friend Nameless, but he did know, from the time he left Africa, that he was journeying towards Nameless, and he now knew that he was very near to Nameless.

Nameless didn't know that his old friend was anywhere near *him*, though, had he observed conditions that evening, he might have wondered why he was sitting up an hour later than usual. He was seated in one of the pews of his prosperous little workmen's dining-rooms—a little gold-mine his wife relations called it—and he was smoking and looking at nothing.

He had added up the till and written the copies of the bill of fare for next day, and thee was nothing to keep him out of bed after his fifteen hours' attention to business. Had he been asked why he was sitting up later than usual, he would first have answered that he didn't know that he was, and would then have explained, in default of any other explanation, that it was for the purpose of having a last pipe. He was quite unaware that he was sitting up and keeping the door unlatched because a long-parted friend from Africa was seeking him and slowly approaching him, and needed his services.

He was quite unaware that he had left the door unlatched at that late hour—half-past eleven—to admit pain and woe.

But even as many bells sent dolefully across the night from their steeples their disagreement as to the point of half-past eleven, pain and woe were but two streets away from him. The mackintosh and dungarees and the sharp white face were coming nearer every moment.

There was silence in the house and in the streets; a heavy silence, broken, or sometimes stressed, by the occasional night-noises—motor horns, back-firing of lorries, shunting at a distant terminus. That silence seemed to envelop the house, but he did not notice it. He did not notice the bells, and he did not even notice the lagging step that approached his shop, and passed—and returned—and passed again—and halted. He was aware of nothing save that he was smoking a last pipe, and he was sitting in that state of hazy reverie which he called thinking, deaf and blind to anything not in his immediate neighbourhood.

But when a hand was laid on the latch, and the latch was lifted, he did hear that, and he looked up. And he saw the door open, and got up and went to it. And there, just within the door, he came face to face with the thin figure of pain and woe.

To kill a fellow-creature is a frightful thing. At the time the act is committed the murderer may have sound and convincing reasons (to him) for his act. But time and reflection may bring regret; even remorse; and this may live with him for many years. Examined in wakeful hours of the night or early morning, the reasons for the act may shed their cold logic, and may cease to be reasons and become mere excuses.

And these naked excuses may strip the murderer and show him to himself as he is. They may begin to hunt his soul, and to run into every little corner of his mind and every little nerve, in search of it.

And if to kill a fellow-creature and to suffer the recurrent regret for an act of heated blood is a frightful thing, it is still more frightful to kill a fellow-creature and bury his body deep in an African jungle, and then, fifteen years later, at about midnight, to see the latch of your door lifted by the hand you had stilled and to see the man, looking much as he did fifteen years ago, walk into your home and claim your hospitality.

★

When the man in mackintosh and dungarees walked into the dining-rooms Nameless stood still; stared; staggered against a table; supported himself by a hand, and said "Oh!"

The other man said "Nameless!"

Then they looked at each other; Nameless with head thrust forward, mouth dropped; eyes wide; the visitor with a dull, glazed expression. If Nameless had not been the man he was—thick, bovine and costive—he would have flung up his arms and screamed. At that moment he felt the need of some such outlet, but did not know how to find it. The only dramatic expression he gave to the situation was to whisper instead of speak.

Twenty emotions came to life in his head and spine, and wrestled there. But they showed themselves only in his staring eyes and his whisper. His first thought, or rather, spasm, was Ghosts-Indigestion-Nervous-Breakdown. His second, when he saw that the figure was substantial and real, was Impersonation. But a slight movement of the part of the visitor dismissed that.

It was a little habitual movement which belonged only to that man; an unconscious twitching of the third finger of the left hand. He knew then that it was Gopak. Gopak, a little changed, but still, miraculously, thirty-two. Gopak, alive, breathing and real. No ghost. No phantom of the stomach. He was as certain of that as he was that fifteen years ago he had killed Gopak stone-dead and buried him.

The blackness of the moment was lightened by Gopak. In thin, flat tones he asked, "May I sit down? I'm tired." He sat down, and said: "So tired. So tired."

Nameless still held the table. He whispered: "Gopak ... Gopak ... But I—I *killed* you. I killed you in the jungle. You were dead. I know you were."

Gopak passed his hand across his face. He seemed about to cry. "I know you did. I know. That's all I can remember—about this earth. You killed me." The voice became thinner and flatter. "And I was so comfortable. So comfortable. It was—such a rest. Such a rest as you don't know. And then they came and—disturbed me. They woke me up. And brought me back." He sat with shoulders sagged, arms drooping, hands hanging between knees. After the first recognition he did not look at Nameless; he looked at the floor.

"Came and disturbed you?" Nameless leaned forward and whispered the words. "Woke you up? Who?"

"The Leopard Men."

"The what?"

"The Leopard Men." The watery voice said it as casually as if it were saying "the night watchman."

"The Leopard Men?" Nameless stared, and his fat face crinkled in an effort to take in the situation of a midnight visitation from a dead man, and the dead man talking nonsense. He felt his blood moving out of its course. He looked at his own hand to see if it was his own hand. He looked at the table to see if it was his table. The hand and the table were facts, and if the dead man was a fact—and he was—

his story might be a fact. It seemed anyway as sensible as the dead man's presence. He gave a heavy sigh from the stomach.

"A-ah... The Leopard Men ... Yes, I heard about them out there. Tales!"

Gopak slowly wagged his head. "Not tales. They're real. If they weren't real—I wouldn't be here. Would I? I'd be at rest."

Nameless had to admit this. He had heard many tales "out there" about the Leopard Men, and had dismissed them as jungle yarns. But now, it seemed, jungle yarns had become commonplace fact in a little London shop.

The watery voice went on. "They do it. I saw them. I came back in the middle of a circle of them. They killed a nigger to put his life into me. They wanted a white man—for their farm. So they brought me back. You may not believe it. You wouldn't *want* to believe it. You wouldn't want to—see or know anything like them. And I wouldn't want any man to. But it's true. That's how I'm here."

"But I left you absolutely dead. I made every test. It was three days before I buried you. And I buried you deep."

"I know. But that wouldn't make any difference to them. It was a long time after when they came and brought me back. And I'm still dead, you know. It's only my body they brought back." The voice trailed into a thread. "And I'm so tired. So tired. I want to go back—to rest."

Sitting in his prosperous eating-house, Nameless was in the presence of an achieved miracle, but the everyday, solid appointments of the eating-house wouldn't let him fully comprehend it. Foolishly, as he realised when he had spoken, he asked Gopak to explain what had happened. Asked a man who couldn't really be alive to explain how he came to be alive. It was like asking Nothing to explain Everything.

Constantly, as he talked, he felt his grasp on his own mind slipping. The surprise of a sudden visitor at a late hour; the shock of the arrival of a long-dead man; and the realisation that this long-dead man was not a wraith, were too much for him.

During the next half-hour he found himself talking to Gopak as to the Gopak he had known seventeen years ago when they were partners. Then he would be halted by the freezing knowledge that he was talking to a dead man, and that a dead man was faintly answering him. He felt that the thing couldn't really have happened, but in the interchange of talk he kept forgetting the improbable side of it, and accepting it. With each recollection of the truth, his mind would clear and settle in one thought—"I've got to get rid of him. How am I going to get rid of him?"

"But how did you get here?"

"I escaped." The words came slowly and thinly, and out of the body rather than the mouth.

"How."

"I don't—know. I don't remember anything—except our quarrel. And being at rest."

"But why come all the way here? Why didn't you stay on the coast?"

"I don't—know. But you're the only man I know. The only man I can remember."

"But how did you find me?"

"I don't know. But I had to—find you. You're the only man—who can help me."

"But how can I help you?"

The head turned weakly from side to side. "I don't—know. But nobody else—can."

Nameless stared through the window, looking on to the lamplit street and seeing nothing of it. The everyday being which had been his half an hour ago had been annihilated; the everyday beliefs and disbeliefs shattered and mixed together. But some shred of his old sense and his old standard remained. He must handle this situation. "Well—what you want to do? What you going to do? I don't see how I can help you. And you can't stay here, obviously." A demon of perversity sent a facetious notion into his head—introducing Gopak to his wife—"This is my dead friend."

But on his last spoken remark Gopak made the effort of raising his head and staring with the glazed eyes at Nameless. "But I *must* stay here. There's nowhere else I can stay. I must stay here. That's why I came. You got to help me."

"But you can't stay here. I got no room. All occupied. Nowhere for you to sleep."

The wan voice said: "That doesn't matter. I *don't* sleep."

"Eh?"

"I *don't* sleep. I haven't slept since they brought me back. I can sit here—till you can think of some way of helping me."

"But how *can* I?"

He again forgot the background of the situation, and began to get angry at the vision of a dead man sitting about the place waiting for him to think of something. "How *can* I if you don't tell me how?"

"I don't—know. But you got to. You killed me. And I was dead—and comfortable. As it all came from you—killing me—you're responsible for me being—like this. So, you got to—help me. That's why I—came to you."

"But what do you want me to do?"

"I don't—know. I can't—think. But nobody but you can help me. I had to come to you. Something brought me—straight to you. That means that you're the one—that can help me. Now I'm with you, something will—happen to help me. I feel it will. In time you'll—think of something."

Nameless found his legs suddenly weak. He sat down and stared with a sick scowl at the hideous and the incomprehensible. Here was a dead man in his house—a man he had murdered in a moment of black temper—and he knew in his heart that he couldn't turn the man out. For one thing, he would have been afraid to touch him; he couldn't see himself touching him. For another, faced with the miracle of the presence of a fifteen-years-dead man, he doubted whether physical force or any material agency would be effectual in moving the man.

His soul shivered, as all men's souls shiver at the demonstration of forces outside their mental or spiritual horizon. He had murdered this man, and often, in fifteen years, he had repented the act. If the man's appalling story were true, then he had some sort of right to turn to Nameless. Nameless recognised that, and knew that whatever happened he couldn't turn him out. His hot-tempered sin had literally come home to him.

The wan voice broke into his nightmare. "You go to rest, Nameless. I'll sit here. You go to rest." He put his face down to his hands and uttered a little moan. "Oh, why can't I rest? Why can't I go back to my beautiful rest?"

★

Nameless came down early next morning with a half-hope that Gopak would not be there. But he was there, seated where Nameless had left him last night. Nameless made some tea, and showed him where he might wash. He washed listlessly, and crawled back to his seat, and listlessly drank the tea which Nameless brought to him.

To his wife and the kitchen helpers Nameless mentioned him as an old friend who had had a bit of a shock. "Shipwrecked and knocked on the head. But quite harmless, and he won't be staying long. He's waiting for admission to a home. A good pal to me in the past, and it's the least I can do to let him stay here a few days. Suffers from sleeplessness and prefers to sit up at night. Quite harmless."

But Gopak stayed more than a few days. He outstayed everybody. Even when the customers had gone Gopak was still there.

On the first morning of his visit when the regular customers came in at mid-day, they looked at the odd, white figure sitting vacantly in the first pew, then stared, then moved away.

All avoided the pew in which he sat. Nameless explained him to them, but his explanation did not seem to relieve the slight tension which settled on the dining-room. The atmosphere was not so brisk and chatty as usual. Even those who had their backs to the stranger seemed to be affected by his presence.

At the end of the first day Nameless, noticing this, told him that he had arranged a nice corner of the front room upstairs, where he could sit by the window and took his arm to take him upstairs. But Gopak feebly shook the hand away, and sat where he was. "No. I don't want to go. I'll stay here. I'll stay here. I don't want to move."

And he wouldn't move. After a few more pleadings Nameless realised with dismay that his refusal was definite; that it would be futile to press him or force him; that he was going to sit in that dining-room for ever. He was as weak as a child and as firm as a rock.

He continued to sit in that first pew, and the customers continued to avoid it, and to give queer glances at it. It seemed that they half-recognised that he was something more than a fellow who had had a shock.

During the second week of his stay three of the regular customers were missing, and more than one of those that remained made acidly facetious suggestions to Nameless that he park his lively friend somewhere else. He made things too exciting for them; all that whoopee took them off their work, and interfered with digestion. Nameless told them he would be staying only a day or so longer, but they found that this was untrue, and at the end of the second week eight of the regulars had found another place.

Each day, when the dinner-hour came, Nameless tried to get him to take a little walk, but always he refused.

He would go out only at night, and then never more than two hundred yards from the shop. For the rest, he sat in his pew, sometimes dozing in the afternoon, at other times staring at the floor. He took his food abstractedly, and never knew whether he had had food or not. He spoke only when questioned, and the burden of his talk was "I'm so tired. So tired."

One thing only seemed to arouse any light of interest in him; one thing only drew his eyes from the floor. That was the seventeen-year-old daughter of his host, who was known as Bubbles, and who helped with the waiting. And Bubbles seemed to be the only member of the shop and its customers who did not shrink from him.

She knew nothing of the truth about him, but she seemed to understand him, and the only response he ever gave to anything was to her childish sympathy. She sat and chatted foolish chatter to him—"bringing him out of himself" she called it—and sometimes he would be brought out to the extent of a watery smile. He came to recognise her step, and would look up before she entered the room. Once or twice in the evening, when the shop was empty, and Nameless was sitting miserably with him, he would ask, without lifting his eyes. "Where's Bubbles?" and would be told that Bubbles had gone to the pictures or was out at a dance, and would relapse into deeper vacancy.

Nameless didn't like this. He was already visited by a curse which, in four weeks, had destroyed most of his business. Regular customers had dropped off two by two, and no new customers came to take their place. Strangers who dropped in once for a meal did not come again; they could not keep their eyes or their minds off the forbidding, white-faced figure sitting motionless in the first pew. At mid-day, when the place had been crowded and late-comers had to wait for a seat, it was now two-thirds empty; only a few of the most thick-skinned remained faithful.

And on top of this there was the interest of the dead man in his daughter, an interest which seemed to be having an unpleasant effect. Nameless hadn't noticed it, but his wife had. "Bubbles don't seem as bright and lively as she was. You noticed it lately? She's getting quiet—and a bit slack. Sits about a lot. Paler than she used to be."

"Her age, perhaps."

"No, She's not one of these thin dark sort. No—it's something else. Jus the last week or two I've noticed it. Off her food. Sits about doing nothing. No interest. May be nothing; just out of sorts, perhaps ... How much longer's that horrible friend of yours going to stay?"

★

The horrible friend stayed some weeks longer—ten weeks in all—while Nameless watched his business drop to nothing and his daughter get pale and peevish. He knew the cause of it. There was no home in all England like his: no home that had a dead man sitting in it for ten weeks. A dead man brought, after a long time, from the grave, to sit and disturb his customers and take the vitality from his daughter. He couldn't tell this to anybody. Nobody would believe such nonsense.

But he *knew* that he was entertaining a dead man, and, knowing that a long-dead man was walking the earth, he could believe in any result of that fact. He could believe almost anything that he would have derided ten weeks ago. His customers had abandoned his shop, not because of the presence of a silent, white-faced man, but because of the presence of a dead-living man.

Their minds might not know it, but their blood knew it. And, as his business had been destroyed, so, he believed, would his daughter be destroyed. Her blood was not warming her; her blood told her only that this was a long-ago friend of her father's, and she was drawn to him.

It was at this point that Nameless, having no work to do, began to drink. And it was well that he did so. For out of the drink came an idea, and with that idea he freed himself from the curse upon him and his house.

The shop now served scarcely half a dozen customers at midday. It had become ill-kempt and dusty, and the service and the food were bad. Nameless took no trouble to be civil to his few customers. Often, when he was notably under drink, he went to the trouble of being very rude to them. They talked about this. They talked about the decline of his business and the dustiness of the shop and the bad food. They talked about his drinking, and, of course, exaggerated it.

And they talked about the queer fellow who sat there day after day and gave everybody the creeps. A few outsiders, hearing the gossip, came to the dining-rooms to see the queer fellow and the always-tight proprietor; but they did not come again, and there were not enough of the curious to keep the place busy. It went down until it served scarcely two customers a day. And Nameless went down with it into drink.

Then, one evening, out of the drink he fished an inspiration.

He took it downstairs to Gopak, who was sitting in his usual seat, hands hanging, eyes on the floor. "Gopak—listen. You came here because I was the only man who could help you in your trouble. You listening?"

A faint "Yes" was his answer.

"Well, now. You told me I'd got to think of something. I've thought of something.... Listen. You say I'm responsible for your condition and got to get you out of it, because I killed you. I did. We had a row. You made me wild. You dared me. And what with that sun and the jungle and the insects, I wasn't meself. I killed you. The moment it was done I could a-cut me right hand off. Because you and me were pals. I could a-cut me right hand off."

"I know. I felt that directly it was over. I knew you were suffering."

"Ah!... I have suffered. And I'm suffering now. Well, this is what I've thought. All your present trouble comes from me killing you in that jungle and burying you. An idea came to me. Do you think it would help you—do you think it would put you back to rest if I—if I—if I—killed you again?"

For some seconds Gopak continued to stare at the floor. Then his shoulders moved. Then, while Nameless watched every little response to his idea, the watery voice began. "Yes. Yes. That's it. That's what I was waiting for. That's why I came here. I can see now. That's why I had to get here. Nobody else could kill me. Only you. I've got to be killed again. Yes, I see. But nobody else—would be able—to kill me. Only the man who first killed me.... Yes, you've found—what we're both—waiting for. Anybody else could shoot me—stab me—hang me—but they couldn't kill me. Only you. That's why I managed to get here and find you."

The watery voice rose to a thin strength. "That's it. And you must do it. Do it now. You don't want to, I know. But you must. You *must*."

His head drooped and he stared at the floor. Nameless, too, stared at the floor. He was seeing things. He had murdered a man and had escaped all punishment save that of his own mind, which had been terrible enough. But now he was going to murder him again—not in a jungle but in a city; and he saw the slow points of the result.

He saw the arrest. He saw the first hearing. He saw the trial. He saw the cell. He saw the rope. He shuddered.

Then he saw the alternative—the breakdown of his life—a ruined business, poverty, the poorhouse, a daughter robbed of her health and perhaps dying, and always the curse of the dead-living man, who might follow him to the poorhouse. Better to end it all, he thought. Rid himself of the curse which Gopak had brought upon him and his family, and then rid his family of himself with a revolver. Better to follow up his idea.

He got stiffly to his feet. The hour was late evening—half-past ten—and the streets were quiet. He had pulled down the shop-blinds and locked the door. The room was lit by one light at the further end. He moved about uncertainly and looked at Gopak. "Er—how would you—how shall I——"

Gopak said, "You did it with a knife. Just under the heart. You must do it that way again."

Nameless stood and looked at him for some seconds. Then, with an air of resolve, he shook himself. He walked quickly to the kitchen.

Three minutes later his wife and daughter heard a crash, as though a table had been overturned. They called but got no answer. When they came down they found him sitting in one of the pews, wiping sweat from his forehead. He was white and shaking, and appeared to be recovering from a faint.

"Whatever's the matter? You all right?"

He waved them away. "Yes, I'm all right. Touch of giddiness. Smoking too much, I think."

"Mmmm. Or drinking.... Where's your friend? Out for a walk?"

"No. He's gone off. Said he wouldn't impose any longer, and'd go and find an infirmary." He spoke weakly and found trouble in picking words. "Didn't you hear that bang—when he shut the door?"

"I thought that was you fell down."

"No. It was him when he went. I couldn't stop him."

"Mmmm. Just as well, I think." She looked about her. "Things seem to a-gone wrong since he's been here."

There was a general air of dustiness about the place. The table-cloths were dirty, not from use but from disuse. The windows were dim. A long knife, very dusty, was lying on the table under the window. In a corner by the door leading to the kitchen, unseen by her, lay a dusty mackintosh and dungaree, which appeared to have been tossed there. But it was over by the main door, near the first pew, that the dust was thickest—a long trail of it—greyish-white dust.

"Reely this place gets more and more slapdash. Why can't you attend to business? You didn't use to be like this. No wonder it's gone down, letting the place get into this state. Why don't you pull yourself together. Just *look* at that dust by the door. Looks as though somebody's been spilling ashes all over the place."

Nameless looked at it, and his hands shook a little. But he answered, more firmly than before: "Yes, I know. I'll have a proper clean-up tomorrow. I'll put it all to rights to-morrow. I been getting a bit slack."

For the first time in ten weeks he smiled at them; a thin, haggard smile, but a smile.

# *The Thing in the Upper Room*

BY ARTHUR MORRISON

A shadow hung ever over the door, which stood black in the depth of its arched recess, like an unfathomable eye under a frowning brow. The landing was wide and panelled, and a heavy rail, supported by a carved balustrade, stretched away in alternate slopes and levels down the dark staircase, past other doors, and so to the courtyard and the street. The other doors were dark also; but it was with a difference. That top landing was lightest of all, because of the skylight; and perhaps it was largely by reason of contrast that its one doorway gloomed so black and forbidding. The doors below opened and shut, slammed, stood ajar. Men and women passed in and out, with talk and human sounds—sometimes even with laughter or a snatch of song; but the door on the top landing remained shut and silent through weeks and months. For, in truth, the *logement* had an ill name, and had been untenanted for years. Long even before the last tenant had occupied it, the room had been regarded with fear and aversion, and the end of that last tenant had in no way lightened the gloom that hung about the place.

The house was so old that its weather-washed face may well have looked down on the bloodshed of St. Bartholomew's, and the haunted room may even have earned its ill name on that same day of death. But Paris is a city of cruel history, and since the old mansion rose proud and new, the *hôtel* of some powerful noble, almost any year of the centuries might have seen the blot fall on that upper room that had left it a place of loathing and shadows. The occasion was long forgotten, but the fact remained; whether or not some horror of the *ancien régime* or some enormity of the Terror was enacted in that room was no longer to be discovered; but nobody would live there, nor stay beyond that gloomy door one second longer than he could help. It might be supposed that the fate of the solitary tenant within living memory had something to do with the matter—and, indeed, his end was sinister enough; but long before his time the room had stood shunned and empty. He, greatly daring, had taken no more heed of the common terror of the room than to use it to his advantage in abating the rent; and he had shot himself a little later, while the police were beating at his door to arrest him on a charge of murder. As I have said, his fate may have added to the general aversion from the place, though it had in no way originated it; and now ten years had passed, and more, since his few articles of furniture had been carried away and sold; and nothing had been carried in to replace them.

When one is twenty-five, healthy, hungry and poor, one is less likely to be frightened from a cheap lodging by mere headshakings than might be expected in other circumstances. Attwater was twenty-five, commonly healthy, often hungry, and always poor. He came to live in Paris because, from his remembrance of his student days, he believed he could live cheaper there than in London; while it was quite certain that he would not sell fewer pictures, since he had never yet sold one.

It was the *concierge* of a neighbouring house who showed Attwater the room. The house of the room itself maintained no such functionary, though its main door stood open day and night. The man said little, but his surprise at Attwater's application was plain to see. Monsieur was English? Yes. The *logement* was convenient, though high, and probably now a little dirty, since it had not been occupied recently. Plainly, the man felt it to be no business of his to enlighten an unsuspecting foreigner as to the reputation of the place; and if he could let it there would be some small gratification from the landlord, though, at such a rent, of course a very small one indeed.

But Attwater was better informed than the *concierge* supposed. He had heard the tale of the haunted room, vaguely and incoherently, it is true, from the little old engraver of watches on the floor below, by whom he had been directed to the *concierge*. The old man had been voluble and friendly, and reported that the room had a good light, facing north-east—indeed, a much better light than he, engraver of watches, enjoyed on the floor below. So much so that, considering this advantage and the much lower rent, he himself would have taken the room long ago, except—well, except for other things. Monsieur was a stranger, and perhaps had no fear to inhabit a haunted chamber; but that was its reputation, as everybody in the quarter knew; it would be a misfortune, however, to a stranger to take the room without suspicion, and to undergo unexpected experiences. Here, however, the old man checked himself, possibly reflecting that too much information to inquirers after the upper room might offend his landlord. He hinted as much, in fact, hoping that his friendly warning would not be allowed to travel farther. As to the precise nature of the disagreeable manifestations in the room, who could say? Perhaps there were really none at all. People said this and that. Certainly, the place had been untenanted for many years, and he would not like to stay in it himself. But it might be the good fortune of monsieur to break the spell, and if monsieur was resolved to defy the *revenant*, he wished monsieur the highest success and happiness.

So much for the engraver of watches; and now the *concierge* of the neighbouring house led the way up the stately old panelled staircase, swinging his keys in his hand, and halted at last before the dark door in the frowning recess. He turned the key with some difficulty, pushed open the door, and stood back with an action of something not wholly deference, to allow Attwater to enter first.

A sort of small lobby had been partitioned off at some time, though except for this the *logement* was of one large room only. There was something unpleasant in the air of the place—not a smell, when one came to analyse one's sensations, though at first it might seem so. Attwater walked across to the wide window and threw it open. The chimneys and roofs of many houses of all ages straggled before him, and out of the welter rose the twin towers of St. Sulpice, scarred and grim.

Air the room as one might, it was unpleasant; a sickly, even a cowed, feeling, invaded one through all the senses—or perhaps through none of them. The feeling was there, though it was not easy to say by what channel it penetrated. Attwater was resolved to admit none but a common-sense explanation, and blamed the long closing of door and window; and the *concierge*, standing uneasily near the door, agreed that that must be it. For a moment Attwater wavered, despite himself. But the rent was very low, and, low as it was, he could not afford a sou more. The light was good, though it was not a top-light, and the place was big enough for his simple requirements. Attwater reflected that he should despise himself ever after if he shrank from the opportunity; it would be one of those secret humiliations that will rise again and again in a man's memory, and make him blush in solitude. He told the *concierge* to leave door and window wide open for the rest of the day, and he clinched the bargain.

It was with something of amused bravado that he reported to his few friends in Paris his acquisition of a haunted room; for, once out of the place, he readily convinced himself that his disgust and dislike while in the room were the result of imagination and nothing more. Certainly, there was no rational reason to account for the unpleasantness; consequently, what could it be but a matter of fancy? He resolved to face the matter from the beginning, and clear his mind from any foolish prejudices that the hints of the old engraver might have inspired, by forcng himself through whatever adventures he might encounter. In fact, as he walked the streets about his business, and arranged for the purchase and delivery of the few simple articles of furniture that would be necessary, his enterprise assumed the guise of a pleasing adventure. He remembered that he had made an attempt, only a year or two ago, to spend a night in a house reputed haunted in England, but had failed to find the landlord. Here was the adventure to hand, with promise of a tale to tell in future times; and a welcome idea struck him that he might look out the ancient history of the room, and work the whole thing into a magazine article, which would bring a little money.

So simple were his needs that by the afternoon of the day following his first examination of the room it was ready for use.

He took his bag from the cheap hotel in a little street of

Montparnasse, where he had been lodging, and carried it to his new home. The key was now in his pocket, and for the first time he entered the place alone. The window remained wide open;-but it was still there—that depressing, choking something that entered the consciousness he knew not by what gate. Again he accused his fancy. He stamped and whistled, and set about unpacking a few canvases and a case of old oriental weapons that were part of his professional properties. But he could give no proper attention to the work, and detected himself more than once yielding to a childish impulse to look over his shoulder. He laughed at himself—with some effort—and sat determinedly to smoke a pipe, and grow used to his surroundings. But presently he found himself, pushing his chair farther and farther back, till it touched the wall. He would take the whole room into view, he said to himself in excuse, and stare it out of countenance. So he sat and smoked, and as he sat his eye fell on a Malay dagger that lay on the table between him and the window. It was a murderous, twisted thing, and its pommel was fashioned into the semblance of a bird's head, with curved beak and an eye of some dull red stone. He found himself gazing on this red eye with an odd, mindless fascination. The dagger in its wicked curves seemed now a creature of some outlandish fantasy—a snake with a beaked head, a thing of nightmare, in some new way dominant, overruling the centre of his perceptions. The rest of the room grew dim, but the red stone glowed with a fuller light; nothing more was present to his consciousness. Then, with a sudden clang, the heavy bell of St. Sulpice aroused him, and he started up in some surprise.

There lay the dagger on the table, strange and murderous enough, but merely as he had always known it. He observed with more surprise, however, that his chair, which had been back against the wall, was now some six feet forward, close by the table; clearly, he must have drawn it forward in his abstraction, towards the dagger on which his eyes had been fixed.... The great bell of St. Sulpice went clanging on, repeating its monotonous call to the Angelus.

He was cold, almost shivering. He flung the dagger into a drawer, and turned to go out. He saw by his watch that it was later than he had supposed; his fit of abstraction must have lasted some time. Perhaps he had even been dozing.

He went slowly downstairs and out into the streets. As he went he grew more and more ashamed of himself, for he had to confess that in some inexplicable way he feared that room. He had seen nothing, heard nothing of the kind that one might have expected, or had heard of in any room reputed haunted; he could not help thinking that it would have been some sort of relief if he had. But there was an all-pervading, overpowering sense of another Presence—something abhorrent, not human, something almost physically nauseous. Withal it was something more than presence; it was power, domination—so he seemed to remember it. And yet the remembrance grew weaker as he walked in the gathering dusk; he thought of a story he had once read of a haunted house wherein it was shown that the house actually was haunted—by the spirit of fear, and nothing else. That, he persuaded himself, was the case with his room; he felt angry at the growing conviction that he had allowed himself to be overborne by fancy—by the spirit of fear.

He returned that night with the resolve to allow himself no foolish indulgence. He had heard nothing and had seen nothing; when something palpable to the senses occurred, it would be time enough to deal with it. He took off his clothes and got into bed deliberately, leaving candle and matches at hand in case of need. He had expected to find some difficulty in sleeping, or at least some delay, but he was scarce well in bed ere he fell into a heavy sleep.

Dazzling sunlight through the window woke him in the morning, and he sat up, staring sleepily about him. He must have slept like a log. But he had been dreaming; the dreams were horrible. His head ached beyond anything he had experienced before, and he was far more tired than when he went to bed. He sank back on the pillow, but the mere contact made his head ring with pain. He got out of bed, and found himself staggering; it was all as though he had been drunk—unspeakably drunk with bad liquor. His dreams—they had been horrid dreams; he could remember that they had been bad, but what they actually were was now gone from him entirely. He rubbed his eyes and stared amazedly down at the table: where the crooked dagger lay, with its bird's head and red stone eye. It lay just as it had lain when he sat gazing at it yesterday, and yet he would have sworn that he had flung that same dagger into a drawer. Perhaps he had dreamed it; at any rate, he put the thing carefully into the drawer now, and, still with his ringing headache, dressed himself and went out.

As he reached the next landing the old engraver greeted him from his door with an inquiring good-day. "Monsieur has not slept well, I fear?"

In some doubt, Attwater protested that he had slept quite soundly. "And as yet I have neither seen nor heard anything of the ghost," he added.

"Nothing?" replied the old man, with a lift of the eyebrows, "nothing at all? It is fortunate. It seemed to me, here below, that monsieur was moving about very restlessly in the night; but no doubt I was mistaken. No doubt, also, I may felicitate monsieur on breaking the evil tradition. We shall hear no more of it; monsieur has the good fortune of a brave heart."

He smiled and bowed pleasantly, but it was with something of a puzzled look that his eyes followed Attwater descending the staircase.

Attwater took his coffee and roll after an hour's walk, and fell asleep in his seat. Not for long, however, and presently he rose and left the café. He felt better, though still unaccountably fatigued. He caught sight of his face in a mirror beside a shop window, and saw an improvement since he had looked in his own glass. That indeed had brought him a shock. Worn and drawn beyond what might have been expected of so bad a night, there was even something more. What was it? How should it remind him of that old legend—was it Japanese?—which he had tried to recollect when he had wondered confusedly at the haggard apparition that confronted him? Some tale of a demon-possessed person who in any mirror, saw never his own face, but the face of the demon.

Work he felt to be impossible, and he spent the day on garden seats, at café tables, and for a while in the Luxembourg. And in the evening he met an English friend, who took him by the shoulders and looked into his eyes, shook him, and declared that he had been overworking, and needed, above all things, a good dinner, which he should have instantly. "You'll dine with me," he said, "at La Perouse, and we'll get a cab to take us there. I'm hungry."

As they stood and looked for a passing cab a man ran shouting with newspapers. "We'll have a cab," Attwater's friend repeated, "and we'll take the new murder with us for conversation's sake. Hi! *Journal!*"

He bought a paper, and followed Attwater into the cab. "I've a strong idea I knew the poor old boy by sight," he said. "I believe he'd seen better days."

"Who?"

"The old man who was murdered in the Rue Broca last night. The description fits exactly. He used to hang about the cafés and run messages. It isn't easy to read in this cab; but there's probably nothing fresh in this edition. They haven't caught the murderer, anyhow."

Attwater took the paper, and struggled to read it in the changing light. A poor old man had been found dead on the footpath of the Rue Broca, torn with a score of stabs. He had been identified—an old man not known to have a friend in the world; also, because he was so old and so poor, probably not an enemy. There was no robbery; the few sous the old man possessed remained in his pocket. He must have been attacked on his way home in the early hours of the morning, possibly by a homicidal maniac, and stabbed again and again with inconceivable fury. No arrest had been made.

Attwater pushed the paper away: "Pah!" he said; "I don't like it. I'm a bit off colour and I was dreaming horribly all last night; though why this should remind me of it I can't guess. But it's no cure for the blues, this!"

"No," replied his friend heartily; "we'll get that upstairs, for here we are, on the quay. A bottle of the best Burgundy on the list and the best dinner they can do—that's your physic. Come!"

It was a good prescription, indeed. Attwater's friend was cheerful and assiduous, and nothing could have bettered the dinner. Attwater found himself reflecting that indulgence in the blues was a poor pastime, with no better excuse than a bad night's rest. And last night's dinner in comparison with this! Well, it was enough to have spoiled his sleep, that one-franc-fifty dinner.

Attwater left La Perouse as gay as his friend. They had sat late, and now there was nothing to do but cross the water and walk a little in the boulevards. This they did, and finished the evening at a café table with half a dozen acquaintances.

Attwater walked home with a light step, feeling less drowsy than at any time during the day. He was well enough. He felt he should soon get used to the room. He had been a little too much alone lately, and that had got on his nerves. It was simply stupid.

Again he slept quickly and heavily—and dreamed. But he had an awakening of another sort. No bright sun blazed in at the open window to lift his heavy lids, and no morning bell from St. Sulpice opened his ears to the cheerful noise of the city. He awoke gasping and staring in the dark, rolling face-downward on the floor, catching his breath in agonized sobs; while through the window from the streets came a clamour of hoarse cries: cries of pursuit and the noise of running men: a shouting and clatter wherein here and there a voice was clear among the rest—"*Al'assassin! Arrêtez!*"

He dragged himself to his feet in the dark, gasping still. What was this—all this? Again a dream? His legs trembled under him, and he sweated with fear. He made for the window, panting and feeble; and then, as he supported himself by the sill, he realized wonderingly that he was fully dressed—that he wore even his hat. The running crowd straggled through the outer street and away, the shouts growing fainter. What had wakened him? Why had he dressed? He remembered his matches, and turned to grope for them; but something was already in his hand—something wet, sticky. He dropped it on the table, and even as he struck the light, before he saw it, he knew. The match sputtered and flared, and there on the table lay the crooked dagger, smeared and dripping and horrible.

Blood was on his hands—the match stuck in his fingers. Caught at the heart by the first grip of an awful surmise, he hooked up and saw in the mirror before him, in the last flare of the match, the face of the Thing in the Room.

# *The Monkey's Paw*

BY W.W. JACOBS

## I

Without, the night was cold and wet, but in the small parlour of Laburnam Villa the blinds were drawn and the fire burned brightly. Father and son were at chess, the former, who possessed ideas about the game involving radical changes, putting his king into such sharp and unnecessary perils that it even provoked comment from the white-haired old lady knitting placidly by the fire.

'Hark at the wind,' said Mr. White, who, having seen a fatal mistake after it was too late, was amiably desirous of preventing his son from seeing it.

'I'm listening,' said the latter, grimly surveying the board as he stretched out his hand. 'Check.'

'I should hardly think that he'd come tonight,' said his father, with his hand poised over the board.

'Mate,' replied the son.

'That's the worst of living so far out,' bawled Mr. White, with sudden and unlooked-for violence; 'of all the beastly, slushy, out-of-the-way places to live in, this is the worst. Pathway's a bog, and the road's a torrent. I don't know what people are thinking about. I suppose because only two houses in the road are let, they think it doesn't matter.'

'Never mind, dear,' said his wife, soothingly; 'perhaps you'll win the next one.'

Mr. White looked up sharply, just in time to intercept a knowing glance between mother and son. The words died away on his lips, and he hid a guilty grin in his thin grey beard.

'There he is,' said Herbert White, as the gate banged to loudly and heavy footsteps came toward the door.

The old man rose with hospitable haste, and opening the door, was heard condoling with the new arrival. The new arrival also condoled with himself, so that Mrs. White said, 'Tut, tut!' and coughed gently as her husband entered the room, followed by a tall, burly man, beady of eye and rubicund of visage.

'Sergeant-Major Morris,' he said, introducing him.

The sergeant-major shook hands, and taking the proffered seat by the fire, watched contentedly while his host got out whisky and tumblers and stood a small copper kettle on the fire.

At the third glass his eyes got brighter, and he began to talk, the little family circle regarding with eager interest this visitor from distant parts, as he squared his broad shoulders in the chair and spoke of wild scenes and doughty deeds; of wars and plagues and strange peoples.

'Twenty-one years of it,' said Mr. White, nodding at his wife and son. 'When he went away he was a slip of a youth in the warehouse. Now look at him.'

'He don't look to have taken much harm,' said Mrs. White, politely.

'I'd like to go to India myself,' said the old man, 'just to look round a bit, you know.'

'Better where you are, ' said the sergeant-major, shaking his head. He put down the empty glass, and sighing softly, shook it again.

'I should like to see those old temples and fakirs and jugglers,' said the old man. 'What was that you started telling me the other day about a monkey's paw or something, Morris?'

'Nothing,' said the soldier, hastily, 'Leastways nothing worth hearing.'

'Monkey's paw?' said Mrs. White, curiously.

'Well, it's just a bit of what you might call magic, perhaps,' said the sergeant-major, off-handedly.

His three listeners leaned forward eagerly. The visitor absent-mindedly put his empty glass to his lips and then set it down again. His host filled it for him.

'To look at,' said the sergeant-major, fumbling in his pocket, 'it's just an ordinary little paw, dried to a mummy.'

He took something out of his pocket and proffered it. Mrs. White drew back with a grimace, but her son, taking it, examined it curiously.

'And what is there special about it?' inquired Mr. White as he took it from his son, and having examined it, placed it upon the table.

'It had a spell put on it by an old fakir,' said the sergeant-major, 'a very holy man. He wanted to show that fate ruled people's lives, and that those who interfered with it did so to their sorrow. He put a spell on it so that three separate men could each have three wishes from it.'

His manner was so impressive that his hearers were conscious that their light laughter jarred somewhat.

'Well, why don't you have three, sir?' said Herbert White, cleverly.

The soldier regarded him in the way that middle age is wont to regard presumptuous youth. 'I have,' he said, quietly, and his blotchy face whitened.

'And did you really have the three wishes granted?' asked Mrs. White.

'I did,' said the sergeant-major, and his glass tapped against his strong teeth.

'And has anybody else wished?' persisted the old lady.

'The first man had his three wishes. Yes,' was the reply; 'I don't know what the first two were, but the third was for death. That's how I got the paw.'

His tones were so grave that a hush fell upon the group.

'If you've had your three wishes, it's no good to you now, then, Morris,' said the old man at last. 'What do you keep it for?'

The soldier shook his head. "Fancy, I suppose,' he said, slowly. 'I did have some idea of selling it, but I don't think I will. It has caused enough mischief already. Besides, people won't buy. They think it's a fairy tale; some of them, and those who do think anything of it want to try it first and pay me afterward.'

'If you could have another three wishes,' said the old man, eyeing him keenly, 'would you have them?'

'I don't know,' said the other. 'I don't know.'

He took the paw, and dangling it between his forefinger and thumb, suddenly threw it upon the fire. White, with a slight cry, stooped down and snatched it off.

'Better let it burn,' said the soldier, solemnly.

'If you don't want it, Morris,' said the other, 'give it to me.'

'I won't,' said his friend, doggedly. 'I threw it on the fire. If you keep it, don't blame me for what happens. Pitch it on the fire again like a sensible man.'

The other shook his head and examined his new possession closely. 'How do you do it?' he inquired.

'Hold it up in your right hand and wish aloud,' said the sergeant-major, 'but I warn you of the consequences.'

Sounds like the *Arabian Nights*,' said Mrs. White, as she rose and began to set the supper. 'Don't you think you might wish for four pairs of hands for me?'

Her husband drew the talisman from pocket, and then all three burst into laughter as the sergeant-major, with a look of alarm on his face, caught him by the arm.

'If you must wish,' he said, gruffly, 'wish for something sensible.'

Mr. White dropped it back in his pocket, and placing chairs, motioned his friend to the table. In the business of supper the talisman was partly forgotten, and afterward the three sat listening in an enthralled fashion to a second instalment of the soldier's adventures in India.

'If the tale about the monkey's paw is not more truthful than those he has been telling us,' said Herbert, as the door closed behind their guest, just in time for him to catch the last train, 'we shan't make much out of it.'

'Did you give him anything for it, father?' inquired Mrs. White, regarding her husband closely.

'A trifle,' said he, colouring slightly. 'He didn't want it, but I made him take it. And he pressed me again to throw it away.'

'Likely,' said Herbert, with pretended horror. 'Why, we're going to be rich, and famous and happy. Wish to be an emperor, father, to begin with; then you can't be henpecked.'

He darted round the table, pursued by the maligned Mrs. White armed with an antimacassar.

Mr. White took the paw from his pocket and eyed it dubiously. 'I don't know what to wish for, and that's a fact,' he said, slowly. 'It seems to me I've got all I want.'

'If you only cleared the house, you'd be quite happy, wouldn't you?' said Herbert, with his hand on his shoulder. 'Well, wish for two hundred pounds, then; that'll just do it.'

His father, smiling shamefacedly at his own credulity, held up the talisman, as his son, with a solemn face, somewhat marred by a wink at his mother, sat down at the piano and struck a few impressive chords.

'I wish for two hundred pounds,' said the old man distinctly.

A fine crash from the piano greeted the words, interrupted by a shuddering cry from the old man. His wife and son ran toward him.

'It moved,' he cried, with a glance of disgust at the object as it lay on the floor. 'As I wished, it twisted in my hand like a snake.'

'Well, I don't see the money,' said his son as he picked it up and placed it on the table, 'and I bet I never shall.'

'It must have been your fancy, father,' said his wife, regarding him anxiously.

He shook his head. 'Never mind, though; there's no harm done, but it gave me a shock all the same.'

They sat down by the fire again while the two men finished their pipes. Outside, the wind was higher than ever, and the old man started nervously at the sound of a door banging upstairs. A silence unusual and depressing settled upon all three, which lasted until the old couple rose to retire for the night.

'I expect you'll find the cash tied up in a big bag in the middle of your bed,' said Herbert, as he bade them goodnight, 'and something horrible squatting up on top of the wardrobe watching you as you pocket your ill-gotten gains.'

He sat alone in the darkness, gazing at the dying fire, and seeing faces in it. The last face was so horrible and so simian that he gazed at it in amazement. It got so vivid that, with a little uneasy laugh, he felt on the table for a glass containing a little water to throw over it. His hand grasped the monkey's paw, and with a little shiver he wiped his hand on his coat and went up to bed.

## II

In the brightness of the wintry sun next morning as it streamed over the breakfast table he laughed at his fears. There was an air of prosaic wholesomeness about the room which it had lacked on the previous night, and the dirty, shrivelled little paw was pitched on the sideboard with a carelessness which betokened no great belief in its virtues.

'I suppose all old soldiers are the same,' said Mrs. White. 'The idea of our listening to such nonsense! How could wishes be granted in these days? And if they could, how could two hundred pounds hurt you, father?'

'Might drop on his head from the sky,' said the frivolous Herbert.

'Morris said the things happened so naturally,' said his father, 'that you might if you so wished attribute it to coincidence.'

'Well, don't break into the money before I come back,' said Herbert as he rose from the table. 'I'm afraid it'll turn you into a mean, avaricious man, and we shall have to disown you.'

His mother laughed, and following him to the door, watched him down the road; and returning to the breakfast table, was very happy at the expense of her husband's credulity. All of which did not prevent her from scurrying to the door at the postman's knock, nor prevent her from referring somewhat shortly to retired sergeant-majors of bibulous habits when she found that the post brought a tailor's bill.

'Herbert will have some more of his funny remarks, I expect, when he comes home,' she said, as they sat at dinner.

'I dare say,' said Mr. White, pouring himself out some beer; 'but for all that, the thing moved in my hand; that I'll swear to.'

'You thought it did,' said the old lady soothingly.

'I say it did,' replied the other. 'There was no thought about it; I had just—What's the matter?'

His wife made no reply. She was watching the mysterious movements of a man outside, who, peering in an undecided fashion at the house, appeared to be trying to make up his mind to enter. In mental connection with the two hundred pounds, she noticed that the stranger was well dressed, and wore a silk hat of glossy newness. Three times he paused at the gate, and then walked on again. The fourth time he stood with his hand upon it, and then with sudden resolution flung it open and walked up the path. Mrs. White at the same moment placed her hands behind her, and hurriedly unfastening the strings of her apron, put that useful article of apparel beneath the cushion of her chair.

She brought the stranger, who seemed ill at ease, into the room. He gazed at her furtively, and listened in a preoccupied fashion as the old lady apologized for the appearance of the room, and her husband's coat, a garment which he usually reserved for the garden. She then waited as patiently as her sex would permit, for him to broach his business, but he was at first strangely silent.

'I—was asked to call,' he said at last, and stooped and picked a piece of cotton from his trousers. 'I come from "Maw and Meggins".'

The old lady started. 'Is anything the matter?' she asked, breathlessly. 'Has anything happened to Herbert? What is it? What is it?'

Her husband interposed. 'There, there, mother,' he said, hastily. 'Sit down, and don't jump to conclusions. You've not brought bad news, I'm sure, sir' and he eyed the other wistfully.

'I'm sorry—' began the visitor.

'Is he hurt?' demanded the mother, wildly.

The visitor bowed in assent. 'Badly hurt,' he said, quietly, 'but he is not in any pain.'

'Oh, thank God!' said the old woman, clasping her hands. 'Thank God for that! Thank—'

She broke off suddenly as the sinister meaning of the assurance dawned upon her and she saw the awful confirmation of her fears in the other's averted face. She caught her breath, and turning to her slower-witted husband, laid her trembling old hand upon his. There was a long silence.

'He was caught in the machinery,' said the visitor at length in a low voice.

'Caught in the machinery,' repeated Mr. White, in a dazed fashion, 'yes.'

He sat staring blankly out at the window, and taking his wife's hand between his own, pressed it as he had been wont to do in their old courting-days nearly forty years before.

'He was the only one left to us,' he said, turning gently to the visitor. 'It is hard.'

The other coughed, and rising, walked slowly to the window. 'The firm wished me to convey their sincere sympathy with you in your great loss,' he said, without looking round. 'I beg that you will understand I am only their servant and merely obeying orders.'

There was no reply; the old woman's face was white, her eyes staring, and her breath inaudible; on the husband's face was a look such as his friend the sergeant might have carried into his first action.

'I was to say that Maw and Meggins disclaim all responsibility,' continued the other. 'They admit no liability at all, but in consideration of your son's services, they wish to present you with a certain sum as compensation.'

Mr. White dropped his wife's hand, and rising to his feet, gazed with a look of horror at his visitor. His dry lips shaped the words, 'How much?'

'Two hundred pounds,' was the answer.

Unconscious of his wife's shriek, the old man smiled faintly, put out his hands like a sightless man, and dropped, a senseless heap, to the floor.

## III

In the huge news cemetery, some two miles distant, the old people buried their dead, and came back to a house steeped in shadow and silence. It was all over so quickly that at first they could hardly realize it, and remained in a state of expectation as though of something else to happen—something else which was to lighten this load, too heavy for old hearts to bear.

But the days passed, and expectation gave place to resignation—the hopeless resignation of the old, sometimes miscalled, apathy. Sometimes they hardly exchanged a word, for now they had nothing to talk about, and their days were long to weariness.

It was about a week after that the old man, waking suddenly in the night, stretched out his hand and found himself alone. The room was in darkness, and the sound of subdued weeping came from the window. He raised himself in bed and listened.

'Come back,' he said, tenderly. 'You will be cold.'

'It is colder for my son,' said the old woman, and wept afresh.

The sound of her sobs died away on his ears. The bed was warm, and his eyes heavy with sleep. He dozed fitfully, and then slept until a sudden wild cry from his wife awoke him with a start.

'*The paw!*' she cried wildly. 'The monkey's paw!'

He started up in alarm. 'Where? Where is it? What's the matter?'

She came stumbling across the room towards him. 'I want it,' she said, quietly. 'You've not destroyed it?'

'It's in the parlour, on the bracket,' he replied, marvelling. 'Why?'

She cried and laughed together, and bending over, kissed his cheek.

'I only just thought of it,' she said, hysterically. 'Why didn't I think of it before? Why didn't *you* think of it?'

'Think of what?' he questioned.

'The other two wishes,' she replied, rapidly. 'We've only had one.'

'Was not that enough?' he demanded, fiercely.

'No,' she cried, triumphantly; 'we'll have one more. Go down and get it quickly, and wish our boy alive again.'

The man sat up in bed and flung the bed-clothes from his quaking limbs. 'Good God, you are mad!' he cried, aghast.

'Get it,' she panted; 'get it quickly, and wish—Oh, my boy, my boy!'

Her husband struck a match and lit the candle. 'Get back to bed,' he said, unsteadily. 'You don't know what you are saying.'

'We had the first wish granted,' said the old woman, feverishly; 'why not the second?'

'A coincidence,' stammered the old man.

'Go and get it and wish,' cried his wife, quivering with excitement.

The old man turned and regarded her, and his voice shook. 'He has been dead ten days, and besides he—I would not tell you else, but—I could only recognize him by his clothing. If he was too terrible for you to see then, how now?'

'Bring him back,' cried the old woman, and dragged him toward the door. 'Do you think I fear the child I have nursed?'

He went down in the darkness, and felt his way to the parlour, and then to the mantelpiece. The talisman was in its place, and a horrible fear that the unspoken wish might bring his mutilated son before him ere he could escape from the room seized upon him, and he caught his breath as he found that he had lost the direction of the door. His brow cold with sweat, he felt his way round the table, and groped along the wall until he found himself in the small passage with the unwholesome thing in his hand.

Even his wife's face seemed changed as he entered the room. It was white and expectant, and to his fears seemed to have an unnatural look upon it. He was afraid of her.

'*Wish!*' she cried, in a strong voice.

'It is foolish and wicked,' he faltered.

'*Wish!*' repeated his wife.

He raised his hand. 'I wish my son is alive again.'

The talisman fell to the floor, and he regarded it fearfully. Then he sank trembling into a chair as the old woman, with burning eyes, walked to the window and raised the blind.

He sat until he was chilled with the cold, glancing occasionally at the figure of the old woman peering through the window. The candle-end, which had burned below the rim of the china candlestick, was throwing pulsating shadows on the ceiling and walls, until, with a flicker larger than the rest, it expired. The old man, with an unspeakable sense of relief at the failure of the talisman, crept back to his bed, and a minute or two afterward the old woman came silently and apathetically beside him.

Neither spoke, but lay silently listening to the ticking of the clock. A stair creaked, and a squeaky mouse scurried noisily through the wall.

The darkness was oppressive, and after lying for some time screwing up his courage, he took the box of matches, and striking one, went downstairs for a candle.

At the foot of the stairs the match went out, and he paused to strike another; and at the same moment a knock, so quiet and stealthy as to be scarcely audible, sounded on the front door.

The matches fell from his hand and spilled in the passage. He stood motionless, his breath suspended until the knock was repeated. Then he turned and fled swiftly back to his room, and closed the door behind him. A third knock sounded through the house.

'*What's that?*' cried the old woman, starting up.

'A rat,' said the old man in shaking tones—'a rat. It passed me on the stairs.'

His wife sat up in bed listening. A loud knock resounded through the house.'

'It's Herbert!' she screamed. 'It's Herbert!'

She ran to the door, but her husband was before her, and catching her by the arm, held her tightly.

'What are you going to do?' he whispered hoarsely.

'It's my boy; it's Herbert!' she cried, struggling mechanically, 'I forgot it was two miles away. What are you holding me for? Let go. I must open the door.'

'For God's sake don't let it in,' cried the old man, trembling.

'You're afraid of your own son,' she cried, struggling. 'Let me go. I'm coming, Herbert; I'm coming.'

There was another knock, and another. The old woman with a sudden wrench broke free and ran from the room. Her husband followed to the landing, and called after her appealingly as she hurried downstairs. He heard the chain rattle back and the bottom bolt drawn slowly and stiffly from the socket. Then the old woman's voice, strained and panting.'

'The bolt,' she cried, loudly. 'Come down. I can't reach it.'

But her husband was on his hands and knees groping wildly on the floor in search of the paw. If he could only find it before the thing outside got in. A perfect fusillade of knocks reverberated through the house, and he heard the scraping of a chair as his wife put it down in the passage against the door. He heard the creaking of the bolt as it came slowly back, and at the same moment he found the monkey's paw, and frantically breathed his third and last wish.

The knocking ceased suddenly, although the echoes of it were still in the house. He heard the chair drawn back, and the door opened. A cold wind rushed up the staircase, and a long loud wail of disappointment and misery from his wife gave him courage to run down to her side, and then to the gate beyond. The street lamp flickering opposite shone on a quiet and deserted road.

